D1497982

# THE

# CASSIQUE OF KIAWAH

## A COLONIAL ROMANCE

# WILLIAM GILMORE SIMMS

# THE

# CASSIQUE OF KIAWAH

A

# COLONIAL ROMANCE

By William Gilmore Simms

*Introduction by* David Aiken

Magnolia Press
Gainesville, Georgia

Reproduced from the Redfield edition of 1859

Introduction copyright 1989 by David Aiken

Published in a limited edition in 1989
Magnolia Press
P.O. Box 2921
Gainesville, Georgia 30503

ISBN 0-916369-12-9
Library of Congress Catalog Card Number: 89-060291
Published in the United States of America

## A NOTE ON THE TEXT

In my prolonged search for a copy of *The Cassique of Kiawah*, I consulted *The National Union Catalog of Pre-1956 Imprints* and discovered very few copies in some twenty rare book collections. I was astonished at the scarcity of the book, and after examining as many copies as possible, I was appalled at the poor condition of the surviving texts. At last I discovered a reproducible first edition at the South Caroliniana Library. I am indebted to the Library Director, Dr. Allan Stokes, for his generosity and cooperation. Without him this edition would never have been. The text and F. O. C. Darley illustrations in the present edition are unemended exact reproductions of the 1859 J. S. Redfield edition of *The Cassique of Kiawah*.

David Aiken
University of Georgia

# Introduction

*The Cassique of Kiawah* is a lost masterpiece. Very few copies of this, the rarest of William Gilmore Simms's 34 works of fiction, have survived. Simms scholars, who have located copies of *Cassique* to read, often acclaim it his best. A result of the mature Simms's life-long devotion to literature, *Cassique* showcases his considerable talents as a novelist. It also demonstrates a number of the major ingredients found in American popular fiction. The plot, setting, characterization, and perspective all combine to make *The Cassique of Kiawah* one of the great works of American literature. The publication of this edition, the only reissue in over a hundred years, is a first step in reclaiming one of our national treasures.

The *Cassique of Kiawah* is the second of Simms's two Colonial Romances. It was preceded by *The Yemassee* (1835) which was published by Simms in his youth, widely read in his lifetime, and proclaimed his best novel for years, largely because it was the only one in print. Unlike *The Yemassee*, *Cassique* was never widely distributed. Its original publication was less than two years before the War Between the States broke out in Charleston Harbor, and the entire nation turned its attention elsewhere. When the War ended, Simms's New York publishing house J. S. Redfield was folding as a business. The novel was not published again until after Simms's death. In 1884 the New York publishers Dodd, Mead came out with a short reissue, which was to be the last until now.

The *Cassique of Kiawah* has all the popular trappings of a romantic adventure story: an exotic and historical setting, an abundance of suspense and action, a broad-shouldered hero, not one but several love triangles, pirates, sword fights, a battle on the open seas, an Indian massacre in a virgin forest, and even a duel between the mighty opposites of two cultures and races. It is a rousing and edifying tale filled with historical information and beautiful descriptions of an unspoiled American landscape. Paul Hamilton Hayne,

Simms's fellow poet and younger contemporary, said that *"The Cassique* is so rapid in movement, so adroit in disposition of events, so picturesque, dramatic, and true in minutest detail to the period and people introduced, that, for my part, I have perused it a dozen times over with undiminished interest."[1]

Throughout the novel Simms keeps the reader in a high state of anticipation. The reader is satisfied aesthetically and emotionally as the pieces of the plot fall into place with the characters sorting out their relationships and moulding their futures. We follow this suspenseful plot, assured that the omniscient narrator will keep events in order and pause periodically to comment on significant happenings, on the spiritual and moral conditions of the characters, and on the exotic world in which they live. But the narrator is not didactic. He establishes a unique relationship with the reader, one that grows as the novel progresses. Functioning sometimes as a producer, sometimes as a friend, often as a satirist, and finally as a kindly father, this philosophical narrator carries us on a journey into a far-away world that is strangely more contemporary than historical.

Any comments might well begin with a close look at the title. The word *Kiawah* refers to an Indian tribe and to the lands they inhabited, but the novel is not another *The Last of the Mohicans*, nor is Simms a Southern James Fenimore Cooper. The Kiawah were Cusabo Indians, a small but picturesque group of tribes settled along the western half of the Carolina coastline in the early days of the province. The narrator, in beginning his story, asks the reader to imagine this coast prior to the coming of the white man's civilization. He portrays nature "hallowed" by God, idyllic and unfallen, before human misuse and abuse. The time is 1684 when the "amiable English" lived in "feeble colonies" surrounded by the "red man" and bordered by the Spanish, an "ugly neighbor" to the South.

The novel features a cassique. This strange term, originally Indian, refers literally to an Indian chief. Europeans settling in South Carolina adopted the word as a special title. John Locke, who divided Carolina gentry into classes, used cassique as one of his classifications. Like the English titles *Lord* and *Baron*, the Carolina title *Cassique* was sometimes conferred by colonists upon a landed aristocrat responsible for governing a plantation modeled on a feudal barony. The term, then, became associated in white culture with political sovereignty.[2]

Although we meet the Indian cassique, Cussobie, we study his white counterpart, the English born and bred Edward Berkeley. He has come to Carolina with a charter from Charles II to establish a landed barony similar to those in seventeenth-century England. Edward is a man of fashion from London, a man of wealth, who acquires from the King 24,000 acres on the Kiawah River fifteen miles above Charleston. He is a rich landed proprietor, a member of the Carolina nobility and a man of character, who disdains petty vanities, shams and tricks. Thus the novel presents two literal cassiques: the English Edward Berkeley, and the Indian Cussobie. Their paths will cross on more than one occasion since our narrator is especially interested in cassique qualities, which he ultimately interprets as more related to character than to race or aristocratic title.

This historical romance describes the halting progress of Edward's barony and of the infant city of Charleston, a mirror of Western civilization transplanted into the howling wilderness of Colonial America. Impediments to the survival and success of the new society are many: some are outside, like the hostile Indians and the marauding Spaniards; but most are within the early settlers themselves. The narrator believes that man's capacity to work mischief is a constant which he takes with him even into this Edenic garden. Defects of character are found wherever man goes, even in our heroic past. The conflicts in the novel rise out of character faults. Greed, foolishness, vanity, and deceit become obstacles to personal fulfillment and social accomplishment. Every civilization must deal with the passion and depravity of its individual citizens.

This mysterious world of Kiawah is one in which human conduct makes a difference. Without the influence of some worthy leader, the tiny settlement of Charleston will surely be destroyed.

Into this beautiful garden and embryonic culture sails the privateer, Harry Calvert. This young Englishman, who is the lost brother of Edward Berkeley, comes burdened with his own passions and is the apex of several love triangles. He must settle a conspiracy aboard his own ship and deal with a city government which labels him a criminal. Yet, as the novel progresses, the reader witnesses Harry's triumph over personal problems and his emergence as the savior of Charleston. Through his efforts the little settlement is spared the folly of pirates, the slaughter of foreign invaders, and the butchery of savages. The narrator spotlights the heroism of Harry Calvert who embodies the skills and attributes of a spiritual cassique.

Harry is a mythic hero of epic proportions. Historically, epics celebrate heroism, and to Simms a romance was like an epic: it celebrates characters of stature in American settings that are wild and wonderful. Best known in his day outside Charleston for his romances, Simms defines the romance in his Preface to *The Yemassee* by emphasizing its epic qualities, especially the celebration of great characters.[3] In Harry Calvert, Simms creates an epic character as large and powerful as the ideal Homeric warrior. Harry has "Herculean proportions . . . and lofty freedom" and possesses "brave simplicity and dignity" (112). He is bold, free, sensible, and courageous, with an eager temper and a generous mood. His valor affects the fate of cities, nations, and races. As a leader, he commands his ship and crew with the authority of an Odysseus. As a fighter, he embodies the courage, military skill, and prowess of an Achilles. As a speaker and master of debate, he mirrors the persuasiveness of the greatest classical heroes. His gentleness echoes Diomedes, and his devotion to family is similar to Hector's. He has the *virtu* and *aristeia* that make him mighty in both battle and peace, and he is Simms's ideal hero of the American Colonial period.

Biblical influences on Simms's understanding of character cannot be overemphasized. Contrary to general opinion, religion appears to have been an integral part of Simms's life and art. Due to the scarcity of documents surviving the War Between the States, the only confirmed church membership of Simms is in St. Paul's Episcopal Church, Charleston, an evangelical off-shoot of St. Michael's and St. Phillip's. In 1867, three years before his death, Simms's name is included on a list of 84 communicants in the Parish Register. Even William P. Trent, who denies Simms's church affiliation, acknowledges the author's "basic beliefs in Christianity."[4] Furthermore, anyone who reads Simms is immediately aware of the immense influence of Biblical religion upon him. In "Literature of the Bible" Simms claims the Bible has made society more humane and modern literature more truthful: "The Bible has furnished to modern literature topics of peculiar grandeur, and thoughts of rare beauty . . . of One God, the cause of all things . . . eternal, unchangeable, supremely independent, perfect in nature, and infinite in all his attributes." Simms continues, "Open the page of inspiration before man's eye, and what a host of glorious truths and ennobling ideas . . . The nature and attributes of the Eternal Spirit, his boundless power, his spotless holiness, his inflexible justice, man's responsibility . . . are truths blazing on every page of the Bible."[5]

Simms's use of the Bible in *The Cassique of Kiawah* is focused on character. Biblical concepts of heroism center around the notion of personal integrity and truthfulness of character. In *Cassique* Simms juxtaposes his honest characters who speak forthrightly, on one hand, to his deceivers and hypocrites, on the other. In this Colonial Romance a man's word and honesty of character is the litmus test for personal integrity. The admirable characters, no matter what social station they hold, are honest, truthful, loyal, and trustworthy—Jack Belcher, Zulieme, Gowdey, Edward, and Harry. The villains and frauds, on the other hand, are deceivers—conspiratorial and hypocritical—the society ladies, Sylvia, Joe Sylvester and Gideon Fairchild, Sam Fowler, the governor, the hostile Indians, Molyneaux, Mrs. Charlotte Anderson, and Mrs. Masterton. Additionally, Simms rates his deceivers, beginning with the Puritan hypocrites and socialites, who covet money and fine ornaments, moving through the political hypocrisy of Governor Robert Quarry and the English Charles II, to Molyneaux's conspiracy, Mrs. Charlotte Anderson's almost satanic deception of Harry and Zulieme, coming at last to deceit between brother and brother, and mother and daughter. The narrator's moral evaluation of a character ultimately comes down to whether or not he tells the truth to others and to himself.

By the time Simms published *Cassique* he had travelled to the North many times. He had, no doubt, heard more than a few comments about the uniqueness of Southerners in general and about Southern gentlemen in particular. The nineteenth-century view of Southerners as aristocrats was common, although many disagreed about what made up the essence of aristocracy. Some who looked at the South from an outsider's vantage point claimed Southern aristocracy was based either on bloodline or wealth. Simms's narrator, however, affirms that the true gentleman is determined not by blood or possessions, but by character. *The Cassique of Kiawah* is essentially an investigation into the importance of character.

At the heart of Simm's notion of high character lies a commitment to honesty and personal integrity. The world of Kiawah sanctifies these personal and social values. The model for high character is the Biblical God who, as the prophets remind us, is righteous, just, and loyal. Above all, He is the God who is faithful to His word. Personal honesty, integrity, and commitment are but the imitations of divine attributes. To find this Biblical God in the depths of one's soul is to transcend the deceit and vanity of the world, simply because the God within is the same God who reigns beyond in Heaven above.

The potential greatness of individual character is the essential theme of *The Cassique of Kiawah*. Harry Calvert, a swashbuckler who transcends his mould, is Simms's chief illustration. All the others in the novel, including his brother Edward, are measured by their relationship to him. He overcomes foolishness, greed, slander, disloyalty, betrayal, and superior odds. He must tame his shrewish wife Zulieme, confront his treacherous lieutenant Molyneaux, deal with the hypocrisy of Mrs. Charlotte Anderson, counter the attacks of the Spanish and hostile Indians, endure the policy changes of King Charles II, and settle his own emotional obsession with Olive, his brother's wife. Upon his efforts and industry does the survival of the Charleston settlement depend as well as the safety of those in his own charge and care. The hero of *The Cassique of Kiawah*, then, is an English privateer who manages against great odds to save himself, his family, his ship and crew, an entire settlement, and (with the narrator's help) perhaps even the reader.

Simms, who thought the whole purpose of civilization was to create sovereign persons embodying the deepest and richest elements of culture, believed that a culture's literature should preserve the old verities. His model for the hero of *Cassique* is based on the deepest roots of Western culture — the ancient classical and Hebrew ideals of personhood. Harry Calvert is Simms's perfect hero, because he is a blending of the classical and Biblical interpretations of successful character, an embodiment of the ideals of the epic hero and the Biblical man of integrity. Periods have existed in Western culture which were unique blendings of these deepest roots. Milton's seventeenth- century London, which existed in the same historical period as that in which *Cassique* is set,was based on such a blending. So too was the Charleston of Simms's day. Its amalgamation of Greek and Hebrew cultures was apparent in the conscious and tacit combination of the oldest and deepest strains of Western culture. Simms takes both of these ancient Western traditions and blends them into a uniquely American hero — a character who solves problems directly and risks his life fighting for what he knows is right. In spite of his melancholy, Harry Calvert embodies a feeling of self-worth and a sense of moral obligation. He is building authentic culture. He is an Englishman making a new world in the wilderness. He is a self-ruler, an independent man. He is a sovereign self. *Cassique*, then, is a study of heroic personality, and heroic personality becomes a model for sovereign selfhood, which Simms sees as the basis for significant culture.

Simms was also strongly influenced by Anglo-Saxon culture and literature. He was an advocate and defender of English society, and especially the values of English literature. We see that influence in *The Cassique of Kiawah*, which is full of appeals and references to English literature and ideals. Simms's hero, we note, resembles Shakespeare's Prince Hal, the ideal English monarch who displays courage, temperance, wisdom and fortitude. Both Shakespeare's Prince and Simms's early American Harry embody personal excellence and a sense of social justice. As Shakespeare's history play *I Henry IV* is a work whose meaning is found in the hero himself, so is the notion of cassiqueness the focus of meaning in Simms's novel. Just as the ideal English prince is virtuous and moral, so also is the Colonial Harry Calvert, who makes his people good because he himself is good. Both heroes inspire us by example to be like them.

Echoing Shakespeare's assessment of England in the history plays and of Providence in *Hamlet*, Harry says to one of his trusted friends: "England is too important to the world's safety and progress, not to find a special Providence interposing in her behalf" (199). The reader gradually surmises that Harry himself may be the spiritual guardian of the tiny American settlement in the hands of a "special Providence." Harry's approach to adversity illustrates both his princely qualities and his special role. Faced with overwhelming odds — the "gathering of the Indians on Savannah," "the cunning and hostility of the Spaniards," the treachery of intimates — Harry gives advice to Governor Quarry that echoes Prince Hamlet's "Let be": "Keep cool; be calm . . . . Why should I rage? Why tremble? The arrow flies, whether we weep or sing . . . Be cool, sir, and wait events, and do not force them" (410). And before his deadly duel with Molyneaux, Harry gives his treacherous lieutenant one last chance to be honest and confess his malice. So even when the hero takes human life, he does not attack first.

In *Cassique* Harry's competence as a sailor and captain is recognized by all. We see him skillfully elude the English warships *Dragon* and *Thunderbolt,* and sail on to safe harborage in Stono Bay. His skills clearly surpass those of the English captains: the rosewater aristocrat Sir Everard and the punch drinking Pogson. We are never led to doubt Harry's devotion to England. Just prior to his heroic efforts against the Spanish dons, Harry will not fire upon the pursuing English ships. Superior commander that he is, Harry displays his authority again and again, as in the Indian "battle of Kiawah, one of the most sanguinary of the thousand fights of the old colonial periods in our English settlements" (587). He leads fifty of his men over land to the Barony of Kiawah, deploys them to strategic locations, and knowing himself to be greatly outnumbered by the Indians, he manages the fighting in such a way as to take full advantage of European weapons. His single combat with club and tomahawk against the mightiest Indian of all is Harry's climactic heroic act.

Harry is a romantic sufferer in the best English style. In spite of the sentimental stereotypes — the domineering mother, the shrewish wife, tears, swooning, natural depravity and innate innocence — *The Cassique of Kiawah* succeeds as a novel of sentiment. This aspect of the book centers around the various love triangles, some genuine and others satirical. Harry's love for the Anglo-Saxon Olive is as tearful and melancholy as any nineteenth-century story of woe. Harry resolves his love conflict, but Olive is not so strong. She loves one brother, but is married to another. Her tale is one of high romance filled with pity and suffering. She faints many times, both day and night. Sleep, food, and drink are of no interest to her. She grows thin and wastes away. Her eyes become terrible to look upon, and she turns deathly pale. She prefers solitude to company, and wanders alone, wailing and moaning. Her spirits grow feeble, for she suffers from the malady of love and melancholy. Her distress, sorrow, and sadness are all the products of falling hopelessly in love and then breaking her vows, largely because of the treachery of Mrs. Masterton, who is the real snake of death and destruction in the Edenic garden of Kiawah. Alas the woe, alas the loss, alas the depravity of mankind. No medieval Knight's tale wrings out more pity and grief. The total effect of the sentiment, both genuine and satirical, is to stress the human side of Harry, his suffering and melancholy, as well as his mythic qualities. Sentiment, then, is not an object in itself, but is a means for enlarging the hero.

Lieutenant Molyneaux's love suffering, a counterfeit version of Harry's true sentiments, is feigned to seduce Zulieme. Languid, sad, and wretched he appears, all because of his love affliction for his captain's wife. But the vain lieutenant meets his match in Harry, who gives him every opportunity to become honest and truthful. Their final confrontation only serves to heighten Harry's greatness. Harry honors the young man's last request and buries him at sea, wrapped in a mattress so that the sharks will not lacerate his vanity.

Molyneaux's pretenses are only a slightly higher hypocrisy than the posturings of the cavaliers Keppel Craven and Cornwall Cavendish. These dandies share similar designs on Zulieme and remind us "what admirable courtiers England can send forth" (353). The airs of these fops transplanted from the court of King Charles II, along with Molyneaux's feigns, are only a small part of Simms's splendid satire which is scattered throughout *Cassique*. As Paul Hamilton Hayne says of Simms's acknowledged ability to portray character: "Few men have ever comprehended human nature more thoroughly, and he could not refrain from caricaturing its weaknesses, although there was never a drop of venom in his heart."[6] Although some of his best satire is of the aristocratic pretensions of Mrs. Charlotte Anderson, Simms does not limit himself to social satire. He often displays his ability to caricature the weakness of human nature and shows himself very adept at mocking the personal passions of vanity, greed, lust, and envy. Like some of the English satirists he admired — especially Thackery and Dickens — Simms is a master at creating characters who embody human weaknesses. Simms's satire, though, is only another way to point to the potential greatness of true character.

Mrs. Charlotte Anderson's masquerade ball is the perfect vehicle for social satire. It represents the human propensity to feign, to mince, to pretend, to destroy. It is Simms's symbol for the worst of civilization: a superior feeling and destructive hypocrisy which is fashionable, the self-deception that our blindest concoctions are true. It illustrates the narrator's claim that our reasoning is a strumpet when based on false assumptions and vain commitments.

Into this social world of masquerading, pretending, and vain striving for false and superficial ends, Simms inserts the child-like Zulieme. She, who earlier was a thorn in the side of her husband's flesh, becomes in the middle of the novel a medium for social satire. She is young, innocent, and foreign; and thus she can observe the hypocrisy and greed of English colonial society: the hypocrisy of her hostess, the ludicrous deceptions of fops, and the manipulation of the colonial council. From her point of view, the narrator can comment on some of the ills which threaten civilization more than invaders or savages. Simms uses Zulieme in *Cassique* in much the same way Clemens uses Huckleberry Finn in his satire of life along the Mississippi: she is an outsider with a sound heart viewing a civilized world of deformed values and actions. The best efforts of Mrs. Anderson and her gallants to compromise the virtue of Zulieme come to naught when the Spanish beauty intuits the nature of those who would betray her husband and chooses instead to remain faithful to him, even though doing so means being out of fashion. Mrs. Anderson's campaign to corrupt Harry's young wife provides ultimately a way for Zulieme to demonstrate her simple intuition and loyalty.

Charlotte Anderson's attempts to persuade Zulieme to revel in unbridled freedom are not unlike Sam Fowler's earlier arguments for piracy when he compels some of Harry's crew to adopt The Jolly Roger. Her arguments against the bonds of marriage and fidelity in relationships echo Satan's arguments in *Paradise Lost* and illustrate the perversion of logic in the service of rebellious intellect seeking to elevate self and to subdue others. Zulieme gives expression to old fashioned righteousness when she says, "I don't . . . care a bit about [Keppel]; and I'm very sure if Harry thought he was making love to me, he'd wring [Keppel's] neck" (435). At the climax of this *bal costume* are three gallants — drunk and vain — fighting over a married woman, whose good heart and devotion to her husband make her an impossible prize to win. After the satire of the masquerade ball, the narrator gives his intimate reader a marvellously realistic description of Charleston in 1684. The location and setting of this gala affair, after all, is a bit primitive, again reminding us to put social pretensions in perspective: today's envy and fashion will be tomorrow's scorn and pity.

At the beginning of the novel, Zulieme fights to master her husband. She is by habit spoiled, flighty, flirtatious, and contentious. She wants only to have fun, and her values are definitely worldly. Simms gives us an eighteenth-century image of fickleness when he paints the foolish young shrew swinging in the forest, surrounded by admirers. Although music and dancing stimulate her Spanish blood, her heart and head are not wanton or lacking in virtue. She will flirt to music, but slap a partner who dares to kiss her, or argue with a hostess who counsels infidelity. As the novel progresses, Zulieme matures and concentrates on keeping her marriage vows rather than on competing for domestic dominance.

At the end of the novel Zulieme becomes in her own right a heroine. As childish as she is, she has the intuition to perceive the significance of her husband, and the devotion to be loyal to him. This growth in her character is a result of the taming influence of our hero. Harry is Zulieme's model of manhood, and compared to him no foppish gallant from a European court measures up. Before the city council at the governor's residence, she bravely offers her life for her husband. She has learned that she cannot dominate him, and she has chosen not to betray him either by committing adultery or by revealing his whereabouts. Her loyalty to Harry is even more commendable than her instincts. Zulieme's greatest gift to Harry, and the sign that she is maturing, is a personal secret she will tell only him. The novel, like many a romance before it, ends happily with the good news that Zulieme and Harry are going to start their own family.[7]

The narrator is in many ways the main character of the novel. He functions at times like a supreme director, staging the entire drama. He dresses and places the characters, introduces and explains them, giving an abundance of information as if to actors preparing to play their parts. He manages his characters and our relations to them. His skillfulness illustrates Simms's dramatic sense and reminds us of the author's life-long devotion to the theater.

Sometimes the narrator functions as an historian. "This is a history," he says, and so he educates the reader, telling about the "humble little colony on the banks of the Cooper and the Ashley" (134). The narrator tells us about the nobility, the aristocrats, the fashionables — the palatines, landgraves, cassiques, barons. Especially at the end of the novel is the narrator an historian, as in his descriptions of the battle of Port Royal (532) after the Spanish sack and destroy the Scotch colony of Beaufort. He is equally informed about Indians and their habitat and habits, as when he explains the necessity of moving "Indian file" through the forest (542). As historian he labels the fierce battle on the Barony of Kiawah "The War with the Stono Indians" (587), which — he reminds us — may be read and studied in history books. The narrator's own history, though, deals with how the famous rover Harry Calvert saves the colonial settlement from destruction. As in all his historical works, Simms models many of his characters and events on history.

Simms's narrator functions in yet another way. This overriding and controlling intelligence is witty and wise. He has lived long and looks at the world through the perspective of common sense and traditional morality. He develops an intimate relationship with the reader, and will even interrupt an exciting narrative because it is time to go to bed (426). He understands human nature, and by looking carefully at the world and by making his conversational judgments, he both delineates and clarifies. His omniscient intelligence, unlike Harry's, does not fail. He is truthful, honest and moral, and quickly we learn to trust him and accept his account of the action and characters. He hovers over the sovereign rover like the Master Sovereign over the world, and his wisdom is the final manifestation of cassiqueness.

Throughout the novel the narrator is distinguished by his fierce love for truth and honesty. He perceives the multi-dimensions of his characters; then he portrays them realistically. When Zulieme early in the novel acts like a spoiled and pampered child, the narrator tells us so without ambiguity. Similarly, when she begins to mature, the narrator is present to comment on the achievement. His satiric humor is focused on human nature and its ubiquitous bent toward deceit. Amid the personal subterfuge and the mincings of society, the friendly narrator reveals the source of his satire: "Give me honest flesh and blood, I say, to all these things of paste and putty!" (430). His outrage at deception in all its manifestations — both socially and personally — is the motive of his satire. His insight into society and human nature is not from the point of view of an outsider trying to understand, but rather from the perspective of a friend who looks closely at people and does not always like what he sees.

In the middle of the novel, the narrator comes to the heart of his point about character and human nature. He begins Chapter XXXIII by discussing the vaunted "distinguishing attribute of man" — reason. But, he argues, reason is only a "hound that hunts for us the game which our lusts and appetites, and vanities and ridiculous ambitions, are perpetually starting". In "the great farce of Society" hardly "a single person" builds his reason upon the truth. Instead, "the passions, using reason as a tool, cut the throat of human wisdom" (315). Reason is the tool of our vanities and our passions: one of the narrator's chief insights into human nature. Thus our civilization for all its flaunted greatness is no higher than our best individuals. Through his guidance as narrator and the interaction between himself and the reader, this complex presence develops the heroism of Harry Calvert into a model of ideal personal existence and autonomous selfhood. In this manner the spiritual, and consequently true cassique of Kiawah, finally becomes an image of the sovereign self as understood and interpreted by Simms in 1859.

The narrator shares the Anglo-Saxon belief in European supremacy. He talks about the superiority of the Anglo-Saxon — tall, straight, muscular, noble, and dignified in appearance. At the top is "the genuine English mould . . . the most beautiful of all living models" for manhood (24). The English excel also in moral capabilities — superior to the red and the black savage, as well as to the Spaniard.

One of the acute social problems in nineteenth-century America was ethnic diversity in the North American population. The cultural and racial conflict between the Indians and the European settlers underlies the whole novel. Simms's Colonial Romances are two of the finest books about Indians written in the nineteenth-century. *The Yemassee*, which Thomas Nelson Page thought was Simms's best book, and *The Cassique of Kiawah*, one of the great masterpieces of nineteenth-century fiction, were both written when the Indians, for all practical purposes, had been removed from or exterminated in both the North- and Southeast. Simms's narrator in *Cassique* expresses grief over this calamity. He indicates the problem with colonial Indians was that they inhabited land the Europeans wanted to civilize — "the life of civilization usurping the domain of the savage" (206). Because the culture of the Indians was primitive, they were ultimately overwhelmed by technical superiority.

Edward Berkeley — voicing the English interpretation of and solution to the "Indian problem" — speculates about the nature and destiny of the aboriginal Americans, the wild man of the forest, as European civilization spreads: "There is a nature which the great God of the universe designs for each several place and people. The wild for the wild; else would it never be made tame. But when, in the great forests, the wild beasts shall all be subdued or slaughtered, will the wild man rise to higher uses? Hath his humanity a free susceptibility for enlargement and other provinces? Shall he feel the growth in his breast and brain, of higher purposes? . . . If it may not be thus, then must he perish, even as the forests perish; he will not survive the one use for which all his instincts and passions seem to be made! It is, perhaps, his destiny!" (513-14).

Immediately we see the self-destruction of the Indian boy, Iswattee, who was consecrated by his people to achieve a "national revenge" upon the white people he had come to serve. The young boy is hopelessly torn between his loyalties. His "nauseous decoctions" and black and crimson liquors brewed in superstition do not provide a solution to his conflict. Simms is compassionate towards the Indians, whom he knew and understood as well as any other nineteenth-century American writer. In *The Cassique of Kiawah*, Simms expresses grief over their destruction.

Simms clearly states that the notion of the dominance of European civilization, associated with the white race, is a national belief in Manifest Destiny, not just Southern. The exploitation of Indians was an old business "practiced . . . from the Plymouth rock to the capes of Florida; by the Pilgrim Fathers as by the Cavaliers; and, indeed, the example of setting the red men at loggerheads, slaughtering the warriors, and selling their wives and children into slavery, was set by the virtuous people of Massachusetts Bay, who justified it from Scripture, in numerous delectable texts, at the cost of the heathen" (589).

The most racially "superior" character in the novel is the Puritan Gideon Fairchild, who boasts his "blood's the nateral, white, pure blood of 'the pilgrims,' that come out of the Mayflower — genooyne Saxon, without a cross. The family of Fairchild was about the first that ever planted a foot on the Plymouth rock," (422) so says the good New Englander, who is constantly searching for a way to make a profit. In Gideon Fairchild, Simms satirizes the greed and hypocrisy of Puritans who would "buy the scalps of the warriors, and sell the souls of their women and children -- bodies, rather; the souls wouldn't bring a stiver in any good Christian market!" (411). Gideon, who is employed by that other virtuous Puritan, the religious hypocrite Sylvester, feels superior to "the red, painted devilish sons of Satan — the Injins" (419) as well as to the black slaves.

In order to escape Harry's imprisonment in *The Happy-go-Lucky* Fairchild elicits the help of the slave girl Sylvia, whom he promises to marry after they have escaped to freedom. The gullible Sylvia learns the hard way about her Northern deliverer, who not only "ignores his promise of marriage" but also schemes to sell the simple girl for a profit. With such good blood in his veins, the best "in all Plymouth, and Massachusetts to boot," it just wouldn't do "to cross it . . . anless for a good consideration." He was, as the narrator reminds us, "decidedly opposed to negro slavery" in the abstract, "but there is, as every virtuous Christian knows and understands, a very substantial difference between a slave to keep and a slave to sell" (421).

Simms's conception of heroism and sovereign character in *Cassique* depends no more on race than it does on wealth or blood. The characters who follow Harry do so, not because they are slaves to a white man, but because they recognize and acknowledge his superiority — a genuine heroism rarely achieved among ordinary men. Regarding race, Simms makes the point that the notion of white superiority in the nineteenth century was American, and not just Southern. But Simms is arguing for something deeper than racial equality: the philosophical narrator in *The Cassique of Kiawah* is committed above all to a notion of greatness of character, a belief in individual autonomy and personal sovereignty, the major commitment of Western culture that has grown out of our deepest roots. If Simms failed to apply that ideal equally to all races, then he was reflecting his times. What is most important, though, is that he grasped fully the standard and commitment, and understood its origins. If Simms's application of the model was restricted according to contemporary insight, he certainly did not blur the clarity of the standard nor confuse its significance and depth. Simms's vision of the essence of sovereign selfhood is much clearer than many contemporary perceptions, and by reading him we come to understand better who we are and where we are going.

In 1859 when Simms published *The Cassique of Kiawah*, Charleston was alive with secessionist talk. Simms, who all his life had defended the South, was very much aware of deep social problems that lay at the heart of American society. He understood culture conflicts between European whites, on one side, and primitive American Indians and Africans on the other. He understood conflicts between races. His satire of social foibles reflects both his analysis of and remedy for social evils. But even more acutely, Simms was aware of the natural degeneracy of individuals, and he

fully understood that people have a propensity to be greedy, irra-
tional, and deceptive.

In spite of seemingly insurmountable social, cultural, and
personal strife, Simms had faith in the power of individuals to solve
problems caused by deep human differences.  The leaders and
saviors of society, though, had to be heroic, sovereign men and
women who possessed above all else the power of integrity.  What
society needs is men like Harry Calvert, epic characters who could
perceive the truth, overcome insurmountable odds, and deliver the
fledgling settlements of mankind from the destructive forces of
passion.  The appearance, purpose, and character of Harry Calvert
is not unlike that of Simms himself, a man straining to save his
beloved home from destructive forces of greed and hypocrisy,
attitudes frequently attributed to the North in the 1850s.  Part of the
great appeal of *Cassique* is that it records the beliefs of the South's
leading literary figure in the Western model of human nobility and
integrity, rather than in the ideal of materialistic profit.  One of the
single most important ideas throughout Simms's fiction is his belief
in the power of the sovereign self.  In *Cassique*  the fullest embodiment of that idea is the hero.  In Harry Calvert, Simms incorporates
the oldest and richest beliefs about the Western notion of personhood and adapts them into a popular type of swashbuckling hero
salted with sensitivity and sentiment, a uniquely Southern creation
of stout proportions.

Simms's Charleston was rich in tradition and learning. It was
based on the oldest classical, Biblical, and Anglo-Saxon traditions.
These rich threads were woven into the fabric of Simms's world and
imagination.  Not only the coterie of writers of distinction who
centered around Simms and met regularly at Russell's Bookstore,
but also the whole city was alive with learning and culture.[8]  He was
dedicated to the old values and to the South.  Classical and Biblical
literature, Shakespeare, Milton, and English customs all find their
way into Simms's best work.  *The Cassique of Kiawah* illustrates
Simms's devotion to these ideas and values.

Like any masterpiece, *The Cassique of Kiawah* is a multidimensional book. It is enjoyable to read on numerous levels and deserves a place in the highest ranks of nineteenth- century American fiction. Like *Moby-Dick, The Scarlet Letter, Walden*, and *Leaves of Grass, The Cassique of Kiawah* was published in the last decade of national innocence. Never again would America be quite the same. *The Cassique of Kiawah* is one of the last great records of the beliefs and convictions of Old America. It should be recognized today as one of the great documents of a lost culture.

*The Cassique of Kiawah* triumphs as a romance, as a story of adventure, and as a novel of sentiment. Into these popular forms of nineteenth-century fiction Simms pours great insight about the nature of man and society. Much of his thought is the result of a life-time dedication to literature. By 1859 Simms had mastered his craft as a writer and had lived over fifty years observing human nature and character. He was a mature and proven author. He had absorbed his culture and was greatly committed to Western civilization as transported and nourished in nineteenth-century Carolina. He had come to embody our culture's deepest beliefs about the nature and dignity of man. He was able to create great literature to both illustrate and illuminate those beliefs.

As an epigraph to *The Cassique of Kiawah*, Simms wrote a personal poem to W. Porcher Miles. He signed this dedicatory sonnet on April 2, 1859. A year later, at his own expense, he published the same poem as one of three hundred in the *Areytos* collection. Porcher Miles was a professor of math at the College of Charleston, a member of congress, and an old and dear friend. In the poem, Simms indicates that he has dedicated the novel to Miles because of his friend's devotion and loyalty, especially during a twelve-day crisis in September 1858, when Miles sat with Simms at the death bed of two of his young sons who had caught yellow fever: Sidney Roach Simms, who died September 22, 1858, at the age of eight; and Beverley Hammond Simms, who died the following day at the age of six. By all accounts, this loss of his sons was a crushing blow for the famous author, one from which he was very slow to recover. In a letter to his friend Hammond, he says that he is so heart broken over the loss that he cannot write.[9]

Referring to these two boys in an earlier letter written on July 25, 1857, Simms says, "Sydney is puny," but Beverley Hammond "is a stout, powerful, good humoured rowdy Saxon."[10] In the same letter Simms says, "I have just laid the keel of a new romance." That book was *Cassique*. Between the laying of the keel and the death of the boys occurred fourteen months. Another seven months passed before Simms submitted the novel for publication in New York.

Simms had developed the habit of reading and writing as a child when he was often solitary, moody, and even wretched about the conditions of his life: the deaths of his mother and two brothers, his own poor health, and long separations from his father.[11] Thus at an early age Simms learned the art of self-therapy through writing. Reading books and writing became a way for him to adjust to family and personal problems. Young Simms's first library was a candle-lighted box into which he crawled at night after curfew during the years he was being cared for by his maternal grandmother, Mrs. Gates. She was a strict woman, about the age of Simms's father, who managed her grandson's life and inheritance. Performing psychological therapy on himself was a skill Simms learned as a youthful orphan. It was a well-formed habit by the time Simms practiced it as he finished writing *The Cassique of Kiawah*. This novel, seen as a resolution of a private grief, illustrates how a great writer, through the power of imagination and spirit, can mould a masterpiece from personal calamity.

The key to this most personal level of *Cassique* is the dedicatory poem to Miles. The tone of the sonnet and the tone of the narrator of the novel are similar: a calm acceptance born in the withstanding of some of life's worst crises, a tranquility of spirit derived from making peace with a world that allows the death of children.

From the first word of the novel, "Suppose," the narrator challenges the reader to use his imagination to enter a "hallowed" land which has not been polluted by man, an eternal, spiritual world that "is as full of bliss as of beauty," where "Love may readily find a covert, in thousands of sweet places of refuge, which God's blessing shall convert into happiest homes." This world of Kiawah is "circumscribed only by the blue walls of Heaven, and watched by starry eyes." Into this world "Death himself never comes but wrapped in fragrance and loveliness" (12). By entering this mysterious world, the reader becomes marvellously refreshed, if he has eyes to see and ears to hear. Simms's imaginary world of Kiawah is the Garden of Eden, the American landscape before the coming of the white man's civilization, and a spiritual world of the eternal present.

Into this setting emerges a host of realistically drawn characters displaying the vices of vanity, greed, hypocrisy, and treachery. This same Edenic, colonial, and spiritual home of the Presence — this hallowed balm to the human spirit — is also the home Simms creates for his two sons who had just died of yellow fever. He pictures them having grown into young men. The elder son becomes an original settler, and the younger becomes the sovereign savior of Charleston. The eight-year old Sydney is transformed into the stately Edward. Beverley Hammond, the stout Saxon boy, is transformed into Edward's younger brother, Harry Calvert. These "precious boys," as Simms calls them in the dedicatory sonnet, become young men through their father's gift of imagination and embody the virtues a loving father would want to instill in his children. The narrator invites the reader to observe the young men, who look, we note, like Simms himself, becoming legends, larger than life, carving out a culture within the formidable wilderness. They are idealized, epic in proportion, as any father might wish his sons to become. The privateer Harry, who is a protective spirit, incarnates some of Simms's deepest beliefs about heroism and personal sovereignty.

Our guide through this layered setting is the narrator, who takes the reader into his spiritual world that he dates in the first years of Charleston. At times the narrator is father to his children. He humanizes the legend. The initial idealized and dreamy portrayal of Harry prepares us for the reprimands, the gentle warnings, and the loving rebukes. Playing the role of kind father to his children, the narrator offers the wise advice and counsel the grieving Simms would never be able to share with his own lost sons. The romanticized portrayal of his boys, through the wisdom of the narrative voice, changes into realistic analysis, even satire. Sometimes he is proud of his children, and sometimes he chides. This wise narrator satirizes romanticism, and at times he satirizes his own children, and sometimes even himself.

To the reader, the narrator is above all a dear friend. He is a confidant who summons the reader as an intimate, a tolerant voice of wisdom and gentle irony. He maintains an intimacy that instills confidence, a sense of justice, and a tongue-in-cheek humor. He befriends the reader from the first, and asks him to suppose and imagine. Why create beauty where it isn't? Because, he explains, beauty speaks of the mystery of eternity. There is life in death, he counsels. The death of Simms's sons creates the life of Simms's tale. Simms, the grieving parent, gains insight and inspiration in the creation of the tale, which he then shares with his readers. With confidence and intimacy, the narrator counsels and patiently waits. Simms's tribute to Porcher Miles, his "More than friend/Beloved evermore," is to embody the spirit of his dear friend in the wise narrator of the novel.

Clearly Simms knew what it was like to watch the dying. Long before Elizabeth Kubler-Ross, Simms offers a realistic appraisal of dying, notably in the description of Olive. The narrator's description of the suffering Olive goes far beyond the typical sentimental fascination with death and indicates an acute awareness of death and dying that comes only after days and weeks at the bedside of dying people. As her infirmities increase, Olive's mind becomes more clear and her spirit "was at one with that joy of peace which reposes on assured hopes and the purest affections, and harmonizes every doubt in faith" (521). The musical death of Olive is in marked contrast to the howling and whooping of the savages in battle.

Harry's request for Olive's son suggests a conflict Simms himself lived through as a youth, when his father left him in the care of his maternal grandmother and traveled to the Southwest to seek his fortune.[12] Edward's objections to Harry's raising the youth echo what must have been Mrs. Gates's reasons for breaking her promise to Simms's father to return the boy after the father was established:

Edward says he does not want to lose his son, and he knows that if Harry takes him, he will lose him. In the novel, there is a happy ending for Harry, who in spite of losing Olive's son, has good reason to hope for one of his own from the faithful Zulieme.

Olive and Zulieme are paired heroines. This pairing is only one of many harmonies in the novel. In appearance, Olive is very English — tall, straight, and fair — while Zulieme is the quintessential type of the Spanish zequita. Simms's own first wife, the blue-eyed, golden-haired Anna Malcom Giles, died February 19, 1832, after their brief four-year marriage. The romance and marriage were "doomed from the outset by Anna's lingering tubercular illness."[13] She was the love of his youth and a haunting presence throughout his life. In his poetry, Simms records feeling her presence years after her death.[14] Their only child Anna Augusta is mentioned often in his letters, and he was passionately attached to this child until his death. It is very likely that Simms had his first wife in mind when he portrays Olive, who in spite of her significance in the life of Harry Calvert, seems dead even before she dies. The wise, fatherly narrator accuses Harry of believing a lie when our hero feels that he cannot love his living wife Zulieme because he committed himself previously to the shadowy Olive.

The dark-eyed, dark-haired Chevillette, whom Simms married when she was 18 and he was 30, is a prototype of Zulieme. Simms's second wife had the "face of an angel," with large dark eyes. She "sang sweetly, and played upon the piano and the guitar,"[15] echoing Zulieme's interest in music. Simms made a home and a life with Chevillette. Reflecting Harry's indebtedness to Zulieme and her father who provided the *Happy-go-Lucky,* Simms inherited the plantation of Woodlands from Chevillette's father, the place that became "his delight and refuge until the end of his days."[16] Simms's portrayal of Zulieme is one of the triumphs of the novel and illustrates his mastery at depicting female characters.

Harry's love for Olive while being married to the beautiful Zulieme probably reflects yet another area in which Simms mirrors the tensions and dynamics of his own life in his writing. Harry's resolution to be both faithful to, and responsible for, Zulieme to whom he feels indebted, and also to love her as a woman, is a development the wise, fatherly narrator commends. Very likely, then, Simms was using his art as, among other things, serious therapy — an opportunity to vent pent-up difficulties and to objectify intense and profound emotional experiences.

In *The Cassique of Kiawah*, William Gilmore Simms has created a masterpiece that depicts a notion of heroism within the trappings of nineteenth-century popular fiction. The concept is present throughout the novel, but focused on the hero Harry Calvert. It is a notion that builds on the deepest traditions of Western culture — classical, Biblical, and Anglo-Saxon. Simms made ample use of the machinery of romance: paired brothers, dark-light heroines, and love triangles. But he imbues these romantic props with his own life and experience. The dream world of his imagination and his own personal life overlap, and the one is enriched by the other. Losing two sons within hours, being a husband and father, having two wives — and many other personal experiences — become a layer that he places over his novel. Edward and Harry are Simms's romantic creations of Old Carolina heroes; they are also images of Western heroism as Simms perceived it; and they are finally enduring tributes of a father to his lost children. As a final tribute Simms bestows a sovereign selfhood on his "precious boys," not only by imagining them as adults in the mysterious world of Kiawah, but also by making them heroes of personal greatness. Such is the grieving father's tribute to his lost sons.


David Aiken
University of Georgia

# Notes

1. Hezekiah Butterworth, *A Zigzag Journey in the Sunny South* (Boston: Estes and Lauriat, 1886), 176. Butterworth, who was the Boston editor of The Ziggag Series and *Youth's Companion*, solicited a Hayne article on Simms, which he then published in both organs. Butterworth printed an abridged version of Hayne's sketch in *Youth's Companion* [59 (January 21, 1886), 19-20.] and the whole piece in *Zigzag*.

2. The *Fundamental Constitutions*, believed written by the noted British philosopher John Locke (1632-1704), envisions the Carolina settlement as a feudal society with an hereditary aristocracy, appointed initially by landed proprietors. Landgraves were the highest ranking nobility, and cassiques were next. The *Constitutions* were never adopted, although they left their mark on the colony.

3. Mary Ann Wimsatt, *The Major Fiction of William Gilmore Simms* (Baton Rouge: LSU Press, 1989) briefly discusses *Cassique* as a romance balanced with social realism. Her statement of the framing of the novel is worth quoting: Simms "employs the clash, well documented in seventeenth-century history, between England and Spain over their New World possessions. Earlier in the era, Charles II of England had commissioned privateers like Simms's hero Harry Berkeley to prey on Spanish ships. The Treaty of Madrid, however, had brought peace and had guaranteed to England the safety of her American holdings; royal decree therefore branded privateers as pirates and outlaws. Simms's use of piracy as a subject allows him to exploit the charm and danger of a picturesque occupation, to hint at crime, and yet to stress that his hero is at bottom far more virtuous than the government that condemns him" (186).

4. *William Gilmore Simms* (New York: Houghton, Mifflin and Company, 1892), 366.

5.  *Southern Quarterly Review,*  13 (January 1845), 103-123.
"Literature of the Bible" is a review-essay which begins by praising
*Harper's Pictorial Bible,* a book reviewed by Simms one year earlier
in Critical Notices of *Southern Quarterly Review* [9 (January 1844),
257-264)].   Neither the review-essay or the Critical Notices is
signed, but internal evidence and a January 26, 1844 letter to George
Frederick Holmes indicate Simms's authorship [Mary C. Simms
Oliphant, Alfred Taylor O'Dell, and T. C. Duncan Eaves, eds., *The
Letters of William Gilmore Simms* (Columbia: University of South
Carolina Press, 1952), I, 399].   Hereafter cited as *Letters*.

6.  "Ante-Bellum Charleston," *Southern Bivouac,* I (October 1885),
12.  Hayne's sketch of Simms is in the second of a three-part essay,
appearing in the September, October, and November issues.

7.  For a different interpretation of Zulieme, see Anne M. Blythe,
"William Gilmore Simms's *The Cassique of Kiawah* and the Principles of His Art," *Long Years of Neglect:" The Work and Reputation of William Gilmore Simms*, ed. John Caldwell Guilds (Fayettev-
ille: The University of Arkansas Press, 1988), 37-59.   Blythe's
review of the publication history of *Cassique* and her notes are
especially worth reading.  This  article is the first serious criticism
devoted exclusively to *Cassique*.

8.  Jay B. Hubbell, *The South in American Literature 1607- 1900*
(Durham: Duke University Press, 1954), 568-571.

9. "Oh! dear Hammond, weep for me! I am crushed to earth. I have
buried in one grave, within twelve hours of each other, my two brave
beautiful boys, Sydney, & your little namesake, Beverley Hammond, two as noble little fellows as ever lived.  It was a dreadful
struggle of 12 days with one, & nine with the other.  It is a terrible
stroke of fate, leaving us almost desolate.  I feel heart broken, hope
crushed, and altogether wretched.  I can write no more.  God's

blessing upon you & yours" (*Letters,* IV, 93).

10. *Letters*, III, 504.

11. *Letters*, I, lxii.

12. *Letters, I, lx-lxi.*

13. *Letters*, I, cxlviii.

14. I am indebted to James E. Kibler, Jr., in conversation, for many insights into Simms's poetry. *The Selected Poetry of Simms* will be available in 1990 from the University of Georgia Press.

15. *Letters*, I, lxxvii.

16. *Letters*, I, lxxviii.

# WORKS OF WILLIAM GILMORE SIMMS

### Uniform Edition, 12mo. Illustrated by Darley.

PRICE $1.25 EACH.

———•◦•———

## *REVOLUTIONARY TALES.*

I.—THE PARTISAN. A ROMANCE OF THE REVOLUTION.

II.—MELLICHAMPE; A LEGEND OF THE SANTEE.

III.—KATHARINE WALTON, or, THE REBEL OF DOR-CHESTER.

IV.—THE SCOUT; or, THE BLACK RIDERS OF THE CON-GAREE.

V.—WOODCRAFT; or, THE HAWKS ABOUT THE DOVE-COTE.

VI.—THE FORAYERS; or, THE RAID OF THE DOG-DAYS.

VII.—EUTAW. A SEQUEL TO THE FORAYERS.

———

## *BORDER ROMANCES OF THE SOUTH.*

VIII.—GUY RIVERS. A TALE OF GEORGIA.

IX.—RICHARD HURDIS. A TALE OF ALABAMA.

X.—BORDER BEAGLES. A TALE OF MISSISSIPPI.

XI.—CHARLEMONT. A TALE OF KENTUCKY.

XII.—BEAUCHAMPE; or, THE KENTUCKY TRAGEDY.

XIII.—CONFESSION; or, THE BLIND HEART.

———

XIV.—THE CASSIQUE OF KIAWAH. A COLONIAL TALE.

XV.—THE YEMASSEE. A ROMANCE OF SOUTH CAROLINA.

XVI.—SOUTHWARD, HO! A SPELL OF SUNSHINE.

XVII.—THE WIGWAM AND CABIN.

XVIII.—VASCONSELOS. A ROMANCE OF THE NEW WORLD.

XIX.-XX.—POEMS — DESCRIPTIVE, DRAMATIC, LEGENDARY, AND CONTEMPLATIVE. With a PORTRAIT on Steel. 2 volumes, 12mo. cloth. Price $2 50.

THE CASSIQUE OF KIAWAH

THE

# CASSIQUE OF KIAWAH

A

## COLONIAL ROMANCE

By WILLIAM GILMORE SIMMS, Esq.

AUTHOR OF "THE YEMASSEE" — "THE PARTISAN" — "GUY RIVERS"—
"SCOUT" — "CHARLEMONT" — "VASCONSELOS" — ETC., ETC.

"I pray you let us satisfy our eyes,
 With the memorials, and the things of fame
 That do renown our city."            SHAKESPEARE.

REDFIELD

34 BEEKMAN STREET, NEW YORK

1859

SAVAGE & MᶜCREA, STEREOTYPERS,
13 Chambers Street, N. Y.

TO

# HON. W. PORCHER MILES, M. C.

O FRIEND ! who satt'st beside me in the hour
    When Death was at my hearth ; and in my home
    The mother's cry of wailing for that doom,
Long hovering, which, at last, with fatal power
Descended, like the vulture on his prey,
    And in his talons bore away our young ! —
    Thou know'st how terribly this heart was wrung :
Thou cam'st with watch and soothing, night and day,
No brother more devoted ! — More than friend,
    Belovéd evermore, — behold me thine ! —
    Yet have I little worthy that is mine,
Save love, and this poor tribute ; which must blend
With memories of thy watch, and of our pain,
And of those precious boys, we both have watched in vain !

W. GILMORE SIMMS.

WOODLANDS, S. C., *April* 2, 1859.

THE

# CASSIQUE OF KIAWAH.

---

## CHAPTER I.

### SCENE OF ACTION.

"Away! away!
Once more his eyes shall hail the welcome day;
Once more the happy shores without a law."—BYRON.

SUPPOSE the day to be a fine one — calm, placid, and without
a cloud — even such a day as frequently comes to cheer us in
the benign and bud-compelling month of April; — suppose the
seas to be smooth; at rest, and slumbering without emotion; with
a fair bosom gently heaving, and sending up only happy murmurs,
like an infant's after a late passion of tears; suppose the hour
to be a little after the turn of noon, when, in April, the sun, only
gently soliciting, forbears all ardency; sweetly smiles and softly
embraces; and, though loving enough for comfort, is not so oppressive in his attachments as to prompt the prayer for an iceberg
upon which to couch ourselves for his future communion; supposing all these supposes, dear reader, then the voyager, running
close in for the land — whose fortune it is to traverse that portion
of the Atlantic which breaks along the shores of Georgia and the
Carolinas — beholds a scene of beauty in repose, such as will be
very apt to make him forgetful of all the dangers he has passed!
  We shall say nothing of the same region, defaced by strifes of

storm and billow, and blackened by the deluging vans of the equinox.

> " Wherefore tax the past,
> For memories of sorrow ? wherefore ask,
> Of the dark Future, what she grimly keeps
> Of terrors in reserve ?"

Enough for us that the Present holds for us delicious compensation; that the moment is our own, exclusively for beauty; — that the charm of the prospect before us is beyond question; at once prompting the desire to describe, yet baffling all powers of description.

Yet why describe? — since, as Byron deplores —

> " Every fool describes in these bright days."

And yet, the scene is so peculiar, so individual, so utterly unlike that kind of scenery from which the traveller usually extorts his inspiration, that something need be said to make us understand the sources of beauty in a region which so completely lacks in saliency, in elevated outlines, in grand mountainous masses, rugged defiles, and headlong cataracts. Here are none of these. All that you behold — sea, and forest-waste, and shore — all lies level before you. As you see, the very waters do not heave themselves into giant forms, wear no angry crests, leap up with no threatening voices, howl forth nothing of their secret rages! We reject, at this moment, all the usual adjuncts which make ocean awful and sublime; those only excepted which harbor in its magnitude, its solemn sterility of waste, its deep mysterious murmurs, that speak to us ever of eternity, even when they speak in the lowest and most musical of their tones.

In what, then, consists the beauty of the scene? Let us explain, and catalogue, at least, where we may not be able to describe. You are aware, dear readers, that you may set forth, on a *periagua*, or, if you like it better, a sloop, a schooner, or a trim little steamer; and, leaving the shores of Virginia, make your way along those of the Carolinas and Georgia, to Florida, almost entirely landlocked the whole voyage; all along these shores, the billows of the sea, meeting with the descending rivers, have thrown up barrier islands and islets, that fence in the main from its own invasions. Here are guardian terraces of green, covered with dense forests, that rise like marshalled legions along the very margins of the deep. Here are naked sand-dunes, closing avenues between, upon which you may easily fancy that the fairies gambol in the moonlight. Some are sprinkled with our southern palm-tree, the palmetto; others completely covered with this modest growth; others again with oak, and pine, and cypress; and there are still others, whose deep, dense, capacious forests harbor the red deer in abundance; and, skirting many of these islets, are others in process of formation; long stripes of marsh, whose perpetual green, contrasting, yet assimilating beautifully with the glare of sunlight on the sea, so relieves the eye with a sense of sweetness, beauty, freshness, and repose, that you never ask yourself the idle question, of what profit this marsh — its green that bears neither fruits nor flowers — its plumage that brings no grateful odor —its growth without market value? Enough, you say or feel, that, in the regions where you find it, it is a beauty and delight.

And so, you navigate your bark through avenues of sea between these islets and the main; through winding channels where the seas lie subdued, their crests under curb, and resting in beds of green and solitude, only tenanted by simple herds of deer, or by wandering pilgrims of the crane, the curlew, the pelican and duck.

Beyond, the great ocean plain stretches wide and far; and even when it rolls in storm, and its billows break in fury along the islet shores, not half a mile away — all here is safe! On either hand, the sheltering nook invites your prow; quiet harbors open for your reception, and offer security. Here, the creek that creeps like a shining serpent through banks of green; here, the bay that has been scooped out in a half circle, as if purposely to persuade you to harborage — are both present, affording refuge; the great oaks grow close down by the ocean's side, and hang over with such massive shadows, that you see the bath and the boudoir together. You have but to plunge in, and no Naiad takes offence; and, lifting yourself to the shores by the help of that great branch that stretches above the water, there you may resume your fig-leaves with impunity, assured that no prudish eyes have been shocked by your eccentric exhibitions of a nude Apollo!

There is a wondrous charm in this exquisite blending of land and water scape. It appeals very sweetly to the sympathies, and does not the less excite the imagination because lacking in irregular forms and stupendous elevations. Nay, we are inclined to think that it touches more sweetly the simply human sensibilities. It does not overawe. It solicits, it soothes, beguiles; wins upon us the more we see; fascinates the more we entertain; and more fully compensates than the study of the bald, the wild, the abrupt and stern, which constitute so largely the elements in that scenery upon which we expend most of our superlatives. Glide through these mysterious avenues of islet, and marsh, and ocean, at early morning, or at evening, when the summer sun is about to subdue himself in the western waters; or at midnight, when the moon wins her slow way, with wan, sweet smile, hallowing the hour; and the charm is complete. It is then that the elements all seem to harmonize for beauty. The plain of ocean is spread out, far as the eye can range, circumscribed only by the blue walls of Heaven, and watched by starry eyes, its little billows breaking with loving murmur upon the islet shores — these, silvery light, as swept for fairy footsteps, or, glowing in green, as if roofed for loving hearts; trees, flowers, fragrance, smiling waters, and delicious breezes, that have hurried from the rugged shores of the Cuban, or the gradual slopes of Texas; or farther yet, from still more beautiful gardens of the South, where Death himself never comes but wrapped in fragrance and loveliness :—look where you will, or as you will, and they unite for your conquest; and you grow meek, yet hopeful; excited, yet satisfied; forgetful of common cares; lifted above ordinary emotions; and, if your heart be still a young one, easily persuaded to believe that the world is as full of bliss as of beauty, and that Love may readily find a covert, in thousands of sweet places of refuge, which God's blessing shall convert into happiest homes. Go through these sweet, silent, mysterious avenues of sea and islet, green plain, and sheltering thicket, under the prescribed conditions, at early morning or toward the sunset, or the midnight hour, and the holy sweetness of the scene will sink into your very soul, and soften it to love and blessing, even as the dews of heaven steal, in the night-time, to the bosom of the thirsting plant, and animate it to new developments of fruitfulness and beauty.

And the scenery of the main partakes of the same character, with but the difference of foliage. It spreads upward into the interior, for near a hundred miles, a vast plain, with few inequalities of surface, but wondrously wooded. If, on the one hand, the islets, marshes, and savannahs, make an empire of sweetness and beauty; not less winning are the evergreen varieties that checker the face of the country on the other. Here are tracts of the noble live oak, of the gigantic pine, of the ghostly cypress; groves of each that occupy their several provinces, indicating as many varieties of soil. Amid these are the crowned laurel, stately as a forest monarch, the bay, the beech, the poplar, and the mulberry, not to speak of thousands besides, distinguished either from their use or beauty; and in the shade of these the dogwood flaunts in virgin white; and the lascivious jessamine wantons over their tops in sensuous twines, filling the air with fragrance; and the grape hangs aloft her purple clusters, which she trains over branches not her own, making the oak and the hickory sustain those fruits which they never bear!

And so, in brief transition, you pass from mighty colonnades of open woods to dense thickets which the black bear may scarcely penetrate. At the time of which we propose to write, he is one of the denizens of these regions; here, too, the panther still lurks, watching the sheepfold or the deer! Here the beaver builds his formidable dams in the solitude of the swamp, and the wolf and the fox find their habitations safe. The streams are full of fish, the forests of prey, the whole region a wild empire in which the redman still winds his way, hardly conscious of his white superior, though he already begins to feel the cruel moral presence, in the instinctive apprehensions of his progress. And birds, in vast varieties, and reptiles of the ground, "startlingly beautiful," are tenants still of these virgin solitudes. The great sea-eagle, the falcon, the vulture; these brood in the mighty tree-tops, and soar as masters of the air; the wild goose and duck lead their young along the sedgy basins; the cormorant and the gull scream across the waters from the marshy islets; and are answered, with cooing murmurs, from myriads of doves that brood at noon in the deep covert of bristly pines. The mock-bird, with his various melodies, a feathered satirist, who can, however, forget his sarcasm in his passion; the red-bird and the nonpareil, with softer and simpler

notes, which may be merry as well as tender, but are never scornful; the humming-bird, that rare sucker of sweets — himself a
flower of the air, — pioneer of the fairies — that finds out the best
flowers ere they come, and rifles them in advance; and — but
enough. Very beautiful, dear friends, to the eye that can see,
the susceptible heart, and the thoughtful, meditative mind, is the
beautiful but peculiar province to which we now invite your
footsteps.

But, as we can not behold all this various world at once, let us
persuade you to one fair locality, which you will find to contain,
in little, all that we have shown you in sweeping generalities.

You will suppose yourselves upon a well-wooded headland,
crowned with live oaks, which looks out upon a quiet bay, at
nearly equal distances between the waters of the Edisto and the
Ashley, in the province of South Carolina. The islets spread
between you and the sea, even as we have described them.
There are winding ways through which you may stretch your
sail, without impediment, into the great Atlantic. There are
lovely isles upon which you may pitch your tents, and take your
prey, while the great billows roll in at your very feet, and the
great green tree shelters you, all the while, from the sharp arrows
of the sun. You look directly down upon what, at the first glance,
would seem a lake: the lands appear to enclose it on every hand;
but there is a difference, you see, in the shade of yonder trees,
from those on the islet just before us, which is due to the fact that
an arm of the sea is thrust between; and here, on the other hand,
there are similar differences which denote a similar cause. But
our lake, or bay, is none the less sheltered or secure, because it
maintains such close connection with the mighty deeps. Faintly
afar, you may note, on the south and west, that there are still
other islets, keeping up a linked line with that which spreads in
front, and helping to form that unbroken chain, which, as I have
told you, spreads along the coast from the capes of Virginia to
those of the Floridian. The territory of the Floridian is under
its old Spanish master still; an ugly neighbor of our amiable
English, who tenant, in feeble colonies, these sylvan realms upon
the verge of which we stand. The period, I may mention here,
is the year of Grace (Grace be with us!) one thousand, six hundred and eighty-four. Our English colonies of Carolina are less

than thirty years old, and their growth has been a slow one. The country is still, in great degree, a solitude!

The day — an April day — is one of those which good old Herbert so happily describes, by its moral aspect, as

"A bridal of the earth and sky."

In truth, it is very sweet and beautiful, repose its prevailing feature — repose upon land and sea; a smiling Peace, sitting in sunshine in the heavens; a healthy, life-giving breeze gushing up from the ocean, in the southwest, and making all the trees along the shore nod welcome and satisfaction to the river; and new blossoms everywhere upon the land; all significant of that virgin birth which the maternal summer is about to receive from a prolific spring, which God has hallowed for the uses of Humanity.

We muse as we look, and say, with the poet —

"Here all but the spirit of man is divine."

And, as yet, we may venture to say that the spirit of man is hardly so corrupt here — hardly so incongenial with earth's vegetable offspring — as greatly to shock by the contrast. Man — the white man at all events — is hardly here in sufficient numbers, massed and in perpetual conflict, to be wholly insensible to the modest moral which is taught by nature. No doubt we shall have enough of him in time. No doubt we shall be forced to behold him in all his most dark and damning colors, such as shadow the fairest aspects of his superior civilization. But he is not yet here in sufficient force or security to become insolent in his vice or passion.

"But the red man," say you. "He is here." Ay, there are his scattered tribes — they are everywhere; but feeble in all their numbers. He is a savage, true; but savage, let me tell you — and the distinction is an important one, arguing ignorance, not will — savage rather in his simplicity than in his corruptions. His brutality is rather that of barbarism than vice. He wanders through these woods at seasons; here fishing to-day — to-morrow, gone, leaving no trace; gone in pursuit of herds which he has probably routed from old pasturages along these very waters. For a hundred miles above, there rove the tribes of the Stono and the Isundiga, the Edisto and the Seewee, the Kiawah, and the

Ashepoo, all tributaries of the great nation of the Yemassee. You
will wander for weeks, yet meet not a man of them; yet, in the
twinkling of an eye, when you least fancy them, when you dream
yourself in possession of an unbroken solitude, they will spring up
beside the path, and challenge your attention by a guttural, which
may seem to you a welcome; or by a *cri de guerre*, which shall
certainly appear to you the whoop of death!

But, at this moment, the solitude seems intact. There are no
red men here. The very silence — so deep is the solitude —
seems to have a sound; and, brooding long on these headlands
without a companion, you will surely hear some voice speaking to
all your senses — perhaps many voices; especially if you do not
use your own. Your ears, that hunger naturally for human
sounds, will finally make them for themselves. Nay, you will
shout aloud, in your desperation, if only in search of echoes.

And, as if the better to satisfy us of the wondrous means of
shelter and security in this world of thicket and seclusion — adding to the natural picturesque that of the moral — even as we
fancy this realm of solitude to be unbroken, there *is* a sound!
There are strokes of the paddle; there are human voices. A
canoe shoots out from the thickets to the east. It emerges from
a creek, which opens so modestly upon the bay that the entrance
to it remains unseen. The vessel is of cypress, one of those little
"*dug-outs*," which the red men scooped for themselves with shells,
after having first charred with fire those portions of the timber
which they designed to remove. It skims over the waters like
an eggshell, carrying three persons as lightly as if it had no
freight. Two of them, one a man, the other a boy, work at the
paddles — not oars; the instrument is a short one, working close
at the side of the boat, even as the sea-fowl uses her feet. The
third, a man also, gray with years, sits at the stern, his head hanging forward, his eyes brooding on the bottom of the canoe. They
are all red men. He at the stern is evidently a chief. He wears
a sort of coronal of feathers, and a gay crimson coat, hunting-shirt
fashion, with yellow fringes, evidently the manufacture of the
white man. There is a belt across his shoulders, from which
hangs the tomahawk; another about his waist, which secures his
knife; his right hand grasps bow and arrows, though the former
remains unbent, and the latter lie bundled together innocuous in

their rattlesnake quiver. The man who paddles is a common Indian, one of the *vileins,* of poor costume and mean aspect. The boy is habited somewhat like the chief, with crimson hunting-shirt, and belt about the waist, but he carries neither knife nor toma-hawk. A bow and arrows suited to his youth lie behind him at the bottom of the boat. He may use them at yonder turn of the bay, where you see a little flock of English ducks plying their beaks along the sedgy shallows.

The canoe passes out of sight, winding through the sinuous passages of yonder marsh; and for a moment the silence resumes its sway along the shores.

But, almost as soon as they disappear, another party comes upon the scene. And he is a white man. He glides down to the headlands, looking out upon the bay, from the deep shelter of the thicket on our left. From this covert he has watched the progress of the canoe; and there were moments when it swept so closely to his place of watch, that it would have been easy, in the case of one so lithe and vigorous of frame, to have leaped into it at a single bound.

The stranger might be thirty-five or forty; a hale, fresh-look-ing Saxon, with a frank, manly face, bronzed rather darkly by our southern sun, but distinguished only by traits of health. His face is somewhat spoiled for beauty by an ugly scar upon one cheek. He is armed with knife and pistols, which he carries in his girdle. His dress is that of the sailor, loose duck trowsers, a round-jacket, a hat of coarse straw with broad blue ribbons round it, in which sticks an earthen pipe of some bulk, with a stem of Carolina cane. In his hand he carries a ship's spyglass, which seems to have done service.

Following the " *dug-out*" of the red men with keen eyes as they sped, he continued to trace their progress with the glass until they were wholly covered from sight by the dense marshes of the creek. Then, thrusting his glass beneath his arm, he turned away, making a sort of moody march along the shore.

" Blast the red rascals," quoth he musingly, " I can make noth-ing of them. That creek leads out to the sea. But there are islands they can stop at, and I suppose mean to do so. There is Kiawah, and a dozen more, that they may work up to in such a light-going craft. Well, we may look for a plenty of 'em soon,

now that fish begin to bite. But I want to be off before they
come. I've no belief in the redskins anyhow, and want to keep
my own skin sound. Don't want to be stuck full of arrows;
don't want to be fried alive in pitch-pine. A Spanish dance
rather, with a score of pikes at the rear, to keep one in motion
where there's no music!"

And the sturdy Englishman, for he was a genuine John Bull
and of a good order, took the pipe from his hat-band, replenished
the mill from his pocket, kindled his tinder, and throwing himself
down in a thicket, proceeded to smoke, taking out his pipe occasionally to soliloquize. We gather up some of his random talks,
as they may help us in our own progress in this veracious
history.

" No, I've no faith in these redskins. They're at peace, they
say. Oh yes! and will smoke any quantity of tobacco in their
calumets, making their treaties and putting away their presents.
But it's a sort of peace that don't pay for the parchment. Just
so long as the colony's strong enough to lick 'em, and no longer,
will they keep the promise. It's only when they see that they
can't outnumber you — when they can count a bagnet for every
bow — that they've any Christian bowels for peace. I wonder
what chance I'd have here, in this lonesome spot, if these three
redskins now had come upon me napping. Wouldn't they have
been working in my wool, without saying ' By your leave, brother'?
The red devils! call *them* human? I'd as soon trust a monkey,
or a sucking tiger, in the matter of human bowels and affection!"

And the soliloquist lapsed away, after this speech, into that
dreamy sort of condition, which tobacco is so well calculated to
inspire, in which the mind is rather disposed to play than work,
or, at all events, in which it rather broods than cogitates. His
pipe exhausted, he rose, emptied the bowl of its ashes, stuck the
stem into his hat-band, braced his leather girdle closer to his
waist by a notch, and, after a long gaze out upon the sea, saun-
tered away slowly into thicker woods.

As we follow him, we see that he makes his way through a sort
of labyrinth. Such thickets afford at all times a temporary cover;
but he so wound about in the present instance, took up so many
clues, and made such circuits, that, did we not follow him so

closely, we should never, of ourselves, be able to track his progress to his fastness.

This lies in a still deeper thicket which stretches down to a creek. Here he has a den which a bear might select, fenced in by a close shrubbery, overshadowed by great trees, vines interlacing them, and, as it were, wrapping them up into a mass which never allowed a sunbeam to penetrate. Art has done something to make the place snug enough for shelter from the weather. There is a rude hut of poles, covered with bark; within it, there is a box, an iron pot, a gridiron, and a jug. An old tarpaulin hat and coat hang from the same branches. There is a light shotgun in a cypress hollow; and, from all you see, you conclude that our solitary has arranged for an abode that seems destined for continuance awhile, and has been in use perhaps a month or two already.

From this cabin he detaches hooks, line, and tackle, for fishing, and takes his way down to the creek. There, snug in close harbor, lies a skiff, of European build, light enough for a damsel to manage. He embarks, glides down the stream, finds his way into the bay already described, and, crossing toward a recess made by the projection of two arms of the marsh, proceeds to anchor and to cast his line. The position he has chosen is one to render him safe from any shaft or shot from the shore; and we must not forget to mention that his light gun lies convenient across the thwarts of the boat. Satisfied that he has taken all due precautions, he yields himself eagerly to the sport before him.

He may have been thus engaged for more than an hour, when he started up suddenly, and his whole countenance assumed an expression of intense interest. A dull, heavy sound was heard reverberating along the waters.

" A shot!" he cries, " and from a brazen muzzle."

His line is instantly drawn in — his anchor. He no longer heeds the fish. He has had some sport. There are twenty shining sides that glisten at the bottom of the boat. There are sundry innocent victims that seem very much out of their proper depths of water and security. But, now, he gives them neither eye nor thought. His lines are in, his paddles out; his lusty sinews are braced to eager exertion. He speeds once more across the bay, passes up his creek of harborage, fastens his skiff to the

shore under close cover, leaps out, leaves his fish behind him, and,
catching up glass and gun, hastens once more to the headland
where we first encountered him.

" 'Tis she !" he exclaims, after sweeping the southwest passage
with his glass.   " 'Tis the 'Happy-go-Lucky' at last.   Thank
God !   I'm sick enough of this waiting.

Following his glance, we see the object which occasions his delight.   A small vessel glides through the distant channels.   Now
we catch a glimpse of her whole figure; a low long brigantine,
that seems to carry admirable heels.   The next moment, her
white sails and slender masts only gleam above the sand dunes
and the marsh.   Now she disappears behind a forest; and anon
emerges, running by a sand dune.

Our solitary runs up a tree that juts out appropriately on the
headland.   He seems to have used it before for such a purpose.
He climbs like a cat; is evidently a sailor; is up, aloft; and, in
a moment, a white streamer is seen waving from the tree !

The scene grows animated with a new life.   There is no longer
solitude.   That one brave vessel, "walking the waters," *is* "a
thing of life."   How beautifully she comes on ! — seems rather to
fly than to swim; darts through the narrow channels, as if certain
of her route; and breaks into the bay, with all her canvass belly-
ing out under the embraces of the western breeze, as if Cleopatra
herself were on deck.   And one, not unlike, and not less beautiful
than Cleopatra, *was* on her deck at that moment.   But of *her*
hereafter.

Our solitary shouts joyous from his tree.   Well may he shout.
It is with love that he shouts.   She is his pet, his favorite; he
loves the gallant vessel, as if she were a bride.

And she is a beautiful creature.   Even in the sight of us simple landsmen, who know nothing of her peculiar virtues, how she
sails; how she can eat into the very eye of the wind; how clean
are her heels; how easy her motion; what storms she has borne
and baffled; what seas she has traversed; over what foes triumphed; what wondrous ventures made; — even to us she comes
on as a beautiful creature, all ethereal — a thing of light, and
life, and flight, and perpetual motion !   Her hull, long and narrow; her tall, rakish masts; the vast spread of canvass which she
carries, and the elaborate grace of her spars and motion — these

strike even the inexperienced eye, as in proof of her speed and beauty. She has a grace of her own; but you see, too, that there are soul and skill in her management. You feel that there are courage and conduct; that there is a master-spirit on board, who wills, and she walks; who shouts, and she flies; who will carry her forward when the seas are wildest, and train her on to the fearfullest encounter with superior bulk, even as the swordfish darts to the encounter with the whale! Even we simple landsmen can see and conceive all these things as we gaze on the beautiful creature, while she flings the feathery spray from her bows.

But the eyes of the seaman glitter as he beholds, and there is a tear from those of the rough old salt, while ours do but smile. His heart is in it. She is the creature of his affections. How he envies the happy chieftain who sways the movements of his painted beauty. His glance follows every plunge which she makes through the pliant waters; and as she comes round upon the breeze, without a word or voice, and darts forward, as an arrow from the bow, straight for her harborage, he shouts — he can not help but shout. He can no longer keep silent: he shouts as he glides down the tree, and rather drops from it than descends.

"Hurrah! God bless the Happy-go-Lucky! hurrah! hurrah!"

The vessel makes her port. Our solitary is on the edge of the cove to which her prow is bent. He is there to catch the rope ere it touches earth, and hurry with it to the tree where he makes her fast. The bolts rattle, the sails descend, and, with scarce a ripple, she glides into the mouth of a little creek which has gratefully felt her form before. Her masts mingle with the tall pines that brood over on either side, so that it shall take very keen and curious eyes to detect her presence. A voice, clear, sharp, and musical, is heard from her decks: —

"Well, Jack Belcher, you see we have not forgotten you."

The tones were affectionate.

"God bless your honor, and your honor's honor! May you live for ever, and die at last in the 'Happy-go-Lucky'! All's well, your honor."

## CHAPTER II.

### THE HAPPY-GO-LUCKIES.

" *Touchstone.* And whither with you now ?   What loose action are you
bound for ?   Come !  what comrades are you to meet withal ?   Where's the
supper ?  where's the rendezvous ?"                              *Eastward Hoe.*

" Quoth he" — the ancient Marinere — " quoth he, there *was* a ship !"

BUT a more famous ship, in her day, than ever floated muse of
Coleridge, was she, the " Happy-go-Lucky" of the Spanish seas
and the year of grace 1684.   Of a remote period to ours, she
was yet not very unlike in build, nor perhaps inferior in performance, to the famous Baltimore clippers of the present time.
" Long, low, rakish," in her structure, she carries a cloud of canvass,
under which we have her seen leaping forward with an impulse
which, in a heavier sea and under a livelier breeze, would have
buried her bowsprit in a continual crush of foam.   In the smooth
waters of the bay beneath her, she glides like some graceful sea-
bird, exulting in the consciousness only of a pleasurable excitement.   Yet, docile in her sports, she has only heard a shrill
whistle, and almost silently her white wings fold themselves up to
her sides, and with scarce a ripple of the wave, and without farther effort of her own, she passes to her covert among the pines,
and her masts are lost among their shady tops of green.

She is a cruiser.   You may guess that from her build, her
world of canvass, her speed, her size, if not from the long brass
cannon working upon a pivot amidships, and the six brass muzzles that grin significantly with open jaws on either side.   She
has the capacity for mischief, clearly, whatever be her character.
Gently rocking in the narrow lagune where she seeks her rest, it
is permitted us to behold something more than her simple outlines.
Her inhabitants now tumble into sight on every hand ; a goodly

number of vigorous sea-dogs — somewhat more numerous, it would seem, than are absolutely necessary to the working of so small a craft. They constitute a crew, which, we may see at a glance, are to be relied upon when blows are heavy. There are scarred veterans among these fellows, motley enough — English, Irish, Dutch, French — an amalgam of nations, which, elsewhere, are rarely to be found working amicably together. Yet here, they seem fused, as by one strong presiding will, into a congruous community. The most casual eye may detect each national characteristic, in shape, look, tone, gesture; yet here they blend together harmoniously, under a common authority. They are docile enough, most of them — nay submissive; yet there is a sort of freedom, too, amounting to a social license, which forbids the idea that either of these has sunk his individuality in his obedience to authority. You hear them laugh and jest together; there are some who sing out aloud, as if to test the healthy capacity of voice and lungs; and, not unfrequently, a broad, corpulent, aggressive British oath breaks upon the ear, like the roar of a bulldog, from the lips of some surly islander, who fancies that unless he swears, and can hear himself and make others hear, he forfeits something of the natural independence of his breed.

You see, next, that these fellows are all picked men. They are rough sea-dogs, no doubt, but sturdy, cool, hardy, stubborn; capable of good knocks; giving and receiving; who have been already trained and tried in a severe apprenticeship. They are fit fellows for a cruiser with a roving commission. And such is that borne by the "Happy-go-Lucky."

As we traverse the decks, we find proofs of a late visit to regions farther south. There are piles of West India fruits strewn about; pyramids of orange, guava, and pine, secured in the nettings around the guns, showing a more innocent species of artillery than belongs altogether to the other aspects of the ship. The "Happy-go-Lucky" has probably looked very lately into Jamaica and Barbadoes; has had a squint at Porto Bello, a bird's-eye view of Havana; and may have enjoyed a loving wrestle with some of the good brigantines of these latter places, in which they have found more fruits than those which lie carelessly strewn on deck. *Quien sabe?*

But these piles of fruit implied, in the present case, neither want of cleanliness nor confusion.   In a twink, our cruiser will be cleared for action; and, in the matter of cleanliness, never were decks kept under " Holy Stone" regimen more rigidly than hers. Her captain, be sure, is something of a martinet; and the nice, trim condition of his ship would, we fancy, have seemed a very idle object to the bluff, less fastidious sailors of the previous generation — the days of Van Tromp, and Drake, and Cavendish. It needs but a glance to assure yourself that our cruiser is under the management of one who is no mere sailor; who brings some taste into exercise along with his duties; who has grace as well as valor; and can, doubtless, dance a galliard with courtly ease, in the very next hour after making the dons of Mexico foot it to the most vexatious sort of music.

But let us see him more nearly.   He is the same person who first welcomed our solitary, Jack Belcher, at the moment of their mutual recognition.   The latter personage has bounded on board the vessel, the moment her sides grazed the shores, and we see that the hand of his superior is extended him, with a frank and hearty freedom that speaks quite as much for friendship as authority.   Our solitary wrings it with warm affection.   There is some love between the two, be sure.   The superior speaks good humoredly : " Well ! tired out, Jack, eh ?"

" Tired enough, your honor — but only of the waiting, not of the work."

" What ! you 'd rather be dancing fandangoes with the Cuban barefoots, eh ?"

And there was a momentary flash of merriment in the blue eyes of the speaker — but momentary only, for the next instant a cloud seemed to pass across his face.

This was a handsome one, of the genuine English mould ; perhaps, for manhood, the most beautiful of all living models.   His features were all noble, decided, and symmetrical.   The *tout ensemble* exhibited boldness, freedom, sensibility ; a prompt courage ; an eager temper ; a generous, though perhaps irritable mood.   It was full of blood as well as character ; big veins swelling on his forehead, while the sanguine temperament declared itself, in warm flushes, through a skin somewhat deeply bronzed with the intense fervor of the tropical sun.   He had the light brown hair and blue eyes of the Saxon ; the great frame, large as well as vigorous ;

the erect carriage, the fearless look and demeanor of the Norman; and just enough of thought and care in the general expression of his face, as to lift the merely physical manhood into the dignity of intellect and authority.

Some care sate upon his cheek, and might be guessed from the gradually growing lines about the mouth; which was nevertheless distinguished equally by its youth and beauty. The broad and elevated brow, large but not massive; the quick, intelligent, and frequent kindling of the eye, looking out blue and lively; but, like an April sky, subject to very sudden changes; the prominent Roman nose; the full, round chin; sweetly expressive, yet very decisive mouth; — all declared for characteristics, which, whether we regard the opinions of Lavater or Gall, impress us, through the features, with the conviction that we stand in the presence of a brave, manly soul, having truthful sympathies, and a will that must everywhere assert command.

His person, as we have intimated, was framed in the very prodigality of nature — tall of height, broad of shoulder, and equally athletic and symmetrical. He was probably thirty years old, may have been thirty-five; but, if we make due allowance for the effects of care, strife, and authority, in situations of great responsibility, we shall be more safe in assuming him to be no more than thirty. He was clad very simply in loose duck trowsers, and wore a sailor's jacket, but these were of very fine materials. His bosom was ruffled in fine linen, curiously embroidered; a scarf of blue, worn loosely, and secured by the sailor-knot, was wrapped about his neck. A white Panama hat of ample rim and high conical crown, of the time of Charles the First, covered his head, and was encircled with a light-blue sash. He wore boots of yellow tanned Spanish leather. A baldric of blue silk, hanging over his shoulders, contained a brace of pistols, of rather long barrel, wide mouth, and richly-wrought stocks, inlaid with silver. He carried, at this moment, no other weapons.

You have the man before you, as he appears to us, shaking the hands of one whose approach, address, tone of voice, and general manner, show him to be a personal retainer, a faithful follower, an old long-tried friend, no less than a subordinate.

"And so, Jack, you have had a taste of the maroon? How long have you been here waiting?"

2

"But thirteen days, your honor; but it seems an age — more than a month, certainly. I left Charleston——"

"Not yet, Jack — wait a little longer."

And,'as he spoke, the face of the superior was overcast with a graver expression. He was approached, at that moment, by another person, who will demand our special attention, even as she coerced his.

"She! a woman!" Yes. Our rover, the "Happy-go-Lucky," is richly freighted. Feast your palate upon the choice fruits of summer and the sun, which you see about you; your cupidity upon the choice bales of silk and merchandises of East and West, which are hoarded in the hold below; but let your *eyes* feed upon the beautiful creature who now challenges our attention.

Very beautiful, indeed, is she, after the Spanish fashion. We said something of Cleopatra in the preceding chapter. That name is suggestive of but one ideal; and she who glides before us, and lays her hand intimately upon the captain's shoulder, and looks up with such a brilliant tenderness into his eyes, embodies that model in perfection. She is not a large creature as Cleopatra may have been — nay, *petite* rather — but full bosomed, with every look speaking passion — music's passion; the sun's passion; the passion of storm and fire upon occasion, ready to burst forth without warning and spoil the sky's face, and rage among the flowers.

She is brown with a summer's sun; her beauty is of the dark; like a night without a cloud, far up in the sky, flecked with solitary stars. Her features are not regular, but, in their very caprice, they harmonize. Her large black eye dilates at every glance, reveals every emotion, however slight, and passes, with the rapidity of lightning, from smiles to tears; from tenderness to a passion, which may easily be rage as well as love! It is keen, restless, jealously watchful, intense in every phase. The nose is small, but capable of sudden dilation; the lips voluptuous, pale, and soon shaken with a tremulous quiver, whenever the feelings are touched. The brow, whiter than the rest of the face, is marked by two blue veins above the eyes, that become swollen at a moment's warning. It is not high, nor massive, nor yet narrow; the eyebrows are thick and black, the lashes long; and when the orbs droop, in the languor of satisfied emotions, they form a beautiful and glossy fringe fit for hiding the fiery jewels that burn beneath.

An easy susceptibility to all emotions; a sleepless intensity of mood, whatever the direction of the will; great energy of passion; an ever-watchful jealousy; feelings that have never learned to brook control or denial; a temper not often accustomed to restraint; these are traits, all visible at a glance, to him who can look through the features, in partial repose at present, to their natural susceptibilities, and the moral atmosphere in which the owner has grown to womanhood.

Her person, though small, is perfect, well rounded, neither too full nor slender; a model, in short, for that style of beauty which was hers. And every movement was graceful. She swam rather than walked. Her little feet were never heard, in the thin, open slippers which she wore. Her costume was of a light, gay green silk; her bodice of the finest texture, embroidered openly in front, and leaving the large, well-formed bosom to its own free swell, under the pressure of perpetually striving emotions. Her dress, though embroidered, and decorated besides with little cords of gold and purple, that crossed the white openings in the silken dress, was worn loosely, rather after a Grecian than an Italian or Spanish fashion; sufficiently showing the perfection of the form, without absolutely defining it; certainly without embarrassing, or tending in the slightest degree to curb its movements.

Hair — such a mass, all raven black, which, loosed, would sweep the earth behind her as she went — eyes, mouth, form, complexion, — all seemed to carry you back to the gay season when, in the halls of Zegri and Abencerrage, the maidens of Granada borrowed lustre from the sun to light up the darkness, and made the moon and stars tributary to passions which could tolerate no stronger light, but which luxuriated in such as theirs.

Verily, she was of Moresco, quite as much as Spanish blood; and you are sure of this when you hear her called "Zulieme." A little poniard in a sheath of green embossed leather, with richly-jewelled hilt, worn in her girdle, seems to help the faith in her Moorish origin. She is dark, but comely, like the beauty sung by Solomon; and that wise person was understood to have quite an eye for a fine woman. She was evidently of the order which he preferred to crown with flowers and music.

But — but! ah! — *but* hereafter.   There will be a time for the qualifications — to-morrow, and to-morrow, and to-morrow!

*Now!*  We see nothing but the beautiful; a sensuous beauty — a thing solely for the eye : such as Canova makes of that exquisite idiot whom he calls " The Venus."

And, in all her beauty, costumed as we have shown her, Zulieme approaches her lord, and, with one hand on his shoulder, and her great black eyes peering into his, she exclaims, in tolerable English, just sufficiently broken and imperfect to show that she is of another nation, and to occasion a pleasant interest by the discovery — she exclaims : —

" Why, Harry, how is this?   Molyneaux tells me that this is not Charleston!'

" I should say not, Zulieme.   This is a wild region, uninhabited almost, except by savages."

" But why have you put in here, Harry?"

" It is necessary," he answered, somewhat coldly.

" But why necessary?   What is to be done here?   Molyneaux says that there is nothing to be done here; that there is nobody to see, nobody to trade with, and I want to go to Charleston.   I would n't have come this voyage had you not promised me I should go to Charleston.   Molyneaux tells me——"

" Tell me no more, if you please, of what Mr. Molyneaux has told you; and if you are wise, Zulieme, you will take your future information, as to *my* purposes and conduct, from no other lips than my own."

" But I am not wise, Harry, and you sha' n't make me wise; and how, if nobody tells me anything but you, and you never tell me anything!"

" I tell you *all*, in respect to myself and my proceedings, Zulieme, which I deem it proper for you to know.   Who undertakes to tell you more, in this ship, assumes a privilege which I shall certainly arrest at the earliest moment."

The gravity had become severity.

" Oh! do n't blame Mr. Molyneaux, now; if anybody is at fault, it's me.   1 asked Mr. Molyneaux, and he answered; and there's no harm in that, Harry."

" I do n't know *that!*" was the answer, slowly spoken, and with the air of one who muses upon some other subject.

"Yes, but you *do* know, Harry; and when *I* want to know something, I *will* ask, and somebody *must* answer."

"Ask of me, then, Zulieme."

"Well, but you won't answer me always."

"Then, it is not proper that you should seek from another the information that I refuse. You ought to know, in such cases, that the knowledge you seek is withheld for some good reason."

"But why — what reason? And why should Mr. Molyneaux know things that I mustn't know? I'm your wife, Harry, am I not?"

"You *are* my wife, Zulieme," was the gravely-spoken answer; and the manner did not show that there was any satisfaction felt in making the acknowledgment; "and as *my* wife, Zulieme, you must content yourself with what *I* am pleased to tell you of the affairs of this ship. Mr. Molyneaux is an officer of this ship; and my wife must learn to know, if he does not, that his duty is to keep its secrets. If your business were the management of the vessel, then it would be your right to know; but——"

"Oh! I don't care about the ship's affairs, Harry; it's my own affairs; and I ask you why you put in here, in this wild place, when we were to go to Charleston? It was to go to Charleston that I agreed to leave New Providence. You told me that we would go there; and you promised to stop at Cuba, yet you never stopped, or only for a moment, and I never had a sight of Havana, and you know what I wanted to see there. Ah, the dear Cuba! the sights, and the bullfights, and the dances! And nòw, it seems, we are not to go to Charleston——"

"Who says that, Zulieme?"

"Why, Mr. Molyneaux said——"

A stern, impatient look and gesture cut short the communication; and the eyes of the captain glanced quickly and angrily from the lady, in the direction of a person who stood near the companion-way, and who seemed, at that moment, to have the ship in charge.

This was Mr. or rather Lieutenant Molyneaux, so often referred to by the lady. He was a young man, probably the youngest in the vessel, of middle size, slight build, but apparently of great activity. His face, which was turned toward the parties at the moment, was effeminate, smooth, even boyish; but its expression was that of careless daring, amounting to effrontery. He belonged to the proverbial " order of the Bashful Irishmen." There was a half smile upon his countenance, as his eye met the glance of his superior, which seemed significant with a peculiar meaning.

" Did you call, sir?" he asked, somewhat indifferently, as his eye caught the expression in that of his superior.

" No, sir — no! — and yet I did call, Mr. Molyneaux. One word, sir."

The other approached at a moderate pace, though without any apparent interest. As he drew nigh, the captain said: —

" Mr. Molyneaux, you will please understand that it is not by any means necessary that you should communicate to anybody but myself the courses and direction of this ship. She may steer east, west, north, or south, and all on board must submit without question, or expectation of answer, to the orders which I give on this and all other subjects. No answer, sir, if you please. I have no purpose to converse now; only to inform, that we may prevent mistakes in future."

The slightest possible smile might be seen upon the lips of the lieutenant as he touched his hat and receded. But a fierce, passionate stare on the part of the lady betrayed equal astonishment and indignation, and threatened a sudden outbreak.

" How, Harry, do you mean that Mr. Molyneaux is not to answer my questions?"

" Exactly! He is to answer no questions, of anybody, in relation to the working of this ship, its course, objects, or interests. These are sacred even from you, and do you not attempt to persuade any officer to a neglect or breach of duty. Ask *me* what you want to know, and if it be proper that you should know, *I* will answer you."

" Look you, Harry, none of your haughty ways with me. I won't stand it. You sha'n't treat me as if I were only a child. I must and will know, Harry. You said positively we were to come to Charleston, and if you hadn't said that, I never should have consented to leave Providence. You promised me, Harry, to carry me to Havana and Charleston both, and now you bring me here to this wild heathen country, where there are wolves and tigers, and the red savages. I say, I will know, Harry, whether you mean to keep your word, and carry me to Charleston."

A very angry expression crossed for a moment the face of the superior. You could see that it needed little for a storm — a sudden burst of thunder; but he subdued the tempest with a severe exertion of will, and in tones not merely sober, but even gentle, though firm, he answered: —

"Zulieme, no more of this at present; whether I shall go to Charleston or not, depends upon intelligence which I am to find here."

"And from whom, Harry, in this savage place? You are only cheating me, I know."

"You saw the person who met me from this shore? But, it does not matter. It should not. It should be enough for you, Zulieme, that I have answered you. I do not relish this too close questioning. You must learn to believe what I tell you, and submit."

The lady pouted, and stamped her little feet impatiently; her companion scarcely heeded it, as he went on: —

"No more of this impatience, Zulieme. Be content with the assurance that I have duties to others, in fulfilling which, I am obliged to put in here — which *may* carry me to Charleston — probably will; but which may require that I shall steer in any other direction. And, as my wife, you must understand that my duties involve yours, and must learn to submit, without complaint or question, to the necessities which I have to recognize. Go below now, or amuse yourself on deck — do what you wish — while I see Jack Belcher, and procure the information which shall decide my course."

"And I say again, Harry Calvert, that you treat me like a child!" exclaimed the spoiled beauty, passionately.

"Ay, and you *are* a child, Zulieme! What else! what else!" This was said very gravely and sadly, but gently, even tenderly.— "But go below, and beware how you make me appear ridiculous in the sight of these rude men. There are eyes upon us, which must see in me nothing but the master. Do not let your folly undo my authority!"

"But why may I not go on shore, Harry?" changing her tone in an instant. "Why not have supper under those great trees, and fruits, and music? Oh! it will be so pretty, and so nice, Harry."

"Yes, to be sure! — why not? Do so, Zulieme. Give the orders, and set your maid to work. Call Phipps to help. Phipps! Phipps!"

Phipps was the cabin-boy.

And, so speaking, Captain Calvert was moving away, when the lady caught his arm:

"But is there no danger of the red savages, Harry? They say your savages of Carolina are a fiercer race than ours. They eat Christians, don't they?"

"I have already got a scouting party in the wood, Zulieme, under Lieutenant Eckles. There is no danger. Belcher has been here, alone, for more than a week."

"Oh! how frightful! and nobody with him! Oh! I should prefer the savages to the silence of these lonely woods. But, go 'long, Harry. Go 'long, now; while I set Sylvia and Phipps to work. We shall have such a nice supper, and music, and a dance."

And she lilted and warbled as she spoke. Then calling, "Sylvia, Sylvia!" to the maid below, and clapping her hands, with a shrill scream for Phipps, the lady, in a moment after, darted down the companion-way, seeming altogether to forget, in her new fancies, that she was the unhappy proprietor of one of those wretched husbands who refuse to answer impertinent questions.

Mr. Molyneaux glanced at her retiring figure; his eyes then followed that of the captain. The latter joined Jack Belcher on the headlands, and proceeded with him into the thicket and out of sight. Upon the lips of Mr. Molyneaux there sat the same smile with which he had met the sudden and stern glance of his principal. It was cool, quiet, full of effrontery and self-esteem. Yet, how feminine were all his features. And how should he — so seemingly effeminate, and evidently the youngest person in the ship — how should he have risen to the rank of second officer?

That smile told the whole story. Girlish though he seemed, he had that degree of audacity and resolution which could carry him through scenes from which greater frames and tougher sinews, and more hardy-looking persons, would have shrunk in dismay. And he would go into the *melée* as to a feast. And the very effeminacy of his person deceived his enemies. Under that girlish and delicate exterior, he concealed powerful muscles and well-knit limbs, and a lithe activity, which, in the moment of danger, left nearly all others behind!

But why did he smile as his captain went from sight? What is the secret in that sinister expression? And did his superior feel, or fancy, the occult meaning which it seemed to cover?

It did not please him, evidently. There was an instinct at work, no doubt, which made Captain Calvert feel that there was something unpleasant in that smile of his second officer. But he is not the man to brood over the occult. And he has other cares on hand at this moment; and, forgetting the whole scene just over, it was with some eagerness that he joined Jack Belcher on the shore, and bade him lead into the thick cover of the forest.

2*

# CHAPTER III.

## AGONIES OF A LOST HOPE.

"Tidings have come to me that on my house a bolt hath fallen at midnight, and left ashes, where I had left delights, in precious babes, and one that watched them."

JACK BELCHER led the way for his superior into that close covert where we have followed the former once before. Here the captain threw himself down upon the little sea-chest which carried all Jack's stores, while the latter leaned against one of the great trees that helped to pillar and roof his sylvan habitation.

"Well, Jack," said Calvert, impatiently, "you have seen the governor? Does he write?"

"No indeed, sir; I think he's a little afraid of putting things to paper. He's scary! — says 'the devil's to pay!' that the king's been bullied by the Spaniard, and our business is to be stopped altogether. There's to be no more winking at our work in the West Indies. The Spanish embassador demands that when an English sailor shouts out, 'No peace beyond the line,' he's to be tucked up, out of sight, in a jiffy, and made to swing, just where you find him, whether on sea or land. There's to be no more fair trading on any account, and the governor seems half disposed to close accounts with you for ever."

The fellow paused.

"Well — well! go on."

"Well, sir, there's little more to tell you. I had some work to get to a private talk with the governor. But when I showed him your ring, and gave him the letter, he let out free enough. Only, I couldn't get him to write. He says the council watches him. But he'll wink, I'm a-thinking, and not look too closely where he shouldn't. That is, if your honor takes care to give him the right kind of eye-water."

"Yes! yes! I understand him! But how are the citizens? You went among them? You saw Stillwater and Franks?"

"All right in that quarter. Stillwater says the governor's a cross between a fool and rogue. He has the conscience for the trade, but wants the pluck. Frank says: "Come on; there's just as good custom now as when the king had Christian bowels. As for the people, I see no difference. *They* don't see the harm or the wrong in riddling a Spanish galleon, or, for that matter, a Frenchman; they hate 'em both, and look upon 'em, sensibly, as natural enemies. They will buy whatever you've got to sell, and ask no question about the sort of flag you pulled down to get at the goods. I don't see that you'll have any trouble from them."

"Then we've nothing to fear from the governor. If such be the temper of the people, Quarry will give us no trouble. As for Charles Stuart, he's a fool. As if the Spaniard and Frenchman were *not* the natural enemies of England. As if every captured galleon was not gain of strength as well as wealth to us. Fool! fool! like his father; and, like him, bought and sold, to the shame and loss of England. But what said the governor to my coming into port?"

"He hemmed and hawed — said it was very dangerous; he couldn't say; *you* might take the risk if you pleased, but 't was your own risk. He couldn't say what would be the upshot of it; he said council was monstrous prying into the business."

"Any armed vessel on the station? — king's ship, I mean?"

"I know, sir. No, not that I could hear. The Lime, Pearl, and Shoreham, were all on the Virginia coast; the Phœnix and Squirrel at New York; the Rose at Boston; the Winchelsea—"

"At Jamaica, we know — and so is the Adventure; did you hear nothing of the Scarborough?"

"She's a thirty-gun ship? There was a report of one that had been on the coast, but I didn't get her name. It's certain there was no king's ship on the Carolina coast when I left; but the governor said one might be expected soon. He was scary enough, and talked a good deal about character, and responsibility, and dignity, and his office, as if he hadn't buttoned 'em up long ago, and covered 'em out of sight with Spanish doubloons. I reckon there's some change in the council, sir, that makes him so scary; there's one person in the council now, sir, that wa'n't in it before;

and the name is one, sir, that'll raise your hair a little. It's a Major Berkeley.

"Major Berkeley!" cried the captain, starting up and approaching the subordinate.

"Yes, sir; but what Berkeley I couldn't find out. I couldn't get to see him, and the governor never told me of him at all. Of course, I thought directly of your own brother, and how curious 't would be if he was removed to Carolina. But I could find out nothing but this, that he's an Edward Berkeley too; they call him Sir Edward, seeing that he's made a cassique, or lord, in this country, and he's got a family — wife and children!"

" Edward Berkeley! and wife! and — did you say children?"

" Yes, sir, he's got children — or a child — one or more. They told me wife and children."

" Children! and by her! O God! and I have lived for this! and Olive is a mother! a mother! and her children are not mine! And what am I, and where am I! after all these struggles, this toil and danger in a doubtful service; denounced by the laws; deserted by my sovereign; an exile — perhaps an outlaw! Ah! God! But *this*, *this* might have been spared me!"

And our cruiser strode the wood as he thus passionately spoke, and his fingers were thrust into his hair and clenched with violence, while his whole frame shook with the convulsions of his soul.

" Don't, sir; don't, your honor; don't take on so, dear master. It may not be your brother, after all."

" 'Tis he! I feel it! They were wedded, I know. That ancient Jezebel, her mother! She has done it all. She has torn us asunder for ever. Olive's heart was mine — mine only. But what are hearts to selfish mothers? What a woman's heart to a mother's ambition? What a younger brother's heart, when he who claims the birthright requires its sacrifice? It is he — it is Edward Berkeley; and he is come hither now, having robbed me of all that made life precious, perhaps to rob me of life also — to bring me to an ignominious death! Poor Olive! with thy depth of soul, with thy singleness of passion, to be thus bartered. And — children too! His children! his children! Oh! Edward Berkeley, thou hast robbed me of something more than life!"

" Master, dear master, remember — you have now a wife of your own."

" Ah! do I not know it, Belcher? Great Heavens! and such a wife! a doll! a painted baby! a poor child-creature, whose very smile mocks me with a cruel memory of all that is lost to me for ever. True, Olive was lost ere I wedded her. Yet why should I have wedded *her?* Better to have made the heart live on the bitter memory. Yet, there was excuse. I owed much to this child's care of me. And in what madness of soul did I seek in another the recompense for that most miserable loss!"

" Alas, your honor, is n't it too late now to—"

" Ah! as if that were not the worst agony of all! There is the venom in the wound. It is too late. No more, Jack! no more! Olive Masterton has children, and they are not mine; and these children will beget that love which did not beget themselves. I must not think. Poor, poor Olive! But I will see her! I will see her once more!"

" Oh! sir, better not!"

" I *will* see her, if I die for it! I can not help it. The Fates, if she is indeed in Charleston, have thrown her in my way. They decree that we shall meet once more. I will gaze upon her face, though she may not see mine. I will startle her soul with my voice, though I may not listen to hers. I will look upon the face of her child — her child! Oh! Olive Masterton, hadst thou been firm, strong, devoted — hadst thou kept thy faith, and had faith in mine — this had never been! The cruel arts of thy cruel mother had never prevailed to tear our hearts asunder, to blight hope and heart, and yield thee, and yield me, to embraces which are loathsome to both. Ay, loathsome to thee, I swear it; unless, indeed, thou wert all a lie, like that artful fiend, thy mother!"

" Master, dear master!"

" Oh! Jack, I am weak — weak unto death!" cried the strong man, throwing himself upon the ground, while a deep groan issued from his chest. The faithful follower hung over him.

" Dear master, give not way."

" I will not, Jack. I will be strong. It is too late. Ay, something is too late. But, I must and will see her. Do not fear me, Jack, I will be calm — calm as the grave when it closes its heavy jaws over the wreck of best affections. Olive! Olive Masterton!

thou hast crushed me to the earth, in thy own wretched lack of love."

"Oh! Master, she lacked not that! But what could she do? You .gone — lost, perhaps — and that old one at her from morning till night.' A mother too! and so cunning. You don't think what the poor girl had to suffer. I know something of it, master. I heard — I saw! and it isn't for a young ,girl to stand a mother's prayers and pleadings long. And they were very poor: and you don't know how they were made to feel it — and they who had been used to live in such grandeur."

"Ay! she was sold; and that Edward Berkeley should be the man to take advantage of her poverty, her dependency, her mother's arts, and my absence."

"Oh, sir, as I'm a living man, I don't believe your brother ever knew of your love for her."

"He must have known — must have heard!"

"He might suspect, but I don't think he knew, and that old hag never let him know. She kept the truth from him. I'm sure of it. You recollect, he was on the continent all the while when you were with her. You were gone before he came home."

"But my letter?"

"Ten to one he never got it. You never got any answer. Oh! sir, do not suspect your brother."

"Why was the marriage so hurried, before I could return?"

"'Twas his passion, sir, and the mother's arts. Besides, 'twa'n't so much hurry, either, since you remember, we were eleven months getting across from Panama, owing to your dreadful sickness."

"Ah! that horrid time! and its more horrid consequences! 'Twas the terrible news from England that broke me down, and made me deplore the cares that saved me in spite of that pestilential fever. And then it was, that, in a fatal hour — in my despair and vexation on the one hand, and in a false notion of gratitude on the other — I committed the worst of all my errors: gave my hand to this foolish child; married a woman who could' move passion, but not love — a toy, not a woman; a mere trifler with the heart that would like to honor — if nothing more — like to believe her worthy of some sympathy, if not of mine."

"But she loves you, sir. Believe me, sir, she loves you!"

"Ay, perhaps, as far as she can know to love; but what a child — how weak, how vain, how frivolous! a continual caprice, that vexes even in its fondness; that makes you revolt, even when passion most persuades to tenderness. Ah! Jack, I have sacrificed a solace in a frenzy. I might have cherished pride even in disappointment. I have shut myself out from the consolations which a cherished faith might have brought me even in moments of despair. What had I to do with a child passion, when I was sure of a noble woman's love?"

"But that was lost and gone, my dear master."

"No! I had lost a hope, but not the life in which the hope had birth. I had lost the woman I had loved — not her affections. Her heart was mine — never less mine than when she was wrapt in the embraces of another. And upon this I might have lived. To brood upon the precious memory would have been a solace, when passion could proffer none. And that I should be so led by passion — I that had suffered in such a school of suffering! — that a mere whim, a caprice, a fancy, should have led me thus into a bondage whose galling chains eat into the very soul, and make every thought a torture."

"'Twas gratitude, sir — 'twas a good feeling that made you marry the señora."

"Tell me nothing of gratitude, Jack Belcher; as if any gratitude should justify such a sacrifice — justify vows which neither can keep or value."

"Oh, sir, I do think the señora loves you. She's true to you, sir."

"Ah, yes! to be sure she's *true!*"

"How she did watch your sick-bed! how she did nurse you when your life hung upon a thread — when even I gave up — when nobody had a thought you could live, and only thought how to save you pain in your dying hours! How she watched and hoped through all, and was never wearied; and kept bathing your head and hands in the vinegar; and kept the cooling plantain-leaf upon your forehead; and, when her mother said you would die, who wept and swore you shouldn't die; and who made all others bend to her — and she still nothing but a child. Oh! sir, that was love — and it saved you; and though she hasn't the ways of our English, yet, sir, I do think her heart is full of love for you, and she's as true to you, though she does vex you so much, as any woman of England could be."

"No doubt! no doubt! But oh! Jack Belcher, though I feel and believe all that you say, yet it brings no relief. There is no consolation in it. Better were she wholly the idle butterfly creature that she séems; better false, hollow, heartless, as she is vain, vexing, weak, and capricious. Then, I could fling her off — whistle her down the wind with scorn — and surrender myself wholly to the bitter memory of that early passion, which was a truth, a faith, a sweet reality of love, no matter what the denial and the loss, instead of fruit and blossom! But leave me for a while, Jack. I must be alone. Let me lie here in the solitude. I would think — think until I forget, if that be now possible."

"Will you take some of the Jamaica, sir? It's a good thing for a solitary man."

Jack's ideas of solace had something in them very decidedly English. He honestly believed that the seat of the soul is the abdomen, and that Jamaica was the divining power which could reach it.

"No, thank you, Jack. Nothing. Leave me for a while. Join me in an hour, when I shall be better able to talk with you of ship's affairs."

The subordinate said no more, but, with a look that still lingered, the faithful fellow made his way out of the thicket, leaving his superior to brood, with what philosophy he might, over the rash impulses which, in a moment of weakness, had led him to voluntary fetters, which now, to use his own strong phraseology, were eating into his very soul. He had simply done what is done by thousands daily —

> ——— " Had embraced
> The shadow for the substance, in his passion;
> And been requited, for the wretched folly,
> By thorn in pillow, which forbade all sleep
> To thought — all waking into Hope at dawn."

## CHAPTER IV.

### LOVE AFTER A FOREIGN FASHION.

> " Call you this love ?
> This phantasy, this sighing, these sad looks !
> Oh fie !  Love 's like the zephyr to the roses,
> That comes with happiest wing, and sings at meeting ;
> Meeting and parting sings, and so dreams joyous
> Of still fresh meetings with as happy flowers."

It is part of youth's business to sport and play, dance and sing, just as certainly as to work and grow.  The work and growth depend quite as much upon the play as the food and nurture. And we must not look too severely upon exuberances which belong to the instincts.  We must let youth rollick at due seasons, just as we suffer young colts to kick up their heels upon a common ; and we must not see too austerely that this kicking up of the heels, whether of the human animal or the young horse, is calculated to exhibit them in uncouth or ridiculous attitudes. Don't vex yourself, or others, about their attitudes.  It is the kicking up which is the essential performance ; the grace will grow afterward, as a due consequence of the familiar exercise. To us who are no longer in the gristle, whose limbs are solidly set, and grow daily more and more uncompromising, there is, no doubt, something quite as impertinent as awkward in this rollicking of young creatures.  But, dear brother, now growing grisly, if not ungraceful, be sure, while you rebuke the absurd antics of boyhood, that you are not governed quite as much by a secret envy, which deceives yourself, as by a fastidious feeling of the proprieties.  Be sure, before you sermonize, that you would really refuse these antics, even if you could practise them ; that it would be no satisfaction to you to leap backward forty years or more, and rejoice in the hop-skip-and-jump, the somersault, or even the

bruising-match and buffet of yonder urchins, whom you now regard with such solemn gravity, as emulous only of the doings of
apes and monkeys.  Boys have to go through a certain portion
of ape-and-monkey practice and experience before they can be
men ; and we have only to take care that they are duly exercised
in man-practice also, so that they do not finally grow into the
exclusive fashion of the beast !

And girls are boys, with a certain difference, and women men !
And they too must pass through a certain amount of rollicking ;
and our only solicitude in their case is that they should not show
quite so much of their heels as the tougher gender.  Just see that
their figleaves are a fraction longer ; and if you make some difference in the cut and fashion of skirt and small-clothes, you will
probably put as much curb on the young creatures as they need
in the rollicking season through which they have to pass.

And if the silly monkeys insist, for their part, on flinging up
their heels to the sound of music, don't fancy, for the life of you,
that the disparagement is to the heels, however much it may be
to the music.  If the fiddle can time the paces of these wild colts ;
if heels can be made to work together harmoniously ; be sure that
there is much less chance of their being cast up in each other's.
faces.  And, one thing let me tell you — the more you encourage
the shaking of the legs, the more you discourage that incessant
wagging of the tongue, which is apt to become a scandal to the
sex, in teaching all the arts of scandal.  In brief, innocent sports
are absolutely necessary to the preservation of innocence ; and
the heart depends quite as much, for its continued purity, upon an
occasional flinging out of legs and arms, as upon your stale saws
and owl-like maxims.  All that we have need to do, to guard
against danger, is that the sports shall be simply those of young
limbs needing exercise, stripped of all conventional adjuncts, by
which we teach something more profound than exercise, and more
mischievous than the contredanse and pugilism.  To the pure all
things are pure, even the heels of colts and the claws of kittens ;
and we have only to see and keep them to the mere rollicking,
without suffering this to become tributary to the sensualism at
once of thought and blood.  And so you shall see that dancing
does not mean simply hugging and squeezing ; and that you are
not reconciled, by a foreign fashionable name, into those practices,

which, in the plain vernacular, mean anything but dancing! Of course, this is doctrine meant only for animals of English breed — that stern, intense, savage Anglo-Norman nature, which goes to its very sports with a sense of morals, and justifies its pursuit of happiness by a reference to duty. It is otherwise with light flexible natures like the Italian and the French. To these, sport is its own justification, and sufficiently satisfies of itself. But when we, of rough British origin, undertake their habitual exercise, we are apt to get drunk upon them. The fire rages in the blood, and rushes to the brain, in our intensity of temperament, and the game which we have begun in play is but too apt to end in passion.

We have said all this, dear reader, in order that you should be properly prepared to look upon a little child's play — a colt rollicking — without feeling your sense of dignity too much outraged. Remember, too, we are in a wild land, where European law scarcely touches us with a feeling of reserve or caution. Our *dramatis personæ*, also, though of all European stocks, are of rather irregular practice, and will, no doubt, show you many rules not to be found in Gunter. Don't let these things cause any misgivings. It is your policy to see something of all the world's varieties — to see how Humanity demeans itself in different situations; and you are wise in just that degree in which you recognise all human practices, irrespective of the laws laid down by your little parish conventionalities. Thus warned, if you blunder, sagely or savagely, in your meditations, the fault is none of ours.

Our Zulieme has no sooner heard that she is in a place of safety, where she can rollick upon dry land without dreading the loss of skin and scalp, than she begins to fling out her heels. She lilts, she sings, she screams, claps her little hands, and dances, and forgets that she has a master.

"Sylvia! Sylvia!" she half shouts, half warbles, as she darts down into the cabin.

"Phipps! Phipps!" — and Sylvia appears, a thick-lipped negress, mulatto rather, with a turbid current running through veins and skin, great eyes, a flat nose, and glossy black hair of that wiry and frizzled character which, to some eyes, may possess a peculiar beauty. In the hands of some modern novelists, who are ambitious equally of taste and eccentricity, she might become a heroine, calculated to provoke the raptures of a Prince Djalma. To others, of more philanthropy than taste, she would appear the ideal of a much-wronged race of hybrids, who would be more esteemed for their charms could an eccentric philosophy succeed in disturbing the natural instincts of a superior civilization. But poor Sylvia lives at a period when taste was more proper and natural, and philanthropy more sane, and so we describe her as she appears to all about her — an Abigail of very vulgar attractions, with all the cunning of her class, sly, deceitful, somewhat clever, and ugly enough for trust, as the waiting-maid of "milady."

Phipps is a brisk cabin-boy, of British bulk and character, sixteen years old, sprightly enough in his province as a knife-cleaner and actor of all work in a cruiser's cabin, without any very salient features, moral or physical, his nasal prominence excepted. This *is* a nose, an unquestionable proboscis; an ample rudder to a round, fair Saxon face of good fleshy rotundity.

They both show themselves at the summons of the lady. They are both pleased to obey a call which promises pleasure. There is to be a supper and a dance on shore. Phipps plays the fiddle: Sylvia feeds with appetite; has as great a passion for dancing as her mistress, though scarcely so graceful of movement; and both are particularly delighted with the idea of a rollicking on shore.

And they go to work with an impulse which makes preparation easy. Fruits, and sweetmeats, and solids; plates, knives and forks; flasks of ruddy wines of Canary and Madeira, are transferred in a twink from hold and cabin to the shelter of green trees. Blankets, nay cloaks, and rich *couvrelits*, are spread upon the turf, and hung from the branches; and soon you behold the fair Zulieme seated in state under a natural canopy of oaks and cedars. And anon you behold the sailors, in clean toggery, beginning to group themselves about the area, though at a respectful distance from the queen of the fête. They are never indifferent to sports which relieve duty; and they are not superior to the vanity which for ever feels conscious that other eyes are looking on. So you note that their duck trowsers are of the whitest; and some of them sport red sashes about the waist, in which their pistols and knives shine with recent furbishing. And they wear jaunty jackets of blue, and green, and crimson ; and their hats of straw are wound about with shawls or handkerchiefs of quite as

many colors; and these are of silken stuffs, such as would have
been held rare and rich enough in the days of old Queen Bess.
And you need but look into the eyes of these several parties, to
see, as Phipps tunes his fiddle in a recess of the wood, and the
notes come faintly to their senses, that they meditate shaking legs
themselves, presuming, no doubt, on indulgences which have not
been denied before.

And at the feet of the beautiful Zulieme you see the Spanish
guitar, thickly inlaid with pearl, and ebony, and silver, in vines
and flowers, while a broad scarf of crimson floats around it in the
breeze, which said scarf will anon encircle the neck and shoulders — white and bare enough in her present costume — of the
beauty of the feast. She has made her toilet for the occasion.
She has an eye, with all her childish simplicity, to what belongs
to such an occasion. She knows that all these rough sailors admire; that they too have eyes; and failing to figure, as she designed, in the *festas* of the Cuban, she is not unwilling to receive
the homage of a ruder class of worshippers.

And so she glows in green and crimson, and her hair wantons
free, only sprinkled with pearls, which contrast exquisitely with
her raven tresses; while, wrapping her neck in frequent folds,
and dropping down upon her bosom in a gorgeous amulet, with
pendant diamond cross, they serve to show how much whiter is
the delicate skin which they do not so much adorn as illustrate.
Her dress, open enough for the display of a very admirable bust,
is loose enough in skirt for the perfect freedom of an exquisite
figure. A cincture of green and gold, with diamond clasp, encir-
cles her waist, and her jewelled poniard secures the clasp, the little sheath forming the rivet which brings the opposing eyes of the
clasp together.

Zulieme has not forgotten the first of her lessons, — the one
taught most easily — the one always taught by a fond, foolish,
adoring mother, — that she is, in truth, very beautiful; and that
the sole object of dress is not, as vulgar people think, to conceal,
but to adorn and properly develop the person; and, as she now
sits before us, we are again reminded of Cleopatra —

"Cleopatra, lussuriosa,"

swelling with all the consciousness, not only of a most voluptuous

beauty, but of the masculine eyes looking on, that drink in provocation at every glance, and grow momently more and more bewildered with the intoxications of passion.

To the class of beauties which Zulieme represents, the possession of the fascination is nothing compared with its exercise upon
the victim. It loses half of its charm in their own eyes, unless
they feel that others grow blind beneath its spells. And when
vanity and voluptuousness grow together, who shall measure the
extent of insanity to which their proprietor will speed? It was
fabled of Circe, that she transformed her worshippers into brutes.
But the fable properly implies that they were brutified by the
fascination, which, in its own growth of passion, had lost all power
to discriminate in the choice of its worshippers, and had ceased to
consider the difference in the quality of the homage, or whether it
was accorded by brutes or men. Circe was willing enough to
exhibit herself to beast as well as man; and, like her, our Zulieme
was perhaps quite as well pleased with the admiration of Jack Tar
as that of her own liege lord, his superior and hers — the stern,
half outlaw, but noble Captain Calvert.

"But where is my lord, the while?"

We could answer. We have seen where and how. But of his
griefs, or of any griefs, our lady asks no questions. The feast is
spread. The viands are about to be served, and Lieutenant Molyneaux sits at the feet of the lady, hands up the cates, and serves
her with hands and eyes. He too, always studious of his personal appearance, is habited with care and taste for the occasion.
His figure, though not massive, is a good one. He prides himself
equally on the having, and the making, of a leg. Charles Molyneaux
is something of a courtier. He has dressed himself, making as near
an approach to the court costume of that day as possible. For
example, his neat figure is clad in silk stockings and small-clothes.
He wears a diamond buckle at knee and instep. He has on a
richly-flowered vest of silk; and the frills of his shirt protrude
six inches from his bosom. His silken cravat is of dimensions
which suit rather a levée at St. James, or St. Cloud, than warm
weather and the woods of Kiawah. His coat is of brocade, such
as Bolingbroke wore at the court of France. It is of Paris cut
and so, a sufficient model, of course, for all the courts of Europe.
Mr. Molyneaux is a person of conventional tastes. He does not

suffer himself sufficient freedom, to consult that better propriety, which makes good taste superior to all convention. In one respect, however, he left Nature to her own decencies. He wore no pomatum or powder in his hair; but this forbearance was not his merit. These commodities were neither among the ship's stores nor his own. He possessed a naturally fine shock, which, let go free, had grown into very copious love-locks, which did not misbeseem the days of Rochester and the effeminate style of his own face. His complacency is such as not to suffer him to suppose that any costume would misbeseem *his* person!

And, sitting at the feet of the gay lady, he played the courtier in speech, and look, and action, no less than in costume. He taught his eyes to languish, looking deathly things into hers. His tones were subdued sweetly to those murmuring accents which lovers suppose to be fitly adapted to honeyed sentiments; and the compliments whispered to her now, and at other periods, were of that equivocal sort — half serious and sentimental, and half playful — which the young coquette hears with a thrill, and responds to with a sigh; and which the fashionable world considers a very natural, proper, and wholly unobjectionable method of conversation: Passion feeling his way; gradually insinuating; not offending all at once, but so preparing his advance that the mind is gradually corrupted, and not apt, when final offence is given, to show itself offended at all. It is, indeed, wonderful how rapid is this progress of safe insinuation in such cases: she who drinks, tasting none of the poison, so infinitesimal is the dose, and so sweet the draught; but, drinking so frequently that all the veins are filled in brief season, and the poison finally makes perfect lodgment in the heart. Of course, where there are many lovers, there is a corresponding growth of obtuseness; passion itself no longer finding stimulus, from too great a familiarity with this sort of provocation, and flirtation serving then to gratify the vanity of that passion which has no other appetite. It is curious, indeed, how cold and sterile vanity contrives to render all other passions.

Poor Zulieme! she was a flirt from mere vanity and vacuity of thought. It was easy for her to smile and play; very pleasant to be played with; very grateful to be taught that she had her own fascinations, and that wisdom, in her case, might very well be dispensed with. She had been made beautiful — made to appear beautiful — and so, to appear beautiful was her great duty in life ; and to receive the continued assurance that she was the beauty that she had been taught to think herself, and was doing the proper business for which she was made, was, of course, calculated to put her mind at rest on all disquieting subjects. That her husband did not seem to care whether she was beautiful or not, was not so much a cause of solicitude as of vexation. It only showed him a wrong-headed, inappreciative person, who really did not know what the uses of a husband are!

But Lieutenant Molyneaux gave no such offence. He was shrewd, quick, selfish; had those arts in perfection which teach how to take advantage of another's weakness. He soon sounded the shallows of poor Zulieme's little heart and head: thought so, at least; but was mistaken partly. She was a pretty idiot, vain and capricious; a spoiled child, insolent as lovely; charming without an art, but charming only as a plaything. But, as Molyneaux was wont to say —

"It's a plaything, after all, that a man most wants. Let a man take a wife who will; a plaything for me! and why not another man's wife?"

There was no good reason, as the world goes, why not! His comrade, Lieutenant Eckles, whom you see also in attendance, not far from the beautiful Zulieme, but not at her feet; a young man of inferior intellectual calibre to Molyneaux, but more certainly moral; a good-looking fellow, too, but by no means beau or courtier; he had some misgivings in regard to the policy, if not the propriety, of his comrade's practice. More than once, on the present voyage, he had shaken his head gravely at the presumption of Molyneaux in respect to the captain's wife: not, however, committing the absurdity of reproaching his morals, but only warning him against the dangers of his course.

"Look you, Molyneaux," he was wont to say, "for all that Captain Calvert seems so indifferent about these liberties you take with his wife, I'm sure he don't like it."

"Likely not, Eckles — but *she* does."

"I think that likely, too; but don't you see that you're in shoal water all the time, and can't say when you'll be among the breakers."

"Pooh, Eckles! shall one drink his can the less because of

that? Shall I refuse fruit lest I be sick to-morrow? I am not such an ascetic; no, nor such a fool. I am for taking the pleasure when and where I find it, without asking myself whether there be a thorn lurking for the fingers."

"You will feel it prick when you least expect it; and the wound will, some day, make you feel that the pleasure was a little too dearly paid for. The captain's a terrible fellow when he rouses up!"

"What do I care, so long as I do my duty? The world's a sort of feast, where men gather to get food which they relish. I find mine here and there, and do not ask who is the gardener. Enough if, when I pluck and eat, my appetite smacks its lips. As for the captain's rages, none know them better than myself; but I fear no man that ever stepped a quarter-deck, and he knows it! But you are mistaken: I take no liberties with his wife that are not the custom of the Spaniard. We dance together, and before his eyes.

"Ay, but he's an Englishman; and what the Spaniard sees no harm in, the Englishman winces at. And dancing's one thing, but regular hugging another. There's that fandango, for instance, which you and she are so fond of. Would you like to see your wife carrying on such a game with another man?"

"When *I* marry, my wife may carry it on if she pleases. But, so long as I have my senses, and know what other men's wives are, you will not catch me putting my neck into the halter. I am quite satisfied with another man's wife at a fandango."

"Very well, perhaps, so long as *he's* satisfied; but if it's the captain, be sure to keep your heels in running order, if he happens to break loose. He's not suspicious, not jealous; he's got too much pride for that, I'm thinking; but if ever he thinks you grow saucy, and go too far, he'll make no more bones of breaking your bones than he would of cleaving a Spaniard to the chine. I can tell you there's not a man in the ship but sees and says you go too far, and will be brought up some day by a taut rope and a short turn. It's one thing to dance with the lady; but to do it as you do, with so much unction — to bring her up to your bosom, and squeeze her so closely, and keep at it so long — it neither agrees with the captain's bile nor with the music. You don't keep proper time, Molyneaux; and devils seize me, if any husband will keep proper temper long, if the thing goes on. For my part, if 'twas my wife, I'd soon have you ashore, broadsword to broadsword."

"And get your skull split in the performance."

"That might be.  But, in a case of that kind, you'd find even me an ugly customer; and as for the captain, let me tell you, clever as you are at fence, you wouldn't stand three minutes before him. He'd beat down all your guards before you could say 'Jack Robinson,' and slice off head or arm, making clean work of it, not leaving you chance for a single prayer.  Now, do you look to it. The captain begins to grow a little restiff; the wife's a silly creature, who can't see; and your very impudence will help to shut your eyes and open his, where a wiser fellow would never be suspected, by keeping wide awake himself."

"My dear Eckles, do you never suspect yourself of being tedious.  Other men would only think you envious; but the envy is forgivable; the dullness never."

"You are the most conceited ass, Molyneaux; and your ears will bring you to the pillory.  I envious! and of you, I suppose? Oh, that a man's calf should turn his brains so completely!"

The young men were both dressing for the *festa* when this dialogue took place: Molyneaux was drawing on his silken stocking, and stroking the limb with evident complacency.  Hence the reference of his companion to the particular member.  The sarcasm of the junior member fell innocuous on the ears of his senior; in fact, provoked his laughter only.  He was too well fortified by self-esteem.  It was an additional tribute to the merits of his legs. But this must suffice for clues.in this progress.  Meanwhile, return we to the *festa*.

Molyneaux served the cates and viands.  Zulieme shared with him, helping him in turn.  Eckles, more respectfully apart, was rather a spectator than participator in the scene.  He ate and drank, it is true.  He had a genuine English appetite.  The sailors were dispersed in the woods, making merry after their fashion, little groups of them forming under so many trees, and drinking, eating, and gambolling, like young donkeys in a pleasant pasturage.  Very soon, finding her mistress absorbed in his gallantries with Molyneaux, Sylvia took herself off to a social circle of more freedom, among her favorites of the crew.  Phipps was not so modest as to suppose that he could draw off with safety;

and Lieutenant Eckles, though feeling himself *de trop*, was yet, for this very reason, unwilling to withdraw. He sat; looked on uneasily; rose and stood about; was sometimes spoken to, and sometimes spoke; but formed no essential member of the *tableau*.

And the rich wines of Sicily and Madeira were soon put in circulation; and the joyous Zulieme seemed to yield herself wholly to the intoxication of the scene. Her bright eyes sparkled back to those of her cavalier. Her lively tones answered to his subdued and sentimental ones.

But it was somewhat disquieting to him that she should talk merrily, in answer to his saddest murmur; that there should be nothing sad either in her looks or words. She was a little too much the child, at play, for him. He could better prefer a little more of that Anglo-Norman intensity which conducts so readily from play to passion.

But where should Zulieme learn that sentiment which is the due medium for such transition? It was neither in heart nor head; and the hopes of any progress on the part of our *roué* could be predicated only of her exuberance; the loose, familiar habits of her race; her ignorance of all concentrative passion; her butterfly caprice and infantile restlessness. Such a character naturally baffled the usual arts of the courtly gallant. He relies upon the use of a conventional sentiment of which she had never learned the A B C. That sort of eloquence — a compound, in which fancy relieves, yet reconciles us to passion; which is enforced by sadly-searching glances; soft, low tones, melting into murmurs — all these, the more common agencies in such a game, were wanting in their wonted potency, dealing with so light a creature. She was willing enough to sport on the edge of the precipice, but only because she was so totally ignorant of any precipice in existence. Sin is usually a thing of great intensities, by which one is hurried onward in repeated provocation; the merely loitering nature is as frequently diverted from sin — that is, the sin of passion — as it is from positive virtues, by its mere caprices; and Zulieme Calvert, *née* Montano, was one whom the sound of a fiddle could divert from a death-bed — whom the grateful occupation of costuming herself for a festa, where she was to be seen of many lovers, would suffice to win from the embraces of the most ardent whom she herself preferred over all the rest.

How shall Lieutenant Molyneaux beguile such a nature to a moment of serious thought of love? for he can only prevail by inspiring her with some such mood.

Well, he spoke of love, of hearts naturally twinned by Heaven, denied by man; afflicted with mutual yearnings, but with great barriers of convention between: not insurmountable, however, thank Heaven! Love will find out a way — why not? Is love, decreed of Heaven, to be denied of man? Shall these mutual hearts be defrauded of their mutual rights? And what are these barriers that rise up to conflict with the purposes of Heaven? Are they not pretexts and impediments of merely human artifice? And shall those who have Heaven's sanction upon their affections — shall they submit to these human artifices?

Such was the sort of stuff, of an ancient fashion, which the roué finds stereotyped to his hands in the old romances, with which our amorous lieutenant regaled the ears of Zulieme Calvert, in the effort to arouse her fancies. The case was, of course, put abstractly.

And he looked so languid and sad, so wretchedly interesting, while he said it, that poor Zulieme sighed too, and looked very wretched herself for a moment, and said:

" 'Twas, indeed, very sad and very cruel, Mr. Molyneaux; and I wonder why people do submit to such denial. I'm sure I wouldn't. If I loved a gentleman I'd have him, and he should have me, and I'd no more mind what mamma said than I'd mind Sylvia. But I don't think such things happen often, lieutenant. I don't think love makes one so wretched. If it did, 'twould be no better than grief or melancholy. Now, when I was in love, I was always the gayest creature in the world. I told everybody. I had a hundred friends, and we talked of it all the time; and we made songs about it, and dances———"

" Dances !"

" Yes! we made dances about it; and one played the gentleman, and the other the lady. And oh! you should have seen us: how we bowed to each other, and sidled by each other, and smiled and looked up, and sighed and looked down; and then, on a sudden, the gentleman seized the lady in his arms, and drew her up to him, and gave her such a kiss. Oh! I vow, when I was in love, or only playing love, it was the most joyous time of my life.

and I was never so gay — so happy. Love never made me wretched."

"But was this when you married the captain? He did not court you in that way, did he?"

"Oh! no! — poor fellow, he couldn't do much courting, any way. When I first saw him, he was half dead. Father brought him home. He was wrecked, you know, and cast away; and he and Belcher travelled over the isthmus, till he was taken sick, and brought to our hacienda. And he was so sick! He hardly knew anybody; was out of his head; could see nothing; and talked all sorts of things about England, and fighting, and a lady whom he called Olive. It was always Olive — Olive, Olive! And he spoke so softly and sweetly, and I could see that he was a handsome man, and a brave, though he was so feeble. And so, when he called *me* 'Olive,' I answered him; and I nursed him; and he was so pleased, and I was so pleased to nurse him. He was like a doll, and I washed his face and bathed his head, and I combed his hair, and all that did him good; and when he was raving, he kissed my hands, and called me his dear Olive, and I let him call me so, and answered him, and never told him that I was not Olive, but Zulieme. And I sang and played to him on the guitar, and when he got better we played together. Oh! he was a great doll for me, and it was in playing together that we made love and carried on our courtship. It was very funny. Such plays as we had — such rompings! And I taught him how to dance our Spanish dances; and he sang with me — he's got a beautiful voice for singing; and I chased him through the orange-groves, and found him out where he used to hide himself; for he loved too much to hide himself among the thick groves; and he looked so sad when I found him; but I cheered him up, and he would smile, and sing and dance with me, all so good; till, one day, he started up in a sort of passion, and looked very grand, and said I should be his little wife; and I said, 'Yes, why not? it will be so funny to become a wife.' And so the priest married us. But he's changed since then — he is not funny now. He's so serious, and so cross! — all you English are so cross and quarrelsome."

"But *I* am not."

"Oh! yes, you are, though you do try to please me and make me happy."

" Ah, Zulieme, what you call love is very different from what I mean. I could teach you a better sort of love — more sweet, more precious — which would fill your soul rather than your eyes; for which you would be willing to die; for which, alone, one who knows what it is would be willing to live !"

" Do teach me, then. I'd like to know every sort of love. I suppose it's different in all countries; but I don't think you English know much about it; at least, I don't like your rough, hard, quarrelsome sort of love. It seems to me as if you are always angry when you love. There's Harry, now — why, when he made love to me, it was like a tiger. I didn't know but he wanted to eat me. And when he spoke of love, even before we were married, it was as if he spoke of some great sorrow and trouble; for he groaned, and clasped his head in his hands, and then he would start, and dash out into the groves, and almost run, till he got into the thickest part, where the sun never shines."

" I would teach you another sort of love from his," responded the courtier in low tones, looking sadly sweet, with that intense stare of the eyes, which, with a slight dash of melancholy in the gaze, makes the usual ideal of devoted and inveterate passion, among professed artists.

" Oh! don't look so wretched !" cried the lady, flinging a handful of Brazil nutshells into his face. " It's enough to scare love out of the country to look so while you talk about it. Don't you — you hurt me."

He had seized her hand, and would have carried it to his lip, when a guttural sound, rather a grunt than groan, aroused him to the consciousness that there were other parties on the ground. With a fierce glance he looked around, and met the ominous visage of his brother lieutenant, who, fearing lest the scene should too greatly shock his own, or the modesty of some other party, sent forth the doleful ejaculation, which had arrested the gallantries of our cavalier. Molyneaux could have taken him by the throat.

" Oh! you had reason to groan, Mr. Eckles," said the laughing lady; " for such a doleful picture as Mr. Molyneaux made of himself was absolutely distressing. Now hear me tell of love: when you love, you must look sweet, and bright, and happy; you must sing, and you must dance; and go together into the groves, and get oranges, and bananas, and figs, and nuts; and then have a chase, and pelt one another as you run, till you're ready to drop with laughter, and only shake it off to dance. For you mustn't laugh out when you're dancing — only smile; you need all your breath, you know, if you want to dance beautifully. But, hark! Phipps has gone off with his fiddle, and the sailors are at it. Hear what a shouting and shuffling: and that Sylvia, she's gone, I vow, and I suppose she's footing it with the best of them. How funny! Come, let's go and see."

And she sprang up, gathered up her skirts with one hand, grasped the arm of Molyneaux with the other, and crying to Eckles, "Come, Mr. Eckles, won't you?" she lilted away in a capering motion, which required that Molyneaux should adopt a new step, somewhat difficult to his execution, in order to keep time with hers. Eckles slowly following, with uplifted hands and eyes, the three soon buried themselves in the deeper woods, where a more inspiriting and less pathetic action was in progress.

# CHAPTER V.

## SIMPLY, LEGS AT OUTLAWRY.

" The piper loud and louder blew;
 The dancers quick and quicker flew;
 They reeled, they set, they crossed, they cleekit,
 Till ilka carlin swat and reekit," &c.—*Tam O'Shanter.*

SAILORS ashore have a proverbial character for rollicking.
So, too, is High Life Below Stairs matter for the proverbialist.
Colts on a common, boys in the holidays, girls at a match or
merry-making: fools all, you say. Oh, ridiculous moralist! throw
off your cloak of wisdom for a while, as Prospero does his magic
garment, and relieve your shoulders of the dignity which should
break any camel's back. Do not require us to apologize for these
silly ones, because you claim to be wise or virtuous. " Shall there
be no more cakes and ale," because you have come to your inheritance from Solomon? Sessa! let these children slide; and stop
your ears at the uproar, but do not complain, lest Apollo stretches
them for you to the dimensions which he gave to those of Midas.

Great is the uproar, wondrous the antics, measureless the fun,
among our rollickers on shore! Is it Bo-peep, Hide and Seek,
Hunt the Slipper, or only a new fashion of the fandango? The
apes — the urchins — the grimalkins — the donkeys! what are
they after? What a charivari! Jack Tar, Ben Bobstay, Jim
Bowline, Bill Bowsprit, Mike Mainsail, and a score besides, are
all busy in a merry contest for the hand of Sylvia, that model
among mulattresses.

And all this to the perpetual clang of Phipps's fiddle; and the
yell and laugh chase each other through the woods, till every
sleeping echo, starting up in terror, screams it out again from
swamp and thicket!

And Sylvia, how she runs, and skips, and bounces! What legs she shows! They toss her about, the Jack Tars, from hand to hand, like a bird from the shuttle; yet, with catlike agility, she keeps upon the wing, and out of all clutches. There! Ben Bobstay has her — no! she slips through his fingers. At the very moment when he shouts, " Shiver my timbers, but I've got her," she breaks loose and skips away, with a joyous yell of her own, that sufficiently testifies her sense of freedom, and her own fun in the chase.

She rather likes this rough usage; is evidently nowise disinclined to " the situation;" and takes good care not so far to distance the pursuer as to discourage his pursuit. Sylvia, poor thing, is neither fun nor man hater; and, in the absence of other people, held the tarry-breeches folks to be quite passable, and by no means to be despised. She is sufficiently removed from her own set to have no dread of vulgarity. And this humble self-estimate is always a commendable virtue among our colored Christian brethren. We commend her example to her race, especially at this philanthropic era. Let them not despise the whites too greatly because they have so especially won the admiration of the Caucasian world. Let them sometimes condescend to a dance and fling with their ancient master, if only to show that they do not pride themselves upon their elevation beyond the usual scale of humanity!

Sylvia is just now a model, not only of modesty, but agility. But the odds are against her. Sailors have great virtues in their legs also, and there are twenty pair now busy to circumvent her one. Ah, poor Sylvia! Jim Bowline, this time, has got the weather-gauge of her; Bill Bowsprit, with great arms stretched wide, is ready to cut her off from port; and that famous reefer, Jack Tar, has taken her amidships; *i. e.*, around the body.

Ha! no! Bravo! Bravissimo! She eludes the pack.

" Well done, Cutty Sark !"

What a leap was that, involving prodigious muscle, and a liberal display of legs!

But it is a last effort. She flags. They surround her. She can no more escape; and, encircled by their outstretched forms and arms, she is constrained to join in the fandango.

Never was there such a scene. It is at its height when the

3*

Señora Zulieme, attended by her cavaliers, comes upon the ground.

Zulieme is ready to die of laughter. She cheers, claps her little hands, and finally, in a very convulsion of merriment, flings herself fairly upon the shoulders of the more courtly of the two lieutenants, and screams her laughter. And, taking advantage of *her* "situation," perhaps misconstruing the action, Molyneaux wraps her in close embrace, and snatches a kiss from her mouth!

The act is requited, quick as lightning, with a slap, laid on his cheek soundly, and with all the breadth, and weight, and muscle, of her little hand. And she tears herself away from his clutch, and says, very coolly — as if the girl simply resented the impertinence of the forward boy —

"Look you, Molyneaux, don't you try that again, or you shall have it harder. I don't like such play. I won't have it."

Play? Molyneaux looks confounded. He never meant it for play. He can not well understand her. Molyneaux, you are to remember, is only a cavalier, not a philosopher. He was trying to teach her serious things, however, and she takes it all for fun; but for a sort of fun for which she simply has not a bit of taste. What a strange sort of education she has had!

The kiss was seen, was heard; and so — much more certainly — was the slap!

And the horse-laugh of Eckles, followed by that of all the sailors, echoed throughout the circle, and somewhat diverted the merry crew from the humors of Madame Sylvia.

Molyneaux, with red face, shot a thunderbolt from his eyes at Eckles, which only made him laugh the more.

But the sports went on. Phipps's fiddle was working wonders; and, as if wholly forgetting kiss, slap, and all offence, Zulieme, laughing all over, threw herself into an attitude, winning, voluptuous, graceful, stretched out her arms to Molyneaux, and challenged him into the charmed circle; and, not slow, the lieutenant leaped forward, wondering still at her capricious temper — ice and fire by turns — and joined in the passion-feeding movements of the fandango.

This was Zulieme's great accomplishment. In this she excelled all her sex. Her whole person was suited to it. Exquisitely modelled, lithe, graceful; her tastes harmonized wondrously with her person, to exhibit all its charms, in the most capricious and voluptuous movement. Every limb consorted with the action. The whole contour of her figure was developed, in all its symmetry, roundness, beauty, ease, and freedom. And the expression of face, eyes, mouth, speaking to and with each several gesture, combined to make the successive movements so many studies for the artist; each constituting a scene to itself, but all happily blended, so as to form a story of eager passion, with all the fluctuations of love, in the usual caprices of young and amorous hearts. Looking at her, you are reminded of what Ulysses says of Cressida: —

> " Fie, fie upon her!
> There's language in her eye, her cheek, her lip;
> Nay, her foot speaks. Her wanton spirits look out,
> At every joint and motive of her body.
> Oh, these encounterers, so glib of tongue,
> That give a coasting welcome ere it comes,
> And wide unclasp the tables of their thoughts
> To every ticklish reader! — set them down,
> For sluttish spoils of opportunity,
> And daughters of the game."

But we should be doing Zulieme injustice were we to apply this language to her. She deserves it in appearance only. Were she a Greek, or an English woman, it might be true. But it is not in her heart or her passions that *her* offence lies. It is because she possesses " wanton spirits," not wanton desires, that she plays the voluptuous one. It is with her just so much play — nothing more. She is an actor, and in her part of the play. In our present sense of the word, she is not voluptuous. She is, in fact, rather cold than passionate. Her blood dances to the intoxication of music — not her head or heart. The dances suffice her — are sufficiently compensative in themselves, conduct to nothing, and rather relieve passion than provoke it. The character of such a woman is not an uncommon one, even with the sterner Anglo-Norman nature. She will suffer the passionate embraces of Lieutenant Molyneaux in the dance, but not otherwise. She will float with him in the languor of soft music, or dart and bound to his persuasions, when the violin discourses with enthusiasm; but if he ventures to kiss her, she will slap his face! There is something serious in kissing which she will not suffer; none in dancing, waltzing — though these sometimes demand pretty close hugging — none in fandango, or castanets; none, in brief, in the fashions of her country, which train the sexes to familiarities, through these media, which, in the case of other nations, more intense and of colder climates, would inevitably awaken all the storms of passion.

And thus it is, that, while the blood of Lieutenant Molyneaux courses through his veins like a lava flood, the bosom of Zulieme Calvert beats as temperately as if she lay at ease in her verandah, while the sweet breezes of the southwest swept over with an ever-fanning wing, waiting upon the drowsiest empress that ever sate on the cushions of apathy.

Lieutenant Molyneaux broke down in the dance. But there was no breaking down in Zulieme. She challenged Eckles to the encounter; caught him by the arm, forced him into the ring, and soon laughed merrily, as, after a series of horrible leaps, bounds, and "*cavortings*," he succumbed also, throwing himself down upon the sward, and declaring himself "all a jelly!"

Zulieme leaped into a grapevine; swang; called for her guitar; played awhile; and, while she played, Molyneaux placed himself behind her, and with officious hands upon her person, kept lady and swing in gentle motion; and with all this, she took no sort of offence.

But, anon, she tired of the guitar and swing; leaped down, turned to Molyneaux, forced him anew into the waltz, and betrayed as much grace, elasticity, and vigor, as before.

We are free to state, that, however grateful to our lieutenant, to be able to grasp hand, and arm, and waist, and to feel her warm breath upon his cheek, he was himself troubled with a shortness of breath, and a heaviness of limb, which made his movements almost as awkward as those of his junior officer, Eckles.

And even while they thus swam and danced together, in that wild, warm, fantastical movement of the American Spaniards — an exaggeration of all that is wild and voluptuous in the dances of the Spaniards in the old world — in the regions Biscayan or Andalusian — there came other spectators to behold the scene.

On the edge of the little amphitheatre, thus occupied, suddenly stood Harry Calvert and his faithful follower, Jack Belcher. The former leaned against a tree, with folded arms, and watched the scene for a while with a gloomy but vacant aspect. He had emerged from the sylvan recess of the latter, ere he had approached him, and found Belcher in waiting. The more violent emotions of the captain were then subdued, but a deeper tint of sadness had overspread his countenance; and, as now he gazes upon the voluptuous and fantastic sports of his wife with his young and amorous lieutenant, it is, perhaps, quite pardonable in his faithful follower to assume that some portion of the ferocious sadness of his features may be caused by the lady's levity, to call it by no harsher name. And, almost unconsciously, Belcher says to him — as it were apologetically —

"It's the custom of the people, sir; she means no harm."

"Surely, she means no harm! It is all child's play. Songs and dances — fools and fiddles. Surely, no harm. Surely not, Jack."

And, speaking thus, Harry Calvert turned away, almost contemptuously, and moved slowly out of the woods.

Was it pride, was it indifference, that rendered the captain heedless of this loose indulgence of festivity on the part of his wife — these freedoms of her sex, so unfamiliar to English eyes, which, in spite of his apologies, revolted those of Jack Belcher? or was it obtuseness? Had the sensibilities of his master become so callous, or brutified, that he neither saw, nor cared to see, how eager was the embrace of Molyneaux, how heedlessly Zulieme yielded herself to his embraces? He could see the satyr in the eyes of the former — what was it in those of the latter which made him indifferent? Perhaps he knew her sufficiently. Perhaps — but wherefore farther supposes? Enough, that he says, moving off, with Belcher close following:—

"A child, Jack — a mere child. Child's play all. Happy that there is neither thought nor memory to stir up passion, or make it bitter! Zulieme is simply a happy child."

And the two walked together along the shores; and their farther talk was of the ship, cargo — anything but love or woman. And, as they went, the darkness came down, and the moon shot up into the heavens, and the stars stole out; and fires were lighted in the woods where the revellers still lingered; and while Zulieme strummed the guitar, and sang some of those wild ballads, Moorish or Castilian, in which the latter language is so prolific, the merry Jack Tars turned their dancing into a drinking party, and the clink of the cannikin served to *soberize* their antics, in gradually bringing them into the province of drunkenness! We have no homily for the occasion. They were less virtuous in those days than we in ours.

Meanwhile, not an ear heard the dip of that paddle which slowly traced the windings of the marsh on the other side of the bay — not an eye beheld that "dugout" of the redman, as it slowly swept along under cover of its green fringes, a mere speck in the moonlight, across the bay, and into the very creek where our cruiser lay at her moorings. But a little while had elapsed, when the sharp, snakelike eyes of the Indian warrior watched the revellers as they lay, or sate, or danced, or slept, around their fires; never fancying that, even then, there was one near who made nice calculations of the number of white scalps which might be taken, were there with him, instead of one, but a score of his lithe and active warriors!

And the two redmen stole away from their place of espionage in the gorge of the forest, and behind its thickets; and soon the little dugout, which had been simply attracted by the shouts of the revellers to see, stole once more quietly out of the creek, and took its course for the open bay. But, this time, not without observation. Calvert and Belcher were upon the headland as it went. The keen ears of the former heard a sound of paddles; the keen eyes of the latter detected the slight dark speck, as it rounded the opposite point into the full blaze of moon and starlight; and the summons :—

"Who goes there!" was only a moment quicker than the pistol-shot which aimed to punish the insolent refusal to answer.

That pistol-shot, ringing clear over the creek and forest, brought the revellers from the thicket. There was prompt pursuit. But the canoe of the redman was nowhere to be found. Belcher then reported that which he had before discovered, and rightly divined this to be the same canoe which he had seen several hours before, steering for the unknown island of Kiawah.

"The Indians are not here yet in any numbers, sir, but it's well to look out for them, now that fish have begun to bite."

"Nay, 't will not need. We shall be gone to-morrow."

At this moment, our captain and his follower were joined by Zulieme and Molyneaux, closely accompanied by Eckles, Sylvia, and the rest. The pistol-shot had served to end the revel. Of course there were a thousand agitating queries, which were soon answered, but without satisfying anybody. When Zulieme found that nothing could be known, she was all reproaches to her lord.

"To break up the dance just when it was so delicious. I was so happy. And why, Harry, didn't you come and dance with me, instead of this Molyneaux? He's so slow, and he wears such tight breeches, that he can do nothing in them. Now, Harry, *you* can do so much better, and you wear such loose breeches, and *you* can stand it so much longer!"

Calvert smiled sadly, as he chucked her silently under the chin. Belcher noted that when Molyneaux presented himself, his master smiled again; but he fancied, this time, that it was quite another sort of smile — that there was something sinister in it — which, had *he* been the object, he should not have wished to see. And Belcher had his own cogitations in respect to this difference of smile.

"It's one thing for the *señora* to be free in them Spanish fandangoes; but it's a very different thing for such a person as Lieutenant Molyneaux to have the freedom too. Oh, yes, indeed! That's a difference! *She's* not thinking at all: but what's *he* thinking about all the time? Oh! I know him — and I reckon the captain knows him too. His thinking, indeed! The goat! the monkey! But let him look to it. I remember that sharp smile of Harry Berkeley — Calvert, I should say — from the time when he was only knee-high to a cocksparrow; and when he smiled so through them half-shut eyes, there was mischief in it; and he's one to work with a word and a blow; and the word is just so much thunder, always after the flash."

Like all favorite body-servants, Jack Belcher had his omens and memories together.

# CHAPTER VI.

### CLEOPATRA IMPATIENT.

> " Oh, we are children all,
> That vex the elements with idle cries,
> For playthings, that we throw away anon,
> Seeking still others ; which not satisfy,
> But mock us like the rest.   We would be wise,
> And are but wanton."

PROMPT in execution as resolve, the captain of the " Happy-go-Lucky" had ordered that, with the dawning, that clever little cruiser should be got ready for sea.

Zulieme was awakened ere the dawn by the rattling of bolts and chains, and the weighing of anchors.   She started up from, no doubt, very pleasant slumbers in that luxurious cabin, and found herself alone.

That cabin !   Cruisers, privateers, pirates, are all understood to have luxurious cabins.   This is the conventional understanding, among your writers of prose fiction.

And there is reason in it.   Such snuggeries as they must be, in such long, low, dark-looking craft as these generally are, must necessarily imply boxes for cabins, such as would better suit the physical dimensions of elf and fairy than stalwart men of Saxon brood.   And, being thus small and snug, why not lavish upon them the nice tastes which commend the cottage, and reconcile us, through beauty and neatness, to the absence of vastness and magnificence ?   Besides, having the wealth, why should not privateer, or cruiser, have a taste ? and these being their homes, why not make them as cheerful and attractive as we are all apt to render our cabins when dwelling on dry land ?   Something, too, of the compensative must be sought, in this respect, for the absence of many of the comforts, to say nothing of the ease and freedom, which we can only seek upon the shores. There will, accordingly, be found huddled together in the cabins of the merest seadogs a variety of treasures, such as we rarely find, in any similar space, in other situations. There will be luxuries at waste, gauds and gems, toys of art and fancy, and appliances of enjoyment and ostentation, such as will be apt to confound the sight of the landsman, even when he shall happen to be born in the purple. The privateers, *quasi* pirates, of the days of *good* Queen Bess were famous for their ostentatious habits and indulgences. There was Cavendish, for example, who entered the British ports with silken sails, as well as streamers, and got himself knighted, just as he showed himself a man of taste and splendor, as well as a man of blood. Stars shine famously on a crimson ground, and the blending, *or* with *gules*, has never mortified the pride of any nobility, ancient or modern.

There is no difficulty in reconciling these anomalies of taste and mood in the character of those who trace back to the northern vikings. Enough, that most cruisers of the good old times, when " there was no peace beyond the line," found it easy to discover a propriety in such combinations of voluptuous glitter with the most savage outlawry.

And the taste has hardly died out in the present day. At all events, our cruiser of the " Happy-go-Lucky" was sufficiently familiar with the practice of the preceding generation, and sufficiently approved it to continue its exercise: though, by the way, we are to admit that much of his present display was due to the simple fact that the fair Zulieme was his passenger. (Query — why *passenger*? why not *passager*?) The magnificence was rather hers than his. His cabin, hardly more than twelve feet square — an empire to himself alone — was necessarily so decorated as to be specially pleasant in the sight of his wife. He did not stop as to the necessary expenditure. Everything, exquisitely little, in that little domain, was exquisitely nice. The furniture, the fixtures, were all of fine mahogany. There were two trim sleeping places, panoplied with gilding and purple. Rich curtains of crimson silk draped the chamber. There was a most exquisitely nice divan, covered also, back and cushion, with silken draperies. There was a pier-table of pearl-inlaid ebony, upon which, in a wicker-work of gilt wire, stood vases filled with flowers, that were now no longer fresh. Bijouterie — chains, and clasps, and medal-lions — lay confusedly on this table; and, something of a contrast, poniards and pistols — enough for two — were oddishly among them. And rich shawls of silk, and fine workmanship, were scat-tered over couch and sofa in rare confusion, mocking taste with mere exuberance and splendor. And there were gay shining. weapons, cimeters and pistols, that hung in racks against the wall; and a lamp, feebly striving to give forth its fires, swung suspended from the ceiling, the glasses that environed it being of thick cut crystal. Altogether, the snuggery, if small enough for the fair-ies, was richly enough garnished and decorated for the more vo-luptuous genii of Eastern fable — the djinns of Gog and Magog dimensions.

And there, starting from sleep as the heavy chain falls upon the deck, Zulieme found herself alone.

She did not conjecture that the cabin had, that night, enter-tained no other inmate than herself. Her lord had strode the decks, or slept upon them, through all the watches of the night. But you are not to suppose that this occasioned her any concern.

To wrap a morning-gown of silk about her shoulders; to fling a silken turban over her head; and thus in *dishabille*, with black hair dishevelled, to dart up the steps of the companion-way, and hurry to the quarter-deck, was the work of but a moment, calling for no single interval of reflection, with any creature so child-ishly impulsive.

Harry Calvert, with arms folded, eyes half shut, and looking inward rather than outward, sombre as a thunder-cloud — hardly conscious of anything but that he was obeyed — did not see her approach, till he felt her arm on his shoulder. He acknowledged her presence with a start, then turned away, and strode to the opposite side of the vessel. She followed him.

" Why, what's the matter, Harry ?"

" Matter! what matter! Nothing's the matter! Don't you see we're at sea ?"

" Yes : but where bound for, Harry ?"

" Charleston."

" Oh! I'm so glad. So you were only plaguing me all the while."

" Plaguing you! *I* plague you ? Why should I plague *you*,

Zulieme? Why plague anybody? Do I look like a man to engage in monkey-tricks?"

And verily, none might reasonably think so, judging from his brows at that moment.

"Oh, don't think to scare me, Harry, with such a face."

"Scare you?"

"To be sure — scare me. If you don't want to scare me, why do you look so? Boo! There's for your sulky faces. I'm sure I don't mind 'em, Harry; and now that we're really to go to Charleston, you may blow yourself up into a thunder-storm as soon as you please."

And she hummed and lilted as usual, swept across the quarter-deck on light fantastic toe, then darted back to him, and with hand again on his shoulder, asked —

"But how long, Harry, before we get there?"

"It may be half a day, Zulieme — it may be never!

"Now, that's too sulky. Why will you talk so? Half a day? I must go and begin to get my things ready."

And she disappeared under a new impulse. He gave her but a single glance, then turned away, and looked out upon the dim waste of sea, now growing white in the increasing light of morning, as, shooting out between the green islets that guard the mouth of the Edisto, our cruiser made her way into blue water.

With a fair wind, indeed, it needed but a few hours to bring the ship to the Charleston entrance, and, in the case of one of such light draft, into port. But, for the present, our cruiser kept the offing, and hung off and on, under cover of the shores, her masts hidden behind stripes of pine forest.

And so she kept till twilight.

Meanwhile the eager and giddy-souled Zulieme, with all the impatience of a child bent upon its day of pleasure, had roused up Sylvia, and set Phipps in motion, preparing to go on shore.

The cabin was soon a scene of wild confusion. Trunks were rummaged and emptied. Silks and satins, gowns and garments, skirts and laces, covered couch and cushion. She made her toilet with care; sat in deliberation on each article of costume; chose and rejected each in turn, until Phipps was beside himself, and Sylvia in despair. More than two hours were thus consumed: and when she ran again upon deck, to ask more questions, she left

to her Abigail the task of restoring to order a wardrobe, ample
enough for a princess of the blood, which, had she tried, could
scarcely have been thrown into a condition of more admirable
confusion. But Sylvia was more patient than her mistress; and
in two hours more she had contrived to render the little chamber
once more habitable. It was not long before our captain drove
her headlong from it; flying himself from the perpetual questioning of the fair Zulieme on deck.

The restless señora had utterly failed to extract any satisfaction
from her lord. She next had recourse to Molyneaux. But,
whether he really knew nothing of the purposes of his superior, as
he alleged; or whether he had taken counsel of prudence from
the warning remonstrances of Eckles; or whether, as is more
probable, his impudence led him to adopt the policy of piquing
the lady into a better recognition of his own importance; he had
suddenly become exceedingly shy of his communications. She
could get nothing from *him !*

And so she petted and pouted through half the day; would eat
no dinner — a circumstance, we are constrained to say, that had
no sort of influence upon the appetites of either of the lieutenants.
Zulieme was somewhat consoled as she saw that her lord ate as
little as herself. She was soon again upon deck, especially as
she heard the ship in motion. But the prospect was as little
grateful as before. The "Happy-go-Lucky" seemed to be exercising herself, simply in a purposeless progress; to and fro; in
the precincts of the port which she seemed coy to enter, yet wist-
ful of the approach. It lay inviting enough before her. Sullivan's island, then well wooded, lay on one hand, and her eye
could trace, in the clear atmosphere, the white houses in the city,
some six miles off in the west. It needed not an hour to reach
the goal. And that hour — that six miles — were these to be
the barriers between her impatience and its object? And why, if
not to enter, had they come hither, and thus far? Who will answer?

The captain kept his cabin. He had already been employed
through certain weary hours, writing, reading, examining, and
preparing papers, with a wilderness of them spread upon the table
before him. A savage silence, save for the sounds made by his
pen, and the rustle of unfolding sheets, prevailed throughout the
chamber. He seemed vexed, wearied, uneasy, striving, it would

seem, to concentrate upon inferior objects those thoughts which were marvellously willed to wander. While thus engaged, Zulieme had sought him repeatedly, but in vain; failing to secure his attention, and only provoking. him to signs of impatience which, with some effort — a fact she scarcely perceived — forbore to express itself with harshness and severity. She failed entirely to wear or worry him into a revelation of his objects.

"Tell me, Harry Calvert," said she, after repeated intrusions, "what's the use of all these foolish papers? And why can't you wait to do them till you get to Charleston? And why, now that we've got here, why do you wait at the door, as if wanting permission to go in? What's to prevent? Molyneaux says there's water a plenty and wind in the right quarter, and that it only needs an hour to be at the docks. And don't you see I'm all dressed and ready to go ashore? I shall die if you keep me another night at sea. And I *won't* be kept. Do you hear me, Harry?"

He had hardly heard a syllable; but he answered, "Yes, I hear," — but without once looking up.

"Harry Calvert, you are a great sulky cayman; and I'm only sorry that I ever saw you."

He seemed to hear *that*, and answered, very soberly, while still continuing to write —

"So am I, Zulieme, very sorry."

"What do you mean by that? you great alligator man! I tell you, Harry, I'm sorry I ever nursed you, and made you well; for you don't care if I die here, in your vile vessel. Oh! you've cheated, and deceived me, and made a fool of me, Harry Calvert, and I hate you! — I do, Harry, and I never did care about you; and if I told you so, I lied. You hear me — I tell you, I never loved you, and I lied when I said so."

It is charity to suppose that the person thus addressed never heard a syllable of this grateful assurance. He simply nodded his head approvingly, and went on writing. She looked at him a moment with a stronger expression of indignation than she had yet shown, then rushed again on deck to the courtly lieutenant.

"Look you, Mr. Molyneaux, didn't you tell me there was nothing to prevent our going to Charleston?"

"No, señora, I did not."

" But I say you did !"

" You misunderstood me, señora.   I said that neither wind nor tide prevented."

" Well, that's the same thing."

" No, ask the captain."

" Ask the great bear and the grand cayman.   He's a brute and monster, and won't hear a word I say.   Now, I ask you, if the wind and water serve, what's to keep us here — what prevents our going in ?"

" Nothing, but the captain.   He says 'no,' and the wind and water must wait on him."

" But *I* won't."

" Ah, Zulieme, a beautiful woman like yourself may do what she pleases."   And the lieutenant smiled very dutifully, as he looked up and said these words in very subdued accents.   " You can will and others must wait."

" How's that, when here I can't get any of you to stir and carry me to Charleston ?   Don't tell me such things, and don't you call me beautiful, when you don't mind a word I say.   Ah ! before I was married, everybody minded me.   Now they all treat me just as if I were a troublesome child.   I wonder what I ever got married for.   I'm sure I'm sick of it."

" You have reason," said the courtly lieutenant, with tones of sympathy, and looking into her face with the utmost tenderness.

" That I have ; and I'll never come with Harry again, though he begs me on his bended knees.   I'd have died here, if I hadn't had you to amuse me.   But tell me, Molyneaux, why don't Harry go up to Charleston ?   What's the reason ?   *Don't* you know ?"

He answered her only with a very annoying, provoking smile, which seemed to say, plainly enough —

" Well, yes, *I do* know, but *you* are not to know."

So she understood the smile.

" But I will know, Mr. Molyneaux."

He smiled still more knowingly, and shrugged his shoulders.

" Now don't you make that impudent motion again.   I won't have it.   You mustn't treat me so, I tell you."

Molyneaux was suddenly seized with a feeling of profound

duty, and grew busied with certain charts of the old Spanish geographers.

Just as suddenly, she pulled the great sheets from his hands, and scattered them about the deck.

" Now, I say, listen to me and answer."

Stooping and picking up the charts, with great placidity, Molyneaux looked up and said, in subdued tones, softly and insinuatingly —

" Ah, señora, would you treat the captain so ?"

" And why not, if he will not answer ?"

The courtly lieutenant shook his head in denial.

" Better not try it, Zulieme, while he is in his present humor."

" But I will try it !  What do I care for his humors ?"

" Nay, señora, I do not suppose that you *do* care much ; but, I know you would never dare do to him what you have just done to the poor lieutenant of this ship."

The wilful creature darted below on the instant.  Looking after her, with a cunning smile upon his countenance, Molyneaux caught the eyes of Jack Belcher fixed steadily upon him.

" Did that fellow hear me ?" quoth he to himself.  Then, a moment after, with a reckless air, and half aloud, " If he did, I care not."

He was not quite so indifferent as he said.  Still less was he indifferent to the events which were probably, even then, going on in the captain's cabin ; but he concentrated his whole regards now upon the charts which he had gathered up from the deck, and seemed heedless of everything besides.

Meanwhile, all below was silent to the ears of those above ; and yet, to those who had witnessed the scene, the feeling was one of suspense and anxiety.  The ears of Molyneaux, however seemingly indifferent, were watchful.  So were those of Jack Belcher. *He* had heard every syllable.  Though of coarser clay, and inferior education, yet his instincts, improved by love for his master, were just and sagacious.  He could see — he suspected — the mischievous purposes of Molyneaux.  He could also suspect their source.  He would have given much to be able to go below, and interpose, if necessary, in the scene which he anticipated.  But he dared not.  He pitied the silly child, who, in a false relationship to his and her superior, was thus made a tool for mischief in the hands of one who could easily make it appear that his whole course was natural enough, if not absolutely proper. We may readily understand how he should be uneasy — how Molyneaux himself should be anxious — about the result of this ridiculous proceeding.

But no sounds reached them from below. Yet had Zulieme kept the silly purpose for which she had darted down. She had approached her lord without a word of premonition. With one fell swoop she had swept the papers from the table to the floor, exclaiming —

"You sha'n't bother with these papers any more, Harry. You shall come on deck and talk with me, and answer me all my questions."

# CHAPTER VII.

## SHADOWS ON THE SEA.

"Know that the fates, frail creature, have decreed
Thy bondage to a power that broods in gloom,
While thou wouldst sing in fancy : that will mar
Thy music, which hath taken an April chirp
From nature, and in place of pleasant carol,
Make it a boding omen, still of evil!"

THE act was like a flash — quick as lightning — one for which
not a syllable had prepared our cruiser. He had not heard or seen
her approach — was deeply busied in the work before him, which
seemed to tax all his attention, and to absorb his whole existence.

But with the act he started into terrible consciousness — started
to his feet, thrust the table from before him, and confronted her
with uplifted hand and clenched fingers. His brow was dark like
a thunder-storm ; there was a lurid fire in his glance that seemed
to smite; and the veins grew suddenly corded across his forehead.
The change was instantaneous. Never had Zulieme beheld such
a countenance in man— never such a look from *him*, the powerful man before her. She recoiled from it, as with all the instinct
of imbecility, cowered, crouched; and the broken murmur from
her lips, speaking which she was hardly conscious, attested her
first sense of her own folly and of his rage.

"Oh, Harry! don't — don't strike me."

"Strike you !" was the hoarsely-spoken answer.

"Strike *you!*" and he drew himself up to his fullest height,
and threw his arms behind him, as if fearing to trust his own
emotions. And it was admirable to behold the wonderful effort
which the strong man made — in his pride, in all the consciousness of power — to subdue himself, as Strength ever should in the
conflict with Imbecility. In a moment his countenance had become composed. There was still a quiver of the muscles which

4

the woman did not see. And then he stooped down deliberately and began picking up the scattered papers, as quietly as Moly-neaux had done on a similar occasion overhead. The woman little dreamed that he thus employed himself only to gain time in the struggle with his own passions. She said something, and laughed hysterically, seeing him so employed; then, with sudden impulse, she sprang to assist in gathering up the sheets of paper. And he suffered her, but continued himself, until all the documents were restored to the table. This done, he said — and with a tone so sad, accents so subdued, an emphasis so melancholy, that the simple words had in them a significance which even she could feel, and which no language could define —

"It is *you*, Zulieme."

*He* did not say so, but we may, that, had the offender been a man — any other person, indeed — he would have brained him where he stood. There would not have been a word spoken.

He took her hand. He led her to the divan, seated her, and stood before her. She was now submissive enough to all his movements.

"Zulieme Calvert, you once saved my life; and — you are my wife. God forbid that aught should ever make me forget what you are, what I owe you, and what I am! But, sit here. I must speak with you. It is necessary that I should try, at least, to lift you into some sense of what you are, what I am, and what is abso-lutely necessary between us."

"Oh, Harry, it was all fun."

"Life, Zulieme, is not a funny thing. Men and women are not made for fun. Life is a sad, serious thing, in which fun is very apt to be impertinence. If I were dying on that couch before you, would you think the affair funny? Would it make you funny? Would you laugh, sing, dance, while I lay struggling with the last enemy of man? There are women — wives, it is said — who would rejoice at such a spectacle; but even they would deem it proper to conceal their delight. They, at least, would not *con-fess* that it was funny in their eyes, or try to make it appear so to the eyes of others."

"Oh, Harry, how can you speak so — and to me — when you know——"

"Do I not tell you that I believe you saved my life? do I not avow that I am your husband? Let this assure you that I will not forget, in what I say, what are the relations between us."

"But oh! Harry, to speak of your dying — and that I should be funny!"

"I did not say that, Zulieme. Hear what I do say: when, in your fun, you tore the papers from my table, I was writing my last will and dying testament."

"Ah — Dios! O, Harry! why should you write such things?"

"Because, the very hour that takes you into Charleston, for which you long so much, may take me to the gallows."

She answered with a scream of horror. He soothed her.

"Let this secure me your attention. If you will be funny, Zulieme, pray be attentive also."

"You stab me to the soul, Harry."

"And I must so stab you to the soul, Zulieme, if only to make you feel that you have one. If, in the pursuit of your merest pleasures, your soul becomes insensible to the anxieties and sufferings of those whom you profess to love, of what use to have a soul at all? It is sometimes necessary to bruise the plant to make it give forth its precious virtues; so, to the cold or sleeping soul it needs that we should sometimes give an almost mortal stab, in order that we may make it feel *that* life, of which otherwise it makes no sign. You have seen that I suffer, yet you heed not; you have been told that I have cares, yet you despise them; I have shown you that I command a turbulent people, who would soon cease to obey if I failed in proper authority, yet you wantonly put that authority in danger. But of these things I have already spoken, and always in vain. I will speak of them no longer. I fear, from what I know of you, that the impressions, even of a great terror, will possess your soul only for an instant; that a gleam of sunshine, a bird song, the sound of music, the laughter of a child, the voice of a gallant in compliment — or his hand in the dance — will make you forget that Danger stands waiting at the door, and that Death lurks, looking over your shoulder, as over mine."

"Oh! Harry, what a fool you must think me!"

"A child, Zulieme; but one that can never *grow*. Your whole people are children. You have no voice in the soul, no urgent thought, which compels *growth*. Happy only, if the world's cares and your own resources will let you remain a child — let you sing, dance, sleep."

He paused, strode away, then turned and resumed. She would have spoken, but, with uplifted hand, he silenced her.

"No, Zulieme, you must hear *me* now. You force me to speak. In marrying me, you married a care — I a child. We were both in error. I have brought you into an atmosphere for which you are unaccustomed. You should have married a man who was willing to dream away life, among the plains or hills of the isthmus, between dance and siesta. I am one whom care and thought do not permit to sleep. You are a bird, that, even in sleep, must sing. You are not asked to do battle in the storm. *My* whole life is a battle. Mine is a life of passion. You know not what passion is. You sob and sleep, sing and sleep, prattle and sleep, and sleep comes to you, rounding life with dream, and rousing it only to new dreams with the morning. What had you, poor Zulieme, to do with a stern, dark, careful man like me? I have brought you to 'an experience of care,' to a life of thought, for which you have no sympathy. It was my fault, perhaps, Zulieme, and your misfortune. And so, we live in different worlds, Zulieme, and though we do not part, we never meet. When we meet, your song is spoiled. I make for you a sky in which no bird can sing, unless the hawk, the vulture, the cormorant. Is it not so, Zulieme?"

"I don't know, Harry; only I feel you are saying terrible things to me. I don't want to hear you!"

"But you *must* hear now. The time has come when you must be made to see clearly how vast a space divides us — makes for us different worlds and fates. Your world changes every day, sometimes every hour. Of the fates, you take no more care than the bird. To-day, you would find your sufficient world in Charleston. In that little town of twelve hundred people, you would dance and sing, quite satisfied, so long as there came a crowd to admire, and a good waltzer to be your partner. And so would it be in Havana. To me these are all childish things."

"Harry, don't talk to me any more. I won't dance again. I will never——"

"Nay, that will be to give up your life, Zulieme. Do not be impatient. You have forced me to speak, and you must hear,

and I promise you that I will not again speak to you, in this manner, till you shall again force me. Now, you must let me finish.
I shall never, Zulieme, cease to repent the selfishness and weakness that made me marry you. I should have known the dangers
and the sufferings to which such an alliance would expose you.
I should have known you well enough to see that you were unfitted
for the encounter. And I *did* know it. But I was weak after
long sickness, and you were very beautiful, Zulieme, and very
tender, and you had saved my life by your nursing, Zulieme."

"Ah, Harry, but didn't I nurse you well?"

"No one could have done it better."

"Yet, you are so cross to me."

"Cross! alas, Zulieme, I try in vain to teach you. Cross!
Child — woman! were you any other than you are, I would have
torn you limb from limb, and thrown you, without remorse or
scruple, to the sharks of yonder deep sea."

"Harry! — you horrid Harry."

"Ay, I am tender to you, Zulieme — tender for *my* nature;
considerate of yours. But I must try and make clear to you the
absolute truths in my situation, however impossible to make you
comprehend the necessities of my nature, or of the character of
yours. When we married, I was weak, and sick, and sore, and
mortified. I had suffered a great disappointment."

"Ah! I know — there was a lady, Harry. And I know her
name, too. You called her often enough when you were out of
your head. And you married me, a poor child you say, because
she wouldn't have you. That's it, Harry."

"That's *not* it, Zulieme. The woman of whom you speak was
mine, all mine — heart, soul, voice — all! all!"

"And why did you not marry her, then?"

"I was an outcast, an exile; but seeking fortune that I might
do so; and in this search I was wrecked, narrowly escaped
drowning, found my way to your father's hacienda, and narrowly
escaped dying; and, after seventeen dreary months of absence
from home, she was made to marry another. But, do not force
me upon this, Zulieme. Rather hear what I would say in regard
to the present, and ourselves; let the past bury its own dead.
Enough for me — sad solace that it is — I knew her to be faithful;
feel that she has been betrayed by those who should have been

true; feel that she has suffered like myself; that never pang went
to my heart that did not find its way to hers. Let there be no
more of this. Let it suffice you that I am your husband — that
she is now the wife of another."

Here he paused, strode aside with averted face, and hastily
swallowed a cup of water.

"Your father found me a dying man, almost glad to die. Had
I been conscious when he took me into his dwelling, I had certainly died. Insensibility, however, came to the relief of nature.
and in the very aberration of intellect the animal recovered. It
was with pain only that I grew to consciousness, and your fond
nursing, Zulieme, gave me the first pleasant impression of returning life and health. I do not reproach you; I am grateful. Yet,
a thousand times better had it been, for you as well as me, had
your sire and self suffered me to perish on the burning highways,
ere you took me to the shelter of your hacienda."

"No! no! Harry — no!"

"Ah! you know not yet the end. And how it all must end.
The sting is yet to come. You are of light heart, a bird nature,
and you will not feel it long. There is consolation in that."

"But, Harry — do n't——"

"Stay, Zulieme, hear!

"Your father's protection, your cares, a vigorous constitution,
and, perhaps, my utter mental unconsciousness for the time, saved
my life. Your father helped me with his means. I bought a
share in this vessel. I finally became sole proprietor. I made
her famous. She became the terror of the Spaniard on the seas.
And here, in this and other ports of the English, she was ever
welcome as a Spanish terror. The Spaniards had been *their* terror. They knew them only as enemies; could know them only as
enemies; and he who strove with the Spaniard was to them an
ally and a friend. I was one of these. The English people
knew me as a friend, and when I tore down a Spanish flag I was
hailed by the plaudits of my people. To do this very work I had
the commission of my king; yet, he now abandons me. Bribed
by the Frenchman, bullied by the Spaniard, faithless to himself
and people, my own king sacrifices me to the foes of both. He
disavows my commission; he denounces me as a pirate of the
seas, whom it is permitted to all men to destroy."

"Oh! Harry, I wouldn't fight for him again. Leave these English; they're a hoggish sort of people — leave them and live with our people. And why should you follow the seas, Harry? What's the use? It isn't money that you want. You have enough, and I have enough, and we'll go back to the Isthmus, where no English can ever find us out; and there, O Harry, there we can be so happy. No troubles, Harry; no cares; nothing but dancing and delight, and fruits and pleasures. Let us go, Harry; let us leave this place; and leave the seas; and have no more trouble, safe, high up in the mountains of the Isthmus."

He shook his head mournfully.

"Rather a single year of life, all storm and battle, than the stagnation of such a life. No peace, no calm for me, Zulieme. I can now live only in the storm. This is what I fail to make you understand. My lot is cast on reefs of danger, through seas of storm, with rocks on either hand, and the hurricane for ever on the wing. It requires all my manhood to steer amid these dangers. It is not for me to skulk them. But, though I do not fear them, and will meet them as becomes a proper manhood, I do not find it easy to win merriment from, or seek it while I am in the death-struggle with, these warring elements. And when I am thus wrestling for life, it is not easy to endure the jest, or the peevish humors, of one even who has saved my life! — even a woman — even a wife! a being whom, in moments of thought, we regard as a thing to cherish close to the heart, and not to gaze on with look of less than kindness. Do you see now why it is that I go to Charleston with mood so different from yours?"

"Do not go, Harry — do not! I did not know that there was danger. I'm sure, Harry, I don't care to go there. Why should I care? I can be seen by quite as many people in Havana, and then we have a thousand times better dancing, I'm sure! No! no! Don't go there, Harry. Rather go home, to our old home on the isthmus."

"I must go, Zulieme, though the gallows waits me at the dock! But I will do nothing rashly, Zulieme, unless goaded to it by your passion for the dance, and by the passions of others not so innocent."

"What passions — what others?"

"Enough, that they are unknown to you. In that ignorance is

my security — and yours! You know, now, why I avoid Charleston by daylight — why I hide my vessel among these headlands, and under cover of these pines. With midnight we will run into port; we will run up Ashley river, and harbor there in a well-known place of security. I will go ashore in disguise. You will remain on board till I tell you that you may come forth in safety. You must be content with this. If not — if stimulated by any foolish love of show or amusement you allow yourself to be discovered — it may lead to my ruin. You must rely on me so as to believe that the restraint I put upon you for awhile, is absolutely necessary for my safety."

"Oh, Harry, I will mind all that you say."

"One word more: beware, Zulieme, how you mind anybody else."

"Who else should I mind, Harry, but you? And if I don't mind you always, Harry, it's because you are such a great English bear sometimes; showing such great teeth and such big paws, and not letting a body laugh as much."

And she threw her arms about his neck and kissed him. He loosed himself tenderly from her hold, took her to the cabin-entrance, and put her out — even as one gently puts out of the window the little bird which has flown into his chamber unadvisedly, and which, ignorant of his purpose, is throbbing with terror underneath his hands. But he had scarce done so, when she returned:

"Harry, let me stay here awhile. I can't go up there now."

"Very well. Lie down, Zulieme."

"Yes, yes! That's what I want!"

And throwing herself down upon the divan behind him, while he went on writing, her great black eyes suddenly gushed out with tears.

But she suppressed the sobs.

After awhile, she started up and cried out:—

"O Harry! there was no truth in what you said about the gallows. You only meant to scare me."

"What my danger may be, Zulieme, I know not. It may not be the gallows. It may not even be death. But there is danger."

He now distinctly heard the sobbing. She could no longer subdue it. He rose, went to her, and, bending over her, kissed her tenderly, while he said:—

"Zulieme, I don't think my neck will ever be defiled by a halter. But it is certain that I am threatened with it by my king. By yours I am threatened with the garote. But I am in danger from neither shame, Zulieme, while I have my strength and senses about me, and carry such a friend as this convenient to my grasp."

And he touched the pistols in his belt, and pointed to certain daggers that hung within reach against the wall.

She started up, and drew the poniard from her own girdle, as she cried —

"And I would kill myself, Harry, if harm should ever come to you."

"Zulieme, if ever you hear of me in prison, come to me if you can, and bring with you that pretty toy! But let them not see it when you come. Weave it up in the masses of your hair, and silence all speech of eyes or tongue, that might declare for what you carry." . . . . .

Enough of this scene. Zulieme in half an hour was asleep, and laughing merrily in her sleep, with those fancies which, in the dialogue, she had been compelled to stifle. Calvert looked round, half confounded, half amused.

"What a contradiction," he muttered to himself. "An April creature. In play a very hurricane — in passion a child that sobs itself to slumber only to dream of play! Yet, though feeble as an infant, she is faithful. If wanting in force and concentration of soul, she is not wanting in truth; and if her love be of the sunshine only, it is pure — a shallow brooklet that can satisfy no thirst, but limpid as the light, and gliding openly, always in the sunshine."

And he resumed his writing for awhile; finished, folded up his papers, and hurried on deck, leaving Zulieme sleeping. She only woke, roused by the vessel's motion, to be told that they were already within the harbor and pressing up toward the infant city. Then she sprang upon her feet and joined her lord on deck.

4*

## CHAPTER VIII.

### SNUG HARBOR.

"Now we're in port and safety, let me ask,
　What is your farther purpose?　Spare me nothing.
　In a false pity that still mocks at sorrow:
　What fate do you design for her who follows
　Such a capricious Fortune?"

THE moon had gone down, but the night was one of many stars. The seas were rising, with the winds fresh from the south. The mists of evening had all lifted from the ocean. The land lay defined on each hand with perfect distinctness. The little city which rose between the twin rivers of Kiawah and Etiwan, or as the English called them, the Ashley and Cooper, grew momently more and more plain to the spectator in the foreground. On the right, silent as stars and midnight, the narrow islet lay which we now call Sullivan. Then, it was a well-wooded strip, almost to the beach; but, then, it had but a single dwelling, where a watch was maintained of four men, under a corporal, in a petty blockhouse, defended by an ancient sixpounder of iron. It stood not far from the present fortress. The forests were subsequently cut down, for the very reason that they served to conceal, from the eyes of the city, such cruisers as the "Happy-go-Lucky"—a little less innocent in fact—a pirate craft, which, at one period, lay in wait for ever at the entrance of the port, ready to dart forth on the unsuspecting merchantman. Equally bare of inhabitants, and even more dense in forest, was the opposite shore, now known as James island.

Not a sound of human life came from either side. The guard at the blockhouse slept, no doubt. It was midnight. The city lay buried in deep sleep; and so the progress of the "Happy-go-Lucky" was unnoticed. She clung as closely as possible to the southern side of the harbor, sheltered in some degree by the shadows of the forests. And thus ran the cruiser when Zulieme Calvert made her appearance on deck. Calvert was already there; had, indeed, navigated the craft into the harbor; and was still engaged, knowing thoroughly the route, in steering her for Ashley river. Every officer and seaman was at his post, and a like silence with that of sea and shore, and midnight, prevailed throughout the vessel.

Zulieme crept to the side of her husband with some timidity. She had not quite recovered her confidence in herself — certainly, was not yet prepared to resume her wilfulness after the scene of the previous evening. Besides, she was impressed by the novelty of her present progress, and the new objects which employed her thoughts : thus entering, at midnight, by stealth, the harbor of a foreign state and people, among whom, as she had been told, lurked some angry terrors for her husband. The very silence which prevailed in the vessel, still pressing on her course, was calculated to awe the glib spirits of the thoughtless creature into reverence. And so, creeping quietly to the side of her husband, she watched his progress, as, with a single word, "larboard" or "starboard," or "port" — or a mere waving of the finger — he directed the movements of the helmsman.

"Oh! what is that, Harry?"

She pointed at the mud reef, on which, at this day, stands Castle Pinckney. It lay immediately upon their right. Then, it was but a mud-reef, having on it a single cabin, near which stood a heavy framework of timber, the uses of which Zulieme could not conjecture. It stood out clearly defined in the starlight, as the eye ranged up the Etiwan, a well-known object to the eyes of our English — not so familiar to those of the Spaniard.

Little did poor Zulieme dream of the answer she was to receive. Calvert looked as she bade him, and quietly putting his hand upon her shoulder, said, in impressive but low tones, scarcely above a whisper :—

"That, Zulieme, is the gallows — that is where they hang the pirates!"

And such, in that early day, was the only use of the reef.

"Ah, Dios! Oh, horrid! And just at the entrance of the city! Oh, what a horrid people!"

What Zulieme ascribed to the popular taste, was, in that day, supposed to be the public policy. They hung men then, "*pour les encourager les autres ;*" and the more conspicuous the place, the greater the elevation — the larger the crowd of spectators — the more horrible the writhings of the victim — the more beneficial the example to society.

Whether we are justified in hanging a man as a warning and example, is a question which we do not care to discuss. There are so many crimes which are justified by law and society, that one feels it a mere waste of time, if not of temper, to endeavor to prove their absurdity. We will, accordingly, suffer the poor Zulieme to suppose that the whole practice was the result of pure British taste; a taste by the way, which, however sanguinary, was not a whit more so than that of her own people, whether under the rule of old Spain, or of its creole *progressistas* who succeeded the Castilian. " But the *garote*," says our refined Spaniard, "is surely not the gallows."

But the " Happy-go-Lucky " has left the gallows islet. She is rounding Oyster point — not a fine stone parapet as we now behold, girdling a famous *drive*, but a mere strip of sandy beach, over which the waves are breaking with the gentlest murmur. We are now in Ashley river — the Kiawah of the redmen, a fine broad, poetical stream, an arm of the sea rather than river — here a mile wide, and of sufficient depth to float a seventy-four. The green marshes bound us on either hand. To the left you see the opening of Wappoo. At high-water, our low, light-draught cruiser might pass through it, and make her way, by a back door, again into the Atlantic. But a couple of miles above, and we pass the primitive settlement of Sayle, where the first settlers of Charleston drove their original stakes, little more than twenty years before. But we stop not here. Our vessel presses on, several miles beyond, where the stream narrows, where the marshes grow less vigorously; where the oaks bend down and kiss the waters; and the marl crops out, seeming, in the moonlight, like a marble margin for some green islet in the Adriatic. We glide into the mouth of a creek on the western bank of the stream, which is thickly fringed with oaks and cedars. Here we shall lie snug, secure from any passing scrutiny. Our sails are quietly furled, and the masts of our cruiser are almost hidden among sheltering pines.

By the time that all this was effected, the day had dawned upon river and forest. Watches were set upon the vessel, and the larger proportion of the crew disappeared from sight, seeking sleep either in their bunks, or in the shelter of the woods. Meanwhile, a small scouting party had been sent out, under Lieutenant Eckles, whose business it was to explore the thickets for a circuit of a mile or two all about. It was important to assure themselves that no encampment of the redmen was within the immediate precinct. They might prove as mischievous as a gipsy band in the neighborhood of a hen-roost. Another small party crossed the river, in order to scour the woods along the opposite shores. These precautions taken, Calvert, who had not closed his eyes for thirty-six hours, threw himself down in his berth, leaving Molyneaux in charge of the cruiser.

It was fortunate for our captain that custom had trained him to sleep promptly, as soon as the exigency had passed which kept him wakeful. Habit had made it easy for nature thus to recuperate after excessive toils. He slept, even as the honest laboring man does, as soon as he touched his pillow. But we do not venture to affirm that he slept so peacefully — that he had no dreams. For, even as he slept, Zulieme stole into the cabin and looked steadily into the face of the sleeper. He was murmuring in his sleep; and again did the ears of the watcher catch from his lips, as she had done more than once before, the name of one, to hear which always brought a flush upon her cheeks. She had too often heard it; and that, too, mingled with language of such tender interest, such fond reproach or entreaty, as to awaken in her heart, so far as that could be roused by such feelings, those of distrust, jealousy, and a vexing suspicion, not only of the past, but of the future. She little dreamed that the occasion was rapidly ripening which would mature suspicion into conviction, and convert a vague jealousy into a source of absolute fear, if not hate and loathing. But we will not anticipate.

Enough, that the lips of the sleeper moaned and murmured — that his sleep was troubled — that he writhed upon his couch, under emotions which were now those of tenderness and grief, and anon, by quick transition, of anger and threatening violence. And over his sleeping hours — not many — that erring but beautiful child of the sun brooded with changing moods, drinking in the

while a bitter aliment, which served to strengthen those feelings
which work for the enfeebling of the better nature.   Sometimes,
too, you might note that what she heard served to impel her to
like exhibitions of *her* own secret nature.   Her cheeks flushed,
her eyes flashed, her lips muttered, also, in broken speech, of vexation, or hate, or mortified vanity, and, more than once, you might
see her grip, with nervous hand, the jewelled toy of a poniard,
which she almost always wore at her girdle.   It was only when
her lord subsided into deep slumbers, which naturally fell upon
him in consequence of his long exhaustion, and ceased to writhe
with torturing thoughts, or to moan with mortified affections, that
her muscles grew composed, and that she stole away from the
cabin, not satisfied, but in silence.

She stooped over him, down toward him, as about to kiss him
ere she went, but suddenly drew back, muttering —

"No, I won't!   He cares nothing for *my* kisses.   He shall
seek them before he gets them."

And she ascended to the deck.   There she joined Molyneaux;
and, after awhile, under his assurance that there was no danger
from the redmen, strolled out into a grove of great live-oaks, attended only by Sylvia.   Three hours might have elapsed, when
she returned to the vessel, re-entered the cabin, and found Calvert not only awake, but busily engaged with papers at the table

"You don't ask where I've been, Harry."

He nodded his head, and showed himself incurious.   She was
piqued.

"You might ask.   You might go with me, Harry, and see these
beautiful woods; such great trees, all green, with such mighty
arms!   I've been climbing trees, Harry.   You should have seen
me."

To all this there was only a vacant shake of the head.   She
looked at him with vexation.

"How long, Harry, are you to keep at these papers? and when
will you go ashore with me?"

"If you wish it, *now*, Zulieme."

"Oh, I'm tired now! but if you'll promise me after dinner."

"After dinner be it, Zulieme: I shall have to leave you to-night."

"Leave me, and to-night? and what for, pray?"

"To go to Charleston."

"But if *you* can go there, why can't *I*, Harry?"

"It is necessary, as I thought I had already told you, that *I* should go thither, if only to see if I can do so with safety."

"Well, that seems to me very foolish, Harry."

"Perhaps so, Zulieme; yet it is the best wisdom that I can command under the circumstances. You will suffer me to judge of it, however, in my own way, as it is my neck, and not yours, that is mostly in danger."

"Pooh! I don't believe your neck's in any danger at all. You gave me one fright about that matter, Harry, last night, but sha'n't give me another. I know something, I tell you; and I can see that *you don't want me* to go to Charleston. *I* know. I'm not so deaf that I can't hear; and I'm not so blind that I can't see."

"What do you know?" said he, gravely. "What new discoveries have you made in the last three hours? What have you seen? what heard? What fool, or scoundrel, has been filling your ears, in this little time, with nonsense?"

"Oh! no fool, and no scoundrel — unless you call yourself by these pretty names. But I know what I know, and you get no more out of me."

This was said with a childish sort of triumph, mingled with a look of suspicion and a meaning shake of the head. He surveyed her, for a moment, with a glance of impatience, which had in it something of contempt; but the expression soon changed to one of sadness, as he said, resuming his papers —

"It is hopeless, Zulieme, to keep you in one settled impression of mind. You will not rest till you do the very mischief that I fear. You are warned — God knows how solemnly warned; but the warning passes off, like a bird's song in a drowsy ear, and all exhortation is hopeless. Before I depart to-night, I will give you all the information I can as to what I intend for you and myself. Leave me now, if you please."

"Ah ha! I've vexed you again — and you don't want to know what I know. That's because you're afraid, Harry."

"Perhaps so; but go now."

"Yes, you may well drive me away; for I know you hate me. There's one you love better, Harry. There's that Olive, that you talk of in your sleep."

He looked up.

" So, you have again———"

" Yes, indeed, and you again blabbed all about her."

"I have told you *more* in my waking moments, Zulieme, than I ever uttered in my sleep."

"Ah! but you don't know that."

"I think so. I *meant* to do so. But it matters not how you hear, Zulieme. It is impossible that you should grow wiser from any communication."

"Oh! I'm a fool, of course."

He resumed his labors. She walked round him; he never looked up. Suddenly she clapped her hands over his eyes, and laughed out, though with some effort.

" You sha'n't write any more, Harry."

He offered no resistance, uttered no complaint; but, quietly laying down the pen, seemed resolved to wait patiently her movements. She released him, and, looking over his shoulder, said :—

" Now you could eat me up, Harry, and without salt. Are you not in a fury now ?"

He did not answer. She looked into his eyes. The sad, resigned air which he wore seemed to say — " This foolish creature saved my life; her father's fortunes have repaired mine; I owe her everything; I must bear with everything."

She seemed to read this in his expression.

" Don't look so, Harry, as if you *had* to take it from me, whether you would or no."

" And I *have*, Zulieme."

" Why? If you hate me, Harry, say so."

" But I do not hate you, Zulieme."

" But you don't *love* me, Harry, any more !"

He was silent.

" Yes, I understand it. Well, if you tell me go from you, I'll go."

" Whither would you go ?"

" Anywhere; but I wouldn't stay with one who wants to be rid of me."

" If you desire to leave me, Zulieme, you are free. But you must take the ship. She is rightly yours. She was bought with your father's money."

" Oh! Harry, don't fling that money into my face. I'd rather you'd beat me at once. I don't want the money, Harry. I only want' you to love me as you should."

" Love! Alas, Zulieme, love is not for me now. But if you desire my love, why do you not submit to my wishes? why thwart and strive against me always?"

" Do I?"

" Even now——"

" And when I'm trying to be fond with you, Harry, you call it striving against you. If you had any love for me, Harry, you wouldn't call it so. What am I to do? You don't give me anything to do; and I want to go with you wherever you go. Let me go with you to Charleston, and I won't vex you any more. But if you go and leave me here, what will I be thinking all the time? That they've put you into the calaboose, and are going to *garote* you — gallows you, I mean."

" Your presence might help me to it, Zulieme."

" How? I would fight for you!" And she griped her little poniard with a sudden hand.

" Go, go, Zulieme — I believe what you tell me — believe that you would fight for me with your feeble strength, and perhaps not shrink to die for me; but your presence would only embarrass me in Charleston, and might lead to the very danger that we fear. At all events, I must first see how the land lies. I have friends there. I must communicate with them. If they report favorably, I will take you to the town. Let that content you."

We need not pursue this dialogue. It was resumed at evening, just before Calvert's departure. Zulieme was still very troublesome. It was to his credit that he was still as patient as before. Again she reproached him with want of love; and, without contradicting, he sought to soothe her. In a fit of childish anger she beheld him leave the vessel. Lieutenant Molyneaux entertained a very different feeling; but he concealed it under an appearance of great demureness, and a profound attention to the instructions given by his superior. Under cover of the night, Calvert dropped down the river in one of the small boats of the cruiser. He was accompanied by four men as rowers. To Jack Belcher, who expected to accompany him, he said, briefly, but in significant tones, which reached only the ears of that faithful fellow :—

" No, Jack, your place is here. You will need to watch. I

will be back in forty hours at most.    Should I not, then, remember
my commands.    You know where to seek the boat — the old
creek, the shell bluff landing: the three pines, and the hedge of
myrtle.    In our next trip, I shall need you with me; but not
now.    Good-by, old fellow."

The oarsman put out with a will.    In a few strokes the boat
was out of sight of the vessel, and Calvert surrendered himself
up to his own dark musings, which did not need to receive their
color from the night.

"After all," he thought to himself, "what need I chafe?    Were
she less a child, less foolish, what would it better my condition?
Even were I in no bonds — were I as free as air — of what avail
now, since she, for whom I could wish to be free, is in bonds no
less heavy than mine?    Look which way I will, the cloud rests
upon the prospect; and such a cloud!    I am so deep in despair
that I am above anger."

## CHAPTER IX.

BEN BACKSTAY AT BOGGY QUARTER.

" This is an honest comrade;
One you may trust when danger grows most pressing,
And foes are thickest; loyal, who will follow,
With courage, born of faith that never falters."

THE tide, which affects the Ashley nearly to its sources, was falling, and it required but moderate effort of the oarsmen to send the boat down the river. It reached the precincts of the little town, an hour after midnight; ran into one of the numerous creeks which perforated the land on every side; and we may mention, in order to more precision, that she took shelter in one of those little arms of the river, which, pursuing a sinuous progress, finally terminated in the neighborhood of the spot now occupied by the statehouse, on Meeting street. At that early day, this region was skirted by a marsh along the water, and by a dense shrubbery upon the higher lands. This afforded ample covering for so small a craft; and as the station chosen was out of the ordinary routes of the citizen, and, by reason of strips of marsh and beds of ooze, was not easy of approach, the chances were that, except to a casual eye, she might lie in the snug basin which she occupied for days, or even weeks, without discovery.

We must take for granted, at all events, not only that such was the opinion of our cruiser, but that it was one well justified by his experience. He had found this harborage a safe one on previous occasions, and the boatmen seemed to know what was requisite to make it so. They took care that the cover should be as complete as possible. The tall marshes of the creek sufficed for this; while the channel had always sufficient depth of water to enable them to emerge into the river without waiting for the tide.

The English settlements of South Carolina were, as we have said, begun only some twenty years before; at first, at Port Royal, upon a noble port, famous in colonial chronicle, but where the very facility of access, and the excellence of the harborage, proved at that period, because of these very advantages, the greatest discouragements to the colony. These characteristics, which would commend such a region *now* to a commercial people, were then obstacles to the success of a commercial settlement, planted in such close propinquity to such powerful maritime enemies as French and Spaniard. Easily assailed, they were difficult of defence; and some early experience of harm, very soon after his arrival at Port Royal, prompted Sayle to remove his infant colony to the western side of Ashley river.

Here Sayle died. In the hands of his successors the settlement pined in feeble condition. If, here, they found themselves more safe from invasion of French or Spaniard, they were yet even more liable to danger from the redmen by whom they were everywhere surrounded. The obstacles in the way of their maritime enemies were, also, obstacles to the approach of their European friends; and gradually, between 1670 and 1680, the settlers, individuals first, and groups afterward, passed from the west bank of the Ashley, or Kiawah, to the west bank of the Cooper, or Etiwan; until the government, nearly left alone on the west side of the Ashley, was compelled to follow its people to the east.

After this remove, the colonists received a considerable addition to their numbers from various sources, and accordingly a new impulse to their energies. There was, for a time, some such rush toward the new establishment, as we note daily in present times, when, under the arts of the speculator, the wanderers from the old states crowd to the competition for lots, in fancy cities of the western territories. People came in from North Carolina, and from other colonies still more remote, to the Ashley river establishment; and the mother-state, taking an interest in a settlement which was founded under the patronge of its chief nobility, contributed the help of government to this new impulse. The protestant French were sent out, at the cost of the crown, to manufacture wines, and cultivate the mulberry, and rear the silkworm. Already the foreign visiter to Carolina had reported "five kinds of grape as already *distinguished*," making good wine, which has met with British approval at home; — approved by the "*best palates*" — by "*mouths* of wisest censure," even at this very early period; leading to the prediction, even then, that "Carolina will, in a little time, prove a magazine and a staple for wines to the whole West Indies" — a prediction which we are now disposed to carry to still farther height of fortune, by substituting Britain herself for the West Indies. In no very distant time, she will probably receive her very best wines from the same and contiguous regions. But our purpose now affords little time for prophecy. Enough that we show what was the promise in 1684. Not only does the vine grow here in a native and peculiarly appropriate soil, but the olive, brought from Fayal, has been planted, and is flourishing also, to the great delight of the prophetic settlers and proprietors. These prophecies and prospects, with actual exports of furs and hides, of lumber, tar, pitch, turpentine, &c., to England, and these same commodities, as well as pickled beef and other marketable productions, to the West India islands, suffice to show that the track has been blazed out sufficiently to beguile the discontents and fugitives of Europe, and that they have begun their march, from various quarters, to the new port of promise in the west.

But the colony, in spite of sudden influx of people, and prophetic gleams of promise, is still in its merest infancy. Instead of twelve hundred people (as Calvert estimates) in Charleston, then newly christened — being, nearly up to this period, "Oyster-Point town" — the *whole* colony scarcely numbers twelve hundred whites, distributed sparsely about the Ashley and Cooper, the Edistow, Winyah, Santee, and Savannah; and these, thus scattered, are enforted in block-houses, having mortal dread of their red neighbors, who are too powerful still not to inspire fear. Charleston has its fort also, mounting two big guns; and you may note in its precincts certain convenient block-houses, designed as places of refuge. We have shown, besides, that the island, at the entrance of the harbor, mounts its block-house and its big gun also. This is meant simply as an alarm gun, to be fired when mousing pirates, or Frenchmen, or Spaniards, show their whiskered visages along the coast.

As a thing of course, there is no city. Charleston is but a scattered hamlet of probably eight hundred inhabitants, all told —

white, black, and equivocal. The grand plan of a city has just
been received from the lord's proprietors, but not yet put in execution. The town, as far as settled, possesses avenues and paths,
rather than streets. It occupies but a small cantlet of the present
city, lying pretty much within the limits comprehended by Tradd
and Church streets on the south and west, and Bay and Market
streets on the east and north; and these streets have, as yet, received no names. Above, and in the rear — that is, north and
west — the land is perforated by creeks, ponds, and marshes; an
occasional wigwam marks one of the ridges between, and the
abode of some one of the surliest or poorest of the settlers. There
are, properly, no churches, no marketplaces, no places of amusement, religion, pleasure, trade; all being individual, though but
little of it, as yet, has been the fruit of individual enterprise. The
community has scarcely begun yet to work together as a whole.

Of course, there are lusts, and vanities, and human passions;
many vices, and perhaps some goodly virtues, scattered broad-
cast among the goodly people of the town, even as at the present
day. And of this stuff, we must even make what we can in our
present history. But, also, almost of course, there was a struggling upward of individuals and circles, just as now; striving feebly, according to a poor idiotic fashion, after wisdom, virtue, religion, and money. And these, too, will have their uses in our
sober narrative. These are just the very elements, mixed and
warring, of which all worlds are made; and, whatever moralists
and philosophers may think, it is not for the artist to quarrel with
the very material out of which his proper wares are to be fabri-
cated; and he surely is not to challenge that wisdom which has
provided him with his proper means of manufacture.

From this rude sketch of the first beginnings of the Palmetto
city, you may easily conjecture many things ; — that the dwellings generally, for example, are very rude ; that there is little
real wealth accumulated, whatever the promise in the future ; that
the avenues from place to place are not always in travelling condition ; that piles of lumber obstruct the pathways ; that you
sometimes get from point to point by means of trees thrown
sprawling over creeks ; that "corduroyed" causeways help you over
mudflats ; that, on dark nights, and after heavy rains, the streets
are literally impassable, unless with the aid of guides and lanterns;

that a large proportion of the people are quite as rude as street and dwelling; and that the assortment of character-among them is such as will afford you any variety for selection. Though not yet infested with drones, the town has a few specimens of the idle gentleman; *chevaliers d'industrie* are to be met at certain well-known reunions; there are two or more proverbial places where you will meet "white gizzards" and "blacklegs" — sots and gamesters; already the precincts of Elliott street, then the "Boggy Quarter," are known as a sort of Snug-Harbor for sailors; and among these you will find whiskered bandits who have wrung the noses of the Spanish dons, and levied heavy assessments upon the galleons of Panama and Vera Cruz; and lost no credit with the British world by the exercise of the peculiar virtues of the flibustier.

Well, it is to this very precinct, called "Boggy Quarter," that our hero made his way, stepping out from his boat at the head of a creek which continued its progress sinuously up through portions of Queen and Broad streets, till it spread out in ooze just in the wake of Courthouse and Mill's House. Supposing St. Michael's to have been existing in that day, you might almost have hurled a pebble from its galleries into the pinnace of our cruiser, where she lay concealed in marsh and myrtle. And could you now dig down some twenty feet, you might gather any quantity of this ooze from beneath the foundations of the Roper hospital, on one hand, and the Catholic cathedral on the other. Whether church and hospital are better fortified on a muddy than a sandy foundation, is a question in morals and masonry which we leave to the dealers in such precious commodities as souls and stone.

Well, stepping out of his boat on a cypress trunk that spanned a hundred feet of bog, our captain of the "Happy-go-Lucky" made his way into the town, pursuing an eastwardly course, a point or two to the south, which took him, after no long period, to that Boggy Quarter, Snug-Harbor, Pirate-Hold, which, in more civilized times, and within the recollection of decent people had scarcely a higher reputation, under the more innocent appellation of Elliott street. There may have been twenty dwellings of all sorts and sizes in and about this precinct, chiefly in that part of it where Elliott enters Church street. The latter was the more choice and courtly region. Here dwelt the governor; here, Landgraves Morton and Marshall, Middleton, and other prominent men of the colony, maintained a sort of state in their mansions, and were comfortably lodged according to the standards of the place. It was the court end of the town, and almost its west end also. A block-house stood very near the spot occupied by St. Philip's, and closed up the street in that northern quarter. Another might be seen at the opposite or southern extremity, which fell a long ways short of its present handsome terminus in "the Battery." And — but we must not suffer details of this sort further to interfere with the progress of Captain Calvert. We may have to conduct him and the reader to others before we have done, but sufficient for the scene should be the action thereof, and the approach to the event will necessarily imply such description of the locality as will serve for its proper comprehension. It contents us now to accompany Captain Calvert to one of the habitations of Boggy Quarter, Elliott street, a nest of rookeries ; two or three frame houses huddled together around a square fabric of logs, which in process of time ceased altogether to appear upon the street, and formed a sort of donjon, or keep, to an otherwise innocent-looking habitation, of very rude and ungainly structure. It lay now in perfect silence and utter darkness ; doors shut, windows fast ; everything secure without, as becomes the caution of a householder who well knows that night-hawks range about new settlements as impudently as about those which have been made venerable by the knaveries of a thousand years.

Calvert, armed with an oyster-shell, made himself heard against an upper window.

A head, covered with a red flannel nightcap, was thrust forth.

"Happy" was the single word spoken by the cruiser.

"Go-Lucky" was the countersign, promptly answered, and the head was instantly withdrawn. In a few moments after the door was opened, no word was spoken, the captain entered, and the house was made fast as before.

We must follow the two into the log-house, which was originally built as a block-house, commanding a creek, and was, by the way, the very first dwelling raised in the Palmetto city, by that race whose generations have reared it to its present goodly dimensions.

Following our guide and companion, we find ourselves in a rude chamber twenty feet square.  A lantern burns dimly upon a pine table in the centre of the room.  There are shelves around the apartment, on which you see kegs, boxes, jugs ; these may contain pipes, tobacco, bacon, sugar, and Jamaica rum.  We need not inquire more particularly.  You see weapons, too, such as were familiar to the brawny muscles of that day.  There are a few cutlasses which hang against the walls; a blunderbuss rests upon yonder shelf; you see a pair of huge pistol-butts protruding from a corner in the same quarter, and a couple of long fowling-pieces lean up below them.  Evidently, a clever squad of flibustiers might equip themselves for sudden action from this rude armory in Boggy Quarter.

The host who has welcomed our captain, is clearly one who has been upon the high seas in some professional capacity.  He yaws about with the natural motion of a sea-dog.  He wears the hard, sun-browned cheeks of Jack Tar; you see that his hair is twisted all over into "pigtails," such as constituted, at an early day, a sort of proper style of marine headdress.  A coarse flannel shirt, red as his nightcap, makes his only upper garment, which a riband secures at the throat.  The bosom is open, the muscular breast seeming to have burst all such small obstacles as a score of buttons might present; and his arms are bare, the sleeves rolled up, showing the maritime tokens, ships, anchors, and other cabalistic insignia, deeply ingrained with gunpowder, from elbow down to wrist.  Jack is clearly one who, if he has left the profession, is not ashamed of it.  He is probably on furlough only.

He receives the captain with some warmth, but quite as much reverence, as he draws out a chair of wicker-work from the corner, brushes it carefully with some garment hastily snatched up, and places it before the captain.

"Glad to see your honor.  Been looking for you now three weeks.  Glad you didn't come before, though; you might have missed stays getting out or in; we've had a smart showing of king's ships on the station.  But Belcher told your honor all!"

"Yes; but king's cruisers haven't troubled us much, Ben, up to this time.  What makes you all so scary about them now?"

"Why, for that matter, sir, so long as you're in the ' Happy-go-Lucky,' I don't see as how kings' ships could do you hurt at any time.  She's got the heels of the best of them ; and I know you

5

can fling a shot just as close as the best gunner that ever sighted
a Long Tom. But it's here, when you git into port, that the breakers git worst. That's the say now. There's new orders come
out from council that don't suffer any more fair trading."

" Well, Ben, we've been used to orders from council for a long
time already : and these gave us no great concern, so long as we
had staunch British hearts, here and about, to give cheer at the
smashing of a Spaniard's deadlights."

" That's true, your honor; but they say, now, there's a change
in the great folks here. There's to be better pay to keep 'em
vartuous."

" Not such good pay as ours, I fancy."

" Well, I should think not, your honor; but there's no telling,
when men begin to git vartuous, what pay will satisfy them; and
when they're a-gitting religious, as well as vartuous, they're monstrous strong ĭn their ixpectations."

" But are there any among our friends who are thus raising
their prices to the virtuous and religious standard?"

" Why, yes, sir; it's a sort of fight now twixt the puritans and
the cavaliers, I'm a thinking, which shall git the first places in
heaven. The cavaliers didn't always make a business of it; didn't
set up for it; wa'n't no ways ambitious; but now that they see
that the puritans are a-gitting on so well, they sort o' begrudges
them the advantage; and tho' they drinks the Jamaica out of a
silver mug, jist as they always did afore, yet they've learned to
look over the cup, into heaven, as I may say, jist to see, at least, if
they can't make a reckoning for the promised land. The puritans,
they sticks to the pewter mug, and they says just as long a prayer
over their sinnings as they ever did; but there's signs enough in the
land that they only wants a chance to snatch the silver mug from
the hands of the cavaliers, and go to hell, by the way of heaven,
if it's only to get a look at the country passing. Landgrave Morton's a getting religious, and Landgrave Bill Owen, he's working
hard for it; and Colonel Rafe Marshall, and a few more of our
big men in authority; but whether it's a working for hell or
heaven, there's no telling, in the short reckoning we're allowed
here. Your man here, Joe Sylvester, that's been such a fast trader,
and if you believes him, sich a friend of yourn, he's a sort of pillar of fire; he calls himself so — a pillar of fire by night, and of

cloud by day; and it's amazing to see how he fattens on his var-
tues and religion. He weighs, I'm thinking, a full forty pounds
more than he did when you was here afore, and he's thriving
worse than ever in worldly goods."

"Does he preach?" This was spoken with a sort of holy
horror.

"He hardly does nothing else. He's at the conventicles who
but he, as proud as the proudest for humility. But the preaching
brings in the profit."

"Then I must beware of him."

"Better," said the other, dryly; "for though he's willing, no
doubt, to carry on the bad business, jist as before, yet he'll be
always asking himself what speculation he can make out of God,
jist by giving up all the secrets of the devil. You'll jist have to
calculate for him beforehand, as to the time when he can drive a
trade for your neck in the halter, with the saints and Pharisees."

"Why, Ben, you speak in such goodly phrase, that I am half
inclined to suspect you of a part in the service of the puritans."

"And you've got reason, your honor. Soon as I found out
that Joe Sylvester had got religion and was turned preacher, I
regularly attended sarvice, p'rticlarly if I knowed he was gwine to
preach; for when a man's a rogue, or I thinks him so, to find out,
I jist wants to see the white of his eye, and to hear how he brings
out his sentiments. Ef he's slow, I knows he's calkilating and a
rogue; for a new convart, in his old age, is bound to be fast, if
he's honest; and he won't think of rolling up his eyes when, all
the time, he's thinking of s'arching you to the very soul, through
your daylights."

"Why, Ben, you're a philosopher."

"No, your honor, only a sailor, and a great rogue of a sinner;
but I can't h'ist false colors, your honor — except in the lawful
sarvice of religion and aginst the Spaniards; and that's a part of
good seamanship in privateer life. When I'm gwine to turn
against your honor, I'll show you a flag, and give you fair warning to stand off."

"What you tell me of Sylvester certainly needs some watch-
fulness; but you say nothing of the governor. Has he been
imbibing religion also? Is he really disposed to show himself
zealous under these new orders of council?"

"Not a bit of it, your honor, only as he's watched by them that's got it in charge to see after him."

"Ah! is *he* suspected?"

"I'm a thinking that's his difficulty, sir. There's a new council, there's new men, and you know what the song says —

"'Git a new master, be a new man.'

There's new masters come out for the governor as well as smaller people. As I tell ye, there's Landgrave Morton, who's got active agin of late, and talks strong agin piracy, as he calls it; though, when you will make a British sailor, or British folk generally, believe that there is any law agin licking the Spaniards when you kin, and emptying their galleons, I shall think the day of judgment is mighty close upon our quarters. It's all lee-shore and no water. Then there's Mr. Arthur Middleton, he sings to the same tune with Morton; and worse than all, there's a new cassique one Major Edward Berkeley——"

"Ah! Well?"

"He's got something of a special commission, they say, for overhauling all cargoes, whether silks or silver of the Spaniards, or Injin slaves for the West Indies. He's to wind up both them trades if he kin do it, and they say he carries a pretty high hand with the governor. It's the watch they keeps on him, these three, that's making him squeamish; otherwise, I reckon, he'd show jist as blind an eye, now, to the running of a cargo as we knows he did last September, when you brought in that fine cargo of the Santa Maria — and a better chance of pretty things never come to this market, and a pretty trade we drove of it."

"Well, I must see the governor and Sylvester both, Ben."

"Ef *must* is the word, captain, then you'll keep close hauled on the wind, ready for any weather. Sylvester's a rogue — about the worst, since he's h'isted the flag of religion. He'll do the thing secret, but you'll jist be sure never to let him guess when all the cargo's out. Keep him to the guess that there's a good deal more to come. In the matter of Governor Quarry, you'll have to see him to himself. You can't walk the town with him now, arm-in-arm, as you did a year ago. But I kin git you into his quarters, and nobody the wiser; and if we can blink the moon we kin run the cargo, and nobody to take offence. As for the officers, they might as well be owls for what they see, and crows for all the fighting they'll do. But you must fight shy of the landgraves and cassiques — Morton and Berkeley, and Middleton; they're a most too scrup'lous for safety, 'less we manage with blankets."

"That we can do. The ship's up the river."

" *There's* the danger, ef a king's ship should be coming round. Don't for the whole cargo let Joe Sylvester know where the beauty lies."

"No! surely not; or the governor either.'

"Should they find out, they'd have a king's cruiser upon you before you could say 'Jack Robinson;' and where would you be, should she run up the river after you?"

"They'd find us prepared, Ben. They can hardly find a king's ship strong enough, single-handed, to cripple the 'Happy-go-Lucky;' and I shall take care they do not catch us napping. How many men can you get together at the signal?"

"Enough for camels." (Burden-bearers.)

"The boat will be at Shell bluff when they come. You shall have the signals beforehand. If we have reason to change the ground, you shall know. I will see you again by daylight, when we must get into the governor's quarters without stirring his sentries. I must go now and see Sylvester."

"Why should he have a hand in the job at all?"

"Only to shut his mouth. He would be sure to get from some of your people that you had camels at work——"

"Maybe so, but——"

"I shall assign him the Hobcaw landing, bringing the boat round. He shall be taught to believe that the vessel lies below, behind the island."

"He'll put a watch on you."

"First, you shall put a watch on him, and so muzzle his watch, if you have to ship him. But we must venture something."

"Well, I reckon so."

"This Major Berkeley, Ben — this new-comer, cassique or what d'ye call him — have you seen him? What sort of person is he?"

"Well, sir, yes; and he's a much of a man, I tell you, judging by his looks. He's about your height and heft; a leetle fuller

round about the girdle; a leetle fuller in the face, I think, and he
wears no sign of a brush.  I should think him about thirty-five
or thereabouts.  He's got grayish eyes, and a good roof to his
head, and he carries himself rather grand and stiff; and you kin
see he means something, and is somebody.  I don't reckon him a
person to be free and familiar, but you see he's quite a gentleman
born.  And so they say he is; some of the talk makes him out to
be a nevy or cousin to Sir John Barkeley, one of the lords proprietors, you know."

Calvert heard this description in silence.  When it was finished
he rose and walked the apartment for a few minutes without
speaking.  Ben Backstay rose at the same time, drew forth a jug,
placed pitcher and tumbler upon the table, and got out a silver
bowl heaped with loaf sugar.

"Something after the talk, your honor?"

Without answering, Calvert drew nigh the table, poured out a
moderate stoup of the Jamaica, and, dashing it with water, drank
it off, resuming his silent progress around the apartment.  Ben
Backstay just as silently followed his example in the matter of the
Jamaica.  Then, after a brief pause, seemingly accorded to his
superior's humor, Ben Backstay ventured to intrude upon it:—

"I've been thinking, your honor, that, considering the squeam-
ishness of the governor, and the strict watch of the council, and
the vartuous inclinations of Sylvester, that 'twould be better if we
didn't use my camels or hisn at all in running the cargo."

"How can we do it otherwise?"

"Let the crew shoulder the cargo, and nobody else, and then
one man kin receive it.  Governor and council, and camels, and
the vartuous Joe, needn't know nothing about it, or even guess
that sich a witch as the 'Happy-go-Lucky' had ever been within
soundings for a month of Sundays.  You've got a full comple-
men of men for fighting, as well as working the vessel; and when
they've neither fighting nor working, why shouldn't they take a
take a hand at camelling?"

"I've thought of it, Ben, but dare not trust 'em.  We've got
some doubtful fellows aboardship this cruise, and I've reason to
suspect mischief a-brewing even now, on the part of those whom,
for the present, I am yet compelled to trust.  If I bring the doubtful fellows down to this work, they would be surrounded here by

temptations to betray me. If I brought the trustworthy, I should leave the ship to the mercy of the rest, who would be then encouraged to attempts which they will hardly venture on as yet. The case is one of embarrassments all round, and I see no process but the one that we have agreed upon. Wind serving, I may may make midnight runs, down and up, of the vessel herself, and so empty cargo the sooner. But, if there should seem to be any skylarking along our lines of watch, you have only to make the old signal, and we can caché in the woods, find a storehouse in the thickets of Accabee, as we did once before; you remember?"

" You know, captain, it's a'most time for the Injins to be coming down to the salts. Parties were in town yesterday, and there's a report that they're gwine to be troublesome. Them Westos, and Stonos, and Savannas, that gin us such trouble in Governor West's time, they're a-waking up agin. You may look to find painted faces about Accabee pretty soon now, any how, as the fishing season is begun."

" We must risk the redmen, keeping our watch as close as possible. If we meet with any, we must only bribe and send 'em off."

" Jamaica'll do it, sir. Ef you kin only show 'em a pipe of that good stuff somewhere along the Santee, they'll be off at the long trot before daylight. But, if you mean to see Joe Sylvester and the governor both to-night, captain, it's time to be moving."

" No!" said the other, abruptly. " I have thought better of it. I will see neither of them to-night. We will run a boat-load, at least, before they shall know of my presence. And, whether I suffer Sylvester to know at all, will depend upon the conclusion I come to after I sleep on it. We have some very valuable articles in the cargo, upon which there need be no black mail paid to anybody but yourself, Ben. These I will have at the long cypress at midnight, to-morrow. For these I can bring a sufficient force of my own sea-dogs — the most trusty — for camelling."

" Best way that, sir."

" We'll see how it works. After that I can see the governor or Sylvester — one, both, or neither, as I please."

And so they parted.

# CHAPTER X.

### BIRD'S-EYE VIEW OF THE PROSPECT.

> " We must ravel up
> These tangled threads, nor stop to sort them now;
> But huddle them together in our wallets
> For future uses."

LET us now, dear reader, suppose a few things rapidly, in order that we may spare each other some unnecessary detail. You will please believe that some three days and nights have elapsed since our last chapter. You are not to suppose that these have been left unemployed by the several parties to our narrative. You will take for granted, for example, that the " Happy-go-Lucky" still keeps close in her snug harbor, some ten miles up the Ashley. You will conceive, for yourselves, that Lieutenant Molyneaux has been vigilant in his watch, assisted by his junior officer; that he has his scouts busy about in the woods, keeping a sharp look-out for intruders, red or white; that there is no reproach of *lachesse* at his doors. Whatever his demerits as a peacock, he knows what are his duties, and performs them, perhaps quite as much in compliance with habit as will.

And we must suppose this also of Eckles, and the rest. They work, too, amazingly well, in the hours in which special tasks are assigned them, whether in their scouting duties, or in those more laborious of breaking bulk and transhipping cargo. Several boats, well stuffed with contraband commodities, have dropped down the river, and have been disposed of by Calvert, through familiar channels. These things will seem to you matters of course.

You are also to take for granted, that the life of the " Happy-go-Luckies" up the river, in their then almost virgin solitude, has not been one of unmitigated drudgery. Our captain of the cruiser is an indulgent master. He knows the nature and the needs of man, especially of sailors; and his maxim, in regard to their management, follows scrupulously the rule laid down in the ancient doggrel:—

> "All work, and no joy,
> Makes Jack a dull boy;
> But all joy, and no toil,
> Is sure the best of Jacks to spoil;"—

and so he pleasantly varies the exercise from work to play; from tasks, regularly exacted, to amusements in which every freedom, even to a decree of license, is allowed, consistently with the prosecution of duty, and the safety of the ship.

So you will please understand that our Jack Tars have had and are having their fun; frequent enough, in the shade of those great old oaks up Ashley river. They have planted quite a gymnasium in one of those mighty amphitheatres of forest, which no grandeur of art could ever emulate. You see that swings of grapevine are even now bearing the forms of the fair Zulieme and the brown Sylvia; that our lieutenants are doing the agreeable, alternately, in setting the swing in motion which bears the fairy-like figure of the former; that the sailors amuse themselves in like fashion at a moderate distance, or in other ways equally rustic. Some of them play the tomahawk exercise at twenty feet against the trees, others hurl the bar or pitch the quoit; and you will see not a few of them using Spanish pieces of eight, vulgarly called "milled dollars," in a like manner, the innocent coin being the forfeit to the most skilful or most lucky of the players. And there are sturdy fellows stripped to the buff and squaring off, after the excellent fashion of John Bull, in quarter-staff or pugilism. Crowns are cracked for a consideration, and "facers" are put in with such emphasis as to spoil mazzards, purely for fun. Then there are practical jokes incessantly plied, such as tickle the fancies of Jack Tar, whether on sea or shore. Lubbers (and there are marines on board the "Happy-go-Lucky") are tied in the rigging — that is, taken with a noose — while the parties straddle upon great branches, in search of birds'-nests, for curious specimens of which they have been persuaded to go aloft.

Our ambitious lieutenant refines something upon these antics of Jack Tar. He calls up the violin of Phipps: he excites the pas-

sion of the fair Zulieme for her national dances; he shares with her,
as before, in the fandango; and he makes her temporarily forgetful that her levity has brought the cloud upon her husband's visage, and over her own fortunes. She can not free herself of levity. With a nature so light as hers, a mind so utterly incapable
of care and thought, forgetfulness is as inevitable as the feeling of existence; and the natural demands of her gay summer life
require that she should play, and sing, and flit about, and fly, just
so soon as the shower is over, and the sun comes out. It is the mistake of our lieutenant to suppose that she can be serious enough,
a sufficiently long time, for the purposes of passion. With her, it
is quite enough that she feels lonesome, to begin play. Tell her
that the world is about to tumble to pieces, and she cries out with
a start of terror; but if the world lingers in the process of dissolu-
tion, and she begins to feel dully from the "hope deferred," she
takes refuge in the free use of legs and arms, and, in the convulsions of her own merriment, straightway forgets all those which
are to make "chaos come again."

And while she sings and dances, and wanders off into the
woods, seeking new scenes for sport, gathering flowers as thought-
lessly as Dis, ere she was herself gathered by the grim lord of
Erebus and Night — with Molyneaux ever watchful of her ways,
and meditating, perhaps, as wickedly as Pluto — we are to suppose that the eyes of Jack Belcher, solicitous for his master, maintain as keen a watch over all the parties.

Nor these two merely. There are others on board the " Happy-go-Lucky" who do not wholly surrender themselves to sport and
play; who have mousing moods, and brood, like political spiders,
in dark corners to themselves, spreading their subtle webs on
every hand, the better to entrap the unwary. These, too, seek
close harbors in the thickets, "michin malico," even as Antonio
and Sebastian work together in conspiracy, while their monarch
sleeps on the Enchanted island. And upon these, too, the faithful Jack Belcher has set the keen eyes of suspicion, at least, if not
discovery; and he waits only to be sure, before he undertakes to
help their councils. How far these discontents are encouraged
by Molyneaux, is yet to be seen. But it is known that they are
his favorites, and not in much favor with their captain. For all
of which there are probably good reasons. Enough, in this place,

that Calvert is very far from blind, though it is a part of his policy not to see a moment too soon. He is quite satisfied, for the present, that he has a faithful hound upon their tracks, whom he holds to be quite able to scent them out in all their sinuosities of progress.

We have shown you that all our parties have been busied, each in his department, during the three days which have elapsed since our last chapter. You are to understand that, in this space of time, no less than four boat-loads of very miscellaneous commodities have been "run" into the virtuous bosom of the young city. You will please believe that the commodities so "run" are of very precious texture and quality; that they comprise bales of silk, and other stuffs precious to luxury, fashion, and the fair sex; that there are besides certain bales of cochineal, certain casks of indigo, larger quantities of naval stores, clothing, provisions, goods and wares, which we need not enumerate; then, the more bulky articles are yet to be landed — those only "run" which are most portable and most precious. Of some ten thousand pieces of eight (dollars), the fruits of the same prosperous voyage, and the proceeds of a gallant passage at arms, at close quarters, with a Spanish galleon of very superior force, bound from Porto Bello to Havana, we gather no official report as yet. We may hear something of them hereafter; but we doubt if captain or crew will feel it necessary to report this particular item either to Governor Quarry, or even the virtuous agent, Ben Backstay. It is very certain that Joe Sylvester, the puritan, will never hear a syllable of it.

The arrangements made by our cruiser, and his factotum, Ben Backstay, whose own claims to virtue have been so modest, have all been successful. Our cruiser has done his own "camelling," and the goods are stored in cell and chamber, in the immediate keeping of Backstay. He will distribute them in due season, and through proper agencies. And thus far, that doubtful puritan, Joe Sylvester, has been kept in profound ignorance (at least, it is supposed so) of all that has been done. The first intelligence he will get of the "run" will be the gradual appearance of fine silks and satins, and shawls and stuffs of rich, unwonted patterns, along the fashionable purlieus, which range from north to south, along the avenue, no longer fashionable, which we now call Church street. The fair women of the infant city will do the first work in publishing the transaction to the little world in which they wander. What to them the fact that the stuffs are contraband? nay, that they are won by the strong hand, upon the high seas, in spite of law and gospel; and, while England and Spain professedly keep the peace in European seas, they are here, in this wild hemisphere, as deadlily hostile as in the days of the Armada; while the sentiment, feeling, opinion, among their respective peoples, justify the hostility which their respective governments ignore? The dear creatures see no treason, or piracy, or blood, or violation of law, in the color, the quality, the texture, or the beauty, in the fine manufactures in which they flaunt. Enough that they *are* fine and fanciful, make *them* look fine, and come to them at prices which would cause the eyes of British dames, could they hear, to gleam with envy. The best of them see no harm in this mode of acquisition. They all approve of smuggling in practice; and the contrabandist is only immoral in a very vague and remote sort of abstraction, which disturbs no social piety or propriety.

And they are not to be counted any worse, you are to understand, than the admirable portions of their sex who remain in the mother-country. You are to know that the Palmetto city, even at this early day, has its fair proportion of fair women, representing almost every class in the British empire. No small proportion of its population has recently come hither from Barbadoes and other islands, from Virginia, and the Dutch colony of Nova Belgia (New York). They had lived in most of these places in rather flourishing fashion; had acquired means, and are emulous of the state, dignity, and fashions of the old world. And there are dashing cavaliers among them, with wives and daughters, who can claim kindred with the old families of Europe — with the *noblesse*; who could already boast of that genuine *azul sangre* which is almost as much the pride of the British as of the Castilian race.

And so, already, Charleston (then Charles town) had its castes and classes, its cliques and aristocracies; in which, people, insisting upon their rights of rank, grew rank in doing so, and were guilty of offences against humanity and good sense, such as cried to Heaven: at all events, made them cry ridiculously loud to earth. There were people who were " in society" then as now; who turned up their noses so high, that their eyes failed to recognise the existence of their nearest neighbors. And there were very excellent people, who, in spite of virtues and talents, were dismissed from all regard, even the human, for the simple but sufficient reason that they were *not* " in society." Those talismanic words, " in society," signifying a sort of virtues which are not contained in any catalogue of the virtues which entitle a poor Christian to any place in the kingdom of heaven.

And so, Charleston had its Lady Loftyhead and Lady Highheels, Lady Flirtabout and Lady Fluster, and no small number of a class besides, whom these good ladies universally voted to be no ladies at all. But not one of them, high or low, in or out of society, ever found the moral gorge to rise at the idea of smuggled silks, or even pirate traffic. Nay, the dashing rovers themselves, men well known to sail under the " Jolly Roger" — so the flag of piracy was always called — were made welcome, and might be seen at certain periods to walk the streets of the young city, arm-in-arm with substantial citizens — nay, to figure in court costume at the balls of the Ladies Loftyhead, Highheels, Flirtabout, and Fluster, all satisfied to enjoy the gallantries of the rover without asking to see too closely the color of his hands. And they had their reward for this tolerance of the Jolly Rogers, who could accord none to the classes *not* " in society." Many a smuggled or stolen shawl, scarf, ay, jewel, decorated the person of a noble dame, the gift of the dashing flibustier; won by the strong hand, at the price of blood, in the purple waters of the gulf. And society nowhere, at that period, attached much censure to this mode of acquisition. Robbery on a large scale has been, among all nations, considered only a legitimate mode for the acquisition of wealth; and the natural human sentiment, " *in* society" at least, has usually been persuaded to find the justifying moral, in the degree of peril in which the game of plunder is carried on. He who risks his life in the spoliation, seems to lift his criminal occupation into a sort of dignity, which effectually strips it of the ignoble traits which belong to simple robbery.

But our purpose is not sarcasm. We doubt if the world improves one jot from all the truths which are told it, especially of itself; and we doubt if it can improve under any existing condition; and we half doubt whether it was designed that it should improve, beyond a certain point; and so we do not so much believe in a millenium as in a regeneration. We are but the germs for a new creation, under a new dispensation, and development goes just so far — and there an end for the present.

But, before we leave the subject of the ladies, especially those of Charleston, let it be understood that our captain of the "Happy-go-Lucky" is by no means unknown to fashionable society in that quarter. He has been "*in society*" in more natural, that is, less legal periods. He has figured in the ballrooms of Lady Lofty-head, and Lady Golightly, and other great people. He has paid for his privileges. Lady Loftyhead wears his diamond ring on her finger — Lady Golightly as glorious a pearl necklace, which he threw over her snowy neck, when she was quite willing that he should see, to its utmost depths, how fair and white it was; and it was with Lady Anderson that he contemplated putting the fair Zulieme in the event of his bringing her to Charleston. He has yet to ascertain, in what degree of security he stands in the community — saying nothing of society — before he can venture upon the hospitality of so magnificent a dame.

And he is now in the process of investigation.

He has "run" his fourth boat-load in safety. This comprises all the compact and choice articles in his cargo. This rest will need more *force;* a greater number of " camels;" a greater degree of peril. He may now allow himself to see Mr. Joe Sylvester, formerly one of his most able agents. He will now venture upon an interview with Governor Robert Quarry, whose virtues as a politician have saved him from the sin of pharisaism. The governor does not eschew the society of publicans and sinners.

How Captain Calvert found his way into the private apartments of his excellency, through what agency of Ben Backstay and others, we might make a long story. It will suffice that we find him there, safely ensconced in the chair of Bermuda cane and manufacture, in which his excellency himself ordinarily sits when dealing with vulgar people. But Calvert is none of your vulgar people; and, seen with Quarry, you would say the cruiser is the lord; the governor, a clever adventurer to whom a roving commission has been confided by a master.

The two are together. We have seen something of Calvert already. Of Quarry — but, dealing with a politician now, we must begin with a new chapter.

# CHAPTER XI.

## SOMETHING OF THE POLITICIAN.

| | |
|---|---|
| *Burnet.* | Speak to the card, I say. |
| *Say.* | And I say, rather, let the cards have speech, |
| | While you say nothing.  He is but a dolt, |
| | That lets his game to lie on any card ! |
| *Clare.* | Nay, brother Say, an it but *lie* on the card, |
| | The speech is well enough for such a game ! |

GOVERNOR ROBERT QUARRY, of whom our Carolina chronicles speak in very meagre phraseology, was a courtier; had a fine person — one of the necessities of the courtier — a good face, a graceful, insinuating manner, and certain accomplishments of mind and training, which had conducted him to a certain degree of success in worldly acquisitions.  It was through his merits, as a courtier, that he had reached the governorship of the infant colony of South Carolina, a remote and feeble settlement on the borders of a heathen country, and in near proximity to the Spaniards of Florida, always the relentless enemies of the English.  Such a position required other abilities than those of the simple courtier; but competence to office was no more the requisite in those days than in ours; and the chief merit in office then, as the chief object in its pursuit, was the capacity to fatten fast upon fortune, and to make as rapid stretches as possible toward its attainment. No long time was allowed to anybody; the tenure of office being usually too short, in those periods, to suffer the politician to dilly-dally with opportunity.  He had to feather his nest as rapidly as any other bird of passage.  Whether the courtier before us was properly doing his duty *to himself*, we shall perhaps see as we proceed.  In what concerns his character, we prefer to let Governor Quarry speak for himself.

His person, we have said, was good ; his manners those of a courtier ; easy, deliberate ; rather *staid*, perhaps — rather *too* courtly,
as was the etiquette in those days — too nice and mincing, but
ever according to the rules.    As you see him now, in a private
chamber of his own dwelling (low down in Church street), habited "*point device*," with a pleasant half smile upon his lips, and
that partly stooping attitude which is so natural to a tall man, and
so proper in a courtier ; he shows well enough.    We see that he
would show well in the ballroom ; at a royal *levée* ; in any situation which makes ease of deportment, and flexibility of movement,
and a gentle self-complaisance, essential elements of the *morale* in
society.

But, showing well as a courtier, he shows at disadvantage in
contrast with the Herculean proportions, and the lofty freedom,
the manly, almost *brusque* carriage, the brave simplicity and dignity, of the rover, Calvert, captain of the " Happy-go-Lucky,"
whom we find closeted with him at this moment.

The costume of our rover has undergone some changes since
we made his acquaintance.    He, too, recognises the necessity of a
more courtier-like, a more pacific appearance.    Accordingly, he
figures in a rich black suit, such as was worn by the gentlemen of
the day.    He has great ruffles at his shirt bosom and wrists.    He
wears knee-breeches and silk stockings.    He carries a rapier at
his side.    His hat is steeple-crowned, but of felt or beaver, no
longer of straw or Panama.    And, though it may lessen his freedom of carriage, we are constrained to admit that the costume of
" King Charles's cavaliers," sets off his fine figure to advantage.
He has, we may mention here, been accustomed to appear in it,
and in high places.

How he has found his way into the private apartments of the
governor of Carolina, we may easily conjecture from previous
portions of this history.    He has probably been conducted thither
by Backstay, and in secresy, under cover of the night.    He is now,
at all events, an inmate of the governor's mansion ; and that governor holds in his escritoire an order from the English lords in
council for his arrest and execution — " short shrift and sudden
cord" — as a pirate of the high seas !

Calvert has reason to suspect the fact.    The governor has not
yet permitted him to know it.    But he knows the governor, and

finds his securities in the character of the man, rather than the commission of the official.

That he suspects, has the effect of lifting his proportions. There is a lofty superiority in his manner. His eye searches keenly into that of the governor for the secret of his soul. You are not to suppose our rover a pirate, in our ordinary sense of the character, because the British government has declared him so. The British government has been more of a pirate than its officials. He has had a British commission for his authority, issued at a time when such commissions were frequent enough; when the British people welcomed every injury done to Spain, or France, as good service to the nation; and the *then* monarch of England, himself, has knighted the most brutal of all the piratical captains who ever preyed upon Spanish property, life, and commerce.

"You do not tell me *all*, Governor Quarry," said our captain, quite abruptly; "but I can conjecture what you conceal. You hold a commission for arresting me. Speak out, sir, like a man, and let us understand each other at the outset."

"The fact is, my dear captain, that affair of the ' Donna Maria del Occidente' has caused a precious stir at court. It was a terrible affair, you will admit. A Spanish man-of-war sunk, her captain slain, her crew cut to pieces!"

"It was a fair fight; she was of superior size and mettle, and fired the first gun, the flag of England all the while flying at our masthead. There was no slaughter save what took place in actual battle."

"Very true. I believe it all. But it happened, unfortunately, that Don Jose de—something——"

"Salvador," interposed the captain.

"Yes, Salvador, her commander, who fell under your own cutlass, proves to have been the nephew to the Spanish embassador at our court, and he has been kicking up the very devil on the subject; and, just at this time, it is the policy of our sovereign to maintain a good understanding with the court of Spain."

"Policy!—Ay! policy! The rogue's argument always. But no policy can be proper to the English nation, at the expense of English honor."

"'Ah! my friend"—with a shrug of the shoulder, which would

have been recognised as quite courtly even at Versailles — " this national honor is very good capital in a speech at the opening of parliament, but must not be allowed to interfere with those nice little arrangements which are found to be essential to individual interests.  The king, like the lords, and even such poor common-ers and courtiers as ourselves, needs sometimes to make a waiver of the national credit for the better keeping of his own."

" Ay, he would sell the nation, as he sold Dunkirk.  Oh, for a year of old Oliver once more !"

" Fie ! fie ! my dear fellow — this is rank heresy and treason ! This will never do.  Remember, if only in regard to my honor, that I am the king's official, though under the creation only of the lords-proprietors.  I do not object to your treasonable sentiments at all.  Indulge them if you please.  But, spare my ears ! *I* must not hear.  We are good friends to-day, but what we shall be to-morrow is another matter ; and I will not suffer my neck to be perilled with a halter because you have a loose sort of eloquence in respect to the rights of the crown."

The rover uttered an exclamation of impatience, and strode the floor, as if to subdue a still further expression of offence.  Then turning quickly about, he said :—

" But you do not answer my question, Governor Quarry."

" Which of them, captain ?  If I remember rightly, you have done me the honor to propound several."

" Pshaw ! there was but one.  Have you any authority for my arrest ?"

The governor smiled pleasantly, went to his escritoir, opened it, and handed our rover a heavy piece of parchment.  He read the title as he handed the instrument to the rover —

" For the better putting down of piracy in the colonies, &c."

Seals and signatures attested the validity of the document. Captain Calvert gave it but a glance, then threw it back to the official.

" Well, you have your order, Governor Quarry ; and — I am here !"

And Calvert folded his arms upon his bosom, and planted him-self before the governor.

" May be so, captain.  But, unless you proclaim it from the housetops, I am not to know that you are here.  To me you do not appear a pirate.   I do not know you as the person mentioned in this instrument."

" You know that I am no pirate; that, for all that I have done, I have a commission under the very sanction of those by whom that paper has been signed.   I am willing to be tried for the offences alleged against me.   I will confront kings, lords, and commons, equally, in the assertion of my honor."

" My dear captain, hear to reason.   Such a proceeding would involve a very great scandal.   The treaty with Spain, which we are all bound to respect as the law of the land, is of date anterior to your commission.   That treaty declares all those to be pirates who prey upon Spanish commerce or dominion in America."

" Of that treaty," replied our sturdy rover, " I knew not a syllable.   I only knew that the people of England regarded the power and the people of Spain as enemies of man and God — of all things and objects which are held sacred and becoming. They were the enemies of nations.   They were outlawed by our nation.   If that treaty was on record when my commission was given to me, then kings, and lords-proprietors, and governors, were the criminals.   I am none.   Shall I passively submit to be the scapegoat for such rogues as these?"

" Patiently, my dear captain, and hear me for a moment.   Do you not see that the same policy which conferred your commission, while that treaty was in existence, is still present to maintain you in your course, provided you do not force yourself upon the notice of your judges.   The governor, who is not *made* to see you, while the world is looking on, has no motive for your arrest.   He need not suppose for a moment that you are within his jurisdiction."

" But this will not suit *me*, Governor Quarry.   I have no wish to violate law or treaty; have no desire to screen my deeds from the world's examination.   I have fought with Frenchman and Spaniard — would fight with them to the crack of doom — even as Drake and Cavendish did, and glory in the danger; but only while my country claps hands and looks on applaudingly.   If we are to be sold to Frenchman or Spaniard, I wash my hands of the business.   I have no wish to fight merely *on* sufferance, and to be seized and hung at the caprice of a treacherous court."

" Do not be rash, my dear captain.   The treacheries of court

are like those of love and lovers. They are supposed to plead
their own excuse, by reason of their pleasantries. And yours is
a very pretty business, captain, that somewhat compensates for
all its risks. A very pretty business, I assure you."

"You have some reason to say so, Governor Quarry. By the
way, there are a thousand pieces of eight [dollars] in yonder can-
vass-sack, which I brought hither for you."

"Of course, my dear captain, I can not accept them! That
would be bribery. You are entirely too direct in your approaches,
sapping human virtue: as direct as if assaulting the Spaniard.
You are no courtier, captain."

"Thank God for it!"

"That is as you please. It is, after all, a mere matter of taste.
Now, were I, by simple accident, unassisted, to happen upon that
sack, with a thousand pieces of eight — nay, were it *two* thousand — it would hardly occasion any difference; were I to find it,
I say, in a corner of my chamber, I should possibly, at first, wonder whence it came; but, having no information on the subject, I
should, after a while, come to the conclusion that it was some odd
sum that I had set aside for a special purpose, and forgotten in
the press of other affairs. The novelty of such a discovery would
not diminish the satisfaction that I should feel on the occasion.
It would only provoke certain reflections upon the singular indifference which courtiers, particularly when in official station, feel
in respect to money! How little do we value, how we waste,
spend, consume it, utterly regardless of the source of supply!
It is, certainly, a very profligate life, this of the courtier and
official."

"As you please. Find it when you please. Enough that the
sack lies in your chamber. You will be so good as to appropriate
it; suppose that you are fortunate in unexpected supplies — and
that I have not spoken!"

"Exactly. You are quick in idea. It is refreshing to think
that one is always in the way of discovery; that there are guardian genii, ever watchful, with lamp and ring, so that we shall
happen, every now and then, upon unsunned treasures. And
now, let me tell you, my dear captain, that you will simply need
to pursue your walks, while in Carolina, with the same circumspection which you have thus far practised. You need not show

yourself unnecessarily about town. You will not expect our recognition, unless you specially force yourself upon our official memories. Our people do not so far sympathize with French or Spaniard as to approve of treaties which cut off a profitable trade; and Heaven forbid that I should quarrel with a fortune that lays a sack of Spanish dollars occasionally in a corner of my chamber."

"We understand each other, governor. So far, so good! But, under existing conditions, it will be hardly wise or proper for me to pursue a vocation which has been put under the ban of law. It is quite enough of peril to face death at the mouth of Spanish cannon. To confront him again at the hands of my own people, and through the agency of a public executioner, is a prospect which the bravest man may well refuse to contemplate. This is probably the last of the cruises that the 'Happy-go-Lucky' will make—at least under her present commander."

"What! the gallant Captain Calvert, the terror of the Spanish seas and dons, frightened by false fires? Why, my dear fellow, do you not see that this treaty is all a sham—a pretence—dust in the eyes of Europe? *Here*, I tell you, *that* patriotism which takes the Spaniard by the beard is the very first of virtues!"

"Yet, you caution me how I show myself in the streets."

"Oh! we have to keep up appearances. But this means nothing; all we insist upon is modesty. No one is required to publish his virtues unnecessarily. With this forbearance on your part, no one asks whence the broad gold pieces come which finally find their way into the pockets of the citizen. We hate the Spaniards, but take their *onzas* to our pockets, and him who brings them to our hearts; and neither see the red blood on *their* faces nor on *his* hands! All we ask of you is caution, my dear captain; and suffer your friends to see you only in private, as at present."

"But is it so sure that there is no prying curiosity, which will be at some pains to pluck the mask from the face of secrecy? They tell me of fresh counsellors among you who have been seized with a sudden fit of zeal, under an overwhelming flood of piety, and who are for searching out all the sore places of society—all its tender places, at least."

"And you have been told the truth. The council is changed, and such *is* the fervor of certain of its members. Middleton and Morton have had a new impulse, in this direction, in consequence of the presence of Colonel Edward Berkeley, a nephew of one of our lords-proprietors, who has lately moved out to Carolina. He has bought his twenty-four thousand acres of land on the Kiawah, and has been made a cassique of that precinct. As a nephew of Sir William, he is understood to be more in the confidence of the lords-proprietors than any of the rest; and the good lords, specially enlivened, if not enlightened, on the subject themselves, have been at pains to egg him on to a degree of activity which keeps the whole council in a fidget. The king, it seems, has sought to excuse the crown to the Spaniard, by insisting upon the *quasi* independent character of the proprietary governments. He flings from his own shoulders the imputation of sheltering the cruisers against Spanish property, by fastening the offence upon the colonies. And the proprietors have had to undergo the rebuke, in the very presence of the Spanish embassador — and bear it in silence — though they knew, all the while, that nobody had ever given so much sanction to the practice as the crown itself. But that wouldn't do to say, you know; and so our good lords had to curse in secret — had to writhe in passion, with their dumb mouths — while our gracious master read them a very proper lesson touching the laws of nations, the singular love and sympathy which England should entertain for Spain especially, the peculiar vice of piracy, the peculiar beauty of holiness, and the great necessity which existed for compelling the loose and licentious society of the colonies to emulate, in all respects, the virtues of the court and the piety of king and people. Nobody laughed but the Spaniard at this homily, and he only in his court-sleeves, which are made capacious, for the due concealment of honest sentiments. And thereafter his most sacred majesty was to be seen on all-fours, with Louise de Querouaille and the other dames of the seraglio in the same comely attitude, hunting a poor butterfly, who might have been pirating on bosoms that were sufficiently open to all sorts of invaders. But, ridiculous as was the sermon to all those who knew the king, our worthy lords-proprietors were not permitted to defend themselves. It is not allowed at court that truth shall save the subject, to the scandal of the crown or the courtiers; and the rule is a good one. So you see what stimulates the sudden zeal of our council, in this matter of piracy, just at this moment. You also see, I doubt not, that no one need give it further heed than simply to forbear all unnecessary publicity in what is properly a very private practice."

The captain shook his head.

"This will hardly suit me, Governor Quarry."

"Pooh! pooh! why not? What need of further scruples? See this commission. It instructs me to seize, and try, and hang you —nay, to hang you without trial, as soon as I can catch you; but I fling it into my drawer, and there it lies harmless! While no one sees that *I* see you, and knows that *I* know you, and can assert that I have had you in my power, I feel no necessity for looking up the commission, nor need you feel any apprehension because you happen to know that there is any such document in existence."

Calvert was about to answer, but arrested himself, and walked slowly for awhile up and down the chamber. His meditations, during this interval, we shall deliver hereafter. When he did speak again, it was with an abrupt change of subject.

"What sort of man is this Colonel Berkeley? I fancy I have seen him."

"Very likely. He was a man of fashion about London for a few seasons. He is a man of wealth — has bought, as I told you, twenty-four thousand acres on the Kiawah, some fifteen miles up on the western banks, and is preparing to put up a baronial establishment. He is a handsome fellow, but cold and stern — not exactly repelling, but standing much upon his dignity; affects state and authority, but seems a discontent. Something has soured him. He is, accordingly — probably — ambitious."

"Has he a family — wife, and — children?"

"Wife and one child, I think."

"Are they — *here?*"

"Not in town. He has built log-cabins, for temporary use; and, except when business calls him here, or on council-meetings, we seldom see him. He lives well, though in seclusion; is perpetually doing something, will make his establishment a grand one, and, if he carries out his plans, the barony of Kiawah will be a model family-seat."

Calvert asked, seemingly without caring for the answer, in respect to the actual locality of the contemplated barony, and other matters relating to the habits of the proprietor, and the character and condition of the family; to all of which the governor replied, without supposing that the querist had any interest in the answer. The questions of the rover were put with an abrupt carelessness, as if for the satisfaction of a mere momentary curiosity. Had the interest of Quarry been greater in the subject-matter, he would have seen that this abrupt manner of the questioner covered deeper emotions than belonged to simple curiosity. He would have detected, in the slight tremor of his voice, in the utterances of his last words, and in its deeper tones — always deep and sonorous, but more so now, as if with effort at suppression — that the subject stirred some of his sensibilities more thoroughly than any other which had been discussed between them, not excepting that which would seem to be the most important of all — that which threatened his safety.

They were yet speaking, when a carriage was heard at the entrance. Quarry peeped through the window, and said :—

"It is Berkeley now! We must put you out of sight for awhile, my dear fellow. This way. You will be snug here, and in safety."

And he led him to the adjoining chamber, and closed the door upon him.

"I am in a trap now, should that man prove treacherous," was the soliloquy of Calvert. "But he will hardly prove so, so long as it is profitable to keep faith. No! I must only not suffer him to know that my occupation ends with the present cruise. He must still be kept in expectation of other canvass-bags, to be found unexpectedly in the corner of his chamber."

His soliloquy was interrupted by the sudden reappearance of the governor, dragging after him the sack of dollars. With a pleasant chuckle, he said :—

"Suffer this to remain with you a space. It is a waif — something I have found; I should not wonder if it turns out to be Spanish pieces of eight — possibly something still more precious! It is right pleasant, certainly, to be in the way of fortune! But the world need not know that one is lucky; nothing so much offends it. The 'happy' are those only who 'go lucky,' my dear fellow; and the world envies the happy man, as if he were perpetually in the way of other people. — But Berkeley enters. You may listen, and hear all that is said. Pray, do so. It may somewhat concern your own fortunes.   Listen for another reason.   He is something of a curiosity ; is antiquated in his notions of virtue ; believes in human perfectibility, and speaks of humanizing the Indians, and putting them in the small-clothes of civilization, as if it were any concern of his, yours, or mine, whether men go to the devil or not!   We are wiser, and know that the best way to take care of a race is to see that one does not himself go bare !"

6

# CHAPTER XII.

### GLIMPSES OF THE CASSIQUE.

"A man of earnest purposes, he bends
  His head with speechless prayer; and in his toils,
  Lives in becoming sense of what is self."

CALVERT answered the politician only with a look of indifference that might as well have been contempt. "Ay," thought he,
as the other went, "such is, no doubt, the moral by which you
live. But, unless Edward Berkeley be wonderfully changed since
I last knew him, he is as much superior to you in wisdom as he
is in virtue. Alas! how I loved him! How great, I fancied,
was his love for me! Yet has he stepped between me and hope
— thrown his larger fortunes between me and happiness, and cut
me off from all that was precious in the heart's sunlight. Oh,
Edward Berkeley! there is but one thing that shall move me
truly to forgiveness. I must know that you have sinned against
me in ignorance; that you knew not, when you passed between
me and the object of my first fond affections, that she was so precious in my sight. And I would fain believe it; and it may be
so! Jack Belcher is shrewd and sagacious—honest as well as
shrewd. He will have it that you were ignorant. You knew not
of the ties that bound her to me—to me only—that woman
whom you now proudly call your own! Be it so; and I can forgive *you!* But for her? What plea, what excuse can she make
for her cruel abandonment of the younger for the elder son!

"Yes, it is he!" he murmured, as the voice of the visiter reached
him from the adjoining chamber—"the same clear, manly tones.
Surely there can not be meanness, or falsehood, or fraud, under
such a tongue."

He stepped to the door which opened into the other chamber.
An irresistible curiosity to behold the visiter—to employ sight as

well as hearing — moved him to explore the crannies of the door, in the hope to gratify this feeling; but the door had been made fast by Quarry as he went out. Our captain could *see* nothing. But every syllable spoken within came distinctly to his ears. There was no reserve on the part of either speaker.

The governor was all civility. His *rôle* was evidently that of conciliation. The cassique of Kiawah — a rich landed proprietor, one of the newly-constituted Carolina nobility, under a system which only made bald recognition of the crown rather as an abstraction than an absolute power — and the nephew of one of the landed proprietors, supposed not only to represent his will but to be his favorite — such a person was to be conciliated. The governor was very courtly, accordingly — quite solicitous; his smooth accents, and polished speech, and adroit compliment, all being judiciously employed — just saving sycophancy and servility — to persuade his visiter into a pleasant frame of self-complacency, which is the process when dealing with all effeminate minds.

This was Quarry's mistake. The cassique was by no means a man of effeminate mind. He was no courtier, and disdained the petty vanities of society; had no artifices himself; was a person of direct, manly character, grasping at power and performance, and nowise accessible to shams and shows, and the mere tricks and trappings of convention. He endured the courtly preliminaries of Governor Quarry, though with some unexpressed impatience.

" Yes, I am settled, after a fashion — hutting it, for the summer, in log-cabins. These we have made tolerably comfortable. I would have found them so, under the naked poles; but Lady Berkeley and her mother have been used to a different life, and, with all my pains-taking, the contrast must still be a prodigious one, their present with their past. I had to combine the house with the fortress, as you know, and the enclosures require to be a sort of court of guard, rather than simple fences. They will give us temporary refuge, and may be covered by musketry from the block-houses which occupy the four corners of some fifteen acres. The dwelling in the centre is itself a ' block ;' and, with the neighboring offices, all at hand, the fences, the palisades all complete, and the gates up, twenty men may keep them against five hundred of the savages."

" That reminds me, my dear cassique, to ask if the redskins

have been seen in your neighborhood lately. I have advices from the frontier that they are moving down in our direction in rather large divisions. The hunting-season is temporarily over, and the fishing begun. This necessarily brings them to the watercourses and the seaboard, out of the interior. And I know not that this should occasion any anxiety. But they are reported to be more numerous than usual. It is suspected that they bring with them tribes which hitherto have lived wholly in the interior, and there is also said to be some discontent among them — some complaints about lands and trespassers — to say nothing of that common subject of complaint, that the English do not make their presents sufficiently frequent or sufficiently large for the wants of the children of the wilderness. They are, by-the-way, as greedy in their desires as a—"

"As a courtier," replied the other, completing the sentence just as Quarry halted for a proper comparison.

"Thank you, yes — exactly. A good hit, my dear colonel. Ha! ha! ha! But we, who have sunned ourselves in royal favor, must not quarrel with the world's sneer. But to return to our red men?—"

"Thus far," said the cassique, "I see nothing to apprehend. I see very few of the tribes as yet. Some stragglers have shown themselves at the barony, and been fed. They gave no trouble. I am in treaty with one of the chiefs of the Stonos and Sewees for his son, whom I propose to employ as a hunter to supply me with venison. He is a mere boy of sixteen, upon whom I design an experiment. I wish to see if I can not detach him gradually from the life of the woods. My purpose is ultimately a more extensive one — the gradual diversion of the tribes from barbarism to the civilizing tasks of culture."

"Ah, my dear cassique, you are nursing philanthropy in defiance of all experience. You might as well warm the frozen snake at your fireside, and hope that its gratitude will take the venom out of its fangs. There is but one safe course with these savages. It is that which the New-Englanders employed. Buy up the scalps of the warriors, and sell the women and children to the West Indies. This is our proper policy."

"But this, you are aware, is positively forbidden by the lords-proprietors."

"The Lord send them a better wisdom! Here are these tribes about us, pretending peace, yet your laborers have to carry the shovel or axe in one hand and the musket in the other."

"Ay, because they have been much more free with musket than with axe or shovel. Had they been content to clear and cultivate we should have had little trouble with the red man. I, at least, shall try the pacific and humane policy, and see what will come of it."

"May you live to see! But take my counsel: in taking up the spade, do not put down the musket."

"Oh, I shall adopt all proper precautions. My fortress shall be well garrisoned. I am now looking out for laborers, who shall be gunmen also. Should you hear of any, who will answer in this twofold capacity, pray secure them for me. What advices lately from England?"

"None: we may look for the 'Swallow' packet daily."

"Is it not strange neglect of us, that there are no war-ships on our station? Here we have the most stringent orders for putting down piracy, yet not a vessel-of-war sent us. They seem, all of them, to crowd about New York and Boston, where they are quite out of the track of the pirates of the gulf. This should be the station of one or more, if we are to do anything efficiently. We have no land-force here for resistance to a single cruiser, which, if insolent, or defied, might boldly enter our harbor, and batter the town about our ears, and we scarce able to bring a gun to bear upon her, or to marshal the smallest battalion in our defence."

"Ah! luckily, most of these pirates are of good English breed. They devour the dons only, and this is so much good service done to the colony."

"We must not say that, Governor Quarry, regarding the existing treaty with Spain, and our orders from the proprietors. This last affair of the rover Calvert—the destruction of the 'Maria del Occidente,' a royal vessel—has made the matter a very serious one, and compels us to adopt a much more strict and national policy. By-the-way, should you not make proclamation of the tenor of your last instructions against piracy, and offer a reward for the apprehension of this rover Calvert?"

"There were no policy in that. With neither ships-of-war nor troops in hand, we could only hope to effect his apprehension by stratagem, in the event of his putting into our port again, as he has boldly done before. To make public proclamation of what he may expect, if he returns, will be most effectually to defeat our own object, and keep him off. Our true policy is to lie low, keep dark, and close upon him when he least expects it."

"You are right. That, in our present condition of weakness, is the only course we can adopt. We must have one or more men-of-war cruising on this station. And yet this rover will be more than a match, I fear, for any of our ships single-handed. He is a good seaman and a fearless scoundrel. The circumstances of that savage fight, were it in a good cause, would suffice to make him a hero. I confess that I share in all our British antipathy to the Spaniard, and in all our admiration of the hardy valor of our Norman breed; and when I heard the particulars of that affair, though out of the sanction of law, I rejoiced that the ancient spirit of the Drakes, the Raleighs, the Sandwiches, and Cavendishes, was not extinct among our seamen. Had we in our king's ships such brave fellows to command as this rover Calvert, Britain would never be made ashamed before Spaniard, or Frenchman, or Hollander. But it is your courtiers, sir, who play the devil with our marine. Here are they, men of the land altogether, too frequently taken from the command of cavalry, sent on board to manage ships and fleets — men of silk and filagree, who do not know a ship's stern from her taffrail, and are just as likely to go into action stern foremost as head. I scarce know one of them now in command in America whom I should not dread to see, yard-arm to yard-arm, in a sea-fight with this 'Happy-go-Lucky.' Our brave sea-dogs have given place to court-monkeys and the powdered popinjays whose only merit seems to be in their ready adoption of all the frills and furbelows of France."

"My dear cassique, you are quite too severe upon our macaronies. These powdered monkeys will fight."

"So they will. But we need conduct as well as valor, and we can have no conduct without the capacity, and this depends upon the hard school, the apprenticeship of seven years, which trains them to the use of every faculty and every art, so that they shall in action work rather by will and intuition than by thought. It is the lack of these that has made us succumb to Dutch, French, and Spaniard, in turn; and but for these unlicensed rovers, who assert the manhood of the nation in spite of its laws, the honor of Britain would too frequently lie upon a puppy's sleeve, for every daw to pluck at. I would it were that the British crown were honestly at war with France and Spain, so that we could legitimate the valor of these cruisers, and appropriate their gallantry to the country's honor. As it is, I should grieve to see this fellow Calvert strung up to the gallows, when, as a mere deed of valor, his crime would rather merit star and garter. But we must beware how we mock at law. Law is the most sacred thing known to society. The moment we hold it in irreverence, that moment we open all the floodgates of license, and Anarchy pours in her conflicting torrents to the breaking down of all the securities that keep the race from ruin."

"Ah! true, and very eloquently spoken, my dear cassique," answered the governor languidly, with difficulty suppressing a yawn. "Law is a very important matter in society. We, who hold offices of such high function, ought never to forget the laws —no! Of course, we must bring these pirates to the gallows— this fellow Calvert especially; though, I confess with you I should much rather see him commissioned in a king's cruiser, and doing a still larger business among the Spanish galleons."

Enough. There was more said; there was some business done between the parties. Papers were exchanged and signed. Money was confided to his excellency by the cassique. There were notes taken touching the Westo and other tribes of red men in the immediate precinct, who had already given the colony some trouble. But we do not care to state more than absolutely concerns our narrative.

The cassique of Kiawah took his departure, and the governor suffered Calvert to emerge from his retreat.

## CHAPTER XIII.

### SHOWING PROGRESS BUT NO ACTION.

> " We must bait awhile,
> For a new journey — pause and look around,
> Ere we depart anew through unknown paths."

" WELL, my dear fellow, you hear what the cassique of Kiawah has to say in regard to your case.   You see that, but for the Spanish influence at court, we should have no trouble at the hands of public opinion, either here or at home.   You have the popular sympathies.   Here, were the citizens alone concerned, you might walk the streets in broad daylight.   As the matter stands, you must needs be cautious.   Our honor, my dear captain, requires that we should hang you up, without benefit of the clergy, should you force upon us the knowledge of your presence !   And there is no need that you should do this.   You are not one of those macaronies who insist upon their proportions being seen — who are never satisfied unless they can spread broad tails, peacock-fashion, and scream aloud, in advance of their approach, the claims that they possess upon public admiration.   In short, my dear captain, the business is a good one — *to be continued* — with only that degree of modesty which forbears to trumpet to the world the extent of our profits."

" I see — I see !" was all the answer Calvert made to this speech. He proceeded abruptly :—

" I should like to have seen this cassique of Kiawah.   There was something in his voice that persuades me that I have seen him before.   What's his age — appearance — seeming ?"

" Some thirty-five — a fine-looking fellow ; not unlike yourself in build, though not quite so tall — say five feet ten ; and, by-the-way, it struck me, when we spoke of him before, that there was a something of likeness between you — a something, I know not exactly what, in the cut of the jib — pardon me the nautical comparison — a something in nose, and eyes, and mouth, very like between you. No disparagement in the comparison, let me tell you, for our cassique has quite a nobleman look and bearing."

"His voice is peculiar."

"Deep, sonorous, something sad. The fact is, his voice makes me think that he has a thorn somewhere in his side that pricks keenly. He's one of those restless men, for ever engaging in something new, whom I always suspect of some secret grief. He is feverishly active; works at all sorts of schemes — never stops work — and is somewhat wild in his choice of labor. Why the devil should he work, and so restlessly, if there be not some irking barb in his vitals? He is rich, does not seem to value money — certainly does not work with regard to the money profits; could live at ease, enjoy himself, and let us enjoy ourselves, if he pleased. Why should he bother himself with the reform of Indians, new experiments in culture, introduction of large stocks into the country, and fine varieties, which these very savages will be sure to slaughter nightly in his ranges?"

"Nay, I see not why he should not be moved by philanthropy."

The governor lifted his eyebrows with a ludicrous stare.

"Do you believe in that sort of stuff as a motive?"

"Yes, with insane people."

"But he's none of your insane ones, I tell you. He's devilish shrewd, methodical, calculating, in spite of all his nonsense of philanthropy."

"He has a wife, you say?"

"Yes, and child."

"You have seen *her*?"

"Yes — but once, on her first arrival: a pale, sad, silent looking woman."

"But that might have been the effects of the sea-voyage."

"Hardly. No! her looks are habitually sad, they tell me, who have seen more of her than I have. Middleton, who has lands near them, and sees them often, made the same remark to me. My own notion is, that our cassique is something of a domestic tyrant. He is certainly the man to make himself the law to his own household. There is a mother along with them — mother of

the lady—who looks as if she had a tongue in her head; carries
an eye as sharp as a fiery arrow; and wears just the look of one
to whom rule comes naturally, and who would bear no tongue-
music not of her own making.   Between the two, the wife seems
destined to the fate of the tender grain between the upper and
nether millstone."

"Does she ever come to the town?"

"Rarely."

"Yet lives at so small a distance—not twenty miles, I think
you said?"

"Not fifteen!   Oh, be sure, Major Berkeley is lord as well as
cassique.   He keeps the rein tightly within his own hands, and,
so far as his wife is concerned, needs no effort to do so.   It is
otherwise, I fancy, with the old lady, who, I suspect, frequently
catches up the ribands, and puts a barb into the leader.   But we
need waste no more words upon our cassique.   He's shrewd, and
sensible, and authoritative, but I can manage him.   You heard
how cleverly I threw him off, when he would have had me make
proclamation of the reward for your capture?"

"Yes!—you were prompt, and the reason given was a good
one."

"Hushed him directly!   But I must leave you now.   I have
to see some of our Indian traders, who are about setting out for
the Cherokees.   You will lie *perdu* for awhile."

"Till night, when I must go forth to receive a cargo.   You
shall have a supply of fruits to-night for the table of your lady."

"And she will have the honor of receiving you at supper.
Unfortunately, with this vigilant committee on the watch, she will
not be able to find you better company.   You must be as little
seen as possible."

"There could be no company more grateful than herself."

"Ah! you might have been a courtier, captain."

"Impossible!"

"Not a whit of it!   But I do not say you have mistaken your
vocation.   I only wish we were able to put you in a position to
combine the two—yours and mine!   But we are in alliance, and
that is next to it.   Now, take care of yourself.   There's your
retreat, should any one call.   And you will find good liquors in
yonder recess – Jamaica for your fiery moments, Madeira for

your courtly moods, and good sedative brown stout if you hap to be contemplative. As our Saxons were wont to say, 'Drink wael, drink hael,' which I take to mean, 'Drink well, and long life to you,' or something like it. *Au revoir!*"

It was a long morning to Calvert, unemployed and almost uncompanioned, in the solitude of the governor's private chamber. But he had his excellency to himself over a bottle of Madeira after dinner — the latter being served to him secretly by miladi herself, who, however, could give the rover but few moments of her presence. We need not report the further dialogues that day with his excellency. Soon as night set in fairly, our cruiser sallied forth, found his way to Franks' quarters, had a long business talk with that burly personage, and the two went forth together in the direction of the well-shadowed lagune where the boat was expected. But as our captain did not linger here very long, and as he is expected elsewhere, let us turn our steps in a new quarter, where we shall see that due preparation has been made for his reception.

# CHAPTER XIV.

## MRS. PERKINS ANDERSON.

"There's still a place at the board for all of us:
Go forward!—all are masked."

WE are wont to say, with no great sagacity, that the world is made up of all sorts of people. We know that it takes a monstrous variety of all sorts to make up the commonest sort of world. Even our new communities, planted in the wilderness, on the edge of heathen lands, must have their castes, their classes, their shades, degrees, and inequalities. Blackguards, for example, are a necessary element, one of the most necessary. We could not well do without them. There is a great deal of dirty work to be done in new communities—not so much, perhaps, as in old ones—which requires this very sort of agency. In the new communities, we need even a greater degree of ruffianism than mere blackguardism, and are always sure to have it. Your pioneer population are of this latter order in large proportion; and it does not work amiss, and is very far from out of place, when you reflect upon the sort of work which requires to be done. Your fine, nice, polished, smooth gentry, never become pioneers, never explore, never have enterprise, never found new empires, or exhibit those masculine traits which alone grapple with lions and hydras, and cleanse Augean stables! It needs for this a rough, unlicked sort of manhood, the muscle of which is never restrainable by morocco slippers and soft kid gloves. Your ancient Hellenes, Pelasgians, Etrurians, and what not, were blackguards and ruffians at the beginning, just like ours—though they fined down so beautifully, at last, into model poets, philosophers, and statesmen. Your sturdy old Romans, who first drove their stakes into the Seven hills, were admirable scamps, every man of them, to whom robbery was a glorious sort of manly exer-

cise, and rape only a pleasant step upward — the first great stride
made — to a most wonderful civilization! Smith's people, when
he founded Jamestown, were great rapscallions; and the puritans,
shod with holiness, though covered with hypocrisy, were the most
atrocious barbarians that ever cut throats, bought scalps, burned
witches, pilloried quakers, and sold the women and children of the
red princes into slavery, after they had butchered their papas and
husbands! And all these bold ruffians and blackguards, if you
believe them, do their dirty work for the glory of some God or
other — Jupiter or Jehovah — it matters not much which to
them! This is a necessary fiction of all society at its first beginnings.

And, even as you see, where the tiger rages, and the snake
crawls, and the frog hops, and the obscene birds prey on garbage,
the lacquered butterfly flickering in air, and hear the plaintive
cooing of innocent doves, and forget yourselves in the spontaneous
gushes of song from gay, glad birds of the sunshine — so, in society, even where the ruffians and the blackguards most congregate, you happen upon choice and generous spirits, brave master-
minds of men, gentle as well as brave; and sweet ministers of
love in the guise of innocent women; and gaudy butterflies of
fashion; macaronies, dandies, flirts, and harlots; all breathing one
physical atmosphere, though all at odds; removed from communion of moral by thousand leagues of gulf and desert in society!

And as new society, when a mere offshoot from an old, seeks
always to emulate the mother-circle, so you may take for granted
that, however new, the infant community will show you the same
moral aspects precisely which are most apparent in the old. The
fashion of the garments may be more stale, but the soul of the
wearer will be of the same ancient type. There will be less pol-
ish among the would-be fine; less learning among the would-be
wise; less grace among the fashionable; and less scruple, exteri-
orly, among the ruffianly and scampish. A course of training, in
a growing community, will, however, gradually bring up the standards of the ambitious; the fashionables will refine; and the scamps
and outlaws will adopt garments of greater cleanliness and more
pacific appearance — disguising with hypocrisy the vicious qualities which it is not yet their profit to abandon, or in their power
to overcome. This is the tribute which they will pay to the grow-

ing virtues of the social sphere, which they still in some degree pollute.

Now, we have already hinted to you that, in our humble little colony on the banks of the Cooper and the Ashley, even at this early period, in less than thirty years from its first foundation, we have our castes and classes — our orders of nobility — our aristocracies — our fashionables — and what nots! The patent nobility — palatines, landgraves, cassiques, barons — are such, of course, by law. They are the legitimates. Nobody questions their right to place. The landgrave's or cassique's carriage stops the way, but no plebeian tongue cries aloud! The fashionables follow close upon the heels of these — wealthy parvenues — who, if they can keep and transmit their wealth to another generation, raise them to a prescriptive class also; and these are your noble commoners. This is a history. It is the history in Carolina.

Now, dear friends, do not be surprised when we tell you that, next to our patent nobility, the highest order was that of the Indian traders. The Indian traders of 1684, and down thence to 1770, ranked second to the local noblesse. They did a flourishing business; they ushered in the first merchants. They were bold adventurers, chiefly of the class called Scotch-Irish, who possessed a hardy enterprise, great personal courage; were shrewd, intelligent, and cautious; not learned, but possessed of mother-wit; were greedy of gain, and ready to risk life upon it; but ambitious of social position, and not unwilling to peril for it that which was more precious than life, money! They aimed at something (and this is a right ambition) of social position for themselves and their descendants. They preceded and paved the way for a bold and liberal commercial enterprise, for which they made the forests furnish the *materiel.* The Indian trade, which had already begun to extend to the remote regions of the Choctaws and Chickasaws, seven hundred miles from Charleston, as well as to the nearer country of the Muscoghees, Cherokees, and Floridians — in other words, on every hand — was a greatly profitable one. The simple red man could be won by a knife, a hatchet, a bell, a medal, a tin pan, or a copper kettle, to exchange the choicest furs and skins with his white brother from the East. So profitable was the business, that the governors of the colony, and the chief people, were fain to participate in the trade; and it was rather with the view to this trade that treaties were made with the red men, followed by nominal purchases of that territory, for which the red men themselves could make no title, and which they dared not attempt to occupy. The whites bought immunity, rather than land.

Now, while our hands are in for it, let us tell you, though it be episodical, that these Indian traders, from a very early period, exercised a large influence, not only over the Indians, but in bringing about those events which affected the European struggles for ascendency in America. Could the court of England have cast off, as so many worthless old slippers, their worthless courtiers to whom they confided most of the colonial governments in America, and given their trusts chiefly to these Scotch or Scoto-Irish adventurers, thousands of lives would have been saved from butchery, millions of dollars kept in the treasury, and the miseries which belong to the caprices of an uncertain Indian war upon a wild frontier would have been escaped. The French would, moreover, have been beaten out of the country almost as soon as they appeared in it.

It was in vain that these bold, red-headed adventurers wrote, and memorialized, and undertook to teach, the silken courtiers to whom the colonies were confided, the true state of the case — the true nature of the red men — the processes by which to win their hearts or to subdue their arms. It was in vain that these traders showed them, by frequent examples, how peace was to be made, and war carried on; for they traversed the Indian country with little danger to themselves — avowed that they knew no danger, and never suffered harm, till the blunders of the governors made the white race absolutely contemptible in the eyes of the savage. These white adventurers were found ready and capable to raise an Indian force, in the heart of Choctaw and Chickasaw settlements — to lead the red men successfully against the French on the Alabama, the Tombeckbe, and the Meschacebe — capable of a patriotism which could prompt them to use their stock in trade as presents to subsidize the savages and reconcile them, when their blood was boiling for war, and when the young warriors had already struck the tomahawk in the painted tree. Neither example nor exhortation availed; and most of the bloodshed along the frontiers was due to the gross incompetence of the white authorities — to their vanity, love of show, insolence, and ignorance, which led them to outrage the red men with scorn and insult, and then to recoil, like timid children, at the warwhoop and the painted warrior whom they had aroused, without preparing for the presence which they conjured — incapable of wisdom, strength, or courage, when they had themselves provoked the strife! This much for the Indian traders, whom we must not suffer to be disparaged by a presentation of the simple idea of trade in their connection. On this trade they perilled life, and in its prosecution they exercised a firm will, a noble courage, an energy, vigilance, caution, and shrewd ingenuity, which endowed them finally with a capital of character such as few educational institutions of the civilized world could possibly impart; and they thus raised trade to the dignity of war and statesmanship — to a moral *status* which, *per se*, it never could assert.

Such were these traders from the beginning. In 1684, their number was comparatively small. It grew rapidly, however, far in proportion beyond the growth of the colonies. Between 1700 and 1770, they constituted something like a small army. But their profits were less than in the early period of which we write.

Perkins Anderson was one of the most prosperous of these Indian traders at this time (1684). The governors of Carolina had, severally, a sort of secret partnership with Perkins Anderson for the profits of this trade. They conciliated Perkins Anderson. He, Perkins, was not unwilling to be conciliated. The governor got his profits. The furs and skins came down from the interior, consigned to him or to his agent; and, in the benevolence of his heart, thus softened by certain quarterly profits, the governor lowered his social dignity, and Mrs. Perkins Anderson was graciously welcomed in the parlor and at the parties of Lady Quarry, wife of his excellency the governor. Of course, Perkins was not displeased with this recognition of his wife; but, if the truth were known, he would not have cared a button though a lady of quality never once looked on the lady of the Indian trader. He was too sedulous in pursuit of the main chance, to give much heed to the butterfly enjoyments of your tripping, gay citizens.

Far otherwise with Mrs. Perkins Anderson. She was just the creature for it — to whom such a life had become a sort of necessity. She had graduated for society as an Edinburgh mantua-maker, or milliner, and in this capacity Perkins had picked her up. She was the very person to know something about dress, and to love it. Her costume always came from London. She had the first advices of the last fashions. She set the mode on Ashley river, just one hundred and seventy years ago! We should surely venerate her memory.

She had a laudable ambition to shine in society. She visited the governor's lady; and, though not exactly acknowledged by the Mortons, the Middletons, the Berkeleys, and other folks who claimed to have been born in the shadow of the purple, if not absolutely within its folds, they were yet compelled to hear of her as a sort of rival for the social rule in Charleston. She was at home everywhere in the immediate precincts of the town. It was only at the baronial seats that she had no *entrée*. Whether she cared for it or not is hardly a matter of concern. She made the most of her own province. She gave balls and parties, and had her evenings, just as such people have them now. She knew, too, the value of a supper in conciliating affections and melting granitic pride and moral, and her suppers were a model and a proverb all over town. Mrs. Perkins Anderson was herself a model.

Poor thing! we must not blame her. Perkins was absent some ten months every year, and, when at home, was not exigent as a husband. He had his consolations, and why should she not have hers? He had a wife in each of the tribes — one at Euchee, another at Echotee, another at Tuckabatchie, another at Highwassee, and he acknowledged to half a dozen more — lamenting, to his Caucasian dame, the painful necessity which required that, for his safety, he should take a wife in every tribe with which he traded. And there may have been some truth in his story. It is very certain that, among the red chiefs, sooner than a white brother should go without a wife, each would give his own; and that, too, with a cheerful resignation which was almost Christian!

And it was beautiful to see the cheerful resignation with which Mrs. Perkins Anderson submitted to these dispensations of love, made on behalf of her husband; beautiful the meekness with which she bore his annual ten months' absence; delightful to note how readily she received all his pleas, excuses, and pretences; admirable to see how happily she contrived to console herself under her privation, by cheerfully yielding herself to the claims of society on every side. Verily, she was a model woman.

And now let us show the uses we have for Mrs. Perkins Anderson. She has just returned from a drive that afternoon—"up the path"—that being the fashionable route in those primitive days, when we had no "Battery." But it was a glorious drive, notwithstanding that it lay very much within the original grace of Nature. The road had been simply cut through a forest of live oaks and other noble trees, counting their lives by centuries. Their branches met and interweaved across the road, festooned with moss, and spanned the space between, making a grand Gothic archway, shutting out the sun. As old Archdale (himself a landgrave) wrote, at a later period—"No prince in Europe hath such an avenue in all his dominions."

Well, Mrs. Perkins Anderson had just returned from her evening drive, in her stately, lumbering English carriage of that date, drawn by two noble grays. Her carriage bore a lion for its crest, though what Perkins or herself had ever to do with lions nobody could say. Her livery was green and gold. Her style was admitted to be exactly the thing. The whole establishment was what the English fine-vulgar would call "a dem'd elegant turn-out!"

Well, she had returned from her drive, had left the carriage—was entering her dwelling—one of the best in town, somewhere near the corner of Church and Tradd streets, as we have them now—when she found our "ancient mariner," Franks, awaiting her at the door. At a signal, he followed her into the house, and might have said a dozen words—scarcely more—when he might have been seen backing out of the dwelling, making most formal bows until he was fairly in the street, and the door shut upon him.

These dozen words were of peculiar potency. Mrs. Perkins Anderson remained at home that night—yet received no company. Externally, the house was in utter darkness. The servants were allowed to depart, having a holyday from the mistress in her amiable mood; and, at a certain hour, the door has been opened by the fair lady herself, to admit two sturdy seamen, bearing a basket of such dimensions, that we can recall no fellow to it, save that which enabled Falstaff to escape the keen scrutiny and cudgel of good Master Ford. This was filled with fruits of Cuba, then rare in the market. It may have been an hour later, when the door opened again, and this time to admit our rover, the gallant Captain Calvert.

## CHAPTER XV.

> " To sigh, yet feel no pain ;
>    To weep, yet scarce know why ;
>    To sport an hour with Beauty's chain,
>    Then fling it idly by" —
> This is love, according to Moore,
>    Over which nobody needs to cry !

MRS. PERKINS ANDERSON herself, clad in her happiest style —
bracelets on her arms, brilliants on bosom and finger — received
our rover at the entrance, and hastily drew him into the dwelling.
They walked together through a dark passage, her hands grasping
his affectionately, and leading him on to an apartment in the rear
of the building, which, the shutters all being carefully closed, was
brilliantly lighted with wax-candles.   The room was, for that day
and region, a handsomely-furnished one.   London had supplied
some of its best styles of furniture in the Elizabethan fashion —
great-backed mahogany chairs, massive, such as might befit a cor-
onation ;  and massive tables ;  and a tall clock in the corner, large
enough for the halls of Gog and Magog ;  and great oval mirrors
against the walls, environed with richly-gilded frames, beautifully
carved with leaves of oak, interspersed with golden acorns.   From
these samples, suppose the rest of the catalogue.   A luxurious
chair received the lady, and another of the same pattern, wheeled
in front of her, was occupied by our captain of the " Happy-go-
Lucky."

The lady was frank and joyous, and glowed apparently with
the happiness she felt at the presence of her visiter.

"I am so glad to see you again, my dear captain !   This is a
real pleasure.   You have been so long absent !   But let me thank
you at once for that beautiful present of fruits.   They are deli-

cious. But, to see you again, and looking so well, makes me at once forget the long time of expectation — the weariness of waiting. You know I count you as among my dearest friends, and will believe me when I assure you that I have looked and longed often for the pleasure of this meeting."

And the lady again took the hands of our captain, and smiled most sweetly in his very eyes.

" You are kind," he said, " kind as ever. And I am rejoiced to find that a gay life, constant society, and increase of wealth, have not made you forgetful of old friends."

" How should they ? It is they who make life precious ; show the uses of wealth ; give the charm to society. Now that you are come, we shall have a merry time of it. We have, indeed, a gay circle here — many very clever and interesting people ; we constantly meet, and there is quite a struggle already as to who shall give the gayest parties."

" You are aware that I am forbidden to go into society — parties especially ?"

" Forbidden ! how — why ?"

" My health !"

" Pshaw ! what nonsense ! You were never looking better — never more handsome !"

" Thank you. Perhaps I should say *my life*, rather than *health*, depends upon my not being seen in public."

" Ah ! I understand you. Franks warned me to be cautious, and to send the servants off. But, my dear captain, are not these precautions very ridiculous ? What have you to fear ? what have you been doing ?"

" Nothing worse than I have done before. But the court of England has suddenly grown virtuous, and sensitive to the royal pledges ; and the crown has taught the proprietary lords to translate ' privateer' into ' pirate,' and especially to consider one Captain Calvert a particular offender of the latter class — simply for not pulling down the British jack in obedience to the shot of a royal packet of Castile."

" And why should you ? What ! the British flag go down before a Spaniard ? I hope you sunk her !"

" The very thing I did. But our royal sovereign does not share the spirit of his people, and the Spanish embassador has had influence enough to get me outlawed. So that, my dear Mrs. Anderson, I am in your power: you see how much I rely upon your friendship! You have only to report my presence here to any of the council, and you win a purse of five hundred pounds, and consign me to dungeon and scaffold."

"Ah! with my help, you shall have no worse dungeon than my dwelling—its most sacred chamber. But what fools! Well, one thing is certain: *our people* will never quarrel with you for knocking the Spaniard on the head. You are quite safe with us—"

"Only so long as I keep unseen. I must make a cloak of the night while in Charleston, and lie close by day. I might be safe with your people; but I am warned, by those who know, that it will not do any longer to appear *publicly* among them. Your privy council are already on the watch to snare and take me; and, did they suspect my presence here now, you would soon hear of the proclamation, and this would be followed by the search."

"I am so sorry! I should so delight to have you at my party on Thursday night! What are we to do? I can hardly give you up."

"I must forego the pleasure. But I'll tell you what I can do."

"Well?"

"I have my wife with me."

"What! that little Mexican creature?"

"Yes, I have but one."

This was said with the faintest effort at a smile. The speech reminded Mrs. Perkins Anderson of the superior advantages possessed by her own husband as an Indian trader. And she sighed, as if in sympathy with the sad fortunes of the rover. But, in a moment after, she said—

"And she is here, with you?"

"With your consent, she will be with you to-morrow night. On the strength of your frequent invitations, I have brought her with me this voyage. She begs your acceptance of these trifles."

He handed the lady a packet and a case. She opened both with eagerness. The first contained a shawl—one of those exquisite fabrics of the East which might be spread over a chamber as a carpet, yet could be crushed into the compass of a walnut-shell; the case, as it was opened, flashed out in a blaze from a cluster of precious gems — their spiritual brightness, so glowing and ethereal, seeming to need, for confinement, that beautiful setting, in golden filagree, with which Mexican art, always wonderful in the execution of such works, had contrived to secure and illustrate the gems ; the setting itself ingeniously devising that a golden serpent, with mosaics on his back, should " wear a precious jewel in its head" — should gleam with two precious jewels for its eyes — and, twined about the fair neck of beauty, should rest its gorgeous though monstrous head upon the heaving breast of white below.   So were those jewelled birds, that were meant to sparkle on her brow, to float above her hair, or to perch as a crest upon the bracelets of her arm.

Mrs. Perkins Anderson, though rich and accustomed to show, was absolutely silenced by the astonishing beauty and evident value of the gift.   When she did speak her raptures, it was only to find all superlatives wanting :—

" Superb ! wonderful ! magnificent !   Oh, how beautiful !   I never thought that there could be such exquisite fabrics.   And wought by these Mexicans and Spaniards !   It is wonderful."

Like a sagacious woman, she never once asked our rover how he got them — by what invasion of Spanish towns ; by what fierce fight with galleons or frigates of Castile and Leon.   But she made some modest hesitation about accepting a gift so costly.

" Consider it only valuable as a gift of love, and then, the more priceless, the more it becomes us to welcome and to wear it.   It is such, believe me.   You have cheered many hours of my solitude, Charlotte, and you will no doubt contribute to make happy the young creature, my wife, while she stays with you.   Suffer us to assure you in this manner — for I deal, you are aware, but little in professions — that we have found your kindness much more precious to us than these toys can ever be to any human heart."

He pushed the jewels back to her as he spoke, and she silently gathered them into the case and laid them with the shawl behind her.   Abruptly then, and with a greater degree of earnestness, she said :—

" Your tones are very sad, Harry.   Is it ever to be thus ?"

" I suppose so !"

" No content ?"

" Save in the unrest which, so long as life lasts, must afford me my only refuge from thought and disappointment."

"I would I could do something, Harry Calvert, to make you more cheerful. *Can* I do nothing? Is the heart utterly sealed? Is there to be no freedom for it? And such a heart as yours! Oh, this life! what a thing of contradictions; of ill-assorted associations; of ties that are bonds, not links; and connections that only chafe, and do not cheer! Ah, Harry, what a life is mine! I am compelled to be frivolous, to escape the snares of feeling. I could love! I could surrender myself wholly to the one affection, could I be sure of its faith; but as I am—"

" Charlotte, we have nothing to do with happiness. It comes, or it does not come. It obeys no regulation. It is secured by no plan, no wisdom, no fine scheme of thought, no human policy or persuasion. The very caprices of life forbid the idea of happiness. We are to undergo an ordeal — to work out a certain result — about which we ourselves have no certainty. We are in the hands of a power in which our hands are powerless — which heeds little how we hope, or sigh, or dream, or suffer. We must keep our hearts silent; stifle what we can; resign, as readily as possible, what we can; indulge in few expectations; leave all that we can to the Power whose will is absolute, and before which all our purposes shrink into nothingness. I am not a fatalist, when I believe in the Providence

'That shapes our ends, rough hew them how we will.'

I have erred like the rest, but I am not getting obdurate. I have simply survived hope — at least in all things in this miserable state of ordeal which we call life."

"Alas! what a confession! Survived hope! Why, Harry, even I, who claim to be disappointed also, have not survived hope."

" Have you weighed it?"

" No, Heaven forbid! I simply let myself alone, and employ the day as profitably for pleasure as I can."

" Why, so do I, and so does every man, woman, and child. But who can see far enough ahead to resolve that the pleasure of to-day will not be the pain of to-morrow? Besides, we are beings of different grades. Some swim and sing through life, touching the sands lightly, as some little bird or insect; others, with sterner will, or heavier wing, dive deep, soar high, move rapidly, and with too much earnestness, not to bruise themselves perpetually in the superior violence of their effort. I am of this nature. It is an enviable condition, that of a lightness which takes nothing seriously — which may be bird or butterfly, satisfied with a day's exertion, and singing or soaring only for its little hour."

"And you hold me one of these creatures, Harry?"

"No—"

"You do, Harry Calvert — you do! But you know me not. I live *in* the world — I must live in it — since I have hardly a home. What is here? Beauty, you will say — grandeur even, for such a region — and wealth. I have luxuries — food — trappings — servants — in abundance. But, Harry, need I say to you that I am here in a solitude? I am alone — no home — for I have no companionship."

Our cruiser showed himself a little uneasy. He rose and paced the room. The lady was growing sentimental. Tears were in her eyes as she drew this melancholy picture of human desolation in the case of one who flourished at all the balls of the season. And there was that *empressement* in her manner which seemed likely to compel his sympathies to a participation in her griefs. He did not answer her, but silently strode the apartment to and fro, never looking up. She rose and followed him, laid her hands upon his shoulder, and continued, even more earnestly —

"You do not believe me, Harry!"

"Why not? Who can know where the serpent coils — under what flower? who say how the heart writhes with secret tortures, wearing yet a face wreathed in smiles? I must not judge of your case, having a sufficient knowledge of my own. But why speak of either? Can they be amended?"

"Alas! I know not. O Harry Calvert, I so long for sympathy! This terrible isolation — this waste of feeling — this consciousness that our hearts give forth their waters, as fountains in the desert, with none to see, or seek, or taste!"

"But the very fact that they flow proves life — not unprofitable life. In their own fullness they find content."

"Ah! but they finally cease to flow, finding that they flow in vain. The fountain chokes at last."

7

" Unless an angel comes down at night to trouble it."

" Ah, would the angel come ! But why should this waste be ?
Why should the heart long in vain for the very nourishment
which is its only need and craving ? Why, of all these myriads
whom we *could* love, and whose love one might deserve and requite, should we still sigh in loneliness, thirsting for living waters
of love in vain ?"

It must not be denied that Mrs. Perkins Anderson was a very
interesting woman. Not exactly handsome — scarcely pretty —
she was yet interesting. She had a face which sparkled with animation and intelligence ; she was short, but not bulky of figure,
and she dressed, as may be conjectured, to a marvel. And now,
as she indulges in the pathetic mood, she may reasonably imagine
that she must be irresistible. Certainly nothing can be more unnatural, in the case of a brave and gallant gentleman, than to
refuse his sympathies when Beauty weeps — and when that Beauty
still keeps her youth, and when those tears are enforced by eloquent pleadings of a warm fancy and a somewhat copious thought !
For, though an ignorant woman, so far as early education is concerned — ignorant of letters and science, and scarcely awakened
to the deep truths that lie in art — Mrs. Perkins Anderson had so
lived, and was so susceptible of education, could so rapidly absorb
from life and society, and had such natural gifts, that, upon occasion, she could rise to eloquence.

She was destined to waste it on the present occasion. The
eyes of Harry Calvert settled upon her with a keen and searching
glance. He was no sentimentalist. His deep, earnest tones were
in unison with the stern, cold, troublesome query which he put.

" Of what, really, do you complain, Mrs. Anderson ?"

" Oh, do not, Harry, use an address so formal. We have known
each other too long — have been tried friends too long — for this :
call me, I entreat you, as before — call me Charlotte."

" Well, Charlotte, of what do you complain ?"

" Of bonds — of fetters !"

He was dull of comprehension.

" Of what nature ?"

" I am the wife of one who loves me not."

The question that followed was a somewhat annoying one :—

" Do you love him ?"

"No!" cried the lady, grasping the arm of the inquirer, and looking intently into his face — "no, Harry, how should I? In what should *he* interest me? How should such as he control affections such as mine? He, bent only on the acquisition of money — cold, selfish, indifferent — leaving me lonely—"

"Does he interest you when here?"

"No!"

"Then you are quits; for it is clear, Charlotte, that you do not interest him, or he would remain, in compliance with your wishes."

The lady's cheeks flushed up to her eyes.

"But, Harry, do you hold me incapable of interest in the eyes of a gentleman?"

"Far from it! At all events, you always interest *me*, and never more than when I think you erring and unreasonable, as I hold you now."

"Ah, Harry, that speech should only be made by a lover."

How very sweetly and tenderly the lady smiled as she uttered this courteous reproach! But there was no answering smile on the face of our cruiser. He had long before sounded the lady's shallows. She belongs to a well-known school, who use sentiment, perhaps unconsciously to themselves, only as a cover for passion. She probably deceived herself. We will suppose so, through charity. Many do, no doubt, deceive themselves through some such medium as sentiment. The class is somewhat increasing in modern times, since gradually society has begun to shake off very generally the sense of duty. All idle women, having a certain amount of smartness, and no children to attend to, and no household duties to perform, or devolving all these upon servants, are necessarily in this very danger. There is a gradual growth of morbid sentimentality, which deals freely in this sort of sophistication, but which has its real root only in passion. Our rover is himself a man of passion, but not a rover in this respect. His passion is true, and therefore concentrative. All passions which lack in concentrativeness are morbid, diseased, unresting, and capricious, as those of a ground-sparrow. You may console the broken heart in an hour, by giving exercise to the blood. Captain Calvert was not pleased to echo the lady's sentimentalities — nay, he was rather disposed to probe them.

" Charlotte," he said coolly, but in the deepest tones of his sonorous voice, " I repeat the question — of what do you complain ?"

" Have I not said of isolation, abandonment, indifference, neglect, on the part of him who ought to love me ?"

" But you have just as distinctly admitted that you do not love
him."

" Because he neglects me."

" But, Charlotte, did you ever love him? Think, now, before
you speak. You knew him before you married. He was always
the same person — a person nowise attractive, externally, to a
woman; shrewd and persevering, but not intellectual; nowise refined; totally inelegant; coarse of manner as of structure, and just
as cold, no doubt, and indifferent always. All this, Charlotte, I
have from your own report. Did you ever love this man ? What
was he, or had he, to win a woman's love — your love ?"

" Alas! I was a mere girl, Harry."

" A pretty old one," was Harry's secret suggestion, but he did
not say it.

" You mean, by that, that you deceived yourself in the belief
that you did love him ?"

" Yes," very faintly.

" But, by the same process, you deceived *him* as well as yourself. May not the secret of his indifference be found in the fact
that he has discovered your secret? Now, Charlotte, he was
much more likely to have loved you than you him. *You* had attractions for the eyes of men. *You* had grace, vivacity, delicacy,
and intelligence. You had — and have — such charms as might
satisfy any man of proper taste and feelings. I think it probable
that Perkins Anderson had always a tenderer regard for you than
you for him. Nay, I think he still has. What does his life show
you ? He goes off into the wilderness, leaving you to loneliness
and isolation. Yet he leaves you in abundance; he provides for
you sumptuously before he departs; he raises you to a social state
which affords *him* individually no pleasure; he is pleased to know
that *you* shine in society — is pleased so to crown your home with
delights, and your person with ornaments, as that you shall necessarily shine in society. He, on the other hand, while he denies
himself your society, denies himself all these pleasures which he
leaves to you; he penetrates the wilderness; he perils his life

among the savages; his life is one of daily toil and nightly anxieties: and these toils are taken, and these anxieties borne, *you say*, in the pursuit of gain — but the gain enures to *you!* He sends his treasures home to you; and, should he perish to-morrow, he has already put you in possession of independence. Do you doubt that this has been an object of his care — knowing that his life is at perpetual hazard — that he yet finds his consolation in the fact that he has made ample provision for you?—"

" As if money constituted the ample provisions of life !" the lady said, somewhat scornfully and impatiently — " as if life had nothing else for which to live ! — as if mere bread, and meat, and fine linen, could console a starving heart, nourish a withering affection, requite and refresh the thirsting soul that seeks for love or nothing ! O Harry Calvert, is it from your lips that I hear such approval of the most mercenary aims of life ?"

" Charlotte," said our rover, " I like you too well, am too much your friend, to suffer you to fall into any delusions, either as regards yourself or me. In respect to myself, it will be safe to suppose that I have no sane purpose in life. I peril it for gain, you suppose ; but I fling away all the winnings of the game. My life is profligate ; yet there is no passion which I pursue with hope or expectation. If you will know it, the only passion which I ever entertained, with all my heart, all my soul, all my strength, has foiled and mocked me ; its arrow has shot into my soul, and left nothing but a harrowing venom, that keeps me from sleep as it keeps me from enjoyment. My energies are watchful and restless ever, simply because my hurts allow me no repose. I toil and adventure, not for gain — for nothing, briefly — but because I dare not hope for rest !"

" And is it so, Harry Calvert ?"

" It is so ! And you ?"

" Ay, what of me ?"

" Your unhappiness is more the result of the absence of a true care, than the presence of any earnest anxieties."

" Oh, Harry !"

" It is so with thousands. You must not talk of disappointed passions, unless you can assure me that you have had an object, precious to all your affections ; the first and only always in your thoughts ; a being for whom you could die ; for whom only you would care to live — before I can suppose you to be the sufferer which you persuade yourself you are. There are very few persons who ever meet with such an object. A blind passion, eager for satisfaction, will make — does make — this object for itself; and hence the disappointments of life — which is never to be satisfied with life, simply as it is! Men and women marry, half the time, through restlessness — impatience of their actual condition; not through a desire for happiness — for this is an object which few persons seek. They seek rather the gratification of a desire — seek gold — seek one another — and, would seek more wisely, were they governed in their search always by some honest passion, having an object in its aim which had been already commended to their sympathies and confidence. They too frequently seek in marriage for the object, not for the object in marriage. Some marry for bread and meat, which, having them, and not doubting that they will continue to have them, they persuade themselves that they despise; others seek show, wealth, an establishment; others the gratification of a wanton vanity, or a still more wanton lust!"

"Hush, Captain Calvert — hush! You are quite too free."

"You must not quarrel with truth. It is so seldom you can get it. Well! disappointment waits on most, and all that remains to us is to economize the wreck of our affections; to make the most of our mistakes; to resign ourselves, as patiently as possible, to the fates which we have made. Believe me, you have as yet suffered no disappointment of the *heart*, having not yet fastened all its hopes upon some ideal creature, who has first warmed your imagination and controlled your sympathies through your own conception of a model husband."

"Ah, but I have, Harry!" with a deep sigh, and a look of the tenderest interest — "ah, but I have!"

"It is too late, now, Charlotte, either for that being or yourself, supposing him to be still in existence."

"He is! he is!"

"Better, then, for *your* sake, that he were dead!"

"Oh! why — why? Dead!"

"You can never be the same to him as at the time when you were unmarried to another."

"Ah, but I did not know him then. It was only when I came to know *him*, that I found my present bonds were fetters."

" Still too late for both, since you can no longer bring him the tribute of a virgin heart.    How should he believe you?  how persuade himself that the same fancies which deluded you to wed another, will not, in their caprice, beguile you from him?"

" Never, never, Harry Calvert!    I could die for *him!*"

" Better live for *yourself*," he answered, gloomily.    " Charlotte Anderson, let us not be children.    Let us be friends.    Suffer me to be yours.    As a friend, I should be faithful to you to the last.    As a lover—nay, were I even that particular person whom you had made your ideal—which is, of course, impossible—I should fly your presence as I would the pestilence!"

A deep sigh from the lady, who sank back in her chair at the same moment, responded to his speech.    Her eyes were gushing with tears.    He took her hand, and in softer accents said, touching his own breast :—

" Judge of the wreck *here*, Charlotte, when I tell you that this young wife, whom I propose to bring to you, is one of the loveliest creatures whom your eyes ever beheld.    She brought me wealth, and such devotion as it was possible for such a child-soul as hers to bring : yet would I now, a thousand times, cheerfully give up life itself, to restore her to the condition — the child-place, and peace of mind, in which I found her, and whence, in one of the phases of my insanity, I won her to my arms.    But I can neither stab her with this truth, nor do the cowardice of suicide.    It is no reproach to her charms when I say that I have no joy in them — as, at the same time, I tell you there are no charms for me in life."

" Yet she is a beauty ?"

" Yes !    You will say so when you see her."

" A Mexican beauty ?"

" A *Spanish* beauty, of the purest blood."

" And loves you ?"

" I think so — as far as so infantile a nature is capable of love.    But to *our* conception of that master-passion it is scarcely in her power to rise.    She is a creature all levity.    Give her crowds : she will live in a ballroom ; will dance without resting, nightly — all the night ; loves glitter, music, show ; loves admiration, gallantry—"

" And you fear not to trust her with me ?"

" Why should I fear?"

" Here, such a being as you describe her will have admiration enough, and be liable to a thousand temptations.   There are younger sons of courtiers about town — gallants who have taken their lessons at the court of Charles, and boast of the patronage of the duchess of Portsmouth.   They are handsome fellows — macaronies — dandies; as unscrupulous as handsome; bold and audacious as gallant; and possessed of all the arts which are so apt to ensnare the unsophisticated female heart.   Do you not fear them?"

" No!   In the very unsophistication of Zulieme, I am secure: she is secure.   Her faith in me assures my faith in her.   The very sports of her people, in which she has been trained, are an additional security.   She will not comprehend the language of gallantry, except in the ear of her vanity.   It will go no deeper. Her heart can not be touched."

" She speaks our language?"

" After a fashion — brokenly, but prettily."

" Well, Harry, I will do for her all I can — though I am not suffered to do anything for her husband!"

" You will do for *me*, Charlotte, when you do for her.   Franks will bring her to you to-morrow night.   And now, Charlotte, God bless you, and send you relief from this unrest!   It is the unrest that properly haunts all that lack an object — that lack cares and necessities.   If you had children, now—"

" Children!   Heaven forbid — and by him!   Go, Harry Calvert — go!   You are a man without a heart."

" Would it were so, Charlotte! — But God bless you, and make you wise enough to lose all memories which are troublesome!"

The cavalier was gone.   The lady sank back with a sigh, covering her face with her hands.   We must not ask what are the thoughts and sorrows of one who has no cares.   But, lest the reader should suffer too much anxiety, from what he has seen of her present state of feeling, we beg to mention that, in ten minutes after, she was busily engaged locking the gorgeous necklace which Calvert had brought her, about her fair, white neck; trying the bracelets upon her arms; weaving the diamonded bird-crests in her hair ; and, finally, folding the delicate shawl tastefully about her shoulders, while she walked before the great oval mirrors, watching with delight the beautiful effects produced by these fine gifts.

"It is the loveliest shawl!" she exclaimed, as she reluctantly folded it away in its original case.

7*

## CHAPTER XVI.

### THE CUP—THE KISS!

"It is the heart that consecrates!   No rite
  Is sacred, or makes sacred, save in that
  Where the affections minister, and Love
  With whole heart hallows as the rite enjoins."

WHEN Calvert left Mrs. Perkins Anderson, he proceeded to a
meeting with Franks; and the two together took their way to the
lagune in which the boats of the "Happy-go-Lucky" were wont
to seek safe harborage.   Two of them had arrived, with full cargoes, which were transferred, in little time, on the shoulders of
the seamen, to the secret warehouse of Master Franks.   Among
those who came this time with the boats was Jack Belcher, with
whom, while the boats were unlading, our rover had a long private conference.   That faithful retainer had a minute and interesting report to make.   There were circumstances that made him
uneasy.   He reported Lieutenant Molyneaux as still desperately
attentive to the fair Zulieme; but this was not so much the cause
of his uneasiness.   They had their dances, as usual, and the rough
Anglo-Saxon was not by any means reconciled, by the frequency
of the fandango, to the familiarities which it allowed.   But, as his
superior saw nothing in this to cause apprehension or displeasure,
Belcher forebore reporting fully the measure of his indignation.

But there were more serious matters of suspicion, if not of mis-
conduct, which had rendered him uneasy.   He discovered, or
fancied that he discovered, that the said lieutenant discriminated,
with singular partiality, in the treatment of the crew.   Some of
the sailors had no favor shown them.   To others he was specially
indulgent; and, with certain of these others, Jack Belcher discovered that the lieutenant was in frequent conference, privately, in
the woods.   Some of these men were occasionally missing, and,

on one of these occasions, one of the boats of the ship was missing also.

Belcher reported the lieutenant as arbitrary in a degree amounting to tyranny, giving great offence to the sailors whom he did not favor. He himself (Belcher), though not strictly under the authority of the lieutenant, as the private attendant and body-servant of the captain, had been made to understand that he was no favorite, and would be subjected to his regimen as soon as ever he dared indulge in authority as fully as he evidently desired. It was time, according to Belcher's opinion, that Captain Calvert should resume the command of the ship.

This tallied well with the captain's purpose.

"I shall go up to-night, Jack. You will remain here with Franks, lying close, and submitting to all his precautions."

To what Belcher said of Molyneaux, Calvert only responded with contemptuous indignation in regard to the course of that individual.

"The vain blockhead! Now will he not be content till he gets knocked upon the head. It is a pity, too, for the fellow is as brave as he is impudent, and as good a seaman as he is a puppy in his uniform. But, I have sounded him, and know just where his oars catch crabs. Never you trouble yourself about him, Jack; but give me the names of the fellows with whom he consorts. Some of them I suspect already. Where do you suppose the missing boat went, when she was taken off?"

"To town, sir — where else?"

"Ah! was she so long gone?"

"Eighteen hours at the least."

"Indeed! We must fathom that. Such visits might seriously endanger us. But enough now. Let us rejoin Franks."

When they had returned to the lagune, they found that the landing of the goods had all been effected.

"Franks," said Calvert, drawing him aside, "have you that stout hackney that I used to ride when I was here last?"

'Yes, sir, and as stout a beast as ever."

'You must get him across the Ashley for me by to-morrow, sometime. Who have you now at Oldtown?"

"Gowdey. You remember him — a queer fellow. He lives on the creek, above the town."

" Is he trusty ?"

" True as steel."

" Anybody else at Oldtown now ?"

" Not a soul besides, that I know of.   The Indians have burnt down most of the houses, and the few left are in ruins.   Gowdey has a log-cabin : it was one of the old blocks just on the outskirts. Fort Sayle, they called it."

" I remember.   Have the horse in Gowdey's hands to-morrow. Do not spare any money.   Be sure of it !   I must not be disappointed."

" It shall be done, sir.'"

" Jack Belcher will remain with you, and help to sort and distribute the goods.   He knows all about it, better than either of us.   I leave you, for the present.   To-morrow night, you will receive my wife, and convey her carefully to Mrs. Perkins Anderson.   She is prepared to welcome her.   It is barely possible that I shall come myself.   But let it matter nothing if I do not.   You and Jack can manage everything now."

And the captain of the cruiser stepped into one of the boats, and gave the word for both to move.   They rowed out of the creek, but hoisted sail when they reached the river — the wind being favorable for its ascent — going half the way " wing-and-wing."   It was about two in the morning when the cry was heard from the watchman of the ship, " Boat, ahoy !"   And the answer was made in the deep voice of the captain, who soon scrambled up on deck, and was welcomed by the officer of the watch.

This happened to be Lieutenant Eckles, whose welcome, by-the-way, appeared to be a somewhat confused one, arising from a certain fact which he chanced to know, and from which he apprehended evil to his colleague, the first lieutenant.   But, as Calvert did not seem to notice the confusion of Eckles, we must not anticipate.   The latter, however, showed some eagerness to hurry below, when he had spoken with the captain ; but our rover arrested him promptly.

" Keep your post, sir : you do not propose that I shall take the watch off your hands !"

Thus speaking, he passed below himself, and, entering his cabin suddenly, was confounded, not only to find the lights burning, but to discover the fair Zulieme sitting up, and engaged, with Lieutenant Molyneaux, at a Spanish game of cards, which the beauteous lady was teaching the ambitious Briton. They had heard nothing of his arrival — too much absorbed, we may suppose, and the vessel being head out from the creek where she lay, and the captain entering from forward. A decanter of Spanish wine stood upon the table, and it was evident that Molyneaux had been imbibing pleasure, if not instruction, in more ways than one. It was a natural impulse of guilt that made him start to his feet, in some confusion, at the sight of his superior. He was otherwise bold enough to face the devil.

"What do you here, sir," demanded the captain, "in my private cabin?"

Zulieme answered, with equal coolness and simplicity —

"I asked him in, Harry, to play with me."

"He should have known better than to have accepted your invitation. This is no place for him, and he knows it. But that I know *you* so well, Zulieme, I had cut his throat and yours too. Away, sir, to your own quarters, and see that you do not repeat this offence at *any* invitation!"

The lieutenant glared savagely upon the speaker as he passed out, but prudence prevailed with him for once, and he was silent. Calvert saw the expression of his face, and simply muttered to himself —

"The time is not yet come!"

Meanwhile, Zulieme had sprung up also, her black eyes flashing with indignation, and her little figure trembling with the same feeling.

"And you come, Harry, only to be a brute! Pray, what's the harm of Molyneaux coming to play with me — and when I asked him, too?"

"Harm! — But what's the use? She can never understand!"

"What's that I can't understand, Harry?"

"That among our brute English, my lieutenant has no business, at midnight, in the chamber of my wife. And I repeat to you that, were you any but the woman that you are, I should have not only cut Mr. Molyneaux' throat, but probably yours also."

"You horrid wretch! And why don't you do it? And why am I different from other women, I want to know?"

"I am afraid that I can't teach you, Zulieme. But, you are.

This person, Molyneaux, knew that he was doing wrong, though you did not.  Does it not strike you as possible, Zulieme, that there are men who would like to persuade you to do wrong?"

"And for what?  But that's always the way!  Everything's wrong with you savage English.  But what made you stay away so long?  You've been gone more than five days."

"It might as well have been five months.  You have spent the time happily enough."

"No!  I've only danced and sung, and run in the woods till I was tired, and scared too, for Mr. Molyneaux said that the red Indians were all about."

"You were more safe in their hands than in his, silly one!  But I am about to remove you from the danger of the red Indians, and possibly from other dangers.  Do you still wish to go to Charleston?"

"Oh, dear Harry, is it true?  Will you carry me?"

"Or send you!  You shall go to-morrow night, if you please."

"Oh, why not to-night?"  And she leaped up and threw her arms round the neck of the sombre man, and kissed him; then whirled about, and pirouetted, and threw herself into the intoxicating raptures of her most voluptuous Mexican dances, vainly entreating him, in dumb show, to take the floor.

He looked at her with a countenance that saddened as he gazed.  The savage severity of face had passed off, and his look was now of a subdued melancholy.  It finally melted into a faint smile, which her quick eyes eagerly detected.

"Ah, Harry, now you look good-natured again.  You will really take me with you to Charleston?"

"Either take you or send you.  I have made arrangements for your reception there.  Mrs. Perkins Anderson, an old acquaintance of mine, has invited you.  She is quite a fine, fashionable lady, who sees a great deal of company, and lives in the best style.  Under her chaperonage, you will enjoy the best opportunity of seeing life in Charleston."

"And is she young, and gay, and pretty, and rich, Harry?  Does she give balls and dancing-parties?"

"Ay, she does little else, and you will be in your element.  But I must warn you that, in Charleston, you are not to be known as Zulieme Calvert—not to be known as my wife—better not be known as a wife at all. My name is under ban in Charleston. A price is set upon my head."

"I won't go, Harry — I won't! Those brute English! Oh, no! Let's go anywhere else. Let's go from 'em — go to Havana, Harry — that's a good Harry!"

"Alas! Zulieme, a still greater price is set upon my head in Havana. Here, they will pay for it but in pounds and dollars; there, in doubloons and joes."

"Why, Harry, what's to be done? Better go back to Darien," she answered, in temporary consternation.

"Nay, Zulieme, you will do as I counsel. I told you repeatedly, before, what were the dangers of my life, everywhere; but you are a bad listener. You were angry with me because I did not give you an opportunity at the *festas* of Havana, though you saw how our vessel had to skulk along the coast, and only peep into some of the Cuban harbors. And, though I showed you the *garote* at Havana, and told you that five hundred ounces would be paid by the governor to any one who would help him to adjust its collar to my neck, you heard of nothing but the bull-fights of 'holy week' — the processions and the fandangos which were to follow. As we entered the harbor of Charleston, I showed you the gallows, and you were then told that here the governor was prepared to give five hundred pounds to him who should help him to rope me by the throat to its accursed beams; yet you had previously heard of the gay people of Charleston, and you gave no heed to the hanging of your husband. Well, I have arranged for your enjoying yourself in Charleston without respect to me."

"But we will *not* go there, Harry, or to Havana either, or anywhere, if they hate you, Harry. We'll go back to the isthmus, Harry, where we can dance as we please, and no *garote* and no gallows for either you or me. O Harry, you talk as if I wished you were dead! You brute, Harry!"

"Nay, Zulieme, let it relieve you when I tell you that, in going to Charleston, you do not increase my embarrassments in any way. We shall not be seen together, or known in connection. You shall be introduced, not as my wife, nor as any wife, but as a young lady of Mexican family, friends to Mr. Perkins Anderson, the famous Indian trader; and you are to become the *protégé* of his wife. Now, Mrs. Perkins Anderson is a very fine woman, gay as a lark and frisky as a kitten, who has only one weakness against which I would warn you. She fancies, all the while, that she is wretched as a ground-mole, and gloomy as an owl that knows not where to find a supper. If she tells you that she is ready to die — to commit suicide — you have only to execute some of your most dashing dances in her sight, or to admire her new dresses, and she will forget all her sorrows. Bating this weakness, she is a fine woman enough. Some think her very pretty. She is very showy, very smart as well as showy, and sometimes converses very brilliantly."

" Ah, Harry ! have you long known her ?"

" Yes, several years."

" Ah ! she is your ' Olive,' then !"

He started up, gazed at the infantile speaker very sternly for a moment, and then said :—

" Zulieme, I have begged you never more to name to me that name. Do not, if you would not vex as well as pain me."

" But, Harry—"

" Not a word more !"

" Oh, you savage, Harry !—"

" Enough, Zulieme, that I try to content you with those things which satisfy your heart. In Charleston you will enjoy yourself, especially under the patronage of Mrs. Perkins Anderson. For her sake, as well as mine, my name must be suppressed. She will find you another. I shall see you occasionally. Now, get you to bed, and beware how you again invite other men into the privacies of my chamber. Remember that there are things, purely domestic, which the Englishman, differing from almost all other people, holds to be sacred. You, of all your race, will be the last to understand this ; but let it suffice you that *I* tell you it is so ! An Englishman's chamber is sacred, Zulieme ; his weapons are sacred ; the cup from which he drinks is sacred ! See — this was to me an especially consecrated cup !"— taking up one which stood upon the table, half-filled with wine — a silver cup, richly chased — just such a cup as loving godmothers give to children. . . . " It was the gift of a grandmother to a mother, of a mother to me. Yet has it been polluted this night by the lips of one who, even while he drank, meditated ill to you and me. It shall never pollute my lips again !"

And he crushed the delicate vessel, with all its grouped vines and fanciful figures, out of all shape, into a mass, by a single nervous grasp of his powerful hand!

"Why, Harry, are you mad? What harm has the cup done, and it was so pretty?"

"It is pretty in my eyes no more — it is no more sweet! Now understand, Zulieme, that we English hold domestic things to be sacred; we hold our chambers sacred — our wives; but if they become polluted by other hands or lips, we crush them, however beautiful or sweet once — we crush them into nothingness, even as I crush this cup! Go — now! Sleep, dream, and wake, if you please, to song and dance; but, remember, that the most sacred thing, once polluted, becomes hateful to the sight and feelings of the Englishman."

"You spiteful, awful Harry!" she cried, half-laughing, half-sobbing, as she threw her arms about his neck. She would have kissed him, but he put her away, and hurriedly left the cabin — murmuring, *sotto voce*, as he did so:—

"I know not — I have half a doubt — no matter how innocent she is — that this impudent fellow has polluted her lips, even as he has polluted my cup. I could suffer her kiss as a thoughtless and innocent child; but no — not after his!"

Zulieme called after him, but he did not heed, perhaps did not hear her. For a moment she appeared disposed to follow him; but — "No, no!" she said, half-aloud; "he is in his cross fit now." And, undressing herself, she went to bed, and in a little while had sobbed herself to sleep.

## CHAPTER XVII.

### SETTLING ACCOUNTS.

" *Cassius.* — Must I endure all this ?
   *Brutus.* — Ay ! more !   Fret till your proud heart break !"
                                        SHAKESPEARE.

————" But there shall come an hour,
When Vengeance shall repay the wrongs of Power !"

" AND now," muttered Calvert, " for Lieutenant Molyneaux !"

That officer was on deck.  He had relieved Eckles, and the latter had just turned in; but not before he had expressed his misgivings to his colleague touching the discovery that the captain had so recently made, and the consequences that would probably follow.

" I warned you, my dear fellow," said the good-natured Eckles, " but you are such a d——d conceited blockhead, and so impudent, that you will listen to nothing till your head's off."

" Pooh !" answered the other, " who cares ?   I am as good as any man that ever stood on quarter-deck."

" Say, as great a monkey !   But you haven't heard the whole of it.   There'll be more words to that tune."

" I'm not afraid to trust my ears.   Get to your hammock, Eckles, and shut your own ears."

And Molyneaux lighted a cigar, and began his ordinary paces. Eckles, yawning, disappeared below.

Spite of his expressed confidence, spite of his effrontery, Molyneaux was not without his own misgivings.   His conscience did not sustain him.   But the same conceit and impudence which moved him so frequently to offend, sufficed to strengthen him usually in the encounter with the consequences of his effrontery ; and he nerved himself, with all his resources of blood and vanity, when he beheld the tall person of his superior emerge from the cabin.

Thus armed and strengthened, he could not help the fancy that

Calvert had grown a foot since he had last seen him. His person now seemed absolutely gigantic. He himself (Molyneaux) was a trim, neatly-built, compact young fellow, active in great degree, and vigorous for his gristle; but, with all his vanity, he did not deceive himself with the notion that he could, for a single instant, maintain his ground in a grapple with our rover. He felt that he was good at his weapon; but he knew that so was Calvert — good at any weapon — and so powerful, that, whether armed with rapier or quarter-staff, he was likely to prove a dangerous enemy, no matter with whom he fought.

These things were all thought over, in a moment, by our lieutenant. In truth, he had an awkward consciousness of guilt and offence, irrespective of his presumption in regard to his superior's wife, which compelled a continually-recurring reference to his resources, in the event of collision with that superior. His vanity, his desire of power, his greed of gain, had all combined to involve him in practices which, he well knew, if discovered, would justify his principal in resorting to the most summary punishment. But, as yet, these are secrets. He believes them to be so, at all events, and in great degree they are.

Calvert, however, was growing suspicious; but, with sufficient grounds for suspicion, he had yet no proper clues for inquiry, and no such evidence as would enable him to form a judgment. It was his present policy to look for these clues. And Calvert, proud, passionate, resolute, was yet cool enough, and a sufficiently-trained man, to pursue the search with equal acuteness and discretion. As yet, his purpose was by no means to push the young offender to extremity. He was first to ascertain to what extent the treachery of Molyneaux had been carried, and how many of the crew had been corrupted. He did not doubt that there was treachery, but whether it contemplated mere peculation, or an insane passion after the supreme power, was a question. The former offence might be winked at in a service so indulgent — the latter never! For the former, there were mild rebukes, and restitution would suffice. The penalty of the superior offence lay at the end of a rope, the swing of a yard-arm, or, in the event of resistance, a sudden shot from a pistol, or the heavy stroke of a cutlass. But just now, Calvert contemplated no such necessities. He had first to make discoveries.

He joined the young man where he stood, on one side of the quarter-deck looking out upon the shore.  Molyneaux flung away his cigar at his superior's approach, and braced himself for the encounter, not exactly conceiving in what way it would come.  He was not left in doubt long.  The voice of Calvert was mild in tone, though firm and serious :—

" Lieutenant Molyneaux, I had occasion to use some sharp language to you in my cabin.  You will oblige me by giving me no occasion in future to repeat the language.  My cabin is sacred ; but you are sufficiently well informed, as one of British blood, to know what Englishmen hold sacred.  Your offence consists, here, in the knowledge that you do and must offend.  I should pay but a sorry compliment to your intelligence to suppose you ignorant of this."

" I was invited, sir, by your lady, into the cabin.  She—"

" My wife, Mr. Molyneaux, is one of another nation than ours, and ignorant of our customs.  To respond, as you did, to her invitation, when you knew better, was as great an outrage as if, asking you for education in the English language, you had taught her only words of English obscenity.  You owed it to her as a lady, and to me as your superior officer, as well as gentleman, not to second her in any mistake which she might make, as a foreigner, by a studious observance yourself of the nicest proprieties upon which our people so tenaciously insist."

" But, sir, as a lady, she had a right, sir—"

" Stop, Mr. Molyneaux : it is one of your mistakes that you are too eager to urge the argument of vanity, rather than to justify your conscientious convictions of the right.  Let me state clearly my cause of complaint.  You knew my wife's ignorance of those English customs which we hold to be requisite for propriety, and you encouraged her in her violation of them, in order to take advantage of her ignorance."

" What advantage, sir ?"

" It is for you to answer.  Suppose you do answer me ?  Why did *you* err, sir, violating the rules of the service, as well as our English proprieties — why do a wrong, which you knew to be such — then meanly plead the invitation of a woman ignorant of our laws, ignorant of English customs, to excuse you in your knowing violation of both, unless that you proposed some selfish object to yourself?

" I had no object, Captain Calvert."

" Mr. Molyneaux, I give you credit for vices, but would not willingly. have to reproach you for meannesses also. Suffer yourself to be silent rather than resort to evasion. But I intend to deal with you more frankly. Now, sir, had my wife been an Englishwoman, do you doubt that I had slain both of you, finding you in my chamber with her as I did to-night? I had as surely pistolled you both as I now speak to you! I should have listened to nothing — said nothing — knowing that both of you must have been aware of the natural impropriety of your being found together in such a situation, at such an hour, in such circumstances, during my absence. She erred through ignorance : you can make no such plea. But that I know *her*, sir, and know that your arts can no more affect her natural purity and simplicity than they can deceive me, I should count you equally guilty. I know that you employ these arts in vain—"

" I employ no arts, Captain Calvert! I deny, sir—"

" Then you are playing a fool's game, indeed! But, Mr. Molyneaux, though I feel sure of the purity of my wife — know that she is superior to any arts such as yours — yet, sir, it is not the less displeasing to me that any man should so presume as to approach her with licentious purpose. That she is ignorant of offence, does not lessen your offence; and I now caution you against any repetition of it. I have hitherto been a little too heedless of this thing, rather through a feeling of scorn than indifference. Now, however, that it has come to be matter of talk in the ship, among the common crew, I feel it due to my wife's honor, if not my own, to arrest your further practice of this sort. You will observe a different course from this moment. Do not, I beg you, fall into an error, natural enough to young men of large self-esteem, of supposing that I fear what you might do. There are many occasions of offence which are not necessarily causes of fear. With my wife, I could afford you any opportunities, and still laugh to scorn all your idle efforts, as she would do were she once made to comprehend them. It will surprise you to know, after all your labors, that she has no sort of notion of what you mean, and holds you simply as a playmate, who amuses her. But my own proper pride, and natural sense of dignity and honor, forbid that *I* should tolerate approaches which contemplate an insulting purpose, how-

ever little likely to succeed; and, once for all, I repeat the warning, that, another such offence, and I shall as certainly put you to
death as that I now speak to you!"

"You have entirely mistaken me, Captain Calvert. I have
had no such purposes as you suppose. I—"

"Not another word, Mr. Molyneaux!—you do not help the
matter. I know young men—I know man—I know *you!* Our
business connection is such as to render me quite satisfied with
you as a good seaman, as a clever officer, as a brave young man,
who knows his duty and has the courage to perform it. For these
qualities I need you and respect you. That I have done you full
justice for these qualities, your employment from the beginning—
your elevation, as second officer of this ship—will sufficiently
prove. You owe this promotion wholly to me. I have advanced
you, not waiting entreaty, seeing your abilities with my own eyes.
I have still other services for you, and there is still further promotion if you continue faithful. My purpose, in rebuking, is not
to pain or to degrade, but to *save you.* I understand, of course,
that, in what I have said to you this night, I have somewhat mortified your vanity; and this was also a part of my purpose. It is
upon this rock, Mr. Molyneaux—this rock of vanity—that your
ship is destined to founder. It is this rock upon which most
young men sink their fortunes. I have noted this *your* chief weakness, and lamented it for a long time. I have seen through all the
little arts by which you have fed your own weakness, and it is
time to open your eyes to your self-delusion. If you are warned
in season, you may cure yourself of this infirmity. If, on the contrary, you feel counsel only as offence; if your vanity still prevails over wisdom; if you too impatiently seek your ends; if these
ends really contemplate only the temporary enjoyment and the
gratification of self-esteem—your career will be short, and the
end shameful! I have now sufficiently warned you. It is for
me an effort to do so, and should argue to you a degree of interest
in your behalf which should rather awaken pride than offend vanity. It would be easier for me, I assure you, to brush off an
offender than seek to cure him. And now, sir, to the business of
the ship."

We have forborne the various interpositions made by Lieutenant Molyneaux, in which he sought to excuse his offences, or to

evade the conclusions of his superior, or to assert his self-esteem. We pass them by, very much as Calvert himself did, and for the same reason, as discreditable pleas and evasions, put in at the expense of his manhood. He was not prepared to join final issue with his superior; and a sense of guilt is, in a young mind, a necessary source of weakness. But his vanity stimulated him to replies which were only to be urged at the cost of character and pride; and to all these Calvert refused to listen, and so may we. We need not report them, at all events.

Nor did Calvert wholly mistake the nature of his lieutenant, so far as to suppose that the same vanity would suffer him to grow wiser after the rebuke. He knew the man too well to believe that anything short of severe penalties, actually enforced, could do any effectual service in bringing him back to a right consciousness of his true relations with the world about him. He rightly conceived that all which he said would be wasted upon blind ears; but he had his own policy in his exhortations, and their very severity on *one* subject was calculated to render the young man obtuse to those more searching inquiries which his superior had to make in other directions. Had Calvert said nothing to him touching his presence in the cabin, Molyneaux must either have supposed him grossly insensible to his honor — which he could hardly be — or too deeply interested in other matters, in which the guilty man was a participator, to suffer him to attach a proper weight to this. Briefly, to forbear in the present instance, might have led Molyneaux to suppose that his forbearance was a blind, concealing his scrutiny into other offences, quite as flagrant, and much more dangerous in their consequences. To dwell on this, as the captain had done, and with so much severity, was, in short, equivalent to saying to him, " This is my only cause of quarrel or complaint."

So Molyneaux construed it; and, conscious of so much more offence, yet undeveloped and apparently unconjectured, he was quite willing for the present to escape so easily. But the language, tone, and manner, of his superior, stung him to the quick; and, though he endeavored so to compose his muscles, and regulate his tones and words, and subdue his passion, as to answer with moderation and almost with humility, the hate all the while was growing in his heart, in due degree with his efforts to suppress its exhibition.

Calvert read him through; understood all the workings of his mind; smiled a bitter scorn as he listened to his replies; and said to himself, at the close :—

" He will not be saved! But my time is not yet come — nor his. We can both wait!"

And so he proceeded to talk, as it were indifferently, of the affairs of the ship; taking a minute report of everything that had been done in his absence, even to a list of the names of parties engaged in the several tasks of scouting the woods, fishing, loading and unloading, and of the crews employed in conveying the boats to town.

" Any signs of Indians ?" he asked.

" Yes, sir, but not within five miles. They do not seem to have found us out yet. There is a new plantation settling, about five miles below where they have been in considerable numbers."

" Keep your scouts busy still — your best men — and have a squad of three or four of them on the other side of the river, with a boat in cover, directly opposite, night and day. Let them report to you nightly. Have you had any men missing — any off without leave ?"

" No, sir.

This was said boldly.

" Keep your eye upon the boats, so that none shall be missing without your knowing it. The danger is, that some of these blockheads will be running down to Charleston, where a reward is offered for every mother's son of them! We may, in fact, very soon have to change our quarters. You have an inventory of all the goods sent down, the number of loads, and a receipt from Franks for all delivered ?"

" Here it is, sir."

" Very well. I will examine it by daylight. The light articles are nearly all gone, I suppose ?"

" Two more boats will carry them, sir."

" We shall then have to devise a plan for discharging the heavy, so as to avoid this tedious process, which would consume weeks for us. In fact, the boats can hardly be used for the purpose. But of this to-morrow. Good-night, Mr. Molyneaux."

" Good-night, sir."

And the captain went below without lingering.

"Now, d—n his blood!" broke from the lieutenant, as he shook his clenched fist toward the cabin when the rover had disappeared. "But I will have it out of his heart yet! Oh! she is too pure, is she?—too virtuous, eh? Of course, I can not succeed! He feels quite safe, does he, on that score? Ha! ha! ha! This is the way in which these d——d silly husbands deceive themselves. Well, we shall see! It is a defiance—a challenge! We shall see! If I am to be taunted on that score, by —— I will see if I can not revenge the taunt! Too pure—too immaculate! Ha! ha! As if there was ever yet painted daughter of Eve who could resist the right persuader! We shall see! *She* shall make me sweet atonement for all this; and he!—ay, if I do not have it out of his heart's blood, then curse me for a coward who has no red blood in his own!"

8

# CHAPTER XVIII.

### LOVE-POWDER.

"Make me a potent filter that shall work
    Upon his passionate senses, till I grow
    His moon of fancy, and with queenly power,
    Such as pale Hecate holds upon the sea,
    Rouse all the fervid billows of his heart,
    Till they flow up to mine."

Scarcely had Calvert shut himself within his cabin, when Sylvia, the mulattress, crawled out from a cupboard which had concealed her under the stairs of the companion-way, and stole up to the deck, where she joined Molyneaux.

He had corrupted her. This was one of the discoveries which Belcher had made, leading him to suspect Molyneaux of other treacheries; but he had failed to communicate the fact to his superior, for the reason, probably, that Calvert had given rather indifferent attention to all the reports which had been made him in respect to his lieutenant's intimacy with Zulieme. But unquestionably, now, the mulattress was in the pay of the lieutenant.

She approached him without preliminaries, he being ready to welcome her communications; showing that the understanding between them had been sufficiently well matured. In her negro *patois*, which we do not care to adopt, she began thus:—

"We are to go to Charleston. He told her so to-night. They had a long talk; and she's to change her name, and live with a Mrs. Anderson; and she's to go to balls and parties every night; and there's to be fine times; and who but she?"

And so the Abigail rambled on, in a loose manner; contriving, however, to report very fully all that Calvert had said to his wife in respect to her abode in town.

"But had they no quarrel?"

"Oh, yes! but he smoothed it all over, easy enough, as soon as he let her know that she was to go to Charleston. That's what she's been dying for. She so loves to be dancing in a crowd of people!"

"But what said he about my being in the cabin?"

"Oh, he told her he'd kill her if she was another woman. But I do n't see the sense of that. And she was spunky, and told him to kill her, and she did n't care how soon; and she called him a brute-beast of an Englishman; she did! She did n't pick the words, but said 'em just as they come up. She ain't afear'd of him, to be sure. When he says 'dog,' she says 'cat;' and if he shows his teeth, she's ready for a scratch, any day. Lord, how she does give it to him sometimes!"

"It was a pretty bit of a quarrel, then?"

"It did me good to hear it, for he's such a dog-in-the-manger, and he'd put his foot on her if she had n't the spunk. And I do n't see why she should n't say what she pleases, when she brought him all the fortune."

"To be sure — why not? That's right! So you think there's no love lost between them?"

"As for the love, there's no saying. If there's any between 'em, she's got it. He do n't love nothing! But, somehow, she has a sort of liking for him, though she does scratch."

"But *liking* can't last long, if it's 'cat and dog' between them."

"No, indeed; and she'd rather be dancing with you, a thousand times, than sitting down at 'dumby and doggy' with him."

"But what was the upshot of it all? How did it end?"

"Oh, she hugged him and kissed him after he told her she was to go to town; but there was a good deal of sobbing and crying, and cross words, first."

"Did she weep?"

"Yes, a little. It was a sort of scream and sob. Then she hushed up, and laughed out; and he told her she was a baby, and maybe kissed her; and so he told her to go to bed, and then he came up to you."

"Did he say anything of me?"

"Not much; only that he would kill you and kill her, if he ever caught you in his cabin again. 'T was then she called him a brute-beast of an Englishman."

"Rough words, Sylvia."

" Was n't they?  But he made all smooth when he told her
that she was to go to town."

" But if she likes me, Sylvia, what makes her so eager to get
away with him?"

" It 's the balls and dances, I tell you.  It 's not to go with him.
*He 's* not to go with us.  He 's to send us to Mrs. Anderson, in
the boat."

" Ah! he 's not to go with her?  What 's he to do with himself?"

" Stay here, I reckon."

"I do n't like that!  What would he stay for?  He 's not
wanted here.  I can see to the ship."

" I do n't know.  That 's what he told her."

" What more?  Did you pick up any more?"

The mulattress simply repeated what had been said already.

" Well," said Molyneaux, " when you get to town, I shall probably send some one to you: if I can, will come myself.  You must
find out all you can; keep an eye on both of them; let me know
all you hear; and keep talking to her about me.  You know how
to do it."

" Do n't I!  Oh, she thinks you a mighty fine man — a handsome man—"

" Ah! she does?  Well?"

" She says you have a most beautiful figure."

" Ah! she sees that — she *says* that?"

" Yes, indeed; though she says 't ain't so mighty as the captain's."

" No — thank God, I 'm not an elephant!"

" No, indeed, you 're not so big.  Now, she says, if you only
knew how to dance—"

" What!  I do n't know how to dance?"

" That 's what she says of all you English, except the captain.
Now, he can dance Spanish, and so lightly, though he 's so large
and heavy.  But he learned among our people — and he 's so
active!"

" Not more so than I am."

" You think not?"

" Certainly not!  I 'm as light and active as any man in the
British islands."

"Ah! is it possible?"

"I can run as fast, bound as high, jump as far, hop as long, as any man of my size in Britain."

"I'm so glad to hear it! She likes to see men doing these things. But you don't dance so well as the captain. She says so."

"I don't know how that can be. I've never seen *him* dance."

"Oh, he never will dance now. That's one thing she quarrels about. He won't play with her now as he used to. If he would, I'm sure you'd stand no chance. But, because you play with her, she likes you."

"Well, if she likes me, I don't care much whether it's because of my heels or my head. Liking can grow to loving."

"That it can!"

"And I'm sworn to have her."

"And so you can!"

"You must do your best, Sylvia. There's a dollar for you. Tell me everything, and you shall have more. Do all that you can to make her love me, and I'll pay you well. And if I get her, my girl, I'll make you rich."

"If we could only give her a powder, now—"

"A powder! what's that? what for?"

"A powder to make her love you."

"I've heard of such; but that's all nonsense."

"Nonsense! I tell you it's true. We've got powders at Darien that'll make the eyes of a man or woman fasten upon a person as if they could see nothing else; make 'em dream of 'em every night, and always such sweet dreams; make 'em hunt after 'em, as a dog hunts after the deer; oh, make their hearts feel for nothing else but them!"

"Why don't you give her one of these powders, then, on my account? I don't much believe in what you tell me, but you must try everything."

"So I would if I had the powders. If I was at Darien, now, I could soon get 'em. But they're made out of roots that grow only in our mountains. And you have to look for 'em at night, and when there's no moon, and that's dangerous. But when you have only the roots about you, in your pocket, and walk side-by-side with the person you want to love you, they'll almost grow to you. They can't leave you for a moment, without pain; and they're happy as soon as they can get to you again. I do think that the captain had some of those roots in his pocket, when they first brought him to our hacienda; and that's the reason that my young mistress took to him so mad as she did."

"There's reason in that. I wonder if he has any of them about him still!—But it's all nonsense. No use to talk about it. You must do what you can, Sylvia, without the love-powder. Now, I'm a good-looking fellow—a handsome fellow: you can say that, surely; and don't let her forget it. Look at that leg."

And he stuck his foot upon the gunwale, and stroked his calf complacently.

"There's a leg for you, Sylvia!"

"Yes, indeed; if you could only shake it **Spanish fashion**."

"Oh, d—n the Spanish fashion! I can shake it Irish fashion, you fool, and that never failed to please a woman yet. Don't forget *that*. Do you hear?"

"No, indeed."

"Well, what can you say against my face — my figure?"

"Say against 'em, sir? Oh, bless your eyes, who can say anything against 'em?"

"Well, but what can you say *for* them, Sylvia? That's the true question."

"Well, sir, every woman sees a man with just her own pair of eyes. Now, if 'twas for myself, I like your face and figure so well, that, if you was to ask me, I'd have you to-morrow, and jump at you too. And so, I reckon, would my mistress, if she was only a free woman; for she says you're a handsome fellow, only you can't dance Spanish."

"I'll *make* her a free woman, by all the holies! Remember *that! Tell* her that! Let her but say that she loves me, and I'll go through blazes to set her free from this infernal bondage! As for the dancing Spanish, let her know that my legs — and you see them — were made for dancing Irish. Let her find a pair of Spanish calves to match with these, and I'll admit that there's some virtue in these d——d Spanish dances; but, till then, an Irish jig for me, whenever good legs are to be shaken. Go, now, Sylvia. There's another dollar for you, my girl. Keep it up — do you hear? The drop of water will wear away the stone; and the right word, said at the right time, and at all times when you get a chance, will wear down a flinty heart. Keep your ears open, and your tongue only for me."

While this scene was in progress, ignorant if not indifferent, Harry Calvert was keeping painful vigil below. He did not sleep — did not seek for sleep — was busy with books and papers. He read and wrote alternately for two hours. Then rising, putting away books and papers, he approached the berth where Zulieme slept — slept like a child — just as heedless of the morning as if it were never to dawn again. The strong man gazed on her sleeping features, in a stern and meditative silence. What was she to him? Were she lying there in the absolute embrace of Death — as she was in that of its twin-sister, Sleep — he would probably have been as sadly calm a spectator. What was she to him? We have heard already. But, though indifferent, he would not have had one breath of heaven too roughly to beteem her cheeks. Not a harsh thought, not an ungenerous feeling, not a hostile fancy, filled his heart or mind toward her. True, she was but a child in his sight — erring, weak, silly — a creature quite unsuited to his needs as to his nature; but whose was the fault that she was here?

"That is the grief," he murmured, as he gazed. "Did I not, from the first, know that she was only the feeble, thoughtless creature that I have found her? Knowing this, what had I to do with her? Why did I pluck her from her proper home — from the simple bed of security in which she had grown — beloved, watched, nurtured tenderly, and honored — when I could not love or honor, could hardly watch, and certainly not tenderly nurture? I must not cast her off, nor scorn her, nor rate heavily her offences, nor treat her with indifference! She must not feel, at my hands, meaner measure of care and kindness than I have had at hers — than she herself has always got from those of fond, foolish mother, and idolizing, doting father. Love is impossible. That I feel! But, for the rest — the care, the kindness, the protection, the indulgence — these she must never lack! Were she guilty, now! — But, no! Who that looks upon that sleep so placid, childlike, satisfied — the lips slightly parted, the brow unruffled, the breathing regular and soft like that of an infant, and the bosom so sweetly

heaving — shall doubt that he looks upon the sleep of innocence?
Ah! she is sobbing in her sleep — a half-stifled sob — a slight
convulsion of feeling, spite of sleep, as if the memory were busy
recalling those sharp words of mine to-night. Sleep on, poor girl,
sleep on! I will not question your purity, though I may your
prudence. Shall I chafe because you are ignorant of vice — of
*those* passions that make vice a necessity — that make jealousy
and suspicion the necessary guardians in a world consciously corrupt? No, no! Sleep on: I will endure it as I may!"

She woke, and threw out her arms.

"Harry — is it you, Harry? Ah! you dear brute Englishman,
why don't you come to bed? You know we are to go to Charleston in the morning. Ha! ha! Harry."

And she sighed, and lapsed away again in sleep.

# CHAPTER XIX.

## ZULIEME IN CHARLESTON.

> " Put on our state,
> Our bravest; we are here among the best,
> And we must bear us as becomes the beauty
> That ignorant wonder still has made us known:
> We 're here but to be worshipped."

ZULIEME was awake by daylight, but only to be disappointed. She did not start for the city quite so soon as she expected. Morning came, and no departure. And Calvert was absent, no one knew in what quarter; in the woods somewhere; but whether with or without an object, who could say?

Zulieme was in despair! But by noon he came — unexpectedly as he went; and it was then understood that it was only after night, availing himself of the tide, that he meant that the boats should drop down the river.

To wait for hours! Oh, what a trial to the eager heart of youth! But the night, with grateful cover, came at last. The boats were manned, and Zulieme summoned. Her trunks were already on board; and she herself had been ready, as we have seen, some twelve hours before. She, too, passed on board. She gave her hand cordially to Molyneaux, and Eckles too, as she left the vessel — though the don, her husband, was at hand — and spoke her farewell with all the freedom of a child.

" Good-by, Mr. Molyneaux — good-by, Mr. Eckles," she cried to them, with *naïve* accents — " good-by! Don't you forget me! I'm going to town, you know, where we shall have dances a plenty, but I sha'n't soon forget those funny ones we have had in the woods."

" That's not very sentimental, Molyneaux," muttered Eckles in

8*

the ears of his brother-lieutenant. "She don't break her heart at parting with us, my boy!"

And Molyneaux seemed to be of the same opinion, for he answered very churlishly to his brother-officer, and in rather saddish accents to the senora. But there was still a scene in reserve, not in the programme. Sylvia was about to step on board after her mistress, when Calvert arrested her.

"Back, girl! we want none of you. You will remain here."

"Oh, missis, they won't let me come!"

"Harry," cried Zulieme, hearing the anguished cry of the Abigail, "I must have Sylvia."

"Impossible, Zulieme."

"But I can't do without her, Harry. Don't tell me impossible!"

"You must try, Zulieme. I wouldn't have her long tongue among the townspeople for half our cargo. Do you forget that we have secrets there, Zulieme?"

"I can't help it: Sylvia must go. Who is to dress me and tend me?"

"She can not go, Zulieme."

"Then I won't go! for I can't do without her, Harry."

"I'm sorry for it; for you must stay, then!—Back the boats, fellows."

"But, Harry, why can't Sylvia go? You are so cross always!"

"I have given you the reason already, Zulieme. The secrets of the ship must not be blabbed about the town."

"But she won't blab, Harry. I promise you!"

"You promise! Answer for yourself, Zulieme. You will have enough to do! As for trusting anything to such a parrot, I can't think of it. Come, Zulieme, decide! Will you go, or stay?"

"And Sylvia is not to go?"

"No, as I'm a living man!"

"You're a monster! Never mind, Sylvia: I'll bring you fine things."

"You are content to go without her?"

"I suppose I must be. You try all you can to make me miserable. You're such a brute Englishman, I wonder why I ever married you!"

"So do I, Zulieme—very much, and very often. But, speak

quickly. The tide is running down fast. I do not compel you to go, Zulieme. If you can't do without Sylvia, don't go — don't leave her."

In a subdued, sobbing voice, Zulieme cried out:—

"Good-by, Sylvia! You see how it is! He won't let you come."

"O my missis! what I going to do without you?"

"Take your amusements, Sylvia. Dance all you can."

"Oh! oh! oh!" sobbed the disconsolate Abigail, as the boats swept away down-stream; while Zulieme repeated for the twentieth time:—

"You try all you can to cross me, Harry Calvert, and make me miserable. I'm sure I wish I had never seen you!"

"It was, indeed, a great misfortune," he responded, in very sober, serious tones, and not reproachfully, only painfully.

"To *me* it was, Harry Calvert — to me, to me only!"

"Surely: who else? It was to you, Zulieme, I repeat, a very great misfortune."

"But it need not be, if you were not the great bear of an Englishman that you are! If you'd try, I'm sure you could make me happy."

"I'm afraid not, Zulieme. But, indeed, I do try as well as I can, and as far as I think it proper. But how could you suppose that I would suffer that wench to go with you to the city, where you are to bear another name than mine, when you know that she has the tongue of a jay, and the wriggling propensities of an eel? She would never rest till she had blabbed everything. Be content! You will have better 'tendance with Mrs. Anderson than Sylvia could ever give you. She will find you half a dozen better maid-servants, each worth a dozen of Sylvia."

But we need not hearken further to this (however interesting) domestic difficulty. Enough, that the decision of Calvert deranged some of the plans of Molyneaux — for the moment. Of these, hereafter.

The boats swept quietly down the placid, poetical river, now veering to one and now to the other bank — each side presenting, with pleasing alternations, some fairy-like glimpses of the shore, crowned everywhere with green umbrage, and the headlands sometimes overshadowing half the stream with the great branches of their ancient oaks. At length, a blazing pile of pine-fagots, raised upon a knoll of earth, drew the eyes of the party to the western banks. In the rear of this pyre stood a dark, square mass, which Calvert instantly recognised as the ancient " Block-house" commanding the creek at " Oldtown." This pyre was his signal. He knew that Gowdey was on the watch, and that his horse was in readiness. Franks had punctually fulfilled his orders.

Without a word, having the tiller in his grasp, our rover turned the head of the boat directly for the ancient landing, with which he was quite familiar. As the boat darted into the little creek, Zulieme cried out:—

" Why, Harry, what's this? Why do you come here?"

" Here I leave the boat, Zulieme."

" But you mustn't leave me. You must carry me yourself to Mrs. Anderson, Harry."

" Impossible! But I have arranged everything. Have no fear."

" Oh! don't you tell me to have no fear. I will have fear; I will be afraid. You send me among strange people, Harry Calvert, and who ought to introduce me but you?"

" My dear Zulieme, you are already introduced, and Mrs. Per-kins Anderson awaits you. She knows you, and I have tried my best to make you know her. I have told you that she's a fine, fashionable woman, and gives balls and parties, the very finest in Charleston; that she's sentimental, and flirts with perfect grace; that she's very sweet-tempered, being young, rich, and surrounded by admirers. So much for her. You will find that all I've told you is true, and that she eagerly expects you, and will know you at a glance. I've told her that you dance to perfection; that you like nothing so well in the world as dancing; that you will dance all night; dream all day of dancing all night; awaken only to work out your dreams; and that you would not give a fig for life itself, unless with the privilege of using your legs to the sound of the tambourine; that you are disappointed in your husband only as he is not content to be a dancing-machine for your exercise."

" That's as much as to say you've told her I'm a fool, you great English cayman! But I'll not go to her house — I won't go a step — unless you go along with me; that's flat!"

" As you please, Zulieme. It is impossible that I should go with you to-night. That, too, is flat! You will at least accompany the boat, and either land in Charleston, and go to Mrs. Anderson, or keep quiet in the boat till its return, when you can go back to the ship."

"No! I'll do neither, since you won't go with me. I'll go with *you*. I'll see where *you* go to-night. I'm too great a fool to go to Mrs. Anderson's! I'll show you that I can do without dancing. *I* love dancing! when I care nothing about it in the world, except when I've got nothing else to amuse me."

To this determined speech Calvert gave no attention. It probably entered his ears and passed through them. With the tiller in his grasp, he kept the boat in the narrow passage up the creek, through green tracts of marsh on either hand; and, as she reached the landing, he adroitly brought her round, so that he leaped with an easy spring upon the shore, sending the vessel off fully ten feet with the effort.

"Why, Harry — Harry, I say! — do you really mean to leave me, you brute monster? Oh, I wish I had never, never, never seen you!"

"Good-night, Zulieme," he cried, as he disappeared in the thickets; "go to Mrs. Anderson's, and fear nothing. Don't be foolish. Good-night!"

She screamed after him, but he made no answer. He was gone. She fairly sobbed out her afflictions. But the case was past remedy, and she was soon reconciled. Before the boat had quite emerged from the creek into the river, she had got up her guitar, and, what with tuning and tinkling, for the benefit of the oarsmen — one of whom had taken the tiller on the captain's departure — she contrived to forget her trials long before the little vessel reached her destination. Calvert knew her resources.

In little more than an hour after he had left the boat, she had entered the lagune, and passed on to the obscure landing-place, in the rear of the courthouse of the present city. Here Franks and Jack Belcher were both in waiting. They both received the fair Zulieme with the deference becoming the wife of their superior. Franks she had never seen before. They escorted her promptly to the dwelling of the fashionable lady, who was in waiting to welcome her. This she did with the ease, grace, and gayety, of a woman of fashion.

"I'm so happy to see you!" and she embraced and kissed her,

and drew her into the brilliantly-lighted parlor, and hurriedly devoured her with all her eyes.

"Bless me, Zulieme," she cried, in a sort of rapture, "you are the prettiest little creature — quite a fairy! Why, you look like a mere girl — a child: nobody would ever take you to be a wife."

"Oh, don't call me a child!" said Zulieme impatiently. "Harry calls me a child and a baby, and treats me just as if I was a doll. Don't you do so. I don't like it."

"Oh, I speak only of your size and looks, my dear. It's no discredit to be thought young, my dear. Everybody knows that we grow older as we grow, fast enough; and, for a woman, it's a great thing to keep young as long as possible. For my part, you could not please me better than by fancying and calling me a girl."

Zulieme's eyes opened wide.

"The great, fat chunk of a creature!" was her unuttered meditation. But Mrs. Perkins Anderson, with the natural facility of a fashionable woman, allowed her companion no chance to speak.

"What a sweet face is this of yours, Zulieme — so very delicate and feminine! And those eyes — how black, and how they dilate! And your hands how small, and your feet! You are, I insist, a little fairy, and look nothing like a wife. And, by-the-way, you are not a wife here. Remember that! Of course, Calvert has told you? You are to be the Senorita Zulieme de Montano, of Florida. You will make a great sensation. Our young dandies and macaronies are very fond of Spanish beauties; and you will be a belle, and they will suppose you a fortune! Nobody can think you a married woman. How long have you been married, my dear?"

"Oh, a long time — more than a year!"

"That *is* a very long time. Alas! Zulieme, I have been married ten; and ten years of married life is an eternity. But, come; we must have supper, and then to sleep. You must be tired."

And she wrapped her arms around the unresisting stranger, and drew her into the supper-room, exclaiming as she went:—

"What a fairy! what a creature for the dance! Oh, what dances we shall have!"

"And I so love dancing!" murmured Zulieme.

# CHAPTER XX.

## OLD GOWDEY.

"How much of wisdom lies in a good heart!
And so we work by nature up to thought,
If we are honest, truthful, to ourselves
Steadfast in virtuous action, to the laws
Obedient, and to God resigned in all!"

OF "Oldtown"—"old Charlestown," the nest-egg of the present opulent state of South Carolina, there is now scarcely a single
vestige. All is level. Even when visited by our rover Calvert,
it was a place of ruins. The old block-house excepted, hardly a
house remained. What time and neglect had spared, the red men
destroyed. They had applied the torch to all that the white settlers had abandoned—not much, it is true—and our rover trod
among beds of cinders overgrown with weeds. At the present
day, we have hardly a trace of the locality. The whole space is
occupied by fertile plantations, in which cotton is eloquent in behalf of civilization; even if civilization, forgetting its wisdom in
its philanthropy, forbears all argument in behalf of cotton. The
future compensates, though it does not restore; and we have no
reason, surveying the present fertility, to deplore the overthrow
of the old experiment. Calvert is not philosopher enough to anticipate the wondrous future; and may be allowed to feel some
saddening sensations as he passes over the ruined site of the infant
colony. We, too, even at this day, with the virgin blooms of the
cotton in our eyes even as we write, are not wholly superior to
that sentiment which deplores that the nest of the eagle should be
abandoned without some memorial to declare whence she took her
flight! We recall with interest the feeble colony of Sayle, seeking safer harborage in this seclusion from provoking foes than
Port Royal, where he first sought to plant, could possibly afford.

And here, for several years, the little settlement grew; having charge of that small nest-egg of a future civilization, which was finally to develop into a proud and potent state!  Here, from this frail hamlet, we have seen great patriots, and sagacious statesmen, and mighty warriors emerge, doing great things in various seasons, and rising into noblest heroism in the hour of storm and danger.  And we can not forget, and should not, how this infant heart beat, in this lone region, with all those pulses of courage, and self-denial, and faith, and virtue, which men were decreed to honor in coming times — to love and honor, without once asking where these beautiful virtues were first cradled for renown!

But the hour passes.  Calvert has little time for reflection upon the vicissitudes of place; and we, who are his biographers, must not suffer him to go from sight.

He glides through the thicket, he winds about the creek, he reaches the knoll where the pyre still blazes to guide his course, behind which looms up the block-house, no longer surrounded by its guardian pickets.  These are all gone.  The square fabric, of hewn and mortised logs, well put together, and crenelled for musketry, stands alone upon the knoll.  Time has begun to work upon it also, though the hand of man has striven to neutralize the rapid progress of decay.  Were it daylight, you could see where new timbers have been let in, replacing the rotten; where certain rents have been patched up with plank; showing human caution to be still at work.

There still peeps out, as you see, the muzzle of an iron cannon, which covers the whole range between the fortress and the creek.  Governor Quarry has deemed it politic to set this outpost in some little order.  It serves to admonish the red men in the neighborhood, and, in the event of their proving troublesome, it will give due notice to the townspeople of their hostilities.  One bellow of that old six-pounder will rouse the citizens, and make them buckle on their armor; and though the post be occupied, at present, only by a single man, he will suffice for the purpose of alarm.

He is an old soldier in Indian warfare — a picked frontier-man, with a passion for solitude which makes him prefer the encounter, single-handed, with the savage, rather than lack in the proper elbow-room which he loves.  But he shall tell us all about himself.

There were no signs of life within the log-house as Calvert approached it. It was, as we have said, a square tower of logs, some forty feet on every hand. On the side facing the river, at an elevation of ten feet, the gun, raised upon a platform within, thrust out its muzzle through a porthole, which looked down upon the creek. Holes were pierced, on a line parallel with this embrasure, for the use of musketry. The entrance was upon the south, overshadowed by a sort of barbacan, from which the garrison might shoot down upon assailants at the gate below. This gate was of heavy slabs of oak, plated crosswise with other slabs, and almost covered with the spikes which were used to bind the two faces of the door together. The tower, for such we may call it, was some twenty-four feet high; it was roofed and terraced, a cement of tar and sand having been employed as a coating. Within, the building consisted of two stories. In the lower, occupied by the six-pounder, Gowdey did his cooking on the ground; never troubling himself as to the escape of the smoke, which found its way through the porthole, or the *crenelling*, or slowly floated into the upper story, which was his sleeping-place. There was no chimney.

But Calvert had not yet found his way in. All was still as death as he approached the entrance. Here he drew a silver whistle from his pocket, and sounded. A voice from the barbacan called out, immediately after, the single word " Happy !" to which our rover answered, " Go Lucky !" Then, assured, Gowdey descended, and the heavy gate of the fortress swung wide to admit its visiter. It was carefully closed behind him. Uncovering a dark-lantern, which served only to make the darkness visible, Gowdey seized with one hand the wrist of Calvert, and conducted him to the foot of the ladder by which they were to mount to the upper story. This, when they attained, they found more fully lighted by another lantern, the rays of which were wholly unseen from without. A scuttle in the roof, open always in clear weather, afforded the inmate light and air; for, though apertures had been pierced around the room for the use of firearms, these had all been covered—for what reason we know not—with a strip of planking. This could be easily torn off, and the place restored wholly to its original purposes.

Our solitary had seemingly few comforts. His bed was spread

upon the floor, a simple mattress.   There were boxes about the
room, and kegs, and odds and ends of simple furniture, stools and
benches.   A rifle and long ducking-gun, pistols, and a couple of
grains for fishing, with rods, and nets, and lines, and tackle, were
to be seen standing in the corners or suspended from the walls.
There was one great oaken table, upon which stood pewter plates,
knives, forks, and coffee-pot.   But we have no need for further
catalogue.   Enough that the chamber of Gowdey was not ill furnished in the eyes of one who had been hunter, fisherman, trapper,
and Indian trader by turns, and who still continued the two former
employments with all the zest of his early manhood.

"You have forgotten me, Gowdey, I suppose," said Calvert, as
he shook the hand of *the garrison.*

"Forgit your honor?   That's impossible!   Certainly not, when
Franks sends me a jug of Jamaica every now and then, and a trit
of tobacco, and tells me that they come from you."

"I told him to supply you."

"And many thanks, your honor.   The Jamaica's a great help
to a vartuous memory ; and, with my pipe a-going, it's won'erful
how much a man's shet eyes kin see, deep down in long-gone seasons.   Lord love you, sir, I don't think I kin forgit anything, so
long as there's any Jamaica in my jug and tobacco in my pipe!
Tobacco's a most blessed, heavenly invintion, your honor, for refreshing a bad memory.   It's so quieting to the heart, and brings
such sweet, orderly thinking to the head!   It's the next thing,
sir, to a famous sleep, with a dream all the time of being jist where
you wants to be."

"Well, Gowdey, so long as I can provide it, you shall have
your tobacco and Jamaica.   But it's so long since we had met—"

"Going on three years only," interposed the other.

"And three years are an eternity in this world of strife and
change."

"It's nothing to an old man of seventy."

"Are you seventy, Gowdey?"

"And one over, your honor."

"You hardly look more than fifty."

"No—perhaps!   And I haven't the feel of more ; and I kin
follow a buck all day, and be spry for a turkey by dawn, jest as
well now as if I wasn't quite fifty.   And ef 'twant for this stiff-

ness of the arm"—lifting his left—"and that's another sign to make me remember you—"

"What about your arm, and what had I to do with it, Gowdey?"

"Why, Lord, sir, 'thas never been the same arm to me sence that famous shirk-fight—don't you remember, sir, in Port-Royal harbor? Why, sir, your honor, ef I never supped your Jamaica, and never snuffed your tobacco, that arm is always ready to 'mind me of that fight, and how you saved me from the jaws of that devouring sea-divil. I would have been but a mouthful in his jaws, ef it hadn't been for you! And it's not every man—no, sir, your honor! not more than one man in a thousand—that would jump overboard into the deep sea, to help a poor fellow out of sich a jaw. When I thinks over that time, and how you dived under the beast, and cut into his lights and liver with your knife, jist when I was a-gasping and looking for my death every minute, on my back, and onder his double row of saws, I forgits tobacco and Jamaica, and thinks of you! I've got his skin presarved, there in the corner, as a bit of good luck to fishermen."

"I remember, now—I remember."

"I reckon you do! How kin you forgit? That, I say, your honor, is about the most valiantest thing that ever you did, though they do cry up your fights with the Spaniards. I hear you licked a great don out of his breeches, and sunk his ship; but that fight with the shirk was, to my thinking, the most desperatest thing that a human mortal ever did do in his sober senses. And you jumped overboard to do it when not a man stirred a peg; and, but for you, I was clean gone, for I could do nothing my one self, and the one gripe of the shoulder that the brute beast give me was a taste of the etarnity of swallow that he had in that maw of his'n! I wouldn't have been more than a morsel in his jaws after that, ef 'twant for you. Oh, I sha'n't forgit it, captain, so long as I have a feeling of crawling flesh about me!"

"Well, Gowdey, we'll say no more of that escape, which was certainly a lucky as it was a narrow one; and I rejoice at my agency in the matter, as at one of the few good actions of my life. I prefer, now, that we should talk of other matters, more agreeable to yourself."

"Lord love your honor! as ef anything could be more grateful than getting out of the shirk's mouth, though by the skin of the teeth."

"Yes, in one sense, it was certainly most grateful to you, as in another sense it was to me."

"In all senses, your honor."

"But you are on dry land now; and, though I do not see many signs of prosperity about you, yet I prefer to think of you, and should like to hear that you are as prosperous on dry land as you are safe."

"Well, your honor, that's soon said. I'm as prosperous as I cares to be, and perhaps more so than I desarve. I have enough and to spare; and that reminds me, your honor, that I've got a little cold supper here for you — some pretty fine fish and a can of Jamaica—"

"Not just yet, Gowdey. Go on with what you were saying. You have enough—"

"And to spare! And that, I may say, is pretty much all that a man needs in this world, and perhaps in any other. I get a trifle of five pounds a year, which keeps me in powder and shot, for keeping up this old block; and I airn a trifle more by fishing for the townspeople; and sometimes I pick up a buck or a turkey in the swamp, or a brace of ducks in the ponds, and that's all grist to my mill; and then I do a little job, at times, for Franks and other people, and they pays me well: and altogether, sir, I'm as well fed, and clothed, and liquored, as a single man wants to be in this country, where the cold don't bite too keenly, and where the warm comes to me natural, like the sun to the corn."

"But you have to work for all this, Gowdey, and pretty hard work too; and, at your age, my good fellow, the heart, head, and body, all equally ask for rest and ease."

"Lord, your honor forgits I passes for only fifty. But work, sir, is a great sweetener of bread and meat; and to airn one's money, makes money a more decent and respectable thing than ef I got it and gave no sweat for it! And so, you see, I don't feel the age, and I don't fear the work; and I find myself so well as I am, that ef I was to be better off, I'm afeard I'd be worse! I'd be gitting sick; and, ef anything could scare a poor sinner like myself, it's the idee of being sick — to lie on one's back and to want water, when every j'int in my body would prefer Jamaica;

to swallow doctors' stuff, when the venison-ham, hanging from the wall, seems to cry, ' Come make a steak of me, and be young agin !' And to think that, maybe, I should git sick with nobody to give me water, or physic either, and then, Lord knows what! That's the consideration, your honor, that sometimes pops into my head, and sets it all over aching with the thinking of what's to happen."

" Ay, and sickness *will* come, Gowdey."

" When sickness comes to me, your honor, I'll make up my bed, and wrap up, and lie down for the last sleep ! I sha'n't take physic, and I kin do without the water for awhile, and no venison-steak will do me good."

" Nay, my good fellow, that will be next door to suicide."

" I don't think so, your honor. For you see, living the sort of life I live, there's nothing but old age to make me sick, and, for that disease, Death is the only doctor. I'm an active man, and does well in the open air ; work strengthens me after a good sweat, and my food is always sweet, and I never over-eat and never over-drink myself ; and what's to make me sick but old age ? I never was sick an hour in my life, and I've kept moving always. It's this moving always and moving fast, your honor, that keeps a man hearty. Sickness kaint catch him. It's your slow people that the fever catches and the agy shakes ; and it only shakes 'em to show how they ought to shake themselves ! That's my doctrine, your honor, and, ef it's true, you see that, when I takes to my bed, I'll need no doctoring. Pay-day's come, and Lord send me the feeling to believe that I kin square accounts with my eternal Creditor, and git an honorable discharge from all my debts !"

" Yet, Gowdey, there must be something melancholy in this solitary way of life. Have you no people — no kindred ?"

" Not a living human as I knows on ; not a chick nor a child. Ef I had, your honor, they should be here, and I'd work the mus-cles harder, but they should lie on a softer bed than mine. But I haint got 'em, and I don't miss 'em. When I was a younger man, I did ; and then I felt how hard it was to be alone. But I'm usen to it now. Men who live, like me, all their lives in the woods, gits out of liking for what you call society. They l'arn to love woods, and thicks, and trees, and rivers, and lakes ; and they gits a quick ear for the cries of birds and beasts ; and they some-

how finds company in very small and sometimes strange matters.
The woods and trees, and even the waters, git to be friends after
awhile; and you talks to them, and you think and believe that
they talks back to you. A cast-away sailor on a desarted island
will git to an acquaintance with every rock and tree that he sees
daily, and l'arn to love 'em, and want no better company. And
so, an old woodman like myself — why, sir, here in this old log-
castle, I'm a-convarsing all day, at the lookout, with something or
other, and studying the set of a tree, and the shape of a cloud, and
the shades of green in the woods as the sun and winds pass over
'em, so that I make out a sort of argyment for them, and myself
too. But there's more than that, your honor. There's the company of blessed spirits, that are always about us, night and day,
doing something — we do n't know what or how — to help us on,
and keep our hearts up, and make our road easy."

" Spirits? Did you ever see a spirit?"

" Yes, your honor; I'm sure of it, though I do n't know for
sartain that one ever did cross my sight. But I've felt it. I
feels very sure that they keep my company. There's something
tells me so. It's in my heart or head; it's in all my veins; it's
my holy belief. And sometimes I think I hear voices; and there
are sounds that stir me up till my heart beats like a strong watch;
and my hair rises naturally, without any thinking of mine — without any warning: so that I know that they are about me."

" But you have seen nothing?"

" Well, I kaint say yes, your honor, but I kaint say no. I've
never had a spirit to stand before me, and face me outright; but
I've felt 'em flash beside me, when I've been in the deep thick,
jest like a flash of a wing — jest like a bird passing."

" 'T was a bird, no doubt."

" No, your honor! My gun p'ints naturally at the flash of a
bird's wing, right or left; and you know I'm an old hunter, and
ought to know what s a bird and what's not. There's not a red-
skin in the woods but will tell you Ben Gowdey knows every bird
that flies. But I hear sounds and I see shapes, when it's growing dusk; and at night, in this old log-castle, I kin hear whispers
in the very room, when its deep midnight; and — but, Lord love
your honor, it's easier to believe than to prove; and ef you were
to ask me all day, I could only tell you that I believe for myself,

but kaint make the thing clear to you. But it stands to reason. I had a father and a mother, like every other man; and I had brothers and sisters, but it so happened that I hardly ever know'd one of 'em; they all died off when I was not knee-high. And I have reason to believe that they were goodish people enough — poor, and sinning now and then, as is the natural case with poor folks, put to it pretty hard by a hard world; but, as the world goes, I reckon they were goodish people. And the little brothers and sisters, not six years old, what was to make them bad? Well, they all naturally feels a feeling to help me on smoothly, and to make me journey safely; and so, I reckon, they are about me. And I'm glad to think so, for it does me good, and keeps me as good as human flesh will let me be! And I'm sure it's they that flash across my sight; and they whisper in my room; and, I tell you, I've had, more than a hundred times, a something whispering in my ear, 'Do n't!' — and sometimes, jest as often, another whispering that said, 'Do!' — and I know it that, jest as I listened to them voices, I got on smooth and safe, and felt the better for it."

"I can't quarrel with your faith, Gowdey, and still less am I disposed to find fault with your philosophy."

"Oh! 't aint philosophy, your honor. I'm not conceited enough for that. It's only the reason, and the common sense, and the natural truth."

"Perhaps so. Certainly, if such are the fruits of their interference with you, the spirits deserve this privilege of visit. But, are you not disturbed by other sounds? Do not the Indians sometimes rouse you up at midnight?"

"Not they! They'd feel it in all their bones, and they know it. They're mortally afear'd of the six-pounder; and they all know what a nice rifle-bead I kin draw upon red skin or white, ef they come too close to the garrison. But they'd like to do it, ef they could, and so I'm good at watch, and knows my time; and am jest as good a scout in the woods as the best of them."

"Are any of them in the neighborhood?"

"They're beginning to come, and some are never gone. Some of them, the Stonos and the Sewees, live almost altogether on the salts. The Yamasees keeps a-moving up and down in the winter, but gits back to the Ashepoo and Pocotaligo, and all along the salts, in fish-time. All these people a'most belongs to the great

Katahbah nation, and the tribes come and go, according to the
season, from the seacoast to the mountain-country and back agin.
There's a sort of trade between them.   The seashore Injuns carry
up shells, and clay pots and pans, and cane-reeds for arrows, and
gits flintstones for hatchets aud arrow-heads, and war-clubs, from
the up-country people, in the way of barter."

"Have you seen many this season?"

"Not many.   But they're about, I hear, and coming along
daily.   In a month's time or so, the woods will be thick with 'em,
all along the rivers.   And I'm sorry to see it."

"What! they lessen your chances at the game — thin the
game—"

"It's not that, your honor; there's a plenty for all of us.   But
I'm afear'd the Injuns are guine to be troublesome agin.   They
have not been whipped bad enough yet, and never was there any
people so apt to forget a whipping soon.   They were pretty sassy
before they went off last autumn, and, from what I then seed, I
was dubous of what was to come.   From what I hear, I reckon
there'll be some of the mountain-tribes coming down along with
'em this season; and ef they do, we may calculate to hear the
warwhoop somewhere about the settlements this summer.   Well,
now you see, jest at this time, when they're most sassy, comes a
new council, and they've got the notion in their heads that all these
redskins are a sort of natural Christians that only wants a leetle
sprinkling to become convarts to our religion, and grow into honest, sober, home-keeping Christians.   But water aint going to do
it, your honor — no, nor soap and water, nor all the preaching
from London down to Vera Cruz.   It's whipping, and hard work,
and l'arning how to eat good bread and meat well cooked, and gitting a taste for vegetables as well as venison: this is the way to
teach a savage how to git religion.   The cook-pot is a great con-
varter of the heathen —that and the whipping-post."

"Rather novel doctrines, Gowdey."

"Oh! I knows the beast, your honor, and kin count every spot
on his hide.   These council-men, they knows nothing.   Here's a
new man, a Colonel Berkeley, a nevey of the Lord Berkeley,
they say, and he's bought ever so much land, jest above us, some
seven or eight miles up; and they've made him a lord, too — a
'cassique,' they call it, which is Injun for a 'lord;' and he's one

of the council-men; and he says they've been too hard upon the Injuns; and he's brought out orders that we're to captivate and sell no more of them, but to have treaties with 'em, and trade with 'em, and treat 'em like brothers. And pretty brothers he'll find them! He's having them at his plantation that he's a-settling, and he's feeding them; and he'll have enough of 'em before he's done with 'em. They'll feed on him all they can, and he'll never content 'em so long as he's got anything left; and when he won't give any more, they'll take; and the first fine chance, when they sees that his barony's full of good things, they'll make a midnight dash at 'em, and he'll never know his danger till he feels their fingers in his hair. They'll raise his scalp for him before they're done with him. But you know the varments as well as I do."

"And has he no notion of all this?"

"No more than a child! I've talked over the whole thing to him, and told him what he may expect. But he says it's all our fault; that we treated the Injuns badly, and made 'em what they are; that they're 'Nature's noblemen,' and only need good treatment to be good fellows and good Christians. He's sat here with me by the hour, talking over the matter — and jest, as I may say, talking like a man in a dream. His head is full of projects. He's always at something new. Now he's for draining all these swamps — he says they'll make the best meadows in the world; then he's for great cattle-ranges and sheepwalks; and for making wine out of the grapes, and says he kin supply all England with wine better than they git from France. Well, the upshot of all will be, that he'll break, and go to smash, and the Injuns will take his scalp and burn his barony. They'll first begin upon his sheep and cattle, and he's got a smart chance of both already from England; and then they'll finish with his family. They'll eat and burn him up."

"But does he maintain no watch — no garrison?"

"Yes: he's got some raw English laborers with him; and the carpenters are at work, and he's got his block-houses and we'pons-of-war; but he don't know the savages how they work a traverse, and they'll all be surprised and cut off. And it's a mighty sad thing to think upon, your honor; for this Colonel Berkeley seems a mighty fine sort of person — honorable, and smart enough, and full of work; he's got a hand for a-most anything, and is jest

9

about as eager at a new beginning as any boy that ever broke loose out of school. I'm to git him an Injun lad for a hunter; and I've agreed for one, the son of an old chief of the Sewees — old Mingo, as we call him, but the Injuns call him Cussoboe. He's the chief of that tribe. I expect him every day. The colonel wanted to hire me to do his hunting; but, at my time, your honor, I won't go into any new contracts. I'm for paddling my own canoe."

"It is to this barony of Colonel Berkeley that I'm to go to-night, Gowdey, and you must direct me how to find it."

"I'll *guide* your honor, if you please. It's easier to do that than to direct you."

"Have you a horse?"

"As sleek a marsh tacky as you ever crossed."

"Franks sent you a horse for me?"

"He's here and safe — hid and hoppled in the thick, alongside of my own."

"Well, Gowdey, I shall be glad to have your guidance. How long will it take us to get there?"

"A short two hours."

"Then, if we start three hours before day, it will answer. Now, understand me. This is a secret expedition. I am not going to see Colonel Berkeley, and do not wish to be seen by him or any of his people. I wish to hover about for awhile, concealed closely, seeing everything if possible, myself unseen. He is, you are aware, a member of the privy council, and exercises a large influence upon the deliberations of that body. I need not tell you that I am compelled to keep dark."

"Yes, I've heard! — that bloody fight with the Spanish don! Well, for my part, I only wish you had sunk a hundred of 'em. Those bloody Spaniards are the natural enemies of all true Englishmen; and the king and lords-proprietors do n't know what mischief they're a-doing, when they tie up the hands of our valiant cruisers. But they hain't ruled you out of law altogether, captain."

"You may earn five hundred pounds, Gowdey, by showing to the governor, or this Colonel Berkeley, where to lay hands upon me!"

"And I'd airn hell and damnation along with the money, your

honor! Surely, sir, your honor believes in the honor of Ben Gowdey?"

"As in my own — and thus it is that you see me here to-night."

"God bless you, sir," grasping and squeezing his guest's hand, "and your visits and honor to this poor old hunter! We must drink together on that, your honor; and now for that bite of supper!"

## CHAPTER XXI.

### NIGHT-RIDE TO KIAWAH.

" Thou dark grove,
That has been called the seat of melancholy,
And shelter for the discontented spirit—
Sure thou art wronged; thou seem'st to me a place
Of solace and content." — THOMAS MAY — *The Heir.*

WE shall say nothing of the supper. It was clean, of course, and simple; the Jamaica was employed, and its virtues acknowledged — though neither Calvert nor the hunter professed to be bottle-holders. While they ate, they talked; that is to say, Gowdey talked: and when did you ever meet old hunter yet, or old fisherman, that was not fond of his own music, except when on duty? At such a time, the hunter and fisherman are as sacredly silent as if in waiting for the delivery of an oracle. They revenge themselves, subsequently, for this reverential abstinence, when, having no game, they only seek a victim!

But, now, Calvert encourages Gowdey to speak. He wiles him, gently and gradually, to the subject of Colonel Berkeley, the cassique, who, by-the-way, is something of a curiosity to our hunter. He admires his energy, his courage, the boldness of his projects, the dignity of his bearing, and, so far as he knows it, the worth of his character. His manliness and unaffected simplicity are especially themes for his admiration. He has no vulgar pride.

" He will sit, jest as you do, captain, for hours, with an old hunter like myself, and ask questions, and listen quietly, and never take pains, every now and then, to let you see that he thinks himself the better man! And, though I think he's quite wild in some of his calculations, and rather more likely to do harm than good — as when he thinks to tame these red savages, and convart these marshes into grand pasturages, and make wine out of these grapes to beat all France — yet he's so manful and courageous in it all, that I can't help liking him. And, another reason, he's all the time trying *to do!* It is n't to *make* money. Ef you believe me, your honor, I do n't think this cassique, as they call him, cares a copper whether he gits anything out of all his workings for himself. But he looks out upon the marsh, and says, 'If I could conquer it from the sea, and make it green with grass!' And he says, 'Think of all these forests, Gowdey, supporting their thousands of sheep!' And then he looks at the grapevines everywhere, and cries out, 'All Europe shall drink of the wine of Carolina!' Them's grand idees, your honor, and them's the idees of Colonel Berkeley. He's got no sort of little meanness in all his nature. He's for taking the rough world, jest as you see it, and making it smooth for man! He's a-blundering, it's true; for you see he comes to Carolina, not knowing much about it, with all his grand English *idees;* and he kain't git quite right till he l'arns all about the actual sarcumstances of the country. But give him time, and he'll do. Now, what do you think? Here he's imported thousands of English brick, to build his houses and chimneys, and his tiles of clay, into a clay-country, where there's the best clay in the world, and more firewood, so I've hearn himself say, in this single county, than in all Great Britain! When he'd seen the Injun clay pans and pots, he kicked the piles of brick at the landing with his feet, and said, 'What a fool I was to bring these things here!' He'll l'arn, but what's the expense? I'm afraid it'll be no less than his scalp."

"But have you not warned him of the treachery of the Indians?"

"Till I'm tired; but he'll have to l'arn them, jest as he l'arned the clay and bricks. And *they'll* soon teach him. Nothing but downright war with the redskins will save him. And who knows but they may begin on him? They're jest as apt to begin with the man they feed on, as on any other person."

"He is making a great place of his barony, then?"

"Give him five years, and it'll be famous."

"Have you seen his family?"

"Yes, sir — his wife, and one child. They've had but one.

But her mother's a-living with him, and there's a girl about thirteen—"

"Her sister — I suppose."

"I reckon; but I don't know.   They call her Grace."

Calvert involuntarily nodded his head in the affirmative.   And here, for awhile, the conversation flagged.   It was resumed, somewhat abruptly, by the hunter:—

"You're asking me, your honor, 'bout the cassique.   Now, there's one thing that's struck me ever sence I first sot eyes on him; and that is, that he looks mighty much like you.   I thought of you the moment I seed him.   He's not so tall as you, and I reckon he's five years older; but you've got the same complexion, the same sort of eyes and face generally; and you're both quick as a breeze, and always a-doing!   And when you walk, there's the same sort of lift in the shoulders; but it's mostly when you're a-setting that I sees the likeness.   You sort o' square off broadly when you set; and your hands rest on your thighs; and you set your head pra'd; and your eyes look through the man you're a-talking to; and your mouth is shut close — pressed tight, I may say, as if you was a-thinking, 'I may have to fight this man yet;' and you are apt to speak sudden, quick, onexpectedly; and then the speech comes short, and the voice is deep, as if it come from the chest, deep down, and it sounds like a bell!   There's a great deal, mighty like, that you've got atween you; and ef he's got the heart that you've got, then, ef ever you git into a quarrel, I wouldn't want to be the looker-on, for I loves *you* and I likes *him:* for, as sure as a gun, there'd be one death, and prehaps two, from the fight.   He'll fight like blazes, I reckon, for he gathers himself up all the time, as ef he was going into battle.   Everything's in airnest that he does.   I reckon ef he was to go into push-pin, he'd made a real life-sort of business out of it."

"I shall be curious to see and know him, Gowdey; but that's impossible, just now, when he's of the council, and I am under ban of law as a pirate."

"Does they give you that name, captain?   And only for licking the Spaniards!   Blast 'em, for the bloodiest fools! as ef every Spanish ship that we blowed out of water wasn't a help to us in these poor colonies.

"A nation only goes to ruin, Gowdey, under the management of cowardice, ignorance, and treachery; and when a king himself betrays his own people, Gowdey, to say nothing of his own dignity, then the disaster enures to the whole race, and to the most distant times."

"And is it the king, your honor?"

"Ay, the king! who, corrupt himself, corrupts justice, corrupts his chief men, corrupts the people; makes office a fraud; makes nobility a shame; makes a people bankrupt of honor as of fortune. But England is too much the care of Heaven to suffer this rule of imbecility very long; and, I tell you, this king will be removed — will die by the hands of God or the hands of man, or there will be another bloody revolution, such as brought his father to the block, to relieve his people from the dangers of his misrule. God will interpose before it be too late! I am sure of this as if I had seen it; for England is too important to the world's safety and progress, not to find a special Providence interposing for her behalf, in a condition of so much doubt and danger. I could feel tempted to prophesy that the hand of Fate is upon him even now!"

"And I'm sure I sha'n't care how soon! The fact is, captain, when a man gits to rambling over a great forest-country like this, he begins to think, 'How's it that we're to have a furrin sovereign?' and then he gits a step further, and axes, 'What's the use of having a king at all?' It's mighty sartain that a king of England, living cl'ar away over that great breadth of ocean, ain't of no sort of use to us here; and the *use* of a king, I reckon, or of any sort of officer, is jest about the first question that a reasonable white man ought to ax anywhere. It's the question that we puts, you know, when we ax after the man: 'What's he good for — what kin he do? Kin he fight, or counsel, or plan, or build, or work, or trap, hunt, fish — work in some way — doing for himself and other people?' Oh, a new country, like ours, is jest the sort of school where we gits rid of ridiculous notions about governors and men. It's not what the man wears, but what he does. And no crown upon his head, and no gold stick in his hand, no epaulette on his shoulder or star upon his breast, or beautiful ribands and buttons, can save a poor skunk of a fellow from disgrace, that ain't got the right sort of stuff of manhood in him. But I'm a

poor old fellow, that ain't nobody but a hunter and fisherman —
that prehaps ought not to talk about such mighty *idees*."

"Mighty ideas you may well call them, Gowdey, and such as
are destined to shake the world some day. But the time is not
yet. They are ideas which will grow here, in this wild country;
are the natural ideas of such a country, and can hardly take root
anywhere else. — But, is it not almost time for a start? I would
have you conduct me within sight of this cassique's barony, and
then leave me. I shall find the way back to-morrow night, and
shall expect you to carry me over to the town in your boat. Of
course, everything must be secret — to ourselves."

"I know, sir — all right! Say the word, and I will git the
horses. But ef you are to be out there all day, lying close, and
seeing nobody, how will you git provision?"

The cruiser showed a snug wallet which he carried under his
hunting-shirt. His costume, by-the-way, had been changed to that
of the American woodsman.

"All right, your honor! I see you do n't forgit the commissa-
riat."

Gowdey went out, and, soon returning, reported the horses to
be in readiness. A stoup of Jamaica concluded the session, after
the usage of the country; and some three hours before the dawn,
the two were upon the road. You are to understand, however,
that, letting out Calvert first, then bolting securely the massive
oaken door upon him, Gowdey, with rope and tackle, let himself
down from the upper story. By a mysterious process, the secret
of which he never suffered out of his own keeping, the rope was
concealed from sight immediately after, and not available to any
one who might wish for it in his absence. Gowdey prided himself very much upon his machinery.

And thus making his house secure, he mounted his marsh
tackey, and led the way through the forests. The trail was a
*blind* one, affording "a short cut" to a point which might have
been reached by a more open but more circuitous route. The
one chosen was at once shorter and more secret. They rode in
silence; policy dictating forbearance to the inveterate tongue of
the old hunter, while our cruiser preferred to indulge in meditations of a nature too delicate to share even with the most trustworthy comrade.

And while Gowdey rode on before, as guide, Calvert discussed in his own mind the subjects of their recent conversation. His thought naturally reverted to the account given of his brother.

"This was not the wont," he mused, "of Edward Berkeley! His habit was wont to be calm, quiet, subdued; grave rather than earnest; thoughtful rather than intense; fond of revery rather than action. How could this change be wrought in him so suddenly, in the short space of three years? Can he be the same person? Can it be my brother whom all these men describe to me?—so like, yet so unlike? I can not doubt that it is he! But how unlike the man he was, ere this dark cloud passed between us; ere we were separated by this terrible chasm which we may not leap, even in eternity! Just so long are we separated. For, if the affections are to survive the grave; if the precious sentiments — those which bring life and verdure to the soul — pass with it into the spheres of the future; if, there, the beloved ones remain to us, still loving and beloved — what must be the future to *us* — to him, to me — but separation for ever? And she! — shall I behold *her* in other worlds, nor claim her as my own, even as in this? Shall the wrongs done us here, not be righted there? Shall he there find a law, and exercise a power, which shall still work for us denial and bitterness, as here? — the forfeiture of all that precious hope on which both of us fed so fondly? — that hope which was never to bear its fruit! Shall there be no atonement, no redress, for this wrong, this robbery, this wo?"

And the strong man groaned aloud unconsciously, as the bitter flood of memory and thought rolled its deep waters over his soul.

"Anything the matter, captain?"

Calvert roused himself at the question, and shook himself free of his revery.

"No, Gowdey — only such matter as makes a sad thought too strong for a sad heart!"

"Ah! well, your honor, there's no medicine in one's pocket for the heart of another. It's only to be a man, and that means one who knows how to carry a camel's load on a poor pair of human shoulders. A great secret, I reckon, ef one could l'arn it! But — psho! psho!"—lowering his voice — "I see a light yonder in the woods. It looks like a camp-fire. Ef you'll let me, captain, I'll jest git down, hitch 'Hop-o'-my-Thumb' to this sapling,

9*

and take a peep at that fire. You know I'm a sort of scout of the garrison when I'm on this kind of night-riding."

He had alighted and hitched his nag ere he had done speaking.

" Ef you'll jest wait a bit here, captain, I won't keep you long; but it's needful to you as well as me that we should see about this 'campment here. We may have to lead our horses for a bit, or turn out of the track into the bushes t'other side, so as not to make the ears of bad-tempered outliers open too big as we go."

The consent of the rover was anticipated by his guide, who soon disappeared in the bushes; and, while he " scouted," gradually nearing the fire which had excited his curiosity, if not alarm, the thoughts of Calvert carried him back to the subject upon which he had been musing a few minutes before.

" What has caused this change in Edward Berkeley? What but guilt! It is the demon that has fastened upon his soul. It is conscience which is busy. He *knows* that he has done me wrong. He has basely taken advantage of my absence, to usurp my rights. His passions have got the better of his truth, of brotherly love, of justice and honor; and, these gratified, he begins to feel the stings and arrows which are to avenge my wrongs! Hence these labors, these wild speculations, this incessant, restless excitement, which make the wonder of all who see! He shall feel more, ere his experience ends. He shall feel life pall upon him, and excitement wear away, and hope lost, and love a fiend, and passion finally a hell!"

Something correct, but not all correct, Calvert. It may be that Edward Berkeley shall thus suffer, but not so much from the goad of conscience. At present, his true tormentor is the demon of unrest — born, certainly, of hopes unsatisfied; of torments felt; of doubts and anxieties; of a dream unrealized; but not of the sense of a wrong done to a brother! No! no! — he knows not that yet. Let us acquit him of *that!* He is not so much sinning as sinned against; he has been deceived; is not willingly a deceiver. But let us not anticipate.

Harry Calvert sat moodily upon his horse, waiting the return of Gowdey, but hardly conscious that he waited. His chin rested upon his breast; his eyes were closed; his thoughts striving in chaotic provinces in which he could as yet find no light. He was roused by the voice of Gowdey:—

"As I thought, captain! Injuns — a few Sewees, or Cusso-boes — a small party. I made 'em all out, and they never guessed it. Ha! ha! Give me a white man, after all, for good scouting. It's curious, captain, one of this party is the chief of the Kiawahs — old Cussoboe; and ef anybody had a raal, natural right to be called ' Cassique of Kiawah,' it's him; for he's been, to my knowl-edge, high chief of all the river, and this part of the country, which is the Kiawah country, for a matter of ten years, and it may be twenty. Well, here's Colonel Berkeley, that comes here under English authority, and buys the land from under the red king's foot, and takes away his very title! The two chiefs will meet to-morrow, I reckon, on a sort of treaty, and I know something about it. Old Micco Cussoboe — that is, King Cussoboe — is on his way to the barony now, I reckon. He's jest stopped, like a cun-ning savage as he is, to eat and drink up all he's got, and get a new supply out of the white men. They're all sound asleep now, but you'll find 'em all wide awake by daylight, painting them-selves up, and putting on their bravest coats, and hats, and feath-ers, to make a show when they come before the white chief. 'T would be a fine thing ef you could see it all; and maybe you will, for it's jest as like as not that the *white* cassique will receive his red brother in the open air; though that's not the *court* way among the Injuns, as long as they've got a house to hold council in. And now, your honor, if you say so, we'll make another start to be jogging."

"Go on, Gowdey."

And they rode as before, Gowdey now silent, and Calvert medi-tative, and still on the same subject:—

"Yes, we *are* alike — and Heaven spare us the meeting as enemies! It is as this keen-sighted hunter says: such a meeting will be the death of one or both! Let us not think of it. No, Edward Berkeley, though you have done me this wrong — though you have made me, as yourself, the victim of a never-ceasing ago-ny of unrest — let there be no strife between us! I, at least, must grow madder than I feel now, before I lift fratricidal hand at *your* bosom!"

We sum up thus a long, wandering train of thought and feeling, in which our rover's fancy conjured up nothing but spectres of wo and evil.

The precincts of the barony of Kiawah were at length reached. There were the openings of the forest; there the settlements — there the forest, black in its density and depth of green. Gowdey pointed out the several localities in detail, as far as they could be noted in the imperfect starlight. Some twelve or fifteen acres had been cleared, an occasional group of oaks alone excepted. At right angles stood four block-houses, *cornering* the clearing. These were to be points of defence, made of squared logs, pierced for musketry, yet designed as lodgings for the workmen. In the centre was the mansion, a framed house on brick pillars, with wings of logs, in which the family resided. The rest was rapidly advancing to completion. The whole square was to be picketed; the outhouses and offices, occupying a line between the several corners, to be pierced in like manner for musketry, yet susceptible of use for ordinary domestic purposes; the doors and windows looking into the court, which was a sort of *place de la garde*, a *plaza d'armas*, but answering for the purposes of court, and grounds, and garden. Here and there a very fine old oak, or pine, or cedar, sometimes clumps of each, had been suffered to remain. Everything as yet was rude, and in a perfectly chaotic state. Log-heaps, piles of brush, remained unburnt; piles of brick and lumber obstructed the pathways. Everything denoted progress and performance, but in just that state when the eye looks dissatisfied over the whole disordered spectacle. The region chosen for the settlement was a long, narrow ridge, running down to the river, where it terminated, some three miles distant, in a bluff. The front of the estate, upon the river, occupied little more than a mile; but it gradually stretched on either hand, as the survey ran inland — as may be supposed, when we know that the barony comprised twenty-four thousand acres.

"Enough, now, Gowdey. I see the ground, and know where I shall harbor. To-morrow night, if nothing happens, look to see me some two hours after nightfall, when I shall expect you to paddle me across the river. You need remain no longer. Good-night!"

"Rather, good-morning, your honor, for the day will soon be upon us. Well, sir, as you say so, I'll leave you. I'll look for you, and be ready. You've got a good hiding-place, and I know that you've the experience to make use of it. I don't fear that anything will happen. As for me, I mean to j'ine that Injun camp. I know 'em all, and I reckon the cassique here will want my help to-morrow as an intarpreter. I'm good at their lingo; and I'm a leetle curious to know what's going on. I reckon it's about an Injun hunter. The cassique wanted me to do his hunting, but I've got too old to follow any man's whistle. This old chief, Cussoboe, wants his son to l'arn English ways; and he agreed, some time ago, that, when they came back from the hills, the boy should hunt for the cassique. It's gitting quite common for the big men to have Injun hunters. But the idee's not a good one. I see trouble in it. But that's not my lookout. After I've given good warning, a shut mouth is the sensible notion. And so, your honor, I leave you; and God prosper your s'arch, whatever it may be!"

And so they parted — Calvert seeking the forest, where he hid his horse, and Gowdey the camp of Cussoboe.

# CHAPTER XXII.

## MOTHER AND DAUGHTER.

"The grace of fortune still must have its foil:
  The bliss may come in showers: but there shall be
  Ever a bitter poison in the cup
  Shall qualify the working to delight!
  We shall have palaces too, and goodly ones;
  But there still sits a mocker at the board,
  To shake a skinny finger at our pomp,
  And give our proud mortality to shame."

IN-DOORS or out of doors? Which way shall we look? With-out, the cassique is busy with the workmen. You hear the griding of the saw, the clink of the hammer, the heavy, dull stroke of the axe. And every sound declares for life — the life of civiliza-tion usurping the domain of the savage.

Within! Ah, within! Is it life here? It is the peculiar prov-ince of the woman. And why not life, even though there be no strife, no bustle? Life asserts itself no less sensibly and keenly through pain and silent suffering than through the clamorous voices that speak for human performance.

Wealth is here, no doubt. But the realm is a simple one. All the appliances and appurtenances are rude. Compared with the European houses of our settlers, the contrast is almost ludicrous. Log-houses — squared logs, it is true — a great waste of timber — massive enough — looking like rude castles — show, nevertheless, but uncouthly in European eyes, reared as our cassique and his family have been, in the grand old homes of England. And this central fabric, which is designed to be especially well finished — in which our Carolina nobleman means that his family shall dwell — what is it but a plain structure of pine and cypress? Large enough, certainly — four rooms on a floor; a great hall of reception, thirty by twenty-four; dining-room, of the same dimensions; a grand passage through the centre; a parlor for the ladies, somewhat smaller than hall and dining-room; and a library opposite! Chambers above, in a second story; wings contemplated, giving other chambers. Well, yes, from a distance, you will say this is a stately mansion, of good dimensions for comfort; and, if you have seen none but the American world, it will be a big fabric, rather grand of size and ample of accommodation, and supposed to represent very superior wealth.

The enclosure which is staked off, partly fenced — picketed, rather — confirms this idea. And there *is* wealth, the standards of the country only considered; and our cassique has prepared to lodge his family well, with equal dignity and comfort. We are to suppose a certain portion of the dwelling-house to be habitable, if not finished. Some of the rooms are lined and panelled with cypress-plank; the chimneys are all built; the furniture is there, all fresh from England, of a rich, massy character — hardly in keeping, however, with the otherwise naked simplicity of the dwelling. Clearly, the dwellers here have need to congratulate themselves that their lot has fallen upon pleasant places.

But, are they happy?

Even this question may be thought an impertinent one. We are of those who think that we have got very little to do with happiness. We have a certain destiny to fulfil, certain duties to perform, certain laws to obey, and vicissitudes to encounter, with such resources of courage as we have — energy, industry, and patient submission, with working; and, these laws complied with, we are to trouble ourselves no further about the compensative in our lot. This is a matter which must be left to God. He will settle our accounts, and make his award; and, whether this be happiness or suffering, is not a concern of ours, though it makes a wonderful difference in the degree in which we may relish life.

Indeed, so certainly is all this true, that our instincts all recognise it; and though we are told that the pursuit of happiness, in our own way, is an inalienable right, yet nobody actually proposes it to himself, at any time, as the object of his endeavor. Men do not deliberately seek happiness at any time. They seek money, seek power, seek indulgence, the gratification of one passion or another; but no one proposes to himself any scheme by which he

contemplates the realization of Eden or Arcady.   We all aim at
very inferior objects, and perhaps rightly.

And how should we pursue an object, in the possession of
which we have no guaranty?   Can there be any happiness in ill
health, in perpetual toil and anxiety, under the caprice of fortune ;
the caprice of wind and weather; the knowledge that the most
precious hopes and affections lie everywhere, at every moment,
exposed to the spoiler — to death, disease, loss, pain, denial, defeat
— those hungry wolves that prey upon humanity — those mocking
phantoms that delude it to despair !

No ! we have nothing to do with happiness.   He who pursues
it pursues a phantom.   He who finds it becomes a coward, perpetually dreading death and disaster.   A certain object — lawful,
proper to our sympathies, natural to our condition, our strength,
and resources — this is what we may and should reasonably pursue ; and this is attainable by all those who bring honest purpose,
and judicious aim, and manly working, to bear upon the object of
desire.   Even Love must be moderate in its aims, and we must
not expect too much from marriage.   Men are not heroes all, nor
women angels ; and if the parties will only bear themselves toward
each other like honest men and women ; be faithful and fond, with
reasonable expectations of care and reverence, honor and respect ;
gentle solicitude on the one hand and manly protection on the
other — we shall perhaps find it a goodly, comfortable world
enough : nor need we then trouble ourselves about the ideal condition which we figure under the word " happiness."   The vulgar
mortal finds this to resolve itself into mutton one day, and roast
beef and plum-pudding another ; in the exhibition of new toggery
and trinkets ; or, as Zulieme Calvert was apt to do, in the fanciful
twirling of very flexible limbs to the inspiriting entreaties of tambourine and fiddle !

But were our cassique and his women-folk as happy as they
might be, in the circumstances of their condition, and under the
qualifying definitions of happiness which we have given?

That is the question !

Well, you have heard of the cassique, and what people think
of *him.*   You have seen him already in one brief interview.   Look
at him now, among yonder workmen.   We show him to you a
week in advance of Calvert's visit.   See the energy with which

he throws himself into labor : see the frightful intensity with which he concentrates will, and thought, and muscle, upon the tasks before him ; watch the eager impulse, the stirring mind, the restless impatience ; hear the sharp, stern voice of authority, angry because dull labor is slow to comprehend, and a sullen mood stubbornly resists instruction.    Note him, as he hurries to and fro — now on foot, now mounted — hurrying this way, straining that ; and now busy with the builders, now with the hewers ; and anon with the ploughmen, as they drive their shares through the newly-cleared lands — striving, by dint of extra exertion, to repair the loss of previous time — the business of " breaking up" having been begun rather late in the season.    And now observe him, as, in a state of physical exhaustion, he flings himself down upon the naked earth, trying to rest the animal man, while the mental, with keen eye and impatient thought, chafes at the demands of the poor body for needful hours of repose !

" Well," you will be apt to say, " at least this man's nature is satisfied.    He is working in his vocation, *con amore ;* he is one of those men who can not help but work — who derives his enjoyments from his employments — the greatest mortal secret."    And, to a certain degree, you will resolve correctly.

But, follow him now, as he starts up and passes into the dwelling.    Note his countenance as he enters the house.    See how it alters in aspect.    You have seen it wear, just now, a variety of changes in a brief space of time.    There was authority asserting itself ; there was thought engaged in a problem ; there was eager zeal growing angry at some vulgar retardation ; there were qualities of mind and temperament, all declaring themselves by sudden and startling transitions.

But these disappear the moment he penetrates the dwelling. We now see that a sudden cloud has passed over his brow, which declares for some deeper working of the more secret nature. There is sadness as well as solemnity in that cloud.    There is a gloomy shadow upon that spirit which the intellect does not offer to disperse.    It is a settled expression of anxiety, verging on apprehension, for which the mind prepares no medicine.

And you note that, when out of doors, and in contact with his workmen, his carriage was rapid, eager, and without that reserve, that staid dignity and measured movement, which vain men usually maintain when dealing with the vulgar; yet, the moment he approaches his dwelling, his movements become slow, his carriage more erect; he seems to brace himself, with effort, as for an encounter. He has put on his armor of pride and dignity as if for the meeting with a foe.

Can this be the case? And what are the relations of this lord with his family?

Let us look within. Let us see how these women carry themselves, ere the cassique appears. There is a tell-tale look or action, a tone, a word, which, where there is a lurking sorrow, will declare something of the secret; and women are better tell-tales of the heart than men.

They occupy, mother and daughter, the parlor in the rear of the dining-room, which has been assigned especially to their use.

The Honorable Mrs. Constance Masterton is about fifty years of age, and, though carefully dressed, is not remarkably well preserved. She may have been a pretty woman in her youth. She has few traces of beauty now. The skin is sallow and wrinkled, the cheeks sunken; she is lean and tall, and, but for a piercing black eye, still full of fire, keen and searching, the sharpness and severity of her visage and the turbid yellow of her skin would make her absolutely revolting.

She is a woman of dignity. She is stately in her air and manner, and, as we have said, studious of her dress. She carries herself haughtily. She has a hard, hard heart; her training has been that of a convention which gave the heart no chance; her manners have all been formed artificially. She knows no nature inconsistent with the rules of her circle. She has had no life but that of society. She was one of those ridiculous people who claim always to be "in society" — to be "the society" — and who affect to despise all other classes — who do not, in fact, acknowledge any other as in existence. She believes only in her own "charmed circle" — one which the natural man would never esteem a charming one. Books are not among her objects. She never read one in her life. Music she recognises only as essential to the proprieties of the household, even as cushions and sofa are regarded as a material part of the furniture. *She* knows no more of music than a mule. Her tastes were limited to costume simply, and this was prescribed by a French *artiste*. Such was she in her English home. There, she was poor withal, in spite of all this social pretension; and in that melancholy situation in which the social vanity is ever at a painful conflict with the conventional necessity. She was a schemer, accordingly; and never did poor demagogue, with large appetite and small wits, labor, with more vulgar agents of trickery, for office, than did she to maintain the social position from which poverty had compelled her to descend. In the exercise of this faculty, she had shown herself sufficiently dexterous. She had shuffled off a younger son with nothing, and contrived to secure the elder, with a fortune, for her eldest daughter. She had large practical wisdom; was a woman of shrewdest policy.

And that daughter? — Olive Berkeley!

As a general rule, dear reader, we should expect the children to inherit the aspect, the habits, tastes, and characteristics, of those from whom they descend — those, at least, by whom they were trained and educated. But the contradictions between children and parents sometimes confound us. We might reconcile them, possibly, were we in possession of all the facts. But, in the present case, one portion of our criteria escapes us. Olive Masterton had a father, but of *him* we know nothing. Was she like him? Perhaps! She was certainly very unlike her mother.

But her mother had educated her, and the poet tells us —

"Just as the twig is bent, the tree's inclined."

Another, more certainly inspired, says: "Train up a child in the way he should go, and when he is old he will not depart from it." And so, too, we may say, generally, of those who are trained up in the way in which they should *not* go. But there are cases — individual and rare exceptions, we admit — in which Nature shows herself paramount to all other influences, whether of training, or tyranny, or simple education. We suspect that Olive Masterton was one of this description. Nature certainly had done not a little to neutralize the misteachings of the mother.

Physically, the daughter was quite unlike her mother. She was tall, it is true, but in this respect father and mother may have been alike. In all other respects, they had little in common. The mother was a brunette — dark of complexion and of eye. And, though called "Olive" — why we know not — the daughter

was a blonde, perfectly fair, of transparent skin; light, lively blue
eye; and the most delicate auburn hair, that floated wild, in free
ringlets, over head and bosom. She was, as is natural to this
temperament, inclined to be full and plump; but there were good
reasons why she was not so at the date of our history. Something
of care and thought, of anxiety and disappointment — the heart,
briefly, had been at conflict with the temperament; and she is
now thin, pale — very pale — and spiritless. The change had
been very great in eighteen months. Before that time, there had
been few creatures of the same class who could be described as
more perfectly beautiful — more round, and plump, and fair, bright,
and blessing, and elastic — a thing of joy and beauty. There
were certainly fewer still whom we can conceive more loving or
*loveable* in character. Gentle, generous, ingenuous — frank and
impulsive — graceful and accomplished — fair and beautiful —
Olive Masterton was as unpresuming as if she had not a single
one of these excellences — as if her mother had never taught her
one lesson of her own. Convention, and her proud, ridiculous
mother, had equally failed to spoil the liberal handiwork of Nature, however much they may have succeeded in perverting it
from its sweet and proper destination. Olive was one of those
who could and did pass through the infected district with a talismanic power, carrying away no single taint upon her pure, white
garments.

But you see that something has gone wrong with Olive. She
is a wife and a mother — young wife, younger mother — yet, as
you see her there before you, not eighteen months a wife, you
doubt if she be a bride; you do not doubt that she is not, in any
sense, a happy one!

She sits at the tambour-frame — at one of those pretty, trifling,
slight sorts of work, so grateful to the feminine nature, so graceful
in feminine fingers, which, under a pretext of employment, affords
opportunity for reveries — which may, or may not, be pleasant!
She seems unconscious of her occupation. Her eyes are half-
closed; her whole air is listless and indifferent; it is very evident
that her thought is far away, and not satisfied with what it finds
in its wanderings. Her face is not merely pale — it is marked
by a deadly marble whiteness; her cheek is colorless; her form
thin to leanness. When she looks up, at the voice of her mother

her large blue eyes dilate with a vacancy of gaze which pains you to behold. Young wife, young mother, but with no young heart, or hope, or fancy. Her glance tells you, if not her cheek, that she has survived all those sweet treasures of her youth.

Her mother watches her with an eager, sharp, dissatisfied sort of interest. She, too, is engaged in needlework; but she lays it down frequently in her lap, and fixes her eyes upon her daughter. Her tall, spare figure, sitting erect in the old Elizabethan chair of massive mahogany, is a good study of pride, antiquity, and self-complacency, assured dignity and satisfied importance. In some respects she is not entirely assured. She is no longer the ruler of her daughter, though she still maintains the natural ascendency of a mother; but she has a fancy that, were hers the only authority, she could very soon cure Olive of that brooding melancholy, of which she begins to be exceedingly distrustful. The attempts which she makes to this end are of a kind rather to annoy than to relieve the mind of the sufferer. How should she — the vain, weak, ridiculous old creature —

> ————— "minister to a mind diseased,
> Pluck from the memory a rooted sorrow,
> Raze out the written troubles of the brain;
> And with some sweet, oblivious antidote,
> Cleanse the *sick* bosom of that perilous stuff
> That weighs upon the heart!"

Alas! like too many of our poor, vain family of man, she can better make sick than well; more certainly pain than cure; rather poison than find the antidote: and, so far as her callous conscience works, that old woman begins to doubt whether she has not done this very thing! It is surely some cruel poison which has made that young creature, once so happy, now so perfectly "a creature of the wo that never moans; dies, but complains not!"

"Olive, my child, is there to be no end of this?" said the mother, rising and approaching the daughter. The tones were reproachful, not conciliatory.

"What is it you wish, mother?" answered the young wife, hardly conscious of the question, and looking up with eyes of great humility; that is, if the utter absence of all animation can be well signified by such a word.

" What do I wish? I wish you to shake off these melancholy humors; to be yourself, my child; as you were of old, when your spirits were gay as any bird's, and your face as smiling as any sunshine."

" Ah! mother, if 't were as easy to do as to wish—"

" And why not? 'T would be quite easy, if you'd only try— only make an effort."

" And why should I make an effort, mother?"

" Why? Why have you not everything in the world to per- suade you? There's your child — your husband—"

" No more, mother, I implore you! All this pains me — does no good."

" But there must be more, Olive. You owe it to the cassique to wear a more smiling, a more pleasant, a more grateful aspect. What has he not done for you? what is he not doing? Here you have every prospect of a beautiful, a splendid home—"

" Would to God, mother, that he had left us to the enjoyment of our poor cottage and our simplicity!"

" Indeed! In other words, to poverty and obscurity—"

" Welcome obscurity!"

" And I say, ' No,' my child; and I shall ever congratulate my- self that you had the wisdom to choose so wisely as you did."

" I choose!"

" Surely, you chose!"

" No, mother, spare me that accusation. It was *your* choice, none of mine; and my hourly thought is one of the deepest self- reproach that I was submissive when I should have been resolved; weak — oh, most pitiably weak — where I should have been strong! But, please you, say no more of this. You have done your work, irrevocably done it, and I am — what I am! Is it not enough that I have submitted to your will?"

" My wish, my child, not any will of mine. Your own will, you know—"

" It matters nothing now."

" But, my dear, it matters everything. Do you suppose it pleas- ant to the cassique, who is doing everything for us, that you should meet him with such lack-lustre eyes always, such pallid cheeks, such a spiritless air, such a wobegone countenance?"

" Can I help it, mother?"

" To be sure you can, if you will try. It only needs that you pluck up resolution."

" I do — to keep from drowning ! I should sink quite, but that I do try, and pluck up a sort of resolution. But I can do no more. I do this only because I would, if it were possible for me, make my husband happy. I do not reproach him."

" You reproach *me*, then — me !"

The young wife was silent. The mother confronted her.

" Yes, Olive, you reproach *me ;* and that is, I say it, the height of ingratitude ! You reproach me because I saved you from the embraces of a beggar—"

" Mother you promised me !—"

" Yes, I did promise you never again to speak of that poverty-stricken reprobate ; but you also promised me that you would try to show yourself grateful for the blessings—"

" Blessings ! Ah, mother, do I not seem to enjoy them ?"

" It's your own fault if you do not. Here's plenty ; here's wealth ; here's servants, any number. Is it money you would have — dress, luxury, splendor ? You may have them all."

" All for peace, mother ! I would give all for peace — for sleep."

" And whose fault is it that you have not peace ? What's to trouble you ? You have nothing to apprehend. You have only to will, and have — command, and be obeyed ; and, I do say it, your husband is one of the best of men."

" He is, and that is enough to rob me of peace ! — that he deserves so much, and I can give so little — nothing, in fact, of what he deserves and desires most."

" You don't try, Olive ! You prefer to sit, and mope, and weep, when your duty is to stir about, and be cheerful and smiling. Trying will do it — only try !"

" I have tried. Oh, do not ask me for further effort !"

" Olive, it's all perversity ! And when I consider the poverty out of which he brought us ; the plenty which we now enjoy ; the dignity to which he has raised you—"

" Oh, mocks, mocks, mocks ! — mocks all, and frauds, mother — where the poor heart sits naked and disconsolate in the solitude, scorning the pomp which is wasted upon the wasting frame. Mother, no more of this. You only make it worse !"

"Make it worse? As if I did not know what was best for my own child!"

The daughter shook her head mournfully, but said nothing. How much might she not have said upon the theme? The mother was not so forbearing.

"Yes," she continued, "I ought to know, who've reared you from the cradle. I say it's mere perversity that makes you go on so; makes you prefer to be miserable when you might be so happy."

"Strange perversity indeed, mother, preferring misery to happiness! Have you found it so easy to procure happiness?"

"That's nothing to the purpose. Here are you, I say, with everything to make *you* happy — plenty, every way; wealth and servants; and a good husband, a nobleman of rank; one of the first men in this country; who is as kind to you as man can be to woman, and one of the most loving, if you'd only suffer him; and with one dear, beautiful child: and yet you sit here, pining and trying to be wretched, when you should have a smile for everything, and be singing your happiness from morning to night and from night to morning. And what's the pretence for all this? Why, that once, when you were a foolish, inexperienced child, you made a ridiculous engagement—"

"Which you then approved, mother."

"Well, I didn't know, then, what I knew afterward — that you might have a far better man."

"No, mother: a richer, perhaps, but never a better!"

"And I say that makes a mighty difference. It's one thing to have a husband that can keep you in state and comfort, but quite another to be married to poverty, and want, and shame—"

"Not shame, mother!"

"I say shame, Olive Berkeley — shame: for what is Poverty, always, but a thing that must hold down its head, and walk humbly through dark passages, and feel all the time that the world is running over its neck? That's shame; and that would have been your portion if you had married Harry Berkeley. And if, as you say, it is *I* that have done it — well, I say it's something of which I might well be proud, and for which you ought to be thankful. And what's the difference between the men, if you come to that? Isn't the cassique as fine a looking man as his younger brother?"

Olive answered nothing to this.

"Isn't he almost as young; quite as handsome; quite as wise and learned; as brave and graceful; isn't he as noble and generous; and doesn't he, in fact, look almost as much like him as if they had been twinned together?"

"Alas! mother, he looks too like him. He reminds me of *him* for ever!"

"Well!—"

"Well—but I know that he is *not* Harry!"

And a gush of tears followed; and the young wife, hearing her husband's footstep in the passage, rose hastily and left the room— but not before the cassique, entering, discovered that she was in tears. She did not look up — hardly noted *his* appearance; but he, quickened to keenest scrutiny by his own anxieties of heart, detected all her emotions in the one passing glance which he caught of her convulsed features as she went. In the face and manner of the mother he distinguished the proofs of recent controversy; of vulgar authority; of a harsh, ungenial censure; of a temper too little ruled by thought or sensibility to permit her to become a consoler or counsellor for a bruised and suffering spirit.

"Madam," said he sternly, "I could wish that you would say nothing to Olive on the subject of her sorrows, whatever they may be. I know not what they are. I can not decipher this mystery; nor, it appears, according to your admission, is it in your power to do so. You allege to me that you know nothing of her present cause of grief."

"To be sure not, my son; but—"

"To attempt to cure the disease of which we know nothing, must be to hurt, not to help; and we may kill the patient in the fond attempt to save. You will permit me once more to insist that you make no such attempt. Do not pry into her mystery. You will only aggravate her suffering, as, I am sorry to tell you, is invariably the case, after your conversations with her. As her mother, you are naturally solicitous; but solicitude here requires forbearance. We must be content to wait upon her moods, to watch their changes; and leave it to herself to suggest the means by which we may bring succor to her mind or body. Once more, madam, I repeat the wish, the injunction, that you will not again

10

trouble her on the subject of her afflictions. Leave them to time
—leave them to me, madam, if you please."

And, saying these words, not waiting for any answer, he withdrew from the apartment; and, hurriedly moving now, left the
house, to rejoin the workmen without.

The mother shot an angry glance after the son-in-law. Had
she but dared, she would have given him a precious tongue-volley
as he went. But the virago was always subdued in the presence
of this stern man, who never addressed her one gratuitous word;
whose words were always direct, even as fiery arrows sent headlong to the mark; whom she felt 't would be dangerous to trifle
with. She well knew that the slightest disposition to pass between
him and his wife, or his will, would insure her immediate dismissal
from his house.

"Leave it to you, indeed!" she muttered; "as if you could
better know than me what is my child's trouble, and how to cure
it! Well I never let him know of that engagement! He shall
never know! No, no; that would be terrible! He'd never forgive me that! But I *must* make Olive sensible to reason. She's
just throwing away happiness and fortune. I know this man so
well, that, sooner than stand this sort of life another year, he'd
break loose from everything. And if, in his fury, he was to demand the truth from Olive, she'd be just as like as not to tell him
every syllable. She hasn't the sense to keep her own secrets or
mine. And if she was to do that, what would become of her—
and me? He'd swear that we deceived him! No, no!—I must
bring Olive to her proper senses, before it's too late. He's
becoming sterner and more keen every day. He must not be
driven too far. *She* must be driven rather."

We shall see something yet of this driving process on the part
of our loving mother!

## CHAPTER XXIII.

### THE SHADOW ON THE HOUSE.

"*Doct.*            Not so sick, my lord,
As she is troubled with thick-coming fancies,
That keep her from her rest.
    *Macb.* Cure her of that!"            SHAKESPEARE.

THE cassique had gone back to the work without. It was with spasmodic energy that he sought relief in employment. The refuge of his soul lay only in throwing off all his nervous energies, by the exercise of all his physical faculties, in the most desultory occupations. But the mind — how did that employ itself the while?

It is surely not difficult to conceive his suffering. A proud man, noble, disinterested, generous, impulsive, has set his heart upon an object; fancies that he has won it; and, in his moment of greatest exultation, finds the fancy a delusion!

He has somehow been the victim of a deception. Was it his own, or whose? Has he deceived himself by his own vanities and desires, or has he been the subject of management? An Englishman is very apt to suspect the latter. All the Old-World convention teaches intrigue and management in the affairs of the heart.

But whose has been the management? Not the wife's, surely. Of that he is satisfied. He knows not her secret — is too noble to pry into it: enough that his wife *has* a secret, which troubles her, and which she does not communicate to him. It is enough for him to know *that*. He cares to know nothing more. His knowledge is already most mournfully sufficient.

*That* proves to him estrangement — want of sympathy. " We are *not* one," he mournfully utters to himself. " But is she guilty?

Has she deliberately lent herself to a fraud upon my affections?
No! It is only to look at her. She, too, has been the victim.
If, in evil hour, she has lied to me, she is paying for it now the
dreadful penalty. The pang has struck home to the heart. There
is no doubt that she is quite as wretched as she has made me.....

"How is it that I saw nothing, suspected nothing?... Now, that
I look back upon our courtship, was there anything to encourage
me? She was ever shy and shrinking; ever denying me opportunity. And, fool that I was, I construed even her reluctance
into modest favor! Should I not have known better? Was it
favor? Does it now seem like favor? Was it not rather coldness, indifference, aversion? Oh, how blind I have been in all
this affair!....

"Was she not heart-whole then? Her mother assured me —
never were assurances more solemn. But — she is her mother;
and — I know *her* now, if I do not yet know Olive!... And she
was reared in that accursed set of the Clives and Saxbys — all
hollow, corrupt, selfish, and artificial; and all poor and pretentious! Ah, I have been a rash and headlong fool!....

"But did I not, even then, separate Olive from them? Did I
not then see, and assure myself — I thought I did — that she had
suffered no contaminations — had escaped their corruptions? She
was pure, simple, unaffected; had no ambition to shine; preferred
solitude to gay society; went not with the dancing fools and monkeys; seemed always most frank, most ingenuous, and delicately
honorable.....

"And — I have not been deceived in her. She is such now.
I doubt her in nothing — save that she has a secret, which she
keeps from me — in the core of which lies all her care! Could I
ask — demand — this secret? Ay — she would declare it. I
doubt not but she would declare it, as truly, fully, fairly, devoutly,
as if in the presence of her God! She might dread to do so! —
But I must not seek to know. It were base to seek, despotic to
demand it.

"Nay, dare I seek? How could I bear to learn that secret?
Whither would it lead? There lies the danger! Olive is not
only my wife, but the mother of my child — my son — he who
must bear the name of my fathers!....

"On every side the cloud hangs heavily. I must not seek to

pierce it; but there's a terrible presentiment that racks my soul. I shall know the truth ere long; and then — God give me the needful strength to endure it! God preserve my manhood!"

And, tearing himself away from thought, as from his direst enemy, he darted with desperate zeal to toil. He himself grasped axe and hammer; seized upon the implements, in the very hands of the workmen, and exhibited to their confounded senses the spectacle of a gentleman who could plan and execute at once — could exhibit such skill and strength as we are wont to consider unsuitable and anomalous when united in the same person, and he a gentleman.

But we must turn from him again to Olive. That day, she declined appearing at dinner. The cassique took his seat silently, ate little, listened patiently to the harangues of his mother-in-law, and, without answering, rose and disappeared. The mother followed soon from table, but took her way to the daughter's chamber. Another lecture, the avowed purpose of which was love.

"You must take exercise, Olive. You must go out and walk with nurse and baby. Come, get ready. I will go along with you."

Olive thanked her, but declined.

"Olive, my child, you are killing yourself."

To this the daughter made no answer, save with a smile — a smile of such a sort as seemed to say, clearer than any words —

"And that were scarce a sorrow, mother!"

It was the luckless nature of this woman, which never suffered her to rest herself, or permit rest to her victim. Under the pretext of soothing, she pursued the daughter. Soothing, indeed! When did a cold heart cheer a sorrowing one? She only worried her; and when the grieving woman pressed her temples with her hands, with a sudden expression of physical pain, then the good mother knew that there was headache to soothe, and other vexing ministries to be performed, when all that the sufferer prayed for was to be at peace — to be let alone. It was a positive gain to the excellent mother, when, at supper-table, she could report to the cassique that his wife's sufferings were now certainly physical.

The husband rose immediately, went to the chamber, looked in only, and said, in the gentlest and most solicitous accents:—

"You are unwell, Olive — can I do anything for you?"

"No, thank you. I simply need repose."

"You shall have it, Olive."

He returned to the table, and said quietly: "Olive would sleep. You will oblige me not to seek her again to-night."

And this was all. If the mother made any answer, the cassique did not hear it. In a few minutes after, he retired to the library, where he sat reading half the night — reading, or lost in those meditations which left Thought stranded on a desert shore!

The next morning there was a change in Olive, but hardly for the better. There was an increase of nervous energy, but it seemed to lack direction. The mind, though elevated a little, seemed to wander in object. The eyes were bright, but it was with a flickering sort of light, that seemed to argue confused and excited fancies. She was restless throughout the day, and this restlessness was construed by the mother into improvement. The judgment of the cassique was more true. He regarded her with an increased earnestness, but said little, and not a syllable on the subject which distressed him. In the afternoon, Olive walked out with nurse and baby. The mother and younger sister followed in search of them. They were found in a great live-oak wood, which stretched away more than a mile and a half in the direction of the river. It was a noble grove, shady, cathedral-like, the ancestral trees of which might have been growing five hundred years — a glorious avenue for contemplation.

Olive wandered in this wood with vacant look and manner. She simply answered when addressed; then fitfully, and with the air of one whom her own voice startled. Even the mother began to think there was something wrong; and this made her somewhat more cautious than usual in her communications.

The next morning the same symptoms, with decided increase. There was as much wildness of air and manner, with more of a spasmodic energy. Olive was still singularly restless — passing from chamber to chamber — engaging momently in some new occupation, and abandoning each in turn almost as soon as taken up. It was noted by the cassique that there was at times a feverish quiver of her lips; a sudden start, upon occasions; an anxious looking round her, as if in obedience to some call, or in expectation of some approach. But, when spoken to, her replies were simple, artless, unaffected, to the point, and, if possible, still more subdued in tone than usual.  The mother observed that she not unfrequently essayed to speak with her when they were alone together ; would begin a sentence abruptly, as if under some ungovernable impulse, yet as suddenly arrest herself in the utterance ; her eyes cast down, on the instant, with a sort of dogged resolution, upon the work in her hands.  Several attempts which the cassique made to speak with her — always in the gentlest tones — were met by an absolute recoil of manner, amounting to repulsion, on the part of the sufferer.  She seemed especially to shrink from his approach.  He consulted with the mother.

" She is either about to be very ill, or she has some oppressive weight upon her mind."

" Oh ! there can be no weight upon her mind ; and I hardly think that she is ill, Sir Edward.    In fact, for the last two days, I think she has been gaining in life and strength."

" Losing in both, *I* think, and during this very space."

" Oh, no, sir !    She has twice the energy and animation now that she had three days ago."

" Twice the restlessness, madam.    There is a strange, hurried wildness in her eyes, which alarms me ; and, if you perceive, she shrinks from *me* with something very like aversion."

" Dear me, Sir Edward, this is a most absurd notion ! — pardon me for saying so.    Olive is a creature of great sensibility — too much sensibility — and she's liable to sudden changes of mood."

" I have frequently heard you say, madam, that she was always very equable, cheerful, animated, full of natural gayety—"

" And so she always was—"

" Till I married her, madam !"

" Oh ! your marriage, I'm sure, had nothing to do with any change, Sir Edward."

" Yet it seems strange that it should take place at that very time."

" No, indeed, Sir Edward, you are quite mistaken there.    It was a full six or eight months before that, when she began to be less cheerful, and to look saddish and melancholy."

" Yet you say there's nothing on her mind ?"

" I'm sure I know of nothing !    I don't see what there should be.    Olive has always been tenderly nurtured, and the good fortune which has attended her, Sir Edward — the fact that she is the honored wife of a person of your wealth and nobleness—"

" Enough, madam, on that score. The only question now is, as to her ailment. What is her cause of suffering? Is it of the mind or body? Not that I care to know, Mrs. Masterton, except with the single desire to help and cure. I have listened to you with deference, but I can not resist the belief which assures me that she labors under some painful burden of the mind or heart—"

" The heart, indeed! No, no! all's right in that quarter. Olive is a loving, true, devoted wife."

" I confess, madam, I have not found her a loving one. I have no reason to doubt that she is a true one. But I am forced painfully to feel that I have never had from her any such proofs of sympathy as could persuade me of her love; and latterly, the pain of this conviction has been greatly increased by what seem to me evident signs of aversion."

" What an idea!"

" It is one, madam, which forces itself upon me, at all hours, and with no encouragement from me. I do not welcome it, madam!"

This was bitterly spoken.

" Oh! dismiss it, sir; it does Olive great injustice. She loves you, sir; yes—"

" I wish I could believe it; but do you know, madam, that I can not help the further thought that she exhibits a similar aversion to our child — her child and mine; that the little innocent wins nothing of a mother's love; that she puts him from her, if not with aversion, at least with indifference; never dandles him in her arms, never sings the mother's lullaby in his ears, never puts his little mouth to hers with a mother's heartfelt fondness."

" Lord bless me, Sir Edward, how blind you seem to have been! Why, I have seen her do it a thousand times — kiss him, and hug him, and dandle him, and sing to him, by the hour."

" You have been more fortunate than myself, madam. She has never done these things in my presence; and I fancy you must deceive yourself, at all events, in the frequency of these endearments. Seeing as I have done, madam — and I have been a keen because a grieving watcher — I infer the worst from this unnatural condition of mind and heart. I confess to you it moves me sometimes to the terrible thought that it is because Olive Berke-ley loathes the father, she denies her love to the child — she loathes him as loathing me ; or, if not this—"

"Oh, Sir Edward, I am astonished at you! It is really too monstrous! How can you, sir—"

"Hear me, madam. There is but one other alternative; and that is—"

"What, sir, what?" finding that he hesitated.

"Another suspicion, scarcely less terrible"—and here his voice sank into a whisper—"that my wife is on the verge of insanity!"

The mother began to cry aloud, when he seized her wrist with an iron gripe :—

"Not a word, madam, for your life! Not a whisper of *this* to mortal! It is in *your* ears only that I breathe it. To suffer *her* to hear either of these terrible conjectures of mine, would be fatal — would be her death, madam — her death!"

"O my God! Oh, Sir Edward, these are most horrible suspi-cions!"

"Horrible, madam! Ay, hell is at the core of either — hell! hell! Enough, madam : be silent! No officiousness now. I *com-mand* that you forbear my wife. I shall send to town for a phy-sician. Doctor Lining is said to be a man of skill, though God knows I look for little succor at any hands!"

10*

## CHAPTER XXIV.

### ESPIONAGE OF THE BROKEN HEART.

"Bring me the joy in secret — let me drink
The little lonely rapture that earth yields me,
Where none can see! Oh! thousand times more precious
As secret! none can envy me the store,
The little store of love, which makes the substance
Of any life for broken hearts like mine!"

THE despatch was prepared and sent off for Doctor Lining; and
the brave cassique, suffering but strong, hurried out again to his
workmen — and grasped their tools, and smote, and hewed, and
sawed, and planed, to the surprise of all — and as all, no doubt,
thought, in a fond pursuit of happiness! Ah, that pursuit of happiness! Certainly, if that had been his object, he has pursued it
with shut eyes. And what sort of happiness, for herself or daughter, has the Honorable Mrs. Masterton aimed at? And poor
Olive, she had pursued nothing: she had only *been* pursued, and
surely not by Happiness!

With evening, Doctor Lining came. The cassique's carriage
had met him at the landing, and brought him on, post-haste. He
was an excellent gentleman, knowing his profession thoroughly as
it was at that day known. He was naturally intelligent, and well
read — a fair sample of the average home-education of professional
people. Of his skill, nothing need be said here. Learning is one
thing, skill another; and medicine, like religion, poetry, and most
of the liberal arts and professions, demands a special gift from
Heaven.

Olive had retired when the doctor came. The mother presided
at the supper-table. But nothing was said of Olive's case. The
cassique very prudently resolved that Lining was not to appear as
a physician; only as a friend, about to revisit the mother-country,

and seeking the cassique simply to receive his commissions. Such was the pious fraud as agreed upon between them.

That night, when the Honorable Mrs. Masterton had retired, the cassique and the doctor conferred together in the library. Colonel Berkeley — or, as the courtesy of the country styled him, because of his cassiqueship, Sir Edward — was one of those downright, direct, resolute sort of men, who allowed himself no circuitous processes in his objects. Heedless of the pain, he laid his own and the case of Olive fully before the physician.

"I do not deceive myself, Doctor Lining, and must not deceive you, in respect to the condition of my wife. I regard her as in danger of becoming a lunatic."

"Good God! I hope not. What are your reasons for this fear?"

Berkeley made a full report of all the suspicious circumstances.

"She does not nurse her child?"

"No, sir: her health affected her milk; and, by the advice of Arbuthnot, we employed a healthy wet-nurse, and she has been relieved of this duty. No evil consequences have happened to the child."

"The necessity, however, was an unfortunate one. The maternal duty might have been a means, and — but go on, sir: I would first hear your particulars. We can think over them afterward."

"It is perhaps necessary, doctor, that I should go into details that do not seem immediately to bear upon the case. But, I am uneasy in respect to this very point, because doubtful of the cause of my wife's sufferings; and one way to mislead a physician is to suppress facts which may be important."

The doctor nodded affirmatively.

"It becomes neeessary, then, that I should reveal a small family history, beginning with my first acquaintance and marriage with Miss Masterton."

"If *you* think it necessary," said Lining.

"Surely: on no other account. I saw Miss Masterton, then a young lady, after my return from the continent. Our families had been intimate, and I had seen her in childhood, but not to remark her particularly. When I came back from the continent, she was a blooming girl of eighteen. I was charmed with her manners, her person, her intelligence. I sought her, saw her frequently, and my visits and attentions were encouraged by her mother. Olive herself was reserved toward me. At first, she received me with frank and cordial welcome; with pleasure, as I fancied; but, as my attentions increased, she became shy. I persevered, however; and, to make a long story as short as possible, my proposals were made, through her mother, and, after some delay, were accepted. Some further delays, urged by herself, as I have reason to believe, prevented our immediate marriage. That finally took place; and, after the birth of our son, we removed to Carolina."

"There is nothing in all this, Colonel Berkeley."

"No, sir: but I soon discovered that my wife, though submissive, was not genial; though gentle, not fond; not, seemingly, susceptible of fondness; reluctant in my presence; silent; finally sad; and, with every day, growing more and more taciturn, more fond of solitude, more reluctant to respond to me in any way. I was not harsh, not imperative; never said a hasty word to her; tried to soothe and conciliate; strove to please. I was always met with coldness — a measured coldness — which was sadness also — and which has recently become, as it seems to me, aversion."

"That is a strong word! May you not deceive yourself?"

"No, sir! I have weighed all the facts with the utmost caution and deliberation. That she is wretched, I see; that she makes me wretched, I know! That she grows more wretched, more estranged daily, more insensible to my cares, more listless, heedless, indifferent in everything, is apparent to every eye. When I first knew her, she was plump and round; she is now reduced to a skeleton. She was young, bright, blooming, when I first came from the continent; she has lost bloom, and flesh, and brightness, almost from the moment of our marriage. Once she was cheerful; now she wears the look of one to whom life can offer nothing; who has no hope. Appetite, spirits, animation, all are gone. Latterly, from being utterly passive — sad, to such indifference, that I verily believe had I smitten her, she would never have lifted hand to protect her face — nay, would have smiled gently at the infliction — now, she has become restless, wandering, capricious; easily startled, nervous; with a restless light in her eyes, which is painful to behold — to me the most startling of the signs that trouble me."

And so he proceeded, till he had concluded the details which he conceived important; not omitting that statement — in which he differed with Mrs. Masterton — that Olive appeared entirely regardless of her child, and gave it no proofs of her affection.

"That, certainly, is a most singular circumstance. But I will not say anything of the case, colonel, till I have seen the patient. It is understood that I am not to be known as her physician. She must simply be watched and studied. I will devote myself to that to-morrow."

"It may require several days, doctor."

"Fortunately, the town is just now so healthy, that I can spare the necessary time.

The conversation flagged, even over a bottle of Madeira, and the parties then retired for the night.

With morning, began the watch and study. Olive little knew the *surveillance* to which she was to be subjected. She had arisen as usual. Her face, air, manner, tones, all exhibited the aspects which we have already reported as characteristic of the three preceding days. There was the same flushed impulse, the same restlessness, caprice, incertitude; the same wild, spiritual brightness of eye; and certainly a great increase of general excitement. But the physician, introduced as Mr. Lining, a friend of her husband, about to revisit Europe, did not occasion any emotion after the first introduction. She scarcely seemed to heed him. And this afforded the doctor a good opportunity for studying her. He did so with a silent inquisitiveness which she had no reason to suspect. The cassique contrived frequent occasions for him.

You must see our boy, Lining! My Lord John will expect you to make a full report. Bring in 'Young Harry.'"

At the words, the wife started, and looked about her wildly.

"Young Harry, with his cuisses on!" continued the cassique, in the proud tones of the father. "He is a brave-looking fellow, is he not? See what a brow he has! From the first, he looked like a dear brother whom I lost — a wild, manly, noble fellow — and he bears his name; and every day seems to strengthen the likeness. I shall be satisfied if he grow like Harry Berkeley."

A deep sigh closed the speech, but it issued from the lips of Olive Berkeley. Every eye was turned toward her. She lay back in her chair. Her own eyes were shut. She had fainted.

The cassique darted to her, and raised her in his arms tenderly. The mother was officious, till pushed away by the doctor. He sprinkled some water upon the face of the unconscious woman — called for hartshorn, which was luckily at hand, and soon witnessed her revival.

"Take her now to her chamber."

When mother and daughter were withdrawn, and the cassique and physician remained alone, the latter said musingly —

"Of what were we speaking, colonel?"

"I know not! I have forgotten everything. Her suffering, doctor, her most inscrutable suffering, takes from me all power of thought and observation."

"Nay, not so bad as that. This fainting-fit is probably not a bad symptom. It would be terrible were she without emotion; and that was what I feared from your statement. But what *were* we talking about?"

The cassique did not answer. Lining resumed:—

"The child — ah! yes; and the name. You have a brother named Harry, Sir Edward?"

"*Had*, doctor."

"Ah!"

"A noble fellow — bold, brave, daring, full of soul and spirit; but the waves are over him."

"Ah! he was lost! How long, may I ask, since the event?"

"We know not. He was nearly three years gone from England when I was on the continent. He had a passion for the sea; became captain of a West Indiaman; afterward took out a private commission against the French and Spaniards, and made so many captures, that he came to own a privateer. She was lost, somewhere along the Spanish main. This must have been about the time of my return from the continent. We received advices, soon after the event, which left no doubt of his fate."

The doctor mused, but made no further inquiries on this head. Scarcely had the dialogue ceased between them, when, to the surprise of all, Olive reappeared, followed closely by her mother."

"She *would* come, sir."

Olive interrupted the mother with a smile, and with such seeming composure and strength as to increase the general surprise.

"I felt so much ashamed of my temporary weakness, and so much better, that I resolved not to play the invalid."

The husband smiled; the doctor mused. The latter saw, what the former did not—so much was he pleased with the unwonted event, a smile from Olive—that her presence, smile, and speech, were due to an extreme effort—a will rising into utmost earnestness, in obedience to some exigent motive.

And what was that motive? "*Quien sabe?*" says the Spaniard. What the cassique said need not be repeated; the doctor said nothing, but meditated much.

And throughout the day, Olive continued to sustain herself, in a somewhat more cheerful strain than usual, but by what the doctor rightly conceived to be an extraordinary effort of will. There was excitement as before; great unrest; frequent uneasiness; a nervous sensibility to sounds, especially of the human voice; and an anxiety that prompted a frequent looking around her, as if for some expected approach. And there was now to be seen occasionally a sudden crimson flush over the marble whiteness of the cheeks, which passed away, as with a flicker, almost the moment it appeared. And there was still a glazed fixedness of the eye, which was intensely and spiritually bright.

Lining noted all these symptoms. He had every opportunity. The cassique devised as many methods ss possible for leaving her in his presence. He showed him over the whole house, not excepting the chambers, and required her to assist.

"My uncle will inquire about everything, and you must be able to answer. I hope, when it is shown how easily I can transfer the comforts of an English to a Carolina home, to beguile him out here also, where he can properly fill the dignity of the palatinate. He will be our lord-palatine, if he will come out.— By-the-way, Olive, do let Lining see your collection of Indian curiosities."

They were shown.

"And now, Olive, can't you give Lining some music? Nay, for that matter, give *me* some. I have had none for a long season. The fact is, Lining, we have had such an infernal clangor of hammer and saw, that music would have been only so many 'sweet bells, jangled, harsh, and out of tune,' enveloped in the perpetual din! But now—what say you, Olive, my dear?"

And she rose passively, without a word, and went to the harpsichord, of which she had once been the mistress.

" Will you sing, Lady Berkeley ?" asked Lining.

" Excuse me, sir ; but I can not trust my voice to-day — scarcely my fingers."

The chords were struck : the hands swept the keys — slowly at first, then with rapidly-increasing fervor as the symphonies rose, following out the caprices and gradual swelling of the human pas- sion which made the burden of the piece. It might have been a battle-piece, though it expressed only the conflicts of one poor, suffering human heart.

Did she play from memory, or was it a *fantasia* of her own? None of the hearers knew; and, playing on, she said nothing; while the instrument, from a sad complaining — a merely plaintive sighing forth of a secret sorrow — rose to a wail, a wild burst and outbreak of a mortal agony, which at length set its prison restraints all at defiance.

And they could see the breast of the player heave in concert with the strain, while her head gradually uplifted, and her dilating eye seemed to rest upon a far corner of the ceiling — rapt, as it were, with some unexpected vision. She no longer watched the keys of the instrument. She no longer seemed conscious of the persons present. But, suddenly, the music changed; the notes fell ; the high, passionate tones gave way to vague, faint, faltering pulsations, rather than beats, varied with occasional *capriccios*, in which a mocking spirit seemed to be at conflict with a broken one : and so the strain fell — no longer gush, and burst, and wild flight of music, but its tear, its sigh, its broken, faltering accent, in which you read the history of defeated love, departed hope, the wreck of a beautiful dream of stars and flowers, and the thick night closing over all ! Then suddenly it stopped, and nothing was heard but a low, ringing echo through the apartment, as if the escaped soul only lingered, moaning ere it went, from the once-beloved abode !

And there was a strange thrill that passed over the frames of the two strong men. They felt the unnatural power of the strain. Was it simply art ? Was it not rather the inspiration of a pas- sionate wo, which gladly seizes upon the stricken one, as the only mode of expression and relief?

And Olive — her brow is still uplifted. Her eye rests still upon the remote ceiling. Her fingers fall suddenly with weight upon the keys, and the crash which follows startles her out of her fancies. Her eyes sink down. She sees the cassique and the doctor gazing wistfully upon her; and, with a slight flush upon her cheek, she rises, bows, and leaves the room.

"It is a curious case, colonel, and not to be judged rashly. We must see all that we can, yet our watch must be unsuspected. You must warn her mother on this point."

Of course, the scrutiny was difficult, but it was pursued with industry, and was sufficiently cautious. Olive did not seem suspicious, but she was shy; and, though her general deportment continued pretty much the same throughout the day, as we have already described it, she seemed to be somewhat more than usually inclined to obey her mother's injunction "to make an effort." Whether it was because of the presence of a visiter, it was evident that she was disposed "to try," and behave with a closer regard to conventional requisitions. There was nothing remarkable in her conduct; only in her appearance, the tones of her voice, expression of her eye, and the frequent wanderings of her thought, as exhibited in her general manner.

So dinner passed.

In the afternoon, Olive had disappeared. The nurse had taken out the child, "Young Harry," into the great avenue of oaks of which we have already spoken; and, whether she knew the fact or not, thither Olive had also gone. Her movements were conducted slyly. She had left the gentlemen, as she thought, too deeply engaged in the library to be conscious of her absence. So, too, she believed her mother to be in her chamber, when, slipping out of the back door, she stole off to the thicket.

But they were all on the alert.

It was in the deepest and shadiest part of the grove, that, watching from a thick covert, the Honorable Mrs. Masterton beheld the young mother busied with the child. She had taken him from the nurse, who had wandered a few hundred yards farther on. Olive tossed the child in her arms, sat with him upon the ground, kissed him repeatedly, and hung over his shiny round face with the deepest interest, perusing every line and feature. And between the kisses and this study, big tears fell from her eyes upon the blooming, red cheeks of the infant, while broken murmurs — "My Harry! my Harry!" escaped her unconscious lips.

Mrs. Masterton, as she saw this, could not help saying, very audibly —

"How I wish Sir Edward could only see this!"

A low voice behind her said:—

"Hush, madam!—not a word! He *does* see! Now, madam, steal away, as I shall do, and do not, for the world, suffer yourself to be seen."

The cassique, accompanied by the physician, stole back to the house, with a heart even lighter than his steps. He was disabused at least of one of his most cruel apprehensions. The doctor encouraged him.

"She weeps; she loves the child; has emotions; is not indifferent. But it is evident that these joys of the mother are sought only in secrecy. There is some secret anxiety—there is some suspicion; and this argues—"

"A want of sympathy with those about her!" answered the cassique, and in rather gloomy tones, completing the sentence which Lining seemed reluctant to finish.

"Precisely so!"

"But, whether the discovery of the cause of this will enable us to do anything by which to relieve her mind from this tension?—"

"If she could be disabused of the cause of suspicion—"

"Yes, and that depends upon a knowledge of the suspicion itself."

"You must beware how you question her, Colonel Berkeley."

"Yes!—you are right. That should never be done by me. It would be something worse than bad policy. It would be an abuse of the relationship between us. The confidence of man and wife must be involuntary. To attempt to force it, on his part, would be a base and unmanly despotism. That it is not *given* here, Doctor Lining, is the most humiliating annoyance which I have been called on to bear. I must endure it as I may!"

"Time, my dear colonel, is the best medicine. Give her that, and she will do you justice. What sort of woman is her mother, and how can she aid you?"

The cassique answered with a gravity and sternness that looked a little like ferocity. Laying his hand on the wrist of Lining, he said:—

"She is a fool, sir, with an empty head and a cold, selfish heart!

She is, I fancy, at the bottom of all this mischief; but in what way
I can not conceive. I have had to check her in a frequent attempt to exercise an authority in my house, and in regard to my
wife, which is at variance with mine. I have had also to warn
her in regard to a system of annoyance, practised on Olive, since
she has been in this condition; the silly mother having no real
conception of the daughter's danger, and perhaps contributing to
it all the while by the perpetual prying, and questioning, and
counselling, of a very restless and ridiculous tongue. She is one
of those fools of society with whom hearts are nothing; who would
sacrifice all the best sympathies — ay, virtues — to the empty
pomps and miserable exhibitions of social vanity, and what is called
' high life' ! You know the animal as it exists in English society :
she is one of its most absurd specimens."

When the unconscious Olive came in from her ramble, her
mother was safely in her chamber, and the gentlemen still con-
versing in the library. She met them at supper, where nothing
remarkable occurred ; Lining still keeping a vigilant watch, while
Berkeley was at pains to maintain the deception which proclaimed
the former to be a simple guest, on his return to Europe.

The next day the doctor took his departure. He encouraged
the cassique to hope everything from time. He could do no
more. He could only counsel equal forbearance and solicitude.
The symptoms of Olive, that day, were the same. They seemed
to increase after the doctor left, but not in any degree to produce
apprehension. It was a sufficient source of anxiety to the cassique that they continued. At all events, something had been
gained. He had seen her caressing " Young Harry" as only a
loving mother could caress ; and he was so far satisfied.

# CHAPTER XXV.

### LURID GLEAMS THROUGH THE DARK.

'There is a something haunts me, most like madness,
  As reason comprehends it.  But the presence
  Is not the less a presence to the spirit,
  As it 'scapes human touch!  The immortal vision
  Makes itself evident to the immortal nature,
  When the coarse fingers stiffen into palsy,
  And can grasp nothing!"

BUT, that night!

Alas for her, the suffering woman, the victim to a false system
and a falser heart!  Alas for him, the brave, noble man, lied to,
and defrauded of his peace and hope — of all that is precious to
the soul and sympathies — by the same base, pernicious system,
the same false, vain, worthless agency!  Alas for the world which
never sets out honestly in the pursuit of happiness; which only
seeks for shams; which ignores the affections, in behalf of the
vanities; and sacrifices the soul, that was designed for heaven, in
the chase after things of earth — and oh, so earthy!  Alas! alas!
we may well wring hands, and weep over these terrible sacrifices,
made daily, ay, hourly, on the altars of false gods — frogs, and
toads, and apes, and monkeys — baser things even than ever were
those set up by African and Egyptian!

Lining gone, and the cassique alone, he busied himself, as usual,
with his workmen during the day, and at night gave himself up to
solitary reading and reflection in the library.  His family gave
him no succor, no companionship.  Those blissful evenings of
which he had dreamed, of rural happiness and sweet content in
the primitive forest; cheered with the smiles and songs of love;
a calm of heaven over the household, and a brooding peace, like a
dove in its happy cote, sitting beside his hearth and making it

glad with serenest joys — these were dreams which he no longer hoped to realize.    His wife evidently shrank from his companionship.    She was never at ease when alone with him.    She would sing if he required it, but not speak ; would answer meekly to his questions and demands — listen with seemingly attentive ear to all he said — but make no responsive remark.    She had no voice echoing to that frank one, speaking from his heart, which had ever striven, but how vainly, to find the answering chord in hers !

Yes, he knew that she could speak — well, gracefully, thoughtfully, and with equal truth of sentiment and sweetness of expression.    He knew that she had taste and fancy, which are in themselves always suggestive.    He knew that, in addition to a good natural intellect, she had gathered stores from books, which, if her mind were allowed free play, would make her a charming companion.    He remembered that she was so considered by all ere she became his wife ; and was painfully reminded by this fact that he, too, had found her so, in the days of his first intimacy with her, and before any suspicion was entertained that he sought her for his wife.    The cruel inference forced itself upon him irresistibly — "It is I who have changed her thus !"

Yet how had he changed her ?    Not, surely, by harshness of usage ; not by lack of sympathy ; not because of any failure of his own heart to bring out the secrets of hers.    He had no self-reproaches on this score.    He felt that he had always been gentle, soothing, solicitously heedful of her needs, her possible wishes, her happiness and comfort.    The further conclusion was inevitable :—

"It is only because of a lack of sympathy with me.    She never loved me.    She must have loved another ! .... But why did she consent to become my wife ?"

Here, thought brought him again to the probable conclusion :—

"It was submission to a mother's will.    That cunning, cold, selfish, calculating woman has done it all !    And there is no remedy !    God !    what a prospect lies before us both !    What a waste of life, of affections, of soul, and thought, and feeling ! — a gloomy waste, over which we must travel together, without speech or hearing between us — all in silence ; not a flower by the wayside ; not a fountain in the desert ; nothing to refresh — death in the privation through which we live, and death the final goal !    And she will die !    she will die !    Whatever this secret struggle in her

soul, and however caused, she can not endure it long!   She will
die !"

Such were his musings in the library till the deep hours of midnight closed in upon him.   Then, with a sense of weariness rather
than sleep, he retired to his chamber.

It was hers also.

The simple world in which our cassique lived had not yet
reached that degree of graceful domesticity which allows husband
and wife separate apartments ; and, with gentle footsteps, Colonel
Berkeley proceeded to Olive's chamber without waking a single
echo.

A dim light was burning in the chimney-place as he entered.
He approached the couch where she was sleeping.   She slept, but
not profoundly ; at least, she showed herself restless.   Her arms
were occasionally tossed about her head, and sighs and faintly-
murmured accents escaped her lips.   He watched her for awhile,
then undressed himself quietly, and with the most cautious movement, so as not to disturb her repose, laid himself down beside
her.   But not to sleep.

An hour passes ; her sleep seems to deepen, but she is even
more restless than before.   He hears the occasional murmur from
her lips, accompanied sometimes by a wild movement of her hand.
At lengh he distinguishes her broken syllables.

No ! no ! do not, dear mother — do not !   I pray you, no more
— no more of this !"

This was all.   What could it mean ?   What did that mother
propose to do, which was so painful to her child ?

The cassique closes his eyes.   He would not hear.   At least,
he will not listen.   But the accents reach him still, more earnestly
expressed, with keener feeling, and a still sadder pleading.   They
are rendered distinct now by reason of their increasing intensity :

" You will kill me, mother !   I do not believe it !   I tell you
he lives ; and I must live for him — for him only !   I can never
be another's.   I will die first !"

A cold sweat covered the brow of the cassique.   He raised
himself on one arm.   He could not help but listen now.   The
matter was too full of significance, as involving his own peace
quite as much as hers :—

" Tell me nothing of these things, mother.   Why should they affect us? To be sure, we are poor. But why should you make me poorer? Why rob me of that faith which makes me smile at poverty? I care for nothing beyond. His wealth is nothing in my sight. Society!—But what to me is the crowd and noise which you call 'society'? Peace, rather—let me be at peace, dear mother, if you would not drive me mad!"

The cassique groaned audibly; but the sound did not disturb the sleeper. Her voice became freer—her language more impressive:—

"Well, he is dead! You have rung it in my ears so often, that the sense deadens. I do not see now so much meaning in what you tell me. He is dead—dead—dead! In the deep sea— wrecked, drowned; and I shall never be his wife—shall never see him more! Well, you see I understand it all! You need not tell me that again. I can say it to myself, and it does not pain me. But it sounds horribly from your lips. It makes you look hateful in my sight. Don't you say it again, mother—do you hear?—if you would not have me hate you! *I* will say it for you. He is dead—Harry is dead—and I shall never be his wife! There! are you satisfied? . . . .

"But"—after a short pause—"is that any reason why you should force me to be the wife of another? Is there any sense in that? Let him die, too; tell *him* to drown! Yes, let us both die and drown in the deep sea! It's just as well we should. It can't be so dreadful, since *he* was drowned in it. And the song tells us the same thing. No, it can not be dreadful."

Here she sang, without effort, in the lowest but sweetest and clearest tones, the ballad from "The Tempest:"—

> " 'Full fathom five thy father lies,
>     Of his bones are coral made;
>    These are pearls that were his eyes:
>      Nothing of him that doth fade,
>    But doth suffer a sea change
>    Into something rich and strange!'

" Ah !——"

A deep sigh ended the ballad—a long-drawn sigh—and the lips closed for a space. There was silence for awhile in the chamber; but not for long. Her lips again began to murmur. Then there was a sort of cry, something between a laugh and sob, and she spoke out audibly :—

"Said I not it was all false? I knew it all the while. He is *not* dead! There was no drowning! He lives! He comes for me! I shall see him again! I shall be his wife — *his* wife — no other's! Ah, Harry, dear Harry, you are come! They told me you were dead, Harry — that you were dead and buried in the deep sea. But you are come at last. They shall never part us again!"

And she rose in the bed, in a sitting posture, threw out her arms, clasped the cassique about his neck, and their eyes met, and she stared fixedly into his, and, throwing herself upon his bosom, murmured fondly —

"Dear Harry, you are come at last!"

Her eyes were open wide, full — looking with dazed stare into those of her husband. But their sense was shut. At all events, the illusion was complete; and she suffered him to lay her back upon the pillow, which he did very gently; while, still looking into his eyes, or seeming to look, she murmured repeatedly :—

"You are come — you are come at last, my Harry! I knew that you would come!"

The cassique could bear it no longer. He rose, dressed himself deliberately, and went forth. She was again asleep — contentedly, it would seem — for her lips were closed : her murmurs for the time had ceased.

The unhappy husband had heard enough. There was no longer any mystery. His own thoughts had led him to a right conjecture; and her unconscious lips had confirmed it in the intensity of her dreams. Nature had compelled the utterance of those agonies of thought and feeling, in her sleep, which in her waking moments she would have died sooner than *he* should hear.

All was confirmed to him of despair. He walked the woods during the weary hours of that night. At morning he ordered his horse. He summoned the mother to the woods as soon as she had risen — led her to a deep part of the thicket, and, confronting her with a brow of too much sorrow for anger, he said to her :—

"Madam, you have betrayed your daughter to her ruin! You have deceived me to mine! You have been false to both! You assured me that there was no other preferred suitor to Olive Masterton. You solemnly affirmed her entire freedom from all ties; that she was heart-whole, until she had been sought by mine! And you knew that all this was false."

" False, Sir Edward ?"

" Ay, madam, false as hell ! Nay, madam, do not assume that look of virtuous indignation. It does not suit you to wear it ! It would become me better, whom you have so terribly deceived, but that indignation is too feeble a sentiment to him who has begun the lesson of despair. You have crushed that poor child's heart, madam ; you have trampled upon mine ! She will die, and you will have murdered her ! She has death now in her heart ! Fortunate only, thrice fortunate, if madness shall so usurp the functions of the brain as to make her insensible to the agonies of a prolonged dying !"

" Really, Sir Edward, these are monstrous charges. I should almost doubt your own sanity. Pray, sir, what are your discoveries, that you venture to charge such heinous crimes to my account ?"

" Ask your own conscience, madam ! You assured me of Olive's freedom !"

" Well, she was free ! There was a person, with whom she had formed some childish engagements ; but he died before you returned from the continent. I think, sir, you will admit that the tie, slight as it was, between them, was fully broken by that event."

" Even that, madam, I am not prepared to admit. It would have made some difference to me, at least, to have known the fact. This you withheld from me. Nay, madam, more : you denied that her heart had ever been committed."

" Well, sir, even in that I see no reason why you should question my truth. A childish entanglement, such as Olive's, does not necessarily imply the committal of the heart."

" Perhaps not necessarily, perhaps not at all, in that convention in which you have had *your* training, madam."

" My training, sir ! And what should be my training ? My family, Sir Edward Berkeley, I take leave to say, is quite as old, and as fortunate in its connections and society, as were ever those of the houses of Berkeley and Craven."

" Perhaps so, madam ; it is a subject upon which I do not care to waste a syllable. Enough that you assured me solemnly that your daughter had committed her affections neither in fact nor in language ; that she was totally free, and had always been so."

" I certainly never attached any importance to the childish en-

11

tanglement of which I have spoken; especially when it had been ruptured by the death of one of the parties—"

" Stay, madam.   This engagement, which you describe as child-ish, had continued up to the moment when I addressed your daughter.   She was then eighteen—an age when we are apt to suspect that the affections may be quite as tenacious of their ob-ject as they are fond and warm in their conception of it.   You may remember, madam, that I was especially anxious on this point, and shaped my questions to you emphatically in respect to *any* committal whatsoever of your daughter's heart."

" So you did, Sir Edward," the lady answered, querulously; " but these are questions of course with all young men—all of whom have a notion that if they have not been a first object in a girl's fancy, they are robbed of some of their natural rights.   But people of experience know the absurdity of such a notion; and know that girls rarely marry the persons whom they happen to fancy in their teens.   It is the fancy only, not the affections, that makes their prepossession; and it is for this reason that thought-ful parents are required to be so vigilant in giving the proper guidance to their daughters in all affairs of the heart.   It should be enough, Sir Edward, for *you*, that I took proper heed to Olive; seeing that she did not fling herself away upon a worthless person, and that she was provided with one of whom the whole world of English society had but one opinion.   I have no reason to regret the choice I made for Olive."

" Better, madam, a thousand times, that you had suffered her to make her own choice!   Your appeal to my vanity does not lessen one atom the agony you have forced into my heart.   But tell me, madam, who was the person with whom Olive had this *childish* entanglement?"

" You do not know that, then?" she exclaimed, as inadvertently as exultingly.   " Then you will permit me to be silent, Sir Ed-ward.   You will never hear it from me!"

" Mrs. Masterton, when I was so urgent with you touching any previous engagement or committal of Olive, I had a serious rea-son for it.   Rumors had reached my ears that there *had* been an engagement—that one was actually existing then—between her and one whom I loved as dearly as I could have loved any wo-man upon earth!   That was my poor brother Harry.   His death would have made no difference in my conduct in respect to one whom I should have conceived to be his widow! She would have been sacred to me. I should have been satisfied, in such a case, to stand in relation with her as a most loving and faithful brother —nothing more! I was therefore urgent with you on this point. And this was the very point upon which you deceived me. Never did human being speak more confidently than yourself. Never were asseverations made with more solemnity. I hinted at my brother's intimacy with the family. You spoke of him as one little known, who had not been seen for long seasons; who had taken but little interest in your family, and scarcely knew anything of Olive."

" You put it too strongly, Sir Edward."

" God be my witness, if I say one word too much! On this point, madam, I was very urgent. The mere doubt, arising from the simplest rumor, was enough for me. Charmed as I was with Olive, had I not received your assurances to the contrary, I had foregone all my own pretensions. I should then have honored her as my brother's betrothed—as his wife—as a dear sister, who should have had my life if she desired it, but never a single avowal which would have brought pain to her bosom. If you have deceived me on this subject, as you have on others, Mrs. Masterton, then may God forgive you—I can not! I will not curse, will not spurn you. You are a woman, but—and even now you can somewhat relieve me. Say, madam, tell me, for mercy's sake—tell me that my brother had no interest in the heart of Olive Masterton!"

The cold, selfish, high-bred woman did not scruple at a lie.

" As God hears me, Sir Edward, Harry Berkeley was not the person!"

" Yet his name was Harry, too?"

" Yes, his name was Harry, too!"

" A singular coincidence!" replied the cassique; then added: " May God forgive you your other offences, madam, only as you have spoken truth in this matter! You have, at all events, taken one sting of agony from my soul!"

He turned away abruptly as he said these words, and hurried to the covert where his horse awaited him—leaped upon him, and disappeared for several hours. As he went from sight, the Honorable Mrs. Masterton drew a deep sigh, as of relief. She had gone through a severe passage; but her stubborn, rigid nature never shrunk from the pressure put upon it.

"How could he have found it out?" she demanded of herself. "Yet how fortunate he did not find out the whole! He shall never hear it from me that Harry Berkeley, his own brother, was in truth his rival! And I must see that Olive makes him no wiser. She is fool enough to tell everything!"

And she chuckled aloud with the grateful conviction that she had been able to lie successfully.

But her day was not yet ended. At breakfast, when the cassique did not appear, Olive asked —

"Where is he?"

"Rode off an hour ago, very fast — I suspect to the city."

"He is gone for the day, then?"

"I suppose so."

"Ah!" — and the exclamation was a sigh of relief.

The servant was in waiting, and no more was said at the moment. But when the mother retired to her own apartment, Olive suddenly made her appearance. Her eyes were wild with light; her cheeks were slightly flushed; her whole appearance indicated increase of excitement.

The mother was struck with some alarm. She remembered what the cassique had said: "She will die! Happy if madness do but usurp the functions of the brain, so as to relieve her from the long consciousness of dying!"

"Why, what's the matter, Olive?"

The young wife looked about her suspiciously, closed the door, and locked it; then said, approaching her mother with great eagerness, while her eye glittered almost fiercely :—

"He is *not* dead! He lives — Harry Berkeley! — he lives! He has spoken with me. I have seen him face to face!"

"You dream, Olive! What can you mean? The thing is ridiculous. The man you speak of has been dead, I tell you, more than eighteen months."

"And I tell you, mother, that he is not dead! He lives. You have deceived me — betrayed me — oh, how dreadfully betrayed me! O mother, mother! how could you wrong me so?"

The mother was almost stupefied by the successive assaults

upon her—doubly bewildered, as she had been so solemnly
warned by the cassique in what manner she spoke to Olive, lest
she should drive her to madness. And this was madness! Of
Harry Berkeley's death by sea, Mrs. Masterton, to do her justice,
had no sort of question. But, uncertain what to say, lest she
should increase the mental infirmities of her daughter, the wise
woman of good society was yet compelled to say something, however little to the purpose.

"I betray you, Olive? I deceive you? Was ever so cruel a
charge brought against a mother; and a mother—I am proud to
say it—who has done everything for her child?"

"Yes, indeed, you have done for me! What made you tell me
such a falsehood? Who told you that Harry was drowned?
Where did you get that letter?"

"From Ivison. He wrote it. He knew the facts. He was
one of the survivors in the long-boat. He saw the pinnace go
down, with all in her."

"He lied to you, mother! The pinnace did *not* go down—
I'm sure of it. Harry escaped to the shore. I know it now!
Hark you!"—and she bent forward, and whispered—"it is a
secret yet—a secret—and we must study what to do with it.
But Harry *is* alive! I have seen and spoken with him, nightly,
the last five nights!"

"Seen—spoken with him, Olive! And where, pray?"

"In my chamber! He comes and wakens me out of my sleep;
he sits by me, and talks to me, and wraps me in his arms so
fondly! Oh, yes, he loves me as much as ever, though he reproaches me that I have been false to him. But I told him all.
I laid the blame on you; told him how you had sworn to me that
he was lost in the deep sea; that the great ocean had gone over
him; that I should never be his wife—that I should never see
him more. Then he said to me, as I have so often said to myself,
'But why should you, Olive Masterton, become the wife of another?' Then I answered him—yes, I answered out, mother—
though 'twas all said in a whisper, for shame—shame for *you*,
mother—then I answered: 'It was for the cassique's gold, Harry!
I was bought and sold, like an African from the Gold-coast, though
they did not call it selling—they only called it marriage!' I told
him it really was not marriage—only a sham; and that, in my

heart, I had only one husband, and that was himself! And he forgave me, mother, and took me in his arms, and said I was in truth his wife, and the other marriage was all a sham!"

"My child, you have been dreaming. This is nothing but a dream."

"Mother, I say I saw him face to face, as close as your face is now to mine! He was in the bed with me! He took me in his arms, and laid me down upon the pillow; and he had been talking with me long before. I knew that I was not dreaming. I was broad awake. It was like no dream! It was all a reality. Yes, mother, my true husband, Harry, is alive!"

We may readily conceive what were the arguments used by the mother to persuade her that she dreamed.

"How could he be here, Olive? how get into your chamber? The cassique was here—has slept with you every night. Nobody else could enter your chamber. If Harry Berkeley were living, he would never dare to do so."

"Harry Berkeley would do everything, mother, to protect his wife."

"But you are *not* his wife, Olive! He might love you, and you love him; but he has no lawful right in you. You are married to his brother; you are the lawful wife of the cassique; and, if Harry Berkeley were living, he would know that, and would know that it would ruin you for ever were he to come into your chamber. Only think, Olive, if Harry were living, and the brothers were to meet—do you not see that they would fight? They would take each other by the throat; they would draw deadly weapons upon each other; and there would be murder; one or both of them would be slain!"

"O my God, mother! what do you tell me? Yet it is true! They would butcher each other; and you, mother, would be the cause of it all! Can it be possible that I have only been dreaming? And everything was so real, so actual, and so sweet! My poor head, how it aches with thinking!"

"You must go to bed—must lie down, my child, and try to get some rest. And remember, all the while, what a dreadful thing it would be for the cassique even to guess that you had loved his brother, and he you!"

"What! did you not tell him, mother? You promised me you would."

" Yes, but I was not such a fool! What was the use, my child, when we knew that Harry was dead?"

" I can not think him dead. I feel him all around me. I seem to breathe the same air with him; I seem to hear his voice at moments; and, sometimes, to catch the bright flash of his great blue eyes. Oh, no! it is impossible to think him dead. You have made me doubt something, but not that he is living still."

" You must lie down, my child, and try to sleep. I will give you some drops to compose your nerves. But not a word of this dreaming to the cassique! Forget these fancies. They are mere delusions of the brain. You have been strangely excited for the last few days."

" Yes, I will lie down. I feel sure he will come to me again, mother, if I lie down."

" That should prove that you only dream these things, Olive. If he comes now, it will be in spirit only."

" His spirit! Oh, if it be so, I do not fear! The spirit of Harry Berkeley shall be more welcome to Olive Masterton than any living man. I will lie down in *your* bed, mother: I do not wish to see the cassique again."

" But he is your husband, my child."

" Oh, mother, I feel that I am the wife of Harry Berkeley only!"

The mother led her off to a couch, and gave her a composing draught, and watched her while she seemed to sleep. But she had only shut her eyes upon the daylight, in the fond hope of recalling the vision of the night.

# CHAPTER XXVI.

### THE WHITE BIRD.

—————— " Now shall we see,
That, in this fair simplicity, there lies
Some subtle policy.   So spiders weave
Their silken snares, that spread about unseen,
Take the unwitting victim to his fate." — OLD PLAY.

SUCH was the condition of things, at the barony, when Harry
Calvert made his night-ride to the precinct, in company with
Gowdey.   It was the night of the day when the cassique had
brought her offences home to the Honorable Mrs. Masterton;
when Olive's reproaches — faint and few as reproaches, terrible
thrusts as the simple utterances of a wo-stricken heart — had smitten heavily, though almost with as little profit as her lord's, upon
the rocky nature of the world-wise mother.   She was stunned,
rather than subdued or convinced.

Had her loving purposes, on her child's behalf, been really so
mischievous in result?   How should *she* think so?   Surely, but
for the peculiar perversity of that child's nature, they must have
been productive of the very best sort of human happiness — according to *her* definition of the word, which comprised little beyond
ample fortune, and a fine social establishment in the *beau monde*.

But, leaving her to work out the worrying problem as she may
— leaving her lovely victim to the hallucinations in which lay at
once her danger and her delight — let us follow the steps of the
cassique.

His policy is to stifle the pangs of heart in the employments
of his head.   He must work down the demon of Unrest and
Thought! and Will must subjugate Sensibility.   With the dawn
he had gone forth.   The first gleams of sunshine found him busy,

with a score of workmen around him, and his own hands grasping square and rule.

He was thus employed when almost surprised by the embassage of the Indians, whose camp-fire had been discovered by Gowdey the night before, as described in a previous chapter.

An embassage of the red men is no ordinary affair. They have a great sense of their dignity. The cassique knew enough of the character to recognise the claims of its vanity. He was desirous of conciliating the race. He had philanthropic purposes, to lift, and ennoble, and civilize it — if he could. He had dedicated no small sums of money to this purpose, some thought, and much patient painstaking. He had laid in stores of such commodities as the red men most desired. These were to be used as presents. He had already given much: he was prepared to give more. But, first, he must receive them in such state as became his dignity and their own; the latter consideration by far the most important, and necessarily involving due regard to the former.

He hurried back to the dwelling the moment he was apprized, by a runner, of the approach of the cassique — the Micco Cussoboe — the great chief of the Kiawahs — and hastily put on the uniform of a British colonel. Clothed in scarlet, with rich facings, *chapeau bras* on his head, and long-sword by his side, he too was a chief, and he came forth properly accoutred for the reception of his brother-noble.

But we have no intention of making a scene of it. It will help us nothing in our narrative. The reader must fancy, for himself, the reserved airs of the red man and his followers; the lofty carriage, the imposing manner, the grand speeches — which Gowdey helped to translate — and the gifts of strouds, blankets, bells, beads, knives, and hatchets, with which the white cassique of Kiawah proceeded to gratify, at the close of the orations, the cupidity of his copper-colored namesake and visiter. The belts of wampum, symbols of treaty, amity, and commerce, were interchanged, with a state and grace becoming higher potentates.

The white cassique, with proper policy, humored the red one to the top of his bent. He could have smiled many times during the proceedings, but his heart was too full of its own peculiar cares.

That he should go through the scene at all, having his own agonies to endure all the while, was no small proof of his strength

11*

of soul, and the brave will which he brought to bear upon, and crush down, the keen, sharp, incessant struggle of his sensibilities.

But the embassage was not one simply of courtesy. It contemplated a special business, for which there had been a previous understanding between the parties. The red cassique of Kiawah came, in fact, to apprentice his only son to his European namesake. "How apprentice," you ask, "and to what occupation?" To explain this will require but few words.

It is perhaps not generally known that the custom had been for some time adopted, among the wealthy settlers of the white race in the Carolinas, of hiring experts from among the red men, to hunt for their families and procure their game. The red chief Cussoboe, hearing of the want of our cassique, had voluntarily offered his son for this purpose; and the boy, only sixteen years old, had been hurried through the usual Indian novitiate which prepares for the toils of manhood, in order to meet the known wishes of Colonel Berkeley.

This novitiate of the red man? A few words on this subject.

In the complacency of our civilization we rate the red men somewhat below humanity. At all events, we give them credit for a very small advance beyond the condition of the mere barbarian. And yet, setting aside the bias of our peculiar convention, we are, probably, in one respect, wanting somewhat in the wisdom of the red man. Our discipline of the young, contemplating the relative duties of the two races, is scarcely so exacting, so proper, or so elevated, as theirs. We shall make no comparisons, lest we make ourselves odious: and we admit, *in limine*, that the larger complications of civilization embarrass the subject of discipline in a degree which the red man scarcely feels; and civilization contemplates objects which do not enter at all into his calculations. But, regarding only what are his, he undoubtedly has a better idea of propriety, and the mode by which his ends are to be attained, than we have reached, with all our gains of learning and science, and in respect to the variety of considerations which press upon our cares.

The red man has two great studies before him. He is to be the hunter and the warrior. His life is thus simplified, as narrowed down to these occupations. How to train himself and son for these? Hardihood, dexterity, cunning. fleetness of foot, firm-

ness to endure, inflexibility in trial, a steadfast purpose, a strong
heart, a cool head, deliberate courage, and a steady aim — these
are the objects of his education, training him equally for the two
employments of his life. He is schooled even more severely than
was the Spartan. His pride, from childhood, is brought into play,
and made to stimulate all his proper faculties. He longs to emulate the great hunter, and circumvent the bear, and trap deer and
turkey, and transfix the flying game with his unerring arrows;
and so, from eight to fifteen years, the naked urchins of the tribe
are engaged in every exercise which can increase the volume and
elasticity of muscle, the strength of legs and arms, the quickness
and farsightedness of eye, the subtlety of pursuit and snare, the
agility of movement, the rapidity of flight, the dexterity of aim
and action, and the cool, resolute purpose to achieve and to endure.

At fifteen, just when the moral nature begins to stir with discontent, the lessons rise, so as to appeal to the spiritual and im-
aginative faculties. At fifteen, there is a new ordeal, when the
priesthood interpose and take up the training, just where the
merely physical development is supposed to be sufficiently compelled by habit.

We do not, of course, deem it necessary to dwell upon certain
incidental lessons which have been imparted in the meantime.
These are preparatory, a part of the training, though they may
seem to have been delivered without any apparent consciousness that the boy is listening. Wild songs are sung, of ancient
braves, in his hearing; tales are told, of wondrous deeds of daring
and endurance in the past; and traditions are transmitted, of such
as, from extra developments of character, have risen to the rank
of demigods, and shine in the mythology of the red men as brightly
to their imaginations as ever did the Thesean and other mythic
heroes in the imagination of the Greeks. Of course, we do not
propose to compare the two races, though some of the red men
might well challenge the comparison with Greek or Roman fames.
But their hero-deities, having no poet, have no record — none, at
least, which can spell our senses into fond allegiance. We will
suppose that, from eight to fifteen, the Indian boy has eagerly
listened to thousands of such legends of myth and hero.

At fifteen, all his early training of the *physique*, and its tributary faculties of sight, and smell, and taste, and touch, and hear-

ing, together with those lessons which have wrought upon his
imagination and superstition, are appealed to, by a new and peculiar process, which is training also; and the boy is solemnly dedicated to the Great Spirit and yielded to his hands, and made to
go through an ordeal which brings into exercise all that is spiritual in his nature.

This process is but imperfectly described, in our language, as
the initiation of youth for manhood.   In one sense, it is this.   It
is the taking on of the *toga virilis.*   It is the assumption, for the
first time, of the responsibilities of life.   But it is something more.
It is a sacrifice, a consecration, an invocation—a religious rite,
the higher purpose of which is to place the neophyte within the
immediate care of the Great Spirit; to commend him to special
favor; and to procure, if possible, such a visitation from the Deity
as will prefigure to him the particular *rôle* which he shall adopt
in the vague future which lies before him.

He is expected to dream dreams, and to see visions; each of
which is to have a special purport to his mind.   In the Yemassee, and the kindred dialects of the Kiawahs, Edistohs, Cussoboes,
Stonoes, Sewees, Ockettees, Accabees, and other tribes, occupying
or ranging through the same precincts, this ordeal was called the
*Beni-as-ke-tau;* among the Muscoghees, it was *A-boos-ke-tau;*
and the several Indian nations had, each, its peculiar name for a
ceremonial which was common to them all.

According to Gowdey, and no doubt many others of the whites
who knew the habits and character of the red man, it was the
formal introduction of the boy to the Indian devil!

But, to the process itself:—

The youth, having reached the proper age, say fifteen, and
promising to be worthy, by reason of the progress he has made in
the sports and exercises which are meant to harden properly his
*physique,* is suddenly withdrawn from the tribe, and conducted to
a region of extremest solitude.   With the nations of the interior,
this was chosen among lonely dells in the mountains, or deep
thickets of the forest, remote from the travelled routes.   Along
the seaboard, according to the season, it was in the depths of the
swamp, or on some desert islet, which was consecrated to this
especial purpose.

Here, after various exorcisms of the priest, he was left with a certain meagre allowance of food, carefully measured for a limited space of time — varying, according to the different usages of the tribes, from seven to twenty-seven days. The food left him was just in sufficient quantity to preserve life. He was left weaponless. He had nothing but coarse meal of the maize, and water was always convenient; he might drink what he pleased of that. In addition, he had provided him certain quantities, duly measured out, of bitter roots, which are emetic in their property. These are sodden in water, and he drinks of the water at morning and evening. When he has vomited freely, he partakes sparingly of his allowance of meal. Having thus fed and physicked himself, with the occasional countenance of the priest, for a space of five days, he substitutes for the emetic roots those of another sort, which have the effect of intoxicating: in fact, from the description given of their properties, we may suppose them to resemble those of the oriental *hacksheesh*, the preparation from hemp. They produce delirium, if they do not temporarily madden.

Then the visions follow. And these visions have a divine import, which the young man must carefully remember. They embody the mystery, and the moral, and perhaps the model, of his future life. They present to his mind the ideal which governs his aims and aspirations ; and from these he detaches, for special worship, the chief object which fastens most tenaciously upon his fancy.

We can well understand how and why it is that, with little or no food, and under the constant appliance of medicine which exhausts the system, and then, with an imagination wrought to intensest activity by the intoxicating potion, the boy should see wondrous things in his visions, and that these should exercise most potent influences over his mind in all succeeding years. The only wonder is, that he should escape from madness.

And you may trust these Indian boys, alone, to carry out faithfully all the duties prescribed to them. They know the object of the ordeal. Their ambition has been raised to the occasion. They are eager for the trial, and never fail in its requisitions. They would die sooner than skulk. In the meantime, should the boy meet another, undergoing the same novitiate, he neither touches nor speaks with him. They are left wholly to God: they will commune with no meaner being. Ablutions and lustrations fol-

low, and a copious sweating process closes the ceremonial, when
the priest reappears, and performs certain mystic rites, and the
mockasons of manhood, prepared for the occasion, "*esta-la-pee-ca*,"
are fastened upon his feet, and he is armed with a new bow, belt,
and arrows, which we may suppose to have been prepared by the
young women of the family.   They are consecrated by the priest,
and the boy usually receives a new name, which is temporary,
and to be changed with his first remarkable achievement to one
which is significant of the event.

The reader will suppose us to have abridged this description,
cutting off many minor details.   We have given the main features
and objects of the ceremonial, and these must suffice.

We enable him to understand now why we have introduced this
description here, when we recall to his memory the scene, in the
first part of this veritable history, in which honest Jack Belcher
detected the Indian canoe on its passage to the sacred isle of
Kiawah, and when subsequently the alarm was given to the same
personage, in company with his superior, Calvert, when they discovered the same Indian canoe so nearly athwart the hawser of
the saucy cruiser, the Happy-go-Lucky.   The inmates of that
canoe were the chief Cussoboe, the priest, and the favorite son,
just brought back from Kiawah, the latter having gone bravely
through his ordeal of seven days, the usual term of the novitiate
among the Yemassee.

"How came he — the Spirit?" was the first query of the cassique to the nearly-exhausted boy.

"An-he-gar; lac-o-me-ne-pah."

"Ha! the little white bird?   Saw you no great wings?—no
eagle?   Was there no wolf that howls—no panther that springs?
Heard you no cry as of the bird that tears the throat?"

The boy gasped out only the one response —

"An-he-gar; lac-o-me-ne-pah!"

"What hast thou to do with little white bird?   It is not for
thee.   I would have had thee see the great sea-eagle; better
the panther that leaps, or the wolf that howls; or the great bear,
whose embrace is death!   But so the Great Spirit hath spoken!
And who shall say, 'Wherefore this speech?'"

This was all said in the dialect of his people.   The philosophy,
as spoken, was unexceptionable; but the gloomy brow of the chief

was scarcely in unison with the uttered sentiment. He was troubled. He walked away dissatisfied.

But he soon returned, and, with great effort, shaking off his dissatisfaction, he proceeded to some of the final ceremonials, such as the fastening on the mockasons and belt, and arming with bow and arrows. And then the whole party walked away together to the beach, where the boat awaited them.

And even as they walked, there lay in the path before them a long, beautiful white feather, as if just fallen from some snowy bird in flight. And the boy reverently stooped and picked it up, and fastened it within the fillet that encircled his brows. And he murmured in low tones, as he did so —

" An-he-gar ; lac-o-me-ne-pah."

The father heard the words, and again he frowned; for it did not please him that the image which had made the deepest impression on the boy's mind should be so insignificant of character. But the lad had gone bravely through his ordeal; and, though feeble, he carried himself erect; and his eye was bright, and his bearing calm and resolute. So the chief made no reply to the words, and no comment upon the action. In fact, whatever the symbol vouchsafed the boy in his visions, it was of sacred origin; and the faith of the red man rarely questions the wisdom in the ultimate designs of the Deity, though it may be that it conflicts with his own pride and the calculations of his policy. It appeared to do so in the present instance, and Cussoboe was troubled. He had a cunning policy, a profound purpose in view, which required that the boy should exercise the highest attributes of manhood; which contemplated for his future, and that at an early period, tests which would tax his strength to the utmost, and trials which should demand his best courage.

In brief, the boy was dedicated almost as solemnly as Hannibal; and long, searching, and severe, was the examination by which, subsequently, the sire sought to probe the nature of the son, and raise his mind to the height of those duties which were in reserve for his future execution.

But we must not anticipate. Ostensibly, he was simply apprenticed to the great white chief as a hunter of the deer and turkey. The terms of this compact were all understood between the parties, prior to their present meeting. It only remained to the English cassique to bestow his gratuities upon his dusky brother. This was done, and the liberality of the one even surpassed the expectations of the other.

But Colonel Berkeley was careful, among his gifts, to bestow no weapons; and this was a disappointment to the chief Cussoboe. He might not have been so placid under this disappointment, but that he meditated schemes which would supply hereafter all present deficiencies of this description.

It was in the midst of this scene, and while Cussoboe was eagerly clutching and putting aside the coveted gifts — robes, shawls, knives, bells, blankets, and a score of " what-nots" besides — that a bright, fairy-like creature, an English girl, fair as a new-budded rose, and fresh as morning, pressed in between the spectators, and made her way into the circle. This was Grace Masterton, the sister of Olive, the wife of Berkeley, a tall girl of twelve or fourteen years, perhaps; a light, graceful creature, whose eyes sparkled with impulse and kindled with every imagination. Scarcely did she appear, when the Indian boy murmured, as if unconsciously —

" An-he-gar ! — lac-o-me-ne-pah !"

And his eyes were fastened upon her face with a long, meditative gaze. And she, too, regarded him with keenest scrutiny for a few moments, when the English cassique, noticing her presence, said to her :—

" Grace, my dear, this is the young Indian hunter, who is to bring us venison. You must treat him kindly, my child. He is the son of the cassique."

" To be sure I will, brother," replied the girl, promptly. " I like his looks. He's handsome, though so red. He shall play with me. I can go with him into the woods."

" You shall teach him English, Grace, when he's off the hunt. Won't you like that better? He knows nothing of our language yet, I fancy. Ask him, Gowdey, if he understands what we say."

The interpreter translated for the parties. The boy replied in his own tongue :—

" I hear the strange bird singing in the woods of Kiawah. 'Tis the white bird that sings. It is sweet to the ears of the young hunter, but he knows not what she sings. He will listen closely, till he learns."

As the interpreter rendered this speech, the girl, with the utmost frankness and simplicity, as if the answer was quite sufficient for friendship, crossed over to where the boy stood, his eyes bright and watchful, and, suddenly taking one of his hands in her own, said :—

"I like what you say, red boy, and I like your looks. You shall play with me, and tell me all about the woods, and I will tell you all about the English and England; and I will teach you how to speak with me, so that we may understand each other. And you shall hunt for me, too, and shall catch and bring me a beautiful smart young fawn—a young deer, you know : you must n't shoot it, mind you, nor hurt it, but catch it in a snare, and just bring it to me so ; and I will put a collar round its neck, and hang my silver bell to it, and it shall follow me about wherever I go. Will you not bring me the beautiful little fawn, red boy ?"

When she spoke, the boy started, as if from a dream. But he did not withdraw his hand from her grasp, and he looked reverently in her eyes, as if trying to comprehend her speech ; but when she stopped speaking, he could only murmur as before, but now looking to his father —

"An-he-gar ; lac-o-me-ne-pah."

"He calls you the white bird, Miss Grace, the little white bird that sings. *Anhegar* is the Yemassee for little white bird."

Such was the translation made at the moment by Gowdey.

"Ugh! ugh !" with a nodding head, was the commentary of Cussoboe ; but he looked on with great gravity, apparently not much pleased with the scene.

"And what is the name of your son ?" asked Berkeley.

The question was understood by the chief, but he was not so successful in conveying his reply, though he attempted one in English. Gowdey came to his assistance.

"The chief says, your honor, that the boy has no proper name yet ; that he can have no good name till he makes one. That 's Injin custom, your honor. What they call him now is not a name to last. It 's to be taken off, he says, but not till he 's made a mark for himself ; that is, a *totem*. If he should have a stiff fight with a bear, now, and take his hide, they 'd call him by some name that means ' The boy that skinned the bear ;' or if 't was war-time, and he took a man's scalp, the name would tell all

about the affair.    Now they call him '*Iswattee*,' and I don't know
well what that means; but the nearest I can come to it is, 'The
tree put to grow.'    For short, they call him 'Iswattee;' and I
reckon that's the name he means you to call him."

"Ugh! ugh! Iswattee — good boy Iswattee.    Shoot dear, kill
bear; good boy Iswattee.    Hunt for white Micco.    Heap kill —
heap catch!    Good hunter is young chief, Iswattee."

We spare the reader more of these details.    The ceremonials
were ended.    Cussoboe had made up his piles; had clutched the
hand of the English cassique with a hearty gripe, seemingly of
good will; then suddenly turned away for the forest, leaving his
treasures behind him, but under the guardianship of his followers.
None seemed to remark his going except the boy Iswattee.    He,
suddenly, as if starting from deepest revery, took the track after
his father, and followed him in silence to the adjoining thickets,
which were close at hand, and in which both of them were soon
buried out of sight.

CHAPTER XXVII.

THE QUIVER OF ARROWS.

"Here, boy, is the commission for thy work:
So many days, and the great peril demands
Thy instant, swift, decisive, and sharp stroke!
Be true as vigilant; for thy duty here
Is a most sacred service to thy people,
And the Great Spirit that watches o'er their weal."
THE SEMINOLE—*a Play.*

YET, though buried in the thicket, the chief and his son did not pass wholly from human sight. They had left the groups, European and Indian alike, which had made the assemblage gathered for the occasion. But other eyes than these were upon them.

Harry Calvert harbored in the very thicket to which they directed their steps. From the edge of this thicket, approaching as nearly as he might with safety, he had watched the whole proceedings. Now, as the cassique and his son drew nigh, he receded stealthily into yet deeper thickets, taking care not to lose them from sight. Not that he felt much, or any curiosity, with regard to their movements. In observing them, he simply obeyed those instincts which had been habitually exercised by the life he led, and the vigilance which its necessities had rendered natural to his mind. He had been a warrior and hunter himself with the red men, and knew much of their ways. It was only the habitual employment of his wits, in the absence of every duty, that he should fathom their purposes. He had a motive in this, by-the-way, in consequence of what Gowdey had reported to him of the doubtful fidelity of the red men in the precinct.

Cussoboe suspected no such *surveillance.* He led the boy into the wood, never once looking behind him, and not doubting that the son would follow. Having reached a supposed place of shelter and security, he paused, and awaited the youth. The latter drew nigh, and Calvert, from a clump of bushes, could behold the scene, though too remote to gather what was spoken. He saw that the cassique spoke with solemnity; that his action was imposing and dignified. He saw his hands lifted to heaven at one moment, and in the next laid on the young man's head.

The latter stood motionless and attentive. The father then pointed to the settlement of the English cassique; and finally, unfolding his robe, he produced a sheaf of arrows, which he numbered with his fingers. From this sheaf he detached a single shaft, snapped it in twain, and, this done, he looked about him until he found a living tree which had a hollow in its trunk. Into this hollow he thrust the sheaf with its remaining arrows, and with his hatchet made a single stroke across the bark, on the side of the tree opposite the cavity. The two then moved away together to the edge of the wood. When there, they separated — the boy taking his way to the settlement of his new employer, the cassique skirting the opening, but keeping in the cover of the thicket, until he had joined his followers a few hundred yards below.

They had loaded themselves with his merchandise, the gifts of the white man, and were now waiting for the coming of their superior, as at an appointed place. In a short time they had disappeared from the scene, moving away as calmly and indifferently as if they had not left behind them the hope of the tribe; as if heedless of the new toils to be forced upon him — his isolation among foreigners — the tenderness of his youth — the temptations and dangers to which he was exposed among those whom his people, whatever the appearances they maintained, undoubtedly regarded as their enemies.

Harry Calvert had been able to behold the scene already described; and, though he heard not a syllable, he yet fully conceived its purport. He waited in his hiding-place until the red men were certainly gone, and at a distance, when he readvanced to the edge of the opening, which revealed the new settlement, and satisfied himself that all there were too much occupied to interfere with his own actions. He returned to the thicket, found the tree in which the sheaf of arrows had been deposited, and drew it forth. He found it tied with the skin of the rattle-snake!

Such a quiver, so encircled, is, when formally despatched by one tribe to another, a solemn declaration of war. And even now, though unsent, it had a peculiar significance, which Calvert well understood. He counted the arrows, and restored the sheaf to its hiding-place. Then, gathering up the fragments of the shaft which had been broken, he retired still deeper into the thickets, till he reached a little *branch*, or brooklet, upon the banks of which the canes or hollow reeds, of which the arrows were made, grew abundantly. He gathered one of these, as nearly like, in size and appearance, as possible, to the one which had been broken; trimmed it with his knife to the same shape and measure, and inserted it within the sheaf with the rest. This done, he resumed his scrutiny of the plantation and settlements of his brother.

In this scrutiny, he consumed the better part of the day. He noted all the bearings and relations of the several buildings, the courses of the streams and woods around the place, and made himself familiar with the various paths or avenues which seemed to lead to and from it. For hours he watched the buildings from such points as afforded him the best survey. He could distinguish the workmen at their several tasks, and his brother among them. He could see much—everything, indeed, which would have been necessary had he been making a *reconnaissance* in contemplation of assault.

But he was still unsatisfied. His eyes never once rested on the object which was most precious to his sight—which he came especially to see!

But there was one sight which worked keenly upon his sensibilities. Toward sunset, he beheld the nurse, with the child, enter the great grove of moss-bearded oaks—a Titan family, hoar with eld, and with branches large as the shafts of other trees—which ranged along one side of the whole settlement; a natural avenue such as no prince of Europe might boast.

He could not doubt that this infant was the child of Olive. "It should be mine! it should be mine!" was the half-choking murmur from his lips. His first impulse was to dart forward and tear the infant from the arms of its bearer. But with a shudder he arrested himself, turned away for a moment, and then one big tear rose into his eyes, and, slowly gathering, rolled down upon his cheeks. He dashed it off hurriedly, as if ashamed of the momentary weakness; and now continued to watch the infant, but with a sterner feeling, deeply imbued with bitterness, which, however brought no emotion into play upon his face. And thus he watched, with a sort of stony stare, until child and nurse had disappeared.

With night he rode back to Gowdey's castle, at Oldtown on the Ashley. Gowdey was in waiting for him. The old man had shaken off his red companions in an hour after the embassage was over. Calvert told him what he had seen, of the interview between the chief and his son. He told him, also, what he had done, in substituting a perfect for the broken arrow.

"Ah! captain, I see you knows the red devils as well as myself. You've got the count of their arrows, I hopes; for, jest as sure as a gun, the day when that last arrow is broken is the day for sudden mischief."

"Yes; here's a memorandum in pencil. Score it, Gowdey, in fire-coal on your walls, so that you too shall remember. We shall have to make our preparations against that day. I shall be able to do something. That this chief, Cussoboe, means mischief, there can be no doubt. That this boy is to be made an agent, some way, in effecting some special and important object, against a particular time, is equally beyond question. Now, what is *he* to effect? Have you thought of that, Gowdey?"

"Well—no! I don't really see. He's so young—he's not more than sixteen, I reckon; and then he's a sort of hostage, you see."

"An Indian boy at fifteen is five years older than a European boy at the same age."

"In the woods, he sartinly is."

"And his life is in the woods only. What we call civilization and society are here mere impertinences. The manhood of the forests is the best manhood *in* the forests, and this boy is already trained with a Spartan education."

"I can't say, captain, that I altogether understand that 'Spartan.'"

"Ah! true. Well, Gowdey, the Spartans were a sort of Indians in their day, who trained their children to a hard life, in order that they might be strong, selfish men. But this must not divert us from what we were saying. This boy's tender years make no difference in this matter. He will do what his father requires. His father will not require him to do anything which he is not able to do, provided he can bravely make the attempt, and has the hardy courage to pursue it."

"That's true, sir."

"Now, Gowdey, it is a mistake to suppose that the boy is in the situation of a hostage. The very business for which my bro— the cassique, I should say — employs him, gives him perfect liberty. He ranges the woods at pleasure; is absent and returns when he pleases; and, unless locked up, can execute any appointed mischief that lies within his strength, courage, and opportunities."

"That's sart'inly true, your honor."

"Now, the question occurs, what can the cassique, his father, expect him to do, which he could not do himself? Nothing, unless the boy, from peculiar opportunities allowed him by the situation he holds, can obtain access to objects and places which his father could have no pretence to seek."

"That seems quite sensible, captain."

"If, then, as we believe, these red men meditate treachery, the objects with which this boy is put to Colonel Berkeley will be, to gain some advantages which are desirable to the insurgents. What are these objects? The boy has free access to the whole domain of Colonel Berkeley. He may be able to open the gates and doors at midnight; may be able to get possession of arms and gunpowder—"

"Ah! that reminds me — that old rogue Cussoboe, though the cassique gave him a smart chance of everything that he wanted, he was not satisfied, and he asked for a gun for himself, one for his brother, and one for the boy. He made quite an argyment to the cassique, after them guns! 'T was lucky the colonel fought shy of that, though he didn't actually refuse."

"There, then, lies the danger. Now, Gowdey, in my examination of the place to-day, I note that there is a strong log-house without windows. It struck me, as you had already told me that Colonel Berkeley had a large supply of guns and ammunition, that this log-house was really the armory and magazine."

"I *know* it is, captain."

"I thought so, Gowdey. But now, mark you: this log-house, or armory and magazine, is at least one hundred and fifty yards from any of the other houses."

"Yes, and he told me the reason for putting it so far off. It was the danger from explosion."

"I thought that likely. But, do you not see that, as there is no covered way from the dwellings to the arsenal and magazine, it would be impossible to get to it, from the houses, in the event of a sudden assault? The red men have only to cover the space between, and nobody can cross to get the weapons. The door, too, of this log-house, though fastened by the best lock ever made in Europe, I can blow open with a pistol—I can pry open with an axe! It only needs a resolute and numerous enemy, and the place is incapable of defence. To make it even partially secure, there must be a covered way, a double row of pickets, from the chief dwelling to the door of the armory, completely enclosing that, and the houses must all be fenced in with pickets. This, with the force which Colonel Berkeley can now muster, can all be done in a few days. He *must* do it. You must see him, Gowdey, to-morrow, and urge the matter upon him."

"Lord love you, captain! he'll never hear to me. He's got a notion, as I told you afore, that these red devils are real humans, and never would do wrong ef they worn't pushed to the wall. Now, ef you'd see and talk to him—"

"Me! You forget, Gowdey, that I am not the man to let myself be seen by one of the proprietors, or council, just at this time."

"But I don't reckon he knows you."

"I am bound to take for granted that he *may* know me, and to keep out of his sight, for a time at least. I shall see—nay, *seek* him—when the time comes, and it is proper to do so. I may say to you that it is my purpose to seek him. I have something to say to him which concerns us both very nearly."

"Ah!—"

"Yes! But, in the meantime, we must not suffer him to be murdered. *You* must see him, and warn him of his danger. Nobody can do it better. I can understand that it will be difficult to disabuse him of these notions of which you speak. He has a hobby of philanthropy; and hobbies, unless well bridled, invariably fling their riders. We must make him put a strong bit, though for a season only, on that which he rides. You *can* do this. You must go to him, and warn him of his danger. Tell him that you *know* there is an insurrection of the red men on foot. You *do* know it. *I* know it. You feel sure, from what you know of the character and habits of this people — from what you yourself have seen, and from what I have told you — that there *is* an insurrection on foot."

"I could swear it on Holy Writ."

"Swear it to him, then! But beware how you offer to argue with him, or give him the testimony upon which you ground your convictions. He will never comprehend your proofs or mine. He knows too little of the red men to understand the significance of such actions as satisfy us of the danger. His very prejudices will make him undervalue your arguments. But you can impress him with your solemn asseverations. You have but to tell him that you *know* the fact, but refuse to give your evidence. You can easily find an excuse for being silent."

"Yes, I can do that."

"Meanwhile, I will warn the governor, in person. You must have an increase of force for your garrison — half a dozen stout fellows at least, though twenty would not be too many. Can you not pick up a score or two of brave fellows who can stand fire?"

"I reckon, captain, if I had the money. But the governor—"

"You shall have it! We must not wait upon governors and councils: they move too slowly for this case. Before they could organize a corps of rangers, there would be a hundred scalps taken. Pick up a score or two of strong fellows within the next three days. Get them into the block-house secretly. It is of the first importance that your enemy should never know where you are, or how strong you are. The red men probably know how weak you are now. I have no doubt that you will have some of them seeking to procure admission here, on some innocent pretence, just to find out the weakness of the place."

"They've been at me already, hallooing to get in."

"But only one has shown himself?"

"Only one — that's sart'in; but I guessed as how there was twenty others in the woods."

12

"Well, do you get a score of stout fellows. I will provide others, and will send over Jack Belcher to you to-morrow. I want him here, and he can co-operate with you. How are you off for weapons?"

"Enough for a few men only."

"You shall have enough for a dozen; and what your governor fails to do, I shall supply. You will communicate to him, however, as if you knew nothing of me; and let him give you orders for the men, if he will. That will guaranty their pay. But, whether he gives you this guaranty or not, get the men, and I will find the money for six months' pay. Contract for that time at least. That will carry you through the harvest. In all probability, Colonel Berkeley is himself the cause of this contemplated insurrection."

"As how, captain?"

"He has awakened the greed and appetite of the red men, by the ostentatious exhibition of stores, which tempt their cupidity, which they esteem beyond all things, and by the little prudence with which he guards them. He has numerous cattle which range all about him. He will awake some morning to find all their throats cut, even before his own. I counted, in one enclosure, not less than twenty-six of the finest Irish graziers—"

"By-the-way, captain, the very best sort of hogs for the swamp-ranges! With their long legs, they don't mind bog or distance; and they're sich gross feeders, that nothing comes amiss. But, captain, you're a most wonderful man. You've seen to everything."

"Ah, Gowdey, my seeing doesn't take the mote out of my own eyes!"

The sudden change in the voice of the speaker; the deep pathos conveyed in those few allegoric words; the utter rejection, in tone, manner, and thought, of that tribute to the vanity of the superior, which the humble man probably designed—and innocently too—to convey in his complimentary language—all combined to reveal the presence of a great grief, perhaps an incurable one, which hitherto Gowdey had never supposed to exist in the heart of Calvert.

"Is it so, then, master?" said the former; and these insignificant words, in themselves so meaningless, enforced by the tremu-

lous accents of the speaker, conveyed volumes of the most touching sympathy.

"Master, is it so?" and, repeating the sentence, the old man
grasped the hand of the young one, and the big tears gathered in
his eye.

"It is so, Gowdey."

"Then God forgive you, and give you peace, master!"

Master! How that word would revolt, at this day, the vanity
of inferiority! Yet it conveyed then, in the mouth of that speaker, no degrading acknowledgment. It was simply the speech of
an honest affection, paying tribute to a noble superiority, that did
not suffer forfeiture of a perfect manhood in the indulgence of the
greatest of human griefs. It was a just tribute of an honest heart
to a genuine heroism.

"It is so, Gowdey!"

"And is there no help?"

"None! none!"

"O captain, have faith! Look up! that's all that's needful.
And you may even shut the eye when you're a-lookin' up. The
faith is apt to see better when the eye is shut. It's the faith that
cures the hurt, and gives sight to the blind man!"

"Enough, Gowdey! Let us sleep now. You must take me
across the river before the dawn."

# CHAPTER XXVIII.

### THE DESPATCH.

"Hard rides the messenger of Law, but Fate
    Rashes, with keener spur, the steed's sleek sides,
    That hurries in pursuit." — *Old Play.*

By the dawn of the next day, Calvert was safely sheltered within the close chamber in the dwelling of Governor Quarry. It was too late that night to disturb the household of Mrs. Perkins Anderson, and agitate the repose of a wife so little nervous as the fair Zulieme. It was enough to find a welcome from the accommodating Governor Quarry, to whom, without committing himself in any way, or revealing his own personal purposes and objects, Calvert made known all his apprehensions of the hostile intentions of the red men.

"Really, my dear captain," said the governor, "you are growing nervous. I do not suppose that the Indians have any good feeling toward us — far from it; but I have myself had no evidence which might confirm your statement. So far as I can hear, they are uniformly pacific; have been quietly getting their maize and peas into the ground; and working as usual (precious small is the degree of work, I grant you) upon their little planting-tracts. Upon what do you found your opinions?"

"I have given you no opinions, Governor Quarry. I assert positively that the red men are preparing for mischief. I state a fact which I will not argue."

"But your facts must be founded upon something; you have evidence for this assertion?"

"Surely, but it is of a sort which I am not prepared to impart. The revelation of my facts involves other interests."

"But, unless I have some evidence — alleged proofs of the

facts, at least — upon which I can found the apprehension, how should I alarm the council? how move them to agree upon the organization of the rangers? Rangers are expensive luxuries, captain, and the colony is a poor one."

"Can you exercise no discretion as governor? — since, if you are to wait upon the dilatory debates of a council, you are likely to send your rangers out only to gather up the scalped heads of your colonists."

"Are you really serious?" asked the governor, now becoming serious himself.

"Never more so in my life!"

"But, do tell *me* upon what you ground these suspicions?"

"That I can not well do. If your council be as ignorant of the nature of the red men as Europeans generally are, what I hold to be conclusive proofs would be to them wholly insignificant. If you yourself can not act in the matter, I should despair of your council doing anything in season. If your scattered colonists up the two rivers, especially here to the south as far as the Savannah, could only be advised by runners to be on the alert; your frontier block-houses strengthened against surprise; patrols of good skill in woodcraft sent out, especially in Berkeley and Colleton counties; and all done without beat of drum, and with the utmost secrecy — then you might hope to avert the danger, or meet it successfully. But what is done should be done quickly. I doubt if you will have more than three weeks for the work. Why should you not assume the responsibility, keeping all the measures secret for a while? It would redound wonderfully to your credit after the event."

"But most atrociously against my credit if the event should never take place. It would fasten a debt upon the colony which the council would never sanction. No, no, captain; unless you give me what the scouts call 'Indian sign,' and enough of it, I can take no steps such as you propose."

"Who keeps the block-house at Oldtown? Have you a garrison there?"

"A single man only — an old sea-dog, trapper, hunter, all sorts of a scout — named Gowdey."

"Does he report nothing?"

"Nothing. I have hardly seen him for a month. He has

been to me twice or thrice during the last six weeks, but I left him to my secretary. I was quite too busy myself to see him; and the old trapper carries with him usually such a strong odor, such an 'ancient and fishlike smell,' that my nostrils resent his presence as they would the precincts of a pest-house. My olfactories keep him from my auditories."

"You may be too nice for safety," answered Calvert, gravely. "Take my counsel, and see him, and hear what he has to say; at least, seek all the information that you can from your scouting-parties; and bring your council to frequent and early meetings as soon as possible, and on any pretext. In the course of a few days, I may be able to put such evidence before you as may even suffice for their enlightenment."

"My dear rover, the council are more likely to fancy danger from a very different class of people than the red men. Do you know that they have a most pernicious habit of treating of privateering as if it were piracy! It is because of this lamentable perversity of opinion that I have not sought them, or cared to see them, since you have been in the precinct. They scarcely speak of anything else; and it has been to me matter of real rejoicing that Berkeley and Morton are busy with their several baronies, and that Middleton has gone pioneering somewhere about the Santee, so that I am temporarily relieved of their discussions as to the proper mode of treating a certain notorious offender, whom they familiarly style 'the pirate Calvert.'"

"Take no heed of me, I pray you. I can put myself in safety at any moment."

"Are you quite sure of that? By my soul, but I am not! I must take heed of you. Read that, and you will see that your former agent, Master Job Sylvester, or Stillwater — still water, you know, has a proverbial depth, if not darkness — is disposed to look after you, since you will not look after him. He has not only grown virtuous, but patriotically suspicious. He is busily so; and assures me that he has good reasons for believing you to be even now in town."

"Indeed!"— and Calvert read the letter, only to lay it down quietly.

"What! you despise its dangers? You treat with contempt the virtuous citizen who tells me that, 'having seen the errors of his ways,' he is prepared 'to make amends for his past errors,' by bringing to the gallows his old associates! Do you not see that he tells us in one sentence that he is moved by the fear of God and the love of the law — or is it the love of God and the fear of the law? — perhaps. But you see where he somewhat modestly asks if there be not some five hundred pounds offered for the capture of 'this most nefarious sea-robber, Harry Calvert?' Oh! a most precious rogue is Master Job Stillwater, but not the less a good, virtuous citizen for all that. He is true to his eastern education, which accommodates itself to God whenever the transaction is profitable; and to the law, after he has made it sufficiently malleable. I confess to you, I somehow fear this virtuous fellow. He has latterly grown so good as not to be quite willing that anybody should live by vice but himself. All such animals have a rare instinct in finding where other foxes take cover. Beware of him."

"I shall!"

"But how have you offended him?"

"By withdrawing all trust from him. I sent Belcher to sound him and others some time ago. You may remember the time, for he had a communication for you."

"Yes, and I warned him of your danger here."

"Precisely. So did Franks. But the counsel of Sylvester was bold and encouraging. He was particularly careful to give a bad account of your excellency's courage and of Franks's honesty. And Belcher found out that, withal, he had grown pious. I so far resolved to respect his piety as to subject him to no more temptations. Accordingly, he was suffered to know nothing of my coming or presence."

"Ay, but he knows something now; at all events, he suspects. He is invited to confer with me in person, and to report the evidence upon which his suspicions are based. I must, of course, give him every encouragement; but shall not object, my dear captain, if, in your own chamber, your ears should happen to be keen enough to obtain any useful knowledge for yourself."

Three hours later, this promise was realized. Sylvester — or, as the governor persisted in calling him, Stillwater — was punctual to his appointment, and Calvert was an unsuspected witness.

Stillwater was a person of many preliminaries, and somewhat circuitous in his progress to an end. We shall abridge these to our limits, confining him and ourselves as strictly as possible to what is absolutely necessary to our narrative. He was careful to confess his previous connection with the pirate, but that was only while piracy was an innocent practice. The moment that God and his majesty Charles II. had discovered its heinousness, from that moment Stillwater felt a change of heart. But he felt that it was not enough for him to shake the sin from his own skirts; it was incumbent upon him to pursue to justice those who continued to indulge in the crime: and when he learned that there was a proclamation of his majesty which rated the offence so high as to offer five hundred pounds for the capture of the chief offender in these parts, he, with becoming virtue and loyalty, resolved to merit his majesty's approval and reward. Accordingly, when Jack Belcher, the emissary of the infamous pirate Calvert, came to him some months ago, as had been his wont on previous occasions, to make arrangements for the sale in Charleston of the plunder which the pirate had made, he, Job Sylvester, with the cunning of the serpent and the innocence of the dove, gave him every encouragement to come, and bring his wares to the customary market. And he, Sylvester, had laid his virtuous snares so happily, that he felt cock-sure of making the pirate a captive, and getting possession of the piratical vessel and all her crew and cargo.

"But you never told me of this, Master Job!" quoth the governor. The pious rogue had his answer:—

"The moment hadn't come for it, your honor. I waited for the time. The time has come at last; and you see me here, ready to finish the good work."

"Ah! you can lay hands, then, on this pirate and his vessel now? He and she are here, do you say?"

"I've got such evidence, your honor, as makes me certain. The town's full of new goods, which never came from England. Franks is working in secret day and night. There's Spanish fruit fresh in the market, and we've had no direct arrivals from Havana or the West Indies for more than a month. Then, strange sailors have been seen about town at night; and, what's more, there's a strange woman staying at the house of Madam Perkins

Anderson, a Spanish woman — you've heard of her, for she's a famous figure to see; they call her the *Señorita de Montano*, and all the young bucks are after her. But I'm pretty sure she's no other than the mistress of this pirate Calvert."

" Ha! what makes you sure of it?"

" I heard something about this woman before. He calls her his wife. I got it from one of the sailors, long ago, that he's married to a Spaniard."

" Perhaps she is really his wife, if connected with him at all. Why should you suppose her his mistress?"

" Oh, your honor, it's not charity to think that these pirate-captains ever call in the church when they splice. They haven't the virtue for that. They're loose livers, and have a wife — of that sort — in all the ports where they trade. But I got a hint of the whole story more than a year ago, from one of the sailors — he was a Spaniard himself, and knew all about it — who worked aboard the Happy-go-Lucky. The woman's his mistress, be sure, and she's here, and he, I reckon, is not far off. And the ship's somewhere about; though, this time, they haven't run her into the place where they always took her before. But the goods that fill the market, the fruit about town, the strange sailors that are seen here by night, and this Spanish *señorita* — how should they get here, when there's been no arrivals from Havana and the West Indies? They come in the Happy-go-Lucky, sir; and I'll have 'em all in a bag, if so be your honor will give me the needful help when the time comes."

" And what do you need, Master Job, for this patriotic service?"

" Well, your honor, I want a despatch express to New York, to bring on the Southampton frigate, and the Scarborough, or any other of the king's ships that are on that station; and, until that's done, I don't want to make any stir, unless we can be so fortunate as to bag the captain, when he's off the vessel and skulking somewhere about town. Once we can get his head into sack, we can find out all about the vessel."

" A most notable idea. You are decidedly right. You are an old trapper, Master Stillwater, and the despatches shall be ready for you when you please."

"Right away!  Now's the time, your honor."

"This very day, if you think proper!  Can you procure me a good express — a safe, hard-spurring fellow?"

"I've just got such a man, your honor: Gideon Fairchild — a good man — a brand, like myself, plucked from the burning, and now a shining light in the meeting-house!"

"You know him thoroughly, Master Job?"

"Like the A, B, C!  We learned our letters together in Connecticut.  He's had his falls, your honor.  He's been a sinner, even as I have been a sinner.  But the Lord has been pleased to send his holy grace to both of our wretched souls, and we are re-deemed by his mercy.  Gideon Fairchild won't let the grass grow to his horse's feet; and he's been the route many times before, when he went on no such virtuous business."

"Let him be ready by three o'clock.  The despatches shall be prepared for him to the governor of New York.  Is there any-thing more that should be done now?"

"Not — just — yet, your honor!  Might I ask your honor if the reward says 'dead or alive,' in the case of this pirate-captain?"

"Alive!  alive!  We want him for an example, Master Still-water.  Remember that!"

"It might be much easier to kill him than to take him," said the pious convert.  "He's quick to fight, and mighty heavy-handed."

"Oh, don't be so bloody in your piety! at least, don't defraud the gallows of its prey."

"And — your honor — what's the reward for the capture of the pirate-ship?"

"Salvage on the cargo, Master Job, is, I take it, the law on that subject.  For the rest, leave it to the generous bounty of his majesty's counsellors, to determine the proper reward for those who shall render him so great a service as the capture of this for-midable pirate."

"And there will be salvage, your honor, on the ship, as well as the cargo?"

"Why, Master Job, your loyalty takes a very voracious aspect!  But, even here, you will not be disappointed.  You will have your reward.  But such a vessel, with such heels as the Happy-

go-Lucky, is more than likely to take her place, once in our possession, among his majesty's own cruisers."

"And she'll do credit to the service, your honor. She's got
the heels of them all. I'm humbly thankful, your honor. Gideon Fairchild will be in readiness, punctual, at three o'clock.
It is a long ride, but Gideon will find a spur in his loyalty
and conscience, your honor; and I can answer for it that no
despatch ever sent before, ever reached so soon as that he
carries."

"If it *ever* reaches!" was the unuttered thought of his amiable
excellency, who had his own reasons for doubting the success of
Gideon's mission.

"Well," said he to Calvert, when Sylvester was gone, "you see
where you are. What will you do?"

"Can your excellency have a short missive conveyed from me
to Franks within the next half-hour?"

"To be sure. Of course, it is your own private affair, and under seal."

"Surely. Even the messenger need n't know you are in the
business."

And Calvert scrawled a few lines in a billet, which he sealed
and put into the governor's hands.

"It is possible," said Calvert, rising, "that Jack Belcher is
somewhere waiting. I fancy I heard his whistle from yonder
orange-shrubbery. If your excellency will suffer me, I will answer."

The governor nodded; and Calvert, applying a silver whistle
to his mouth, sounded three *mots*, and then a fourth, after a pause.
The governor walked out of the chamber to the lower story and
the back-door of the house, taking the billet with him. He returned without it.

The despatches were ready at three o'clock. The governor
read them to Master Job Sylvester. They were very emphatic,
and particularly urgent. Nothing could be more emphatic, or
more satisfactory to our patriotic citizen; and, at half-past three,
Gideon was on the road!

At half-past six, he was knocked from his horse by sundry un-
civil persons, who took from him money and despatches. He
was fastened again upon the horse, his legs tied together beneath

the belly of the animal, his hands behind him, and his mouth muzzled!

It was midnight before he was suffered to alight: then, lifted tenderly enough from the beast, he found himself hoisted, with equal tenderness, into a boat, and transferred to the deck of the Happy-go-Lucky, in the hold of which we must keep him for a season, cooling his heels and temper together, in a somewhat uncomfortable position.

## CHAPTER XXIX.

### THE DESOLATE HEART.

" The strong man weeps, from sympathy, not fear:
He knows and braves the fate that yet must crush !"
*Old Play.*

BUT we are not to suppose that the dangers of the Happy-go-Lucky, and her valiant captain, were set at rest by this prompt practice. True, Gideon Fairchild was laid by the heels, and kept on short commons, in the hold of the saucy cruiser; and his brother in grace, the goodly Job Sylvester, wist not, all the while, but that he was fast making his way to the king's cruisers at New York.

But Job was not the less active because he had set certain wheels in motion. He was one of a tribe which habitually keeps all its wheels in motion. He was not the person to fancy anything done, while anything which *he* could do remained undone; and the king's reward of five hundred pounds exercised such a potent effect upon his pious fancy as to keep him sleepless in fruitful meditation upon the plans which should render it of easy and safe acquisition. He gave the world credit, now that his cupidity was aroused, for a vigilance, cunning, and energy, like his own; and perpetually trembled lest some person just as 'cute and clever as himself, probably with better luck, should interpose, at a drowsy moment, and rob him of his prey.

No sooner had he got the despatches from the governor, and started Gideon on his route, than he began to reflect upon the readiness with which the former had yielded to his wishes. He suspected the governor — it may be as well said here as elsewhere — and began to feel some doubts of his good faith, when he recalled the facility with which he had obtained his object. He had expected his excellency to evade his application — to make

light of his arguments, and to put him off for a season; and had
already made his calculations that he should have finally to appeal
to some of the members of the council whom he knew to be much
more honest in their desires to carry out the ostensible objects of
the king's proclamation.

That Governor Quarry should have foreborne the formal publication of the government missives against piracy — should have
given no circulation to the fact that a heavy reward had been
offered for Calvert — was, of itself, sufficiently suspicious; and Job
was not the man to be put at fault by any such pretexts as those
which had quieted Sir Edward Berkeley. Of course, his suspicions were rendered lively by a degree of knowledge which he
possessed, through former associations, in respect to Quarry's flexibility of conscience, of which Berkeley and the rest of the council
were either wholly or mostly ignorant.

He was morally sure of Quarry's corrupt practice, and shrewdly
suspected that no small share of the piratical profits had gone into
the pockets of the government official. With this knowledge,
and these suspicions, he was not satisfied to rely upon the governor's good faith, even now, when the promptness of the latter,
in complying with his application, might well have disarmed the
suspicions of less cunning persons. He did not, accordingly, re-
lax his watch or exertions; but, affecting the utmost confidence
in the official, he put on a frankness of speech which, for him,
required no little effort. When he came for the despatches at
three o'clock, he said, in reply to the renewed question —

"What more do you think necessary, Master Stillwater, for securing the pirate?" —

"Nothing just now, your honor. As yet, I've got no clues to
his hiding-place. But, when I'm sure that he's in town, and can
find out where he is, then I shall come to your excellency for the
necessary force for his capture."

When he was gone, and Calvert came forth from the chamber
where he had heard everything, the governor said —

"I fancy I have disarmed that scamp of all suspicions."

"Not so," answered the more sagacious cruiser. "You have
surprised him, that is all. But he has no more faith in you than
before. Surprising him by your promptness, without disarming
his suspicions, has only made him more vigilant. He knows

more than he has told you. When a cunning fellow, who is cold-blooded, as all merely cunning people are, puts on a voluntary show of frankness, he is then most dangerous. In his frankness he is ostentatious. Of course, he has his object in it. You must be more than ever vigilant. He will be communicating with the council. Have you a trusty rogue whom you can put upon his heels? You must have his movements watched. Be sure he will watch yours, and I must relieve your house of my presence this very night."

" Where will you go?"

" Better that *you* should know nothing. I will take care of myself. I will see, too, that *he* is watched."

We need not pursue the conference, which was one simply of details. That night, Calvert left the governor's mansion as darkly as he came. He· soon found another hiding-place under the guidance of Franks, with whom, and Belcher, he had a long conference. With the latter he crossed the river to Gowdey's castle. Here, another conference took place, between these parties; but this chiefly contemplated other matters. Gowdey made a rough map, at the instance of Calvert, showing the topography of all the region lying along the coast from the Kiawah to the Stono rivers, and to the Edisto beyond, and inland up to the barony of Sir Edward Berkeley. The routes were described, their bearings shown, and all the distances accurately given.

" The ship must shift her ground, Belcher. She must run round, in a few nights, to Cooper river; run up out of sight from the harbor; and we must discharge the rest of the cargo in the woods above. But I have told Franks everything on that head. The rest remains for you. You will go with me to-night. Gowdey will let you have his horse. You must see the governor to-morrow, Gowdey, and get his sanction, if possible, for picking up a score of stout fellows. Tell him everything, which you yourself know, which justifies us in suspecting these red men of mischief. If still he refuses to give you the men, get them yourself. Here is bounty-money; and I will see that you have six months' pay for a dozen at least."

At midnight, Calvert and Belcher were upon the road. By dawn they were on the banks of the creek in which the Happy-go-Lucky was harbored.

Calvert's coming was a surprise; even the wonted audacity of Lieutenant Molyneaux failing him for a moment. He had not looked for his superior from this quarter. But, whether Calvert had suspicions or not, he never gave the slightest indication of them. He was simply taciturn; he had no reproaches; spoke of the discipline of the vessel; and gave his orders with regard to her future disposition, only leaving the period of the ship's removal in doubt, to be determined by his further orders through Belcher. But he made a selection of a dozen of his best marines, put them under an orderly, bade them be in readiness for any call, and keep their weapons ready. To both lieutenants he said, at parting:—

"Let these men march the moment Belcher calls for them, and he will assume the direction of the party until he joins me. Let him be implicitly obeyed. Meanwhile, have the ship ready to move with the first wind, and as soon after Belcher brings my orders as possible. You can not be too vigilant, gentlemen. The Indians are growing numerous, and you must watch the land as well as the river. See that your men do not wander. They will be cut off. Of course, you have suffered none of them to go to the city?"

This was said carelessly, affirmed rather than asked. He did not wait for the answer, which he would have found a confused one. The suggestion somewhat agitated Molyneaux. We shall see hereafter, perhaps, that the first lieutenant was even more of an offender than Calvert thought him. But, when Belcher, after they had left the ship, and remounted their steeds, proceeded to certain detailed passages in respect to his dealing with the discontents, Calvert silenced him.

"I know all that you would say, perhaps more than you guess. I have had other agencies at work, and know exactly how far he has gone with the men; nay, I could almost put my hands on the very fellows whom he has corrupted. But *his* schemes are not yet matured. Neither his fruit nor mine is ripe. I shall be able to anticipate all his purposes. He is simply a brave blockhead, whom Nature never designed for a conspirator. But for the men themselves, I could almost suffer the fellow to proceed. He little knows, Jack, how cheerfully I could surrender the little vessel to her fate, and be content to wear out the rest of my poor time in the obscurest solitude of sea, or rock, or forest, that an outlawed heart may find, in which to seek a grave and find rest!"

Belcher would have remonstrated with this woful self-abandonment, but Calvert hushed him:—

"Of what use, Jack? Do you not know me by this time?"

"Oh! sir, is there no hope?"

"Hope is the child's star, which it fain would clutch! I have done with it. I know too much — know all! Life has nothing in reserve. I can no longer deceive myself with any dream of my own: how idle to show me one of yours! I tell you I have grown indifferent to all things in this weary world."

"Oh!" groaned Belcher, bitterly; and then, as if in soliloquy, "O for a grapple, yard-arm to yard-arm, with the biggest cruiser of the dons!"

A sad smile passed over the face of Calvert as he heard the speech, and he answered mournfully:—

"Do you think, because I am indifferent to all things, Jack, that I would not *do* many things — *that* especially? Yes, I could pray for that, as the last act to finish the drama fitly. To fight the dons would be easy; nay, to feel the thrill and passion of the conflict — as I have felt it when I had a hope — that, too, would seem natural enough. Do not suppose that, because I have survived hope, I have survived impulse. I must still, even while I live, work down these restless energies which find their stimulus in the very disappointments which follow every effort. They drive me forward, as a bird before the storm; but I have no aim — there is no port which I would seek: the bark is rudderless — she cares not whither she drives."

Jack Belcher had no answer but a deep sob; and the two rode on in silence through the thick forests. They met with no interruption. When, at length, they had reached a point which Calvert judged to be about a mile from the barony of Kiawah, he stopped, alighted, and motioned Belcher to do the same. He then threw himself upon the sward, and, covering his eyes, lay awhile without speaking. Belcher did not seek to disturb his revery. When he did speak, his tone, words, and manner, conveyed, more fully than anything he had said before, the hopeless apathy of his soul. The mind might be present in its fullest vigor

— the energies of manhood, the courage, the resolve — but oh, how mournful the desolation that seemed to wither up the heart!

"The sun shines, I think, Belcher. The sun shines! There is not a cloud to be seen; and how sweet is the peace of these forests! if we could only sink into the earth, taking root, and spreading out, simply to grow, like these trees, and not to feel anything but growth and sunshine! But such is not for us — not for me. I have no growth, no sunshine; but I have toils to achieve, and perils to encounter, nevertheless. Who shall say when these shall end? It matters little. . . . . . . I think I have told you everything. You will do what I have bidden. If aught happens to me, you know what is to be done. My wife must be cared for. You will protect her. You know where our treasures are secured: I leave you in full guardianship of the trust. To put *her* in safety once more; to save these poor fellows — ay, even the faithless among them, and from themselves — is my first duty. I must do it. I have brought them hither; have done something toward making their present life acceptable; and this life is one which is banned by law. I must put them in safety. I will carry them to the isthmus, provide each with the means of honest livelihood, and — for the rest! — what more?"

"Yourself!" gasped Belcher.

"It will be time to think of myself when I have done for these."

"O my dear master, do not speak so hopelessly! Why should you not share the retreat that you seek for your people? Why should *we* not — your wife, and I, your poor, long-tried servant — why should we not all live together in some quiet retreat upon the isthmus? It is a peaceful world — almost to itself — is solitary enough, God knows, for any sore heart; but the sky is bright, and the air mild, and the fruits delicious, and the flowers beautiful. And the señora too! O my dear master! she is a child, I know, and perhaps will never quite understand you, or any Englishman; but, as I am a living man, and your faithful servant, I do believe she loves you as truly as it is possible for her to love any mortal man. It is not with these Spaniards of the isthmus to feel very passionately: she's like the sky, and the flowers, and the fruits of her country. She's changeable of temper, and she can never answer to a strong thought in a serious soul; but she's true! and, I tell you — I feel it, I know it — she loves you, and none but you, and as much as she can ever love any living man."

"Why, Belcher, you are eloquent."

"No, no, master! only my heart is full, and I must talk out or cry; and — I am doing both."

"We can not turn the leaves of our lives at pleasure, Jack, and *will* what is to be written there. It may be as you say. Did you suppose that I would abandon you or her? No, no! Let me suffer as I may, I will be no savage. I have only spoken to you of my hopelessness; only spoken of things for you to do, should the Fates deprive *me* of the power to do. I hold my purposes subject to my necessities. I see great dangers before me, and many troubles. To save these very men, against their will — this is, perhaps, the worst; but it shall be tried. For the rest — but you already have your instructions. Watch here, while I sleep for one hour. Then leave me, and find your way to Gowdey's castle, and help his preparations. Take charge of the place if he would go to town. I hope to be with you at midnight."

# CHAPTER XXX.

### THE JOLLY ROGER.

"Hang out the sign, the fatal sign of blood,
  Woven while the hurricane sweeps the sea with rage,
  And strews the shore with wreck of goodly ships!
  Now swear beneath its folds; while, overhead,
  In the black sky, the trooping fiends shriek joy
  And welcome to the kindred souls below,
  That swear to bring them homage." — *The Pirate.*

AND, closing his eyes, our rover sank almost immediately to sleep, awaking at the very moment which he had designated. Such is the force of habit with all persons who are accustomed to keep vigil, and are compelled to seize capricious moments for the relief of Nature in her exhaustion.

Having given Belcher instructions in respect to his route, and warned him to guard against all chance encounters, whether with red men or white, Calvert shook the hand of that faithful follower; and, mounting their horses, the two went different ways, Belcher taking his progress toward Gowdey's block-house, and Calvert shaping his route for the barony of his brother.

Once there, he was careful to conceal his steed in the deepest coverts, yet convenient to his reach; then he walked forward till the grounds of the new settlement began to appear through the woods.

His first object was to visit the tree in which the sheaf of arrows had been deposited by Cussoboe. He found a second shaft broken, as he expected. As before, he supplied its place. Then he resumed his espionage upon the premises.

He soon caught a glimpse of his brother, the cassique; saw him, still impetuously busied with his workmen; and, in the course of his watch, noted the Indian boy, wandering about the settlement, accompanied by Grace Masterton; she rather leading him than he her, and eagerly challenging his observation to the thousand wonders, in her eyes, of that primitive world which she now for the first time inhabited.

Let us leave Calvert to this espionage, which shall not profit him greatly, even though he may satisfy that curiosity — if we may describe, by such a word, the mood which prompted him — which was perhaps the only object of his watch. It was a wasting care which possessed him; and his eye grew dim, and his face pale, and his heart sank within him, while his watch was protracted. His was the nature which required great physical exertions to work off the stimulating passions which excited him; and, lacking these, during the hours devoted to this unprofitable employment, his excitements grew momently more powerful, and told upon his frame. His movements were marked by a nervous and irregular energy; his action was spasmodic; he started now at every sound in the woods; he found his fancies active, as it were, in the mood equally of experience and judgment; he felt himself no longer the cool, deliberate master, of either his situation, his resources, or his own moods. It was only when he could throw himself into the interests of others, while planning for his ship, people, or the colony — working in concert with Gowdey and others, in anticipation of danger — that he felt reassured on the subject of his own manhood. More than once a strong impulse seized him to dart forward, join his brother, denounce him where he stood, no matter in what presence, and have any issue with him which should effect a crisis; or to grapple with the tools of the workmen, and lose his intellectual nature in the mere brute exertions of his physical.

We will suppose a week to pass in these employments: by day, in *surveillance* of the barony; by night, in riding to Gowdey's, passing over to the city, or cantering up to the cruiser where she still lay in her snug harborage up the river. The tides happened to be low, however, the winds were ahead, and there were reasons why the Happy-go-Lucky should not yet change her position. When Calvert now visited the ship, he did so on horseback; but he took care to leave his horse in the woods, to approach stealthily, and never appeared on shipboard. His visits were unsuspected, save by one of the crew, who, previously counselled, knew where to expect him, and had learned to distinguish his whistle in the thickets from that of any wandering bird.

From this person our rover gathered a certain knowledge nightly of what was done in the ship. But, though he heard much, he heard not all. There were still some things beyond the scrutiny of Bill Hazard — such was the fellow's name, or *nom de guerre*. The factious lieutenant, Molyneaux, was working in secret, with a degree of circumspection, the credit of which was due to one of his accomplices rather than to his own sagacity. This was an old sea-dog, a genuine pirate, who, having served an apprenticeship among the "Brothers of the Coast," as the pirates called themselves, was by no means satisfied with the less exceptionable practices of one who still claimed to sail under a *quasi* commission of the British crown. He, it may be said here, was the original tempter of Molyneaux. He found him impatient of control, eager for action, anxious to be in sole authority, and especially jealous of his superior. The old sailor took the full measure of his man, and laid his baits accordingly. He found him accessible enough; and, though insinuating his temptations, at first, with sufficient caution, it was very soon easy to speak openly.

Sam Fowler, *alias* "Squint-eye Sam," became the right-hand man, the chief counsellor of Molyneaux, and his agent for disseminating treason among the crew. He had won over a goodly number, though but few were admitted to the more private councils of the two heads of the conspiracy. The plot had been some time in progress, and never standing quite still at any time since its first inception. It had been broached between the lieutenant and Sam several months before, and while they lay at Tampico. But it had never been so thoroughly matured as now, when the captain, and his satellite, Jack Belcher, were so frequently absent. And now, such had been its progress to maturity, that the frequent question, with all the guilty parties, was simply as to the proper moment for firing the train which they had so skilfully laid.

It was a dark night, when Molyneaux made his way stealthily from the ship to the shore, and buried himself from sight among those mighty trees in which the fair Zulieme had roused up all the sylvan echoes, by her joyous laughter, as she danced, capered, swung, when the vessel first ran into her harbor of seclusion.

Here, at a spot which had been already too frequently used for the purposes of conspiracy, he was joined, at intervals, by some five of the more intelligent seamen who had been won over by the arts of Sam Fowler. Each was challenged as he came. He gave no name — only a pass-word; and, squat in the covert, they proceeded to report progress severally, and to discuss the plans of the future.

But where is the chief agent in the treason? Sam Fowler is not present. He is, however, momently expected.

He was even then in the breach of orders; had been despatched to the city secretly the night before, in a skiff, with two stout rowers, on a mission which concerned a variety of illegal interests.

The rogues had stores of their own for which they sought a market. They, too, had emissaries in the town, as well as their superior. They had passions and appetites, for which the town could afford the only proper theatre; and they had a mission to execute, on behalf of Molyneaux himself. All parties were accordingly impatient for the return of Sam; and what discussion took place among them before he arrived, was confined mostly to topics which had been on the *tapis* long before. But, among conspirators, iteration is an essential necessity for confirming them in a purpose which implies no small peril.

At length, Sam Fowler came, stealing through the thickets like a catamount. He soon made his way into the circle. The boat had been left hidden in the rushes a quarter of a mile below. The old sailor took his place among the brethren with the freedom of one who knew his importance.

" Some grog, fellows, 'fore I begin. I 'm as blasted thirsty as the chap as was in Abraham's buzzom. The Jamaica 'gin out five miles below; not a blasted sup after that! And, somehow, 't was short commons in town; I had to lie so close. 'T wan't as it used to be there."

The liquor was soon provided. Conspiracy, and among pirates, is wonderfully helped by its potations. The supply of grog was abundant. Long, and strong, and deep, was the draught taken by the old sea-dog, whose sentences, by-the-way, were so larded with oaths as to render them only in part intelligible. We shall strip them of most of his weeds of rhetoric. When he had fairly concluded his draught, which was taken with exceedingly deliberate *gusto,* and wiped his mouth with a gorgeous bandanna, Sam condescended to enlighten his brethren.

" I 've sold your plate, Jordan ; your silks, Foster ; your tobacco, Rollins. Got the cash for 'em. You shall have it when we empty the boat. Done a pretty good business, considerin' that the honest traders always make out to cheat the free bretheren. And they say prayers while doin' it. But that's no matter, neither here nor there. We ixpects as much : always ixpect to be cheated when the trader makes a prayer while makin' a barg'in. They 're mighty vartuous and religious, on a sudden, in Charlestoon. The old church was bad enough in its goodness ; but these Dissenters, as they calls 'em — and town 's full of 'em — they 're the d——dest rogues that ever lied in the name of God ! It a'most turns my stomach when I has to deal with 'em. I ixpects to be cheated ; but this callin' in o' God to be a witness, as it were, ag'in himself, is worse than any Spanish practice. But there 's no helpin' it. We has to do with 'em, or we can 't trade. Now, Sproulls, the man I deal with, he 's about as good as the best ; but though he grins at his prayers, jest as ef he was a-cheatin' the Lord himself, he can 't no more help prayin' than he can fly. I jest said to him, ' Shut up your oven, and say no more prayers if you please ;' but he kept on jest the same, sayin', by way of ixcusin' himself — ' It 's no use to try, Fowler ; I can 't help it, and it don n't mean nothin' ! It 's only a way I 've got.' And jest so I answered him when he wanted to put a clapper on my mouth for swearin'. Says I, ' Them 's my prayers, and they do n't mean no more than yours. It 's jest a way I 've got.' Then he showed his teeth ag'in, jest like a shark in shallow water among a school of mullets, and we went on with our trade till the cheat was over."

" Did you see Franks and Sylvester ?"

" Did n't I see 'em ! But I was n't sich a dummy as to let 'em see me. Sylvester 's got religion in all his garments : he shakes it out as he walks. His hat 's got religion ; his coat ; his breeches ; the tie of his cravat ; and I think his nose has got a good inch longer and sharper from the new vartue that 's in it ! He 's all over religion ; and sich a sample of it, that there 's no more trustin' him with a trade than trustin' your finger in the gripe of a stone-crab. Franks ain't so vartuous ; but my business was to watch him and make out what I could, without lettin' him over-haul me with his eye. He' as close as he's sharp, as you all know, and I reckon is true to the captain as a trump. Of course, 't would n't do to let Franks or Sylvester know that I was in town ; for I reckon that both of them's in the captain's books, jest as deep as ever. I'm not supposin' that any religion of either will do much to stop a trade if they can make it."

" Did you get sight of the captain?" asked Molyneaux.

" No! and I had all the lights out, too. I tried my best to get into his wake. But he carries no flag. I could n't hear a word from Sproulls, though he was monstrous curious with me, and I reckon was jest as curious with all other persons. It's clear that the captain, wherever he is, keeps mighty close ; and there's rea-son for it. There's a big price offered for him, so I hear tell, though there's no open proclamation yet! Sproulls was quite curious to get out of me what he could. 'Where was the ship?' he asked. 'Over the bar,' was my answer. 'I'm jest sent up with the boat to get medicine, and I took the chance to sell off a little prog.' But that's not enough for him ; and ef he'd ha' had a chance, he'd ha' had a spy at my heels, I'm thinkin', ef 't was only to get wiser on a poor man's secrets. He's curious, that Sproulls. He'll not blow so long as the profit comes in ; but he, too, is gettin' more and more vartuous from what I know'd him a year ago — and that made it only the worse for my barg'ins. He did cheat me worse than ever this time. You'll see, fellows, by the bills, when I settle. There's a sort of fashion of religion now, 'mong all the people in town ; and you get less money and more preachin' for your goods than I've ever know'd before ; but there's a better chance, for that very reason, of finding friends for sich a trade as ours. The more they can make, the more vartuous the business ; they're all hot ag'in the king's proc-lamation ag'in pirates. They say — and that's true — that we're their best friends ag'in the Spaniards. Sproulls said we might come up to the wharf, and nobody would trouble us among the people, though he did confess that the governor and council were sich bloody fools as to talk of minding the king's orders. I reckon, from what I seed and heard, that we might haul up the Happy-go-Lucky right ag'in the town battery, and nobody ever think to p'int a cannon at her. The captain's gettin' scary without any 'casion."

13

" Yes, indeed ; something's the matter with him *here*," replied Molyneaux, scornfully, touching his forehead with his finger. " He could fight once, boys, bravely enough ; but ever since he had that knock-over from the Spanish splinter, he's been weak in the upper story : ay, and in the heart too, or he would n't care a button for the king's proclamation. Why should we fear the king's proclamation any more than we do his cruisers ? We can trip the heels, and, yard-arm to yard-arm, muzzle every gun in her own porthole, in the very best of them ; yes, and give them the advantage over us, five guns a side. But for the captain's cowardice, fellows, we might be gutting the Spanish galleons now !"

" And we will be doin' it soon, too, if other men have their hearts in the right places," said Sam Fowler, significantly.

" The sooner the better !" was the common answer.

" And if the courage be all, men," quoth the lieutenant, " I can answer for one, who will never back out from any don that ever sailed the gulf."

" Ay, indeed !" responded Sam Fowler. " That's all well enough — all right enough, lieutenant ; but there's not enough of it. It's not the dons only that we must n't show our backs to ; it's not the Spaniards only that we 've got to face ! I'm bold to say that ef we are to do the right business, we must muzzle a king's cruiser, and the marchant of any nation, jest as bold as we muzzle a don — and ef only to show that we 're not guine to let ourselves be muzzled by any of 'em. I'm for a free flag of our own, even if we have to hang out the 'Jolly Roger !' Ay ! I'm not afraid to speak it. Run up the 'Jolly Roger,' say I ; and I drink to 'THE JOLLY ROGER' for ever ! Here, boys, is to the ' Brothers of the Coast' — the free life, the black flag, and death to the traitor and the coward that's afraid to fight under the Jolly Roger !"

There was a murmur of excitement. It might be enthusiasm. With some of the parties, no doubt the bold speech of Sam Fowler was in considerable degree contagious. But it is doubtful whether, before this meeting, the conspirators had been prepared to run up the black flag. They had mostly contemplated nothing more than running away with the ship and getting a more flexible captain. To defy the laws of nations openly, and at a season when

the cruisers of Britain and Spain were everywhere on the alert
against piracy, required no little audacity; and it is probable that
the speech of Fowler would have fallen cheerlessly upon the
senses of not a few of the conspirators, had it not been that it was
so promptly seconded by Molyneaux. That unhappy young man,
eager for power, arrogant in his vanity, and not a little warmed
by strong drink, acting upon his highly-inflammable nature, echoed
the toast of Fowler with additions; rising to his feet, seizing the
cup from the hands of the latter, filling it to the brim, drinking its
contents to the bottom, and flinging the vessel over his head into
the thickets, as he cried aloud —

"Hurrah for the Jolly Roger! the Jolly Roger for ever!"

"Your hand upon it, lieutenant!" said Sam Fowler; "but you
need n't wake up the woods jest yet! It'll be time enough for
that when we feel blue water under us. Stand round, fellows
— all round, and j'ine hands! And now, here we are, brothers
of the coast, sworn to one another ag'in all the world. Them
that 's not with us is ag'in us! Swear, fellows! and all cowards
and traitors to the sharks!"

There were no more murmurs. The conspirators were grouped
together in a circle, and joined hands, while Molyneaux stood in
the centre, with weapon drawn, upon which they all swore horrible oaths of fidelity to one another, and to the more horrid purposes of crime for which they stood leagued together. This done,
Sam Fowler suddenly shook out over their heads the folds of the
black flag, prepared for the purpose; dark as night; with a bloody
fringe; and, wrought in ghastly white in the centre, a skull and
crossbones — the usual insignia, in those days, of the pirate banner.

He lowered it among them.

"Every man kiss the 'Jolly Roger!'"

And with a chill probably at the hearts of most of them, each
of them in turn embraced the gloomy flag, and pressed his lips
upon the ghastly emblems of mortality which it bore!

"It's as good as sworn, fellows," said Sam Fowler. "As good
as sworn, I say: all hell looking on, and fires of sulphur lighted
for the coward and the traitor that deserts the flag of the true
'Brothers of the Coast'! We are sworn to one another through
thick and thin; and we're the men to stand by one another, till
all burns blue! But for a time, boys, a keen eye, a quick hand,

and a close tongue! We're not out of shoal water, remember.
But it's only the length of an oar, and there's sea-room enough.
Hearts up — eyes wide — and hands ready! One drink round, I
say, fellows, to the 'Jolly Roger,' at the mast-head of the Happy-
go-Lucky!"

And the liquor went round; and, even as they drank, Sam
Fowler kept the fatal flag in motion over their heads, as if, woven
under some troubled sign, it was supposed to be endued with the
power to exercise a demoniac influence over the souls of those
who had sworn to serve under it.

# CHAPTER XXXI.

## CONSPIRACY.

"He dies, at least! by fraud or force, he dies —
'Tis sworn! His death alone secures the prize."
*The Rover.*

"And now, boys," said Fowler, "get to quarters, one by one, without waking up any of the water-rats. We'll settle our small affairs together in the mornin'. There's a good handful of the king's pictures for all of you. We understand one another to-night. Me and the lieutenant ["I and the king"] have something more to say together, which don't need any help, and has to be settled in private. But it's for the good of the cause; and you knows very well that means the good of all. Git into your hammocks, quiet as you can, without shaking the ship's knees. Who's on the watch?"

"Stoddart."

"He's safe! Well, off with you, now; and we'll have another and a closer talk, to-morrow night, jest here, in the same place."

So Sam Fowler, who, with the habitual dictation of an old sea-dog (and, we may add, an old conspirator and turbulent), found authority easy, when such was the game; and assumed the parole, without any concession, made previously, to the self-esteem of Lieutenant Molyneaux. The latter would have kicked at this assumption with all the fury of a Celt, but that he, too, felt the natural force of an authority which was based upon a superior experience. Besides, he too, we may add, was a little taken by surprise by the decided movements of his coadjutor.

When the rest were gone, and fully out of hearing, and Fowler had satisfied himself, by following them a certain distance, that they were all moving quietly in the direction of the ship, he returned and resumed the conference.

"And now, lieutenant, you're to be captain: that's settled in my mind. What am I to be?"

"First, of course. What else?"

"All right! It's what I looked for. In course, you see what's to be done. We've to run off with the ship the moment we've got all things ready for moving. There's no stayin' here much longer. We'll have the king's frigates down upon us — two, three — for jest so many have they got in New York, and all on the shy. Sproulls tells me that there's been a despatch sent for'ard to bring on the frigates fast as wind and water will let 'em."

"That despatch will never reach! Set your mind easy there. We've got the fellow fast now in the ship's hold, and a terrible praying and psalm-singing does he keep up day and night. The captain's got the despatch. He fixed the whole business, and had the fellow brought here and put under fast locker."

Where the h—l can *he* be, then! I tried my best to get upon his tracks in town, but 'twas no go. Couldn't hear nor see nothin' of him; and no one could tell. Sproulls pumped mighty hard to get it out of me; for I could see he didn't half believe what I said about the ship over the bar. He's 'cute and close, and I'm thinkin' a leetle mixed up with Sylvester. They goes to meetin' together; I knows that. But ef the governor and council are makin' despatches ag'in us, they're not a-guine to stop at that one. We may overhaul one jigger, but what's to prevent 'em sendin' a dozen? The captain may be sly as a fox, but there's a shifting of the wind in town; that's a sign of bad weather ahead. In old times, governor and council had a blind eye for a free-trader. Is it so certain that they haven't got the captain himself somewhere under hatches? There's a squall comin' on! The governor's got wind of us, and the council too, I reckon; and how could they help it, if they wanted to see? The town's full of our goods. Fresh fruits are plenty, though there's been not a single craft — so Sproulls tells me — from any West Injy port for nineteen days before we came. In course, these people ain't fools; and there's rogues enough among 'em to keep 'em from blindness, even if Natur had made the most of 'em the very best of fools!

And so they reasons together; and though they do n't guess where
we are, they know we 're somewhere about; over the island they
reckon, behind the swamp; but able to run in with the tide, every
night, and land a cargo. We can't keep snug much longer; we 'll
have to run for it; and that, too, before they bring on their frigates. 'T would be the stupidest thing in natur' to let 'em catch
us here at anchor, and in a creek in which we could n't swing
round, and in a river where a long-sided craft like ours could n't
go about, under a broadside."

"There's hardly any danger yet, Sam, and we want all the
time we can get. We 've got only nineteen of the fellows
over."

"But them 's the true *men!* As for the others, they 'll jest do
what they sees the boldest men do, once they 're under workin'
orders. You get me together six fellows that are ready, tooth
and nail, and the rest, though they be sixty, will be quick enough
to fall into the ranks."

"Not with such a fellow to halloo them on against us as Harry
Calvert."

"There I 'gree with you. But where 's he to halloo them on?
Look you, captain — so I makes free to call you at once — I 'm
a-thinkin' that Captain Calvert will never pipe our fellows to
quarters ag'in. He 's safe from us, ef he ain't safe from the governor; and, thank the devils, we 're safe from him!"

"You think so! He was here three nights ago."

"And three days have gone since then. Where 's he now?
We hear no more of him! I *knows* that Franks hain't seed him
in all that time. No! I 'm tellin' you jest what 's the reasonable
thinkin'. They 've got Calvert fast. He 's the main one they
strike at, for you see there 's a good five hundred pounds offered
for him one, dead or alive. They 'll be satisfied to have him in
the darbies, and they 'll be pleased to have our trade jest the
same."

"I would n't trust 'em."

"Nor would I! But s'posin' him locked up in cold quarters,
or s'posin' him not locked up, and jest schoolin' about on his own
business, what 's it to us any way? It only gives us the more
chance to get off. We must run, ef we can. Better now, when
we need n't fight for it — when it 's with wind and tide — than to

have a bloody fight of it on the high seas: and we're so far in, that, if we don't move now, pretty soon, it must come to that. The first question is, whether we shall use our heels to please Captain Calvert, or to please me and Captain Molyneaux. I'm clear that we should go for our own dear selves, in preference to a man that jest rules us as he thinks proper, and don't ax us who's pleased besides. He's been a famous captain in his time, but somehow he's only a Dutch lugger now. He's not the man any longer. I'm clear for one thing — cuttin' loose from moorings here, jest as soon as we can, and not waitin' to see where the wind's goin' to come out. If we wait for Calvert, there's so much more to do, and so much more risk in the doin' of it. There's one thing which I wouldn't like to have to do."

"What's that, Fowler?"

"Cut the captain's throat!"

"D—n him! why should you shirk at that?"

"It's not because I love him. No! the devil, no! It's because, whenever the thing has to be done, there'll be more throats to be slit than the one. He's a d——d great fellow in a fight, and he's got the strength of Jolly Cæsar, the great Roman; and he's got the trick of the broadsword and the tomhog [tomahawk], the knife and the blunderbuss, better than any sea-captain that ever stepped a quarter-deck in our day; and he's got some d——d true fellows that'll back him, ef he can call for 'em, 'gainst any force we can bring. Ef we can get off with the ship without his knowing, we mustn't stop to find out where he is. It's enough for us ef he ain't in our way; and that's jest what we've got to do! But, ef we wait for him, we must feed the fishes with him."

"Look you, Sam! Captain Calvert owes me a life. I've sworn to have it. He has wounded my honor; he has treated me with scorn and insult. I will have my revenge."

"You! Fight with *him*?"

"Man to man, breast to breast; a fair fight, and no other man to come between."

"Psho! Captain Molyneaux — so I begs leave to call you — that's all in my eye and Betty Martin. Don't be sich a Judy. A man what's got sich a great business on his hands has nothin' to do with honor and revenge. That'll do for boys. It's all gammon. If you say, now, you 're for slitting his windpipe, at the first good chance, takin' care that you keep your own safe all the time, I do n't say nothin' ag'in it. It 's all right, and a sensible way to sarve out an enemy to the fishes ; but to talk of a fair fight, riskin' everything after we 've got the stakes in our own hands, I 'll never agree to that."

"It must be so, Sam," answered the other, doggedly. "I 'm sworn to it. My honor demands it. He shall give me satisfaction."

"Why, so he shall ; and what better satisfaction than takin' his ship, and leaving him, on a sort of maroon here, where they 'll give five hundred pounds for his head, and where there 's so many who are on the watch for him, day and night, to get the prize-money ? Ef that ain't takin' satisfaction out of him, then I 've no ixperience in sich a consarn."

"Not enough for me. I must crush him — have him under foot — see him at my mercy. My sword must drink his blood !"

"And you mean to give him a fair chance, in a reg'lar hand-to-hand fight ?"

"He shall have nothing less !"

"Then, ef that 's your resolution, hear to mine. We part company. I thought I was dealin' with a man of sense. I do n't risk my neck under the ' Jolly Roger,' with any captain that talks about his honor, and fair play, and all that sort of stuff and nonsense. I 'm sorry, lieutenant, for I think ef 't wan't for this redick-'lous notion, you 'd be the very man for us."

"What ! you abandon me, because I 'm bold enough to take our old captain by the throat ?"

"No, by your leave — no sich thing ! But because you 're for lettin' him take you by the throat at the same time. And do n't I know what 'll happen ef he once does get you in his gripe ? Why, he 'll slit your oozen as easy as he 'd slice an orange. Look you, Lieutenant Molyneaux — I 'd like to call you captain, all the time — it 's a mighty redick'lous bull that won't see the shortness of his own horns. Once hitched with Harry Calvert, you 'd soon enough l'arn the difference 'twixt your'n and his'n. As for a fight with him, man to man, it 's not in you."

Molyneaux was about to protest his skill and valor with all the indignant vanity of a Milesian.

13*

"Do n't be a fool, lieutenant! You 're as brave a lad as I know, and you can use a broadsword as well as most men; but Harry Calvert! — do n't be foolish! That 's not the way! Hear to me. We 'll cut and run, soon as the wind sarves, and we can get off these ceroons of indigo. We 'll be off while Calvert 's ashore, no matter where. We 'll leave him — maroon him, and in good quarters, I reckon. And ef we can 't do that, there 's but one way — and that 's to send him down-stream, swimming like a pig in a gale of wind, with a gapin' throat. Ef we manage that sensibly, we can do it easily; and the rest we can settle at New Providence."

"I would rather fight him, man to man. It 's a point of honor, Sam. Besides—"

"P'int of h—l! What have we got to do with sich redick'lous matters? Look you, lieutenant — if you talk so, I give you up; for all this is jest downright nonsense. It 's business we 're on, now; not honor! It 's part of the business that we leave Captain Calvert to take care of himself, on a coast where he knows all the bearings as well as we do; or, if he comes in our way, and only when he comes in our way, when the word is ' Cut and run,' then we cut him out of it. If you say ' No,' then there 's an end to the trade. We 'll stand off, jest where we was before, and no harm done !"

"You 're hard on me, Sam Fowler. I 've let you have your own way in the management of the affair so far."

"Exactly! and who do you think could manage it a better way ?"

"I do n't deny that. You were as good as born to the business; but here, the very first thing. I want to do for myself, you oppose it. It 's true, I propose to fight: but the fight is mine — the risk all mine. I do n't ask any man to peril his life for me !"

"And that 's the redick'lous part of the notion. Ef you 'd say, ' I must have the captain's heart's-blood,' and call upon the help of half a dozen to make the thing sart'in sure, and without any danger to your own throat, there would be some sense in it. But the other way is no better than a sort of madness. I won't hear to it."

"But, Sam, there 's another reason for putting Calvert out of the way."

" Well, out with it !"

" Zulieme Calvert must be mine.   I love her !"

" Does she love you ?"

" I 've every reason to think so."

" And I 've no reason to think so  at  all.   The woman 's half a fool, I 'm thinkin', and has no love for anything but plays and toys, singin' and jiggin'.   But that 's nothin' to the purpose.   Ef you want  the  woman,  it  do n't  need  any  love  between  the  parties. Take her, ef you can — as you can, and where you can."

" But she 'll never  consent,  so  long  as  Calvert  is  a  living man."

"Then butcher  him  when  you  find  him ;  nobody says ' no' to that ; it 's only against the nonsense of a fight with him, yard-arm to yard-arm ; for in sich a fight he 'll sink you  to  Davy Jones's locker, jest so sure as you come to the grapple !   But who says that she won't take up with you, when you can get her clear of him ?   It 's strange, lieutenant, that a man that 's got sich a good conceit of himself in some things, should be so bashful in others. Now, you 're a fine fellow  to  look at — few quite so handsome ; and you 're young and strong, and can talk that sort of gammon that women likes : and what 's to hinder her preference, if you come turtle over her, when 't other 's out of the way ?   She 'll do it !"

" Do you really think so ?"

" Why not ?   There 's reason enough for it.   I do n't mean to say that she 'll have any love in the business — any more than you—"

" But I do love her, Sam."

" As a fish-hawk loves a mullet !   Well, as you please.   I do n't say one word against your cuttin' the captain's throat, ef it comes easy and in your way, and carryin' off his woman."

" You will lend a hand at both, Sam ?"

" My hand on it !   But remember, we 're not to go out of our way, or take any risks for it."

" I understand."

" You  promise, then, there 's to  be  no more nonsense about a fair fight, and all that ?"

" I promise you.   You shall approve all that I do in the matter."

" Well, that's spoken like a man of sense. And now to more plain business. It's mighty strange I could n't get on the track of Captain Calvert anywhere in town. He's either under the governor's hatches, or he's off somewhere. He's got some secret business on some of the plantations. What if he should think to turn the ship into a slaver? He's scrup'lous, I know, about privateerin' any more ag'inst the dons, now that the king calls it piracy. What's left for him, but the slave-trade?"

" Oh, he'd never think to dirt his fingers with that business !"

" What else can he do? 'T would be a poor business for him; and what with crammin' the hold with cargo, and starvin' the negroes, these eastern people would beat him clean out of sight. He'd be for givin' them niggers room enough, and air enough, and food enough, and good food too, and that would ruin him. His niggers would cost him quite too much before they could reach the market. Besides, it's quite too slow a business for us."

" Yes, indeed ! I'll none of it."

" Nor I. We'll make shorter cruises in chase of fortune. And I can hardly think, ef Calvert knows anything about the business, that 't would suit him. Still, it's curious where he hides himself. I got a squint of Franks, though—"

" You did n't suffer him to see you?"

" Catch me at that ! Belcher I could n't hear of any more than Calvert. They're either stowed away in the governor's locker, or they're at some secret business which we're not to know about."

" May not Calvert be with his wife?"

" Well, he warn't over fond of her company when he had the freedom of it; and it's not likely he'll run his neck into a halter for it now, when he's got so much reason to keep from any sort of a noose. I should only care to know where she is to steer clear of him. I'm more anxious to find Jack Belcher than his master."

" Why him?"

" He knows the hiding-place of all his money; and that's enough to pay for a voyage round the world. We must have the fingerin' of that, lieutenant; and, look you now, that's betwixt ourselves. There's no sharin' that among the crew. It's not prize-money; it's our own right, 'twixt us, before the cruise. Besides, 'twould be mighty foolish to put 'em in flush, at the very start: they'd be desarting, half of 'em. And then, they've got quite enough in the ixpectations, you know; the ixpectations of a Jolly Roger are his best argyments. In course, it's understood atween us that we goes shares, half-and-half, in the captain's treasure."

"That was our agreement."

"Hands on it, lieutenant!"

And they clasped hands.

"There can be no mistake now," continued the old pirate. "We shall both have enough and to spare. All that we want now is to get Jack Belcher under the screw."

"And where *can* he keep when not here? He was here three days ago."

"He's in town, I reckon, though I could n't find him. The captain keeps him busy, perhaps, watchin' over his harum-scarum wife."

"What! he watch her? He never watched her here."

"Did n't he, then? He watched her as close as cat watches mouse. But Calvert did n't fear for *her*. It was you he was afraid of. He's too proud to think that *she* would play him false; but he's too wise not to know what hot blood, in the veins of a young Irishman, might not attempt. Did n't he surprise you together in the cabin? Do you suppose he did n't keep eyes on you elsewhere? 'T was easy for *her* to get out of the scrape, but not so easy for you."

"But I did get out of it."

"You did? You're not out of it yet! Do you think he forgets or forgives so easily? No, lieutenant; if I know man, and this man in particular, you've got to pay for your impudence yet. He's only waitin' his time, till he can take you unawares; and you do n't know how soon he'll be upon you! Nothin' can save you from *his* vengeance, but this plan of ours! Do you take the ship, and let him find *his* satisfaction, after that, any way he can."

"What! do you think I'm afraid of anything he can do? Hark you, Sam; I promised not to seek, or challenge him to single combat, but I did n't promise that I would shirk the fight if he should challenge me. No, by Heaven! I would never submit to that dishonor. I should face him, though I knew that he would slay me at the first passage."

"And hark you, Lieutenant Molyneaux, I say to you that ef I should be at hand, and I saw any sich affair goin' on, I should calculate to put in between you with half a dozen good fellows besides, and save you from any consequences that might do up our present business."

"No, Sam! do not, I entreat you. Should the captain challenge me, the point of honor—"

"Oh, d—n and blast that p'int of honor! I thought we had settled that matter already; and ef we have n't, the sooner we do come to the right sense of our agreement the better. You 're to kill him, ef you can; but not to fight him at all! That 's the reason! We want you; we 've need of you; we can 't do without you; we like you; and blast my eyes, lieutenant, we 'll save you as long as we can!"

"Why, you talk, Sam, as if 't were a certain thing that I must fall, fighting Calvert."

"To be sure you will! Oh, I know, lieutenant, you 've got face and heart to fight the devil; and that 's the reason why I made up to you, as the man to put us all right, in a bold navigation. But, ef you mean that you can stand a fair, up-and-down fight, with smallsword or broadsword, ag'in Harry Calvert, then you 've more of Irish conceit in you than I 'm willin' you should nurse to spoilin'. You can 't do it; and the best thing for you and us is, to slip cable, and get the wind of him while we have a chance. I 'm not willin' to lose more time than we can help, or any valuable life. A few days more, I reckon, will give us a chance at Jack Belcher. Ef he comes here, we must muzzle him somewhere in the woods, and have his secret out of him, though we pull out his tongue with it! And ef his master comes, then we must sarve him in the same fashion. We 've got nineteen strong fellows sart'in, and can get more; and what we can 't get, we can shut hatches down upon, and starve 'em into sense, on bread and water."

"What 's to be done with Eccles?"

"He! We do n't want him, anyhow. He 's a born simpleton. But he 's so easy, that, once out to sea, I reckon we can bring him to anything."

"Did you see anything of *her* — the captain's wife — when you were in town?"

"See! Did n't I? She was ridin' out in a grand coach, with another woman, all in flyin' colors, all the flags of all the nations; four horses in silver harness, and two outriders in green and gold uniforms. She 's the town beauty. I heard more of *her* than I can tell of her: she 's at all the balls and dances; and they talk of her as a Spanish lady, with a mint of money. Sproulls had a great deal to say about her. There was a dozen young rakes, most of 'em noblemen's sons, at her skairts all the time. What 's the best fun of all, she passes for a young, unmarried innocent — a *senorita* somebody — Mountainair, I think — fresh from Florida! Young Cavendish — a lord, they say — is in turtle-fits all the time on her account; and there 's more young lords besides, that she keeps in a sort of gander-heaven."

Molyneaux stirred his whiskers fiercely as he heard this account. The other continued — having his motive in it, no doubt :—

"Sproulls p'inted out to me where she lived — with one Mother Anderson, or Parkins, 't was one or both — and told me all about her! There 's to be a grand, smashin' party at her house on Thursday night next, when everybody 's got to go in masks and disguise-dresses, after the French or Spanish fancy. In town, they talks of nothin' else; and I reckon they 'll use up, for the occasion, all the fine silks, and satins, and velvets, that we 've sold 'em. Calvert got to the right market this time, and helped to make it when he carried his frisky wife down there, under a false name."

The effect of this communication upon Molyneaux was instantaneous. He started to his feet, struck his forehead sharply, and strode a few paces, right and left, under the trees. Sam Fowler seemed somewhat surprised by the effect he had produced.

"Why, what 's the matter, lieutenant?"

"When is that party to take place, did you say, Sam?"

"Thursday next."

"Almost a week off. I must be at that party, Sam."

"How can you, when we may have to weigh anchor at a moment's warnin'?"

"I care not for that : I must be at that party. I must see Zulieme; I must see and speak with her. Everything depends upon it."

Sam expostulated. He had overshot his mark. Whatever his real object, he had not calculated on such an effect from his communication. He now, earnestly enough, endeavored to dissuade his hot-headed ally from his purpose; but in vain. Never was Celt more doggedly determined.

"I will go, if all the devils in h—l stand against me! Do n't think to dissuade me, Sam. I have submitted to you in everything; but I 'll be d——d if I submit in this! I will see her."

"But how will you get there? At these parties, they ax you for your tickets. There 's an invitation and a ticket; and where are you to get one?"

"Ticket! as if any of their nigger-servants could stop me entering a lady's parlor! They won't try it. They 're not very strict at these parties; and when they see a fellow well dressed, presenting himself boldly, they take some things for granted."

"Yes; but when supper-time comes, you 've got to unmask."

"Well, suppose I do n't stay for supper! Do n't you be afraid, Sam: I 've the head for any situation."

"Ef you do n't get your head into sich a sitiation as will make it hard to get it out ag'in!"

"I 'll take the risk."

"I 'll go with you, down to the city at least, and have the boat ready for anything that happens," was the conclusion of Sam, finally giving up the contest. Molyneaux was no longer to be reasoned with, and the old sea-dog was disposed to make the most of a difficult customer.

"I 'll go with you; but a week of waitin'! And how if Calvert comes up in the meantime, and orders us to weigh anchor?"

"Then muzzle him, as you propose! Once in the hold of the vessel, hatches close, what 's to prevent us doing what we please?"

"It may be done — must be done, if it comes to the worst; but we may have to fight for it. Remember, we 've got only nineteen of the fellows dead sure.'

"We must do what 's needful. If he forces us to the worst, his blood be upon his own head! And Zulieme I *will* see! I will know from herself what she feels."

"And ef she grins at you, like a monkey on a high tree?"

"Then I seize if I can, and plead no longer! It will be easy enough to carry her off."

"Ef you can get at her! and that's easy, ef you don't give her a scare beforehand. 'T won't be hard to get her out in the dusk, with some message from Calvert."

"True, true! we must arrange all that. I will have her, by all the devils!"

The conference pretty much closed here for the night. The two conspirators returned severally to the vessel, Molyneaux being last.

## CHAPTER XXXII.

### WOODS HAVE EARS.

> ———"There's a destiny in life,
> That still denies all certainty to Crime,
> And makes its nature mortal !   Be as sure
> As Cunning — that base wisdom of the snake —
> Can make thy infidelity and falsehood,
> And still the Ithuriel spear of Truth will pierce
> Thy meshes, and the crevice in thy armor,
> When least thou thinkest of Fate !" — *Old Play.*

THE forest was once more silent, still as death — a solemn silence which seems to overawe Nature, and check her most courageous breathings.   The conspirators were gone, and by this time probably were all housed safely, and in their several hammocks, in the Happy-go-Lucky, that smart rover, over which they designed to spread the ominous standard of the " Jolly Roger."

But the silence was for a few moments only.   The thicket which they had so recently occupied, was anon conscious of new parties upon the scene, in the persons of two other men who came out from yet deeper hiding-places in the rear.   There they had evidently lain *perdu*, and in a situation which enabled them to take in all the particulars which we have related.   One of the last-comers now spoke, in low but deep accents, the tones of which were significant of greatly-aroused and very painful emotions :—

" Great God of heaven ! is it possible that I have heard all this ?"

The voice was that of our rover himself, Captain Calvert.   The voice which answered him was that of one who has hitherto been unknown to us.

"I reckon, captain, you are now satisfied that I told you no more than the truth."

"Would to Heaven I could believe otherwise, Bill Hazard! I would give a thousand pounds could I convict you of falsehood."

"That you will never do, captain. Your own ears are the very witnesses I wanted. I knew it must reach you at last, for this is the place they meet in nightly. You have heard all I have been telling you for more than two weeks, and something more I reckon; and I'm glad you've heard for yourself; for it's not easy to believe in such villany, in men we've been trusting so long, upon any evidence short of one's own senses."

"Verily, it is not! Yet do me justice, Hazard, and remember that I have always held you faithful and honest in what you said. It was rather a hope with me that you had been deceived, than a doubt that you were honest. I am now satisfied, however painfully, that you have spoken nothing but the truth. Belcher entertained his suspicions, not to the same degree with you, but I would not hear him. Yours is evidence; and it is now mine. All his suspicions, and your statements, have been confirmed by my own senses."

"You know all the parties, captain?"

"No! I am not sure of some two or three of the common seamen. Of course, I know the voices of Molyneaux and Fowler, and I have my guesses at some of the rest. Some of the names were also spoken. There were Fowler, Stoddart, Jordan, Rollins, and—"

"Pearson and Gibbes," answered the other, concluding the sentence.

"But all these were not present. They were only named by the others, as sure."

"And they are sure, sir! These are the very rascals of the ship."

"It may be! Yet the best of men may be involved by a misrepresentation."

"That is true, sir; and we might doubt, if we had reason to suppose that Molyneaux and Fowler could fancy that they were overheard. But they did not, that is certain; and these fellows are just as guilty as the rest."

"Not exactly. Some men are rogues through feebleness. A strong will, in one villain, subdues to villany the feebler nature, in the absence of any better authority. We may hang a miserable wretch for crime to-day, whom a few hours of time, under a good master, would make a worthy citizen. At all events, Hazard, there must be no doubt of the persons in the movement, when they are required to pay the penalty of their crimes. We must have all *that* right, and even then, there will be cases, in respect to whom Justice must take some hints from Mercy."

"That's for you to say, captain. Yet, it's just as well to have your rope round about the man you mean to pardon, the same as him you mean to hang; you've got the first list I gave you, sir?"

"Yes; but there are additions to be made to it. These you can furnish me to-morrow night."

"You don't forget, captain, as I told you, that I had to mix a little in this business myself, before I could get to see so far."

"I remember all, Hazard."

"Thank you, sir. I needn't say, captain, after what you've heard yourself, that what's to be done you'll have to do quickly. You see they're pretty hot on the scent. You've got to make quick preparations as well as strong ones."

"It will need little time. I am already in part prepared for the emergency; for, though unwilling to believe in all that Belcher and yourself told me, I yet felt that every precaution was necessary, and I have not neglected the affair. We shall be ready for these wretches."

"I'm glad, captain, for I was beginning to get quite scary."

"Have you found out where Eccles is?"

"No, sir. I don't think there's anything against him, except he's too blind to many things that he ought to see. He's thick-headed, sir."

"He's weak. And you note that Fowler and Molyneaux both count upon his weakness, to render him willing, when once they've played their game; and perhaps they are right."

"I think so. So far, I think him only easy and blind, and not criminal."

"We shall interpose in time for his safety."

"But that visit of Lieutenant Molyneaux and Fowler to the town, sir? Won't that be apt to give you some trouble?"

" I think not. On the contrary, I see in it a new opportunity for effecting my objects with more certainty, and perhaps safety. These details do not make me anxious, Hazard. The mere danger and difficulty to myself constitute the least part of my anxiety. But, great God! to think that I have trained so many of these wretches for such a life as they deliberately propose to lead! — that the flag of Britain, through my agency, has prepared them for running up the black and bloody ensign of piracy! Have I, in truth, under the roving commission which has seemed to me hitherto a sufficient guaranty, been tutoring these miserable creatures for a life of license; for the flinging off all law, social and divine; loosening the ties of morals, with the bonds of nations, and making the transition easy from the privateer to the pirate!"

" Don't trouble your mind with such a notion, captain! You've done nothing of the kind. This fellow, Sam Fowler, is an old buccaneer. He has twice accepted the king's mercy, and escaped the penalties of former crime only by doing so at the last moment. But the black blood hasn't been, and couldn't be, purged out by a king's pardon. He's so thoroughly a pirate by habit, that, put him wherever you please — in the regular service even — and he'd be at his bloody tricks again in no time, and with the first easy opportunity. And there are two others of these chaps who are just like him — old pirates — regular 'scape-gallowses — sworn brothers of the coast, and most unredeemable villains."

" Who are they?"

" Pearson and Gibbes."

" I will remember them. We must try and discriminate between the ringleaders and the miserable wretches whom they beguile. Of this be sure, William Hazard: the flag of Britain, while I breathe, shall never give place, on that vessel, to the Jolly Roger! No; there shall be one head low — one heart shall be cold for ever — ere your eyes shall see that spectacle!"

" God be with you and help you, captain!" exclaimed the other, fervently.

"And that vain young Irish blockhead! to be so easily won, so readily deluded, in spite of my warnings. my painstaking and forbearance, and by that evil-eyed, miserable, hoary-headed old ruffian! And through what snare? Not gold; he has enough

of that: but through lust, and hate, and envy—all these the children of a mere vanity!—that bubble passion, the first-born with
us, the last to die out of our bosoms, which absorbs and uses all
other passions!"

" It's mighty strong in his bosom, sir."

" Light head, vaporous brain, vain, vicious heart.  And he
would cross weapons with me!  The 'point of honor'!  Honor!
honor!  What a word to be used upon a dog's tongue!  Fool!
fool!  But he shall have the privilege he craves.  His wish shall
be indulged, and let the fatal sisters watch the issue from the
clouds."

" You don't mean, sir, that you will fight with such as he?"

" Will I not!  Yes, boy, in such a case I waive pride, character, authority, all things upon which, in ordinary cases, I should
insist.  I mean to fight with him, point to point, though he bring
a score of bloodhounds at his back.  I will make him feel that I
am his master.  I rejoice that he broods with this desire.  It
somewhat accords with my own.  He has been an offender in
other respects, boy, than those which you report.  But of this I
shall say naught.  Enough that he shall have his wish; and let
his skill and spirit maintain his vanity, if they can!"

Calvert almost forgot the presence of his follower, in the utterance of his passionate speech; but he soon recalled his thoughts,
bringing them, by a strong effort of will, from vehemence to subjection:—

" And now, Will Hazard, my good boy, keep up your watch,
as well and faithfully as you have done thus far.  Note the departure of the boat, with Molyneaux and Fowler; and, just so
soon as they are out of sight, get off with five fellows whom you
can trust.  Let the men be well armed with cutlasses and pistols.
Cross the river to the other shore, and creep down in the shadows till you reach the five old oaks, at the bend of Accabee.
Belcher, or Franks, will meet you there.  Should I arrange anything better in the meantime, you shall hear from me, at this
place.  Fortunately, you have time enough.  There are five days
before this masquerade.  Masquerade!  More fools!  It is perhaps fortunate that there are more fools — that we have this masquerade.  It gives us time.  The rogues will not attempt anything till this folly's over.  So, watch, my good boy, and be in

readiness. You know what I require. Away, now, to the ship! You can enter it in safety?"

"With the next change of watch, sir."

"Do so, then. Fear nothing; I shall neither fail you nor these people. Something I have to digest before I decide upon the game to play. But I will not leave you uninformed. Be sure, at all events, that I shall be ready for them. Neither head nor hand can fail me now. Be patient, and steer prudently, as before. You shall have my signal in proper season. Go, now, boy; you have done well — worthily — as few older men could do. I shall remember you as you deserve."

And the other, Will Hazard, went away as bidden. And the outlawed rover stood alone in the depth and midnight shadow of that Indian forest, his eyes straining through the solid thickness of the woods, and the almost solid density of the night, in the direction of the ship, which he could not see.

"What a man's soul is in that boy!" was his exclamation.

And well, indeed, might he make it. Will Hazard was but eighteen, a slim English lad, with fair face and bright blue eyes and a cheery, laughing spirit, whom no one would suspect of heroism or conspiracy. Yet, had he been tempted by the latter, and, in a simple, almost unconscious matter, was proving himself capable of the former. Such is the modest material of which Nature makes proper men.

But the thought of the boy gave place, in the mind of the rover, to the stronger impression made by the conspirators; and he again spoke, though now in soliloquy, of the vexing trouble which was most his care:—

"O fools! blind fools!" he muttered, shaking his hand still in the direction of the ship — "O fools! as monstrous in stupidity as in crime! Do you think me a dullard, an imbecile? Ye shall, feel me. I forebore ye, and hoped — nay, might have prayed for ye, but that I had as little faith in my prayers as in your virtue! But ye have reached the length of your tether — the term of your insolence and my forbearance. Ye shall soon know me as your judge!"

And again he waved his hand in air, slowly and solemnly, as denouncing judgment.

"Ye can not persuade me now! Ye are doomed!"

So speaking, he turned his back upon the scene, and strode to the spot where his steed was fastened; and while he tightened the girth about the beast, he murmured unconsciously :—

" It has come upon me sooner than I thought, but not wholly unexpected. It has spread farther than I feared, but not too far for arrest. I have been too confident of this people, too heedless of my own duty. But this shall be done. Alas! look which way I will, I see that I have lived in vain!

" And this painful watch by day and night — it profits me nothing. How should it profit? What can it bring, but the confirmation of a great agony, and the certainty of all its stings?

" And yet I have not the courage to forbear the watch whose discoveries must still be wo! Would to God that the struggle were all over! — every struggle — all at once — in one mighty convulsion — one hurricane rage — in which the good ship goes down in the overwhelming shock, and the waves settle over her in placid supremacy. I have spread sail, surely, only for such a fate !"

And a bitter groan escaped him at the close. And, with a sort of desperation, he threw himself upon his steed; and it was only after several irregular bounds, under the fierce pricking of his spur, which bore him into deeper thickets, that he was taught the wiser policy to prick his way rather than the beast. His own impatience gave him no succor, in the effort to dissipate his griefs in the headlong violence of his pace.

# CHAPTER XXXIII.

PETTY REVENGES.

"Methinks I wander in an atmosphere
　All rank with treachery.　There is in the air
　A wooing, silent mischief, which prevails
　O'er the too languid nature, and will glide
　Subtly, to feeble and too gentle natures,
　Until they seize upon the citadel,
　And blight the soul with death !" — *Old Play*.

WE are apt to speak of reason as the distinguishing attribute of man, and to prattle, with wondrous self-complacency, upon its dignity and grandeur. Yet how do we use it? Not one in a hundred of those who thus pride themselves, and prattle, ever employ it with any due regard to the superior interests of immortality, or even of a considerate and becoming humanity We use it rather as a drudge — a dog, with which we hunt down the game that is started by our fancies or our passions — and in this we exhibit ourselves as children only; our toys and sports being scarcely a whit more dignified than those of children, and only more imposing, in our sight, as involving the exercise of intenser passions, which are far less innocent than those which beguile the boy.

Here, for example, in this our true story of real life, we are made acquainted with no small variety of persons — scarcely one of whom, in the ordinary estimates of society, would be called a blockhead. For that matter, a pioneer people never can be blockheads. Here is Molyneaux, who considers himself a monstrous clever fellow, exceedingly smart and well-appointed in his wits. Ask *him*, and, if he answers honestly, and without allowing his habitual modesty to interfere in the delivery of his response, he will tell you that no man was ever more adequately endowed, or

14

trained, than himself, for the greater variety of human and social achievements.

Ask those about him, and they will so far confirm his opinion of himself, as to assure you that there never was a better seaman; that he is bold, vigorous, well-skilled in his weapon; a good leaper, runner, boxer; as able to lift a clever boat out of shoal water as any officer on the coast; and, when he talks, that he says deuced smart things in a smart manner of his own.

He is evidently regarded by all about him as a person much above the ordinary standard of human intellect; and hence we find him second officer of the ship; and, further, that a certain number of the ship's company are resolved to make him first officer, regarding his claims as superior to his present position.

Yet, with all this, we see that the fellow is a blockhead; that he is using his wits, much or little, in such a fashion as will probably get him knocked on the head, with a reasonable prospect that the brains will be so scattered, after such an event, as to be of little future service to their present owner or to anybody else. And yet he uses his reason daily; and prides himself upon the wonderful sagacity with which he shapes his course, so that his aims shall be duly seconded quite as much by his prudence as by enterprise and thought.

But the abuse of his reason lies first in his aims. You see that his reasoning faculties are under bond wholly to his vanity; and, let him reason however cunningly, the first step which he has taken is fatal to the integrity of that very reason which he supposes to be eminently employed all the time.

The reason which we employ to make the wrong appear the right, or to enable us to do wrong, is no longer a faculty to be relied on. Commencing with a lie, all its argument, thus basely founded, must be false, though it may be logical in the last degree, if its first assumption of policy be recognised. We have but to slur over the premise, and we shall see no flaw in the logical progress, step by step, to the inevitable conclusion: but the fraud with which we begin, and with which we subject reason to the uses of a passion, corrupts the entire case; and we have no more real benefit from this most precious human faculty than if we were so many brute beasts, to whom all such endowment is supposed to be denied.

And so with all those whose wilful, wicked, or frivolous passions, coerce the Reason into a mere slave, carrying out the behests of a master; the Kislar Aga of the seraglio; the hound that hunts for us the game which our lusts and appetites, our vanities and ridiculous ambitions, are perpetually starting. Molyneaux, but for his absurd vanity, would be no fool — would have a very fair share of the reasoning faculty — and would probably escape the summary processes which now threaten the health and safety, the integrity and soundness, of a moderately-developed cranium, with a very decent filling up of brains.

You may argue out the case, under the suggestions above given, with respect to the greater number of our *dramatis personæ ;* and you need not confine the application to the persons of *our* drama. Take the great farce of Society — tragedy or farce — they but too frequently mean the same thing — and, of all the performing characters, you find only here and there a single person who uses his reason with respectful deference, and does not tax its exercise in the service of a mere passion, having its premises arbitrarily resolved upon, and looking only to foregone desires for its conclusions. One's vanity, as in the case of Molyneaux, is the grand passion; another's, avarice; another's, lust; another's, gluttony; and so on, through the whole census. The passions, using reason as a tool, cut the throat of human wisdom.

So our Harry Calvert; so our cassique, his brother; so the courtly Robert Quarry, governor of the colony; and so the pious Master Sylvester, *alias* Stillwater : all of these, running as deep as their waters may, and exercising whatever amount you please of the reasoning faculty, have somehow, through some fraudful or debilitating passion, denuded the cogitating faculty of its best virtues at the very outset; and now keep it busy, wandering in a circle, and in movements not half the time so graceful, though quite as erratic, as those of your tabby, who will suddenly dart away from her comfortable couch upon the hearth-rug, and put herself into fever-heat, in the very intellectual chase after — her own tail!

And we must not forget the tender sex, in their assertion of the right to abuse the virtues of this faculty. They, too, strange as it may seem, have a reason for all their follies. Take, for example, the case of Mrs. Perkins Anderson. We have shown you that she is a smart woman as well as a fine one. She is clever, quick, has wit, sentiment, and a sort of philosophy — which serves, at least, to disguise a passion of very doubtful quality so dextrously, that it passes current as a virtue among half of the fashionable circle in which she moves and has her being. Ask herself, or her neighbors, who is the cleverest woman in town, and you are told, "Mrs. Perkins Anderson, undoubtedly!" She lives well, talks well, dresses well, dances well, and so lives as never to tax offensively or in any way inconveniently the community in which she resides. This is a great virtue in society. There is not a member of her circle, not one of those persons who claim to be "in society," who has the slightest apprehension that Mrs. Perkins Anderson will ever need their assistance in anything. If they could fancy, for a moment, that she was in straits for money, they would not consider her half so intellectual. Of course, were she to ask for succor, they would instinctively regard her as a person who had lost her senses. Having no such dreadful apprehensions of danger in this respect, either to her or to themselves, they gladly attend her parties; they vote her a trump among court cards and courtly circles; admire the magnificence with which she provides, the taste with which she presides, and the fine judgment which enables her to select her guests with such discrimination as to prompt each individual thus honored to recognise the propriety of her preference — in his own case, at least!

But we have seen, as well as Harry Calvert, that Mrs. Perkins Anderson is still veritably a fool of the first water. Let us not be too particular in describing the passion or passions — for there are several busy in her case — which keep *her* reason (excellent as the world esteems it) in bondage to a lie! Enough that we say she has not common sense sufficient to let her prosperity be sure. She is in excellent worldly condition; has an accommodating husband, who provides for her magnificently, yet never troubles her to entertain him; yet she will not let herself alone! She desires to make a conquest of Harry Calvert. You, perhaps, fancy that she loves him. Don't make yourself ridiculous by such a notion. She has not a bit more love for him than for Perkins Anderson, though he may better please her *tastes*. But she is wealthy and idle-minded; and all persons in this condition must exercise their brains in some way, and in the provocations of some petty passion. She *fancies* that she loves him, possibly; but the truth is, that she desires to make a conquest. The desire is stimulated by her vanity. This is one of the weak points of the sex, and of Mrs. Perkins Anderson in particular. Even as the young damsel, just rising into seventeen, fancies that she is an outcast and desolate, unless there be some youth, with newly-budding mustache, bobbing about her, as a cork, with a feather in it, bobs along a trout-stream; so these old girls, with nothing to do, continue to long for similar bobs: though the period may have long since passed away when the tenderness of the trout makes it acceptable on the table of the epicure. With idle women this becomes the whole passion of life — a passion of blended vanity and appetite; and this is precisely the case with Mrs. Perkins Anderson. She will waste her smiles and sighs — nay, her caresses — on Harry Calvert; but if Harry will not suffer himself to be caressed, she will condescend to Dick or Peter. She must restlessly wriggle on, in the hope of being precious to somebody. It is a part of her capital, in the society which she prefers, to be recognised as an object still of a most passionate attachment. This is so much food for that vanity which lacks all pretence of honest passion; and, for such persons, a mere flirtation will suffice — flirtation being a sort of moral prostitution which only lacks sufficient courage to be criminal. Not that Mrs. Anderson will not fall, and sufficiently low too, if properly seconded. But she does not *contemplate* extreme cases. She is not too moral for surrender, if vigorously assailed; but she will content herself, if suffered to do so, with the small excitements of the flirtation.

Enough! a flirting fool at forty is sufficiently ridiculous, without needing comment. Harry Calvert knew her thoroughly, and was not to be deluded by her sentimentality. He, however, committed one error — that of piquing her vanity by his disregard of her blandishments. Women do not readily forgive such an offence. It equally mortifies vanity and self-esteem. The one is stung, the other humbled.

No doubt Calvert felt that this was his danger. He knew the sex; few men better. He knew *her*; and he felt that to yield, but a single hair, and he must have laid his head in her lap — another Samson in the embrace of a new Delilah. He was too earnest a man to trifle in a flirtation. He was one of those persons

who, in *affaires de cœur*, are apt to proceed as the lion is said to
do when he woos *his* bride! He knew very well that the lady had
no passion at work more profound than her vanity, and he was
not *willing* to engage in a traffic of the passions at too much cost
to his own. *His* passions were all terribly intense ones; he knew
not how to trifle with them. Besides, they were all absorbed in
one, and that was hallowed! Over its fortunes there hung the
gloom of defeat, disappointment, death perhaps; the storm; the
wreck; the convulsion; and an agony such as would have been
only mocked by such a feeble sort of passion as worked in the
bosom of Mrs. Perkins Anderson! He knew that she could sigh,
and sigh, and yet feel no pain. Sighing with her was only a
pleasant accomplishment; and, when she spoke of her heart's disappointments, he had only to look at her and smile. Certainly
Mrs. Perkins Anderson was in most excellent *physique*. Well
preserved, she had reached that condition of *embonpoint* which
converts a wrinkle into a ridge, and maintains such an adequate
degree of red upon the cheeks as to render quite unnecessary any
resort to Parisian chemicals. He felt that she would survive any
defeat of hope and heart; that her affections were scarcely skin-
deep; and, though he scrupulously forebore to exhibit his fullest
consciousness of her case — forebore to wound and mortify unnecessarily by tone, word, or look — he yet did not hesitate to fling
her off and deny. He fancied that he had done this too gently
to offend; but he did not the less pique and disappoint. That she
felt the pique we shall see hereafter.

  She felt it, and her vanity brought another passion into activity.
It was, however, rather an instinct, than a thought or passion,
which led her to conceive a purpose of revenge. The agent to be
used for this purpose was no other than our poor little giddy-pated
Zulieme Calvert, otherwise known (but only while in Charleston)
as the *Señorita Montano*, a belle of the neighboring Spanish province of Florida; an heiress in her own right; having certain silver-mines and mountains in Mexico; coffee and sugar plantations
in Cuba; and a princely *hacienda*, whither she had resort in spring
and winter, in the life-giving and life-preserving region of Espiritu
Santo (or Tampa bay). These — inventions mostly — owed their
birth and circulation to the fertile genius of Mrs. Perkins Anderson, who contrived, within twenty-four hours after her guest had

reached her domicil, to set these golden bubbles of fancy afloat on the wings of rumor. She had her policy in multiplying the attractions of her house; for the fine lady, though in her own set supreme, had yet certain competitors in society. There were other coarse, fat, vulgar, and ridiculous women about town — of a certain age — whose ambition it was to usurp dominion over all the local exclusives. The Señorita de Montano was admirably designed to provoke the envy and jealousy of all these people.

Poor child! Little did she fancy the uses she was to be put to. Frankly admitting herself to be a fool, and ignoring reason utterly in her own case, Zulieme can not well be brought before our court for judgment, in respect to those absurdities of moral which we undertook to canvass passingly at the opening of this chapter. She was willing to be a child, and to profess nothing beyond. Her humility affords her ample refuge from our judgment. But, by way of *caveat* to the judgment of others, we take leave to say that, if we take the operations of her feminine instincts into the account, Zulieme is perhaps not half the fool which she appears — not half the fool, compared with some of her most self-assured neighbors; for, *entre nous*, an *honest* instinct is not only a safer, but, in all respects, a wiser guide for humanity than a corrupt or perverted reason; and, where there is any feebleness of intellect, it is no small proof of real wisdom to trust nothing to this blind sort of guide, but modestly to content one's self with a lamblike deference to tracks, as prescribed by the good old maternal bell-wether, which we call Nature.

Of course, we can all conceive, very readily, that Miss Montano — the Señorita de Montano — is to be the great feature, the lioness, at the receptions of Mrs. Perkins Anderson. But, as we have hinted, the pique of that lady toward Harry Calvert suggested certain other objects which may not be so obvious to the unsuspecting wits of our readers. Let us make them wiser, if we can; and we can scarcely do this so well as by retracing our steps, for a brief space, to the period of that interview, already reported, between Calvert and Mrs. Anderson, in which the former arranged for the visit of his wife to a town in which he dared not show himself.

We all remember with what savage coolness Calvert received the revelations of tenderness which Mrs. Anderson made on that oc-

casion. When he was gone, and the lady had sufficiently examined the presents of shawl and jewels he had brought her, she put
them away, with a sigh of satisfaction, and subsided pensively into
her cushions — her thoughts divided between the sensation which
these ornaments would produce among her envious friends, and
the disappointment which she felt at Calvert's cavalier indifference to her charms, which, as she fondly conceived, would not
have been so slighted by any other cavalier.

"Cold and insensible!" exclaimed the lady, after some ten minutes of moody meditation.

"He sees how I feel. He knows how much I think of him.
Yet he mocks my affections. In *his* heart he mocks at mine!
His smooth and courtly compliments do not deceive me. Is it
possible that he thinks lightly of me — despises me? Ha!"

And she rose quickly, and stood before the great circular mirror. The survey consoled her. When did it fail to do so, in the
case of vanity — that self-deceiving passion which drinks in aliment from so many thousand deceptive sources? Her eyes brightened:—

"No! it can not be that he despises my affection. Is he dull,
then? Can he not see, for himself, how much more precious
would be *his* sympathies than the most fervid passion of the man
to whom I am fettered? Ah! *he* would say, the man to whom I
have sold myself! Was not that his own sarcasm? Did he not
imply, even if he did not express it? And does he not admit that
he, too, had sold himself? He talks of gratitude as prompting
him to marry this Zulieme; but would he have married this Spanish woman, of whom he speaks as a child — which is almost saying she is a fool — if she had not brought him a golden dowry?
He admits that he loved another, even while he married her! In
what, then, does his conduct differ from mine, and how should he
dare rebuke me for a weakness of which he was just as guilty
himself? He loves another: he avows it, and *to me;* ay, at the
very moment when I am showing my affection for himself! Cruel,
scornful, insolent! He might have spared me that. And she
lives — this other, this preferred one — but where? Not here, certainly. She is lost to him for ever: that he admits. Living, yet
lost! Then she must be the wife of another. Ah! it is not his
*virtues,* then, that make him cold to me. He would no doubt

bear her off from the more fortunate husband, if she would suffer it — ay, if she but showed him, as I have done, how much he was preferred. Who can she be? I must worm the secret from him!"

She again resumed her place upon the cushions. She lay with languid air, at length. But her cheeks were flushed, and her eyes brightened, with the heightening fever in her veins, as, step by step, she reconsidered the details of her interview with the reluctant rover.

"But what a man he is! How noble in form and presence! What an air he carries! — what a haughty yet subdued aspect! what sweet but powerful tones in his voice! what authority in all his words! I could be that man's slave sooner than the honored wife that I am! I could share his poverty with pride, brave his dangers without fear: while now, blest, as he tells me, with wealth, and safe in society, I have no satisfaction in either. That he should taunt me so!

"Ay!" she murmured, with increase of bitterness in her accents —

"Ay! he could refer me to my wealth and position, as sufficient to console me for this wretched life; lacking all sympathy; in which the heart broods over its own loneliness, while the passions gnaw upon it, keeping it for ever bleeding! Wealth, to a wanting heart! Society and fashion, to one who asks only for love's precious aliment! O Harry Calvert! how can *you*, with your own heart denied, commend such wretched food to mine? It is in very mockery that you have spoken, and I will never forgive it!"

She wept at the self-drawn picture of her own wretchedness. For the moment, she persuaded herself that it was true to the life. The quality of reason, warped by the master-passion to its purposes, had rendered her conclusions sufficiently logical to satisfy her thought. She really wept at her own fancied sorrows.

"And this Spanish woman? this *child*, as he calls her! She is pretty, even in his eyes — pretty and gentle; a child, and dependent on him: yet he loves her not! She is not capable of *his* affections; she can not understand *him;* does not suffice for *his* heart — does not know her own! And they have no children — no children, no more than I! Yet he is sure of her; he can trust

14*

*her!* He relies upon her *instincts* for her fidelity; upon her simplicity, forsooth, to protect her passions! Indeed! and he thinks he knows the nature of the woman-heart! We shall see — we shall see!"

And now she laughed, as certain other thoughts rose mischievously in her brain. She laughed merrily.

"We shall try her. He braves the trial. I gave him proper warning. He can not blame *me!* It is he that exposes her to the peril, not I! *I* do not throw it in her way. *I* use no arts, no arguments, to persuade her. *There* is the fruit upon the tree: let her pluck and eat if she will! He himself is willing to conduct her to the garden; he himself shows her the tree; and he turns to me, with cool exultation, and says:—

"'I can trust her safely. Her *instincts* are too childish to be vicious. She will only dance under the tree; she will only look on, while others eat, without any desire herself.'

"And he knows that there will be others to persuade — others of his own treacherous and artful sex — who will help raise her to the branches, so that she may help herself — nay, will brave any danger rather than she should forego the temptation! Well, I will take care that there shall be a tempter: and we shall see if her boasted simplicity of heart will afford her any better shield than mine!

"There is that young Cavendish, a most courtly gallant; as handsome and eloquent as Belial; as impudent as the devil; as licentious as any in the court of Charles; who has been caressed by maids of honor — precious maids of honor! — and he has come hither to escape the consequences of this very free caressing! I have but to whisper a word in his ear, and he will show her where grow the beautiful fruits of perdition! He will conduct her to the tree! Ha! ha! Harry Calvert.

"He shall have opportunity enough. Yea, Harry Calvert, since her *simplicity* of heart is so perfect a security, she shall rely on that wholly. I shall use no watch, no restraint. And what should I care if she falls? what is it to me?

"Yes, indeed, it may be something to me! who knows? Now that he holds her to be so perfect in virtue, her childishness of character becomes a virtue in itself. Infantile simplicity redeems all other defects; and it is by this one quality that she maintains her ascendency over *him*. This lost, he flings her off with scorn. He will do it. He is then justified in her abandonment. The debt of gratitude is obliterated by the stain upon his honor; and she is one, at least, out of my way! His faith in her fidelity makes against *my* passions, even when they show themselves subject to his own. Well, we shall cure his blindness. She shall be tried, at least. Let her go through the trial as she can! Cavendish shall be the tempter; and he is just the man to make his way with such a creature — such a simpleton. He is cunning as a serpent; playful as a kitten; handsome; fashionable; a famous dancer and singer; will carol love like a nightingale, yet mock all the while; and with a mouth always full of the sweetest, fantastical speeches, he is audacious enough for anything.

"If she withstands *him*, she is a miracle of women. We shall see; and when the fruit is eaten, Harry Calvert shall also see! He is not a man whom you can blind through any self-conceit. He can be made to see without needing that I should lift a finger. And see he shall, or I am not Charlotte Anderson!"

Such were the meditations, such the purposes, of Mrs. Perkins Anderson. Do you set her down, accordingly, as a monster? Oh, no! she is only a clever woman, "in society;" having a rage for personal appreciation; ambitious of notoriety to the last degree; seeking it from no matter what sources; easily piqued by disappointment; and aiming at nothing more than — petty revenges!

But in your simplicity, dear reader, you cry out:—

"Petty revenges! Do you call such a crime as she meditates a petty one?"

Yes, indeed! According to the conventional standards to which the good lady is accustomed, it may be held a very petty sort of revenge; really, a very moderate way of resenting a disappointment! For you must remember that people of this description do not regard virtue with any such sublime sentiment of veneration as possesses your unsophisticated bosom. They hardly regard its loss as a matter of evil or regret. It is only the *exposure* of its loss which they have need to fear. They are only too happy to expose each other's sins, while indulging in their own. For themselves, they are not at all solicitous for its safety. The quality has some *repute*, and must be assumed to be in their possession.  What they really and only dread is, the scandal of the loss ; not the absence of the thing itself.  They may think as the lady in the Proverbs—

> "Who eats the fruit without alarm,
> Then wipes her mouth, and — where the harm ?"

They have only to wipe the mouth carefully after the eating, and all's right with the consumer ; for the simple reason that all *seems* right with the world !

With such an appreciation as Mrs. Perkins Anderson had of virtue in the abstract, you may hold her to be quite moderate in the sort of revenge which she proposed to take, at once of Harry Calvert and his wife—the one, for the indifference which he had shown to her charms ; the other, for that most impertinent simplicity of heart by which she was assumed to be less assailable than wiser people.

And to the fall of Zulieme from the grace of innocence, Mrs. Perkins Anderson pledged all her faculties.  All that her intellect could do — her arts, her reason — must be done, to realize that result which was required to bring consolation to her own mortified vanity — her own unsatisfied desires.  But we must reserve the process of her working for yet other pages.

Shall the tempter succeed?  Shall the innocent one succumb?  These are the questions.  They hang over a thousand fortunes daily.  We rise at morning, and the bird sings joyously in the roof-tree, and the flowers smile without stain, all odorous, in the garden beneath our eyes ; and they beguile us to unconsciousness as we walk forth.  We forget the caprices of Fortune ; we think nothing of the Fates !  We, too, sing and smile, not dreaming what the hour shall bring forth ; especially as, with too many of us, there lies a serpent among our flowers—sleek, smooth—who, even if we see it, looks not so much like a serpent, but rather like Mrs. Perkins Anderson : and her we take to be a friend !  She is so sweet, so smiling, so very loving !

# CHAPTER XXXIV.

### INITIATION OF THE YOUNG BEGINNER.

" From silks to scandals ; from the deep-laid plan
 To win free passage to the heart of man ;
 Subdue that rugged despot to the will
 Of one whose sweetness hides a despot still ;—
 To that small play of fancies on the wing,
 The motes of summer and the birds of spring ;
 The chase of butterflies through garden-flowers,
 Or artful games of love in secret bowers —
 Capricious games, where all too conscious grown,
 The woman seeks a province not her own ;
 And now in play and now in passion tost,
 Wins all she seeks, and, winning, still is lost !" — *The Town.*

LITTLE did our poor little Zulieme, in all her anticipations,
fancy the sort of welcome which awaited her in Charleston. Little did she suspect that she was already marked out as a victim
by the cunning of the serpent. She had no more thought of the
*gravity* of the future than a young girl has of her first ball. Of
course, her head swam with excitement. She thought of dances
and dresses, and gay people, and a constant whirl of pleasurable
performances, in which she was to be the happiest actor. But
beyond this she had no single thought, feeling, or desire. She
was a creature of society, who had no relish for solitude. Hers
was an external world wholly, the interior of which she had no
care to penetrate. To pass the hours gayly, and to snatch pauses
of rest under green trees and rosy enclosures, gently waving in
the sweet breezes of the southwest ; to awaken to new strains of
mandolin and guitar, and to the gay prattle of new companions, all
as eager after sport, in sunshine or shade, as herself ; to fill her
little mouth with sun-purpled fruits, plucking them as she desired ;

and to feel herself a favorite of favorite people, though she taxed
them with no greater care than that of providing her amusements:
this was the all of life she knew, or cared to know.   She designed
no conquests, and never troubled herself with a solitary feeling
of jealousy toward those who made them.   But she loved homage
nevertheless, though never seeking to secure it; simply, perhaps,
because accustomed to it from her earliest consciousness, it had
become a sort of necessity with her nature, rather than any craving of her heart.   She no more anticipated the purposes and
policies of the lady of fashion, accustomed in town-life to a perpetual struggle, with equally active rivals, after the means and
objects of social display, than she conceived any idea of coquetry,
conquest, or flirtation.   She had only a child-fancy, which is satisfied to chase a butterfly, and many butterflies!

Still less could she apprehend that she was to be specially chosen as a victim, the better to afford a rival the means of victimi-
zing another.   Little did she dream the subtle mazes with which
social cunning was prepared to invest her heart and person; little
fancy the means which were meant to corrupt the one, and possibly degrade the other.   Had it been possible for her infantile and
unsophisticated mind to conceive the wicked purposes which were
already at work for her reception — the deep, sinister passions
which were to be put in play against her peace and purity — she
would, childlike and silly as she was, have recoiled with horror,
rather than have rushed with delight into the specious and pleasing circle which opened its arms wide for her reception.

But, as Calvert very well knew, she was not a person to conceive of such dangers; and there was no mode which reason might
choose, which could enlighten her understanding upon the subject.
She could be taught only through her instincts and sensibilities;
and she must *live* the experience by which alone she could learn.
She has entered upon the experience already; but her very simplicity is, in some degree, her security — as much against suspicion
as against real danger.

We have seen what was her reception by the interesting Mrs.
Perkins Anderson.   That very clever woman was solicitous to
make the most favorable impression upon her guest.   Of course,
Zulieme expected *kindness*, and a friendly welcome.   But even
her Spanish mode of exalted and superb compliment, which puts

house, home, horses, and servants, all at the disposal of the new-comer, was surpassed in the lavish warmth of Mrs. Anderson's embrace and caresses.   No care was foreborne, no consideration spared, to make the guest feel that she had only to will or wish, and be gratified.   She was stifled with kisses; she was over-whelmed with compliments; and the extravagant raptures of the hostess naturally enkindled all her own.   The former could not sufficiently satiate her eyes, gazing upon the charms of her guest. She was so sweet, so delicate, so exquisite, a little thing; such a fairy; with such eyes, such hair — such a wilderness of hair! With her own hands, Mrs. Perkins Anderson, with the prettiest playfulness, undid the masses of glossy, raven richness, from the tiara of jewels which bound them up, and let them fall to the very floor.   And she made Zulieme stand upon the hair, that she might be able to boast that she had seen it with her own eyes.

And what hands — what feet!   How tiny, and how beautifully formed!

She measured the hands with her own.   She persisted in pulling off the slippers of Zulieme, and her stockings, that she might see the feet!   Such tiny feet!   She half suspected that the girl had been subjected to some Chinese process, and that the feet had been made small at the expense of their symmetry.   But, no! they were perfect — the very feet of the fairy Nymphalina!

"What a sylph!" she cried.   "Oh, how Harry Calvert must love you, dear Zulieme!"

"He love me?   No!   He don't care about pretty hair, or little feet, or little women!" said Zulieme, poutingly.

"Oh! my dear, you must be mistaken.   Harry Calvert's a person of good taste.   He could never be so stupid as to look with indifference upon such charms as yours!"

"But he does!   He don't love me at all."   And the pout grew more positive.

"Indeed! who does he love, then?" curiously.

"Nobody.   He's one of your fierce, fighting, English brutes, as I constantly call him, who takes pleasure in nothing but the sulks.   He's a savage; and so cross, sometimes, that I'm afraid he'll eat me up!   Oh, no! — he has no love in him for any-body."

"I know better!   He *must* love *you!*"

"No, I tell you! He does not. Everybody loves me better than Harry."

"Ah! you don't—you can not think so! But in truth, my dear, one's husband is not expected to be one's lover, you know."

"But why not? Why shouldn't Harry love me as other people love me?"

"Perhaps he loves you much better?"

"Why can't he show it, then, as other people do?"

"Oh! husbands, my dear child, are not expected to do so. They, at least, seem to think so. For they have ways of their own for showing affection, and I suppose these ways may be the better ones."

"I don't think so. I would like Harry to show me as much love as anybody else, and more! But, look you, Charlotte, don't you be calling me child. I begged you once before. Don't you do it again; I don't like it. I'm not a child—I'm a young woman."

"But where's the harm, dear Zulieme?"

"I don't know that there's any harm. But I'm afraid 'child' means 'fool,' or something like it, in your hard English language; for whenever Harry's vexed with me, he always calls me 'child' —'a mere child;' and I know that must mean 'fool,' or something quite as ugly."

"Well, dear, I won't call you so again. But why should Harry ever be vexed with *you?* What do you do, or say, to make him vexed with you? It does seem to me that it would be monstrous to be angry with so sweet a creature as you are."

"And why not? Do you think, because I'm small and young, I can't make people angry? I make Harry angry every day; and he does look so grand when he's angry!—but he frightens me too."

And the pretty child—for child she was, and perhaps would remain so a thousand years—gave a lively narration of some of her most startling freaks, such as had, frequently enough, driven the stern Harry Calvert from his propriety. Charlotte Anderson laughed merrily at the recital, clapped her hands, and appeared wondrously delighted. Of course, she understood the whole mystery, from the simple revelation.

"Excellent, my dear, excellent! How you must have worried

the formidable captain! I can fancy the whole scene: you laughing at the mischief done, and he storming.   Comedy and tragedy
on the same boards.   Ha! ha! ha!   Admirable!"

"It was no laughing matter, I can tell you; though I did laugh
all the time!   But I trembled, I can assure you, even though I
laughed.   I knew he could only kill me, at the most—"

"Kill you!   What an idea!"

"Yes, indeed!   Harry's anger kills sometimes.   He's one of
your terrible English brutes, I tell you; but I know, if I can
only get behind him, and throw my arms round his neck, it's all
over.   And then he pushes me off so gently; and I sometimes
think, he looks so sorrowful, that he's going to cry!   But don't
you believe he cries: he never sheds a tear!   I sometimes think,
if he would cry a little, he'd laugh more!   But he won't laugh,
and he won't cry, and I don't know what to make of him—except
that he don't love me."

"That's the way, I fancy, with all husbands.   They expend
all their passion in winning our young affections, and think, perhaps, they have done enough for us.   Some of them seek other
women, and give them the love that is the right only of their
wives.   You don't suppose, do you, that Harry Calvert loves any
other woman?"

"He love!   No, I tell you!   He loves nobody.   It's ridiculous to think of such as he loving anybody."

"Not even himself?"

"Not even himself!   He fights, so Lieutenant Eccles told me,
just as if he wanted some bullet to kill him.   He runs his head
just where the danger is worst.   And he fears no danger.   I've
seen him myself, more than once, where I thought he was trying
to be killed.   But he don't feel or fear, and nothing hurts him."

"Is he, then, so desperate?   Poor Harry!   But I must not
pity him, if he does not pity you.   Still, I can't do him the injustice to think that he does not love you.   I'm sure he loves you
much more than you imagine.   But he is like thousands who have
the feelings they know not how to show."

"Oh!   Harry could show them if he pleased.   There's no person so quick to feel.   He can change in a moment, like lightning;
and he shows you, very soon, that he feels every change.   He
sees, too, every change in your feelings.   But, Charlotte dear,

something 's wrong with Harry. His heart has had some sad
hurts. He used to speak of a person—"

"Ah ! a lady ?"

"Yes. Her name was Olive."

"Olive ? — ah ! indeed — Olive !"

Mrs. Perkins Anderson had advanced one step in her knowledge.

"Olive — who ?"

"He never told me any more; and that he told me when he
was out of his head with fever, and when I nursed him."

"Yes, I have heard of your nursing. He owes you much,
Zulieme."

"Well, he loved this Lady Olive very much. He told it all
when he was raving."

"*Lady* Olive ? Ah ! — and what then ? What became of
*her* ?"

In a whisper, drawing close to the eager listener :—

"She was false to him ! She ran away with another man, and
Harry never could hear of her again; and since then he 's been
the same cold, passionless Harry that you see him now — and he
loves nobody, I tell you !"

"Not even you ?" with a smile.

"Not even me !" with a sigh.

"But why did he marry you, then, or why did you marry *him*,
if you knew all this ?"

"I do n't know, really ! Somehow, I thought it would be pleasant to be Harry's wife; and he asked me one day, and I said
' Yes.' We were playing in the orange-grove."

"He *playing !* I should as soon think of an elephant or lion
dancing to the castanets."

"Oh, but he can dance, I tell you ! When I said ' playing,' I
should rather say that I was playing with him, and he suffered
it. Now I think of it, it could be no humor of play that he was
in, for he spoke most wofully all the time. He was very sad, and
very changeful; and his man, Jack Belcher, said he was afraid
his master would go mad ! And so I said I would marry him,
and so it was."

"And there was no love in the matter ? You only married
him that he should n't go mad ?"

"Oh! yes, indeed, there *was* love. I love Harry; and is n't he a noble-looking fellow to love? I like to look at him, even though he scares me; and even when he looks at me with a growl, like the great English brute that he is! But what I mean to say is, that he do n't love me as I love him — and, indeed, do n't love me at all! And sometimes I feel as if I could run away from him, and go back to the old *hacienda* at Panama, and never see him any more! Everybody *there* loves me."

"And they will love you here, Zulieme. You will find many to love you as you never were loved before. Nay, you will have to be quite watchful of your little heart; for there are some cavaliers here, who are the very handsomest and pleasantest persons in the world — who dress divinely, and are at the very head of fashion. They come of the best English families; they are familiar with the royal court; have danced with princesses and duchesses; and, no doubt, enjoyed many a stolen kiss from lips that claimed royal blood in every vein, and perhaps had their brute husbands besides. I warn you, you will have to take care of your little heart, or they will teach you how to love as you never knew before; and how to cheat love with the sweetest sort of vengeance! You may find some of these young cavaliers irresistible."

"Oh! I do n't think so. I 've seen many fine cavaliers in my time. I 've danced with hundreds."

"Mexicans?"

There may have been something of a sneer in the tone of Mrs. Anderson, as she uttered the single word. The other seemed to fancy it, for she replied quickly, sharply, and proudly —

"Spaniards! — Castilians, Charlotte; and the most beautiful dressers and dancers."

"Ah! but the cavaliers of the court of the gallant King Charles are, I tell you, irresistible. They 've seen the world of France and the world of Spain, and they 've made the court of England the most gallant of all the courts of Christendom. You 'll see some of them here. And such fine fellows! Why, dear Zulieme, they have no other business than making love and winning hearts. Their days and nights are spent in this employment entirely; and practice should make perfect, you know."

Mrs. Perkins Anderson, whom we do not care to repeat in de-

tail, dilated upon her present theme to the utmost. Her purpose
was to excite the wonder of her auditor, and to familiarize her
mind with those pretty and pleasant freedoms of the sexes with
which the court of Charles had made the whole world familiar.
In this progress she gave an entirely new notion of the privileges
of the sexes, to any which Zulieme had hitherto known.  She
laughed at the authority of husbands as legitimate ; denounced
their tyrannies, as at war with all natural rights ; and the tyrannies of law, which sought to degrade the sex into an inferior condition ; sneered at the marriage-bond as a mere superstition, which
the despotism of the man alone sought to sustain, and in behalf of
which he had subsidized the priesthood, who, as she said, were
themselves sufficiently men to desire all the privileges of the
sterner gender.  She described the delights of that easier sort of
virtue which suffers to both sexes those freedoms which the passions naturally desire. . She insisted upon the legitimacy of the
Passions, as asserting Nature, in opposition to the mere arbitrary
laws of society.  She referred to all the animal tribes, which acknowledged no other law, and were happy accordingly ; and she
found the human race sufficiently analogous with the animal to
justify for it the assertion of a like liberty.  In short, she anticipated a very great deal of the popular argument, now freely in
use, upon these subjects.  The topic is no new one now-a-days ;
nor are the arguments a discovery, on the part of those wise women of the East, who are for setting up for themselves, to the
subjugation of the homelier sex.  The doctrines and the logic
employed are as old as humanity itself, and are the natural doctrines and arguments of the passions, the lusts, and the vanities,
of a people.  Suffer them to decide in their own case, and the
same result is reached in all periods of time — namely, prostitution !

"Marriage," quoth Mrs. Perkins Anderson, "where there is no
love, is only a legal prostitution."

Suppose we admit the fact with the lady — what then ?  The
act of marriage is in most cases a purely voluntary one.  It was
so in *her* case.  Reject, if you please, the religious aspect of the
rite, and regard it only as a civil contract, with all its understood
conditions ; and she is as much bound by it as if the deed were
registered in heaven !

But she was not questioned by Zulieme on this head, or upon any head.    Zulieme was no logician.    The simple girl listened, but with some degree of weariness.    She did not much comprehend the matter, and did not care to do so.    It was enough if she could sport and play.    Beyond this she had no strong passion or appetite, so working in her blood or bosom as to persuade her into any interest in the mental abstractions by which its exercise was to be justified.    It was there; she had it; and it justified its right to be there by its simple exercise, irrespective of all other motive or consideration.    She herself needed no argument which, justifying the passion,- sought really to legitimate its excesses; and, the truth told, she listened, or only appeared to listen, to her experienced Mentor with some degree of impatience.    She thought to herself :—

"All this is very fine, very well said ; Mrs. Anderson is a very smart woman — certainly knows a great many things; but, is she not rather tedious in her eloquence ?"

She had to endure a good deal of it.    When people like Mrs. Anderson fancy they can be eloquent, and are apt at saying clever things, they are very prone to grow wearisome.    The hourly iteration distressed the more capricious mind of Zulieme; and her hostess soon learned to discover when the little Spaniard caught up her jewels and began playing with them, or began to open her trunks and display her dresses, that the period was reached when her homilies should cease.    She was wise enough to stop on such occasions, and begin to play the child herself, rather than the Mentor.

But she contrived, in these repeated talks, to make the ears if not the understanding of Zulieme familiar with the loose social principles which she sought to inculcate as preparatory to her objects.    Her themes were, the wrongs of married women ; the brutality and selfishness of husbands ; the unreasonableness of the marriage rite and bond, as inconsistent with the freedom of the heart.    She taught that love implied perfect liberty, and lost its qualities and character unless this liberty was enjoyed ; that women had a perfect right to correct their mistakes of choice in marriage, and that society required nothing more from them than a modest reserve, which avoided all publicity, in the correction of such mistakes.    And, in these lessons, many others were taught, the details of which might have startled even so obtuse a mind as that of Zulieme Calvert, had they been delivered in less oracular and circumspect phraseology. Mrs. Anderson was a little too metaphysical, in her forms of speech and thought, to descend to the mere instincts of the girl, through which alone could her understanding be reached. The lessons were too frequently thrown away.

But they were given, nevertheless, and enforced too, by the freedoms which the guest witnessed in the household. Of these we shall say nothing at present, unless by an example which occurred during the second week after Zulieme's arrival in town. It was after a long talk, as usual, meant to enlighten the young lady on the privileges which the sex might safely enjoy, if sought on conditions of proper secresy, that Zulieme showed her weariness, as on previous occasions, by opening her trunks and jewel-cases, and getting out her toys. The two were in her chamber. The weather was growing hot. Zulieme was in her simplest *deshabille,* and had thrown herself upon the floor, the better to assort and arrange her wardrobe. Mrs. Anderson was not well pleased that her eloquence should be thrown away, and she was even then in one of her best passages; but, making a merit of the necessity, she accommodated herself to the temper of her guest, threw herself on the floor beside her, and began to examine the dresses with as eager an air of childhood as the other.

But suddenly a thought seized her. A flash of memory opened a new plan of strategics. She started up.

"I long to look at your pretty things, Zulieme. You have so many, and they are so beautiful! But not here; it is so hot in this chamber at this hour. Let us go below to the parlor. It is the coolest room in the house. Guy can bring down your trunks, and we will go over them below. And we must be doing something, by-the-way, toward the masquerade, you know."

She began gathering up the dresses as she spoke, and huddled them back into the trunks; and, seizing upon the case of jewels, she led the way, Zulieme following without apprehension. Guy, an able-bodied negro, was sent up to bring down the luggage. This was brought into the front parlor, a very prettily-furnished room for the time and country, and one of fair dimensions even in modern periods, though the house, like all others in Charleston

at that day, was of wood, and by no means imposing in its size
or architecture.

Very soon, the contents of trunks and jewel-cases were scattered over the whitely-matted floor, and the two ladies stretched
beside them, buried in that study which, to a certain few of the
sex, is supposed to be so very attractive. There was a great
deal in Zulieme's wardrobe to attract Mrs. Anderson. Never was
city *belle*, even in the days of "Nothing to Wear," so well provided with a wholesome variety. Silks and satins, of the richest
hues and most delicate textures, were in abundance. There were
dresses not made up; shawls and scarfs, 'kerchiefs, lawns, and
laces, at every moment caught the eye and provoked the admiration of the fashionable lady.

"Bless my soul, Zulieme, what lots and loves of things you
have! You can never wear them all. Here's enough for a dozen
women, and to last them a dozen years. And it's well that so
much remain untouched. How could you have kept these silks
without making them up? I'm sure I never should have been
satisfied till I had tried myself in every color. That is a great
secret of beauty, my dear. One never knows what will suit a
complexion till she tries. That green will be most becoming to
you. You would be a queen in it; and we must devise something, out of that very silk, for your *bal costume*. You should be
a queen of fairies, and shall be. Dear me, there's no end to
them! Don't tell me that Calvert doesn't love you, when he
furnishes your wardrobe with such extravagance."

"He doesn't furnish me. I just take what I want."

"Take! How? Where do you get them?"

"Out of the stores."

"As we do here: you mean the shops?"

"Shops? no! I mean the ship."

"Oh, I see! I understand. What a grand thing it must be to
get your dresses in that way! No wonder you have so many.
The only wonder is, that you did not take more. If 't were me,
now, I should hardly leave the ship without taking off half her
cargo. But isn't it still a loving husband who lets you take as
you please?"

"Oh! Harry don't care. He don't value these things."

"Or any things: even so nice a little thing as yourself, Zulieme."

"Not a bit! Harry's a strange sort of English brute, you know; but he lets me do as I please with myself."

"But not with him?"

"No, indeed! Sometimes I do."

"Now, if he would let you do as you please with him as well as yourself, one *might* think that he had some love for you. . . . . Dear me, what a glorious scarf! I never saw anything so rich. I should look like a queen myself in that scarf."

"Do!" and Zulieme threw it over her neck; and the portly beauty rose and strode before the mirror with delight. She came back after a few moments, and laid it down with a sigh.

"Hide it from my sight, Zulieme. It is too beautiful — too tempting."

"No! I mean it for you." And she restored it. "Wear it, Charlotte, you do look so fine in it."

"And you mean it for me, Zulieme?" cried the other. "You are so good!"

And the heart of the vain woman half revolted at the *rôle* she had resolved to play, in her relations with the simple creature.

"Yes," said Zulieme. "And here is more, Charlotte, that will better suit you than me. There is a silk: it will make a beautiful dress, and match the scarf. But, somehow, I don't like the shade; it don't suit me now. I wonder why I took it. And here's a maroon. Do you like maroon? I don't. Take that — and that, too, Charlotte."

"No, I won't! You are too generous, child. I won't rob you so!"

"Rob me! Why, I meant several of these things for you, when I came. Harry bade me choose them for you."

"Then they are *his* presents, not yours!"

"Yes! I never would have thought of it, Charlotte. But Harry, he thinks of everything."

"A strange husband, that — your Harry — and not so bad after all."

"Bad! Harry bad? No, indeed! Harry's as good a man as ever wore a hat. It's only that he's such a monster, that I quarrel with him. He's such a great English brute, and so grand!"

Charlotte laughed at the child's contradictions of speech, but did not seek to reconcile them. And so, for awhile, the chat con-

tinued ; passing very soon into a discussion of the several characters from which they might successfully choose for the approaching masquerade, and how the dresses were to be made up.

Into these details, Heaven forefend that we should enter !    We
half forget, indeed, whether we have said enough, in previous
pages, to apprize the reader of that great event with which the
fashionable Mrs. Perkins Anderson was preparing to confound
the simple natives of Charleston.

It was to be the first affair of the kind on Ashley river.    Let
this fact be remembered.    Of course, it was to be a *sensational*
affair ; Mrs. Anderson being resolved, by this one superlative
effort, to take the wind out of all other fashionable sails, and establish her own superior going, as a vessel of the greatest *ton*-nage !
Calvert's jewels, and Zulieme's silks and satins, were calculated,
in great degree, to render the affair successful.

It was while the two were prostrate on the floor, immersed in
these rainbow varieties of silk and splendor — the matting literally overstrewn with colors, and the pair of tongues eager in their
discussion — that the door was opened wide, and, simultaneously
with the announcement of his name, the Honorable Keppel Craven
abruptly made his appearance in the room !

15

# CHAPTER XXXV.

### HEADS OR TAILS.

"We'll take the cast of Fortune on our fate,
    And he who wins shall pledge himself to bide
In friendship with the loser; he who fails,
Do service to the conqueror.  So shall both
Profit, through loss; and gain itself become
Joint capital for those who, paired with love,
Know free division of the common gain." — *Old Play.*

THE Honorable Keppel Craven was a younger son.  He had
nothing beyond his airs, graces, and good looks, of which properly
to boast.  He had no lands, no possessions, no funds, upon which
a creditor could lay hands.  But he was a courtier; not ill-looking, and with all that current change of conversation, about people
and society, which constitutes the sufficient capital for a man of
fashion.

He was not a wit, but he was chatty; not wise, but he had
seen something of a certain sort of pretentious and self-satisfied
world; with scarcely an accomplishment beyond fiddling and
dancing, but these things he could do with very considerable dexterity.  He was impudent as the devil, and almost as much a
gentleman, in the ordinary courtier sense of the term.  He had a
smooth face, with slight yellow mustache, and fine, curling, amber-
colored hair, which he kept well oiled for conquest.  He wore a
profusion of the love-locks of the period, of the tresses of which,
resting upon his shoulders, he was not a little vain.

Suppose him in the well-laced coat and purple and pantouffled
small-clothes of the time; with half-drowsy, half-smiling eyes, and
a fashionable lisp; with long rapier and well-pointed shoes — and
you have the whole of him.

We may add that some irregularities at a gaming-table had been the occult occasion for sending him off to the colonies; and that, as a nephew of one of the lords-proprietors, he had honored Carolina with his choice, in preference to Barbadoes and a market.

The world was his market at the present moment; and his wits and beauties, airs and graces, were the all-sufficient capital with which he had entered it for the nonce.

He had seen Zulieme, briefly, at the ballroom of Mrs. Calder Carpenter, the night before. A whisper of Mrs. Perkins Anderson had brought him, for the renewal of his acquaintance, the next day. He was one of the *irresistibles* of that lady. She was overpowered with his fashionable claims, and conquered by his pretension. It was in full expectation of his visit that she had caused the trunks of her guest to be brought down to a reception-room. She had already enjoyed such a glimpse of Zulieme's wardrobe, that she was not unwilling it should be seen by others. She well knew that it would confirm the hints she had thrown out of the wealth and treasures of her guest, who, it must be remembered, was a damsel, unmarried, unencumbered (save by wealth), and the heiress, in her own right, of half the silver-mines of Mexico!

The bait naturally took, and the Honorable Keppel Craven was an early morning caller.

He was not the only one, we may add, *par parenthèse*, to whom Mrs. Anderson had indicated the same pleasant lures; for she was one of those ladies who always provide, if they can, extra strings to their bows — seeking to secure as many beaux in her string as it can comfortably draw.

But of the full resources of Mrs. Anderson, on her own and the account of Zulieme, we must suffer events and time to make their own report at the proper season. Enough, here, to admit that the Honorable Keppel Craven is not the person whom she especially hopes to secure as an ally in her design upon the simple Zulieme. The most formidable of King Charles's cavaliers, in the sight of Mrs. Anderson, is the Honorable Mr. Cornwall Cavendish, a scion of the noble English family of that name; a gallant even more comely and commanding than Craven; not relying so much on oil and scent, but not the less accomplished in beguiling a young damsel out of the proprieties.

Cornwall Cavendish was, like Craven, a rake-helly and a blackguard, after the genteel school of English fashion; cunning as a
serpent, winning as a dove, and capricious as a cock-sparrow.
They were birds of a feather; and, though the plumage of Cavendish was less showy than that of Craven, he was not a whit
more distinguished for sobriety. They were both birds of prey;
not after the fashion of eagle and hawk, but of the type of those
garden-birds that tear up the seeds as you plant them, and wage
devouring war upon the insect tribes: to whom a glossy, wriggling
worm, if painted outside, is a *bonne bouche;* and who will resort
to a thousand circumventions for the conquest of a golden butterfly
or beetle! They could be earnest enough in such a pursuit,
though, in all other matters, triflers; but the worm, beetle, or butterfly, must be *golden!*

" Either will do !" was the murmured thought of Mrs. Perkins
Anderson, after duly advising both of the prize in her keeping.

" Either will do ! Both have the proper arts for winning their
way with such a creature; and, if they succeed, why, what prevents my conquest of Harry Calvert? He loves her *now,* after a
fashion; respects her, at all events, as he has faith in her fidelity.
She is his toy, no doubt — the mere plaything of his fancy; but
the fancy of such a man requires that his playthings shall not be
common! Their wheels must not be set in motion by the hands
of other men. Let him once see that she is frail, and he whistles
her off with scorn; and then! ay, then?

" He must have refuge in *some* affections — somewhere ! Men
are so far dependent upon women, that, however stern or earnest
— whatever their cares or sorrows — the very proudest of them
must seek a refuge in our sex, whether for passion or play. And
he is not superior to the rest of his tribe. He will turn to *me!*
He has seen that I prefer him; and, however he may disguise
the feeling from himself — satisfied as he is, at present, with this
toy of a woman — the discovery did not displease him. No! his
vanity was interested, I am sure, in spite of his woes and virtues.
And that vanity, so soon as he finds out the weakness of the *one*
creature, whom he now values chiefly for her fidelity, will bring
him to me!

" Ah! I know him — know his sex thoroughly, and do not despair to conquer his stubbornness, so soon as this pretty child is

out of his thought and sight.  Let them carry her off — one or
t'other, it matters not which — and I leave the rest to Fortune!
Harry will not fail me then!  He will not look with indifference
upon a person—"

And the rest of the sentence was supplied mutely, by a gratified
reference to the mirror.

"Ay," she resumed, "I will have him to myself — all!  *He*
is not capricious.  I can love *him!*  I feel that his earnestness
of soul is not a whit superior to mine.  I can appreciate his manhood; can sympathize with his sorrows; can forgive him that he
has ever loved another with so much devotion; and gradually win
him to forget the ruined past, in a present in which he will find a
soul responsive to his own.

"Meanwhile, this struggle for the fair Zulieme binds these two
fashionable cavaliers to *my* circle.  They have been shy hitherto.
They are now mine.  How it will mortify that silly but insolent
Mrs. Calder Carpenter!  How it will vex and worry that stale
old graybeard, that looks like Hecate, just after getting in a new
set of teeth, Mrs. Andrew Beresford!  Anyhow, the affair must
be a success.  I have shot the arrow home: let us hope soon for
all the sports of the chase!"

The hints of Mrs. Anderson to our two gallants were confirmed
by the impressions made by Zulieme herself.  She had taken the
fashionables of Charleston by storm.  Her infantile beauty; her
picturesque costume — for she wore her Spanish dresses, and
could not be persuaded to adopt the English; the piquancy of
her simplicity; the unqualified *abandon* of her manner; her *naïveté*
of remark and reply, and the splendor of her jewels, had effectually done the work: and there was quite a *furore* among all parties, in consequence.  The gallants were wild with feverish hopes;
the leaders of the *ton* coerced to conciliation by the overwhelming advent of wealth and beauty; and Zulieme was a foreigner —
a rich foreigner — a beautiful foreigner: her *prestige* was established in the first hour of her appearance upon the scene!

"'T is distance lends enchantment to the view."  That nobody
could say exactly what she was, or who she was; could refer to
no doubtful antecedents, no qualifying associations; *must* receive
her just as she was, with the luminous halo of the remote and
vague about her beauty: this, itself, was a sufficient cause for the

rapidity with which she produced her effects. And when the beauty and the wealth seemed equally unquestionable, they naturally became exaggerated.

Mr. Keppel Craven was in ecstatics; Mr. Cornwall Cavendish in raptures; both equally eager in expectation, and equally resolved on her conquest.

They returned together from the party where they had encountered this cynosure of love and beauty. They lodged together; and, though understood rivals at the first moment of their discovery of the treasure, they communed together of the prize, and of the manner in which it was to be won. They were not sufficiently deep in passion to be angry with each other. They were only deep in expectation and policy.

They reached their lodgings in a feverish state of excitement; flushed with wine as well as fancy; exhilarated, happy, unapprehensive; and each exulting in the degree of favor which had been shown him by the artless subject of their raptures.

"By Venus the victorious, a prize!" cried Mr. Keppel Craven, as he flung himself, at length, along the cane settee of the chamber, and summoned his servant. Cavendish had entered the room with him, and disposed of his person on a lounge opposite. The servant entered; and Craven kicked off his shoes, while the lacquey cased his feet in gold-and-velvet slippers, and brought him a loose *robe de chambre*, for which he exchanged his silken coat.

"And now, John, bring us a bowl of punch, dem'd strong, and devilish sweet, and piquantly sour! Nothing but punch, Cornwall, after such a night: the sweet, the strong, and the sour — the all of wedlock and the honeymoon!"

"Sits the wind in that quarter with you, Keppel?"

"The moon, rather. I am moonstruck! That Spaniard is my Luna! I will worship her after a witch-fashion, though I ride on a broomstick for ever after!"

"Look you, John, put more of the sour than the sweet into your master's punch; he will have nausea else," said Cavendish, with a leer.

John, by-the-way, is the prescriptive name for an Englishman's body-servant. The fellow who waits on this occasion had been christened Richard. One of his great-grandsons is now a member of Congress, and looks to the presidency.

John, *alias* Richard, grinned and disappeared. The punch was prepared in a jiffy, and strong tumblers of the liquor were soon in the hands of the two gallants.

"The Mexican gold-mine!" quoth Craven; "and the diamonds and diamond-eyes of the new jewel of Golconda, the beautiful Zulieme de Montano!"

"Good! and a fair wind and open sea to the brave fellow who shall carry her off!" replied his companion.

"*Ecce homo!*" responded Craven, as he threw himself back upon the settee, and lifted his goblet in air.

"You, Keppel? you!"

"Why not? That excellent Mrs. Perkins Anderson has already felicitated me upon my progress to conquest."

"Egad! she has been equally bountiful to me. She specially complimented me upon the impression I had made."

"The devil she did! The arch-serpent! Why, Cornwall, had you heard her, you would have sworn that the game was already won."

"And, by Juno — whom I suspect to be something of a widow bewitched — she gave me to understand, in the fullest number of words, that I had proved myself irresistible; and, i' faith, I am free to say that the girl herself told me quite as much — with her eyes, at least."

"With her eyes? Oh, d—n the eyes! I must have it by word of mouth. And 1 could almost swear that she gave me assurance—"

"Oh, d—n your assurance!" cried Cornwall; "if it comes to that, the evidence is absolutely worthless, however extravagant. But your assurance will never do here. You have to win her against a score of competitors; and there are some, I fancy, Keppel, who will hold you to the full stretch of your tether in a love as well as a steeple chase."

"You, for example — eh?"

"Yes, blister my fingers! but I am man enough to do it. Look you, Keppel, don't forget the affair of the lovely Jennings."

"Pshaw! will you never cease to harp upon that affair? You kissed her, *you say:* she boxed my ears, *I know!* But what further?"

"Deponent saith not!"

"For the marvellous reason that you have nothing more to say! But, even the kiss was only secured, I suspect, by Rochester's favor — his contrivance, and her fright. He had been before you, and wanted a cover."

"Suspect what you please, Keppel. Enough that I am satisfied with the degree of happiness I have had with the Jennings."

"Well, that ought to content you, though I fancy you were over-soon satisfied. Still, according to your own admission, you have had enough of happiness for one life. Be content, and leave this prize to me."

"In love, nothing contents while anything is to be won! I mean to yield the prize to nobody."

"Love! what has love to do in the matter?" demanded Craven.

"Well, we use a certain word in the absence of any more expressive. It is love, or it is lust, or it is matrimony — which is another name, I take it, for speculation in the funds."

"Ho! ho! are you there, Master Cornwall? Have with you! You are, then, sufficiently satisfied with this Mexican damsel to share the noose with her — to marry, are you?"

"There is no room for doubt. It seems to me that the proofs are unquestionable. She is doubtless quite as rich as Mrs. Anderson reports her. Did you ever see such jewels? They shone upon her like the crown-jewels — as I have seen them upon the queen, and our own loving duchess."

"If not paste and crystal."

"They are not, I'm sure! I'm rather a judge of what's good water."

"Well, drink your *punch*, and refill. You linger over it as if you thought it water only."

"I might have drunk more freely if I could think it less potent. But your fellow John has made it as strong as the devil!"

"So much the better, Master Cornwall. We are upon an argument that requires strength. I agree with you that this beautiful Mexican wears jewels of the best water. I think it very likely that the report of Mrs. Anderson is in great measure true, and that she is an heiress — not, perhaps, to the extent that she reports, but she's rich enough, no doubt, for either of us; and so devilish pretty, and so piquant, so peculiar, and so *petite* — of evils choose the least, you know — that, like you, sooner than not wear such a treasure, I too am willing to take it — with a noose."

"Ha! ha! — good! It would almost compensate me for my own defeat with the Mexican, to see you 'Benedict the married man.' What a revolution — what a transformation! You would never show your face again in London."

"Would I not? Would *you* not? My dear Cornwall, marriage is a pill, the bitterness of which is soothed by the gilding! and who, in London, does not acknowledge *that?* Why are we here?"

"True, true! That is enough on that head; but—"

"But, my dear fellow, it has not come to marriage *yet*, with either of us; and may not, if we play our cards with proper dexterity. This lovely Spanish creature seems a mere simpleton. She wants love, and may think of matrimony; but how if she is satisfied with love alone?"

"Precisely my thought. Women do not much care for matrimony, anyhow, when they can get love. It is only in our d——d world of convention that too much love and too little matrimony loses a woman position, while making the position of the man. She evidently knows nothing of this. And these Spaniards of Mexico are loose livers at the best. Money will satisfy the Church at any time; and where the Church shows herself unscrupulous, the woman may well use all her liberty. She generally regulates her moral — when a simple creature like this — by that of the Church; and we can surely find many good fathers in God, to grant her absolution, when Love makes his plea with a money-bag in his fingers. I shall dodge matrimony, in this instance, if I can — and as long as I can!"

"But, if dodging will not suffice? — if the simpleton should be sagacious on this one score?"

"Then, dem it! swallow the physic as I may!"

"But you *will* swallow it?"

"If I can do no better. I *will* have this Mexican lady of the mines! I will disembowel her Potosi! I will revel in her charms and ingots! I will end this d——d long, degrading struggle in a sphere, for maintenance in which I lack all the material essentials. It is resolved that, *par amours*, or as a Benedict, I shall possess this fair little prize, worth galleons and millions, the beautiful Zulieme de Montano!"

"Good! I like your spirit; all the better, indeed, as I had just come to the same resolution."

"You, Cornwall? Impossible!"

"Yes, by Jupiter! Look you, Keppel, we are friends, and must remain so; but friendship does not forbid honest rivalry. I am without a guinea, more than will pay off absolute scores from day to day. I can not afford to be generous; but I am willing to be just. Shall it be a fair contest between us?"

"I had much rather there should be none at all!"

This was said somewhat sulkily.

"Ho! there, John! More punch!" — as the fellow appeared — "and a cruetful, sharper and stronger than the last!"

For a few moments, the parties sank into a dubious fit of meditation; but the punch was brought in, and John having disappeared, the goblets were refilled, and the dialogue resumed — Keppel taking the *parole:*—

"A contest between us, Cornwall, may defeat both parties; and I have as much need of the girl's gold as yourself, perhaps more. We have neither of us anything to boast of in the way of surplus funds. Besides, a contest is fatiguing; it exhausts me! You have to be constantly on the watch, and constantly striving. I confess to a preference for that fruit which does not require me to climb the tree; and, if I mistake not, you are not less averse to useless effort than I am. Can we not avoid the struggle?"

"I don't see how. My wits fail to conceive of any plan but the one — that of winning the Mexican if I can, and by any process! I shall try to do this, by all the wits in my power. I am not ill-looking, Keppel; I have *some* wits; I can be clever at an answer; and can do my *impromptu* as well as any man, with twelve hours' notice! I dance, sing, play; and, though I do not relish fatiguing operations of any kind, yet, by Plutus, when a silver-mine is the stake, I shall go through fire and water for it!"

"My resolution too, by Jove, rather than be defeated! Well, it comes to this: we are in each other's way. Now, there was an old mode of removing an obstacle of this sort by resort to a short, sharp cut-and-thrust. But, my dear Cornwall, we respect each other's throats, do we not?"

" Most reverently, Keppel."

" If we both pursue this lady, one or other of us must be defeated."

" Most logical conclusion !"

" You may console yourself with hope, as I do, that the unfortunate will be other than ourself; but, *quien sabe?* as the Spaniard hath it. Who knows? I do not relish the idea of utter defeat, nor do you. I dread, in the conflict between us, that both will suffer. Now, I have a scheme to avoid this danger."

" Ah ! Deliver, my dear fellow !"

" Let us submit it to Fortune, beforehand, to decide which shall woo the damsel first; and he who wins, pays over to the other, within three weeks after marriage, a round sum of ten thousand pounds. Her estates can afford all of that ! With such a sum as this, I should be reconciled to seeing the fair Zulieme de Montana safely locked in your arms !"

" Admirably thought, and declared ! We are to throw the dice for the lady or ten thousand pounds ?"

" Precisely : that is the scheme."

" Good, Keppel ! and the losing party shall help the other, in all possible ways, in the promotion of his object?"

" Granted, with one reservation : that *his* failure exonerates the other, and leaves him free to the pursuit on his own account?"

" A good proviso ! The dice ! the dice ! the dice ! Hither, good John !"

" Do not be too impatient. You are challenging Fate, you know ! Drink your punch ! Think, meanwhile, of your loss."

" My gains rather. The lady with the mines of Potosi, or ten thousand pounds ! Any how, I shall be better off than now ! Summon your man, and bid him bring forth the ivories !"

John, *alias* Richard, appeared at the summons.

" Pen, ink, and paper," said his master, the Honorable Keppel Craven.

" What the devil do you want with pen, ink, and paper ?"

" To reduce the terms to writing."

" By Jupiter, you were born for a scrivener, rather than a conqueror ! But, be it so ! I accept the requisition as a good augury."

Craven wrote : the other looked over the paper.

" You were *not* born for a scrivener, Keppel.   I acquit you of the imputation.   As d——d cramp a hand as that of a York-shire ploughman !   But men of noble blood are not to affect the special virtues of a clerk."

" There : read — sign !"

" All right !" said Cavendish, dashing his signature below the writing.   Craven followed him.

" A copy," said the former.

It was prepared and signed like the former, the order of the signatures only being reversed.

" Will it need a witness ?"

" No ! pshaw ! no !   We shall neither of us forswear the sig-nature.   And now for the dice !"

John appeared as soon as he was summoned, bringing the dice-box.

" Set it down.   Avaunt, fellow ! begone !   We are at study on the fate of nations."

John fled.

" Throw first, Corny," said Master Keppel Craven."

" What ! you begin to tremble, do you ?   And well you may ! I must throw first, you say ?   Be it so !   There is no use in hanging off, when one has agreed upon the play.   And now, help me, ye gods, who second bold hearts and gallant fortunes !   Help, you especially who excel in the snares set for beauty — Vulcan, the net-flinger ! — help me to victory !"

And, even as he spoke, he rolled forth the dice with a violence and effort which were surely unnecessary after putting the affair into the hands of Fate.

" Ha ! ha ! ha !" roared Craven, not able to restrain his mirth. " You are clearly no favorite with the gods.   Three, four, *one !* No great shakes that, Corny !"

" No, indeed !" answered the other, sulkily.   " But, better it if you can, and don't stand grinning like a monkey !"

" Here's at you !"   But the Honorable Keppel, striving to con-ceal his anxiety in a strained laughter, was slow to take up the dice and box.   The impatience of his companion, however, urged him to the throw, which was nervously delivered.

" Venus the victorious !" he murmured, as he let the dice roll gently from the box.   He was the conqueror !

"Three, four, five ! Well, Keppel, you have the mine, and I am to submit to ten thousand pounds !"

"Yes, my dear fellow, and be content. The lesson is your own. For my part, I owe a pair of doves to Venus ! And now sit down, swallow your punch, and let us proceed to the plan of operations."

These we need not examine. The half-drunken rake-hellies continued over the punch-bowl till dawn ; when John, *alias* Richard, came to the relief of the parties, and, summoning the servant of Cavendish, assisted Keppel Craven to his chamber, after having helped his brother-lacquey in a like service rendered to Cornwall.

# CHAPTER XXXVI.

### " HIGH JINKS."

*Puck.* " Then will two at once woo one;
　　That must needs be sport alone:
　　And these things do best please me
　　That befall preposterously."
　　　　　　　　　*Midsummer Night's Dream.*

THE sudden entrance of the Honorable Mr. Craven was a complete surprise to the younger of the two ladies. The wily Mrs. Anderson, who had fully expected her visiter, at that very hour, put on, however, an admirable air of astonishment, which she did not feel.

"Bless my soul, Mr. Craven, is it you? Oh, what a surprise!"

" A not unpleasant one, I trust," answered the cavalier, gallantly kissing the extended hand of the lady. Zulieme looked up, and laughed merrily. She never once changed her position on the floor, or sought to change it. Her surprise was not one of consternation or annoyance. It really did not concern her a jot that she should be caught, by a gay courtier, lying at length along the floor, immersed in silks, satins, and garments of peculiar cut and fashion, for which gentlemen vainly conjecture the names and uses. There were cases of jewels open, displaying their brave contents — thanks to the providence of Mrs. Anderson, whose pretended curiosity had contrived to put on exhibition every article of magnificence and value which Zulieme's trunks contained: and she was rich.

As we have said, that ingenuous young creature never once fancied any awkwardness in her situation; never had the least misgivings of its propriety. Nor need we, at present, entertain any misgivings about her.

Of the mere grace of her attitude we can confidently speak. She lay like another Titania — the Titania of the opera-house, perhaps, but still a Titania. She was grace itself, reclining on luxury and ease; that is, on one elbow, amid a pile of silks, her head lifted, her eyes looking up merrily at the sudden visiter; while an enormous string of pearls, a yard or two in length, doubled over her right hand, fell around her half-naked arm, beautifully harmonizing with the exquisite skin, which was not too dark to be left unenlivened by a warm current of healthy blood.

It must be admitted that, whether she was conscious of it or not, the position of Zulieme was such as to leave exposed something more of her ankles than is usually allowed to entreat the gaze of discreet young gentlemen; and, still further to confess, the dear little Mexican, taking advantage of the growing heat of the season — had thrown off her stockings! Think of that, ladies! It was the natural ankle that shone, white and bare as the arm, upon the eager sight of our gallant, and fixed his eyes irresistibly, as if with fascination. And it was not an ankle to be ashamed of. It was still that of a Titania — exquisite, fairy-like, and worthy to win the smiles of Oberon, even after the third month of wedlock.

Even thus, as natural and unsophisticated, did the Fairy Queen rest, with naked feet and tolerably short petticoat — of green silk, perhaps — beside that type of the universal genius, Master Nicholas Bottom! Even thus did she expose to vulgar eyes those charms which she could only learn to value properly herself when Oberon had found a rival!

For a moment, the Honorable Keppel Craven was at fault. Convention, at least in the simple world of Ashley river, was set at defiance. Was it indifference that kept Zulieme from all show of disquiet or concern — caught in such an attitude, and by a stranger — caught in such a *deshabille*, and by a bold gallant of the court of Charles II.? — and so caught, when Mrs. Perkins Anderson well knew that he was to be there, and *must* have apprized her guest of his coming? Thus did Craven query with himself. And, if indifference, what did this indifference signify? Either she regarded him too lightly to care what he saw or thought — and that was provocation to his self-esteem, which made him feel excessively wicked—or she was a damsel of considerable experience—a very knowing and accommodating one—and had grown rather obtuse in non-essentials!

This thought rendered him a few degrees more wicked in his fancies.

Or the lady was willing to allure him, after an easy Mexican fashion, to a conquest, in which she was prepared to yield, without making the labor of victory a very exhausting one?

At that moment, he had no other theories of the situation than these; and these were all huddled together in his thoughts; each sufficiently provocative, and all encouraging his impudence—which, as Mrs. Perkins Anderson had familiarly phrased it, was that of the devil!

The result was that, even while addressing the señorita, in terms of lavish and courtly compliment, he threw himself gallantly down beside her on the floor, with a grace becoming the best stage Lothario; his rapier so judiciously disposed as not to get between his legs, and his descent made with such admirable balance as not to derange his doublet.

The Honorable Mr. Craven had evidently practised in a school which rendered much flexibility of body a highly-necessary accomplishment.

As he lay upon the floor, beside and fronting the fair beauty of Panama, the picture was a fine one.    Titania had her Oberon! His figure was by no means too large for the Fairy King, who, as a Saxon elf, had necessarily a good *physique*, even for a fairy. And his costume was not inappropriate to the situation : a rich doublet of purple satin, frilled with lace; gay small-clothes of a light texture, purffled and flowered; with silk stockings of a delicate flesh-color; a laced collar; and a steeple-crowned hat, with feather—he was the macaroni of the era, and realized the object of English satire, as found in the nursery-ballads of that very time :—

> " Yankee Doodle 's come to town,
>       Upon a Kentish pony;
>    Stick a feather in his cap,
>       And call him Macaroni!"*

---

* Our author here gives us, no doubt, the original source of our national air; the verse and its music being twinned together and harmonizing natu-

As if taking his lesson from the stereotyped stage-Hamlet, our cavalier adroitly struck off his hat while falling; so that his long locks floated free, and filled the chamber with the fine oleaginous fragrance, then famous, as the "*Delice de la Valliére.*"

The performance was so cleverly done, that Mrs. Perkins Anderson clapped her hands. Zulieme, too was delighted. It was just such a feat as amused her childish fancy, and made her forget everything else.

"Oh, the funny fellow!" she exclaimed, laughing immoderately, and nowise discomfited.

"Funny fellow!" thought Keppel Craven; and he fancied there was something irreverent in the speech, and ridiculous in the idea, at a moment when he was practising the graces. But he smiled through all his doubts.

"Really, Mr. Craven, you should have been an actor. It is very certain that you are a gallant! Ah! I can fancy that you have practised this action a thousand times, at the feet of duchesses and ladies of honor."

So the gracious Mrs. Perkins Anderson. She proceeded:—

"So much for your not rising, Zulieme. But I thank you. It has enabled us to see what admirable courtiers England can send forth."

The laughter of Zulieme again answered her — an irrepressible burst, which she did not seek to suppress. When she recovered from the fit, she exclaimed:—

"Oh! do, Mr. Craven, do it over again! It was so very, very funny!"

"Do it over!" he cried, aghast at the mere idea of the monstrous effort involved in the exercise; and looked vacantly at the speaker. Was she laughing at the absurdity of the thing? An Englishman is peculiarly sensitive to ridicule. But his self-esteem as quickly reassured him. The Honorable Keppel Craven could not surely, by any possibility, do anything absurd! And, if he doubted, the pleased, bright eyes, frank and joyous, of Zulieme,

rally. When the Boston militia first began to parade as patriots, awkwardly enough, and with cornstalk muskets, the English army-bands, on station in Boston, ridiculed their military display, by playing the old English nursery-air of "Yankee Doodle," to their marching. PRINTER'S DEVIL.

satisfied him in a moment after. They had no irony in their glance.

Suddenly, however, she discovered that he had taken his full length upon some of her gayest silks. Her tone immediately changed :—

" Get up, you great English elephant, before you ruin my dresses !— He is on my brocade and satin, Charlotte — my most beautiful gown ! Get up, you great, awkward monster, before I beat you !"

" Beat me !— Your gown !" he exclaimed, looking about him, but not stirring, and curious in a survey of the treasures he endangered.

His movements were quite too slow for the impatient señorita, who first threw her great Panama fan at his head, and then, darting up, proceeded to heap on him a pile of the clothing so copiously accumulated around her.

His head was, in a jiffy, enveloped in a monstrous shawl ; and, we are constrained to report, that one of the equivocal garments, of white linen, was adroitly enough thrust over his neck.

This was too much, even for a younger son. He began now to feel the ridiculous in his situation ; and, with much more quickness and dexterity than his usual languid address and manner would warrant us to expect, he contrived to scramble to his feet, and fling off his encumbrances, all of which he threw right and left, with no scrupulous hand ; his face emerging finally from the envelopes, deeply empurpled by his desperate efforts, and by his growing feeling of the ridiculous in the affair.

The laughter of the ladies was immoderate. Even Mrs. Perkins Anderson, though perfectly conscious of what was due to the dignity of a cavalier of the court of Charles, could not resist the cachinating impulse ; while Zulieme clapped her hands, held her sides, danced, and made the echoes ring with her clear, free, childlike outburst of delight.

But, as she stood confronting our cavalier, looking the very imp of mischief, with her bright eyes flashing, though watery, and her lips parted with her frantic merriment, she looked so provoking, that the Honorable Keppel darted at her.

We must not venture on a metaphysical or psychological subject so profound as to ask what were his purposes in the onslaught. Something of pique, no doubt; something of humor; for the silly fellow was not a *mauvais sujêt.* He was lively and ridiculous, no doubt, but not a savage. But, whatever his purposes, they failed. He shot, like a rocket, to the place where she stood, but she was gone; vaulting, like a gazelle, at a single bound, over a cane settee, and ensconcing herself behind it. Craven eyed the leap, but did not dare to attempt it. She leered at and defied him.

Then commenced a regular chase round settee, chairs, and tables, until at length the honorable gentleman was compelled to confess himself conquered; he yielded the victory, collapsing, like an exhausted butterfly, upon the sofa.

But where was Mrs. Perkins Anderson? That amiable lady, so soon as she beheld the game of " High Jinks" in full operation, vanished. She felt herself *de trop*, and fled with a purpose and a hope. She was, at all events, willing to afford the cavalier a sufcient opportunity for play — or mischief.

But Keppel Craven did not catch and kiss the Mexican, as she fancied he would ; and the excellent hostess came back in season to behold the issue: the cavalier exhausted with his unusual exertions, and no doubt feeling very ridiculous; and Zulieme, neither fatigued nor frightened, and as full of laugh as ever, standing coolly apart, contemplating the exhausted swain, and quietly fanning herself with the great leaves of the fan of Panama.

" I'm done for, demme!" gasped the cavalier. " O thou nimblest of all the elves, lend me thy palm-leaves ere I suffocate !"

" What is it you call me ?" asked Zulieme.

" Elf, witch!—"

" Witch! That means something abominable, I know !" responded our Mexican, while the fire flashed from her eyes.

" Abominable? no ! It means something divine, delicious, and most killing! A witch is a beautiful woman that wins hearts, and laughs at her winnings; a tricksy creature that plays with poor mortal affections — that conquers only to fling away; an angel that comes to fill our brains with dreams of delightful promise, only to mock them with denial ! Ah ! indeed, thou art a witch, more potent than she of Endor. Thou knowest not what a spirit thou hast called up from my soul."

" Now, I know that you are insulting me, in spite of all your fine speeches. For do n't I know that the witch of Endor was an ugly old hag; and do n't I know that the witches were all to be killed; and do n't I know that you Englishmen burnt 'em up? And, after that, do you pretend that you are not calling me by bad names? I have half a mind to knock you with the broom-stick!"

"A regular witch-weapon, dear señorita. But, in sooth, let me teach thee, most beautiful of all Mexican beauties, that, in the divine language of poesy, witchcraft means the magical power of beauty, the spell of an angelic excellence, throned in the eyes and on the lips of a lovely woman, making her potent over devoted hearts. And such is the power which, almost at a glance, the divine charms of thy beauty hath exercised upon mine. I believe thou art guilty of witchcraft; else it could never be that the eyes which have never faltered before all the beauties of the royal court of Charles, should be so humbled before thine. I am lost in amaze at my own feebleness of soul! Once I was a conqueror. I won the worship which I am now compelled to offer. O love-liest Zulieme, beautiful Turk, let me make of thee a Christian, indeed, by persuading thee to bestow mercy upon the poor captive whom the fate of love hath delivered into thy hands!"

"There, again! you are calling me a Turk, as if I did n't know that all the Turks are Jews and idolaters; and, besides, you say you want to make me a Christian, as if I were not already a pure Castilian Christian, while you English are nothing but heathens. I tell you, if you talk so, I will have to knock you! I won't suf-fer it."

"O perversest of all Christian beauties! O most wilful of all Castilian witches! didst thou know enough of the divine speech of the poetry of Albion, thou wouldst know that the epithets I give thee are all loving ones, most considerate of thy charms, thy spells, thy divine loveliness, which lacks only in the Christian vir-tue of mercy for him thou hast taken captive with thy bow and spear!"

"Now, what nonsense are you talking, as if you had ever seen me using bow and spear!"

"Alas! what mischief is in thy hands, when thou usest thy weapons so ignorantly, not knowing that they are in thy very grasp; for dost thou not know that the bow is the very beautiful black arch above thine eyes, and that from the eyes the spear issues which has pierced my heart to the core? and dost thou not see that I am thy captive, since here I lie at thy feet, entreating thee to take me to thy mercy?"

Here the speaker rather slided than descended from the settee, taking an attitude for the occasion, and appearing the graceful suppliant, making such tender eyes at the lady as to disarm any hostility which her doubts of his language might have occasioned.

" Get up, you foolish fellow," she answered, laughingly — not at all displeased at the action — " get up, and do n't be so foolish. You only fall down there because you think you do it so prettily. But I can tell you I have seen other men who did it much better."

" Cruel, that you should tell me this ! So, you have had other men at your feet !"

" Hundreds ; and some quite as pretty little fellows as you."

" Pretty ! little !" cried the cavalier, starting to his feet with sudden indignation. " Do you call me little, señorita?"

And he rose to his fullest proportions, a graceful, rather slender person, of some five feet five. Not above the average of that day in America, certainly — perhaps somewhat below it. In fact, while no one could recognise the Honorable Mr. Craven as a large person, still no one, without prejudice, would describe him as a small one. He did not know, nor did Zulieme herself conjecture, that she had tacitly adopted her own husband as the becoming model for stature as well as manhood ; and that such a standard would distress the ambitious efforts of most of the courtiers of the Charles II. circle.

" Do you call me *little*, señorita?" he repeated, approaching the lady, and towering above her, arms a-kimbo, and head superbly lifted.

" No, indeed ; not when you come so close. You are big enough to eat me up, and look as if you wanted to do it."

She receded from him as he spoke, as if apprehending a renewal of his pursuit. But he had not quite recovered from the previous chase. He was content to use his tongue rather than his feet.

" Devour you ? Yes ! I feel that I could. I have the appetite for it !"

" O monster !"

"Yes: but it is with love that I would devour."

"That would n't make it any more pleasant to me, I can tell you."

"Hear me, beautiful Castilian, while I ask a single question."

"Well, what's it?"

"Have you, amid all your rich possessions, by possibility, such a thing as men call a heart?"

He advanced, and she again retreated, with the question.

"A heart, I say! You beauties are not so apt to believe in the necessity of such a possession, even while you insist upon it. Are you an exception to the common rule? Have you, beautiful señorita, that vulgar essential of humanity — a human heart?"

"Me! a heart? Ha! ha! ha! What a stupid question! No, indeed, no. Why, what do I want with a heart? What should I do with it — or you? I do n't think it's for either of us."

"But, beautiful señorita, you mock, surely. A heart to a woman — a young woman, especially — a beautiful woman, particularly — an angel, a sylph, a fairy—"

He was approaching while he spoke, and she began to retreat, especially as his hands were stretching toward her under the impulse of his eloquence.

"Farther off!" said she. "Talk away, but do n't come a bit closer. I do n't want another run, in this hot weather. And I'm sure you can't stand it. You'd faint, and then I might get scared; and, anyhow, I do n't want to have the worry of fanning you."

"Faint! most probable!" muttered the cavalier, *sotto voce;* the very thought making him begin to fan himself with his hands. But he said, aloud:—

"But you would fan me, should I faint? You have heart enough for that, surely."

"I do n't know: I'd be more like to run. Men have no right to faint before women; they make such ugly faces."

"Ugly faces!" he exclaimed, and again he made a show of darting at her; but she was gone, with a single bound, over the settee, which stood as an impassable wall between them. There she laughed at him, and clapped her hands, and defied him. He had looked with wonder at her display of muscle — and, we may add, ankle — of which she had not thought.

" Really, señorita, you have wonderful powers of endurance —
rustic powers, it is true, but not the less wonderful. 'Pon my soul,
it is well sometimes to pass out of the customary world, if it be
only to observe what muscle is to be found in other regions. Ah,
Señorita Zulieme, were you as loving as you are light; as tender
as you are touching; with as much feeling as activity; as susceptible as provocative — I could — eh! yes, I could—"

" Well, what?"

" Demme! I do n't know what; but—ah! I have it, beautiful
señorita — I could die for you."

" And what good would that do me, I want to know?"

" Well, I could live for you, if you'd suffer me."

" Ah! that's something more sensible. But, would you really
die, if I would n't suffer you to live for me?"

" Heaven only knows! It might be that Nature, which is singularly tenacious of vitality, would enable me to struggle on, in a
seeming existence; but that would not be life. The bloom would
be gone from the rose, the glory from the sky; and one, you know,
might very well be dead after that."

" Well, you talk very foolishly, I think; as if you had been all
your life in a house where the people had all agreed to say nothing that needed any answer. I do n't think that your feelings
will ever be the death of you; and I do n't care at all for such
talk. What do you say, now — you have rested long enough —
what do you say for a *bolero ?*"

" A *bolero !* Heavens! was ever such muscle in a woman?
After that chase? Señorita, I see you have a design upon my
life. *You* would, indeed, be the death of me. Dance a *bolero !*
For Heaven's sake, lend me your fan !"

She handed it to him, with a merry laughter. As she did so,
he caught desperately at her arm. But she was too quick for
him; and, in the merriment which she felt at his defeat, she forgot the offence in his attempt.

" Ah, cruelest of all the Castilians !" he murmured, affectedly.
" There might be some hopes were you a Morescan, of browner
tinge."

" What's that you say?" sharply. " A Morescan? Jews,
again !"

" Oh, nothing! The Morescans were the houris of Granada;

beautiful creatures that came down from the stars, and brought wine and odors for suffering mortals like myself."

"Oh! you want something to drink, and something to smell? Charlotte! Charlotte!"—calling pretty loudly—"here's Mr. Craven going to faint, and he wants some wine!"

"Great Heavens!" cried the cavalier, aghast, and now almost ready to faint in earnest.

"Why, don't you want some wine? don't you feel like fainting?"

"Was ever such a —— creature? So provokingly dull and literal!"

This was all *sotto voce*.

Here, the accommodating Mrs. Perkins Anderson, hearing the outcry, and taking for granted that she had afforded the parties opportunity enough, timelily made her appearance; the servant following soon after, with lunch — and punch — on an enormous silver waiter.

It was with a sincere sense of relief that the Honorable Mr. Craven welcomed the lady and the liquor. He ejaculated—

"Ah! thank you. I was quite thirsty. I was overcome! This most piquant señorita has — a — a—"

And he quaffed a goblet of punch, as if to cool a fever, and finish a period which lacked all natural terminus.

The scene was over; but not the interview. The excellent Mrs. Anderson, when she reappeared, did so in full morning costume. She had taken advantage of her temporary absence to adjust her own toilet. Zulieme was only apprized of *her deshabille* by beholding the fair Charlotte in all "her fine effects."

"Why, holy Mother! Charlotte, here have I been playing with this foolish little fellow, and—look at *me!*"

And she absolutely thrust out her naked feet, in the slippers, while holding her skirts sufficiently high to let the white ankles assert themselves.

"O Zulieme!" exclaimed the modest matron. "What a child of Nature!"

"Child!" muttered Zulieme; "don't you call me so, Charlotte."

And, with finger shaking at the lady, and a familiar nod to the Honorable Keppel, she disappeared.

"Did you ever see so unsophisticated a creature?" exclaimed the hostess.

"With face of brass and muscles of steel!" answered Mr. Craven. "She did me up, in a chase of fifteen minutes."

"What did you chase her for?" asked Mrs. Anderson, with a significant and somewhat knowing smile.

"Eh! why, only to see her ankles!"

"Oh, you wicked creature! I should not have left her to such an able courtier."

"Faith, she was safe enough. She has the legs of an antelope! But, dear Mrs. Anderson, do you really think her so ignorant as she seems?"

"She is a perfect child of Nature. There is no art about her. But she can be taught! and lucky the man who can succeed in winning her young affections. But he must be bold; and the usual courtier-like process will not answer here. She has no romance in her. Sentiment is thrown away upon her: but play, fun, merriment, dancing; a gay humor; great vivacity; perpetual restlessness; and a ready adoption of *her* humors — these are the arts by which to win her heart. Methinks she has given you a chance at hers."

"Eh! heart? Hark ye, my dear Mrs. Anderson: this winning of hearts may be pleasant enough, while the game is doubtful; but the question is, do they pay for the trouble, the exertion?" — Here he fanned himself. "*Mere* hearts—" he continued.

"Ah! true — are of little count at court. But Zulieme's diamonds are something, Sir Keppel."

"If not paste! — yes!"

"Paste! See for yourself. There is not an English duchess who can wear such jewels as these!"

She displayed the glittering treasures to the gloating eyes of the cavalier, who thought of the ankles and the gems together.

"And see how she leaves them about. She values them just as little as I do mine! So much for having them as mere playthings from her childhood. She has played with diamonds as you courtiers with hearts, and values them as little."

Enough, perhaps, was said and shown by the hostess. She was probably not wholly unaware of the game at "High Jinks" which had been played in her absence. She saw that the vanity of the cavalier had been piqued, his cupidity excited; his passions warmed, and his purpose determined. She was now satisfied to

16

let events take their own course, assured that Mr. Craven, at least, would engage in the pursuit as hotly as was possible to his languid nature.

Here, then, for the present, let us stop. Our purpose was simply to show under what circumstances the Honorable Mr. Craven began that acquaintance with Zulieme which was rapidly to ripen into intimacy. And this was destined to have some peculiar consequences.

But we must not anticipate. Enough that the intimacy was very fairly begun; strangely enough, but not in a way to startle the Mexican señora—señorita for the nonce. We may add that it was continued as begun, until our cavalier was regarded as her special attendant. Had it been suspected, by any of those outside the mystery, that the lady was señora, and not señorita, he would have been dubbed her *cavaliere servente*. He rode with her, walked with her, danced with her, and talked with her; but, as Zulieme was rather pert than fluent, Mr. Craven was better pleased to flirt with her, and only dance occasionally. She usually broke him down; when — such is true friendship and a proper holy alliance — Cornwall Cavendish would come to his aid, and take the lady off his hands.

We must do her the justice to say that, in respect to these two gallants, she truly gave neither any proper right to suppose that he was held in highest favor. But never was innocent lady more civil! And both gallants, we may add, began soon to entertain equal hopes, especially as the *bal masque* was in progress.

# CHAPTER XXXVII.

## THE DEAD ALIVE.

"I dreamt my lady came and found me dead!
  (Strange dream! that gives a dead man leave to think),
  And breathed such life, with kisses, on my lips,
  That I revived! . . . . . . . . . . . . . . . .
  Ah me! how sweet is love itself possessed,
  When but Love's shadows are so rich in joy!" — *Romeo and Juliet.*

       ————" Why look you so upon me?
I am but sorry; not afraid." — *Winter's Tale.*

THIS life with all its ridiculous contrasts! Farce and tragedy; melodrame and pantomime; Melpomene and Punchinello!

Here, in one dwelling, you see the chamber of death — the pall and the bier. Before the entrance stands the hearse, that melancholy coach of state. From the chamber ascends the wail of one who will not be comforted. Rachel weeping for her first-born; David, in the mixed agonies of remorse and wo, lamenting the son torn from him as the punishment of his crime. The cloud, black with penal thunders, hangs over the dwelling; and from the midst of it issues a mighty hand, shaking out fiery bolts!

Next door, they have a dinner and a guest to-day, and all the young ladies are agog with expectation. The coming visiter is a *millionaire;* and each one studies, in the pages of the siren, how best to fascinate and fix!

Or, there is a ball to-night, and the fiddles are already in requisition; or, Darby and Joan, no longer placid, are at odds touching the roast; or, the alderman dreams, after a monstrous surfeit, that he is engaged in the labors of Sisyphus. What you will — the contrast is sufficiently ludicrous.

These atrocious truisms! we can not escape them, though we try.

Now, while the amiable Mrs. Perkins Anderson, and the lovely simpleton, Spanish wife, and the Honorable Keppel Craven, are each eager in the chase of their several butterflies, rollicking at "High Jinks" in the parlor, you see the cassique of Accabee, with heavy head resting in his palms; heavier heart, with nothing upon which to rest; moody with a grief for which there is no comforter; his whole life and hope resolved into a settled compact with wo and desolation; disappointment that dries up the sources of hope; defeat that hangs like a millstone around the neck of the spent swimmer!

He strikes out wildly, like the blind wrestler, in the air; and the blows, though they fall upon vacancy, exhaust his vigor. He works, madly enough, when thought becomes too terrible for endurance. But the spectre clings to his side like a shadow. He builds; would improve; has tastes that still plead for gratification; energies that will not suffer themselves to be denied: but these no longer minister to his satisfaction; no longer offer refuge to thought; no longer resupply the fountains of pride, and hope, and pleasure, to his soul.

It is amazing to see how he works, physically as well as with thought; amazing to see what his own head and hands have done, in very few days, in that new baronial domain which he has planted for other generations in the wilderness. His workmen, used to labor, are confounded. He keeps their muscles on the stretch, but with no such tension as his own must endure. And they know nothing of that agony of brain and soul which is goading his limbs to their incessant exercise. He does not groan or murmur — declares no suffering in speech! He is not only building houses, and laying off routes and fences — doing after a merely necessary plan and fashion — he does more: he plans terraces of beauty; is opening artificial fishponds; he will have Art confront Nature in her own empire, and challenge the supremacy. There are gardeners from Holland — which, about that time, was furnishing the general models for landscape-gardening for Europe — but he too will design, at least to such a degree as to modify the formalities of the Dutch taste, and, in bringing Nature to a better knowledge of Art, not suffering the latter to subvert any of those charms of the former which we should only injure in the effort to improve.

And in all these labors, though in everything he exhibits marked intelligence and taste, he performs mechanically. His heart is no longer in his work. His eyes wander from it — wander off perpetually in contemplation of that gloomy thundercloud that overhangs his house and heart. He is looking momently to see it part — to see this hand of Judgment shaking free the bolt which is to strike down work and workman in one common ruin!

Ah! this is very terrible — this picture of the strong man using his strength after a wonted habit, but with no longer love for his work; still fighting bravely with the adverse hosts of Fate, though he well knows that he fights under a doom — that, however long delayed, the bolt *must* fall, and the ruin be complete!

It is already complete. *He* has lost all — all that he holds precious. He can lose no more. His grand hope of heart and life has proved a grand defeat; and the defeat is irreparable!

What remains? The battle is over — so he himself thinks: but it is for him now to bury his dead; to cleanse the field of its bloody trophies; to hide the horrid proofs from sight; and, this done — whither for him? Whither shall he fly? Why fly? He can not escape his own memories — his own consciousness of what has been his hope — what has been the agony in its being — and that it is no more a hope! He can neither fly from Memory nor fly to Hope. The dead Past, with all its horrors, is bound irrevocably to his still living soul!

He broods, even while at work; and if he leaves his work, in the very exhaustion of his physical nature, it is again to brood.

But not over his own griefs and disappointments. No, no! Do the brave man no injustice. His cares are not selfish. He broods over another's fate. Unseen, he watches the victim — ah! mockery to speak it — the victim of his own very love! His strong passion and her weak will have, together, bound her to the rock, and fastened the vulture on her dovelike bosom!

He broods with the vainest question, evermore recurring, what may be done, that she be saved? How save her? — not simply from death and pain, but from that torture which momently threatens her with madness! He has again had the physician to her aid; but art has failed in such a case. He has brought with him neither hope nor comforter; and the brave but anguished man looks on her with eyes of stony fixedness, yet of lightning-like avidity, as if he strove to penetrate the shut avenues of her woman-soul, to see where lay the particular hurt to which Love, denied itself, might yet bring balm, if not healing.

And never was scrutiny more circumspect, as well as keen. She was suffered to see nothing of his eager watch — to suspect nothing of his intense interest and scrutiny; though, perhaps, it does not much matter what she sees, or what she may suspect. In the state of mental *extasie* which prevails with her, she hardly seems to be conscious of external things, or any objects of the mere outer sense. She, too, is looking through a fate-cloud; not for the bolt, but for the receiving angel — the soothing, saving, lifting — who is to bear her to the joy of heaven, or its peace!

If she showed any solicitude — and this was the keenest pang that *he* was required to endure — it was how to escape his eyes, his presence, his companionship, the consciousness of his existence, the recollection of his rights in herself! She taught him this in every movement. He had become, in the acuteness of his own griefs, as sensitive to every mood of *her* soul as to the keen agonies that strove within his own. He shivered, with a sort of horror, at the mournful conviction, which he could not repel, that his simple presence had grown to be a terror to her imagination.

And, though dying, absolutely dying — though this fact was scarcely conceived by any but himself — Olive yet walked about life, apparently unhurt. She could sing — she was now for ever singing, however unconsciously, to herself — and oh, with what a touching, tearful sweetness, bringing involuntary moisture to other eyes! She sang over, one by one, all the sweet love-songs of her girlhood — her childhood even — whenever she felt herself alone. And sometimes she did not seem to heed the presence of others, but sang on, apparently never beholding them, and looking, speaking, singing, just as if she were alone. She sang the gayest ditties, which, as you saw the singer, melted you to sorrow; and sometimes the merest lullabies, which made you smile through your tears, though you wept afterward. And, even as she sang, she walked the house like a spectre; sought commerce with none; walked incessantly, with the strangest restlessness; wandered into the neighboring woods, all alone; strangely satisfied with — nay, feeding upon — their solitude and silence!

The workmen beheld her pass, and shook their heads. She

saw them not — that strange woman — yet hurried by them with a fitful chant or murmured ballad. They knew not that she was dying; yet they felt, by instinct, that she had been struck, heart-deep, by some invisible arrow. They saw it in her dazed and wandering eyes, that seemed looking out, gazing, yet seeing nothing; in the wonderfully white transparency of her skin, the delicacy of which was marvellous in any mortal creature. She ate little, but she had ceased to moan. She did not sigh. Her mother heard nothing but her singing, and the burden of that seemed to say simply :—

"Let me be alone — let me be alone! Do you not see that I am at peace? Don't you hear that I can sing? I am happy now!"

And the mother began to fancy now that she was doing well — that she would soon be better — that the song implied health and increasing strength; and she began to renew her prattle of world-wise maxims and dull commonplaces, you may be sure. And then the poor child smiled; but such smiling! There was no satire in the smile; but it was of such ghastly simplicity and vagueness, that the other was usually silenced by it. There was something in it which terrified her; and she would stop in her speech, bewildered. It was enough for her victim that she would thus stop. The commonplaces of her mother, and her worldly counsels, had grown to an eldritch and ominous sort of voicing in the ears of the child. She dreaded them; they somehow usually checked her song; and it was only when the mother ceased to speak, that she resumed her chanting — chanting it was, a sort of blended sobbing and murmur — and then the silly mother would say to herself :—

"As long as she can sing, she will do. She is evidently growing better and stronger; she will be better soon. Hearts don't break so easily. And what is there in her case to make the heart break? No! she will recover soon. I am glad always when I hear her sing."

The silly old woman! It was the death-song of the swan!

And the cassique watched her all the while — saw everything — understood all. He knew, spite of the song and the smile, that his wife was dying!

His instincts were all alive with this consciousness. But he,

the strong man — who felt himself so strong — who had hitherto
been strong enough for everything — he groaned in spirit as he
now felt himself powerless.   He said to himself:—

   " She will die!   Nothing can save her !"

   And the next thought was:—

   " And I have brought her to this !   However innocent of evil,
or selfish purpose, I have brought her to this.   And I can not
save ; I can not repair.   The bolt is inevitable !"

   And, so thinking, he watched and toiled : watched in agony and
gloom ; toiled in the sunshine without feeling it ; toiled to create
a home of art, and taste, and beauty; while he yet well knew
that she for whom chiefly he had dreamed and designed the whole,
would see, feel, taste, enjoy, none of the delights of life or home
— would appreciate none of these loving cares, which appealed
to no other sympathies than hers.

   Ah ! dear brethren, ye who struggle on gallantly in this mortal
conflict, so trying to — so meant to try — our human heroism, this
is the saddest of all our soul-disappointments.   To love, and toil,
and think, and struggle, all equally in vain : the beloved one will
not see or feel how great has been our care to prove the merit
and the beauty in our love !

   You have made your Eden — the best that you could make —
fitting for the best angel that you know.   You are in possession ;
you would put her in possession.   Yet, somehow, the serpent of
Fate has crept in, and keeps out the dove of Peace, if not of Innocence.   It is the old experience.   The shaft of Ahrimanes has
pierced the egg of Ormusd !

   And, while the eyes of the cassique were thus mournfully at
watch over the progress of that cruel Fate which was thus busy
in the destruction of all his architectural felicities, he wot not of
those other, those kindred eyes, which were quite as keen though
not so well informed as his own, in a like watch over the same
precincts.   There were otner eyes that studied and watched as
intensely, though with less freedom, over the fate of that beloved
object, who seemed so indifferent to every care — eyes full of a
like anxiety, perhaps of even superior agony, to his.   How like,
yet how unlike, but not less intense with passion than his own !

   And those were the eyes of a brother — the brother he had
once loved, but so greatly yet unwittingly wronged; whose heart

of hearts he had so lately understood, but whose wounds, he still
ncied, had all been healed by Death. That, alone, was the con-
-oling thought of Edward Berkeley, when he reflected upon the
defeat of heart and hope in the case of his brother Harry. A sad
sort of consolation, but not to be rejected in such a case, and
where the living wo was of so keen a character.

How little did he dream of that brother's watch, unless from
the clouds! As a spirit, he thought, Harry Berkeley will know
that, wittingly, his brother had never done him wrong. Supposing him still to be an inhabitant of earth, and thus watching,
what would be his emotions! How could he explain — how repair? He would do both, were this possible; for never, in truth,
did brother love more fondly than our cassique.

The deep love, the heart-instincts of Olive, had made her more
conscious, if not wiser. Her fancies, now wholly spiritual, had
conjured Harry Berkeley from his imagined grave beneath the
seas. She felt that he lived. He had brought an atmosphere
with him, into which, though in dreams of the midnight only, her
soul could penetrate. Her thought, though a madness to all others, was with her a conviction. She *felt* that Harry Berkeley
was beside her! In her mind's eye he was ever present. She
heard his voice in the silence of the night. Her soul grew more
seeing as she approached the time when it should cast off all its
impediments of clay. Ah! this divine soul, what an all-seeing
thing it is, if we only suffer it to use its wing!

She was right, even in her sense of the experience that kept her
conscious. The living Harry Berkeley, even now, in yonder primitive forest, keeps watch for her — a loving watch; looks terribly out
on the cassique — mournfully enough, as so terrible: even as the
three melancholy sisters, who are appointed to carry fate in their
foreheads, and to send the shaft at every glance, look over all!

You see them, perhaps, in the deep shadow upon the cassique's
brow; in the wild glare that sometimes gleams out from the eyes
of Harry Berkeley; in the beautiful death, which flickers, like a
star, lily-like and pale, in every feature of the sweetly-spiritualized
face of Olive.

Which shall perish first? They all glide along the precipice,
and below them the gulf is ready! Which shall first succumb
beneath the stroke? They are all, possibly, in equal peril; for

16*

there are deadly passions, busy in the hearts of these strong men, which, with but a change of the moon, a caprice of the winds, or perchance the stars, shall help to do the work of Fate!

Our rover, toiling hourly like the cassique, his brother, with like earnestness of character and energy — toiling, too, more in the behalf of others than his own — suffers from a like sense of isolation and wo; but there is no pang of remorse in *his* passion; and *he* has one solace, which gives him succor — in the sense of indignation!

He has been wronged. He errs, it is true, in the belief that the wrong is done him by his brother. But this makes no difference in the character of the strength which he derives from the conviction. It is certain that he has been wronged; but, whether by *him*, by *her*, or by the mother, matters not. There is an equal solace in the double fact that he can reproach himself with no wrong in the history, and that his own wrongs are certain. They demand a victim!

We must not conceal from ourselves the truth that the demon has entered his soul along with the iron; that the gaunt, famishing passion for vengeance, is muttering within his bosom, goading him on in search after the victim, and with an eagerness which he himself does not conjecture.

But, as now we see him, with ready weapon by his side, the hilt of which he sometimes clutches convulsively, we know that his blood will work upon his brain, to terrible results of action, the moment that the occasion shall occur which shall bid him strike.

He has been busied, with all that calm, methodical will and judgment, which men of action and character attain through habit. He has gone to the hollow tree, where the sheaf of Indian arrows, betokening the gradual progress of an evil purpose to the bloody event, has been hidden away. He has counted the remaining shafts with deliberate care, and knows that the hour of savage outbreak rapidly approaches. He has duly made his preparations for it. He has warned Gowdey, at the block-house, to keep his rangers in readiness; he has given his last instructions to Belcher, who is still in town, as to the course which he is to pursue at a certain hour; and he now calmly reviews the necessities of the whole event, having prepared for it, as well as he might, with his own unassisted resources of mind and money. His warnings have fallen, with little effect, upon the ears of Governor Quarry. And he is in no situation to warn his brother. He will save his household, if he can, without taxing its own resources. He can not do otherwise. Though lost to himself for ever — nay, dying, though he knows not that — Olive Berkeley must be saved — Olive Berkeley and *her* child!

But we have no need here to review his relations, or anticipate his further purposes. Enough that, with his vigilant mind, nothing has been forgotten: and he thinks of ship and crew; the conspirators who would run up the "Jolly Roger;" the simple Spanish wife, who is playing at "High Jinks" with the Honorable Keppel Craven; all the parties dear to his regards or to his revenges — with the stern resolve and the calm judgment with which one, seated on a mount of power, looks down upon the plains, and regulates, without an emotion, the fortunes of the blind multitudes who toil or sport below!

So Harry Calvert, otherwise Berkeley, watched the manor of Kiawah. Great had been the progress of the cassique, since our rover had first begun his watch. Houses had been run up; grounds laid out; pickets and fences erected; order had taken place of confusion; Civilization was asserting itself over Nature; comfort had succeeded to the crude and wild; and, though still rough and rude, the scene already began to exhibit many of the attractions of beauty.

Harry Calvert watched the progress with mingled emotions of sweet and bitter, and with increasing interest. When his brother came upon the scene, or the mother of Olive, then he writhed with a restless feeling of indignation and revolting; then he felt like strife and curses!

But there was an atmosphere over all that tended, in some degree, to soothe this bitterness. The very spectacle of Art laboring to subdue the wild and uncouth in Nature, was itself a spell upon the savage mood. And when manhood was striving in his sight; and the energetic woodman was busy everywhere, laying the axe to the root of the mightiest forms; Labor, like a giant, grappling with the gnarled oak, and the tough, resinous pine, and the towering, gray cypress — admiration naturally got the better of smaller, selfish emotions: and the spectator, not forgetting his own cares, was yet compelled to admit the ennobling influence of a moral power in the objects of his survey; and this consciousness ever appeals gratefully to the like sense of power in our own souls, subduing in some degree their own consciousness of self.

As yet, he had looked in vain for the one presence whom over all he sought. Once, he had got a glimpse of Olive, as he fancied; and she seemed bending her way from the dwelling to the very covert in which he harbored: but it was almost dusk, and, just then, several of the workmen, with the cassique at their head, approached the skirts of the wood, and proceeded to lay off the grounds in that quarter, previous to the overthrow of certain objectionable trees. At this sight, the figure of Olive — if, indeed, 't were hers — disappeared again within the shadows of the house.

He frequently caught a sight of her younger sister, Grace, whom he well remembered; a lovely child of twelve years, tall and fair, and promising to become almost as great a beauty as Olive. And when he saw Grace, she was usually accompanied by the young Indian hunter, whom she tasked to teach her the use of bow and arrow, and how to set snares for squirrels, and traps for birds; and who promised — neglected as she seemed to be by the whole household, in consequence of the superior cares from which all other parties suffered — to become almost as wild as the red-boy of the wilderness. He had snared for her a yearling doe, and was teaching her how best to tame it. It was surprising how completely he himself had already brought the wild creature to docility. It licked from his hand, but could not yet be persuaded to lick from hers; and it thrust its nose into the boy's face, but shrank back when the girl would have kissed and hugged it.

And thus were these two children exercised in the grounds, while Harry Berkeley kept his watch over them on this very occasion. The scene helped, in some degree, to soothe his more savage humors.

He had thus watched through a part of the day, with but few intervals. That melancholy watch! from day to day, profitlessly pursued; to the increase of his unhappy moods; to the wasting of his frame, for he was growing wan and thin; and to the satisfaction, thus far, of no single hope or fancy!

The day was waning. The evening sun was purpling tenderly the great waving pine-tops, and shooting slanting streaks of rosy light over the openings in the forest; and the heart of the strong man sickened sadly as he felt the rapid approach of another night of exhausting meditation and disappointment. At a distance, on the opposite quarter of the opening, he sees the workmen busy with beams and timbers. His brother is not visible. The girl and the Indian boy have also strayed away to a field which is waving in rye — one of the few grains, aside from maize, the culture of which had yet been attempted at the barony. The murmurs of life and toil, removed from the immediate precinct, had almost ceased to sound in the ears of our rover. The squirrels were leaping about him, suddenly appearing to feed at sunset, and no longer disturbed by the workmen. And he, too, depressed by the scene — by its silence, by his own weariness of watch, by the disappointment which had hitherto attended it — was about to turn away, take his horse, and canter off to the ship, which he needed that night to visit; when he suddenly felt his whole frame thrill with a strange and mixed emotion, as a sound, half song, half murmur, touched his senses.

Looking up, he beheld Olive moving slowly through the grove toward him. Her hands were clasped and lifted up, and swayed aloft in air; while her eyes were raised also, her head resting slightly on one side, as if she were gazing through the tree-tops. And thus, with glances that sought nothing below, she came toward him, her lips still parting, unconsciously, in song and murmur.

She was clad in white, a loose, simple dress, as unstudied as that of the Grecian damsel, going to the spring for water, in the days of Iphigenia and Andromache. And how wondrously beautiful she looked in that simple, white costume! Her pale, transparent skin; the ecstatic elevation of her dark-blue eyes; the exquisite purity and delicacy of air, carriage, manner, all betokening a perfect grace; and so spiritualized — so utterly free from earthly taint — that, without seeking to define thought or consciousness to ask, "What is this that approaches me?" — Harry Berkeley felt awed, subdued, hallowed; every human emotion schooled, in sudden subjection, and even shame, as if, indeed, a spirit stood before him.

He moved not. He was spell-bound by the long-desired but unexpected sight!

She came on, meanwhile, unseeing; her eyes still looking upward; her lips still murmuring, in song; no, not song — something like the dreamy chant of revery, when the lips part and we know not, and there is a speech that rather reveals an emotion than a thought, or sentiment, or wish, or care.

It did not occur to him — nay, he had not the power — to stand aside, and let her pass. He stood, frozen as it were, beneath a wondrous presence ; and her course was arrested only when she was actually in contact with his outstretched arms, which he lifted involuntarily as she drew nigh.

Then, her lips ceased to murmur. Then, her eyes were let down ; and, as she saw him, she cried out, and threw herself upon his bosom, with a faint, short sobbing, intermingled with the broken words —

"It is no dream — no dream. I know 'tis he ! — my Harry ! my Harry !"

He wrapped her instinctively in his close embrace — close — close — even as the dying man grasps convulsively, and with agonizing tenacity, the dear form which he feels he is about to lose for ever. He had but a single word —

"Olive !"

And this was spoken in such low, murmured tones, that it is doubtful if she heard him. But her lips answered to him still :—

"I knew 'twas you ! I knew that you would come !"

"Death should not keep me from you, Olive."

"No, no ! I knew that, Harry ! I believed you when you told me so before. But I did not feel you then, as now. And you left me so soon ! You would go ! Why did you go ? I have been looking for you the last three nights ; and oh, how I have kissed the pillow where your head had lain !"

He was bewildered at these words. He would have gazed into her face for explanation, but that was buried in his bosom. She never once looked up ; and, as she continued to murmur, with a sort of sobbing joy, brokenly and with such sweet pathos, he felt that her mind wandered — that she labored under some strange illusions ; while her evident frailness of form, as she clung to him — the thin, wan fingers, as she grasped his neck — too plainly declared her physical decline.

"Did you think that I would desert you, Olive ?"

"Desert me ? You ! — never ! Oh, no ! I knew better. But you were dead ! Ah ! that was the dreadful thing. Drowned in the deep sea — in the great ocean! The big, black billows tumbling over you, until you sunk, sunk, sunk — down, down, down — so that I might never see you more!"

"And you believed this, Olive?"

"Oh, yes! I knew, at first, it was all true. But, afterward, Harry, I could not feel you dead! And when I heard you calling to me from the waters, and when you came and took me in your arms by night, then I knew that they had told me false! I knew it was no dream. I had you again; had you in my arms — close to me, and your warm kisses were upon my lips — and they had no taste of death. But, O Harry, you did stay away so long!"

"I am come now, Olive — I am come at last; and we shall never part again!"

"No, no! never part again! Beware of that, Harry. Don't leave me again, Harry; for you know not what they say to me when you are gone. And sometimes they make me believe it all, it is so like the truth. But I have you now, and you will never again leave me, Harry? No more partings! We shall have everything safe now, and happy! No horrid drowning — no death — no storms — no seas; only the sweet willows at dear old Feltham."

"My poor, poor Olive!" was the exclamation, groaned rather than spoken, by Harry Berkeley —

"My poor, poor Olive, you have suffered sadly, but I am come! I am here, Olive; and I am a man! You are mine — I yours; and let me see the man, or woman, who shall torture you again! O God, would I had come sooner!"

By this time, Harry Berkeley was wiser in respect to the condition of Olive Berkeley. He saw that she was doomed: he knew not that she was dying! Yet he somehow felt that a great thundercloud overhung her life and his own. He bared his bosom to the bolt; he defied it. There was a proud, imperious, if not triumphant spirit, that seized him — strange to say, almost as the natural consequence of his discovery of her real condition. It was a sacred madness. She was doomed; and he — reckless as despairing! He lifted her from his bosom — held her off — gazed with a long, passionate *vehemence* in her eyes, and cried —

"Yes, by the God who sees, you are mine — mine only, Olive Masterton!"

"Berkeley — Berkeley.  You forget, Harry."

"Olive Berkeley, you are mine only!  From this moment you are mine for ever!  They have lied to you.  But they shall lie to you no longer.  The woods of Feltham — the sweet old willows!  Come — come, Olive!  It is Harry that says, ' Come!' "

"Dear Harry!"

He shared her frenzy.  The one look which he had taken of her wan face seemed to madden him.  Again he clasped her to his bosom, and she sank upon it unresistingly.

"Ay, ay! to the Feltham willows, Olive.  We shall be happy now."

"O Harry, yes — so happy!"

"Come — come!"

And he bore her away, not heeding that she lifted no limb — that she hung heavily upon him — by this time, seemingly, as wholly unconscious of his grasp as he was of the burden which he bore. He seemed to be governed by a wild and desperate impulse.  It was as if, suddenly put in possession of his treasure, and dreading that it should be torn away from him, he was resolved to bear her away — to lose no moment of precious time in doing so ; and, thus feeling, if not thinking, he put forth all the gigantic strength of his frame, and, lifting her wholly from the ground, strode at once for the deeper thickets where his horse had been tethered.

He did not think ; he had no deliberate purpose.  The impulse was one of a wild and headlong frenzy, the creature of long-pent-up passions, now working with ungovernable sway, and rejecting wholly the mastery of reason.

"Yes, you are mine now, Olive — mine for ever!  Let me see who shall cross our path!  They have wronged us long enough ; we shall baffle them now.  We will go free, to a new life, to hope and happiness, my love.  You do not doubt me, Olive? — do not fear me?  Are you not mine, mine only, my beloved?"

"Oh, yes, dear Harry — you know! you ought to know!  We shall go back to the Feltham willows, dear Harry, and then there shall be no more death — no more drowning.  Ah! they can not cheat me now."

And, even as she spoke, she moaned feebly.  The painful sound seemed to move him with a fearful rage.  He said, bitterly :—

"They shall atone for this!  *He* shall atone!  My poor Olive, how they have crushed you among them! The dove among hawks and vultures! But let me find them. You are safe now. I will carry you far. You shall have peace, my beloved — peace at last — and love!"

"Yes, peace — love!" she murmured; and then, as he hurried on through the grove, he felt her head, which had been lifted as she spoke, fall heavily upon his shoulder, and her moaning and speech ceased together.

"She faints. God! if she should die now!"

And he gnashed his teeth, and increased his speed. She was apparently insensible. He feared this; but it only made him hasten onward with his burden, as if he could find no help for her anywhere short of the refuge, with himself only, to which his impulse would have borne her. Never were wits and impulse more unreasoning.

"If I can get her on horseback!" he muttered, between his teeth. This was the one idea. "It is but a moment's weakness. She will recover with the motion, and in a single hour!—"

And his pace was accelerated. He was already at the end of the grove, and she still insensible, when suddenly the faint crying of a child was heard, on the verge of the thicket, and near the very point which he was approaching.

The maternal instincts became immediately conscious. In the same moment, at the first sound of that cry, Olive started into instant life and animation — started to her feet — shook herself free from the grasp of our rover — pushed him from her — exclaiming, as she did so —

"My child, my child! It is my child!" Then, giving him a look of reproach —

"O Harry, how could you do me thus?"

For the first time she stood up, boldly confronting him, her eyes now looking fearlessly into his. His arms no longer sustained her; his hands had dropped by his side; and as his glance rested fairly upon her, he saw in a moment what a cruel mockery it had been, of hope and heart, to think of any mere mortal passion in connection with such a creature. She was no longer a thing of earth. All the spiritual aspect of death shone out in her eyes — in the wan, transparent visage — so sadly wan, so entirely sublimed by sorrow — by a Fate which lifted her above earthly sentiments, if not above mortal griefs, and trampled all mortal passion under foot.    And when she so mournfully exclaimed, with such a full return of reason and consciousness —

"How could you do me thus, Harry?"—

He was stricken with self-reproach, humbled and ashamed.    He might just as properly have borne her to the bier for the bed of bridal, as to think any more of a merely mortal love, in the case of one already consecrated by the stroke of Fate.    The kiss of a mortal passion upon lips thus hallowed for Death, would be profanation.

His excuse to his own conscience was, in his momentary blindness.    He had been goaded by a temporary insanity; hurried away, without thought, by long-suppressed passion, which forbade for awhile the control of reason.    But, now, the first ferocity of passion had gone over: reason was restored by a tenderer feeling, a more generous instinct.    The revulsion left him for the instant paralyzed.    Great drops gathered in his eyes; his lips quivered; he was speechless, save in the sadness, the contrition, the remorse and agony, in his countenance, as their mutual eyes met and dwelt upon each other.

"Forgive me, Olive — forgive!    It was madness!"

So, at length, he spoke, in broken murmurs.

And she, too, spoke again — very slowly, and in the most subdued tones — her eyes still resting steadily upon his face.

"And it *is* — it *is* you, Harry!"

To this he could only answer by a moan, clasping his head with his hands, as if to control the bursting violence with which his brain was throbbing in all its chambers.

"And you do live!    O my God, I thank thee for this — this, at least!    You are — I know it now — you are still in life — still a strong man!    *You* will live!"

"Alas!    Olive, I *do* live.    The more the pity!"

"Say not so, Harry,    You must live; and be not sad—"

"Another plaintive cry of the child, now evidently approaching, half drowned the feeble accents of her voice, and stifled the half-spoken sentence.    She would have turned about to the cry, as she heard it; but her limbs failed her.    The momentary strength was gone; she staggered, and would have fallen, but that he caught her in his arms.

"Carry me to my child, Harry!" was all she could utter.

She sank heavily in his embrace, with these broken words. She had ceased to be conscious, in the momentary recurring of her consciousness. His arm alone sustained her. As he felt this, he exclaimed aloud, in his agony:—

"Olive! Olive! O God, she is dying!—she is dead!"

At this moment, and while he still clasped her to his bosom, in the spasmodic embrace of one who feels that a long-lost treasure has been suddenly restored to him, and fears again to lose it, a voice at his elbow abruptly aroused him to the consciousness of another party to the scene. The voice was subdued, measured, though quivering with emotion; but there was also a compressive sternness in its tones. Harry knew, with the first intonation, from whose lips the accents came. It was the voice of his brother — of Edward Berkeley, the husband of Olive — the cassique of Kiawah!

He turned abruptly, firmly, with set teeth, and confronted the speaker.

The cassique met his gaze with strange apparent calmness. There was no hostility in his looks. Nay, could Harry have exercised sufficient calm of mood to note the expression in his eyes, he would have seen that they were full of sorrow, and not of strife.

But he had heard the tones; and now, as he turned, he saw that the cassique carried a drawn rapier in his hand.

Harry, supporting Olive with one arm, instantly extricated his own rapier from its sheath. In this action, Olive began to recover her consciousness. Her eyes opened slowly, and, staring for a moment wildly upon her husband, she started suddenly to her feet — started forward, and, though staggering, stood up, alone and unsupported, between the brothers, who had each, as by a mutual instinct, recoiled a pace. She beheld the drawn sword in the hands of each. She extended her own hands between them.

"Oh, shame!" she cried; "oh, shame! Weapons drawn, in the eyes of a dying woman!"

And both swords were dropped to the ground. And the cheeks of the two strong men were flushed; and they felt, in whatever degree either of them had meditated violence, all the terrible rebuke contained in that single pregnant speech from the wan, spiritual, shadowy form before them.

It was a scene for the bold dramatic painter.  Both men were nobly-formed creations, framed in the very prodigality of Nature — tall, erect, with well-developed limbs and muscles; graceful and commanding; full of courage; and, without even meditating the conflict, naturally taking their positions for it with the attitudes of the most accomplished gladiators of the days of chivalry. Nor was the costume of either wanting in the requisitions of grace. While Edward Berkeley and his brother, our rover, both adhered to the small-clothes of the day, which showed fully the perfection of the lower limbs, the upper garments had been chosen rather with regard to the ease and freedom of the hunter-life than to the demands of a formal European court.  The cassique wore a loose sort of blouse, which, wide open in front, hung loosely from his shoulders, in his present attitude, like the light cloak of the Spanish cavalier.  Harry, on the other hand, was garbed in the manly and picturesque costume of the forest-ranger — the hunting-shirt of light-blue homespun, with its falling capes and fringes — a garment which, for grace of drapery, and the freedom of movement which it allows, merits preference over all others, as properest for the American costume.

And between the two, thus *posed*, thus habited and confronted, stood the slight, frail, shadowy woman, whose wan visage, transparent skin, and eyes of dazzling, spiritual brightness, seemed to declare her the denizen of a superior world, suddenly descended between the combatants, to arrest their conflict.

We have seen the effect of her first words.  She had power for a few more only.

"O Harry! O Sir Edward!  Let me die; but do not you — brothers — brothers!—"

And she again sank, and again into the arms of our rover.

"Give her to me, Harry Berkeley," said the cassique, as he took her from the unresisting arms of the other.  "Give her to me; but await me here!"

One might almost suppose, from the tones, that the speaker were emotionless.  But he had trained himself to this; he had been schooled to suffer, too long, to yield even at such a moment. His voice was that of a will which embodied authority.  He had shown no surprise when, in the person of the stranger, he had recognised his long-lost brother; he had shown no jealous conflict in his soul at the relation in which he had seen him with his wife ; yet the inference is natural that he had witnessed much if not all of the scene between them, though he might not have heard the language : and unless we suppose, from the circumstance that he approached with rapier drawn, that he meditated violence, there was nothing in his demeanor to argue any such purpose on his part. We may add, from what we know, that, when he first drew nigh, he knew not that the audacious stranger was a brother. Long persuaded of his death, he had no reason to suppose Harry Berkeley to be still a living man.

With the same heroic calmness and diffidence of manner which he had shown throughout the scene, did he take his wife into his arms. And Harry Berkeley, now fully master of himself, exhibited a like firmness of nerve and steadiness of countenance. He yielded her, with one fond, despairing glance, to the arms of his brother. Olive was utterly insensible. She knew nothing of what followed ; and, with the tenderness of one whose heart was full of loving care, and who had no cause of complaint, the cassique lifted his wife upon his bosom, and as he bore her away repeated the injunction —

" Wait till I return."

This was all : there was nothing to show in what mood, or with what purpose, he should return. And with his own doubts still upon him, Harry replied —

" Be sure I will await you, Edward Berkeley."

And as the cassique bore away his precious burden toward the dwelling, Harry picked up his rapier, and, without sheathing it, walked slowly off for a few paces, to the sheltering branches of a great oak, under which he threw himself down.

" Yes, Edward, I will await you ! It is proper that you should meet me *here*, where I have parted, perhaps for ever, from *her !* I will await you, and—"

The soliloquy was arrested abruptly. In his present conflict of mood, there could be no logical conclusion for it. We, too, will await the parties.

# CHAPTER XXXVIII.

## THE MEETING OF THE BROTHERS.

> " Speak you so gently ?   Pardon me, I pray you :
> I thought that all things had been savage here ;
> And, therefore, put I on the countenance
> Of stern commandment ! . . . . . . . . . .
> . . . . . . . . I blush, and hide my sword."
>
> *As You Like It.*

OUR rover lay waiting for some time impatiently beneath his tree.  The cassique was necessarily delayed by the condition of Olive.  It was scarcely possible that he should leave her before she showed signs of recovery.  Even Harry Berkeley could allow for this in spite of his impatience.  But he was not the less impatient for the allowance.  His blood and brain were in wild confusion.

At length the cassique appeared in sight, slowly moving toward him.  We must not, in this place, interrupt the progress of events, by reporting the trying scene of Olive's recovery from insensibility.  We must give ourselves wholly to the things before us.

As Harry saw his brother approach, he rose eagerly to his feet, but did not advance, till he beheld the other pick up his sword. He had not sheathed his own ; and now, poising it lightly in his grasp, he strode a few paces forward, diminishing the distance between them.

The cassique beheld the action of his brother, and his countenance assumed a sadder aspect than before.  He paused — deliberately sheathed his own sword, and came forward, presenting his hand.

Harry gazed sternly on his face ; and, speaking only to the action of the other, said, in the harshest accents :—

" Better take your weapon in it, Edward Berkeley.   Our hands can never again meet ungloved.   It is too late for such peaceful signs.   You have passed the bounds of amnesty.   We must try the last issues !"

" I know not why it should be so, Harry, my brother."

" You know not !   It is then strange enough that you should know anything.   But, before we speak of discord, first tell me, what of *her* — what of Olive — the woman you are murdering ! Does she live ?   Is she recovered ?"

" She recovers — she lives."

" Ah !  God be praised for that !  I shall not, then, have *her* murder, as well as my own wrongs, to avenge !"

" If this is to be taken into the account, Harry," said the other, sadly enough, " I know not how long it will be before you may make your reckoning complete.   Olive Berkeley recovers from her swoon, it is true ; she lives, for the present : but I must not disguise it from you, as I do not from myself, that she can not live very long.   The strings of life are snapping, one by one.   Soon they will vibrate no longer !   She will die, Harry Berkeley — nothing now can save her !"

" And with these tidings on your lips, you think that I will take your hand ?   That I will grasp with friendship the hand of him who has been her murderer !   Edward Berkeley, robber of thy brother, traitorous and dishonest kinsman, it was not enough that thou shouldst carry off all the wealth of thy father, as the first-born to the inheritance ; that I, thy brother, should be driven abroad to perilous venture upon the high seas, in search of fortune ; but thou must glide in between me and happiness — between my heart and its one treasure — and rob me of that which alone could suffice to make my home precious !   Draw, sir, and let your manhood show itself equal to your malice !"

Deep crimson was the flush that suddenly passed over the cheeks and forehead of the cassique as he listened to this language.

But the flush was succeeded by a still more decided pallor. His lips were, for a moment, sternly compressed, as if to subdue all efforts of the rising passion in his blood.   When he spoke, he had obtained a great triumph over himself.   His tones were measured, his words and utterance quite calm.

" These are fearful charges, my brother; terrible, indeed, were they true."

" And are they not true? Are you not in possession of one who was pledged to me, in life and death; and is she not dying in your hands? Couple the cause with the effect; note the history, step by step, as you may, with any honest logic, and the truth is patent. True! Do you dare venture to deny the truth?"

" It is new to me, Harry Berkeley, to listen to such language, from any lips."

" Why listen, then? The sword—"

" There had been a season, Harry, when even *you* should not have challenged me to the sword without the sword's answer. But now—"

" Ah! now! What is it now subdues your courage? What, but your conscience? Edward Berkeley, good swordsman as you are, in such a cause you would cross my weapon only to fate."

" Perhaps; and yet I know not that. But what have I to do with vain boasting, or equally vain reply to your boast, when such a fate as now threatens, hangs over yonder dwelling?"

" Ay!" answered the other, gloomily. " It may well rouse conscience and challenge fear in the bosom of him to whom it is all due."

" Due to me, indeed! But not knowingly, not willingly, as Heaven looks down upon us now! Harry Berkeley, impatient brother of mine, the greatest of my pangs now, after the one which follows that impending fate, is, that I should hear such language from your lips; listen to such accusations; and be taught that they are made by one who, after a twenty years' experience, should know me so little as to entertain such fancies. True! God of heaven! has the brother of my childhood and happy youth — when we were both happy — has he yet to learn the qualities of one with whom he has slept and sported for nearly twenty years? This is my great regret; the very dagger to my heart of pride. What! have I been so utterly void of demonstration, or character, that, without question, you should think of me such thoughts?"

" Ah! you declaim it well! But this will never answer. Say, are you not *here*, and in possession of one whom you know to have been my betrothed?"

" I know it *now!* I knew it not, a month ago."

"Ha! impossible! I happen to know better. This tale will never answer. Enough; I say the thing is impossible."

"Why, yes, Harry; it must be impossible to you, in such a mood as yours, when you make it my offence that I was born before you; that, by law, I have a certain family inheritance. When such are my imputed offences, what hope have I that any proofs would satisfy my accuser? He forgets that he has shared with me the profits of this very inheritance; that my purse has ever been his own; that his first outfits for fortune were under my advances of money; and that I have never said him 'Nay,' when from boyhood to manhood he had a craving or a plan, a need or a pleasure, which implied the free use of money. May God curse the wealth which is to deprive me of a brother's faith — the affections of a kinsman!"

"Now, by my soul, Edward Berkeley, but it confirms all my belief in your crime, when you plead your benefits, your bounty, in justification of your wrong-doing."

"Plead? My benefits! my bounty!"

"Ay, plead! what else? You tell me of your purse, and how I shared it; and how, as boy and youth, I had wants and appetites, to which your wealth has ministered. And this, in reply to my charge that you had basely stolen from me the one only jewel to which, in all my poverty, I had clung as keenly as to life. She was my life! I have had none since!"

Again the warm crimson overspread the cheeks of the cassique. Indignation and mortification strove together in the expression of his face.

"O Harry Berkeley," he said, "this is very, very cruel. How vexatiously do you pervert my speech!"

"Yes; you remind me of your benefits — of what I owe you! That is, you have given money to a boy who wanted toys — to a youth who had appetites for pleasure; you have given freely, ungrudgingly; and you tell him so! It is true; you have so given. But, thank Heaven, I am able to 'quite you the amount of this giving, ten times told! You shall have it, every farthing."

"Harry! Harry!"

"But, what did I not give *you*, in return for these benefits — this liberal allowance of money? I gave you faith, sir — the generous faith of a most unselfish boyhood. I opened to you all my

17

heart; I confided freely in yours. You had, from me, the fondest deference, the most uncalculating confidence, the most brotherly love, unmixed with envy, jealousy, or any other baser metal
of the passions. Your money did not buy these! It was your
love, your truth, your equal confidence and faith. And where
were these when you wronged my absence? Suppose me worthless, ungrateful for all your gifts, forgetful of your benefits: should
this justify you in the usurpation of my rights?"

"I did not! By the great God—"

"By all the gods, you did! You seized the moment of my
greatest misfortune—my wreck upon the seas, and the dreary
absence which followed it—to insinuate yourself into the affections of the woman who was pledged to me—the only woman I
had ever loved! By cunning arts, you overcame her weakness;
roused her vanities by your temptations—your wealth, your title;
played upon her poor, weak, woman-heart; dazzled her eyes—"

"Stop, Harry; and whatever else you may say in your madness, forbear all reproach of Olive Berkeley! Not a word of
censure upon her! She was weak, no doubt; weak where, would
to God she had been most strong; but mean vanity, lust of wealth,
pride, pomp, or power, never weighed one moment in her bosom.
*She*, at least, was free from all such sin."

"What is it, then, that you call her weakness?"

"She had no proper power—no will, perhaps—when she heard
that you were dead, to resist an authority under which her infancy
and childhood had been always trained. The fault (and there was
fault) was none of hers. She must not suffer censure from your
lips or mine."

"Ah! I thank you, Edward Berkeley, for this, at least. It
restores *her* to my thought, to my heart, as she was before—a
pure, loving, faithful, and devoted woman. Olive! Olive! it is a
great gain to my soul that I can still think of you as in that first
morning of our youth, when neither of us had dread of wreck.
But, how much more the wrong and shame of those who have baffled the hopes and crushed the hearts of both! Yes, Olive, I
might have known, in your wan visage and breaking heart, that
you were only a victim! But you shall not be unavenged!—
Weak, say you, Edward Berkeley?—weak as a loving, simple-
hearted, tender woman! But whose was the wily art to abuse

this weakness? to win this weak heart from its faith? to deceive her with false tidings of my death? to torture her life by incessant practice, until, through sheer exhaustion, she sank into submission to a fate at which her whole soul revolted — a fate which has brought her now, as you admit, to the very verge of doom? Who, but you, and that wretched old beldame, her mother?"

"False! false! *I* am guiltless."

"Yes; you joined wits together; laid your snares; practised your arts; lied, cajoled, vexed, worried, until you triumphed — triumphed in the utter overthrow of the fairest, gentlest, loveliest of all God's creatures. Your money and rank bought that miser-erable old woman, whose passions, nursed by vanity, had no life save in public show. The strong will of the strong man; the cun-ning arts of the selfish old woman: these combined to overawe, to overcome the timorous young thing, till you had her tangled in your snares, fettered in your meshes, trembling under your des-potism, and, in utter despair at last, yielding submission, through utterly-exhausted faculties and a wretchedly-bewildered brain! And lo! the fruits — madness, and a closely-impending death! Acquit Olive, as you do, and such is the history, such the damna-ble crime; and all the guilt is yours!"

A cold sweat covered the pallid brows of the cassique. The vehemence of our rover had been irresistible. And such *was* the *apparent* history. On his lips, it was but too plausibly stated; and the cassique shuddered as he heard.

"It is a terrible picture, Harry Berkeley, which you have drawn; and I feel there is too much in it that is probably true! This is what crushes me. For, though myself guiltless, I fear, from what I *now* know, that such have been the arts practised to subdue the faith of Olive Berkeley, and cause her to yield to my wishes. I have been made to win by a practice in which I did not share."

"Ah! and who not guilty, if not you? Knew you nothing of these processes? Was Olive's such a clear, frank, noonday con-senting to your prayers, that it never once struck you that it was an enforced business? Can you tell me that she smiled gratefully when you came? that her eyes seemed to hunger for your com-ing; that her lips welcomed you with fondest falterings of speech, Oh! there are thousand signs by which one detects the passion

lurking in the purest virgin heart, and giving encouragement to
the bashful wooer.  All of these you saw?  You were not a simpleton ; not blind with self-conceit ; no mere boy, laboring under a
bounding impulse of the blood?  You could see, could hear, could
understand, that child-nature — so unsophisticated, so true in every gushing emotion, thought, feeling, fancy !  You were not deceived.  Had you these signs, proofs ? — for such signs speak as
certainly for the ingenuous young heart as any that shine from
heaven, or pass before our eyes on earth.  Ah ! you had these
proofs, Edward Berkeley, all, ere you ventured to say to yourself, 'This woman loves me ?'  Surely, you never, with your
pride, your manhood, would descend to a traffic in hearts, in
which you were willing to have a counterfeit passed upon you !"

"Were I to say to you, Harry, that I had such proofs — now,
with my present thoughts and convictions — I should speak
falsely.  But, when I sought Olive Masterton in marriage, I fondly
fancied that I had these proofs.  No ! my pride alone would never
have suffered me to take a counterfeit passion to my breast."

"Never ! never !  You could never have believed that you had
such proofs."

"I had *not*.  I am willing *now* to admit that I had not.  Yet,
I loved, and was willing to believe !  I was deceived by others ;
I was too easy, too willing to be deceived by myself.  That was
all *my* fault.  Now that I look back, I wonder at my own self-
deception.  Olive was simply passive.  The proofs that assured
and lured me were such as cunning could suggest to passion."

"And whose the cunning ?"

"It is enough for me, Harry, to disclaim the cunning as mine.
I used no arts, except those which should commend myself to a
beloved object ; none but such as I thought, and still think, legitimate to use.  That others were used, I now believe ; but it is
not for me, Harry, to declare or denounce the guilty.  Enough
for me, to disclaim all part in the guilt.  I had no doubt of
your death ; but you were not spoken of, or thought of, in this
connection.  I fancied, when I proposed for Olive, that her heart
had been touched in no serious manner : that she had been an
object of attention, had reached my ears ; but no such object ever
presented himself to my sight ; and the assurance given me was,
that there had been no obligation between her and any other

party.  I am satisfied now — even before any word from you — that all this was false; that there had been an engagement: but even then, even when I had made this discovery, I never dreamed that you had been the object of her affections.  This discovery was reserved for a more recent period.  It was then made involuntarily by Olive herself, under circumstances too sacred to speak of.  Whatever subterfuge or cunning was employed to bring her to my wishes, Harry Berkeley, as God hears me at this moment, I knew nothing of them.  I was as innocent of any false practice with Olive Masterton as she with me!  That she was practised upon — that we were both practised upon, selfishly and dishonestly, even as you describe the practice — I am now too well satisfied.  It is my great grief that I was the gainer — if, indeed, it be gain — by this false practice; that so much that you have said is true!  But I, too, have been the victim.  Do you think that I would have married any woman whom I should have to love in vain?"

An incredulous laugh, full of bitterness, answered this assurance.  For the moment, the speaker had no other answer.

"You may laugh, Harry, as you will.  But I have lived too long in vain, to be moved by this treatment.  It is matter of more moment to you than to me, that you should continue to nurse this demon of doubt.  If I loved Olive Masterton — if I tried all arts to win her — sacrificing truth, and faith, and magnanimity, as well as honesty — I am terribly punished for the fault!  She will soon be lost to us for ever.  She has long since been lost to *me!*  For months have I known, not only that she loved me not, but that my presence was a pain to her, and a loathing!  If I have sinned against you, my brother, I have got my reward.  My punishment is inevitable.  If I could reproach myself, as you now reproach me, I should entreat your sword to my throat; nay, my brother, be prompted to use my own!  The demon has urged this in my ears a thousand times, and with reason, for, of a truth, life is to me a dreadful weariness!"

"Edward Berkeley, I would to God that I could believe you!  How I have loved you, can be said by no lips better than by yours; it will not now be said by mine.  I believed you all truth and honor.  I would have trusted you with mine — with life, love, everything — ay, even with Olive !  And to be betrayed by you !"

" I never betrayed you, Harry."

" Stay, Edward Berkeley. Do not suppose me ignorant. My emissaries have been busy. I have heard the truth. There was one person, at least, who told you of Olive's engagement, and the claims of your brother."

" Never!  Who ?"

" Old Walter Hern!  You saw him; you spoke to him of Olive and her childhood, and he told you of our betrothal."

" He did not."

" What! old Hern lie — that good old man — the faithful steward of our father for forty years ?"

" Did Hern tell you, in so many words, that he had told me these things?  I honor his truth no less than you.  If he said this, I should (but for my own conscientious conviction that I could not so have erred) be staggered by the assertion."

" He said to Jack Belcher that he had told you all."

" He did not!  Belcher has jumped to his conclusions, and the old man has spoken vaguely.  I have no doubt that he would have spoken out, but for a false notion of delicacy.  Certainly he would have done so, but for the account of your death, when he had no further reason to see embarrassment in my marriage with Olive.  O Harry, would to God that the old man had spoken out!  But he never did.  He dealt in hints and inuendoes, the amount of which was that Olive, at some time past, had been interested in another.  This was all that I could comprehend, and upon this hint I pressed Mrs. Masterton with the keenest inquiry. I have already told you what was her answer."

" The miserable hag!"

" It is possible that, could I now recall all that Walter said, in his shrinking, timid, doubtful manner, I should have the clue to what he meant.  With my subsequent knowledge, all might be made clear.  But the old man, though he spoke of another attachment, of secret meetings—"

" Not so very secret.  You might have heard it from a dozen at Feltham."

" But we were not at Feltham.  I did not meet Olive there. Her mother and herself were in lodgings at London."

" Ha! London — waiting your arrival."

" But never once, though Walter hinted a betrothal, did he or any one give me the slightest reason to suppose that you, my brother, were the person who was thought to have preceded me in the affections of Olive."

" But should not the mere hint of the betrothal, no matter to what person, have served to check your pursuit ?"

" It did—"

" Not very long."

" O Harry ! be not so coldly and unjustly incredulous.    It did check my pursuit ; for I should be the last man to seek so ready a *fiancée*.    But I had the most solemn assurance from the mother of Olive that there was no truth in the report.    She admitted that there had been some attention from another ; that, for awhile, she fancied Olive to be impressed, but she was mistaken ; that there had been no engagement, no impressment ; and that the affair was all over, long before."

" Jezebel !   And you never once conjectured that the other party was your own brother ?"

" Never, as I hope for mercy !"

The eyes of Harry Berkeley deliberately addressed themselves to those of his brother.   He searched them piercingly, and with a keen intensity, which seemed resolutely to probe the soul through them to its most secret depths.   Those of the cassique were open to the scrutiny as frankly, fairly, broadly, as were the soft, blue skies overhead.   They shrank not from the search ; they recorded the truthful utterance of his lips ; there could not be a doubt of their veracity ; and Harry Berkeley, however reluctant to believe — however still dissatisfied as hopeless — could not fail to be impressed.   He lifted his rapier-point slowly from the earth, and sent it home with force into the scabbard.

" We have played together, Edward," he said, very slowly and sadly, " as loving brothers.   We have had, for long, pleasant seasons, but a single life between us.   Your money has been mine ; you have never given it grudgingly ; and if I suffered myself to reproach you as the first-born of my father, believe me I never once envied you your better fortune, not even when I strove to make myself independent of it.   O Edward, it was the bitterest pang to me of all, when I felt compelled to think that you had passed between me and all my hopes, and all that my heart held precious, by means of that wealth !"

" And *how could you* think that, my brother? — how, at least, think that I could do so knowingly, wilfully?"

" Could I think otherwise, in possession of such evidence?"

" No evidence — nay, that of your own senses even — should have sufficed to make you believe that I could wrong you, in the face of such an experience as ours.  Ah! Harry, this is among the keenest pangs of my soul.  What should I not require to believe *you* false to *me*, to honor, and the sweet, pure lessons of our sainted mother!"

" Speak not of her *now*," said the other, in husky accents.  " She, at least, is spared the sight of our mutual disappointments."

" True; and yet how glad and grateful was her hope!"

" She is at rest, thank Heaven, and can feel no disappointment now."

" Unless in sympathy with us!  O Harry Berkeley, if I had ever wronged you in this matter, or in any matter, you have a revenge such as no sword-stroke of yours could ever inflict.  Look at these locks, prematurely gray, yet how little am I your senior! I tell you, I now live for nothing — have lived in vain!  I struggle — strive; for I have turbulent energies that I must keep employed, lest, like wolves, in the shape of passions, they turn upon and rend me.  But, save for this, I exercise mind and muscle to no end.  I have no longer a purpose in my work, as I no longer have a living hope in my soul.  Hope and ambition are dead within me.  She for whom I could have striven valiantly and nobly, she is heedless; can not heed even if she would; and, too well I know, would not if she could.  Of that I am too painfully assured.  Loving her as I do, Harry, would to God, for your sake and hers, I had never seen her!  Would to God I could restore her to you now!  But prayer is now vain.  She will die, Harry — you have seen that — Olive will die!"

" Ay! to both of us!"

" And it is well now.  She could live for neither.  She has not lived for me; and it may give your heart a sad satisfaction now to know that her life, such as it has been, has been wholly yours. I know it now, too late — too late!  Harry — it is something very sacred — but hearken."

Here his voice sank to a whisper, and he drew his brother aside, taking him by the arm :—

" Harry, all the secret of her love for you has been delivered to me, by her own unconscious lips, in her midnight dreams, and when her senses seemed all to wander. Think of that, Harry: how awful! O Harry, though I shuddered to hear the cruel story, yet a strange fascination bound me to her side, and I was made fatally wise in regard to her fate, and mine, and yours—all so terribly bound up together! Alas! we have all been cruelly betrayed. She is not the only victim. She has passed the crisis. She is now beyond all trial of the Fates!"

" You do not tell me that she is — dead?" was the question of our rover, in hoarse but subdued accents, as if under a sudden shock, which made him recoil from that embrace which his brother had unconsciously taken about his neck.

" No! oh, no! She still lives; but the worst pangs — those of the soul — of its first consciousness of wreck and ruin — are all over. And still she suffers in the body. But the life of her mind, now, is resolved into mere dream."

" Yet she grew to consciousness, when standing here between us. That one speech, that action—"

" Was probably the last effort of the lingering mind. All is delirium now, and vacancy. She will probably never again know us, except in the last struggle which looses the silver cord of life."

" Edward, I would be near her then. I must, I tell you — must catch her last look, hear her last murmurs, see the light go out of her eyes. I feel that she will know me then. I must be present."

" Go to her now; be with her always—to the last. She may linger thus for weeks: she may sigh out life in an hour."

" No, not now! I can not see her now! Edward, my brother, when I waited for you this evening, I fully thought that there could be no explanation between us save one — that of the sword. I felt, my brother, that I could slay you; felt sure that, having so wronged me, you would strive probably to slay me. I have had dire and desperate thoughts, Edward! Forgive me these thoughts; forgive me that I could so easily forget our boyhood, and our boyhood's mother, as to meditate your death. But, it was a madness, my brother, rather than a thought! I have been a madman for a long season, and have done the maddest things."

17*

"Tell me of yourself, Harry," in low, sweet accents; and the hand of the cassique gently stole once more about the neck of our rover.

"No, no! nothing now. There will be a better time for this, when we meet under a canopy of cloud, with the badges of stately mourning all around, and the signs of death staring the life out of our own eyes. Ask me then, when we are standing, perchance, over the bier of — of — ay, Edward, the bier of Olive Masterton — ask me then. It will be a proper time. We must part now."

"Whither would you go, Harry?"

"Whither? As the winds drive! What matters whither?"

"But you will go with me? Be with me now, Harry, since Fate so thoroughly restores you to me! Come with me; all here is yours. I and mine are yours, Harry! — Olive, too, is yours!"

And the brave cassique covered his face with his hands, while deep sobs broke from his lips. Harry Berkeley turned away abruptly, as if to depart; possibly to subdue his own emotions.

The other pursued and clasped him in his arms.

"Let us not part now, Harry. Go with me!"

"No, Edward, not now. I must go elsewhere: I have duties."

This was said very calmly, as if the passions had been all subdued. The cassique clung to him.

"Duties! What are you doing? how came you here? whence — why? and where have you been these many, many months? I have so much to hear, Harry!"

"And I so much to tell — if it will bear telling, or if I could speak! But it will only pain me to do so, and scarcely please you. Let me go now, Edward. Another time! There is time enough for all. — Hark! some one calls."

They both looked about. The nurse, with the child in her arms, rapidly approached them and addressed the cassique.

"O sir!—"

"What's the matter?"

"My lady, sir — she's raving, worse than ever. Mrs. Masterton begs you to come."

"Will you go with me, Harry?"

The other strode to and fro. Then quickly—

"No, Edward, not now; not while she raves. But there will come an hour when I shall be with you."

" Why not see her now? Perhaps—"

" See her—now! and while she raves! I that have never seen her save when her soul was placid as that of an angel! See it now in storm! No, no; God of heaven, save me from such sight! 'Twould madden me, too, Edward Berkeley, and I should forget that we have spoken in words of peace—"

" And love, too, Harry!"

" I should forget all, but her wrongs and my own. I will not see her now. Enough that I have seen her: and such a wreck of love, and happiness, and beauty! Away! Go you, Edward; go quickly!"

" I must. Yet, O my brother, say that I am forgiven the unconscious share I have had in this threefold work of wo! Though guilty of no treachery, I feel that I too have been weak and miserably blind. I have suffered my own passions to cloud my senses and baffle my reason. But for this, all would have been well with all of us!"

" Ah, no more! Hell's curses upon that she-fiend!—"

" Curse not, Harry!" very solemnly. " Even at this very moment, Olive—"

" Ah! go to her, Edward."

" You will now grasp my hand — we may now embrace, dear Harry!" was the pleading, faltering speech of the cassique; and the brothers fell into each other's arms! One violent grasp — one close, passionate embrace; the big tears gathering from both eyes; heavy, choking sobs, bursting from both bosoms; their manly frames trembling with the emotions of their souls — and they tore themselves asunder.

The cassique sped toward the dwelling, never once looking behind him. Harry watched him as he went. Then, as he turned, he discovered the nurse with the child close beside him. Confounded by what she saw, the woman had lingered. She had witnessed the parting embrace of the brothers — heard their passionate language; they wholly forgetful of her presence.

The moment Harry Berkeley beheld her, he said —

" Ha! it is Olive's child!"

And he took the infant quickly, but tenderly enough, from the arms of the nurse. He held it aloft, and gazed in its soft blue eyes. And it smiled upon him, and cooed with its little lips.

And he felt how like it was, in feature, to himself. Giving it back to the nurse, he murmured —

"It is Olive's child — Olive's, but not mine!"

Then, without further look or word, he turned away, and with rapid strides soon buried himself in the thickets. In a few moments he was upon his steed, and going at a rapid pace through the forest.

# CHAPTER XXXIX.

## COILS, CARES, AND CLUES.

" Coils, which are cares, but grow to clues, if Care
    Will heedfully unwind them, and march on,
    The string in hand, to where the end awaits !
    It is your dullard dodges from his care,
    Nor knows it as a missile, to be caught,
    Aud hurled back to the cricketeer of Fate." — *Old Play.*

RAPID motion, in the case of all persons of highly-sanguine temperament, compels thought; that is to say, in the case of people who have brains enough, at any time, for such exercise ! The mere temperament may be a motor to the reason; a stimulating force, as steam to the engine; but it is not the faculty itself. Such men as Harry Berkeley (or Calvert, for we must still continue to know him by both names) think in action. There is a consentaneous working of blood, and brain, and body, to a common end and object; the only sort of working which is worth. This consentaneous working makes the *action* in the case of the orator. The effect, in that of our hero, who did not pretend to oratory, would be, as in general with most of good Anglo-Norman stock, the stroke and shout together; the eye will be clear the while, affording that greatest virtue in the military man, the exercise of the *coup d'œil;* the judgment will be really quickened, and more admirable, with the sense of danger once awakened.

So it was, that the moment Harry Calvert began to gallop, he began to think. And very various, indeed, were the topics which now pressed upon his thoughts. Ship and crew; brother and wife; his own wife; the machinations of the conspirators among his people; the machinations of the red men against the colony :

all these in turn, and all together, crowded upon his thought and memory — his steed, meanwhile, beginning to suffer under the infliction of the spur.

But the rider did not reason the less closely and correctly because of the fleetness of his motion; and when, after nightfall, he reached the precincts of the creek where his vessel found harborage, he had properly digested all his plan of operations in regard to the subjects most pressing upon his anxieties.

Events were ripening fast to their several issues, and he gathered up all their clues.

He did not go on board the vessel; but, lurking in the thickets, approached on foot, near enough to make his signals, which, after awhile, procured him a secret interview with young Will Hazard, the youth whose adroit practice had first put him in possession of the secret of those who were willing to run up the " Jolly Roger." Having made a final disposition of all the matters between them, he sent Hazard back to the ship, and betook himself to a body of forest in which he had tethered his horse. Here he snatched a few hours of much-needed sleep. With the dawn he was again mounted; and this time, picking his way slowly and cautiously, he descended the country, keeping as closely as he could to the river, until he reached Gowdey's castle, at Oldtown, where he found a late breakfast awaiting him, and old Gowdey eager for his return.

He had given the veteran full employment, nor had the latter neglected any of his commissions. He had manned his castle, in secret, with fourteen sturdy fellows, old sea-dogs, foresters, and craftsmen; men who could put their hands to anything; could handle musket or oar with equal dexterity; and, having passed through most of the roughening processes of life, without having reaped any of the rewards of fortune, were just as ready for new enterprise as the most ardent young fellow of twenty-one.

His little garrison was well armed from the magazine of the Happy-go-Lucky. Gowdey had drilled them after his mixed fashion; the sailor and the forester blending oddly enough in his nature. He had been careful to observe the injunctions of Calvert, and had maintained the strictest secresy in his operations. His fellows had been smuggled in under cover of the night; and while, to all without, the old castle presented its wonted aspect of solitude and feebleness, no one, white or red, could suspect its increase of society and strength.

The creature-comforts had not been forgotten. Preparations were made even for a siege. Casks of bacon, barrels of flour and biscuit, potatoes, and other stores, had been provided, as well as all essential munitions of war, rendering the castle a complete house of refuge for the contiguous country, in the event of any sudden outbreak among the red men.

Nor had the veteran been heedless of what had been going on without. To use his own words :—

" I 've been a-scoutin', captain. Soon as I got these fellows in garrison, and found a man among 'em I could trust, to keep all dark and close, jest as ef I was here myself, I put out, and have had a good smart cruise round about the country. I went off west, to the Stonoe river; then I tuk down the river, among the Stonoes and Cussoboes; and spread out, right and left, to the settlements of the Wadmalahs and Kiawahs."

" Well, what discoveries ?"

" It 's clear we 're to have a risin'! The warriors ain't nowhere. They 're off in the thick somewhere; but where, there 's no tellin'. I skairted two camps of them, both Wadmalahs, but could n't git too nigh; for they had their scouts out, and busy. It tuk all I had of wood-cunnin' to see what I did, and git off without showin' my heels; but I did ! Old Cussoboe was gone above, with all his men. That I got out of an old squaw, for a tin cup I carried. But she would tell me no more. The women in the settlements, I could see, wor oneasy. They had everything ready for a start at a moment's warnin'. So that, I reckon, you wor jest as near right, in your calkilations of a risin', as ever was a man yit that know'd the meanin' of an Injin sign."

" Did you warn any of the whites ?"

" Did n't see many, your honor. I 'm afraid they 'll have to pay for it with their wool, same as ever. When once these traders are on the scent of a good trade, they won't smell even the sulphur of hell's fires, though it 's a-blazin' under their very noses ! I met a Dutchman and three Scotchmen, and each a-horseback, and a great pack behind him; and I says, ' Look you, you 're a-guine to a most bloody market.' And the Dutchman says, ' Himmel! de plut is goot in de market !' When I told him 'zactly what I meant, he answered by showin' a great pistol, and, looking brave enough, said, ' I vill show de red rascals dis leetle gon !' And much would they mind his little gun ! He'd git the arrow through his great belly, out of the woods, and never see the chap that held the bow. The Scotchmen wor all three together, and had a sort of consult about what I told them ; but they had a young fellow who was a kind of leader, and he laughed at Injin fightin', and they all agreed to push for'ard. It seems that a party of seven, with great packs, had gone ahead, and they wanted to overhaul 'em, lest they should take off the edge of the market before they could get up."

" Whither were they bound ?"

" Toward the Savano town, where, they tell, there's a large gatherin' of the Injins — the Westoes, Savanoes, Isundigoes, and Coosaws — for a great ball-play. 'Cordin' to the Scotchmen, there 'll be a thousand of the red-skins, and maybe more, at the gatherin' !"

" Can Cussoboe be off among these people ? Is it possible that he has brought them together with reference to his own object ?"

" I reckon not, your honor. I believe what the old woman says. I reckon he's gone above, to the heads of the Edisto, to bring down the great power of his own tribe, that hadn't come down, and ginerally don't come down, till the corn's laid by ; that is, sometime late in July and the first weeks in August. It's not likely that he'll try to work in more tribes than his own ; for these Injins are greedy after what they can git, and don't want too many to share the sp'ile. And that's one reason why they can't keep together in large bodies for very long : they grudges to give up anything they git. I reckon old Cussoboe has marked out everything, at our white cassique's, for himself ; and that's one reason why he's put his own son there. He'll set the other chiefs of his people to lookin' for their prog in other quarters. There's a small settlement of Scotch and English down upon South Edisto, close to the salts. They haven't been there long ; and I hear there's a bigger Scotch settlement at Beaufort, under a great Scotch lord. Ef the Injins are uprisin', ginerally, they 'll all be cut off, unless they git warnin' in time, and are sensible enough to take it."

" And, in an Indian outbreak, we must always expect a rising to be more or less general. If it takes in only the tribes of one nation, they will suffice for the work of destruction."

" I could n't stretch away fur enough, captain, to give 'em warnin' on the Edisto and at Beaufort. I had, you know, enough to consider and watch *here;* more at home, as I may say. But, ef you think—"

" No! you will be wanted here. We must try and warn them by boats from the sea. That will be safer and easier. I will see to that to-night."

" To-night, sir!" with a smile. " Why, I reckon to-night you 'll be at the grand *fandango* and misdemeanor ball, at Lady Anderson's, in town. There 's to be old fun, and big splinters, and all-tearin' music and dancin' there, to-night! Hain't you heard?—ain't you axed to the music?"

Our rover smiled.

" Well, perhaps I am, Gowdey; and it is possible I may be there."

" 'T will suit you, captain, for everybody 's to go in his own disguisin's, jest as he pleases, and wear what sort of coat suits his idees; and he can kiver his face with a kind of black curt'in that they calls a mask. Ah! I have it now: the party is a masker-adies!—that's it. It's a big word for a sailor, that's got but half a jaw for his speakin', and t'other half for his quid."

" I may look in *upon* the masqueraders, Gowdey, but can hardly be *among* them. At all events, I can snatch opportunity enough, I think, to send off a boat to the settlement at Beaufort. What you tell me of these traders, and the settlements, troubles me. I fear the mischief is more general than we thought it. These settlements are all in danger. They seem to have no sense of it; they have taken no precautions. The authorities here despise the red men too much; and, indeed, having been for some time quiet and peaceable, they have furnished natural reasons why the whites should be lulled into security. This large gathering of the Indians to the south of us, if true, is an imposing fact. It is too late in the season for the ball-play. They have other festivities, it is true—the green-corn dance, and—"

" Oh! there's always some rolly-polly's goin' on among 'em!

They're jest like our white folks, after all. Only let the drum beat, or the trumpet blow, or the fife squeak, or squeeze the Scotchman's bags; or jest fling a handful of pebbles in a tin kittle, and rattle away, and swig liquor all the while; and the monkeys will crowd about the pole from a thousand quarters, and grin, and shake their legs, and catch hold of any partners."

" True enough! But the tribes do not usually congregate in such numbers, so far from their own council-houses, for any ordinary music. There is danger that all these traders will lose their scalps."

" Like enough! I warned 'em to take a good feel of the wool on their sculps, for they worn't likely to feel it very long. But they wor all full of braggadocio, under that young fellow's lead; and, as they all carried pistols, they talked as ef they wor an army."

" Well, we can do nothing for them. But the settlements we may be in season to save."

" Yes, ef you can send right away — this very night — and ef so be they believe you after they hear."

" Lord Cardross is a stout soldier, and his heart's in his colony. He will probably take counsel. We must try, at all events, to make him do so. This large gathering of the Indians, assuming the report to be true, argues something beyond the usual Indian policy. I suspect the Spanish *guarda costas* are again upon the coast, and busy in secret. If so, Beaufort is in danger. They may even meditate mischief here, at Charleston. The place is without good defences. A single brigantine, well officered, could destroy the town in three hours."

" You think so, captain?"

" Think for yourself. What's the value of the palmetto fort which they have at Oyster point? Of what use the mud crescent at the Governor's creek? And if an enemy came through Wappoo into Kiawah, save your own one gun, Gowdey, no other could be brought to bear upon her, and that could do no mischief if she took a position southwest of the town. If I were quite free at this moment, I would run round with the Happy-go-Lucky to Port Royal, and see for the Spaniards myself."

" 'T would be famous fun to git in among them *guarda costas*, and catch the dons nappin'! I'd jest like to have a few cracks at 'em myself, ef only to pay off old scores. They had me nine months, hard at work, with a bracelet on the ankle, at their cussed castle at St. Augustine. I owe 'em the weight of that iron bracelet, in iron bullets, at the rate of nine pounds a day for nine months; and whenever you can say to me, ' Gowdey, come, pay off them scores with the. Spaniards,' you 'll not find an old salt more ready for a new craft or a fresh quid !"

We must not pursue the dialogue, though in its progress between the parties it involved a great variety of details, minor certainly, but all bearing upon the several necessities which concerned the fortunes of the personages in our history. Besides, it consumed the day. Calvert lingered with Gowdey till dark, making final arrangements in reference to the approaching issues; and was then, under cover of the night, paddled over to the thickets of the opposite shore, whence he made his way to the town on foot.

Here, at an appointed place, he found Jack Belcher and our old acquaintance Franks, who were both eager for his coming, and in no little consternation. Belcher had received a private despatch from the ship, reporting the fact that, only the night before, the prisoner, Gideon Fairchild (whom Sylvester, *alias* Stillwater, had procured to be sent to New York, as express, on the part of the governor), had made his escape; as it was supposed through the agency of the mulattress Sylvia, the maidservant of the fair Zulieme, as she too had disappeared from the vessel.

Nothing further was known. There were no clues. Sylvia had been seen in close communication with Gideon, in the hold where he was kept; but how she had effected his release from his irons, and his escape from the ship, nothing was stated. The two had probably got into the forests, and were making, or had possibly made, their way to town — having had ample time for it, even by the longest route.

Here was a danger. It argued great laxity of discipline on board the ship, and our rover now began to reproach himself bitterly for having suffered his private affairs and feelings to endanger the safety of his people; for, once in town, Gideon Fairchild carried a perilous secret, with which the cunning Sylvester could compel the governor to action against the vessel and crew —

which, as we well know, he would otherwise gladly avoid.   And
against this danger even the fertile genius of Harry Calvert had
no remedy.

But he seemed neither surprised nor disconcerted.

"Have you any tidings of a boat from the ship?   Has Molyneaux reached town, or Fowler?"

"Not yet — not that we know."

"Keep a sharp lookout.   You know what is to be done."

To Franks he said:—

"Have you had your eyes on Sylvester?   Has he been to the
governor?"

"No, sir; but he has been out of town, and is out of town now,
I believe."

"Whither did he go?"

"We couldn't find out.   We only believe him absent because
we see nothing of him.   If he left town, he did so between two
days.   He's been very quiet."

"He has outwitted you, I am afraid.   But we must prepare
against him as well as we can.   You have"— to Belcher —"prepared for the arrival of Will Hazard and his party?"

"He's at his place long before this."

"And a good boat's-crew ready at the lagune?"

"Five stout fellows, regular sea-dogs, and well tried."

"Good!   Keep close watch on the approaches from the river,
and upon the house of Mrs. Anderson.   You have provided
masks for all of us, Franks?"

"All, sir."

"Very good.   I shall not fail you.   I shall leave you for an
hour or two.   It is still early.   Let no mouse stir without seeing
it!"

And so he left them, and the two separated on their several
duties.

Half an hour later, our rover was closeted with his excellency
Governor Quarry.   The governor was in good spirits.   These
were soon dashed by the tidings Calvert brought.   But, before
he spoke of those which most affected his own private fortunes, he opened the one topic of most importance to the col-
any:—

"Your excellency has, I fear, taken no steps in regard to

the report I made you touching the movements of the red men."

"What, still piping to that tune, captain?"

"It is one to which you will probably be made to *dance*, when you least expect it! I now beg you to despatch a fly-boat, or *periagua*, with all haste, to the colony of my Lord Cardross, and to another colony of Scotch, said to be in his neighborhood, somewhere along the Edisto, advising them to put themselves instantly under arms against the red men and the Spaniards! I have reason to think that there is present danger from both."

"You are not serious?"

"I have long since ceased to jest."

The governor rose, and stood up before Calvert.

"My dear captain, you are one of the most mysterious men living! Where have you been all this while?—what doing? What keeps you from the sea, now that the chief business is over with which you came into port? for I feel pretty sure, from what I hear, that you have emptied your ship. You have at least filled the town with your goods. The thing is spoken of openly."

"But they have no clue to the ship's anchorage?"

"No! that adds to the mystery. Where have you hidden her?"

"Better that even you should not know. You will the more innocently answer. At all events, you must not expect me to answer all the queries you put to me."

"But how is it that you know so much of the settlements, of those subjects which are so especially my own — the condition of the colony, its dangers, and the red men and the Spaniards? 'Pon my soul, though not much vexed with that verdant passion which poets call ambition, I begin to feel a little jealous of you, with your mysterious knowings in my province."

"Do not suffer any such childish feeling to disparage the importance of what I say. Act promptly upon my report. Write to my Lord Cardross, as cautiously as you please, but still write him, to put his people under arms, and employ all his vigilance, as well by sea as land; and send your despatches this very night. Believe me, there is no time to be lost."

"Well, you do seem very serious, and I do not see but that I may safely adopt your counsel."

" You will be prudent to do so."

" But I hate these perpetual alarms about the Indians. Half the time they make a governor ridiculous."

" Scarcely, unless he makes himself so. You will not do this. You have only to write a plain letter, to the effect stated; adding that the rumors may be groundless, but that the precaution will be proper. You need say no more, except to urge the notorious treachery of the red men; the cunning and hostility of the Spaniards; their frequent invasion; the near neighborhood of St. Augustine to Beaufort; the fact that the prevailing winds are favorable from that quarter; and, further, that you have advices that the governor of St. Augustine has just received an additional force of three new, light brigantines from Havana, each mounting ten guns."

" How know you that?"

" By my own discovery. I crossed them on my voyage hither, and would have fought them, but that my ship was too deeply loaded, and with a cargo quite too valuable, to peril against a force so superior — and the crews of which had nothing to lose."

" But about the red men? How is it that you can hear these things, and I nothing? I have had my emissaries out, too, and they report everything quiet. The traders go and come. I gave thirty-eight commissions to as many Scotchmen only three days ago, to carry on their traffic in the Indian lands, to and up the Savannah, to Echoee."

" They will probably, every man of them, lose his scalp."

" Pshaw, my dear captain! this is being too oracular and prophetic, surely. Come, come, we will hear to evidence, but not prophecy. How is it that you can arrive at these things — you, a mere looker-on — and I, whose very business it is, should know nothing? — I, too, who have my agents and scouts constantly going to and fro!"

" Did they tell you, these scouts, of the great gathering of the Indians on Savannah?"

" Ay, for a ball-play, or some such Indian junketing."

" A thousand Indians, on our seaboard, gathered to a ball-play, and at this season of the year, is by no means a common event. But, did your scouts report that the red warriors south of us were temporarily separated from their women, and were nowhere visible except in secret camps?'

"No! That I did not hear."

"There are many things, my dear governor, which you will never hear, though you had a thousand scouts, unless you were sure of those who know the business. Scouting is a beautiful art. Your Scotch traders have yet to learn it. Had you some that I could mention, they would soon change your notion of the aspect of affairs. I took the liberty to counsel you some time ago to fit up and reman the castle at Oldtown. Did you do so?"

"No, faith, I did not. Old Gowdey came to me also on the subject, and he had suspicions like yours; but I fancied that the old sea-dog only wanted to get an increase of importance and pay—"

"And what did I want, giving the same counsel?"

The governor was taken aback by the question, and answered with some confusion:—

"Oh, zounds, captain! you are too close, too keen, too sharp at logical conclusions. Of course, *you* wanted nothing, except — except—"

"To give advice; to increase my own importance, as old Gowdey desired to increase his, eh?"

"Faith, I confess, such was somewhat my thought."

"I forgive you, my dear governor, especially as I took leave to repair your neglect — I trust, without subjecting your administration to reproach."

"Why, what have you done?"

"To show you what sort of scouts you employ, and what reliance you may place upon their reports, know that the Oldtown castle has been manned with fourteen stout soldiers and sea-dogs, besides old Gowdey; that each of these has his musket, pistols, and a plenty of ammunition; and that the provisions are ample for a siege of three weeks. Yet, though, according to Gowdey's report, no less than five of your scouts have been to see him — called in passing — since this change has been made, not one has seen or suspects it."

"The devil! you say — and — and — my dear captain — you say that you have done all this — engaged all these beef-eaters, in government name, and at government expense!—"

His excellency showed real consternation.   Calvert knew where
the difficulty lay.

"Even so, your excellency.   But here are receipts from all of
them, for six months' pay, the term for which they are engaged;
and here, too, are receipts, all in your name, for the stores of
beef, biscuit, pork, molasses, rum, potatoes, and other commodities, which were deemed necessary for the garrison for the same
term."

The governor took the papers in silence.   He was confounded.
The rover proceeded :—

"You will establish your claim against the colony for so much
advance made by yourself.   You will permit me to say that I
have no claim upon you."

"By ——! Captain Calvert, you are a d——d generous fellow!   D——d generous, by ——!"

"Say no more, please!   I am compelled, however, to say that,
as soon as you can exchange my ship's muskets, pistols, and cutlasses, for those of the colony, I shall be glad to have mine back.
These belong to the ship."

"I shall see to it.   I will send the despatch in a fast fly-boat,
this very night, to my Lord Cardross."

"Better this very hour."

"As soon as you leave me."

"I shall leave you shortly; have very little more to say, now:
and that little is, unfortunately, like to give us trouble — me, at
least.   Your early knowledge of the facts may help you to keep
out of danger."

"Why, what's the matter?" demanded the governor, eagerly,
but with no little trepidation in his tones.   He felt that something
serious was impending.   He knew Calvert too well to suppose
him guilty of a jest; knew, in fact, that when he expressed an apprehension, it was generally founded upon some trouble of more
than common difficulty.

"Why, what's the matter, captain?"

"The watch on my ship has been kept badly, during my ab-
cence from it.   The express-rider — Gideon Fairchild — has es-
saped."

"The devil!   Gone? got off?"

"It would seem so.   He escaped last night.   The discovery

was only made to-day.  He has probably had eighteen hours to make off."

" This is a serious matter."

" To me, perhaps : hardly to you.  I shall have to change my anchorage-ground.  You will have to order out the *posse comitatus*, and create a special police ; nay, despatch an armed force in search after the vessel, and perhaps put the town under martial law.  It will require, for your own safety, after you shall be officially apprized of the intelligence I now give you, to show yourself earnest in asserting the dignity and authority of government.  You will hear of it soon enough.  You must show yourself very resolute and active."

" Where the devil's the fellow Stillwater [Sylvester] ?   I have not seen or heard of him for a week or more."

" He is not in town, I fancy."

" Where the devil can he be ?"

" Ask rather where your members of council are, for I suspect he is even now closeted with Morton or Middleton, or some one or more of them.  If he suspects you—"

" Suspects *me !*   How the devil should he suspect *me ?*"

" I do not say that he does.  But the thing is possible.  He is cunning enough.  He may think you to be lukewarm, at all events, and he *knows* some of the council to be otherwise.  You will probably hear the facts through your council."

" And what's to be done ?" demanded his excellency, greatly chafed, and striding his chamber with seven-league boots of anxiety.

" I have told you.  Keep cool ; be calm !  It will be sufficient that you have due notice.  You must not be taken by surprise.  You will show yourself more eager in pursuit than your council.  Go with them, even ahead of them, in all the plans they may propose, for my capture and the seizure of the ship.  It is possible that they will not attempt this, by any force now in the colony.  It is probable that Morton, who was on the Santee a week ago, has been followed thither by Sylvester ; and I think it likely that, without consultation with you, or any other member of the council, he will despatch Fairchild from that point to New York, with a new commission to bring on the king's ships.  I must prepare for them.  See that you prepare for Morton.  There need

18

be no embarrassment to you, now that you are prepared to know exactly what to do. You will, as soon as the facts are forced upon you, issue your proclamation, and make public the reward offered for my capture."

" By ——, Captain Calvert, but you take it with a d——d virtuous coolness !"

" Why should I rage? Why tremble? The arrow flies, whether we weep or sing."

" And what mean you to do with yourself ?"

" Ah ! better, as I have so frequently said, that you should know as little as possible. I, too, am forewarned."

" What ! suppose I issue my proclamation to-morrow ?"

" You will do no such thing, unless you desire to ruin yourself as well as me. Do nothing, as I said, until the facts are so forced upon you that you can not escape them. Issue your proclamation now, and when Morton, Middleton, and Berkeley, ask whence you get your information, what will you answer? ' From Calvert himself,' eh ?"

" True, true ! But it 's a devil of a predicament !"

" Pshaw ! nothing, governor, so long as we know where the snares lie, and walk like bearded men with our eyes open, and our wits, like keen-nosed hounds, running before us. Be cool, sir, and wait events, and do not force them."

" Where go you now ?"

" Into cover, as soon as possible, as the fox does when she knows the hounds are abroad. I must relieve you of all responsibility, all doubts of my safety, so that you may act with the most prompt decision, at the requisition of your council. Be so good as to send the fly-boat to my Lord Cardross to-night. They must use sail and oar, as they can ; but make rapid headway. As for these Indians—"

" D—n 'em ! If your suspicions be true, that is another trouble !"

" One trouble is apt to devour another ! Considered selfishly, an outbreak of the red men now, should be subject of congratulation. It will divert your people and council from your piratical friends : it will give you and me respite."

" Egad ! that 's likely enough. And, by-the-way, an Indian war will reopen a branch of business which my virtuous brethren in council have been busy in shutting up. It will give us captives for the West-India markets. We must follow the example of our New-England crop-ears, and buy the scalps of the warriors, and sell the souls of their women and children — bodies, rather; the souls would n't bring a stiver in any good Christian market!"

Our rover left our governor to as many sources of consolation as his own soul could suggest. We shall follow his example; but not before we have seen his excellency preparing his despatches, apprizing Lord Cardross of the possible danger from red men and Spaniards.

## CHAPTER XL.

### A NIGHT OF ADVENTURES.

——"Go to, and follow:—
We skip from one to t'other here,
And note their several fortunes."

FROM the stately dwelling of the governor, our rover hastened
to the lowly one of the ancient Jack-tar Franks, in "Boggy Quarter." His route was an obscure one, by Fiddler's Green, Cow-
alley, and Myrtle cove — places no longer known to modern no-
menclature in the same precinct — until he found himself safe in
the obscurities of "Boggy Quarter." Here he obtained a mask,
and such change of costume as he desired to make, should he think
proper to peril his person at the fancy ball of Mrs. Perkins Anderson.

Old Franks had a "curiosity shop" of his own — how collected,
we may conjecture, but are not able to say — and could, at a
pinch, have fitted out a score of masqueraders in their fancy
dresses.

But Harry Calvert, while he twiddled the domino in his fingers,
did not seem eager to habit himself for the evening. He gave
himself up to a sombre fit of meditation, seeing which, old Franks,
with genuine sailor instinct, proceeded to get out the rum, and
sugar, and lemon-juice, and quietly concoct a bowl of punch. He
knew the virtues of punch in vexatious moods. He also knew
that, though our rover was anything but a swiller of liquor, yet,
when in such a mood, he had only to place a can of the beverage
beside his captain, and it would be swallowed unconsciously.
Were he to offer to prepare it, as dull dogs are apt to do, Calvert
would no doubt refuse. The only proper way, as old experience and

a gentlemanly tact had taught him, was the process already adopted. And, having such a profound faith in punch, in all similar cases of head and heart, Franks held himself justified in beguiling his superior to his medicine. His moral in the business was such as any honest temperance society will approve.

But, though Calvert drank, he grew moodier than ever. At length, Franks went forth and left him alone. Anon he returned and made his report.

Lieutenant Molyneaux and the old pirate, Sam Fowler, had reached town in their boat.

"Well," said the rover, not turning his head, "does Belcher know?"

"'T was he told me, yer honor."

"Ah! well!—he knows what to do."

And he relapsed again into his meditations.

Leaving him to these, let us pick up and unwind some of the clues which we have, hitherto, rather laid aside than dropped.

First, then, the mode of Fairchild's escape from the Happy-go-Lucky?

The mulattress was, in truth, the agent. She had pretty much the freedom of the ship. As the maid of Zulieme, a great many privileges had been accorded her. As the spy and agent of Lieutenant Molyneaux, she had succeeded to a good many more. Eccles, the second lieutenant, though really an honest and good fellow, belonged to the numerous family of the "softs." He was bashful in office; and while Molyneaux was present, in authority, Eccles never adequately asserted his own.

Molyneaux had temporarily forgotten his interest in Sylvia, in that more absorbing interest which followed from his intrigues with Fowler. Sylvia, while slighted by Molyneaux, had still the freedom of the ship.

The mulatto is the cross of white upon negro blood. The male mulatto has a share of the quickness of the white man, with little of his solidity or grasp. He has the cunning of the negro, without his loyalty, or strength, or even courage.

The female mulatto has, in excess, all the arts of the male, with a proportionate increase of that dexterity and cunning which naturally belong to the sex. She is fond of toys, capricious of mood, restless of place, eager for change, greedy for show and vanity,

and vindictive in her passion. This is especially true of the creature where the cross is that of Spaniard or Portuguese. If the
father be French, there will be equal caprice but greater playfulness. The Spanish mulattress will be a shade more religious.
The cross with the English gives a more solid character, capable
of greater thought and work. If Scotch, there will be a certain
character of moodiness and sullenness, with a like capacity for
work, and a greater degree of endurance. Descendants of the
Irish cross are apt to approach those of the French in character.
Sylvia was the daughter of a white Spaniard.

She had vanity and religion, appetite and frivolity, superstition
and passion, all huddled up together, in her composition. She
was a fool, of course; but not the less dangerous because a fool.
Molyneaux had slighted her. He had promised to convey her to
town, for which she sighed quite as much as her mistress. He
gave her the freedom of the ship, but so watched, that she could
not get away from it. He found that she could only profit him,
in his proposed intrigue with her mistress, *while with her ;* and,
separate from her, she was good for nothing, and could do nothing. Finding the vessel empty, he simply left it on the shelf.

And Sylvia resented this, after vainly seeking to regain her ascendency. He gave her no credit for her amulets. She might
have been pacified, if he had recognised her charms. But the
mulattress was no beauty. And so, with the sense of neglect, she
grew mischievous. She had, among other petty passions, a most
terrible curiosity. There was a prisoner in the hold, brought in
under mysterious circumstances. She found her way to him.

Gideon Fairchild was a straight-laced Puritan; a rogue by instinct, but a saint by profession. He succeeded in persuading
Sylvia to undo his fetters. He promised to take her to town, to
her mistress; the very thing she most sighed for at that moment,
How he proceeded — by what oily words and phrases, by what
asseverations — we need not say. But it will not surprise you
to hear that, in the darkness of the hold, Gideon did not scruple
to promise marriage to the mulattress. He had one wife already
in Charleston; and there had been a scandal, which insisted that
he had left another in Connecticut. But the latter never looked
him up in Carolina, no doubt for very good reasons; and to the
former he may have meditated no wrong in his promise to the

mulattress. It was probably the only argument by which to persuade her to undo his bonds; and some little latitude must be accorded to a Puritan in durance vile.

Well, they escaped together; and even at his departure from the ship, Molyneaux was ignorant of the fact. Eccles, indeed, knew it, but did not trouble his senior officer with the intelligence. Nor, in fact, had he the chance: all that day, Molyneaux had been busied in adjusting his costume for the night. He had a wondrous wardrobe. Costumes of English cavalier, French marquis, Spanish don, Italian bandit, and (no less picturesque) gallant rover: black hat, like steeple; diamond button; great, black plumage of the ostrich: rich frock, heavy with lace; belt, studded with jewels; slings, for a brace of silver-mounted pistols; sling, for long, glittering cut-and-thrust; diamond buckles for the knee; silken stockings, elaborately clocked; and peaked shoes, glossy with varnish, and gleaming with their buckles also.

What shall he wear? The question is one of proverbial difficulty to an English macaroni, especially when the object is a fancy ball. Molyneaux labors under an *embarras des richesse*. It takes him a whole day to determine; and, though he decides before nightfall, he is still dubious. He decides to be a courtier of Charles II.; but, lest his tastes should change ere he reaches town, he concludes to carry with him an Italian brigand, a Spanish don, and a French marquis. Anyhow, he will wear an *aigrette* of pearl, and a great rope about his neck, of the same precious tears, from the sea of Oman, or the less classical shores of the Pacific.

Sam Fowler, "Squint-eyed Sam," the old pirate, begrudges boat-room to the chest which is required for these precious fantasticals; for Sam's taste is more of the butcher than the tailor order. But Molyneaux makes a point of it, and such a comrade is not to be quarrelled with in a mere matter of taste. And so they leave together the snug nook upon the Ashley, and make their way to "Oyster Point"—a name which, among the vulgar, clung to the good city of the cavaliers a long time after. She had been formally christened "CHARLESTON," after the "merrie monarch."

They reached their destination, a creek which put in somewhere between the present streets Queen and Wentworth, in the very

heart of the modern city, and possibly an eighth of a mile above
that which usually afforded shelter to the skiff of Captain Calvert.
And here, on a little bank of sand, over which hung a single live
oak, skirted by a fringe of myrtle and sea-willows, the gallant Mr.
Molyneaux made his toilet, rigging himself out as a cavalier of
the English court.

He was now ready for the masking.  But he had still to find
his way to the dwelling of Mrs. Perkins Anderson.  For the necessary knowledge he could only look to Sam Fowler; and the
latter, in turn, must refer to his trading-acquaintance, Mr. Ebene-
zer Sproulls.

As both of our parties were eager after their several affairs
— for if Molyneaux looked to the costume-ball for his delights,
Fowler had visions of a famous drinking-'bout, with choice companions, running in his head — they very soon left the boat in the
keeping of the two sailors who had rowed them down.  These
sailors, by-the-way, were among their confederates, sworn brothers
under the "Jolly Roger."  Fowler gave them stern counsel to
keep the boat, lie close under the willows, and obey their signal.

"If you try to git into town, my lads, they'll have you in the
bilboes; and then, be sure, you'll die in your shoes, and that too
with no solid deck to stand upon."

"They've no liquors?" asked Molyneaux.

"Not a drap, yer honors!"  And the two rascals grinned as
they answered in the same breath.

"Well, eyes bright, my lads, and lie close, with a good gripe of
pistols as well as oars.  Remember, the three whistles and a
chirrup!"

And so they were left to the consolations of a dry time on a lee
shore.  The reckless rascals, however, had made provision for
themselves; and, hardly had their two superiors gone from sight,
ere they produced a portly jug of Jamaica, and proceeded to
refresh themselves.  Their providence, and the frequency and
strength of their draughts, rendered the work of Jack Belcher
much easier than it otherwise might have been.  In one hour
after they had begun their potations, they were only half conscious, and nowise capable of using oar or pistol; and in this condition were set upon by half a dozen sturdy fellows, who had them
roped and gagged in a jiffy, stripped of every weapon, and car-

ried off to a closer harborage. Their places in the boat were supplied by two others, who were soon habited in their garments, and better able to perform their duties.

Meanwhile, Molyneaux and Fowler made their way to the habitation of Sproulls. A Spanish *roquelaure*, of great dimensions, though light of weight, sufficed to conceal the gayety of our lieutenant's costume from all vulgar eyes. But they met few persons in the infant city, and no policemen. Not that the town was lacking in its Dogberries. But the mere corporal's guard, then kept on the establishment, did not suffice for more than angel-visits to the several streets.

Our lieutenant found the thoroughfares muddy. There were pools to cross, and quagmires to leap, and ditches which were more easy to penetrate than to pass; and Sam Fowler was something of a blind guide. But all difficulties were finally overcome, and the two reached Sproulls's dwelling in safety, though it was found that the shoes of our lieutenant needed nice treatment and a considerate brush. And Sproulls himself condescended to this labor. He was, or affected to be, full of admiration at the costume of his visiter; and no doubt he was. Besides, Molyneaux was a very pretty fellow, with a good leg, and a well-built and graceful figure. He prided himself with propriety upon his leg. Sproulls was no doubt moved to admiration, in some degree, because of the notion he had taken that the famous rover, Calvert himself, stood before him. Fowler had not named his companion. Molyneaux kept on his vizard, and Sproulls himself had never seen Calvert. He conjectured and concluded just as he wished. Here let us leave the parties for awhile, until it becomes proper to take the principal to the assembly of Mrs. Perkins Anderson.

It is not known exactly at what hour, and by what particular mode, Gideon Fairchild and Sylvia succeeded in leaving the Happy-go-Lucky. But we do know that their escape was made, in the first instance, to the woods on the western side of the river. Here they immediately buried themselves in the thickets, hurrying below with the flight of fear. Two miles below, they discovered an old canoe fastened to a tree in the water by a grapevine. It was leaky, and seemed to have been abandoned as unseaworthy. A broken paddle lay in the bottom of the boat. But this, with a stream so narrow at this point, and so smooth, was suffi-

cient for their purposes. They did not stop to bail the rickety
vessel, but boldly ventured in and paddled across; their apprehensions increasing during the voyage lest the canoe should sink,
for the water gurgled in from numerous seams and cracks. But
they succeeded in getting her into a creek running through the
opposite marsh, and landed safely at a point which tradition still
indicates as near the eastern bank of the " Ten-mile Ferry." But
it must have been above this point, since, according to the " claim"
put in by Gideon Fairchild for " damages" — which may perhaps
still be found in the records of the colonial office — he mentioned
his dreary midnight tramp of *fourteen miles* to the city after he
had crossed the river. But the matter is not of serious moment.
The fugitives crossed in safety, and succeeded in making their
way to the main thoroughfare of the country — a noble avenue,
girdled on both sides by mighty live oaks, hung with moss, and
gigantic pines, the most stately of all evergreens, the growth of
half a century or more, which literally linked their branches
across the track, forming a grand Gothic archway of many, many
miles in length. Old John Archdale, the Quaker governor for a
season, and one of the lords-proprietors, said of this avenue many
years after, that it was such as no prince in Europe could boast.
And for a good reason: it was cut out of the primitive forests,
which the axe of civilization had never dishonored by a stroke !

It was hard work for our fugitives, in the thick woods and
thicker darkness, to make their way from the river to the open
road. Gideon, who pretended to some merits as a scout, but was
at best nothing but an express, was frequently puzzled and in
despair. But Sylvia kept beside him, cheerful through all, and
sometimes helping him forward by a hint, often by a word of encouragement. Her exercises as vaulter, tumbler, and dan   had
admirably prepared her lower limbs for any ordeal on foot, and
she ran beside Gideon without effort, as he stumbled and fought
his way through the thicket, his Puritan restraints frequently so
far forgotten as to allow of sundry explosive expletives, such as
" Odds blood ! ' " Odds flesh !" " Odds zounds !" and " Odds bodi-
kins !" — all so many contractions of the Sacred Name, modifica-
tions of well-known English oaths of the days of " good Queen
Bess."

" You 're swearing, ain't you ?" demanded the gipsy ; " what for ?"

" These 'tarnal thick woods !"

" What ! do you mind the woods ?  I can see like an owl."

" Well, I wish I could light my eyes by your lamp.  I'm tarnation 'fear'd we shall never git out of this thick."

" Oh, yes, we will !  I can get through !  You ought n't to mind that, since your 're out of the hold of that nasty old ship."

" S'blood ! but 't was nasty !  I shall never forgit, ef I live till Methuselah.  I do n't think I shall ever git the smell of the tar out of my nose."

" Well, you 're out now, and that 's something.  It 's better here, and free to go, than stay there without any daylight."

" Odds Bob ! but what 's the freedom here, I wonder ?  There, now !  I had it right slap in my face !  Sich a wipe !—a blasted big airm of the tree !"

Sylvia laughed merrily as her companion, growling the while, extricated himself for the moment, but only to run into a new mesh of entanglement.

" Here, hold my hand," said the girl, " I 'll show you the way."

But his pride would n't suffer this ; and when she laughed again, he growled, fiercely —

" What the dickens do you yell for !  Do n't you know there 's wolves and tigers all about these woods ?"

" *Madre de Dios !* is it true ?"  And the gipsy nestled closer.

" True ! why, you can hear them sometimes a-barkin' in the streets of Charlestoun."

" *Jesu !* holy Mother ! but is it true ?"

" True ! — Ah ! the Lord be praised, we 're in the road at last !"

And the two looked up, and saw the stars shining out fairly through the avenue.

" Yes ! we 're in a cl'ar track now, and that 's a God's mercy."

" But the wolves and tigers, Mr. Gideon !"

" Yes ! do n't you wake 'em up with your infarnal yells ag'in. You do n't know how soon they 'll be on us anyhow.  Stick to me."

" I will !"

" And there 's the red, painted, devilish sons of Satan — the Injins !"

" O *Jesu !* and have you the red Injins so near the town ?"

" Near the town! We've got a good ten miles to go yet; and we may both lose our sculps before we git a mile further."

" But they would n't sculp a woman, would they?"

" Would n't they? Why, why not? What would they want her for?"

" Why, they'd want her to go with one of the warriors; they'd some of them be wanting to marry her."

" And so you think you'd git off that way, while they was a-sculpin' me, do ye?"

" No! but that would be the worst of it for a woman."

" And you'd marry an Injin, would ye?"

" And why not? He's got a good color, jest like mine. But, you know, I'm to marry you, Mr. Gideon."

" Hem! marry me? Wal, I guess we did say something about it, when I was onable to make a contract. Do you recollect anything of sich talk?"

" To be sure, I do! You are to carry me to my missus, you know, and if she says ' Yes,' why, you're to marry me."

" I'm afear'd, my poor gal, that your mistress won't say ' Yes.'"

" Oh, but she will!"

" I guess not. You see, I've been a-thinkin' about it, Sylvia; and, you see, you're a slave."

" Oh! you'll pay missus so much money, you know."

" And whar's it to come from, I say?"

" Why, to be sure, you ought to know."

" But I do n't know. And I reckon, my poor gal, you'll have to give up any sich onreasonable ixpectations."

" But why?"

" For the reasons I tell you, and for other reasons that I won't tell you."

The gipsy began to whine and blubber. But just then, Gideon:—

" Hairk! what's that in the thick? Shet up your oven, gal, and do n't bring out all the painted savages 'twixt here and hell to eat us up! Shet up, I say, and push on, now the track's clear. It'll be broad daylight afore we git to town, ef you do n't walk faster."

The word " savages" sufficed. Sylvia darted forward at a run.

" Why, you 'tarnal ——! would you jest now surrender me up

to the painted varmints, and leave me to be sculped intire? Is
that the way you shows your gratitude, now that I've extercated
you out of that pirate prison?"

Gideon had completely changed the relative obligations of the
parties. In due degree as he began to feel himself secure, did
the sense of gratitude decline within him. We have seen how
decidedly he ignored his promise of marriage. It was necessary
that he should do this effectually before he reached the presence
of the Mrs. Gideon of Charleston. But, even as he felt the necessity of silencing the one idea, another entered his head. He
was not altogether prepared to give Sylvia up to her mistress.
She was a slave to the Spaniard. Why not to him? In the abstract, he was decidedly opposed to negro slavery; but there is,
as every virtuous Christian knows and understands, a very substantial difference between a slave to keep and a slave to sell!
Now, it was very certain that Mrs. Gideon would never suffer
him to keep Sylvia; but he was quite as sure that that excellent
woman would never object to selling her, at a proper market val-
uation. Sylvia would bring, even in that day, as an accomplished
lady's maid, some fifty pounds under the hammer. Now, if Sylvia, reconciled to the denial of her claims, as wife, could be persuaded of the superior advantages to herself of becoming, for a
season, lady's maid to Mrs. Gideon, the next step was easy. Once
recognised, though for the briefest possible period, as the servant
of Gideon, the presumption of ownership would be sufficient. As
for the rival claims of Zulieme Calvert, Gideon knew enough to
satisfy him that he could dispose of them by a very easy process.
He had not been slow to extract from the prattling Sylvia the
evidence that he desired in respect to our rover, the Señorita de
Montano, and the good ship, the Happy-go-Lucky. Sylvia had
left herself few secrets.

With these cunning thoughts running in his head, and which
matured with great rapidity in a brain that cupidity had sharp-
ened as a cut-and-thrust, Gideon, when about half way from town,
concluded to call a rest.

"Let's set awhile, Sylvia, my gal; let's set, and rest. We've
done the worst half of our work, and the rest's pretty easy. A
leetle rest, now, will be good for both."

"Where shall we set? I'm tired."

" So am I. Here's a log, now, jest convenient to the roadside.
I'll jest poke it first, to scare off the snakes, ef there be any.
Thar! set you down, gal."

And the two sat, cheek by jowl. Then Gideon, putting his
hand good-naturedly on Sylvia's shoulder, began :—

" I've helped you out of the hands of them heathen pirates—"

" But they ain't no pirates, I tell you."

" Oh, yes, my gal, they air, though you kain't understand."

" Yes, I can; and I know they ain't no pirates. They're a
rough, nasty set, and she's a nasty little ship, and that's true;
but they ain't no pirates, Mr. Gideon."

" Wal, don't matter; they're nasty, and I've helped you out
of their hobbles."

" You! I was a-thinkin' 'twas I helped you. I could git
away at any time."

" En why didn't you, I wonder?"

" 'Cause I had nobody to ax me to be married, before you
come."

" Ahem! you still talks about that, Sylvia, as ef you had a sort
of right. But I guess I made it cl'ar to you that sich a thing was
all foolishness."

" But you said it."

" A man what's in a donjin, or is a-drownin', ain't answerable
for what he says! That's the law, Sylvia, and it's sense! So,
jest you shet up about the marriage. Marriage, 'twixt us, is only
so much nonsense. It kain't be."

" Why not?"

" Bekaise, you see, I've got a Mrs. Gid a'ready, and the law
won't let me have tew Mrs. Gids; and, what's more, I don't want
'em. Lord save us from sich a happiness! Next, you see, you're
a nigger—"

" Nigger!" starting up. " No more nigger than you, sah!"

" Oh, yes, Sylvia, you've got the blood, and I aint! My
blood's the nateral, white, pure blood of ' the pilgrims,' that come
out of the Mayflower — genooyne Saxon, without a cross. The
family of Fairchild was about the first that ever planted a foot on
the Plymouth rock, and 'twas a foot in a shoe, my gal; for, you
see, old Gid, my great, great, great, gran'ther, was a shoemaker,
and it stands to reason he always took care to have a good pair

of shoes for himself. The blood's the best, I tell you, in all Plymouth, and Massachusetts bay to boot; and 't wont do to cross it with nigger blood, unless for a good consideration. Now, I 've hearn of some of your Spaniards that had a cross of black, or white, or mestizo; but they had, same time, a smart chance of nigger-property and lands. Ef so be you was one of them sort, now—"

"Yer' you, Mr. Gideon, I 'm no nigger. I 've got white blood —a leetle yellowish, that 's all; and ef you thinks your 'n is so much better, look yer, git yourself out of prisoned next time for yourself! See what your white blood's guine to do, to open them iron rings you had about your legs and arms! You ain't forgot that, I reckon."

"Guess not! Wal, you see, I held up the darbies, and you found the key, and, between us, I worked out! That was all you did. I paddled you over the river, and showed you the way here—"

"You!" and the gipsy laughed merrily at the absurdity. She had not seen so much absurdity in his mode of presenting the manner of his escape from the darbies — he holding up the manacles, and she finding and using the key; but, remembering his troubles in the woods, his claims as a guide seemed to her superlatively ridiculous.

"Now," said he, "I 've showed you what we 've done for one another; and I reckon we 're about square. As for a wife, that, you see, is the onpossible thing; it 's like the onpardonable sin of scripter. You see, thar 's a Madam Gid a'ready, and she 'd tear all to pieces before she 'd hear of it; and, what's more, she 'd have you sent back, tied neck and heels, to this pirate-vessel."

"Oh, do n't say so!"

"She 'd do it, by all that 's bloody, or she 'd make everything crack ag'in!"

"O Mr. Gideon, what shall I do?"

"Wal! to do you a sarvice, for the leetle that you did for me, you must mind your eyes, and some few things I 've got to tell you. First, you 'll have to clap a stopper on your jaws, and never let out about our gittin' out of that ship, or what you did, and what I might happen to say to you in my weakness of heart and tribulations of sperit, when them cussed iron clamps was upon me."

" Yes."

" You 're not to say a word about husband and wife, you hear ?"

" Not a word."

" And you 're to go to my house ; and my wife, Mrs. Gideon — a most sweet, sainted vessel of the sperit — she 'll be your missus instead of that painted harlot, what do you call her ?—"

He was interrupted by a scream — a shriek — a yell of disgust and indignation. And the next moment the girl was on her feet, and darting forward down the road like mad.

" Odds 'ounds ! Where are you goin', and at that mad rate, gal ?"

" You 're a brute — a great British brute — that you are !"

" But where are you goin', gal ?"

" To town — to my missus. I 'll not have any missus of your 'n."

" But the wolves — the tigers !"

" You 're a wolf and a tiger yourself ! I won't stay with you."

" But you must. How would you git on in town, ef 't want for me ? You 'd never find your way."

" The road 's a big one."

" But, before you git a mile, there 's a dozen roads ; and, in town, there 's two hundred houses. You 'd never find the right one."

" I 'll go through town, through every street, and holler for the señora. I kin holler — I kin ! Whoo—whoo—whoop ! O se-ñora ! O my lady Zulieme ! Where are you ? I 'm here ! I 'm lookin' for you. It 's Sylvia that 's callin' for you everywhere."

" Confound the b——! She 'll wake up the Injins for true, ef any of 'em 's a-harborin' about. Hairk ye, gal ! do n't be foolish. I 'll see you safe."

" Whoo—whoo—whoop !"

" Was ever sich a bletherin' b——! Hairk ye, gal ! There 's Injins, as I 'm a livin' sinner !"

" Where ?"

He got up to her, and caught her by the arm.

" They 're in the woods, on the right, on the left, front and rear ; and they 'll have your sculp, and they 'll have mine too, ef you do n't put a bridle on your tongue. Do n't be a fool ! I 'll carry you to your missus — the half-witted Spanish fool! I'll carry you safe. Trust me. I was only a-tryin' you. O Lord, presarve us — women's are sich blasted fools!"

The momentary paroxysm was over. Sylvia was quieted by the Indians, though she snapped her fingers at the wolves. She had an infantile dread, as a Mexican, of red fingers in her hair. She was pacified, but only on conditions.

"Ef you talk ag'in the señora, I'll bawl though there were fifty Injins! I must go to the señora. You must take me to her."

"I will."

"And no more about your Mrs. Gideon, or I'll tell all!"

"To be sure not. I'm still as a suckfish."

"And take your fingers off me. I'm not to be your wife."

"No! to be sure not."

And then the girl yelled again, probably at her painful disappointment. "Some natural tears she shed, but dried them soon." In brief, Sylvia was cunning. The arts of Gideon had not suffered him to conceal the dread of his spouse which he felt. In this, Sylvia found her strength and the secret of her safety. Gideon grew complaisant; and if he did not utterly forego his secret purpose of making her a slave to himself, he yet felt that his policy must be reserved for other circumstances. He did not forego it; but he said to himself —

"It will be easier to fix that, when we've got the señora and her bully under government hatches!"

The result was, that the two reached town in safety; and, though still an hour before day, Sylvia made him take her to the dwelling of Mrs. Perkins Anderson. When the servant, after repeated and clamorous rapping with a stick, was roused to open the door, Sylvia darted in headlong, calling for the señora. Zulieme, awakened by the clamor and well-known voice, started out of bed, and threw open the chamber-door. Mrs. Perkins Anderson was also roused, and appeared at the same moment. Great was the confusion. But Sylvia, as each lady stood before her with candle in hand, soon distinguished her "missus."

"O my lady! O señora! it's me — it's Sylvia! I'm come to you all afoot; and there's wolves and tigers, and the red Injins!"

"Where? where?" demanded both ladies, in a breath.

"In the woods! in the woods! But I'm safe now. O my lady, I'm safe here, I know!"

Gideon Fairchild slipped off in the confusion. In the same hour he made his way to the housing-place of Sylvester. He could find that cunning master of fence, though Belcher and Franks could not; and he found him a willing listener.

He had, in some degree, anticipated the tidings of Gideon. He had but just returned from a secret mission to Colonel Morton, one of the most influential of the council of state. But of this, hereafter. We shall see that Sylvester lost no time in availing himself of the swelling intelligence which was brought by Gideon. But this in due season. Let us to bed now.

# CHAPTER XLI.

### ODDS AND ENDS WITHOUT ENDING.

———"Make yourself welcome!
There's that in every true man which makes entrance
Happier than exit."                              *Old Play.*

THE night of Mrs. Perkins Anderson's glory has arrived!
This night she is to outshine all her competitors in the fashion-
able world of Oyster Point.   She is to take the shine out of Mrs.
Artemisia Bluebottle; the wind out of the sails of Mrs. Araminta
Gaylofty; and utterly to outdo and undo sundry other rivals in
fine "society."   She is about to reach her crowning performance.
*Finis coronat opus!*   In other words, she will put the finishing
stroke to her own career.

And you are not to suppose, dear reader, that we use this word
"glory" unwittingly, and without a due regard to its grand significance.   Glory, like wealth, virtue, and other imposing things,
is yet a matter of relative signification.   It has its degrees, and is
to be measured by the usual experiences of people, rather than
by any intrinsic standards of its own.   The society which rates
pleasure as profit, and gawds as gain; which holds a dance or a
dinner to be the chief end and employment of life; and which aims
at no higher social performance than simply to outshine less clever
circles—in all such society, a *fête* like that of Mrs. Perkins Anderson, attempting exhibitions and attractions such as far exceed
all previous aims and achievements, is a thing of glorious anticipation, and, if successful, unquestionably of most glorious result.
Certainly in our little city of the Carolinas, if she succeeds this
time, people will be sure to say, and to think, that the measure of
her glory has been filled!   She so thinks herself.

And this, dear reader, if only with regard to what has been done already, by those about us, not by those remote.

Now, if you are such a judy as to turn up your ridiculous little turnipy nose at the performance, after all, and say, " Ah! they do the thing far otherwise in France and England," we give you up as wholly immaterial! " Oyster Point," or, to speak with more reverence, Charleston, is not exactly Paris or London. Even to-day, when we have a far cleverer and vastly larger circle than at the period of which we write — far more wealth, better education, better tastes, and a better knowledge of what the world abroad has done and is doing — even to-day, I say, we must yet fall within the category of a petty and remote provincial offshoot from European civilization, striving, greatly in the rear, at the emulation of its beautiful follies, and graceful and interesting absurdities of society and fashion. It is " high life below-stairs" at best; though we have some very simple people among us — very good, but distressingly simple — who really delude themselves with the notion that, if the world is not absolutely staring the eyes out of its head to see what we are doing, the world is making a very poor and unprofitable use of its vision!

But, even in spite of such good people, the truth may as well be told. Though nearly two hundred years older now than at the date of our story, Charleston has not overcome, by its own forward progress, the relative difference between the two hemispheres. She is still provincial in her tastes, habits, aims, and performances; and society — that very society which is most apt to boast of its possessions — yet tinkers on, tied to the foreign car of state or fashion, lacking the courage to assert an independent and well-founded standard of judgment for itself. This is the great secret, this of social independence, for all really great achievement, and which we need to-day almost in as great degree as we did two hundred years ago.

Nay, I am not sure that our need is not greater now than then. We now know so much more! We have a superior consciousness. We are not so rude as then, and not so ignorant of the merits of fig-leaves in the way of costume. We are in closer propinquity with Europe than in that early day; lack the courage which ignorance imparts; and dare not assert ourselves independently, in the face of our own consciousness of deficient resources.

Yet, we have our own intrinsic resources, material and mental, if we only knew how, and had the courage to apply them. But we do not! We might show why this is the case, but this is not the place for it. Enough that, so far as we are concerned, it will not do for *us* to sneer at the short-comings, in fashionable or high life, of the daring little colony at Ashley river in 1684. We make better displays to-day, no doubt, but we are not a whit less servile in our imitations of what is done elsewhere. We are but feeble copyists, after all, of the butterfly-tribes in foreign centres; nay, we take much of this at second and third hands; and Paris and London come to us, diluted, through Gotham, and Boston, and the Quaker-city.

We state all this, if only to protect *old* Charleston, in its little social ambitions, from the sneer of *young* Charleston. You are to-day, Mrs. Frill, but a development of Mrs. Perkins Anderson. The tail is longer and broader, and there is something more of fullness about the pin-feathers; but you are birds of the same feather. I do not see that Mrs. Loftyhead, of 1684, differs in much from Mrs. Furbelow, whom I met last week nightly in all the four fashionable sets of the present city, each of which claims to be "the society" of the place. The costume was very much the same. In latitude and longitude of skirt, Mrs. Furbelow had certainly the advantage. Her hoops were twice the size of those of Mrs. Loftyhead; and, so far as toggery was concerned, the palm would unquestionably be carried off by the former. But, to counterbalance all this, compare the women. The natural red and white, the portly proportions, the honest bone and muscle, of the ancient lady, asserted themselves independently of costume: they needed no plea; asked no indulgence; were superior to all the help of art. She could have done without a skirt; whalebone was useless in her case; and paddings about breast and body, and red varnishes upon the cheeks, were never dreamed of. She had an honest English bust, which could beat bravely against the bosom of a true man, in a wrestle whether of love or hate.

Alas, for the fine lady of to-day, the dashing Mrs. Furbelow! It is really pure absurdity to talk of her as a living animal at all. She needs all her skirts and hoops, and paints, padding, and varnish! And her leathery skin, sallow and yellow, and tallow, at *naked* fallow, would, without these helps, provoke nothing but dis-

gust and revulsion.   And chalk and *rouge* help her little.   Verily, let us not sneer at old times, since such creatures as these are
tolerated by the present.   There was more honesty in their arts
as well as in their flesh and blood; and their manners were decidedly better, though lacking in much of the artifice which chills,
and moulds, and *stales* all modern convention.   Give me honest
flesh and blood, I say, to all these things of paste and putty!
And give me the honest expression of a *native* sentiment, however rude or simple, to the stereotyped persiflage of a circle which
is confessedly ignorant of an idea, and lives only in the security
of a well-memorized commonplace.

But, bless me! we are keeping you from the company, here in
the hall; and the music is growing earnest, and the dancing will
soon begin.   And yet, a little while longer, let us delay you here.
We have something to say of the hostess; to let you into certain
secrets, showing why she especially ought to make her fancy ball
a clever thing.

We have shown you, we trust, that Mrs. Perkins Anderson is
a clever woman.   She is naturally a strong woman; quick, sharp,
acquisitive, discriminative; and with instincts that have a hundred
eyes.   She has also blood; and this, with nothing to do, is at the
bottom of all the evils in her character.   She must expend her
superfluous energies.   Lacking regular duties, she will be apt to
do so mischievously, and in consonance with certain very natural
instincts.   This is one of the secret causes of vicious tendencies
on the part of people of wealth, who have also health!   But we
must not be essayical.

Well, Mrs. Perkins Anderson is a clever woman.   She has had
opportunities; and a certain probation of toil, in her early life,
will enable her to do clever things which her neighbors will hardly
attempt.   As an Edinburgh mantuamaker, or milliner, and what-
not, she had acquired sundry experiences in the offskirts of good
society, if only by manufacturing its skirts.   She is a good clipper
and cutter; had been, *on dit*, a *royal* clipper: by which we do not
mean a three-decker or a yacht, but, in literal language, a manu-
facturess of the robes and dresses of certain members of the royal
family; that is, when they happened, in Edinburgh, to feel the
lack of a skirt.   And it may be in London, too, for the lady lived
several years in that pleasant little borough-town, and carried on

—we must use a vulgarism of our moderns — the profession of the *artiste of modes*. But the true secret of her claims to royal favor consists, probably, in her having been employed as a costumer for the theatre, where she made the robes of princes and princesses, lords and ladies, and accordingly picked up some notions at once of high art and high people. This was one of the scandals against the lady, put in circulation in Charleston by the envious Mrs. Golightly — a lady who has left a very large and rather light progeny behind her. No matter how Mrs. Anderson gets her knowledge — she has it; and, with her acknowledged cleverness, you may be sure it will do smart things. She will get up *her* part of this fancy ball with grace, spirit, and effect. She will help such of her neighbors as are willing to ask for assistance. She will devise suitable characters for certain persons, and these she will lesson in their proper personation: she has a talent for this business, and would have made a dextrous manager of private theatricals. She will possibly pass to these, when she has once carried through her masquerade ball successfully.

Successfully? That is according to certain provincial standards. Don't be unreasonable, and expect too much. It is doubtful if, according to the *ideal* standards, we could get up a successful masquerade ball anywhere in this country! It is reported that when Mr. Dickens's visit to New York was in contemplation, and it was proposed to lionize him, one of the leaders of the fashionables of that city said, "Can we make him fashionable?" And this query was but a natural introduction to what followed. Tableaux, from the writings of the author, were chosen, as the most grateful mode of paying him homage; and it was then that the fashionables were compelled to buy his books and study his characters. Dickens himself soon discovered the sort of hands into which he had fallen. He would have found twenty times the intelligence among the weekday, working world, which his entertainers had ignored. So, if you, dear brethren, build upon the people who claim to be "in society," as the parties best calculated to personate the grand and gorgeous in history and the drama, you will find it politic, before you begin, to put them through a course of the primers and Mother Goose. Do not, therefore, be unreasonable in your anticipations, touching the *projêt* of our Mrs. Perkins Anderson.

For, look you, she has but two rooms, twenty feet square, and a piazza, forty feet long, for all her company. The chambers will be used for 'tiring-rooms; and there shall be one of these for the tough, the other for the tender gender. And the supper-table shall be spread in a shed-room; but she will give them a famous supper of solids.

But there is no ice, alas! Ice is a modern invention!

No; but the water shall be cool. It is kept in a sort of "monkeys," a well-known porous vessel of that day, which was greatly in use; and these shall be hung in the trees all around the house, wrapped with wet blankets: and you will, as you drink, be forced to admit that our ancestors might be content to endure to live, even though ice was not invented!

There were no ice-creams, of course; but there were the West-India fruits, sweetmeats, jams, pines, berries, grenadines, all in sirup or crusted sugar. And there were

> "Fragrant jellies, fresh from Samarcand,
> And lucent sirups tinct with cinnamon."

Ay, and ginger shall be sweet in the mouth too, as well as hot. There will be no lack, be sure, of any of the cates and delicacies known in that day and region. Champagne was not; but there was Madeira, and (more popular yet) there were bowls of punch, a rare marriage of the strong, the sour, and the sweet, bringing about such harmonies as were apt to "seize the prisoned soul and lap it in Elysium." And, as the invited guests probably said to themselves and to one another—

"There shall be no want of music;

"There shall be free *footing;* and—

"Supper at twelve o'clock!"—

A very interesting programme, scarcely inferior to that usual at the present day.

We have shown what was the population of Charleston at the date of our history. We have also given some idea of the rude, wild, irregular state of its topography. But a few more words on this head, by way of description, may not be amiss. We have before us now a plan of the infant city, as laid off in 1680. Fancy, then, a great shoulder of bacon, with the knuckle at what is now "the Battery." On the *east* side there is an irregular plat, with *three* main streets running south and north, crossed by four others running east and west. There are lines drawn, which indicate bastions and a wall, encircling the whole. These lines are limits which you will find now all comprised within Market street on the north, Meeting street on the west, Water street on the south, and the Bay on the east; and half of this is a quagmire, and quite unsettled. South, west, north, and east, the ground which the city now occupies is perforated by creeks that stretch up almost to a meeting, from Ashley river on the west and Cooper on the east. We count no less than ten of these creeks, so intersecting the territory between the southern terminus of the city and Calhoun street, which crosses it now nearly at the centre. Between each of these creeks there is a little farmstead; scarcely more than one. Here is a ricefield; here a cornfield; here a vegetable-garden; and here a brick-kiln. The watch-house stands at the southern extremity, wholly beyond call of the citizens. There is a "block-house," with two pieces of cannon contiguous, looking out on Ashley river. There is another watch-house, or court of guard, at the east end of Broad street, where the custom-house now stands; and, at half a dozen points, the sites are indicated for future bastions, which were not raised for ten years after. The great avenues of Meeting and King streets were laid out, and the former opened for several miles into the interior; but, in bad weather, these were almost impassable. All the creeks were bold ones, navigable by boats into the very heart of the town. Their banks were fringed with shrubbery, and sometimes their margins covered with marsh. No wonder that Molyneaux got his shoes muddied! The wonder is, that, in such limits, living so crudely, there should be such people as Mrs. Anderson and Lady Highflier; that there should be balls and parties; that ambition should soar to such a pitch as to achieve a masquerade. It will be seen that Mrs. Anderson was no ordinary woman!

Though giving all help and instruction to every pretty and young, and some ugly and antique damsels — antiques, but not gems — our excellent hostess was especially heedful to instruct her beautiful little guest in the way that she should [not?] go. She had forgotten, had foregone, none of her projects. She had carried out her purpose to caparison Zulieme as Titania. She had persuaded the Honorable Mr. Keppel Craven to don the

19

golden armor of Oberon.   Precious little did Zulieme know of
Titania; but she could frisk and dance like a faerie, and she could
be deceived by a clown!   Now, Keppel Craven was no clown,
though he wore his own ears.   Mrs. Anderson was pleased to say
to him that Oberon was born to conquest; that his part was, not
to fail; that he could *not* fail, with proper audacity; and that, if
he would only comprehend his real attractions, there could be no
apprehensions of failure.   Certainly, her lessons were quite enough
to make him impudent.   She designed that they should make him
more.   Mere impudence may *say* saucy things, and, with proper
encouragement, encountering a weaker object, may be bold enough
to *do* them; but it is the will — the reckless resolve not to fail,
but to carry a purpose through, without heeding check, and despite of hinderance — this was the sort of spirit with which Mrs.
Perkins Anderson would infuse the Honorable Mr. Craven.

The better to help him in his progress, she bestowed her counsels on Zulieme.   When the latter happened to say —

"Where can Harry be?   I wonder if he will come to-night?"
she answered:—

"What matter if he comes or not?   What's the good of him,
or any husband?   Marriage, my dear Zulieme, is only a tyran-
nous bondage, invented by husbands, who seek to keep by law
what they can not keep by love!   Their jealousy and our cowardice are the secrets of this tyranny.   It is against Nature, which
is the proper teacher; and where we feel a liking, there we may
entertain a love.   What! because we have been mistaken in the
objects of our affections, shall we be tied to a hateful object for
ever?   To be sure not!   I'm certain, if I saw anybody to love
better than Perkins Anderson, I'd give him my heart directly."

"But would that be right, Charlotte?"

"Right!   What's right?   Isn't Nature right?   Don't she
know best?   Marriage, where the nature is not prepared to love,
is only—"

But we care not to repeat.   The argument is already well
known, and is in the mouths of a good many strong-minded women.

"Ah! but I love Harry," said poor little Zulieme, with a sigh.

"You!   You love that stern British brute, as you call him?"

"Yes, I do! — I suppose because he is a brute!   I wish he'd come to-night.  I'm sure he can outdance all these people.  That young Craven, though he's a most funny little fellow, can't dance with Harry."

"Oh! don't let *him* hear you call him little."

"But he *is* little!"

"No!  He's of good size enough — not to compare with Harry Calvert, of course — *he's* a sort of monster — but a most superior cavalier.  Ah, what a conquest you've made, Zulieme!  Keppel Craven loves you to distraction."

"He's a fool for it; for I don't love him!"

"Oh, don't say so, Zulieme!  If ever woman loved a man, I'm sure you love him."

"Me!"

"Yes, indeed, and he's such a proper match for you!"

"Match for me!  Why, Charlotte!  And I'm married already."

"What if you are?  Does your being married make you a slave?  Does it forbid that you shall feel?  Can it?  No!  And, if it can't, it's only hypocrisy to pretend that it does.  I tell you, Zulieme, marriage is a cunning invention of the men, the better to make slaves of us poor women!"

"But you're not a slave, Charlotte! and I'm not a slave!"

"But if we should happen to love another man than our husband, Zulieme — we can't help it, you know — shall we be denied to do so?  And doesn't marriage deny it? and ain't that bondage? and ain't bondage slavery?  Ay, we poor women are the merest slaves!  But we are not to submit.  I know that you do love Keppel Craven, and he's worthy of it, and I don't see the harm of it!'

"Well, it's strange, Charlotte.  I don't think I care a bit about him; and I'm very sure if Harry thought he was making love to me, he'd wring his neck!"

"Wring his neck?  Shocking!  Dear Zulieme, you must drop all these horrid phrases."

"But he'd *do* it, Charlotte!"

"Well, if he could, perhaps; because it's the nature of tyranny to enforce its laws by violence.  But, if Keppel Craven loved me, and I him, precious little would I care for its laws, and bonds, and rites!  I'd—"

Enough of this!    Enough for us to know that the true nature
of our little Spanish señora is not understood — even, perhaps, by
those who know her best.    Mrs. Perkins Anderson, at all events,
has been making some mistakes, in spite of all her cleverness.
Zulieme listens to her social and moral philosophy with some coolness, possibly some impatience.    But Zulieme's passions are not
to be reached through her mind.    She could not be argued into
sinful fancies.    Intellectually, she is a thing all shallows — limpid as a brook at play in breeze and sunlight; and her training,
in a secluded *hacienda*, among simple people, has not tended to
enlighten her passions, though it may have increased the spright-
liness of her fancies.    All the morals of Mrs. Perkins Anderson
were wasted upon her; and she thought only of the dance, and
not of the dancer, even though he should be the Honorable Keppel Craven.

Suppose the company to be assembling fast.    There are coaches
at the door.    The "shay" was one of the vehicles of Charleston
in that day, and the "chair;" and these were the most numerous.
Some of the gentlemen came on horseback; none on foot.    The
streets were without sidewalks, and Mrs. Perkins Anderson's
"circle" contemplated no such persons as needed their own legs
for any other than dancing-purposes.    It was, accordingly, a staggering circumstance, when the servant in green-and-scarlet livery
was required to admit our Lieutenant Molyneaux, even though
in the garb of a cavalier, when he presented himself on foot.
Molyneaux came under the guidance of Sproulls, who was talkative, and addressed him all the way as "captain."    That our lieutenant did not seem startled by this title, and made no remark
upon it, was calculated to confirm Sproulls in his suspicion that
he was piloting the famous rover.    But Molyneaux had been
made somewhat familiar with the title by the free use which
the politic old rogue, Fowler, had made of it, in winning him
over to his purposes.    Sproulls was exceedingly communicative.
and pretty free in his comments upon the fine women about town,
who, according to his report, were quite "fast" enough for our
own day.    But his scandals were sufficiently natural to one who
was not admitted within the sacred precincts.    He pointed out
the house of Mrs. Anderson, and stood at a little distance, to see
him enter.    There was some delay in this proceeding.    The house

was already pretty well filled; and the stout negro who officiated as porter was, as we have said, quite staggered to see the stranger present himself on foot. The fine clothes certainly made their impression; but, no horse — no carriage! The fellow parleyed with our lieutenant:—

"But, I say, maussa, whay you hitch you' hoss?"

"Horse? I had no horse!"

"Carriage — shay — den?"

"I did n't ride, fellow! I walked!"

"Ki! maussa! wha' for you walk? You hab ticket for come?"

"Ticket be ——! What do I want with a ticket? Stand aside, fellow! Clear the gangway; and none of your —— palaver!"

The lieutenant suited the action to the word; and, hurling the servant aside contemptuously, with no little emphasis of muscle, he proceeded to enter the house.

## CHAPTER XLII.

"You have displaced the mirth; broke the good meeting,
    With most admired disorder."                    *Macbeth.*

MOLYNEAUX'S proceedings, at entrance, were not of a sort to escape notice. He was rough-handed in his practice: the negro was hurled aside as if he had been a stone. Pompey was a spoiled negro, as are half of the old family-servants of the South. He was a fellow apt to put himself upon his dignity. At the treatment of Molyneaux, so new to his experience, he made lamentable outcry. His mistress was upon the watch. Never lady, about to achieve glory in good society, more vigilant. She was instantly in the piazza. She encountered our lieutenant at the threshold, and with no little stateliness.

"Sir!" said she, haughtily.

"Ma'am!" quoth he.

"Whom, sir, have I the honor to receive?"

Molyneaux was an Irishman and a rover. Whatever the degree of bashfulness which belongs to the one character, it was more than relieved by the boldness which should always accompany the other. In spite of his origin, Molyneaux was nowise wanting in proper self-esteem.

"Madam," said he, "you are, I fancy, the lady of the house. I am a friend of your guest, the Señora Zulieme Calvert. I wish to see her."

"Hush! hush! for God's sake, sir! That name is not to be spoken here." ˙

The language of the hostess was that of trepidation. Our bashful Irishman was evidently wanting in a knowledge of "the ropes."

"Ah! I see; but I am her friend, her old acquaintance."

" Who are you, sir?"

" Why, to tell the truth, madam, I do n't know but that a like caution should forbid me giving my own name. But if you are in the secrets of the Señora—"

" Still, sir, it needs not that I should know yours. But I can guess them. Perhaps, sir, the shortest and best course will be to suffer you to see the lady."

" That's it, madam. There can be no harm done."

" None, sir. Please follow me."

And she took him to the rear of the piazza—in the background—where he could remain unseen by new-comers. She then brought Zulieme to him. He lifted his mask at her approach.

" What! you, Molyneaux?" cried Zulieme, in tones of pleasure, offering her hand. " I 'm glad to see you."

" I knew you would be, señora," responded our bashful Irishman, grasping her hand warmly, and carrying it to his lips.

" But where's Harry, and where's the ship?"

" I have not seen the captain for a week."

" Not for a week! And where is he, then?"

" On a cruise somewhere, which he keeps secret."

" Ah! well — and what brings you here?"

" The felicity of seeing you."

" Well, you 're come at the right time, and I see you 're dressed for the occasion, as if you knew of it."

" To confess a truth, I *did* know of it; and here you see me, as I am."

" Well, now, Charlotte—"

Mrs. Anderson was present during the scene, a silent but not an unobservant spectator.

" Well, my dear, how would you dispose of your friend?"

" Why, to be sure, have him in among the rest."

" But is there no danger?"

" Danger! from what?"

" Danger, madam, is a familiar acquaintance. I have slept with it nightly for seven years!"

Mrs. Anderson thought to herself: " The man's well to look on; he is in courtly costume; he will be a handsome addition to my party; and the very fact that he is unknown, and can not be well suspected by anybody, will make him a lion. But we must make him keep close."

"Zulieme, my dear, there can, perhaps, be no danger, if your friend, Mr. ———?"

A pause.

"Mr. Molyneaux — Lieutenant Molyneaux — next officer to Harry in the ship—"

"If Mr. Molyneaux will be careful not to forego his disguise for a moment."

"Wear my mask all the while, madam, you mean?"

"Exactly, sir."

"Egad, madam, I can do it, and will, if you require it; but I'm not much used to disguisings, and my face, madam—"

He lifted his visor for the benefit of Mrs. Anderson, and by the action properly finished the sentence. The smiling Mrs. Anderson found the appropriate words —

"Is not one that you need be ashamed of."

"'Gad, madam, you have the proper idea!"

"Well, sir, your costume is that of—"

"Sir Edward Molyneaux, madam, who had the honor, long ago, to be a frequent attendant at the court of his majesty King Charles I. He lost his head, madam—"

"Enough, sir. Do not lose yours, if you please. I know enough of your ship and captain to know that you, as well as he, would be in some danger here if discovered. You will exercise the utmost caution. Go in, my love — go in, Zulieme — and we shall follow you. Be pleased not to know your friend, till I introduce him as Sir Edward Molyneaux."

Zulieme disappeared, and, after a reasonable pause, the lady of the house followed her into the ballroom, and was followed in turn by Sir Edward. In this character he was formally introduced to a number of persons, male and female, who were all designated in character. Many of these were known to the party through their disguises; but our Sir Edward was a mystery, and so naturally provoked no small curiosity, especially as he boasted a fine leg, and was altogether a very graceful fellow in his court costume.

Costume or fancy balls are very rarely successful, in any dramatic sense of the term. Very few persons are equal to the im-

personation of marked characters, even where they are acquainted
fully with the biography of him or her whom they represent.
Actors, like poets, are born, not made.   But fine dresses, and gay
humors, and lively music, and our own exercise in the dance, will
carry off an affair of the kind with sufficient *eclat*.   Anyhow, and
with all its defects, a masquerade ball is a great improvement on
that of mere existing society.   There is more privilege, more
piquancy, and so much more variety!   You are to understand
that this of Mrs. Anderson, though pettily provincial in a thousand respects, was yet perfectly delightful, for the time it lasted,
to all the parties engaged in it; and even the Honorable Messrs.
Craven and Cavendish permitted themselves for a brief season to
forget the more imposing conventions of the court from which they
were in temporary exile.

But the affair had its *désagrémens* even to these courtier gen-
tles.   The Honorable Keppel was particularly annoyed at the
cool familiarity which the imposing stranger, Sir Edward Molyneaux, exhibited in his intercourse with the fair Zulieme.   Molyneaux put himself very soon at home; and the very experience
of his rover-life rendered him a confident and presumptuous wooer.
He strode the hall with the same command and freedom which he
exhibited on the quarter-deck, when no sailor dared to pass bè-
tween the wind and his nobility.   He sat beside the lovely Zulieme, the moment a seat became vacant; and more than once he
took her hand, and, toying with her fan, she was seen to rap him
playfully over his fingers, evidently to chide or check some devoted speech.   But she smiled gayly as she did so, and he had
his retort,—would playfully seize the fan, and agitate the atmosphere about her into breezes rather than zephyrs, being but
slightly accustomed to deal with such delicate implements.

"The d——d impudent puppy!" muttered the Honorable Keppel.   "Who can he be?"

"He seems an old acquaintance," replied Cavendish; "but he's
evidently no Spaniard.  I begin to tremble for our guineas, Keppel."

"D—nation, yes!   I must see Madam Anderson."

"The worst is, the señorita seems wonderfully pleased with his
attentions."

"Oh, she's pleased with all attentions!   The kitten appears
hardly to care with what mouse she plays."

19*

"He's no mouse! He carries himself like a bully, a roystering soldier from the Low Countries."

"We must find him out. Ha, for the *coranto!*"

And, so speaking, the Honorable Keppel darted across the room to Zulieme, and extended his hand to take her out. She rose and gave it him, but Molyneaux interposed promptly:—

"How's this? Was I not to dance with you, Zulieme?"

"*Zulieme!*" muttered Craven. "Dem'd free!"

"The next dance," she answered, to Molyneaux; "not this."

Molyneaux growled out some guttural, which had no softness in it, and glared through his vizard at the effeminate courtier as he bore the lady into the area. With an oath, he muttered—

"I should like to wring the fellow's neck!"

"Who's your friend?" asked the Honorable Keppel of the señorita.

"He? why, he's—" and then she paused.

"He's who?"

"Oh, don't ask me! I *do* know, but I can't tell you. But, no matter—he's nobody."

And they whirled away under the call of the music.

Molyneaux followed them round the room, in all their evolutions, like a grim Afrite following a fairy fresh from Yemen; and whenever his eyes met those of Craven, the mutual flash of each showed that their instincts had already made them bitter enemies. But dear little Zulieme saw nothing of this. She was exhilarated; laughed merrily with her partner; yielded herself voluptuously to all the caprices of the dance; went through the *corantos*, the *lavoltas*, the *delicias*, with all the gusto of an eastern *almée*—little dreaming that Molyneaux was writhing with rage, and fumbling the hilt of his rapier, and muttering his prayers that somebody, of the masculine gender, might look at him and sneeze!

But it was soon his turn to dance, and Craven's to writhe. The next dance brought them into the same circle, but this time Molyneaux danced with Zulieme, and Keppel with another damsel. And now was Molyneaux all exultation, for Zulieme was just as full of glee and buoyant fancy as when she danced with Craven; yielded herself just as fondly to his embraces; and scarcely seemed to heed the graceful voluptuary, as he swam, in corresponding mazes, with another fair partner, directly opposite.

But Craven was not so indifferent.

"The dem'd puppy!" he muttered, whenever his eyes met with those of Molyneaux; and when the two danced toward each other, it could be seen that there was a something mutually defiant in their manner. There was a haughty toss of the head on one side, and an insolent bull-fling of the other forward; and the parties each felt as if the occasion were approaching when they must surely take each other by the throat. The awkwardness of Molyneaux in the dance nearly led to this result in the progress of this very round. Whirling Zulieme about, and following her movements very unequally with his own, he found himself entangled with a group, and, setting down one of his feet with emphasis, as if to secure himself steadily in position, he planted the heavy heel on the pointed toe of the Honorable Keppel, who was just then gliding, with zephyr-like sweep, beside him.

We know not what was the exact condition of Craven's toes. He possibly had a corn or two which no delicate surgery had yet been able to extirpate. His pumps were perhaps new, and tight as new. One thing was certain: that setting down of his foot by Molyneaux had been terribly emphatic. The Honorable Keppel writhed under it with a bitter cry; doubled up his body, downward from his shoulders; dropped the hand of his partner — her waist, perhaps — while she went over headlong into another set; the victim, meanwhile, catching up the suffering foot in his hand, and muttering a fearful malediction upon the elephantine hoof that caused the injury.

A hoarse laugh from Molyneaux, which he could not suppress, disgusted the hearers, and even aroused Zulieme.

"You've hurt him!" she said; and he muttered, in reply —

"D—n him! not half enough."

She dropped his arm; and, hearing his insolent laugh, Craven now approached and whispered in his ear —

"You shall answer for this!"

"To be sure, I will; and you shall answer too!" was the fierce reply, a little too loudly uttered, since it reached other ears than those for whom it was meant. There was a buzz about the room, and some confusion. Mrs. Anderson began to fear that her party might fail yet. Craven, with a nice propriety, whispered again in Molyneaux's ear, as he saw the hostess approaching:—

"We understand each other. Let us keep up appearances. Take my hand, that it may seem as if the matter were amicably settled."

And he extended his hand as he spoke, lifted his vizard, and smiled graciously, with a bow. Molyneaux caught the proffered hand with a vice-like gripe which made the other wince.

" Ay, we understand each other !"

The action arrested the confusion for awhile: the dance was resumed; refreshments were served; the chat once more became hilarious; and, leaving the company in a good humor, we will change the scene to the lodgings of Sproulls, where we left Sam Fowler, the old salt and pirate — " Squint-eye Sam" — beginning, with a few kindred spirits, a night of grosser debauchery.

## CHAPTER XLIII.

### THE TIGER BREAKS THE TRAP.

" *Countess.* If thou be he, then art thou prisoner.
*Talbot.* Prisoner? To whom?
*Countess.* To me, bloodthirsty lord;
        And for that cause I trained thee to my house. . . .
*Talbot.* Ha! ha! ha!" SHAKESPEARE.

THERE is always a latent infirmity in crime, that serves finally to defeat the efforts and designs of the most vigorous sort of manhood. Crime, in fact, presupposes a defect of mind, as it does of character. The most vigorous and thinking criminal shall yet be a victim to certain shortcomings of calculation, or some qualifying weaknesses, which shall operate to the ultimate defeat of all his purposes. And if this be the fact in the case of those who are really well and vigorously endowed, what must be the defect in the case of a coarse ruffian like our old pirate, Sam Fowler? This wretch had been lapped in crime and suckled on infamy. He had been made callous by brawls and bloodshed; reckless by self-indulgence and drunkenness. Yet he could conceive great purposes of outlawry, had his ambition for rule, and aimed at a certain control and supremacy over his fellow-men. But, even while he planned conspiracy, which required the utmost prudence as well as the utmost resolution, he was so little capable of restraining his licentious habits, that, though the success of his projects required the greatest sobriety — and while in a hostile city, where a reward was offered for his head — he had not the necessary strength which should keep from drunkenness, nor the degree of caution which might shelter from detection.

So, accordingly, while the vanities of his colleague and superior,

Molyneaux, led him to exhibit his legs at the *bal costume* of Madam Anderson, he (Fowler) regaled himself at Sproulls's, with a villanously low circle, on the strongest potations and the heaviest meats.

Sproulls was in *quasi* alliance with the keen and cunning Sylvester, *alias* Stillwater. It is needless to try and fathom the secret between these two persons. But it is certain that Sproulls was much more decidedly the agent of Stillwater than the friend of Fowler. Whether he wished to acquire a claim on the favors of Stillwater, or that he desired to obtain a clue to the hiding-place of the rover Calvert, matters nothing to us. His motive need not tax our inquiry. Enough that he fancies Molyneaux to be Calvert. He has contrived so to report to Sylvester, and to furnish all the clues to the present employment of the lieutenant. The next matter is to secure Fowler.

This required management. Fowler is an old sea-dog, of vigorous frame, well armed, and of determined courage. A city police is not always equal to a hand-and-hand encounter with a desperado, and it requires a very considerable superiority of force before the attempt will be made. But the preliminaries have been overcome. There is a hot supper — steaks, oysters, and other good things — at Sproulls's den, the locality of which may yet be designated, somewhere in the purlieus of Queen street and the bay. Hot rum-punch is in abundance, and no better beverage is asked for until the period arrives when, the taste silenced, the appetite calls for something more potent still, and the naked rum throws upon his back that champion whose heels the sweetened liquor only served to trip.

Four or five stout fellows have consented to meet Sproulls and his friend in good fellowship. The steaks and oysters smoked from separate dishes. The foaming liquors, hot and cold, went freely round. Sam Fowler sat as sovereign, well satisfied. He had impudence, and a ruffian-like humor; was fond of horse-play; and dealt out the most brutal oaths, as boys fling cherry-stones about. The demureness of his companions, at first, seemed to him the natural tribute of inexperience and inferior spirits to his own superiority. Every brute has his vanity. He found this sort of tribute grateful.

" You'll git bolder, fellows, when you 've ploughed the seas for twenty-five years; when you've tasted the salt of a lee shore; when you've split every sail in a 'norther;' and been so far up in the wind's eye, that you'd only got to stretch out your hand to take the man in the moon by the beard! A week's maroon, now, would make men of you all. A desarted island, without a tree or shrub, and nothin' but a pocketful of biscuit, a gun without a lock, and no way to git your grub but by listening when a turtle grunts, as she's a-marchin' up the sands to drop her eggs! That's the sort of schoolin', to take the pip off a man-chicken's tongue! A week of that sort of idication, my lads, would make something of you all, and bring out the pluck. It's life you wants; and ef you've the heart to l'arn, say so, fellows, and ship with me, outward bound and return v'yage, with shares of eights upon the venture. What do you say to that?"

The cue was to humor the ruffian.

"Well," said one, and then another. "It's monstrous poor sort of life that we lives here — hardly gits our grub, and more salt than sugar in it. I'm clear for any venture that'll give us a chance at a better sort of life."

"Shill have it, my lads. I'll be ready for you. You'll have to sign articles, lads — not much — only to have an understandin' of the tarms, and the rest's easy, and the money sure. I've known three hundred pounds starling per man, out of a single v'yage of two months. Bales always ready for our cargo, and markets right and left, east, west, north, south — everywhere, jest like here in Charlestoun, where the folks sing night and day, even when they're a-prayin'.

"'Come along, ye jolly brothers,
That do range the Spanish main!
Bring us in the precious galleons,
With their gold and silver grain:
Ye've brought us treasure oft before,
So cut and come again!'

"But — fellows! am I to do all the drinkin'? I say drink, though it blows a harricane! You'll never be up to a spankin' breeze ef you don't l'arn the uses of a bottle. Grog's the whole secret of all that's good and lucky: grog's courage; grog's good luck; grog's sense and sperit; grog makes the cargo, and grog knows how to spend it. Drink, I say! By the holy pipers, I'll lay my cutlash over the first nose that I see holdin' off from the punch-bowl! Up with it, fellows — down with it — let's hear it give an honest guggle as it goes down a wide swallow!"

Suppose, in this speech, the action suited to the word. The burly ruffian actually stood up, tankard in one hand and naked cutlass in the other; and, while quaffing the contents of the cup, he flourished the weapon over the heads of his companions.

Now, Sproulls's assistants, though not exactly of the class of Dogberrys, were yet very far from being familiar with the sharp, prompt practice of our ancient buccaneer; and their heads *shyed*, from side to side, as the gleaming cutlass waved to and fro. They eagerly filled their cups and swallowed.

"No heeltaps, you milksops! Drink deep as death and d—nation! I'm not goin' to palaver over punch. Drink, I say!— swallow like a suckfish — swallow, and be gentlemen-rovers, fit for the high-seas, and a ready market! Ef you do n't, I'll make a short swipe of you! Ef you does, I'll know you to be men of good, warm blood — able to write your names under a 'Jolly Roger!'"

He had his will of them; and he laughed in half scorn, half merriment, to see the avidity with which they swallowed — the alacrity with which they obeyed him.

"That's goin' it honest! I like a free drinker. The fellow that skulks his liquor ain't honest. I say, now, write down yer names on that paper! You're entered for a cruise."

And he cast down a paper before them. The fellows looked blank — looked at one another. The task now put before them seemed to promise more peril than the punch.

"What's this for?" said one.

"What's that to you, blast me! Sign!"

And again the cutlass was flourished over the heads of the party. They signed, not daring to stop to read what was written — signed to a man! And the old pirate coolly gathered up the paper, and pocketed it away, as if it had been a deed of value; though he was now evidently too drunk to reason correctly upon any subject. It was habit and instinct that governed his actions.

He chuckled, with all the self-complacency of an ancient despot, when he found them so submissive.

"That's it! all right!" said he; "you're bound for the v'yage. No backin' out now. Sworn to the Jolly Roger. But it's a free life, fellows — pleasure all the time! Nothin' but fun, and fightin', and plenty of liquor; and lots of fine gals at New Providence and all along the keys. It's a glorious life. Fill up, now, I say, and let's drink to the Jolly Roger!"

They filled! he filled! the cutlass flourishing in fearful proximity to every head, and Fowler walking to and fro, as he spoke, with the air of a commander upon the quarter-deck, ready to board the enemy. But, as they carried the cups to their mouths, he stopped:—

"Where's that blasted son of a yardstick? where's Sproulls?"

"He's jest gone for a minute. He'll be back soon."

"He's skulked a matter of five glasses. I'll take the d——d fellows ears off, close to his top! What's he, that he should skulk? Why ain't he here, I say? Who's here to answer for him? Does I come to visit him, and he sneak off and leave me to take care of myself! Nobody to ax me to liquor! I'm a decent man, and can't ax myself: it's for him to ax. I won't drink of any d——d, blasted liquor, when the right owner do n't ax me. I'll shave his ears off, blast me!"

The desperado fairly overawed the proper men around him. The cutlass again flourished about in terrible closeness to their heads. One of them, more bold than the rest, endeavored to pacify him. He said:—

"Sproulls is my friend. He's a good fellow. Do n't mean anything oncivil — would n't for the world. He said he *had* to go. Begged me to do the purlite; and *I* ax you, captain — *I* ax you, in *his* name — take a pull — take a pull with me!"

"D—n his name! Who's he? I'll take a pull with *you*, in your own name. What's *your* name?"

"Jim Atkinson."

"Jim Atkinson? Ah! you've signed"—taking out and trying to examine the paper. "Well, stand up, old fellow; you're a man of size; you've got the inches! I'll take a pull with *you*. Fill up all, fellows. A pull all round with Jim Atkinson. Hurrah for the Jolly Roger! Drink that, boys, ef you wants to be blest."

They drank.

"I've got the benefits! I must be off now. See to the boat. See to the lieutenant. He's a fool! Footin' it with women, when he ought to be drivin' along the coast, and down for the gulf! But, no matter: life's a long day. So long as the liquor lasts, and there's good feedin', no need to hurry. But you're all booked, and we must be off soon. I count on you as my fellows. You shall have a glorious swing of it. Not in your shoes, you boobies! do n't think that! No man need fear the gallows who's got the sense to die a wet death. We'll do it in stockin'-feet! Another pull, my beauties, and then I'm off! I've eat a'most too many of them d——d 'ysters! They're watery. But the punch ain't! Another pull, all round, and hurrah for the Jolly Roger! You'll be all ready at mess-call!"

And every hand grasped the noggin, though possibly none but Fowler emptied the vessel. He did this to the last drop. Then, thrusting his cutlass home, he strode off toward the door.

"I'll give you the sign when it's time to go aboard; not quite ready yit. Git stores in the locker; work the ship round first. You shall know when the time comes. Hard a-port, I say! Hey, there!—a cup! One more cup; and then, a free sheet and a flowin' sea!"

It was with some disquiet that his companions beheld him prepared to depart, and resolved upon it. It was against their instructions that he should be suffered to go. Sproulls's secret words had been emphatic:—

"You'll have no trouble with him so long as the liquor lasts. He'll stop till daylight. Ply him fast. Drink with him, man by man. But keep him till I get back. We must have him fast by the heels. It's a hundred pounds sterling in our pockets; and every man shall have his five pounds, remember that! I'll bring a proper officer, and we can fix him fast when I get back. But should he offer to go, jump upon him, all of you, and get him down, and rope him. You're strong enough, each of you, and there's four of you. Keep him, fair or foul—see that you keep him till I get back."

The instructions seemed quite natural and easy to the hearers when first delivered; but, since then, their humors had cooled. The course of Fowler had been so decidedly desperate, that what seemed to promise so feasibly at the outset, became now quite a hazardous measure. So far from taking the initiative, in keeping him at his liquor, he had rather forced it upon them; and his fear-

ful cutlass-flourishes had not suffered them to prevaricate at their
punch.    They could not play him, and sham their own drinking;
and each felt that his potations had done something toward disturbing his own equilibrium.

Besides, the reckless demeanor of the ruffian; his physical proportions; the dexterity with which he flourished his weapon; and
the discovery which they made of the mahogany-butts of pistols
protruding from his breast—all combined to beget an extreme
degree of prudence on the part of these valiant citizens, which did
not argue any great promptitude, should it become necessary for
them to jump upon him, as one man, and lay him out like a turtle,
on his back.

Still, something must be done.   He was evidently resolved on
his departure; and the fellow who had played spokesman before,
now taking the *parole*, as if warmed by his beverages to eloquence,
began his work as insidiously as he could.

" Sorry, captain, that Sproulls hain't got back time enough to
do his honest drinkin' with you—"

" D—n Sproulls, for a sneak !"

" So say I, too !   D—n Sproulls !   But so long as his liquor
lasts, I 'm for it.   So, what say you, boys, to a pull all round?   I
say, captain, this punch is glorious, and there 's a smart chance in
the bowl yet."

" D—n punch !   The sweet 's too snakish.   Give me the naked
Jamaica !"

The rum was placed before him — a huge, square, black bottle,
containing a gallon.   The pirate filled, taking his rum this time
*in puris naturalibus*.   But the rest began filling from the punch-
bowl.

" H–ll !" he cried; " am I to take the naked creetur, and you
be swizzin' out of the sweetened sarpent?   And you wants to sail
under the ' Jolly Roger,' too !   Blast my peepers, if they shall
look on and see sich infarnal hypocrisy !   There 's for your d——d
wash !"

And, with a tremendous sweep of the arm, he hurled the punch-
bowl from the table, sending the beverage in every direction, and
shattering the vessel into a thousand pieces.

" The naked sinner, fellows !   Kiss the black jug, and show that
you 've got the strength for a fair wrestle with the naked sperit !"

The demonstration was sufficient, and they drank with him. The drunken despot would not allow them to water the liquor; they must take it raw. .Luckily for them, his eyes were quite too humid to suffer him to see whether they filled to the brim or not. The former spokesman, in still more subdued accents, though affecting a frank good-humor which he did not feel, cried out—

"That's right! The sweetened liquor don't do after the short hours come on. Here's to the good ship, captain, and a glorious cruise, a rich cargo, and a ready market!"

"Good!" was the answer, with a gruff complacency. "But what did you say about the short hours? How late do you call it, fellows?"

"Oh! it's not late: somewhere 'twixt twelve and one."

"Twelve and one! I must be off—must see to that d——d peacock! We shall soon be on the ebb of tide. Must be off. Well, fellows, you shall hear my signal soon. Keep your ears on the stretch, and your fingers and feet free. You're good fellows, I see; know when rum ought to be taken naked; l'arn you, ef you don't know. And so, the devil's blessings upon you, my kittens! I'll come for you before he does, and we'll both be sartain!"

And, without waiting any answer, he strode to the door. They all rose, and approached him. The spokesman on previous occasions, Atkinson, gave the rest the wink. He had contrived to whisper them—

"When you see us shakin' hands, then jump upon him, all at once, and bring him down!"

But Fowler had reached the door before Jim Atkinson could reach him. He found it closed, and locked on the outside! So slyly had Sproulls done this, that it had passed unnoticed by all the party. The effect upon Fowler was to endow the ruffian with all his resolution, and some of his habitual readiness and decision. In an instant the effects of the liquor seemed to disappear. He confronted the party, his back to the door, which opened on the outside, and drew a brace of pistols from his bosom.

"What bloody lubber has done this?"

"Done what, captain?" said Atkinson, approaching.

"Done *what!* Do you ask, you blackguard? Stand off, or I'll feed you on bullets which shall last you to the grave!"

And he cocked his pistols. Atkinson stopped short, his hand

extended as for leave-taking. His comrades, meanwhile, were slowly gliding round the table, like himself irresolute. They all had weapons, but produced none.

"Caught in a trap! and of your settin', you d——d fresh-water sneaks! You would harness a shark with spider-webs, would you!"

And, keeping his eyes steadily upon them, and his pistols extended with deliberate aim, he lifted his foot and drove it behind him, with all his force, against the door. The slight fabric yielded at the first blow, and was sent free from bolt and hinges. The way was clear.

"Now move one step toward me, and I'll plaster the wall with your bloody brains! Ho! ho! ho!—a pretty trap! Say to Sproulls, I've taken his measure: I'll cut out his garmints for him! I'll paint 'em red, do you hear! I'll make the sign of the cross on him, so deep, that the priest won't have anything to do! And all that won't save him. I'll—oh, blast him! He sha'n't know what hurts him!"

And he strode forth into the highway, pistols in hand, coolly resolute, steady with the sobriety of desperation; and none of the party dared to follow him. They looked at one another with somewhat of the philosophy of Dogberry:—

"Take no note of him. Let him go, and thank God you are rid of a knave."

Atkinson said, apologetically:—

"I would have taken hold of him, though I died for it; but I've got a wife and children. But why did n't you all jump upon him, fellows, when you seed me offer him my hand?"

"But you was to take his hand, you know, and then we was to jump on him. That was what you told us."

"But when you seed that he would n't shake hands?"

"Then we waited to see what you would do. You was nearest to him."

"But why did n't you git up? Ef you had only pressed about him, I'd ha' jumped on him anyhow."

"And ef you'd ha' jumped on him, we'd been up fast enough."

"And you wanted me to face his two pistols by myself, did you? and I with a wife and three young children!"

"And ain't my life as dear to me as your'n, no matter ef you

had fifty wives and children?    And when I consider 't was only a
poor five pounds that we was to git, after all, I do n't see the sense
of runnin' ag'in a brace of bullets from the biggest-mouthed pistols I ever laid eyes on !"

"They were monstratious big," said a third party.  "They
looked like young cannon.  A bullet from them muzzles would
take off a man's head clean !"

"Well," responded Atkinson, "it's agreed we all did our best.
We tried all we could to stop him.  We made him drunk — I
thought we had him dead drunk.  You seed how he reeled about
when he first got up from the table !"

" But, Lord, how sudden he got quite sober, soon as he found
the door was locked !"

"He's a most powerful villain; he'd be a match for any five
men I ever seed.    I thank God we're well rid of him, and no life
lost !  I do n't feel like takin' up and seein' hung an honest rover
that we 've been dealin' with so long.   I 'm glad he 's off, and we
have n't had the sheddin' of his blood."

"And he the sheddin' of your 'n, Bonney."

"Well, I consent !   I do n't want to burrow in a dog's hole before the Lord calls me !"

And the party soon persuaded themselves that their proceedings had been marked equally by courage and judgment, and would
have been quite successful but for the unexpected and brutal ob-
stinacy of Fowler, who in no degree would contribute to the triumph of their operations.

They had logically reached this result, when Sproulls reappeared, bringing with him another party.  His eye beheld the
wreck of the door; and, as he failed to see Fowler, he at once
conjectured the failure of his scheme.  He listened impatiently to
the narrative of Atkinson, but did not quite agree with him in his
estimate of the courage and conduct they had shown.

"But why did you not follow him and see where he burrows now?"

" Follow six pistols, with mouths as big as a blunderbuss, and
stuffed to the muzzle with bullets !"

"We must be after him," said Sproulls to his companion, "and
see if we can 't do what these fellows failed in."

"No !" replied the other; "we have n't time.  We 've to see
after higher game : we must take care and not lose both."

" You 're right!  Look you, boys, you 've lost a matter of twenty
pounds apiece, lettin' the pirate git off!"

" You only said five apiece; and was I to risk my life for a
poor, pitiful five pounds, and I have a wife and three children
lookin' to me for all they git?"

" Never mind that, my good fellows," said the stranger; " go
with us now, and see that you do better!  I 'll lead you, and not
ask any of you to face a danger that I 'm not willing to face the
first.  We 've got to make another capture; and if we succeed, and
he 's the person we look for, you shall have your twenty pounds
apiece yet!  You know me, I think, and know that I 'm not going
to ask you to do that which I won't attempt myself."

They at once expressed their alacrity.  They knew the speaker.
He had, even then, quite a local celebrity; and was destined to
make himself still more notorious in after-days, in the colonial
*régime* of Carolina.  He spoke with a decided Irish accent; was
a fine-looking, stalwart fellow, in a sort of undress uniform; had
rich, rosy cheeks, fair complexion, blue eyes; and carried himself
like a knight of chivalry.  This was Florence O'Sullivan, then in
command of the twó-gun battery, on the southwest point of the
town; afterward in command of the first palmetto battery, or log-
castle, on Sullivan's island, which takes its name from this very
personage.

He led the way, and all the party followed him into the street.

NOTE. — We have suffered our old pirate to deliver himself freely in his
habitually brutal language; preferring that he should revolt the instincts of
the young, whose more elegant forms of speech, in the dialect of the *flibustier*,
might be apt to persuade.  It is better, perhaps, that we should suffer brutality to disgust the *tastes* — even as the Spartans exhibited their slaves when
in a state of drunkenness — than, by a solicitous forbearance to offend the
tastes, to endanger the morals.  It is the just objection to many of our ro-
mancers and poets, that they drew the portraits of their corsairs and brigands
in such artful colors (suppressing all that might offend the tastes) as to convert the criminal into the hero, and, by appealing to the fancies and mere
instincts, succeeded too surely in corrupting the soul.  Having thus far suffered *our* ruffian to show himself in his true colors, we shall clap a stopper on
him hereafter.

# CHAPTER XLIV.

### A BLOODY STRUGGLE.

"A bloody deed, and desperately despatched!"
                                        SHAKESPEARE.

WHEN Sam Fowler left the house of Sproulls, his first notion
was, to find his way to the dwelling of Mrs. Perkins Anderson,
and endeavor to draw Molyneaux forth.   The fellow had become
doubtful of his securities, suspicious of the precinct, and apprehensive for his companion.   But he had no guide; felt his legs
beginning to be more and more unsteady, as he inhaled the cool,
fresh air of the morning; and, upon second thought, he directed
his steps toward the lagune in which the boat had been hidden.
His selfishness overcame his good-fellowship.

"This chap Molyneaux," he muttered to himself, "is no great
shakes.   We can do without him.   Why shouldn't I have the
ship to myself?   He's a fool too, not thoroughbred, and will be
always after some fol-de-rol or other, sp'ilin' a profitable v'yage!
We can do without him.   Let him git out of the scrape as he can.
I'll wait for him in the boat.   Ef he comes, we're no worse off
than before.   He can be captain of the ship.   I'll be *his* captain; and ef he kicks, we can send him over the side to feed the
sharks!"

Such was his policy and moral.

He took his way to the lagune, and found it.

He gave the signal.   The boat shot from her sheltering myr-
tles, and was run up to the shore.   Two silent figures managed
her.

"Here away, fellows — up to that 'yster-bed!   No need to
muddy one's feet!"

The boat obeyed him.

He stepped in with a yawing, unsteady motion, his brain feeling more than ever the potations he had drunken.

"Put her out, and row for the mouth of the creek, fellows. We shall be safer there, and can hear the lieutenant's signal when he comes upon the p'int. I'm thirsty as d—nation!"

He was obeyed in silence.

"What have you seen, boys? Any strange sail?—anybody here?"

"None, sir."

"None? Well, that's good! They haven't found us out, then! But they've got bloody lights out. There's rats abroad. I've had a narrow escape. Had me on the hip. Got ropes stretched. The d——d punch! Them sweet liquors have snared many a true man. Drink no more of 'em! The naked rum for me!"

And he laid himself back in the stern.

"How's tide, boys?"

"Have the ebb soon, sir."

"Ay, I know'd it. 'Twixt twelve and one, they said. Two now. Ebb at three. D—n the punch! Wish we were safe all, stowed away in our bunks!"

A deep silence followed. The rowers continued to pull out. They were nearly at the mouth of the creek. The Ashley was rolling broad, clear, and fresh, in the growing moonlight. Fowler seemed to sleep. One of the rowers muttered to the other—

"He sleeps!"

"Not yet," was the answer.

"Well, away! avast, there! What do you pipe?" demanded the supposed sleeper.

"Nothin', sir!"

"Nothin' be d——d! Talk out! Why don't you talk? What have you got to say?"

"Nothin', sir!"

"I say nothin' be d——d! Say somethin'! You, Byrd, have talk enough when the humor suits you. Have you no liquor?"

"Not a drop, sir."

"D——d bad lookout! Wish I had brought the black junk. Famous Jamaica. Feel hot and thirsty as h–ll! Ought to have cut one of them d——d throats! Been easier for it. The sneak-

20

in' lubbers! Sich a trap for a strong man! But I'll smoke 'em yet! I'll smoke the d——d town, soon as I git fairly on the quarter-deck! smoke the rats out of their holes! Sich a trap! Sproulls! Jim — Jim Atkinson! Got 'em all down in the ship's articles. Hang 'em for traitors — hang 'em in their shoes — the d——d fresh-water lubbers!"

Here his eloquence was interrupted by a fit of hiccoughing, broken with muttered ejaculations of the same type with the preceding; the sample is sufficient. He finally gave up the effort to speak, and again subsided, with head upon the side of the boat. He was silent. The oarsmen paused in the stroke, and the oars were resting on the sides. Fowler seemed to sleep. He was quiet; the hiccoughs were gone.

"He sleeps now," whispered one rower to the other.

"Not yet."

"But he's so drunk, that it will be quite as easy."

"Hardly! We need risk nothin'. There's time enough yet for an hour."

The supposed sleeper rose up:—

"Why the h–ll do n't you pull?"

"We're at the mouth of the creek, sir!"

"What of that? Pull out, I say!"

"Into the river, sir?"

"Yes — h–ll! To be sure!"

"But the lieutenant, sir!—"

"D——n the lieutenant! I'm myself lieutenant. Shall we stay for him all night, locked up in a d——d cabin with five fellows at one's throat? Pull out, and the lieutenant be d——d! Ef he will burn daylight, shakin' his d——d ridiculous legs at a *fandango*, when he ought to be breezin' it at ten knots straight for the gulf, he may stay for ever! Pull out, fellows, and lay us aboard the Happy-go-Lucky before the dawn!"

They obeyed him, and he again relapsed into silence. The rowers rested on their oars. The boat lay rocking to and fro, steadied in the one spot only by an occasional dip of the oar from one of the parties. Fowler showed himself restless, and, starting up, exclaimed:—

"Look you, fellows, why do n't you say somethin'? and — hello! why do you stop the boat? Why do n't you pull? What do you mean by not talkin'? What's come over you? Where's your report?"

The rowers were silent and motionless.

Fowler sat up, and stared at them. His brain was foggy, but not so much befogged but that something mysterious in their conduct made itself felt.

" Look you, Byrd! — talk, I say !"

And the speech was rounded by a volley of oaths.

" Talk, I say ! Let me hear somethin' I can understand. Talk, though you talk to the fishes only ! Ef you do n't, by —— you shall go to feed 'em !"

Both rowers answered him.

" Heh ! Who 's that ?"

There was something strange in the voice.

" I say, fellows, who 's that spoke ? Was it Byrd, or — or — Cromley ?"

" Cromley, sir."

" A d——d strange croak for Cromley ! Got a frog in your throat, fellow. I must look for it."

And, staggering up, he strode forward and took the first oarsman by the shoulder. The light of the moon, now one third of her course in heaven, was sufficient for the inspection, which, as the pirate made it, he roared out :—

" Ha ! ha ! h–ll and brimstone ! More traps ! — more sarcumventions ! The d——d punch ! But I ain't on my beam-ends yet. You bloody sarpents ! You think you 've got me, do you ! But, thunder and blazes, I 'm not to be laid by the heels by sich chaps as you !"

He had discovered Jack Belcher in the oarsman whom he had taken for Byrd. This discovery revealed his danger. He knew the fidelity of Belcher to Calvert; felt, from his presence, in the place of the hands he had left in the boat, that his treachery was known.

His prompt action kept pace with his words. With the hand which grasped the collar of Belcher, he pressed him over upon the thwarts, while with the other hand he fumbled at his pistols.

The crisis was come. Belcher felt that he had to deal with one who was desperate, and almost as vigorous as desperate. Danger and strife had the effect to restore him, in some degree, to sobriety, and so to a corresponding increase of strength. It was necessary for the assailed party to make powerful exertions. It was not easy to do so in his situation. Not expecting assault from the drunken man, he had kept his seat on his approach; and, as the truth dawned on the mind of Fowler, the outlaw had incontinently thrown himself upon the oarsman, bearing him down backward to the bottom of the boat, from which he was only saved by the lap of his companion. That companion was no less a person than the old salt, Franks; Calvert having found it necessary, in the present complication of his affairs, to put all his *personnel* into requisition. We may here state that the orders of our rover to his two subordinates were, to secure the person of Fowler — not to hurt him — to fetter him effectually; and, for this purpose, the iron handcuffs were provided, and in the bottom of the boat.

Caught suddenly, grasped firmly, and by the still vigorous frame of the old pirate, Belcher was overborne for the moment. Dropping his oar, his only resource was to throw his arms about the neck of the ruffian and drag him down with him. Thus they rolled together — struggled and strove — with rapid movements, which, from their confined and constrained position, were necessarily awkward ones. Both felt that the struggle was for life. Belcher's aim was, to hoist his assailant over the boat's side. This he might have done, could he have obtained the upper position; but Fowler was too heavy of build, still too strong, and had all the advantage of the gripe. Franks, sitting at the forehand-oar, could take no hold; Belcher's position having been between him and that of the pirate. But the old sea-dog watched his chances, seeming altogether quiescent during the struggle.

It was in vain that Belcher strove to throw off his assailant; still more vain, with both hands needed to keep himself uppermost, that Fowler fumbled, at moments, for his pistols or knife. And the strife thus continued; few words being spoken by either party, and Fowler only belching forth an occasional oath, as he felt himself baffled in his effort.

But Belcher was beginning to suffer. His enemy had him by the throat with one hand, his head being borne below the level of his body. The weight of his heavy assailant was stretched upon him. His breathing was difficult. As yet, Fowler showed no signs of suffering. He was working one hand with some freedom. Franks watched and listened. Suddenly the click of a pistol was heard, and a moment afterward the fire. Belcher made a violent effort and threw off his assailant. He was, happily, uninjured. The bullet went into the bottom of the boat, just grazing his side. Fowler, thrown off, lay beside his antagonist, who contrived to cast a leg over him and pinion his lower limbs. Then, as the hat of the outlaw fell off, and he lifted his head, old Franks seized him by his hair, which was long, and plaited into " pig-tails."

"All right now!" quoth the old salt, as he dragged down the uplifted head of the pirate. But the hands of the latter were free. He struck right and left with the empty pistol, inflicting some heavy blows; but he was evidently growing weaker. He felt this; and, dropping the pistol, stuck his hand into his belt, seeking another.

Belcher was too quick for him, and now buckled, with all his weight, close to his body, even as Fowler had succeeded previously in keeping him down. For a moment the ruffian lay quiet, but it was only for a temporary respite from exertion, and the regaining of his strength; and while his two assailants were taking advantage of the pause to recover breath, he began a series of new and most desperate exertions.

"We shall have to kill him," said Franks. "There's no hitching him!"

"Kill him! and why not," muttered Belcher, "as soon kill him as any wolf that runs?"

"Kill!" roared Fowler; and the conflict was renewed with increasing vigor. Then Belcher, with clenched teeth, fell upon him with all his might. Fowler half righted himself, sitting fairly up in the grasp of the enemy. It was a final and exhausting effort. Belcher, in another moment, succeeded in pressing his head over the gunwale of the boat, which by this time had drifted into the middle of the river.

"Help, Franks," quoth he, "while I pitch him over!"

"Pitch him over," said Franks, "while there's so much life in him? He'll sink better after this!—"

And, with the iron handcuffs, which he had caught up from the bottom of the boat, he smote the naked head of the pirate, as it lay over the side — one, two, three, terrible blows — under which you could hear the crunching of the skull; while a horrid shriek went up from the victim. One violent, spasmodic convulsion of the whole frame, and his death-agony was over; and even while he was writhing in the muscular spasms, Belcher seized him bodily, and flung him over into the river.

Then the two survivors drew a long breath, and sat gazing at each other in deep silence. They both felt all the horrors of the scene. They were both exhausted. Franks was the first to catch up his oar, and motion to his companion to do likewise.

"Throw these handcuffs overboard," said Belcher, "and wash the side of the boat."

"We *had* to do it!" responded Franks, apologetically.

"Yes, it was him or us! 'Twas life or death between us. Could n't be helped; the fellow was desperate! And better so, for we could n't have kept him. What could the captain do with him?"

"'T was a maroon shore he meant for him, I reckon. But he might have got off from that, and somebody would have had, at last, to cut his throat; for he was past cure. And, let to live, who knows how many murders he would have done!"

"Yes, it's best so!"

"Yet, I'd rather it had n't been my old hands to do it. I was prayin' that the time was gone by for me to meddle with fightin' and bloodshed. But it could n't be helped."

"And it's over now, Franks! 'T was a hard struggle, and a bloody end. But 't was not to be dodged. Let's pull in now, for I reckon the captain will want all the help he can git to-night. We ain't out of the woods yet."

## CHAPTER XLV.

THE FINALE AT THE BAL MASQUE.

"Oh! I see that nose of yours, but not that dog that I shall throw it to."
*Othello.*

AND, while this tragic scene was in progress on the river, our gallant rover, Lieutentant Molyneaux, was footing it, after a free Irish fashion, in the saloon of Mrs. Perkins Anderson. He had forgotten his piratical comrade in the intoxication of spirit occasioned by his return, at last, after so long a period of denial, to the society of fair women. As a good-figured and well-dressed stranger, of commanding carriage, and wholly unknown — *omne ignotum pro magnifico* — he was the observed of all observers. The ladies smiled upon him graciously. You can always note when the fair sex favors and when it only tolerates the party. They are not apt to conceal; in fact, they can not, while young, easily disguise their likes and dislikes.

Though something of a puppy, Molyneaux did not deceive himself when he came to the conclusion that he had made a favorable impression. Mrs. Anderson was despatched to bring him to more than one fair lady who felt willing to fling him the handkerchief for the dance, if for no longer engagement. And our lieutenant soon established himself on a favorable footing — we mean no pun here — with old and young. His manners gave him the advantage over the confessedly high sprigs of nobility, the cavaliers Craven and Cavendish. They were too apt to insist upon their blood; carried high heads; and, in their intercourse with the best people of the colony, made it very manifest that they were only temporarily condescending to the provincials.

Now, Molyneaux, a better-looking fellow than either of them, and quite as well-habited, was rarely upon his dignity. He was

too vain, and so too eager to conciliate kindly sentiment, to entertain much self-esteem.   A little stately at first — perhaps something awkward because of his stateliness — he soon found himself
at home in the circle, as he found his welcome ; and his manners
sensibly improved.   He was gay, chatty, miscellaneous, frank —
eager to take the floor, and full of *empressement* when in such a
*tête-à-tête* with a fair woman as even a ballroom will sometimes
afford to a judicious couple who have learned to school the tones
of the voice only to the stretch of a single pair of ears.   To sum
up, Molyneaux was vulgarly interesting.   His *empressement*, fatal
to his aristocracy, was yet everything for his popularity.   His
approach won an involuntary smile ; his *bon mots* and sayings
were caught up and repeated.   In two hours he had taken the
wind out of the sails of both his high-bred rivals.

"Who is he ?   What is he ?"

Curiosity grew the more it questioned.   Mrs. Anderson was
charmingly knowing and evasive.   She knew well how to convert
her casual capital into good marketable stock.   With a significant
smile, finger on lip, she would answer the eager questioner :—

"After a time.   You shall know in due season.   Be patient ;
you will not be disappointed."

Meanwhile, Craven and Cavendish began to feel uneasy.   Molyneaux had been doing the gallant to Zulieme with rare energy.
He had been fast growing familiar with some others of the acknowledged beauties about town.   He was making his way with
wonderful rapidity through the circle.

"The dem'd impudent puppy !"

"The dem'd conceited ass !"

"What a vulgar voice he has !   How loud in his tones ! how
boisterous !"

"And, do n't it occur to you, Keppel, that there is something
of the brogue — a twang — a—"

"Yes, by St. Jupiter ! that accounts for it all.   He's a demn'd
impudent Irishman !"

"Ha ! was not Sir Richard Pepper about to come out to the
colonies ?"

"Yes ; but that's not Pepper !   He's too short and too stout.
No ! it's not Pepper ; but who is he, then ?"

"He's certainly from ' Grane Arin.' "

"Yes!  There's no mistaking the brogue."

"And he's a bully!"

"Right, like enough!   But I'll pink his jacket for him if he gives me a chance!"

"He's like enough to do it, Keppel.   The fellow's disposed to be insolent."

"It's the bully art.   But a drawn rapier usually quiets such a temper."

"Come, come ;  no brawls here!"

"Here?  oh!  surely not;  but he must not put his horrid·elephantine hoofs upon my toes a second time!"

"You have a sort of pledge to him already on that score."

"Yes! — but, as we know nothing of the fellow, I shall pursue it only in the event of his crossing my path a second time.   I will surely pink him if he does."

So the friends talked together, *sotto voce*, of the dashing stranger.   So Keppel Craven resolved to act in a certain event.   And so, talking and resolving, the pair eyed the movements of Molyneaux with glances of jealousy and vexation.

And the dance sped, and the promenade ;  and groups formed in the intervals ;  and punches and lemonades were served, with jellies and preserves ;  all that the West Indies, in that day, could provide — that fashion could employ — toward the comforting of the "creature" in good society.

And, as the hours advanced — we are constrained to confess it — the intoxications of such an assembly, added to the intoxicating effects of punch, swallowed *ad libitum,* began to tell upon the brain and the free-and-easy temper of our roving lieutenant. The bashful Irishman began gradually to fling off the sedate restraints of a becoming courtier, as well as of a natural modesty. His voice grew louder ;  the brogue more rich ;  the sentiment more free ;  the levity more audacious ;  and his action began to correspond with the growing license of his tongue and sentiment.   Rude enough before in the dance, his *steps* became wilder, wider, wholly out of the reach of measure and music.   He would lose his partner ;  lose his own circle ;  and find himself throwing a contiguous ring into most adverse disorder.

But his merriment all the while — his free laughter — the good-natured apology which excused his blundering and awkwardness

—were readily received; and his irregularities only provoked the
mirth, not the indignation of the party, if we except the two mal-
content rivals, Craven and Cavendish. They grew more and
more chafed as they perceived that the romping Zulieme looked
on with as much good humor as the rest, and resented none of
those familiarities which our lieutenant now began to bestow freely
upon all with whom he came in contact. His hands and arms
exhibited a restless desire to paw and encircle. Rebuffed, or
turned aside, he would laugh merrily, and address his freedoms
to some more flexible damsel. In the dance with Zulieme, he
would catch and fetter her hands; exhibit the queerest antics;
seize her fan, work it violently toward her face and his own, and
break out into the wildest guffaws. He was evidently fast as-
cending into the excesses which usually distinguished the revelries
among certain classes of the West Indies, with which his experience had been considerable.

While they danced thus, and he capered, Zulieme said to him:
"Look you, you great Irish monster, you are getting drunk!
Do n't you drink any more. I know what 'll come next. You 'll
be for fighting somebody!"

"Who shall I fight? I 'll fight anybody for you, Zulieme!"

"Thank you! But I do n't want any fighting done for me.
I do n't love fighting. When I do, I 've somebody to do my fighting already."

"What! you mean Calvert? Blast him, Zulieme, I 'll fight
him, any day, for you!"

This was spoken with an extreme change of voice and manner,
so sudden and startling, that even Zulieme felt it; and, as she
looked into his eyes — for he had now lifted his visor, and stared
intently upon her face — and as she noted the stern, concentrated
passion in his tones, she withdrew her hand from the fingers which
violently clutched it, and said:—

"You! — you fight *him!* It would be your last fight, then!
Harry would chop you to pieces in a minute! And you talk to
me of him, of my husband, in such a voice, and such language!
And curse him, too! Go! you are a great Irish blockhead and
a brute; and I wish you 'd leave, and begone to the ship!"

"Your husband! Why, Zulieme, that 's a good one! What
do you care for him?"

"Me! what do I care for Harry? Oh, you are the greatest fool! Why don't you go, I say, and leave me? You will be making a fool of yourself here, before long, getting drunk and fighting somebody."

"To be sure, I will! Shall I fight those two whipper-snappers yonder? They seem to be watching us, by St. Jupiter! I'll see what they mean by it. I'll—"

And he was rising, his glances set in the direction of the two English cavaliers.

"No, no!" she cried, laying her hand upon his arm, and grasping it firmly. "Oh, what a fool you are, you great Irish blackguard! Why *did* you come here? Sit where you are, and be quiet!"

"You don't want me to go, then?"

"Oh, yes, go! Go from here, before there is mischief. You'll get into danger, and put Harry and the ship in danger. Why did you come?"

"If I must go, Zulieme, I shall pull those fellows' noses before I go! My fingers are itching for it. I will find out how much tallow goes to the making of a fashionable puppy's nose. It will grease my fingers, no doubt; but I'll take the shape out of the rudder. I'll give it such a twist, that they will never be able to steer by it again."

"If you do, Mr. Molyneaux, I'll never forgive you."

"What! you love that curly-headed chap, do you? Say so, and you send him to execution! It will not be his nose; it will be his throat! Say it, if you dare! Just say you love that fellow!"

"Love him? You are the greatest fool, I tell you! You might as well ask me if I love you."

"Well, didn't you once?"

The scorn rose, like a lightning-flash, into her eyes.

"Yes, as I did my monkey! He was so odd and ugly, he made me laugh."

"Ha! your monkey! Zulieme Calvert, or Zulieme de Montano, whichever you please, those words shall cost that fellow his ears! Ay, they shall cost *you* a pair of ears, too—not your own, for you are a woman; and, hark you!"—stooping and hissing the words into her ear—"I'll have you yet; ay, for that very speech!

Your monkey, Zulieme! Pretty little Zulieme! I shall yet see you, and feel you, hugging and kissing that monkey, much more fondly than you have ever kissed your husband — your royal Harry — your — your — blast him!"

And, without waiting her speech, if she had been disposed to make any, he rose and strode away from her — strode away into the adjoining room, and in the direction of the punch-bowl.

For a moment's space Zulieme was stunned. Her child-nature was horrified by the intense and concentrative bitterness with which the man had spoken, by the ferocious violence with which he threatened, and by the wolfish glare which shot from his eyes. His phase of drunkenness had changed in a moment from the monkey to the tiger development. She looked at him with a vacant stare of terror, thoroughly paralyzed.

But, only for a moment. Scarcely had he left the room, than her attention was roused by seeing Craven and Cavendish following him. These two young men, irritated already with Molyneaux; dissatisfied with themselves — their vanity vexed at the unwonted necessity of playing second fiddle in a circle where hitherto they had been the ruling spirits; curious to see who Molyneaux was; and, with a vague sense of a want unsatisfied, a resentment unappeased, an outrage unredressed; without any definite idea of what should be done, but restless with mixed emotions of a vexing ill humor — they followed him into the drinking-room.

As soon as Zulieme beheld the course which they took, her energies came back to her. She started up, and crossed the room to where Mrs. Perkins Anderson sat, the centre of a group of well-dressed gentlemen, who no longer ranged themselves in the ranks of the youthful candidates for merriment or matrimony; and, drawing her aside, in a hurried whisper, she said:—

"Oh, dear Charlotte, send some of these gentlemen into the other room!"

"Why, what's the matter, dear Zulieme? You seem frightened."

"I am frightened. That great Irish brute, Molyneaux, is drunk, and getting savage. He has been rude to Craven, and threatens him. Send some of these old gentlemen, and let them keep these foolish fellows from fighting."

"Oh, surely, there can be no danger of that. I'll go myself."

"No, don't you!"

"Oh, yes: nothing like a woman to keep the peace between young men. But I will carry some of these gentlemen with me. Mr. Yonge — Mr. Yeamans!"

The two gentlemen came forward.

"Come with me. The Señorita de Montano thinks there is a quarrel on foot between some of our young gallants. Come with me, and give me your assistance should it be necessary."

And quietly, with a composing smile for the circle which she left, the fair hostess tripped out of the room, followed closely by the two gentlemen to whom she had appealed.

Molyneaux was already at the punch-bowl. Two or three persons, of like appetite with himself, were standing nigh, each with a huge goblet in his hands. Molyneaux filled his own, and looked around with a lordly complacency.

"Gentlemen, with your permission, I will drink with you."

"We are honored, sir," was the answer.

"Thanks! Then here's d—nation to land-sharks and water-sharks; to sharks masculine and feminine; to tiger-sharks and puppy-sharks; to beast-sharks and human sharks; to all sharks that — that — don't value good-fellowship, and don't know the honesty in punch!"

"Well, that's a grand toast, and too much for a shark's swallow. Here's to you, sir, and may the punch-bowl never run dry!"

Even as Molyneaux held the goblet to his lips, Craven and Cavendish came upon the scene, gradually approaching the parties. He held the uplifted goblet untasted, and glanced at the new-comers, saying aloud to those around him:—

"I said *puppy*-sharks too, my friends, you remember! That's a breed by itself. It's a breed that follows in the wake of the tiger-sharks. It has a thundering swallow, big as any, but no teeth. It lives on what the tiger leaves. I say, fellows, of all sharks I despise, the puppy-shark is the meanest. I spit on him! He's a suckfish!"

And he spat in the direction of the two cavaliers, never once heeding the fine, well-bleached matting on Mrs. Anderson's floor. Then he swallowed the contents of his goblet at a single gulp.

The action was sufficiently unequivocal. It was understood by everybody, and occasioned some emotion among the other drinkers. Craven and Cavendish did not misunderstand. Both of them were men of blood. They might be frivolous, but they had courage. They paused, however. Blood requires, in the case of any old *noblesse*, of any country, that it shall not descend to its inferiors, except in absolute self-defence. They knew nothing of Molyneaux; and his conduct had been of a sort to show that, whatever of *blue* might be in his blood, he lacked the breeding of the gentleman.

"It is evident," said Craven, in a whisper to Cavendish, "that this fellow means to insult us, and me in particular."

"He is a bully!"

"True; and in London, my dear fellow, I should hire a cudgel-player to punish him. But the case is altered here. These people know nothing of the refinements of a court, and are rather pleased to behold the higher classes subjected to mortification: they will side with the bully. Now, if this fellow will fight, and offers any further annoyance, he *shall* fight. I feel that I can not submit to further trespass. I must punish him. Look about you at the first chance, and find Budgell, who is a gentleman — he was here an hour ago — and Gifford, and one or two others, whom we can trust, to see fair play. We must take care that we keep off all bullies but the one. As for this fellow, I shall spit him like a frog!"

Thus they communed, and in low voices, for a few seconds. Molyneaux laid his goblet down, with some deliberation. He had evidently made up his mind to something. He approached them. But, even as he did so, Mrs. Perkins Anderson, followed by the two gentlemen, passed between the parties. She wore the sweetest smiles; she bowed with the most exquisite graces; her tones were subdued to singular softness:—

"What, gentlemen," said she, "do you fly the ladies for the punch-bowl? Fie, fie upon you! What would be said of such taste at the court of the merry monarch? Do you know the ladies wait upon you for a minuet? Let me have the honor of your arms."

Craven and Cavendish were at once the gentlemen. It is surprising how much a clever woman can achieve against the angry passions of men. She did not take the arm of Cavendish; only that of Craven.

"Sir Richard," she said, addressing Molyneaux, "we can not spare you."

And she passed her arm within his. He hiccoughed, and staggered forward. Her two elderly companions interposed.

"Pardon us, dear Mrs. Anderson, but we desire to make the acquaintance of Sir Richard. Suffer him to remain with us; we will guaranty his future appearance."

Sir Richard was not unwilling to remain. He had reached that mood when woman gives way to wine. The lady bore off the two cavaliers. So far, she was successful. But they were both uneasy. We are not prepared to say that they went through the minuet. It is certain that Cavendish suddenly missed Craven, and went after him. The company, meanwhile, was employed. Zulieme had forgotten her terrors, in the mazes of a new dance, with a new partner. Mrs. Anderson was busied with her circle. It was not long before Craven and Cavendish were both in the room where Molyneaux was expatiating on the delights of a "wet sheet and a flowing sea," half speaking, half singing.

On the appearance of the two cavaliers, he grew sullen. He had been seated; he now rose. In evil moment, the two gentlemen, Yonge and Yeamans, who had begun to suspect that his inimicality was toward the two courtiers, fancied they could reconcile the parties. The error of such an effort is a great one where one of these is drunk, and where the parties have been reared under a different convention. Punch was supposed to be the proper mediatizing spirit. Molyneaux was never insensible to the claims of punch. He was ready at the suggestion of a goblet all round, But, even as Craven and Cavendish entered the circle, the inveterate humor of the drunkard filled his brain; and when Yonge and Yeamans fancied that all was now right and pacific, the rover, confronting Craven, said abruptly:—

"I am to drink with you, am I? Do n't object! But I never drink with a man whose nose is doubtful! I am curious to see what your nose is made of. It looks soapy — greasy; has a look of putty; and — so —"

Without stopping to finish the speech, he seized the nose of Craven with thumb and forefinger, and, putting all his muscle into the performance, subjected the astonished member to such a twinge as was wholly new to the cavalier's experience.

The action of Craven was instantaneous.  Like all true Britons, of good breed, he was practised in the "manly art of self-defence."  In the next moment he addressed a facer to Molyneaux, which drew the claret.

The parties rushed into collision, but were instantly separated. Then, while Molyneaux raved, Craven touched his sword-hilt, and led the way out of the room into the piazza, and thence into the street.

The affair had gone too far for intercession or mediation of any kind.  The elderly gentlemen gave the matter up.  The punch-drinkers followed Molyneaux as a leader: Craven, closely attended by Cavendish, was accompanied by three gentlemen; and all parties drew their swords the moment they emerged from the dwelling.

" Not here !" said one of the party.   " Let us not bring discredit on the house."

And he led the way, all following, to a thicket, which stood by no means remote in that early day, and which was sufficiently far from the dwelling for the purposes of combat.

None of the parties perceived that they were followed by other and unknown persons.  A group of six or eight men had been prowling about the house, sheltered from sight by as many forest-trees.  They may have been curious only; but they followed close in the wake of the combatants, without pressing upon them.

Mrs. Perkins Anderson dwelt, as we have said, somewhere near the present corner of Church and Tradd streets.  It was not much of a walk from this point to the northern terminus of the town, then very much on the spot covered now by the churches St. Philip and the Circular.  There was a tolerably thick wood in this quarter — oak, pine, and cedar.  A few scattered habitations had cut out squares in the woods; but there was still enough shelter for security, and there were well-known openings in which the moon held a sufficient torch for the purposes of strife.

" Not too fast," said one of the unknown party following; " but keep close.  It is a fight, I reckon.  We must see what they are after.  If they stand up for each other, they are too many for us. But if there's a fight, we have only to watch our chance.  Do

you be ready to put in when I bid you.   The stout fellow, that
you see yawing so, is our man.   He is a sailor, and must yaw a
little ; but I reckon it's the Jamaica that wants so much sea-
room."

And this group followed on.   Scarcely had they begun to glide
among the trees, when still another party appeared, taking the
same course.

" To the right, Belcher!   Sweep round for the rear ; and take
cover, as you see me.   Till I move, let no man stir.   Use no pistols, if you can help it ; the bludgeons will answer.   Take no life,
mark you, save in self-defence.   But, when I have my man, throw
yourselves between us and the creek, and retreat with your faces
to the pursuers, whom you can easily keep back with the show
of firearms, till they lose the chase in the thicket by the marsh.
Look to me to take you off in the boat."

## CHAPTER XLVI.

### HOW CALVERT AND MOLYNEAUX MEET.

"Let life be short; else, shame will be too long!"
                                              SHAKESPEARE.

LITTLE did Molyneaux suspect how much, and by how many, he was the subject of consideration at this moment. Ignorant, arrogant, vain, and maudlin, in his ferocious mood, he thought of nothing but wreaking his resentment upon the cavaliers he was about to meet. He dreamed not of the several parties following in his wake; some of them prepared to pursue him to the death, with even more tenacity of purpose, though perhaps less personal feeling, than the Honorable Keppel Craven.

Reaching the sufficient cover of the woods, with a broad space within the enclosure over which the moon cast an adequate light, the antagonists paused, their rapiers already naked in their hands. One of the punch-drinkers, who had somehow tacitly become the second of Molyneaux, met and conferred with Cavendish, who acted for Craven.

"Can we not adjust this matter without crossing weapons?" was the natural question of Molyneaux' friend.

"I do not see how this is possible," answered Cavendish, with English phlegm. "My friend has been subjected to a personal indignity. It is not merely a point of honor; it is an issue of blood."

"We then underlie your challenge," said the other.

"Surely."

"Will the simple drawing of blood suffice?"

"If it shall amount to the positive disabling of one or other of the combatants; not else."

"Then it is the combat *à l'outrance.*"

Cavendish bowed.

The rapier only."

" We have hardly any other choice at present."

" Pshaw, my dear fellow!" cried Molyneaux, staggering forward and interposing, "what's the use of this d——d long palaver? The fellow's got to fight, has n't he; or has the feeling in
his nose quite worn off? Would he have me give him another
tweak?"

After this, there could be no further preliminaries. Craven,
now keenly excited, confronted him. At once the weapons
crossed each other: a moment's pause, when they clashed, clung,
strove together, flashed in air; and were then worked with the
rapid evolutions known to practised swordsmen.

Craven was well taught in the science; had been taught by
one of the best Italian masters of the time. Molyneaux had had
no such master. But he had been in scores of actual conflicts, for
life and death, with Frenchman and Spaniard, on decks already
slippery with gore. The one had the art in nicer perfection:
the other the fiercer passion for blood; the Hunnish thirst for the
conflict; the muscular power; the eye that had learned to look
on death and ferocity with scorn; the rage that makes battle with
an enemy a passion and delight.

If Craven had agility and art, Molyneaux had a reckless fury,
and a physical force, that may have matched them. Besides, the
degree of drunkenness which might have blinded and stupefied
another person of different temperament, was, in the case of his
Celtic blood, a positive assistance. It had not so far advanced as
to enfeeble his *physique*, though it staggered it. He had a formidable brain for punch; and now, yawing still in sailor-fashion,
with his head rolling, but his eyes fixed with a steady, bright
glare, in which the ferocity rose almost to the expression of insanity — and his rage, under the existing conditions of his case,
was very like insanity — it was astonishing how cool and collected
was his play. It was one thing for his brain and blood to be on
fire; but his sword was as sober as it was keen: his practice was
positively refreshing in contrast with the evident fury of his blood.
He came on guard, passed, made his feints, recovered, with the
ease and simple dexterity of one refining in the schools.

Craven felt that he needed all of his own play. Though enraged and indignant, he had none of that wolfish venom in his blood, that tiger-like thirst, which had been all the while at work with Molyneaux. He could be temperate, and was so, without being frigid. He felt that so long as he could maintain his present temper, he was a match for his antagonist; but he also felt, after a few minutes' play, that he had nothing to spare.

And the play went on.

But it was growing to be work. The steady glare of Molyneaux' eyes upon his own warned him that the other was preparing for a vindictive passage. It came, with formidable force. The Celt was pressing upon the Anglo-Norman: the latter receded under the very tempest of thrusts put in — receded, but kept eye and sword firm and steady; and, watching the first cessation of the shower, he himself now made offensive play; and succeeded, by an adroit management of one of his Italian master's favorite feints, in a triumphant lunge which pierced the sword-arm of his antagonist.

It was but a flesh-wound — the hurt was slight, though sharp; and, with a positive roar, like that of a wounded bull, now desperate, our Celt rushed upon the Englishman, beat down his guard, had him at his mercy, was about to send the rapier home to his heart, when he was suddenly caught, clasped by the body from behind, his arms drawn back and fettered by a powerful gripe, which not only prevented his thrust, but deprived him of all capacity for resistance. Craven recovered himself, but lowered the point of his weapon, and, with the instant spirit of the gentleman, interposed :—

"Why do you interfere, sirrah? How dare you pass between gentlemen thus? Stand by me, my friends, and rescue Sir Richard Molyneaux!"

"Sir Richard Fiddlestick!" said the powerful fellow who had our lieutenant, struggling furiously, in his clutches —

"Stand back, gentlemen, and do not let his majesty's servants in the execution of their duty. I am Captain Florence O'Sullivan, commander of the guard, and this is the famous pirate-captain, Calvert; I have the council's warrant for his capture, under his majesty's proclamation. Disperse, and leave this fellow in my hands. You have done him too much honor, Mr. Craven, in crossing weapons with him."

"Ho! ho! ho!" were the only ejaculations of Molyneaux, as he heard these words. They caused him to renew his struggles more violently than ever. Powerful of frame as was O'Sullivan, he had not been able to get him down.

Craven was reluctant to withdraw; but Cavendish, seizing him by the arm, forced him away.

"It is not well for us to be seen further in this business," said he, as he drew him off.

Meanwhile, the punch-drinking companions of Molyneaux disappeared among the shrubbery the moment they recognised the chief of police. Our Celt was abandoned to the officer of justice, whose myrmidons, four or five in number, were now busy in helping to secure the prisoner.

But, with a surprise as sudden and unexpected as his seizure had been to Molyneaux, the redoubtable Captain O'Sullivan received a buffet under the ear from some unknown but well-practised hand — so well delivered, an upraking blow, of tremendous force — under which he dropped down as quickly as the bullock beneath the stroke of the butcher, and lay perfectly insensible! At the same moment, a score of stout sea-dogs, cudgel in hand, made in among the squad of local police, and, laying their staves about them with hearty good will, dispersed Dogberry, Verges, and the rest, in the twinkling of an eye. No need to show the pistols — to spring locks or pull triggers.

Molyneaux was rescued, but too much stupefied by these successive changes in his condition to understand a syllable as yet. But he stood up, freed, and shook himself, even as a great Newfoundland dog just out of the water.

The person who rescued him seized him by the hand:—

"Come, Lieutenant Molyneaux, we have no time to lose. This fellow will recover in a moment or two, and he might trouble us. Let us away!"

"It is Captain Calvert," said the lieutenant, meekly.

There was no answer. Calvert, for it was he, led the way in silence.

Molyneaux was becoming sobered and ashamed.

"Captain Calvert," continued he, apologetically, though with some effort, "I am ashamed, sir, of all this business—"

"Let us not talk of it now."

"But I must talk of it, sir. You have saved me from the gallows, I suppose."

"Very likely," answered the other, dryly. "But, come on!"

And he hurried forward, as if to escape any further explanation.

Molyneaux was piqued, but followed. What else could he do?

They reached the edge of a creek. The solid citizens of the present Charleston, when they look at the marble walls of the new custom-house, will perhaps be surprised to be told that the said creek ran into the city under the piled foundations of the said fabric, and made its way, somewhat sinuously, into the very heart of the town, finding its terminus not far from the present massive structure called at this day the Charleston hotel.

Here, our rover and his lieutenant found a boat, with but two rowers, though the vessel was large enough for a dozen. Into this they got; the captain taking the seat at the tiller, and sounding the little ivory whistle which he carried.

They may have waited some ten minutes before the seamen began to appear. Molyneaux several times attempted to break the silence, by apologetic and atoning speeches, but Calvert *bluffed* him off. He sat moodily taciturn. The lieutenant gradually sobered, and became moody also.

When all the sailors were reported, the boat put off without a word. She was rowed out into the river, and headed up-stream. After an hour's pulling, she was brought to, in-shore, at a point subsequently well known as Hampstead. The whole party, two excepted, went ashore, as if under previous orders of the captain. Here they found themselves upon the banks of the stream, a tolerably high piece of headland, with a thick wood of pines and oaks contiguous.

Among the party here assembled were Jack Belcher and the ancient Tom Bowling, Master Franks. They had, it appears, brought the boat round, having the assistance of four other oarsmen, from Ashley to Cooper river. It was the same boat which had witnessed the fearful strife with the old pirate Fowler, and his final surrender to the fishes.

When fairly landed, Calvert said, abruptly:—

"Lieutenant Molyneaux, we must have some talk together.

Belcher, you and Franks take the men off; keep them distant a hundred yards or so.   If Mr. Molyneaux, after our interview, comes out to you, take him aboard the ship.   Do not inquire whither I go.   Belcher alone will follow, and find me out.   He knows what I design, and will act according to my instructions."

Belcher seized his hand and wrung it with a passionate grasp of emotion, amounting to agony, while his eyes gushed with tears.

" Go, now, Jack, and remember!   Do as I have commanded. You see that the thing is unavoidable."

Saying this, he shook off the faithful fellow, and led the way to the edge of the woods — now Hampstead, and woods no longer.

Molyneaux was mystified.   He felt that something unusual was about to occur, and his guilty conscience made him apprehensive. But he followed doggedly.

When the two reached the edge of the wood, Calvert paused. He was a man of terribly direct purpose — no trifler.

" Lieutenant Molyneaux," he said, " we are now alone together.   I need not say to you that we can no longer sail in company. Your own conscience will tell you why.   I scarcely need add, that we are foes ; that you have long entertained a bitter hostility to me, and that you have done me such wrong, and meditated such further wrong, not simply to my life, but to my honor, that the issue between us must be one of life and death."

" Do you mean, sir, that we are to fight?" answered the other.

" Nothing less, sir !"

" I can not fight with the man who has just saved my life."

" That will not do, sir.   I have saved your life before ; and, even after this, you have entertained a design against my honor. Remember, sir, the last speech you made to my wife, this very night, in which you proposed my death as your dearest hope, and brutally asserted your purpose to compel her to your wishes !"

" Has she told you this ?" asked the other, in husky accents.

" No, sir ; but I have been near her, all this night, as her guardian and protector, and she knew not, no more than you."

" Captain Calvert in the character of a spy !" said the other, bitterly.

" When we have to deal with traitors, Lieutenant Molyneaux, the spy becomes necessary to the safety of the captain, his ship, his crew, his honor, and the well-being of the people he has in charge. Hear me, sir! I have done much for you. I liked you; promoted you; paid you well; fostered you; would have made a man of you. Your wretched vanity would not be content with a part — you craved all! You were not content to be second officer; you wished to be first. You were not content that your captain's purse was yours; you attempted his honor. You have wronged me, and insulted my wife. I need not say, after this, that there is but one necessity before us."

"Why did you save me from the officers of the law, having a purpose yourself to slay me?"

"I saved you from the law, because I had, in some degree, contributed to bring you within its jurisdiction. I saved you, as I would save, or try to save, the meanest scullion on board my ship. You yourself, it is true, by your own disobedience of orders, brought yourself into danger; but I brought you within the sphere of temptation. I knew your weakness, your vanity, yet left you in possession of a degree of liberty and power inconsistent with your judgment. I have done my utmost to save you from the consequences of your folly. This done, I propose to give you a chance for escape from other punishment. You have been pleased to avow your hate of me — your desire to destroy me — and can not complain that I now afford you the opportunity that you crave, on equal terms, your sword to mine."

"I can not draw sword upon you, sir: you have just saved my life."

"Think again, Lieutenant Molyneaux. Think that the same vigilance that has watched over your conduct and safety this night, has been equally exercised in regard to the ship, and that nothing has escaped the eyes of one who feels himself conscientiously bound for the safety of the meanest cabin-boy that works under his command. I know all, sir."

"I know not what you mean, sir."

"God! that a brave man should lie! Know, then, sir, that Fowler, this night, has paid for his crimes with his life! — that I well know all the details of that foul conspiracy by which you and he agreed to seize the ship, and supersede the flag of England by the bloody banner of piracy! You were to run up the Jolly Roger—"

"Enough! enough! It is, indeed, your life or mine!"

And Molyneaux, drawing his rapier in an instant, rushed upon his captain.

The other was not unprepared. The fight was short, but terrific. Molyneaux was run through the body after a few passes. He lay weltering in his blood on the ground, but he had his senses, and, with his senses, a return of proper feeling.

" Forgive me, Captain Calvert, forgive me !   I am rightly punished.   I have been an ass, sir ; a d——d peacock ; a fool, sir — what a fool !   I see it now.   Ah, it is all over !   What a fool I have been !"

" I am sorry for you, Molyneaux — very sorry !   I would have saved you.   But your death was necessary to the safety of the crew.   You would have led them to piracy and the gallows.   I would save them from both.   But, in honor, I felt bound to give you the one chance for your life, which your personal hostility to me seemed to require.   I have no enmities.   I would save you now, if I could.   What can I do for you ?"

" Do ?   Yes ! yes ! I have a mother —I have sisters — in Ireland.   Wexford — Wexford !   Give 'em what is mine.   There is money — much — enough for their wants.   Tell them nothing. Give them the money."

" It shall be done !   What more ?"

" Bury me in the sea ! not here !   Mattress me well.   Well shotted ; so that the d——d sharks do not tear me to pieces !"

We spare the rest.   So the fool died !

Calvert joined the boat's crew, and the body of Molyneaux was carried on board.   That night, according to his wishes, in shotted mattress, he was committed to the deep waters of Cooper river !

21

## CHAPTER XLVII.

" We give this pretty hostage to your keeping." — *Old Play.*

THE body of Molyneaux committed to the deep, at the mouth of that bold creek which is now called Hog-island channel, the boat of our rover shot downward, skirting the mud-reef on which " Castle Pinckney" now stands. Here it was run up close to the reef, and the party went on shore. A narrow stretch of shells and sand afforded them solid footing; and here, it seemed, Captain Calvert proposed a temporary rest, with what object we shall see hereafter.

The spot was a gloomy one enough. The moon was entering a body of dark masses of clouds which were silently heaving up from the west. The morning was close at hand. The tide was at its ebb. The adjuncts of the immediate scene were well calculated to increase the solemnity of the hour, the gloom of the events which had just taken place, and the situation of the party. A ruined habitation of logs, the refuge of some lonely fisherman, was the only sign of life that the spot afforded, and that was of life departed. A more imposing structure, ominous of death in its most terrible aspect, stood at the very verge of the shelly part of the reef, in that gallows whose cruel uses, pointed out to Zulieme when she first approached the city, had called forth her expressions of horror and disgust at the brute ferocity of the English race. There it stood, in solitary significance, and a bit of rope still hung dangling from the centre of the horizontal beam. Calvert surveyed the engine with a stern composure; but, after a moment, he said abruptly to his followers —

" Is there an axe in the boat?"

" There is, sir."

" Bring it, and cut down this gallows!   Let it no more disgrace
the approaches to a town which boasts of human ties and affections.   If the law requires human blood, let it not gloat over
mortal agonies ; let it not ostentatiously mock humanity with the
show of the cruel engine on which it stretches humanity for
death !"

And he stood, sternly watching the proceeding, while one of
the sailors, with vigorous arm and active stroke, smote the up-
rights until ready to fall ; when, lending their united strength, the
party pushed the ominous fabric into the sea.   It was a relief to
all when its skeleton frame no longer towered above their heads,
and they beheld it borne away by the billows, and whirling outward to the great deeps.

Here, in solemn brooding, with a mind intensely exercised with
the numerous and conflicting cares which still rose before it, Calvert sat silent, a protracted watch, which none of his followers
cared to disturb.   Some of them strolled along the reef, and con-
versed thoughtfully — for even the reckless sailor, in such an hour
and situation, can think deeply and sadly ; while others went on
board the boat, and lay at length upon their oars.

Suddenly, the attention of the party was sharply awakened by
the deep bellowing of a gun from the town.   Another and another
followed, in quick succession.

" It is the fort at Oyster Point, sir," said Belcher to Calvert.

" Ay! the ship is coming round."

" She will soon pass the fort, sir — wind and tide are both in
her favor."

" Ay, they can scarcely give her more than a single round ;
and, unless some unlucky shot should cripple her masts, she will
suffer nothing.   To the boat!   We must put off, and make the
signal."

" All hands aboard !"

The boat was off, a few minutes after, and rowing due south.
Soon the tapering masts and broad sheets of the Happy-go-Lucky
were seen sweeping round from west to east — rounding the point
of shoal which, as " The Battery," is now the favorite drive, " Car-
rousel," or " Alameda," and promenade, of the present city.   She
had escaped the shot of the fort with a mere rent in her rigging.

"Send up the signal, Belcher, that they may know where to look for us," said Calvert.

In an instant a light was struck, and a rocket of blue fires went up from the dark bosom of the bay. It was soon answered by another from the ship, which now shaped her course for the little vessel. It was not long before Calvert, followed by the boat's crew, ascended the sides of the Happy-go-Lucky, once more the free rover — once more sole master of his little world; and, as he strode the quarter-deck, he was conscious of security, and a certain degree of elation at having escaped more perils than we have thought proper to put on record.

Eccles, now first-lieutenant, had proved faithful. His former rank was conferred on young Hazard, the loyal emissary on board when Calvert was absent from the ship; a mere boy of nineteen, but precocious, ardent, full of enthusiasm as courage, and too happy to be *doing*, to desire to do wilfully or mischievously. Calvert possessed a rare faculty in the knowledge of men. He took no present heed of the seamen who had pledged themselves to Molyneaux and Fowler. He well knew how they had been seduced from duty; and, their ringleaders cut off, had no reason to doubt that the mere followers would sink back to their ordinary tasks, and do them especially well, if only to prevent suspicion, or investigation of the past. Besides, he was aware that all of the guilty parties were known to Hazard. *His* eye would be upon them for the future.

The Happy-go-Lucky, with a fair wind, at once put out to sea.

But, whither? And will Calvert leave his work undone? Has he left the colony to its fate? — left it to the savages to work out their scheme of midnight murder? — left his wife to the tender mercies of his enemies?

Hardly! We have known his character too long to suppose that he will be unfaithful to any duties or any interests in behalf of which he has given his pledges in his cares. And, as yet, we know not what his policy may be: but we may rest assured that it is one founded on thought, experience, and a knowledge of necessities which have not yet become clear to us; in brief, of the best human wisdom, in such a case as his, as it develops to his understanding. Hitherto, he has proved himself equal to every emergency.

Leaving the rover to his own progress on the high-seas, let us look to other parties in the infant city.

Governor Quarry is somewhat uneasy. He has a guest whose presence is annoying. This is Morton, one of the "proprietary council." Other councillors are expected. Despatches have been sent for Middleton and Berkeley. Morton has hurried down from his country-seat, charged with the secret intelligence of Stillwater. He tells Quarry that, under the exigency, he himself has taken leave to send express to New York for all such ships-of-war as his majesty may have in the waters of that colony. At his requisition, Quarry has issued his proclamation against the pirate Calvert. Florence O'Sullivan has been commissioned for his arrest, with powers to call out the *posse comitatus*. It is positively sworn by Stillwater, *alias* Sylvester, that Calvert is in Charleston. Nay, more; there is an affidavit, by the same immaculate patriot, that the pirate's mistress is in town, *particeps criminis*, and vending contraband goods! Poor little Zulieme a *contrabandista!* and a warrant has been issued for her arrest, even while she foots it with the cavaliers.

We need not wonder that Quarry is disquieted. No wonder that he paces his library, at two o'clock in the morning, very restlessly, Morton present; uneasy, excited, yet compelled to appear not only cool and determined, but especially loyal; with a holy indignation against pirates, and Calvert in particular, as the prince of them! He does not know what will be the upshot of the business. The fact that Stillwater has travelled off to Morton, argues for certain doubts, on the part of that worthy citizen, as regards himself. His own conscience assures him that these doubts are well founded. But how much is known? how much suspected? He believes that Morton regards him with suspicion also. Altogether, his position is a disquieting one; but he smiles, is courteous, outwardly calm, and wonderfully loyal.

He has one little gleam of consolation. At twelve o'clock, just one hour before Morton's arrival, he had received a little scrap of paper, on which he reads —

"Have no fear, though events are ripening rapidly. I shall make myself safe. There will be an uproar, but no discovery that shall trouble you. *Do your duty* as an official. Be no laggard. Do your utmost. Anticipate any and every demand of the coun-

cil. Show yourself as earnest as you please. Issue your proclamation — your warrants. Seek no evasion. Be as hearty, in the
prosecution of the supposed public enemy, as my enemies desire.
Go beyond them in your endeavors. Nothing that you or they
can do will affect my safety. Do not let them affect yours. Be
the governor, in all respects; as much so as the most bigoted pro-
prietaries could require."

The paper was not signed, but the handwriting was known.
Quarry read, and at once consumed it in the candle. He thanked
Calvert in his heart. It was the only assurance that he had. He
obeyed his counsels; and Morton, whom Sylvester had taught to
suspect the governor, was absolutely confounded at his ready loyalty, and the eager earnestness with which he addressed his efforts
to the capture of the outlaws supposed to be in town.

The governor and his councilmen have done all that they could
do. They have sent forth their myrmidons, armed with the proper
warrants, and, as Sylvester supposed, with the adequate force to
carry them into effect. We have seen the issue of their strata-
gems. It was somewhat later when the tidings reached Quarry
and Morton. Sylvester was the first to appear, his head broken
with a cudgel-stroke. He reported the facts, as far as he knew
them, and announced O'Sullivan, the *chef-de-police*, as slain outright. But, hardly had he got through his narrative, when O'Sullivan himself appeared, bloody at mouth and ears, but not mate-
rially hurt. He could only report his failure. He *had* caught
the pirate-captain; but he was rescued by superior force, and the
city police had utterly failed him. The town must be put under
martial law. It was evidently full of pirates.

Even while they conferred together, the heavy booming of the
cannon of the fort added new materials to the excitement.

"It is the fort! The pirate is evidently passing. Heaven
grant that they sink her!" said the patriotic governor.

"The fort," replied O'Sullivan, "is a mere pepper-box. It will
be only a lucky accident if they do her any damage. Tide's running out like a mill-race, and the wind favors. Before they can
load up for a second shot, she will have passed them!"

"Who's in command, captain?"

"Lieutenant Waring."

"Does he know what's to be done?"

" All that he can do, he will do !"

" Let us to the fort, Morton," said Quarry, buckling on his small-sword. He was monstrously relieved by the intelligence which was brought him. It confirmed all the assurances made in his anonymous despatch. He felt now comparatively safe.

They reached the fort, only to obtain distant glimpses of the Happy-go-Lucky ; her white sails spread for ocean, and already six miles from the town ; tide and wind sending her out at ten knots an hour. The fort, of two guns, had succeeded in firing three shots — quite an achievement : one shot had wounded the ship's sails, and, it was thought, another her hull. In other words, the fort was a—a—a—(in modern parlance) a humbug !

So Florence O'Sullivan delivered himself :—

" It's just of no use *here*, your honors ! It should be yonder, on that island, covering the channel ; and, if one is put *here*, it should be on the east bank. Here, you can have but one fling at an enemy, and there's an end."

It happened, not long afterward, whether from this event and counsel or not, that, even as our *chef-de-police* suggested, the fort was built on the island, and he himself put in command.

This was the original of Fort Sullivan, afterward Fort Moultrie — which has a famous history of its own.

It was broad daylight before the party returned to the house of Governor Quarry ; and, with daylight, began the beating of drums, and the array of the *posse comitatus*, and the gathering of the militia. The town was put under martial law. There was a monstrous hubbub.

But something had been saved. The *bal masque* of Mrs. Anderson had been not simply a success, but a sensation ! It was the town-talk for long after !

It rather dashed and daunted the fair and fashionable hostess, however, when, just as her company had departed, and while she was chatting gayly with Zulieme over the events of the night, the door was rudely assailed by thundering raps ; and, as it opened, the civil officers rushed in, laying rude hands on the fair Zulieme, arresting her as a pirate's wife, and a *contrabandista* in her own proper person.

Even as she was, caparisoned as Titania, mask in hand, the dear, silly little creature was made to go, on foot, to the dwelling of Governor Quarry, there to confront the said dignitary, with his solemn proprietary council.

Mrs. Perkins Anderson was not the woman to abandon her guest. Whatever her vices and weaknesses, the woman had a soul! She accompanied Zulieme, resolved to share her fate if necessary. After such a successful party, she felt no little of the heroic in her; felt grateful, too, to her guest, for having helped to make her experiment a success; felt outraged at the official indignity put upon her, and was altogether in a condition of exaltation to say eloquent things even to his sainted majesty himself.

When first arrested, poor little Zulieme was confounded. Never was young sinner so completely taken by surprise. Was it her quaint garments of the Fairy Queen that were guilty? What was it?

"But, I'm a woman, sir!" said she to the officer, as if women had some special immunities for evil.

"Oh, to be sure! I know that! That's what I 'rest you for — 'ca'se you 're a woman. Ef you was n't, would n't have nothin' to say to you, nohow."

And he chuckled with perhaps a notion of some fine official humor in what he had said.

"What does it all mean, Charlotte?" she asked, in her simplicity. There was no terror.

"It means that the governor is a fool, and his council are fools together; that's what it means!"

"Well, that's comin' it big, I must say!" exclaimed the officer. "But come along, miss, unless you wants me to pick you up and carry you. You must go and see them same fools!"

"Must I go, Charlotte?"

"Yes, my dear, *we* must go. I will go along with you! It amounts to nothing, I suppose. It is some nonsense of the governor and his council, who had better be in their beds, as so many old women, than arresting young women as pirates!"

"Ah! it is as a pirate that I am to go to the judge!" And, as she spoke, the little creature rose into dignity and increase of stature. She thought to herself:—

"Ah! they would seize Harry! He never thought they would seize *me*. And why not seize me as well as Harry? I'm Har-

ry's wife. I'm as much pirate, I'm sure, as he is! I'll show
him! — I'm not afraid!"

So the thought ran through her little brain, conferring upon it
a certain increase of consequence. She would show Harry she
was no such child as he supposed!

"Well, let us go, Charlotte!"

And she sank into silence, and passively submitted to the arrest. Not so the fair hostess. She was eloquent with indignation
all the way!

Meanwhile, the whole town was astir. Everybody was abroad.
Everybody saw them in their state dresses. We really forget
what was the costume of Mrs. Anderson, but have a notion that
it was in the character of Zenobia that she did the honors that
night. We will assume that she then walked the street as
'Zenobia,' with the lovely little 'Queen of the Fairies' by her
side.

The news came startlingly to the ears of our two cavaliers,
Keppel Craven and Cavendish. They were just about to disem-
barrass themselves of their fine clothes.

"What, the señorita arrested? What nonsense!"

"And as the wife of the d——d pirate!"

"A *contrabandista!*"

The silver-mines of the one, the ten thousand pounds of the
other, would not suffer them to sleep at such an hour. It might,
it must be, all nonsense — some ridiculous mistake of the police!
At all events, they must do their *devoirs* as cavaliers. They
must be at hand, watchful and ready to assist the demoiselle with
whom they have flirted; pay proper homage to the hostess who
had entertained them so elegantly. So, changing the court for
mere city costume, they hurried off to the governor's dwelling.

When Zulieme and Mrs. Anderson reached the residence of
the governor, it was sunrise. Quarry and Morton were seated
in state, grave seigniors, in all the dignity of their official position, ready for their reception. There was a crowd already collected. Curiosity brought a goodly number. The police was
stronger in the governor's presence than they had shown themselves in the field, and behaved themselves with much more dignity. There was a cloud of witnesses, each prepared to testify to
as many falsehoods as facts; for, in such cases, men become so

enamored of their own conjectures, that the mind insists upon them as facts, and the subservient memory will not discredit them. There was the keen and restless Stillwater, *alias* Sylvester, prowling about like a young shark hungering for his breakfast; and there was Sproulls, whose bloody and bandaged head was a tragic volume of evidence itself; and O'Sullivan was there, with a cheek monstrously blue and green of hue, and one eye so black and bunged, that you might read the whole history of the night in it; and there were many others who had something to say or to show.

The appearance of Zulieme made a decided impression on the company. Her strange but appropriate costume; her *petite* but symmetrical figure; her beauty; and the very childish, infantile simplicity of her features, now lifted into unwonted character by the new sense of importance in her position — were all calculated to produce a sympathetic and friendly interest in her judges, who regarded her with equal curiosity and satisfaction. The governor's courtliness and pleasant smile were not withheld; and the grave, saturnine Morton, lifting his dark brow, gazed intently and with a mild interest on the stranger, who seemed indeed a fairy, fresh from the forests, whom the sun had lovingly kissed, and with whose wanton hair every breeze of heaven had toyed with tenderness.

"Be seated, ladies," said the governor. "We are sorry to be compelled to disquiet you; but we are obliged, by a painful sense of duty, to require the attendance of one of you, at least, in order that we may ask you a few questions which concern the public welfare."

"Answer no questions, Zulieme," said Mrs. Anderson, in a whisper.

Our trader's wife might have done well as a lawyer at this day, when women are about to assert their rights in the courts, as well as in courtship.

"You, Mrs. ———; ah, Mrs. ———"

"Anderson, sir — Mrs. Perkins Anderson," answered the lady to whom the governor was addressing eyes and voice, while unable apparently to recall her name. The lady was somewhat piqued. Her name forgotten! But it is a common trick with the British, when they affect the aristocratic, to forget the names

of comparatively obscure people. His excellency knew that of
our hostess very well. Had not his wife, indeed, visited her—at
least on one occasion? But it was not simply an affectation of
vanity that prompted the governor to forget. It was matter of
policy that he should know as little as possible of the lady with
whom Zulieme dwelt. But the fair Charlotte did not give him
credit for his policy; she ascribed it to official pride, and resented
it accordingly. She was wrong in this instance.

"Ah! yes, Mrs. Anderson. How should I forget! But, Mrs.
Anderson, permit me to say that we have no requisition on *you*."

"No, sir; but the Señorita Zulieme de Montano is my guest,
sir; and I certainly would not suffer her to leave my house, under
this most humiliating treatment, without giving her all the support
in my power."

"Right, madam," said Morton; "and there is no reason why
you should *not* be present at this examination, which I trust will
be found neither hurtful nor disagreeable. We only fancied that
an officer might have committed the mistake of doing more than
his warrant authorized."

The lady bowed, somewhat mollified. The governor proceeded:—

"Your name is said to be Zulieme de Montano, young lady?"
Zulieme bowed.

"Pardon me, *señorita*, but you are a Floridian, I am told."

"A Spaniard, sirs. My father and mother were both of Castile."

"But you are from the Spanish province of Florida?"

"My father has an estate in Florida."

"You are from thence?"

"Last! I was born, and lived long, on the mountains of the
isthmus."

"Suffer me to ask, señorita, if you have always borne the name
which you now bear?"

Mrs. Perkins Anderson gave Zulieme a look. It was enough.
A flush passed over the dark cheeks of the young Spaniard; and
she rose quickly, but with subdued and quiet manner.

"Señores," she said, approaching the governor and his council-
lor—"señores, caballeros, you are gentlemen and lords. You
ask me questions which I do not want to answer. It may do me

hurt to answer them, and I will not lie.   I do not know what you wish to do with me.   But if your laws require me to die, I can die, though I am very young to die.   But ask me no questions to catch my tongue !   If you think harm of me, tell me what is the offence I have been doing.   I have been dancing a great deal since I have been here, and did not know — perhaps there is a law against dancing?   Some people, here, tell me it is a sin, and against the laws of God.   I did not know that.   I don't believe it.   *Our* people did not teach me so.   But it may be against the laws of *your* people ;  and I must die for it !   I confess I have danced a great deal.   If there is anything else that I have done against your laws, tell me, and I will answer.   Do you speak to me what you have heard against me, and what you think of me, and what they tell you I have done.   Tell me all, and I will answer you if I can.   But I will not tell you more than I can, for there may be some snare — some danger to my soul !"

The simplicity of this speech, spoken in rather broken English, had a wonderful effect.   The governor himself smiled, very much amused ; several of the bystanders laughed outright.   Morton looked with a greater degree of interest and pity on the young creature than before.   His stern visage had grown sadly sweet.

" Die !" said the governor — " snare your soul, my dear young woman ?   What could put such a notion into your head ?   As for dancing, it is not yet a criminal offence by our laws ; though, I believe, there are some who fancy that eternal perdition must follow the shaking of symmetrical legs to the sound of lively music.   No ! the charges brought against you — and there are charges — are of very different character."

He paused.

" Tell her what is charged, your excellency," said Morton. " There is no need of any art in dealing with such a child as this."

The governor proceeded with his counts :—

" It is charged, señorita, that you are concerned in a contraband trade—"

" Contraband ?   What 's that ?"

" That you bring goods into the town for sale, without first paying to the government certain dues and duties, in violation of our laws,"

" I bring goods for sale? Me! Oh, sir, I never sold anything in my life. What I have brought here, I have brought to give away."

" I can prove *that*, your excellency," said Mrs. Perkins Anderson.

" It is also charged, my young lady, that you are the wife, or companion, of the notorious pirate, Harry or Henry Calvert, captain of the cruiser called 'The Happy-go-Lucky,' or 'The Almeida,' or the 'St. George's Dragon'—for by all these names the vessel is reported to sail."

Then broke out the woman-soul:—

" Harry a pirate! You are a bad man, for saying it! Harry is a fighting-man, like all you English—"

She was about to add " brutes," for it had become a somewhat familiar epithet with her; but a warning instinct arrested her in the speech. But what she had said sufficed to effect an instant change in all countenances. Mrs. Anderson clasped her hands together in despair; Sylvester and his factotum, the express, Fairchild, lifted fingers and eyebrows in exultation; the governor looked aghast. In an instant, Zulieme saw these changes, and, turning to Mrs. Anderson, she murmured—

" O Charlotte, what have I said?"

" A few words too many, my dear."

" Have I done anything to hurt Harry?"

" Hardly; but something, perhaps, to hurt yourself."

" Ah!" and she sighed as with a sense of relief.

The governor, remembering Calvert's private letter, put on a triumphant air, and, turning to Morton, said—

" It is hardly necessary to ask her any more questions."

" Hardly; though, with the fact of her identity established, we gain nothing. I know no law which makes the wife of a pirate liable for his offences."

" Oh, no! surely not," was the answer—the governor secretly pleased to see that Morton's sympathies were with the woman. " Still, sir, we should probe the matter as far as we can."

The other nodded. " As you please."

" It is very clear, my dear young làdy, that the Harry of whom you speak, and Harry Calvert of the Happy-go-Lucky, are the same person."

" I won't say any more! I am a foolish thing, and do n't know
what I say. But if there's anything against Harry, I 'm ready
to answer it. If he 's a pirate, then hang me, for I won't deny it.
Harry's my own, own husband. He 's been married to me a
year; and you may kill me for him! But he's no pirate; but a
brave, fighting, good, brute Englishman — just as good and brave
as any of you here! There, now! you may kill me when you
like."

Craven and Cavendish looked at each other, and groaned
aloud.

" Ten thousand gone !" muttered Cavendish.

" D—nation, yes! and my silver-mines! Let 's be off, Cav!
D—n all Spaniards, and pretty señoritas, for ever !"

And, following each other, as unostentatiously as possible, they
stole out of the apartment.

" We need inquire no further," said Quarry.

" Of her — no! Call up your other witnesses."

Sylvester, Sproulls, Gideon Fairchild, each gave his testimony
in turn. We know it pretty nearly as they delivered it, allowing
for certain natural exaggerations, in which they coupled with the
facts the usual modicum of conjecture. Zulieme listened to their
details without sign of interest or emotion. She did not see the
drift of much of it, and perhaps did not see the harm in any.
But when, on a sudden, Sylvia, the mullattress, who had been arrested, was also brought in, manacled — for she had darted off at full
speed from the officer, and was with difficulty retaken — and made
to confront her mistress, the little Zulieme rose again, and, looking sternly upon her judges, said :—

" This is my slave, my lords, caballeros, and gentlemen. What
has *she* done? Why is she chained up ?"

" She 's one of the witnesses," replied Fairchild.

" One of the best we have, too," added Sylvester.

" That 's unfortunate," observed Morton, " if she be a slave."

" You a witness against me, Sylvia !" said Zulieme, with the
saddest reproach.

" Nebber, missus! Who say dat?"

" I say it," answered Fairchild.

" Missus, do n't b'lieb dem buckrah! Dey lie fas' as squirrel
climb tree! Look yer, missus — dey catch and bring me yer,

I run; but dey catch me, and put dese heaby tings on my han'. I no want for come. Dey make me come. Ef you say so, I won't tell 'em not'ing."

"There's a way to make you," said Sylvester.

Zulieme looked mournfully at the mullattress, who was now fairly stifled in a sea of sobbing, but she remained silent. Some effort was made to move Sylvia to renew her revelations, but without effect. She was resolved that the proper virtue lay in emulating her lady in taciturnity.

"It needs not," said Morton; "her statement will be valueless as evidence. Let Mr. Fairchild state what he knows, and even what he has heard. This is a purely desultory examination. Stripped of all unnecessary matter, there may be, nay, must be, something which shall be evidence. He can report all the parties to his own seizure and confinement in the pirate-ship; what he saw there; and what he heard the pirates say of themselves. If he includes in it what the slave has said, it will not much matter: let it go for what it is worth."

And Gideon Fairchild told his story. He was prolix in all his details, with the exception of one class of them; he suppressed all the tender passages between Sylvia and himself. He reported only what she had told him of ship, crew, and cargo. She was the one who taught him the true character of the cruiser; the name of her captain; the fact that his wife was in town, and where; in brief, all that she knew.

"O wretch!" cried Zulieme, with indignation.

The mullattress broke out with a cry:—

"O missus, de buckrah lie like book! I nebber tell 'em not'ing; only I bin so want for see you and be wid you; and when he tell me he will bring me to you, and den, when he promise for marry me, and say he lub me so much—"

Here Gideon broke out:—

"It's a most infamous, lyin' wench, your excellency! Me marry a nigger! me! And here everybody knows I've got an angel-wife of my own, and three of the beautifullest children! The nigger's fool-mad, your excellency!"

Gideon was perplexed and perspiring. He looked about him uneasily, lest Mrs. Gideon should be among the listeners. There was a round laugh at his expense, especially when Zulieme, with the prettiest expression of scorn in the world, said to the mulattress —

"And would you marry such a creature as that?"

"Nebber, missus! I 'spise de poor buckrah; I 'spise 'em for true. I only mek b'lieb I guine marry 'em, 'cause I want 'em to bring me to yer, missus."

There was another laugh.

"This looks serious, Fairchild," said the governor, appearing ludicrously grave. "The negress is your own witness! Do you say, woman, that this man promised to marry you?"

"To be sure him promise, maussa."

"It's nigger evidence, your excellency," responded Fairchild; "she's the lyin'est blackguard!"

"If we reject it on either score, Master Gideon, we must reject all that we get from her. I am afraid we shall have to receive it all. We shall have to turn you over to the tender mercies of the churchwardens and — your wife!"

"Do n't say so, your excellency!"

"Whether the negress, *per prochein ami*, would have an action against Gideon for breach of promise?"

The governor was disposed to amuse himself.

Morton frowned, and showed impatience.

"Let us proceed, your excellency."

"We have got through — got evidence enough, certainly, for commitment."

"Commitment! The point is one to require a law-officer. confess, even the identification of this woman, as the wife of the criminal, does not seem to me to establish any offence on her part. I do n't see how we can commit *her*."

"Except, perhaps, as sailing under the pirate-flag — assisting, abetting, aiding, counselling—"

"We have no proof of that fact! We do *not* find her sailing under the pirate-flag. We find her in our municipality, and only know not how she gets here. The statement of the woman Sylvia, a slave, is not to be regarded."

"But a fair and reasonable inference—"

"None, such as this, can be considered in capital cases."

But we need not pursue the discussion, which was somewhat protracted. While it was in full progress, Quarry affecting a very earnest purpose of severity and extreme strictness, Sir Edward Berkeley made his appearance.

As she beheld him, Zulieme started with extreme emotion, and whispered —

"Charlotte, tell me, who's he?"

"That's Sir Edward Berkeley, one of the councillors."

"He's so like Harry! oh, so like! I see he's not Harry — but—"

"Certainly, a great likeness." And the ladies whispered together.

The governor and his councillors retired to consult in another apartment. Sir Edward Berkeley seemed as much interested in the beautiful and artless little Spaniard as Morton had been; and when the governor repeated the suggestion of commitment, he was indignant.

"Commit such a creature as that — and to prison! Fie, sir — fie!"

"Oh! not to prison, surely," said the governor; "but to some custody, in which, while treated well, she will be under watch."

Berkeley shook his head.

"I see no use in it."

"I do not well see how we should do it," observed Morton — "how we should be justified. There is positively nothing against the woman. I have no doubt that she is Calvert's wife — perhaps mistress — but there is no reasonable ground for supposing her to be an active participant in his criminal proceedings. She is a mere child; is evidently without tact or cunning; and with just as little faculty for business of any sort. To employ her, even in the petty practice of the contraband service, would be just as likely as not to ruin all the profits of the trade."

"Yet, you find," said Quarry, "that, at the very time she appears in town, the town becomes flooded with foreign goods of strange fabric and fashion; while the West-India fruits, in great abundance, are to be had — when, as we all know, no West-Indian vessels have come into port."

"I half suspect," rejoined Morton, "that, in the greater number of cases, these make their way in, just as this pirate has done, and lie *perdu* high up Cooper and Ashley rivers. This pirate evidently knew his ground — the soundings, the channel, and the proper places of concealment. We can build nothing against the woman on this sort of evidence. Nay, more; how idle to talk of this woman being the agent and emissary, when your own chief of police and all his officers tell you of the town being full of pirates! Your own proclamation of martial law is grounded upon the necessity derived from this very evidence. And they tell us, moreover, of boats arriving nightly — this is the evidence of both Sylvester and Sproulls — both of whom, by-the-way, seem, in the course of their practice, to have known rather more of these contraband cruisers than becomes honest men."

"Ay, set a thief to catch a thief! But that reminds me to say to you, gentlemen, that the warrant issued for the arrest of the old sailor, Franks, has been returned '*non est.*' He is off, and all his chattels. His house, which was a sort of curiosity-shop, is regularly gutted. He has probably transferred himself, bag and baggage, to the pirate."

"We must not be surprised," said Berkeley, "that there should be so many in the town who sympathize with these pirates. It is a new thing, indeed, among us, to call them pirates. Hitherto, they have been — however in conflict with the laws of nations — the enemies of our enemies only, and sailing their craft under absolute commissions from the crown-officers. The public sympathies, in all the colonies, have been really and warmly with this fellow Calvert, for his famous fight with the '*Maria del Occidente*' — that very affair which the Spanish influence at the English court has succeeded in making an act of piracy, bringing forth the proclamation which we have just published. We must take for granted that there are many here who sympathize with these cruisers. There is no doubt that the town has been full of them; and, with their boats here nightly — their sailors, their agents, in town — it is not necessary that we should suspect this strangely-beautiful little creature of any part in the *business* of the cruiser. She is, no doubt, as she alleges, the wife of the captain, who has presumed upon the sympathies of the citizens to bring her here, that she might enjoy herself, while he and his men carried on their unlawful operations by night."

"I fully agree with Sir Edward in these opinions," said Morton. "Still, the question occurs, 'What are we to do with this woman?' There is *something* in the idea of his excellency, that we should keep her in some sort of custody, for awhile at least; in order, by this means, to obtain some control of her husband. He will, no doubt, be coming to look after her. She is too pretty a prize to be abandoned by a man of taste."

"But where to keep her? Our prison—"

"Oh! do n't mention that, your excellency," interrupted Morton. "We must not talk of prison for this young creature."

"I 'll take charge of her," said Berkeley, with a sudden impulse. "I 'll be her custodian, at my poor forest barony. It will not be easy, on the part of the pirate, to seek her there; and if he does, I have a good stout force of laborers, all of whom I have armed, and he will not find smooth sailing to make his approaches. She shall be treated with tenderness and care, but closely watched. I confess, keeping her here in town, I should almost fear that this pirate, who is bold enough for anything, would have her out of your prison, or out of any private custody, if he had to bombard the place for it."

"And we have seen with what scorn his vessel has passed our fort, and of what small defence the fort is capable," responded Morton.

"Really," said the governor to Berkeley, "your offer relieves us from a dilemma; for, though clear that she should be kept in custody — for awhile at least — I should be unwilling to send her to prison, and should not find it easy to provide for her a proper custodian."

"Well, you are agreed to accept my offer?" replied Berkeley. "I am glad of it! I have somehow conceived a sympathy for this strange little creature, and I should never consent to any harsh means being employed. We must reconcile her to my guardianship. Leave that to me, gentlemen, if you please; and I trust that she will be persuaded to accept my protection."

The council adjourned to the hall where the ladies and the crowd had been left, impatient of the long delay.

Our cassique of Kiawah immediately joined the two ladies.

When Zulieme heard him out, she said to Mrs. Anderson —

"I am to be a prisoner, Charlotte, for Harry? Is that it?"

"Yes, my dear; not exactly a prisoner, if I understand Sir Edward, but—"

"No, my dear young lady, not exactly a prisoner; but an inmate of my family, until the trouble of this affair shall blow over."

" Zulieme looked up, simply, and said—

" I will go with you, señor."

To Mrs. Anderson she added, *sotto voce :—*

" I would not have gone with any other! They should have carried me! But I like his looks, Charlotte. He is so good — so sweet! And he looks so like Harry!"

## CHAPTER XLVIII.

ZULIEME'S FIRST SIGHT OF THE BARONY.

"These humors of the children be not strange."

*Old Play.*

IF we have properly considered the light, lively temperament of Zulieme Calvert, and remember the child-life which she has led, we shall probably be somewhat surprised at the quiet resignation with which she gave up her abode with the fashionable Mrs. Anderson. One would think, seeing her deportment, that she had made no sacrifice. She had no tears. She seemed to have danced herself out. She was subdued and pensive, but very calm. There was a secret power at work in the bosom of the little woman, unfelt before, which sustained her wonderfully. Mrs. Anderson was quite astonished. *She* made many lamentations. We could give a chapter of garrulous speech which she poured forth to and *at* the council of the lords-proprietors, and thrust specially into the ears of the cassique of Kiawah. But we do not affect this sort of eloquence. Mrs. Anderson, judging from Zulieme's seeming stolidity, thought her astonishingly cold. *She* could find tears, as well as eloquence, at their enforced separation; Zulieme neither. What she said was curt and unostentatious, and she even appeared impatient to be gone.

"It do n't matter, Charlotte," she said; "I do not fear what they can do! They can only put me in chains! If they kill me, what then? It'll be just like your brute English. But I won't beg them or pray to them, and they sha' n't see any tears of mine. And I will take care how I talk. They sha' n't hear a word from me which shall bring trouble to Harry. He shall find that I am a woman *now*."

Mrs. Anderson began to think that Harry Calvert knew his ridiculous little wife better than herself. Certainly, she showed her a new phase of her character.

It was only when, just before the carriage of the cassique came to take her away, that Zulieme showed anything like tears or passion. But, though her anger was roused, her firmness was not shaken even then! The occasion was the sudden appearance of Sylvia, the mulattress, who rushed out upon her, weeping and shrieking, and imploring to be taken with her. Then the little woman flushed up with something like fury :—

"Take her away! She shall never go with me again! Oh, the brute! the liar! To tell everything! To try and bring Harry to the gallows! Do, Charlotte, have her flung into the sea! oh, do!"

"No, no! not *that*, Zulieme!"

"Do n't let her come nigh *me!*"

The mulattress flung herself at her feet, and renewed her cries and protestations. The little woman seized a broomstick (what a weapon for a heroine!) and, but for the interposition of Mrs. Perkins Anderson, who was quite scandalized by such an unfeminine demonstration, would, no doubt, have belabored the waiting-maid soundly.

"Well, take her away — send her off — drown her in the sea — give her away — take her yourself, Charlotte, if you will; but never let her show herself to me again!"

And the matter was finally settled after this fashion. Mrs. Anderson agreed, to oblige Zulieme, to accept the gift; and the affair being thus understood, Sylvia promised to silence her affliction. She was not unwilling. In all probability, had Zulieme been anxious to take her, she would have shown herself a discontent. Like her mistress, she preferred town to country life; many people to few; smart company, on *terra firma*, to tary sailors aboard 'ship; and she was already prepossessed with Mrs. Perkins Anderson, and had learned to fancy that Charleston was a very tolerable place, though her tender affections had been so grievously mortified in it by the loose principles of Gideon Fairchild.

It was just as this affair was settled, that the stately carriage-and-four of the cassique of Kiawah, bearing the family crest, with

its French motto, "*Dieu avec nous*," drove up to the entrance —
the cassique the sole occupant.    There were two outriders in
livery.

It was a pleasurable reflection to Mrs. Perkins Anderson that
the carriage of one of the local barons should stand at her door,
no matter what the occasion.    She contrived to delay its waiting
as long as possible ; and for long afterward it was her wont to
say, whenever the cassique was referred to —

" Ah ! he was a fine gentleman.    His coach was frequently at
my door.    He was a favorite here ; and when he came, he seemed
quite unwilling to depart : he made long visits."

We need scarcely mention that, in removing Zulieme, the cassique " did his spiriting" with all courtesy and gentleness.    He
could not altogether prevent her from feeling that she was something of a prisoner.    The fact was patent in that of her removal.
But, neither in look, nor word, nor action, did he suffer her to feel
that she was likely to be annoyed in her *duresse*, or that it would
be other than was quite consistent with her claims as a wife, a
woman, and a lady.    He was tender and solicitous ; awaited her
moods with patience ; and, when he lifted her into the carriage, it
was with the studious observances of the nicest *preux chevalier*
of the time of Philip Sidney.

It is true that Zulieme was somewhat awed by this treatment,
and by the sad looks and dignified grace of the cassique.    She
had been at first a little terrified, when brought before the council.    It was only when she was taught how unwittingly her tongue
had committed her husband, that she recovered her composure,
and became lifted into resolution.    Still she felt an involuntary
disquiet, under the eye of the cassique, which was accorded rather
to his individual than his official character.    But this feeling had
no kin to fear.    Having persuaded herself that she was a hostage
for Harry, and possibly might be a sacrifice, she rose to a sense
of dignity with the sense of danger, which changed, for the time,
her whole demeanor.    Levity had given place to pride ; and it
was rather amusing than impressive, in the eyes of Mrs. Anderson, to see the stateliness and dignity which now, in the bearing
of the little woman, took the place of her former kitten-playful-
ness.    It was really comical to behold such resolved looks, such a
lofty carriage, so much reserve and dignity, in the conduct of one

so very *petite*, and whom she had been accustomed to see only in the character of the ballet-girl.  She could scarcely keep from laughter as she saw it.  She laughed at it a thousand times after.

But the parting took place after many delays.  Tears and many words constituted the demonstration of the fashionable Mrs. Charlotte.  Zulieme had no tears, and but few words; but these were proper, simple, graceful, and dignified.  She thanked her hostess gratefully for her care and kindness, and promised to remember all.  As the two embraced, Mrs. Anderson whispered—

"Oh! what shall I say from you to Craven and Cavendish? They will be so wretched!"

"Say?  Nothing!  What have I to say to them, Charlotte?"

"Ah, Zulieme, they were both so very fond of you!"

"They are both very foolish fellows, then; for I have no fondness for them!  Tell them nothing!"

And when she said this, her little, pulpy lips put on the smallest possible curl of contempt, while her eye looked as coldly and indifferently into that of Charlotte as if she scarcely remembered the parties spoken of.  The amiable hostess sighed gently.  She felt that some of her calculations had been made in vain.  Altogether, the little child-wife was a little problem.  But the two parted, tenderly enough.  Zulieme had absolutely shared her wardrobe with her hostess, who, whatever her weaknesses, whatever the wickedness of her designs — of which Zulieme knew nothing — had treated her with great and affectionate consideration of manner.  They parted, and the cassique lifted Zulieme into the carriage; and, at a wave of the hand, the coachman smacked his whip, postillion-fashion, and the carriage whirled away in a cloud of dust — the two outriders putting their horses into a canter to keep up with the vehicle.

That night Mrs. Anderson received no company.  Mrs. Calder Carpenter did.  But neither Cavendish nor Craven was present.  Of course, there was any amount of scandal and conjecture touching the wonderful events of the previous night and day; but the result of all was favorable to the Anderson.  She had certainly caused *a sensation* — which is always the *ne plus ultra* of the fashionable world — for good or evil matters little!  And, by-the-way, public opinion in Charleston was hardly so unfavorable to Calvert, "the don-destroyer," as to suffer his little wife to be disparaged.  Zulieme had won upon the circles which she had penetrated.

Poor Zulieme! she sat back in the cassique's carriage, perched proudly on her dignity!  Was she not doing penance for her husband?  Was she not a martyr — likely to be sacrificed for him?  The fancy made her very proud!  She was no longer a kitten!  Let us add that there was another reason — which must remain a secret a little longer — which added to her strength and dignity, and which rendered her so indifferent, if not contemptuous, when Charlotte Anderson reminded her of those two popinjays, Craven and Cavendish.  She brooded over this secret of her own — she never breathed it to her hostess even — with no little satisfaction.  Briefly, she had made a long stride, in a single moment, from girlhood to womanhood.  But of all this, hereafter.  It is a secret that will keep.  Zulieme will tell it to but one!

The cassique of Kiawah is already known to us, and we may well conceive that he bore himself toward the little wife of the famous corsair with all proper kindliness.  But it was only when he felt the necessity of soothing her mind, and reconciling her to her condition of captivity, that he began to perceive how awkward his situation was as custodian.  What sort of custodian could he be, with a household in such a condition as was his?  His wife — it was agony to think of her!  Her mother — it was with anger that he thought of *her!*  How could he make his captive comfortable in such condition of his household?  He had not thought of this before.  Born to wealth — accustomed to have his will, and command the service, even as he wished it — he suddenly felt that he had no service, no resources, to meet his present requisition.  His prisoner — a woman, young, seemingly artless, and of peculiar characteristics — would almost be companionless.  He had spoken, in council, from a natural impulse, and without due reflection.  His instincts had moved him.  He had been touched by the child-simplicity of the young wife of the corsair, and had undertaken to reconcile two objects: to keep her in security, from the possible attempts of the corsair himself — who, it was thought, would scarcely venture to penetrate the country; and to keep her from the humiliations of a common dungeon.  He was worried, in no small degree, at the task he had undertaken, and the more he thought of it; but, like a true knight, *sans peur*

22

*et sans reproche*, he prepared to do his *devoir*, and leave the rest to God's favor and the chapter of chances.

As a matter of course, he endeavored to beguile the route for his companion, by gentle and courteous conversation. The region through which they had to pass was not suggestive of agreeable topics. As we know, however beautiful to the eye which is " to the manner born," it was lacking in all salient essentials of the picturesque. It was without *form*, though far from *void*. There were no great heights; no striking inequalities; only vast tracts of forest, with brief stretches of road, so closed in on every hand, that there was no beyond. True, the season was one of flowers and fruits. There are green leaves, a glorious foliage; blossoms that were sweet upon the air; colossal trees, that made cathedral-shadows all around; dense masses of leaf and flower; vines and shrubs: but the eye naturally grew weary of the dead levels and the uniformity, which finally showed as one great waste! Yet had he little else of which to speak; and Zulieme, he soon found, had no eye for scenery. Besides, she had seen the great mountains which divide the seas, Pacific and Atlantic. And he quickly discovered that she had not the soul for that beauty which abounds in the instincts of art. She had had no cultivation, and the original soil of mind had received no seeds from Nature which a genial care could make to grow, as under the mere waving of the wand of Thought. There was no possible point of contact between the souls of the two. Zulieme had no thoughts, no imagination, hardly any fancies; scarcely more than the little bush-bird which hops from twig to twig, and never feels an aspiration to soar. Curious enough in respect to her husband, the corsair, our cassique was yet too much of the gentleman to touch upon this subject. But, as a gentleman, he wearied himself, sore and sick at heart as he was, in the effort to amuse her. But all in vain. She looked kindly into his eyes — almost reverentially. Her own instincts taught her that he was striving to please and amuse; but she could make no response; and he asked himself—

" How is it that education fails us, even when we aim to please, and in the case of those who are evidently so far below us in endowment and acquisition ?"

He did not remember that his own heart was ill at ease, and that his labors were those only of the mind. He did not forget,

it is true, that there was another reason for his failure.  He did
not dare to approach the very topics upon which her own mind
and heart were brooding.   There is a point of contact for all humanity, which will, at some moments, bring together the loftiest
and lowest; but this can only be found where the relations between the parties are such as leave both in comparative freedom.
Here, and now, both were under constraint, and from a variety of
causes.   At length the cassique gave up the effort, and sank back
in the carriage, silent and forgetful.   In his forgetfulness he
sighed, and such a sigh!  No sigh that Zulieme ever heard was
more deep, more expressive of mortal anguish.   She watched
him obliquely, with a growing sympathy; and, with every glance,
she thought—

"How like to Harry!"

She was awed by him, no doubt.   A noble earnestness of character, coupled with an evident sorrow, borne with manliness, must
always compel the respectful sympathies of the pure and ingenuous.   She could give the cassique credit as a noble gentleman,
even while she remembered that he was her jailer; and, in some
degree, she conjectured the truth — that he had become her jailer
only to save and spare her those humiliations which must have
followed her detention in the town.   She watched and studied her
companion in silence, but with a momently-growing sympathy.
He was so sad; his looks were so grand, yet so gentle; and he
was "so like Harry!"   And, even as she watched and mused, the
cassique forgot that she was present — that he had any companion, any auditor; and the deep sigh became a deeper groan, and
the bosom of the strong man heaved with convulsive emotions,
that distended his broad breast and shook his powerful frame;
and, in his anguish and oblivion, the big tears gushed from his
eyes, and he moaned aloud in syllables that startled the keen,
quick consciousness of his companion:—

"Olive!  Olive!   Would to God I could die for thee, Olive!"

"Olive!" murmured Zulieme to herself, looking more earnestly
into his eyes; "that name!"

Another big groan from the laboring breast; and the child-
woman forgot her curiosity in her sympathies, and laid her little
hand upon the cassique's arm, while she said, in her softest manner—

" Ah! señor, my lord — I am sorry that you so suffer!"

He started wildly at the touch and voice.

" Me, child! Suffer! I suffer?"

And he tried to smile; and, in the effort, he became conscious of the big tears still rolling down his cheek; and then his cheek was flushed with shame.

" I have forgotten myself, my dear young lady. Pray, pardon me. My thoughts wandered far away."

" Ah, sir, you groaned so bitterly!"

" It was not well to groan — not wise, nor courteous, my dear young lady; and I feel ashamed that I could so entirely forget your presence. Yet it is, perhaps, just as well that I should do so. It enables me to prepare you for a sad household. I have taken you with me, my child, not to a pleasant abiding-place, but to a safe one — one where you will find little to please or to amuse you; nay, where you may see things which shall sadden your young heart: but you will find protection, and a tender care, which shall not wound or vex you, until such time as the council shall choose to set you entirely free. I wish to be kind to you, young lady, and to hold you under guardianship, rather than in bonds."

" I think I know what you mean, señor, my lord," was the reply, in rather more broken English than usual, " and I thank you, señor, and Harry will thank you too; but tell me how long you mean that I should stay with you."

" Ah! that I can not yet say; for it does not lie with me wholly: but I will do my best, so that you shall be free as soon as it is possible. The trouble lies in this: if free, whither would you go? Your husband is under ban of outlawry. He will hardly come hither. He knows not where you are. He will scarcely venture again to visit Charleston, for the danger awaits him there. Your case is one of great difficulty, unless he can procure the king's pardon, which, for your sake, and somewhat for his own, I shall strive to get for him."

" Harry will not wait for a king's pardon. He will come for me anywhere. Harry does not love me much, but he will fight for me. He is not afraid to come to Charleston. Why, if Harry was so minded, he would bring his ship and fight all the town!"

The cassique mused at the little wife's confidence in her husband's courage and prowess; but the more he mused, the more sure he felt that the corsair would not find it hard to pelt the walls of Charleston about the ears of its people. But of this he said nothing. Only, being something curious, he asked —

"But why do you say that your husband does not love you much?"

"Oh! I suppose he loves me as much as he **loves** anybody" — then a pause — "except one, perhaps."

"And who is she? For it is a lady, I suppose."

"Yes!" — and, this said, the little wife looked into the eyes of the cassique earnestly and sadly, then added — "but I must not tell her name to *you*."

She had almost told it.

"And why not to *me*?"

"Nay, I must tell it to nobody. It is Harry's secret."

"I would I knew your husband, young lady. Though outlawed, I like what I have heard of him. I like him for his deeds."

"Oh! I am glad to hear you say so. You would like him better if you knew him, though he is so grand and proud, and so cold! And then, he looks so very much like you, señor!"

"Like me! Ah! I would I knew him. I will try to get his pardon, at all events."

"Thank you, señor; but Harry will not wait for that! He will have me, I know it, as soon as he can find me. He will take me out of your deepest dungeons."

"Oh! you must not speak of dungeons at Kiawah, my child. It is full of sorrow, and death hangs over it like a thunder-cloud ready to burst: but there are no bonds; and you shall find nothing but tenderness, even if there be no love.... Ha! look there! There is one of our dear little ones of Kiawah. That is my wife's sister and mine — our dear little pet, Grace Masterton. She is a sweet child, but a child only."

And he pointed to a group — Grace Masterton, and the Indian hunter, Iswattee, with a fawn that they were taming by the roadside, within one of the first enclosures of the barony.

"A child! you call that a child?" said Zulieme. "Why, she is as big as me!"

The cassique smiled sadly.

" Yes, but a child nevertheless."

" Let me get out and play with her ! She 's a beautiful creature ; and the red Indian boy ; and the little deer ; oh ! they all together look like a picture I have seen."

" It is, indeed, a picture," said the cassique ; and, at his command, the carriage stopped. By this time, the rolling of the wheels had reached the ears of the group ; and Grace had leaped the fence, and darted toward it, crying—

" Is it you, brother !" Then, seeing the strange lady, she hung back, abashed. The young Indian did not move from his place, but appeared to busy himself with his fawn. He did not even look out toward the carriage, preserving well that stolidity of demeanor — that show of incuriousness — which is the usual characteristic of the red man. But, from the corner of his eye, he had already, at a single glance, taken in the whole party ; and even before Grace had leaped the fence, he had seen that there was a strange lady in the carriage.

For the first few moments, Zulieme had become a child again. She had forgotten her dignity — forgotten the pride which had reminded her, ever and anon throughout the journey, that she was a prisoner — a hostage for her husband. The sight of Grace, a tall, fair English girl, with bright eye and tresses floating free ; the half-tamed fawn ; the Indian boy, in his picturesque costume — fringed hunting-shirt, mockasons, leggins, baldric over the shoulders, fur cap and white eagle-feather, and the long, black, straight hair, which hung down over his neck — this group suggested to Zulieme the idea of play and sport. It was, at least, a relief to escape from the close carriage, and feel herself on the greensward, and under embowering trees ; and she cried out —

" Oh ! let me get out, if you please."

Then Grace seconded the entreaty, saying—

" Oh ! yes, do, dear brother ; let the little girl get out and come with me. I 'm so glad you 've brought her !"

The cassique good-naturedly ordered the door to be opened. But Zulieme had changed her mind. She had resumed her dignities — had been reminded of them all by the one little sentence spoken by Grace.

" Little girl !" quoth she to herself, looking proudly. " Ah ! if they but knew !"

" Will you alight, my dear young lady," said the cassique, musing upon the sudden change in all her features.

" No, thank you, señor; I will go on."

" If you will alight," said he, " the carriage will remain, and bring you up with my little sister, when you are prepared to come.  It is now but a short distance to the settlement, and I would walk among my workmen.  I prefer to walk."

" Do so, señor; but, if you please, I will not now get out."

Then, finding it of no avail to press her, the cassique alighted himself, and lifted Grace into the vehicle, and bade her be good friends of the young lady, who, he added impressively, " is the wife of Captain Calvert."

" Wife !" murmured Grace; and with a curious eye she regarded Zulieme as she took her seat beside her.  And thus, the two together, the carriage drove away.  Then, as they rode, Grace gently took the hand of Zulieme, and pressed it, and said:—

" I am so glad that my good brother has brought you here; for I am so lonesome !  We will be so happy together !"

But, for a part of the ride, Zulieme would not *look* her willingness to be happy, and Grace began to think her strangely churlish.  But the little wife thawed after awhile; and, before the carriage reached the dwelling, she and Grace had become very tolerable companions: albeit Zulieme had sundry returns of her pride and dignity, especially when she thought of her nice little secret; and when she remembered that she was at the barony *on compulsion*, and as the hostage for her husband !

# CHAPTER XLIX.

### ISWATTEE.

"How terrible this duty to be done;
  This trial to be passed!   Yet must I brave it."

THE cassique, meanwhile, having alighted from the carriage, approached the Indian boy, where he stood busy with the fawn, whispering in her ear, and practising those arts of the woodman by which he subdues the wild animal to tameness. And, as he drew nigh, the cassique became suddenly conscious of a great change which had taken place in the appearance of the youth. He perceived that he was grown thin, even to meagerness; that his eyes, though very bright, as ever, seemed to shine forth out of hollows; and that his cheeks were greatly sunken. Now, this change had been growing for some time; but the cassique had been too much busied with his own cares to note those of his forester. He had been content to believe that the boy had been well kept and tendered, and that he performed skilfully his sylvan duties; so that he held it sure that all went well with him. In sooth, if he thought of him, at any time, it was only to wonder at the marvellous skill which he displayed in taking, snaring, or slaughtering, his game. Never once, while he was with the cassique, was the venison wanting to his employer's table; and sometimes he brought home great fat turkeys, and ducks of such size and flavor as might not be equalled in all Europe. He wist not, indeed, that the young man occasionally got help from his brethren; for his sire, old Cussoboe, ever and anon, through some runners of his people, helped him to a buck, or a great turkey, and to ducks which he had himself shot with his arrows, along the great bays and estuaries which lie, in this country, everywhere close beside the sea.

But, now that the eyes of the cassique were suddenly drawn upon the boy, and he saw truly his condition — how meagre he was of frame, how sunken of eye and cheek, and what a deep sorrow seemed to rest upon his visage — he began to fear lest he had suffered some despite at the hands of his people. So he said to him:—

"Iswattee, my lad, what ails you? You look not well. Are you sick? Is there hurt or grievance which I may redress? Tell me, my good boy; and remember, I must be to you a father, in the absence of your own."

So he laid hands upon the boy, and gazed kindlily into his face; and the tones of his voice were sweet and soothing, even as his words were kind. But the boy cast his eyes down to the earth, and did not answer him; only the cassique noted, as if a little shuddering had suddenly gone through his body. And the boy stooped to the fawn, and busied himself with the silver collar, and the bell, which Grace Masterton had put about her neck. Then the cassique could well conceive that something had gone wrong with him; and he more earnestly, but with even more tenderness than before, exhorted him to say wherein he ailed. To this the boy replied abruptly, in the manner of his people, but not, as we should deem, with any purpose to be rude.

"What should ail Iswattee? Iswattee says not, 'Iswattee is hurt — Iswattee is sick!'"

Then he stooped and whispered something in the ear of the little fawn, and at the same moment he pulled her by the forefoot; whereupon — even as he had devised by the action — the little beast sprang away from him, and coursed with all its speed over the meadows. Then the boy as suddenly sprang away after her, leaving the cassique unanswered and alone.

And the cassique mused upon the strangeness of the proceeding; for well he surmised that the boy had so trained the doe to flight, by a trick of whisper, even as the Arab trains his horse. And he said to himself, musingly:—

"It belongs to the race! There is a nature which the great God of the universe designs for each several place and people. The wild for the wild; else would it never be made tame! But when, in

22*

the great forests, the wild beasts shall all be subdued or slaughtered, will the wild man rise to higher uses? Hath his humanity
a free susceptibility for enlargement and other provinces? Shall
he feel the growth, in his breast and brain, of higher purposes?
Will his thought grow, and provide for newer wants of his soul?
If it may not be thus, then must he perish, even as the forests
perish; he will not survive the one use for which all his instincts
and passions seem to be made! It is, perhaps, his destiny! He
hath a pioneer mission, to prepare the wild for the superior race;
and, this duty done, he departs: and, even as one growth of the
forest, when hewn down, makes way for quite another growth of
trees, so will he give place to another people. Verily, the mysteries of Providence are passing wonderful!"

And, so musing, our cassique took his way to the openings of
the barony, where his workmen were all busy in laying off the
grounds — making great avenues, and converting the wild forests into goodly woods. Meanwhile, the Indian boy had sped
from sight, wild as the deer himself, seemingly in pursuit of the
fawn. But her he soon whistled to him, so soon as he had sped
out of call of the cassique; and he carried her back to the barony
in safety; and housed her in the neat little house which had been
made for her; and, having brought her green food, he closed the
door upon her, and departed — stealing away from sight so that
no one knew how he went — and he hid himself in the deep thickets where stood the hollow tree which kept the war-arrows from
which "*he broke* the successive *days*" daily.

From the hollow he drew forth the sheaf, the arrows of which
had become but few. He counted them, one by one, with a sad
eye and slow hand; withdrew one of them and broke it, and again
he counted them. He had not done this before. He had scarcely
need to do so now; for the arrows were now so few, that he might
easily see, at a glance, that his own term of service was about to
close, and that the first fearful trial of his young life was approaching fast. Not two weeks remained to him ere that event. And
that event! It was the thought — the dread of its coming — which
had made him thin and wo-begone of aspect; had withered, as it
would seem, his young life; had taken the lightness away from
his heart, and placed there, instead of it, a leaden sorrow. And,
by the sorrows which he shall show us to-night, shall we learn

what were those which have been robbing him of the healthy vigor of his limbs, and the cheery brightness of his eye!

It has been shown us that he has been consecrated by his sire to a great purpose of his tribe. For this hath he been assigned to a menial service in the dwelling of one whom his people secretly regarded as a public enemy. He is fully conscious of the duty before him. It contemplates a national revenge. It involves treachery, havoc, and murder; and he is put in a position to minister to the terrible object by his keen subtlety and cunning stratagem.

But his nature revolts at the work before him. He is somewhat differently constituted from his people. Though the son of a prince — himself a prince, reared and trained with reference to this very performance — his soul, of less masculine nature than that of his people, shrinks as he contemplates the results of his action. He does not fear death or strife. But his moods are naturally gentle; his fancies are lively; his susceptibilities large; his imagination lofty: he would better make the orator or the poet of his people, than their sanguinary warrior! The red men make their mistakes, even as the whites, in *willing* a pursuit for their sons which is inconsistent with natural endowment. Set aside, suffered to go free, and work out the problem for himself, independently of convention, and Iswattee — " *the tree put to grow*" — might become something of a philosopher — something higher, perhaps — a seer, a poet, gifted with prophetic foresight! Arbitrarily decreed to be a warrior, and to steep his hands in blood, as a sort of baptism of his opening manhood, he shudders at the destiny before him; which, as yet, he sees not how to escape.

His ordeal, which we have already described, has shown us that the spiritual influences which have wrought upon his imagination were not in accordance with the will of his father. The images which wooed him in his dreams were not savage, but gentle and loving. Instead of the raging tiger, the stealthy panther, the stealing and subtle serpent, the thundering cayman, either of which would have gratified his sire, there came to him a white bird, which sweetly stooped to his ear, and whispered him with love! And anon, when he was first brought to the white cassique, whom he was to requite with treachery, he beheld a fair white girl, whom his lips unwittingly called " An-ne-gar!"— whom his instincts taught him was the very creature which had been imaged to his dreaming senses as the bird whose *totem* he should bear!

And, strange to say, this damsel of the pale-races attached herself only to him! Poor Grace! she had no alternative. She had no playmates, no companions of her own age; her mother scarcely noticed her; and her elder sister, dying by sad degrees, hardly conscious half the time, had no thought of Grace, unless when she stood actually beside her!

And so Grace and the Indian boy went together in the forests, until she grew almost as wild as he; and he brought her the young fawn; and he taught her his sylvan arts — how to snare the game and trap the bird; and, in return, she sang for him, and gave him the only lessons which he had, by which to articulate in the speech of the foreign people.

And daily, if he grew not wiser in this strange speech, his heart grew softer, his moods more gentle; and then he began to feel, more and more, how terrible was the duty which had been set him by his sire! And nightly as he came, as now, to do his task — to break the arrow, and mark the day which was spent; as he came to see how rapidly approaching was the period when he should be required to open the doors of the dwelling to the midnight murderer — to steep his own knife and hatchet in the blood of the people who belonged to An-ne-gar, his white bird: nay, when the terrible picture rose before his imagination, of that fair creature herself reft of those beautiful tresses; her white skin dabbled in blood; her bright, laughing eyes quenched in death — then the wretched boy threw himself, in his agony, down upon the brown heather; and, though he broke the arrow, he wailed and bemoaned the destiny to which Indian boy had never before proved himself untrue!

That there should be one, unknown, who should supply, for a time, the broken arrows, and thus compel him to mistake the appointed time, he, of course, knew not; but these substituted arrows covered but a week of time: and now, as he looked upon the sheaf, he groaned in despair; for he discovered that, by *his* count, but thirteen arrows remained of all the sheaf which his sire had given him — but thirteen days of respite — and then the wild cry at midnight; the whoop of death; the sharp arrow; the griding knife; the cleaving hatchet; the wholesale massacre of those whose bread he ate, whose care he felt, whose love he desired most; the murder of the very bird of whiteness and ineffable beauty, which the Great Spirit had commissioned him to take to his heart as its tutelary genius!

But thirteen nights, and then all these crowding horrors! How much more terrible would have been his anguish, had he dreamed that even this respite was not allowed him — that he had not half this time; that his strategy had been baffled by superior cunning; that half of the arrows remaining in his serpent-quiver were false substitutes for others which he had already broken!

But, even with his imperfect knowledge, his misery could scarcely have suffered increase. Having broken the *one* arrow, and restored the sheaf to the hollow tree, he cast himself down upon the earth, face prone in the dust, and moaned audibly. He could moan — the red man can weep, moan, and laugh, like the men of another race, *if he be alone.* But his self-esteem, which is always nursed by solitude, will never suffer a witness of his tears; hardly of his laughter. He is not adamant, though he hides from the sight of the white man — whom his instincts describe to him as a mocking superior — his passionate emotions, his agonies, his fears and tears.

And hot and scalding were the tears which gushed from the young eyes of Iswattee, and deep and sad enough were the great sobs that shook his bosom and burst from his parted lips — as, throwing himself upon the earth, with face buried in the dust, he prayed to the Great Spirit, the Almighty and Eternal Father, whom he so ignorantly knew, to find him some way of escape from the task set him — from the sire of his people! — prayed him to open a path, at least, by which to save the little White Bird and *her* people! And, might we now translate the language of his prayer, it would be seen that nothing more fervent and full of earnest passion ever flowed from the lips of Christian priest or sinner!

But he did not limit himself to prayer. The poor savage, with heart thus growing white, had still a perfect faith in the superstitions of his own people. His faith required penance, an ordeal, as well as prayer; and, with the hope to receive a saving and teaching inspiration, he imposed upon himself a renewal of that exhausting novitiate from which he had only just emerged, when first brought to our knowledge.  He had gathered a supply of the bitter roots of the forest, emetic and narcotic, which the Indian pharmacy had already taught him how to prepare ; and there, night-ly, in the secrecy of the thicket, he built his fires, and in his little pots of clay he boiled his nauseous decoctions.  Nightly did he drink of the liquors, black and crimson alternately, purging his blood and stimulating his brain ; and swallowing daily only such small portions of the simplest food as should sustain life.  Then, retiring into still deeper thickets, he threw himself down in the solitude and darkness, to sleep, and dream, and win from Heaven the much-desired inspiration.  Let us not mock at the simple superstition, in consideration of his simpler and much-confiding faith.  Alas, for the poor boy ! his visions now brought him only to a bewildering confusion of the senses.  The images that visited his dreaming fancies were mingled wildly, and taught him noth-ing.  Ever the white bird was present, conspicuous over all, but it was amid the storm of a conflict, in which his sire and the bird and himself strove at once together.  There were raging wolves ; there were lurking serpents ; the great black bear sometimes would trample on his bosom, and the stealthy panther scream be-side his ear ; but the white bird would come, even then, between him and his fate, and in the flutter of her perfect plumage his aching spirit would be lulled to sleep.  But, from all his visions he won no counsel ; and the morning found him, at every dawn-ing, as doubtful of his future, as unsteady of his purpose, as when he had surrendered himself to sleep the night before.  No wonder the cassique was confounded at the wo-stricken aspect of the boy !

Alas ! fearful as was the trial before him, he was not the only sufferer under the bloody sweat of the spirit, struggling with the fleshly destiny.  The cassique must go through a like ordeal, though under the guidance of a superior nature.  He, too, must appeal to the Great Spirit, and through secret prayer, and in the patient en-durance of a wo that knows no remedy — that can not save — that feels how certain is the doom that crushes the beloved one out of life, and denies that any arm shall save !  He knows that Olive, his wife, is doomed.  He deceives himself in nothing.  He knows that, without knowledge or evil purpose, he himself hath doomed her ; his very love, which would have saved and nourished, and crowned her, as his queen of love, of beauty, of song, and of truth and purity, hath been the bane of her life, and the blast which hath mildewed her beauty. He hath built, and hoped, and prayed, and loved, in vain; and not merely in vain, but mischievously. And now he feels no more the heart to build, or the hope to save, or the taste for the beautiful. His occupation is at an end. The very being for whose blessing he had decreed that the wilderness should blossom as the rose, can see no more, can feel no more, of the charm that dwelleth in sky, or wood, or tree, or flower. The blossoms have perished from her cheeks, and a premature autumn is blowing its blight across her heart.

Yet, though he sees and feels all this, and though his own heart is full of its own agonies, he must come before her with a brow serene, if sad. She sits in a cushioned chair in her chamber when he comes, clad in white, her hands clasped upon her lap, her face wan as the moon upon a wintry night, yet her eyes shining with a supernatural brightness. Her lips are bloodless — whiter than her cheeks. Her long hair falls upon her shoulders, escaping from beneath the white cap, and rests altogether lifeless, that was once all glow and sparkling beauty. And thus she sits for hours, until, in her exhaustion, she will say, "Mother;" and when the miserable mother comes to her, she will only point to the couch, and whisper, "Sleep — sleep! I *must* sleep, mother."

But now, as the cassique returns, he conducts Zulieme to his wife's chamber, and finds her sitting up as we have described. He has met her mother in the hall, who has much wondered to see him bring the stranger, and one so beautiful and young. He is brief in his introduction of Zulieme; and the mother is suddenly haughty.

"I see not," she said, in a half whisper, "how we are to entertain a stranger *now*."

"You are not required to overcome this difficulty, Mrs. Masterton. I beg you not to attempt it. I will instruct Mrs. Pond — my housekeeper — as to what is to be done. I have considered the whole matter."

"But you will not trouble Olive, in her present state, with this woman's presence," she replied, in still subdued tones, seeing that the cassique was actually about to do this very thing.

"It will hardly trouble her; it may soothe. This lady is a

married woman, though very young, and she will be my guest for
awhile; and, while my guest, it is fitting that she should see my
wife. I can not think that it will hurt Olive; it must rather interest her. She may arouse and divert her thoughts."

The Honorable Mrs. Masterton lifted her eyebrows, and her
hands slightly, as the cassique turned away from her to Zulieme;
and finally left the hall hurriedly, and proceeded with all haste to
Olive's chamber. Here she had no sooner entered, but the ma-
licious fool-woman exclaimed—

"What do you think?—he has gone and brought home a
strange woman—a strange woman—and a young one, too—and
you, my poor Olive, so feeble—so—"

"Oh, I pray you, *hush*, mother!" was the plaintive appeal of
Olive; which might not have availed to stop the beldame's tongue,
but that the cassique was so quick in following her footsteps. He
gave her but a look as he entered, and Olive saw that look, if
nothing else. The mother left the room. The cassique approached his wife tenderly, and with a strange, sad humility of
deportment, as if he felt a fear. The look of authority, which had
awed the mother, was changed to one of the meekest and most
submissive gentleness and timidity.

"Olive," he said, "I have ventured to bring you a young lady-
companion for awhile. You will make her welcome. She is
young and artless."

A sweet smile passed over the lips of the dying woman—so
sweet, so soliciting, so bland and blessing, that it won Zulieme in a
moment to her side, where she suddenly knelt down and kissed the
wan, thin hands of the sufferer. Her quick eye caught instantly
the fearful intelligence of death in that strangely-sweet aspect.
She saw that the lady was fast escaping from earth, and that her
spirit was already sublimed for heaven by its own perfect consciousness of the truth. She saw, too, that the heart of the sufferer was desolate; but that, in its desolation, it had grown to tenderness! And the lady was named "Olive." How that name
haunted our little Spanish wife! but, in this case, it was not with
any fear. Surely, this could not be the "Olive" that Harry used
to love! And yet, how strange that the cassique should so greatly
resemble Harry! Zulieme was bewildered, but not forgetful.
Olive suffered her to keep possession of her thin, wan fingers, and

smiled upon her the gentle welcome that her lips did not speak; and with this welcome the wife of our rover was content.

Olive Berkeley had fully recovered her senses. She had passed through a fearful paroxysm; but it left her brain free. In degree as her infirmities increased, her mind had become clearer. She had no more visions of Harry Berkeley. Once assured that he was living — once assured of his actual presence — it would seem that all the mists that had clouded her mental vision had passed away, and the evening promised a sweet, mild, gentle sunset. The skies were growing brighter as the earth grew dim. Life had nothing to bestow, and all the love of which she was now capable was perfectly free. Her spirit was at one with that joy of peace which reposes on assured hopes and the purest affections, and harmonizes every doubt in faith.

Zulieme was soon at home at the barony of Kiawah. She was often with Olive, and talked with her, and grew fond of serving her. She played with Grace, and became a child as she played with the child. But she shrank from the stately mother, whose smile of mixed scorn and vexation usually drove her to the chamber of Olive, or to the playground of Grace, with whom she frequently found the Indian boy Iswattee. But she somehow disliked this boy. He was solemn without cause. She could forgive the gravity of the dying Olive; but such gravity as that of Iswattee she held to be an impertinence. What right had such a boy to look so sorrowfully grand? Alas for the poor Indian! she knew not where *his* torture lay!

Grace suddenly discovered, only the day after Zulieme's arrival, that something ailed Iswattee; and she said to him, abruptly:

"Iswattee, ar'n't you sick? You look so! You must have physic! You must get well. You must go to brother, and get some of that physic he gives to me. It always makes me well. But, O boy! how it will make you tie up your face, it's so horrid nasty! What!" — as the Indian shook his head — "you won't go? But I will myself. I'll tell brother; and he'll mix the physic; and I'll bring it; and I'll make you drink it, you foolish fellow, and laugh to see the face you'll make! But 'twill make you well, Iswattee."

Having now temporarily disposed of the cassique's household, let us look to our rover on the sea.

## CHAPTER L.

### THE DOINGS WITH THE DONS.

"This be one of your circumventions, forsooth! I warrant you it shall end in a broil." — *Old Comedy.*

THE "Happy-go-Lucky" was once more at sea, "walking the waters like a thing of life." But she did not walk according to the desires of her captain. She had head winds. He desired to run down south, but the winds blew from that quarter; and, before he had left the port of Ashley an hour, they came on heavily to blow. To keep her from being blown north, was all that he could hope for; and the labors of the day were all addressed to this object. Incessantly was the little cruiser put about, our rover keeping his eye steadfastly in the direction of Kiawah.

He was troubled. His mind was full of deep anxieties. To be thwarted, even by a straw, when we have set our souls upon an object, is to chafe and madden!

"We have but few days left us," said Calvert to his favorite follower, Belcher, as he strode the quarter-deck. "These accursed savages will be upon them at Kiawah! These murderous Spaniards will be upon them at Beaufort! If this gale last— this wind continue from this quarter — where shall I be? Where I can give them no succor!"

"But," responded Belcher, "have you not had advices sent to Beaufort?"

"Yes, if any faith can be put in the promise of Governor Quarry! But he made quite too light of the danger, as it seemed to me, and has probably done nothing. That a butterfly should be in commission when a mountain is to be heaved up!"

"Oh! no doubt he has done it, sir. He could hardly, if he promised you, have forgotten or neglected it."

" I could hope so — deem so ; for I took care to urge the matter upon him in no moderate terms of entreaty.    Yet all will depend upon his promptness.    He would need to send his despatch by water to Lord Cardross.    One *periagua* might fail.    I should have sent three, in swift succession ; so that if one were swamped, or two, there might be a third chance.    But — and it is not easy to say that any would be in season !    The Spaniards once upon the seas, would take the wind, not heeding any appointed days with the savages ; and this wind, now dead ahead for us, would bring them rapidly on their way.    They might capture and destroy the settlement at Beaufort, without giving heed to the rising of the Indians, even though they had concerted with them for a simultaneous invasion.    In the conquest of Beaufort they would need no help of the savages.    It would be an achievement wholly of their shipping ; and, even with the advices of Governor Quarry, Lord Cardross could not put the place in a state of defence.    His only hope of safety would be in its abandonment, and the escape of his people to Charleston by land.    Then would come the next danger from the savages.    O winds ! winds ! winds ! why do ye baffle me at this perilous moment ?"

And he strode the deck impatiently, heedless of the storm and driving spray.    Then, returning to where Belcher stood, now joined by old Franks, he said :—

" And there is that danger, the uprising of the red men themselves.    We have but a few days more to spare — not six before their outbreak ; and, unless we can get back in season, the scattered settlements will all be destroyed, and their people massacred. There is my wilfully-blind bro—"

Here he checked himself, and looked sternly on his two listeners.    Then, suddenly —

" Does not the wind lull ?"

" Blows harder than ever, your honor," was the reply of old Franks."

" What was I saying?    Ah !    There is the settlement of Kiawah, the new barony of Sir Edward Berkeley — what shall save it, and the thoughtless inhabitants, unless we can seasonably arrive ?"

" But, sir, I myself carried your instructions to Gowdey, and the letter to Sir Edward, counselling him to be watchful."

"Ay, but suppose Gowdey could not get to Kiawah? These red men are now scattered over the face of the country. He might find it impossible to make his way."

"Oh! sir, I'd stake ten years of my life on old Gowdey as a scout."

"Perhaps! But if the cassique will not hear him? If, as has been hitherto the case, he holds these to be vain apprehensions, and still persists in his belief in the good faith of the red men?"

"Then," said old Franks, something vexatiously — "then he ought to feel their arrows! Ef a man's so full of his own conceit, that he won't hear to reason and ixperience, I'm clear he ought to suffer for it."

"Silence, old man! you know not what you say! It is a virtuous error in the cassique of Kiawah. It is an error, no doubt; but it is the growth of a noble heart. Let us not be too free to use God's judgments! Better that men should suffer, from too much faith in humanity, than that faith should die out wholly in the heart of man! No, Franks! let us not speak thus, though we feel that our fellow is blind and weak, and persists in a foolish error. We must save men from their errors, if we can; not abandon them to Fate, because they are foolish."

"But who's the cassique of Kiawah, that he should refuse to listen when wiser men tell him of his danger? He's but a new-comer among us, and pretends to know more of these red-skins than anybody besides. He ought to have the decency to listen to those who know 'em better. Why, sir, to believe in an Injin is like trustin' to a shark. He'll saw through you with his teeth while you're a-ticklin' in his ears. Everybody who knows the breed, knows that you've got to shoot as soon as you can see enough of the copper of the skin to drop a bead upon; ef you stops to ax first what they're a-wantin', it's equal to sayin', 'Come and take my sculp!'"

The captain strode to and fro in considerable vexation; then returning, said to Belcher: —

"Do you know anything of one Ligon? Gowdey has engaged him as a scout for me, between his castle, Kiawah, and the bay where we harbored."

"And he couldn't have got a better, sir; he's first rate: Franks knows him well. 'T was he that showed me the way over the country when I came to Charleston first from Beaufort."

"He's good as a guide, then? Knows all the country along the Stono and Ashley?"

"Like a book, sir."

"He is to meet us at our landing, and to serve us as a guide to Kiawah from that point. We have to pursue the shortest and most secret route, by the Stono upward."

"'Tain't always the shortest that's the safest."

"No, indeed! But these are the very objects that he is to reconcile. Gowdey tells me he can do it."

"Ef anybody can, he can. I'd jest as lief have Ligon as Gowdey, and I'd as soon have Gowdey as any scout livin'."

"Well, if the winds will but chop round to east or north, we shall do!"

And all parties, as if by a common impulse, proceeded, *sotto voce*, to apostrophize the winds, after a well-known sailor-fashion. But, though the gale subsided, the winds remained ahead all day. The air was thick with rain, and so it continued till nightfall. The rain ceased after night, but a heavy mist followed, which continued till ten o'clock next day. The cruiser had probably been driven, in spite of all seamanship, some thirty miles farther north. Such were Calvert's calculations.

At ten, however, the wind had slightly shifted, so as to enable the ship to shape her course a few points nearer. But the airs grew light and baffling. Suddenly, the lookout from the mast-head sang out —

"Sail ho!"

"Where away?"

"Due east, sir."

Here was a new subject of concern. Was this one of the king's cruisers from New York, obeying the requisitions of the council of the lords-proprietors, and sent specially for the overhauling of our rover? It seemed probable.

"Sail ho!" was again the cry from the top.

"Ha! two!" exclaimed Calvert. His hands now promised to be full. His anxieties increased. But the skies thickened again, and into fog. The breeze grew more and more languid. A vast curtain seemed dropped over the whole ocean; objects could not be discerned beyond the ship's length. The unknown vessels were lost as soon as seen. They were probably but five miles distant when first discovered.

"It is easy enough, perhaps, to show them our heels," he said to Belcher, "for there are few creatures so swift of wing as our little cruiser; but we must make our port! We can only run a certain distance. Kiawah must bring us up. We run for Stono. At all events, beyond Beaufort we can not go!"

"We can surely run out of sight of any British cruiser in these waters," replied Belcher.

"Perhaps! yet the 'Southampton' is a fast sailer, and so is the 'Swallow'—she is even faster."

"Yes, sir; but the Swallow can't weigh metal against ours."

"What, Belcher! are you, too, thinking of fighting a king's ship? No, no! we must run from them—elude them, in some way, and make our harbor."

It was neither the Southampton nor the Swallow that they saw; but vessels of even better speed and heavier metal—the "Thunderbolt" and "Dragon;" the one commanded by Sir Everard Holly, a sprig of nobility—a baronet of late creation—a creature of the court, who had never been baptized in salt water, and knew nothing of his business. The Dragon had quite another sort of captain; an old sea-dog, who knew his business thoroughly, but had one infirmity: he sacrificed to Bacchus in the strongest waters. The lookout of the Dragon had caught a glimpse of the Happy-go-Lucky, and she signalled to the Thunderbolt, upon which Sir Everard had his bath prepared and made his toilet. Captain Pogson at the same moment went below, and swallowed a potent goblet of punch. These were so many oblations to Fortune! Both made all the sail they could under the circumstances, duly stimulated by the reward offered for the capture of the famous cruiser, and by the persuasion of prize-money besides. But the fog soon covered the sea, for them as for the Happy-go-Lucky.

The fog lifted again at nightfall; the winds grew more favorable; the stars gradually began to steal out. The Happy-go-Lucky was at once upon the wing. Calvert walked the deck. Suddenly the watch reported—

"Lights!"

"Where away?"

" Right astern! about four miles."

" Shall we extinguish *our* cabin-lights, sir?" demanded Belcher

" No!"

Belcher and Franks were somewhat surprised, and both ventured to expostulate.

" We are but drawing them after us, sir. They both sail well. With our lights in, sir, we might lose them."

" We shall be more likely to do so with lights shown. But they will take the course anyhow. We must *mislead* them *by* our lights."

The king's ships had first caught the favoring breeze. They had gained accordingly; but Calvert soon found—for they continued to show lights also—that they did not gain upon him.

" We can run out of sight of them, if we please; but I would rather beguile them into the gulf. I do not care that they should reach Charleston until our work is over."

" Shall we clap on more sail, your honor?"

" Not a rag! We have enough for our present object."

" The dem'd impertinent!" quoth Sir Everard; " he shows his lights, too! He is very complacently dem'd civil, and we shall knock his dead-lights in for him, I deliberately determine! Do with your dem'd sails what you will"—to the lieutenant—" but put on all you can; only don't let that beast of a tar-coat, Pogson, throw his skirt in our faces. I do not affect the odor from his ship."

" He will pass us, your honor. The Dragon, on this wind, has the heels of the Thunderbolt."

" And can you do nothing—is there no way, by dexterously working this implement here"—pointing to the helm—" or by putting on sails, to get ahead of this unclean vessel? She has a savor such as the ark of Noah must have had, with its very-much-mixed population."

The marine of England, in the time of Charles II., had fallen into just such hands, with few exceptions. The Raleighs and Blakes were extinct.

" We will try, your honor."

" You will greatly try my honor if you do not; ay, and my honor's nostrils, too! Faugh! what a most horrid, onion-like savor!"

But the Dragon would pass the Thunderbolt. Both vessels carried all the sail they could. And so the chase was hotly urged until long after midnight; the pursuing and pursued keeping up nearly the same relative space between them as at first.

Shifting the scene to the Happy-go-Lucky, we find Calvert still on deck, as the stars began to pale in the growing mists of the morning. He seemed to drowse, so silent were his musings. But never mind was more vigilant; never eye more widely awake. At length he said, referring to a previous order—

"Belcher, has the boat been made ready, with the lanterns?"

"All ready, sir."

"We have run so many knots the hour, have we not?"

"My count, sir, exactly."

"In an hour more we shall be off the opening of the Stono. It is yet three hours to daylight. The mists are thickening. It will be dark enough for our purpose. Call Lieutenant Eccles."

The first lieutenant drew nigh.

"Lieutenant Eccles, you will please see to the launch. You have stepped her mast? And the lanterns are all prepared?"

"All right, sir; all ready!"

"Have your tackle all ready to set her afloat when I give the signal."

Calvert mused and strode the deck; Eccles lingered. Soon Belcher came forward.

"The wind will just suit us; quite enough northing for an off-shore course, and the sea is smooth enough. If we can send them wide, after a firefly, but for one hour — ay, half an hour — it will suffice."

This seemed spoken in soliloquy, softly; and no sooner was it spoken, than our rover walked forward, looked over the bows and gunwale, watched the run of the ship, stepped back to the binnacle and noted her bearings, examined his watch, and then — some three quarters of an hour having elapsed since he first questioned about the launch — he said to Eccles:—

"Now, lieutenant, our hour has come. Your launch is ready, your lanterns hung? Lounch the boat, and light them; and you, Hazard, with your own hands, instantly put out the lights of the ship."

The thing was done with that regularity and promptness which marks all the evolutions in a well-managed ship-of-war, and the report made to the captain. In a few moments after, the boat, with lighted lanterns at the top of her mast, was borne away, glimmering and gleaming along the edge of the sea, like a star rapidly losing its fires in the dawn. At the same moment, Calvert seized the helm of the ship from the hands of the seaman, and, under the sudden direction of his arm, she shot aside obliquely into the darkness; shifting her course, and laying her head landward, though as yet no outline of the shore was visible to any eye.

"Our little 'Firefly,'" quoth Calvert to the group beside him, "must make report for us to our pursuers. The wind, as it bears now, and the drift of the sea (the tide now running out) will keep her clear of the land. If she swims but a single hour, she will do her work — she will serve our purpose. We must do the rest. You, Lieutenant Eccles, and you, Will Hazard, get into the rigging, and keep sharp lookout on either hand. You, Belcher, get into the chains, and Franks watch amidships. We shall need all our eyes in this navigation; for though mine are good, and I have been a pilot more than once in these waters, the work is sufficiently perilous and nice."

"Now I see it all," quoth Belcher to Franks, as the two made off together. "These king's ships, ef they be king's ships, will follow the 'Firefly;' and we'll slip into the Stono, and not draw any eyes after us."

"It's dark enough for it," replied Franks. "It's a sort of fightin' in the dark, with the inimy up the chimney."

"It is that! But the captain's got the eyes of an owl! He's great for pilotage. The place he's once seen, or the person, he knows for ever. I'll risk anything on his eyes."

"They're better than mine."

"To your posts, men!" cried the captain.

They were off in an instant.

"Keep the lead going, Lieutenant Eccles!" continued Calvert. "Let them make prompt report."

"Ay, ay, sir!"

"Do you see the lights of the king's ships — how they're steering?" whispered Belcher to Franks, as he mounted the gunwale at the prow, and was stepping into the chains.

" They're steering, I reckon, as before."

" Yes, I think so. Ef they should attempt to follow us, I reckon we shall see them beached before daylight. And the ' Firefly ?' "

" The critter's standin' out to sea, and keeps her course like a sensible thing. Well, Belcher, good luck to him that sees the end of it !"

" Psho ! old fellow, you're scary ! I'm never scary when the captain's at the helm."

" By the deep, *twelve !*" was the sonorous cry of the sailor who heaved the lead.

" She shoals mighty fast, I'm thinkin', said Franks.

" Oh ! the captain knows jest where to put about. He knows all the soundin's. But go you along the sides now, as he told you. He'll know, ef you are not jest where he wants you."

And Franks went toward the captain.

" By the deep, *twelve !*" said the lead.

" Shoalin' fast, captain."

" Just as I would have it, Franks. I think I know where I am now ! Hark, Franks ! are you on the lookout there ?"

" Ay, ay, sir !"

" And don't hear the breakers ?"

" Not yet, your honor. But we shall soon, I reckon."

" Take the wax from your ears, old man ! I hear them now."

" Breakers on the *lee-bow !*" cried Belcher.

" Ha ! Well, as I told you."

" Breakers to *windward !*"

" Good ! We are in the Gut !"

" By the deep, *nine !*' cried the lead.

" Look out, Franks, for the shore-line !"

" I can't see twenty yards ahead, your honor."

" Are you sure you've got eyes at all ! Why, man, do you not see the white line of the breakers on the lee-bow, here, not a hundred yards off ? And here to *windward* do you not hear them ? The dogs are barking on both sides of us."

" Alas ! master, I've no more eyes nor ears for good service."

" You have hands, however, and head, old fellow. Here, take the helm, and work it, at a word, while I look out."

And Calvert ran up the rigging, to the windward side.

" By the deep, *nine !*"

" Starboard your helm !"

" Starboard it is, sir !"

" Steady — so !"

Here an unusual swelling of the sea ! —

" The cross-currents from inshore, of Kiawah, Stono, and Ede-lano !" muttered Calvert. " What water have you got there, Jack ?"

" By the deep, *seven !*"

" Ha ! touch and go ! We can spare little now. Starboard your helm !"

" Starboard it is, sir !"

" By the deep, *nine !*"

" We shall do ! There are two more points that ask for seeing and hearing, and we shall have a floating and free berth. How lucky that the shoaling is so gradual all along this coast ! It needs but eye and ear, and tolerably smooth water, and one may feel his way in safety. Now !"

" Breakers to *windward !*"

" Breakers to *leeward !*"

" Breakers *ahead !*"

" Ah, ha ! Merry dogs these ! — all about us, fellows ! But here is the worst passage. This cursed mud-flat lies just at the channel's mouth ! Now, eyes, ears, all senses, do your duty ! Port, there — hard a-port !"

" Port it is, sir !"

" Helm, there ! Port !"

" Port it is, sir !"

" The old sea-dog, without eyes or ears, is yet all bone and muscle. Once more ! —"

" By the deep, *seven !*"

" Hold on ! What water ?"

" By the deep, *seven !*"

" What water ?"

" By the deep, *six !*"

" Starboard !"

" Starboard it is, sir !"

" What water ?"

" By the deep, *seven !*"

" What water? '

" By the deep, *nine !*"

" Good! All's right now. The worst shoal and bar are passed. We have but one other ugly spot, and now the light thickens. I can see the whole line of breakers. I can trace the shore-line. I note the sand-hills, and the woods. Ah! here we are, at the Marsh. Starboard — steady! Port — steady! Starboard! Keep your course! All's right. Let her head as she goes."

Calvert descended from the rigging, and relieved Franks at the helm.

" You have been prompt, old man, as if you were but thirty-five."

" And you've had the eyes of old Satan, Captain Calvert, I must say it, gittin' through these cussed sand-banks as you did! And, even now, I can't see a good fifty yards before me."

" Never mind, old fellow. The simple secret is this, that your eyes and ears have given out a few years before your hands, your head, or your heart. You have been as quick to answer with the helm as I to speak. But let me have it now. We are on our course, just splitting the last two shoals, and all's plain sailing. But it needs some eye now, if not ear."

The little cruiser was soon established triumphantly in her harborage. There was no more difficulty, and day was about to dawn. Yet, perhaps, no man but Calvert, of all that crew of ninety men, good seamen all, could have carried them through that difficult navigation, in that thick atmosphere. Many times did old Franks and Belcher draw long and anxious breaths, at certain points in the passage, even though both of them felt the most perfect confidence in the captain. They were now all relieved. The little cruiser was in a well-known bay, with plenty of water, and every feeling of anxiety was at end.

" And we have two good days to spare !" said Calvert, exultingly. " But for that lucky shifting of the wind, Jack Belcher, I do believe I should have gone mad !"

The Happy-go-Lucky was now land-locked. No danger that the king's cruisers would attempt to follow, even if they had noted her course, through the sinuous channels which the familiar eye and mind of Calvert had enabled him to penetrate.

The Thunderbolt and Dragon, pressing all sail, pursued the false light, and gained upon it.

"Dem the fellow's impudence!" quoth Sir Everard; "he's not afraid! He absolutely entreats us to close quarters, and holds the light for us. Now shall we have fighting to our hearts' content! But for the unpleasant smell, and the smoke, which occasions the rheum to affect my orbs of vision, I verily believe I should enjoy fighting. I like to hear the guns roar, and see the beautiful flashes! Hark ye, Lieutenant Smudge, is everything in readiness? Have you the gunpowder and the balls, and are all your monkeys in hand? We shall have rare work to do, for, wot you not, this pirate is an embodied devil in a fight! He hath conquered the biggest of the Spanish dons; and, though I give no credit to the Spaniard as a fighting-animal, yet shall we be wise to blow this pirate to the moon at the first broadside. See that you are prepared to do this! I will, meanwhile, regale myself with a quaint scene in my 'Wycherley.' But, advise me when we are upon him."

On board the Dragon, Captain Pogson was more emphatic and more brief:—

"We gain upon her! D—n and blast the fellow! he means to give us work! To show his lights to the last! Clear away, and get ready for action! We are almost within long shot, now."

And he hurried below, to regale himself with a rummer of punch.

Meanwhile, the pursuers clapped on every sail that could draw, encouraged by that wandering light which flickered before them; tossing, ever and anon, drunkenly on the billows, but still gleaming aloft; and steadily going, as if some human will and conduct were guiding at the helm. The boat, thus drifting, swept away along the isles of Kiawah, and by Edings's, even while the cruiser was quietly slipping into her harborage at Stono. The currents and winds favored its course along-shore, and almost within soundings, until suddenly the pursuers beheld the light extinguished.

"Ha!" cried Pogson of the Dragon, which vessel was ahead of the Thunderbolt, "the chase has doused her glim. She begins to feel less saucy! A sharp lookout now, fellows, at fore and top, and stand ready at your guns, every man of you, who would have a hand in the gutting of the pirate !"

But neither boat nor light did they again behold that night; but they kept on, with every sail spread that could draw, the wind speeding them with increasing force, now entirely favorable, until broad daylight, when they suddenly found themselves in the midst of a Spanish fleet of brigantines and *guarda costas*, which had just emerged from the mouth of Port Royal; and, though the two nations were at peace, saluted them with a warm welcome of broadsides.

Then the Thunderbolt, spite of her rosewater captain, discharged her levin; and the Dragon spat her fires, not the less freely because of Captain Pogson's rummers of punch; and, never unwilling, the Spanish craft closed in upon the two English vessels, and poured in their volleys from every side. There were no less than a dozen of these cruisers constituting the fleet, which had just finished its work of destruction upon the little colony of my Lord Cardross at Beaufort. The Thunderbolt had her half-score of assailants, and the Dragon as many; and they hovered about the two English ships as so many wolves about the wounded buffalo. Fortunately, a sufficient space between the consorts enabled them to work their guns without injury to each other; and never did the British bulldog show himself more eager, more fierce, or more formidable, dealing with such unequal force. Fortunately, too, though so numerous, the Spaniards were of smaller craft, and carried less weighty metal; but the inequality was still too great, unless with some equivalent odds of fortune. Sir Everard was a fop and a fool, but he had nevertheless British courage; and, though his olfactories revolted at the smell of gunpowder, his nerves never shrank from the sound of shot. Nor did the frequent rummers of Pogson render him less willing for, or perhaps less able in, the conflict. To it they went like tigers, ranging fearfully on all sides, the Spaniards standing up to their guns like genuine salamanders, as they had been wont to do ere the days of the *Armada*. They were encouraged by their numbers; and this reconciled other inequalities, as between the weight of ships and metal. Three fine new brigantines, just out of Havana, and a score of *guarda costas*, all well manned and armed, were too much for the English ships. But the honor of Britain was not discredited in their keeping. Never was fight more prolonged or desperate. Sails and rigging were torn to pieces, the ships hulled, *guarda costas* sunk, brigantines compelled to draw off and refit; but still the Thunderbolt and Dragon roared and raged, *rampant*, fearfully dealing their bolts, and using their teeth — rending, raging, destroying, though themselves on the verge of destruction!

This the Spaniards well knew. They were, indeed, great sufferers; but the question was one of time. Their numbers were such that, just in proportion to the prolongation of the conflict, were their chances of success. The English must succumb from exhaustion. The light craft of the Spaniards could come on, or sheer off, at discretion. There were always a sufficient number ready to renew the game, and supply the temporary withdrawal of others when the battle grew too hot.

And thus, for six mortal hours, did the conflict go on. Sir Everard, properly caparisoned, in full uniform, stood the fire in the most conspicuous situation. The powdered puppy, spite of his *eau de luce*, and the surly bulldog Pogson, spite of his *eau de vie*, kept their posts, notwithstanding their wounds. Sir Everard was compelled to lie upon the deck; but he had a mattress brought up for the purpose, and from this he gave his orders. Fortunately, he had but one order to give :—

"Fight on, my good fellows, and who knows but you will all be made gentlemen in time!" Pogson was more emphatic :—

"Give 'em h–ll! the bloody Turks! What! shall these blasted Spaniards pull down an English flag? Pitch the shot into 'em, fellows! Plenty of prize-money and grog!"

The second officer in each ship was a staunch seaman, knew his business, and had the requisite back-bone. But the fate of the English ships was certain: they were doomed! They had been terribly handled. They had lost a large proportion of their men slain outright, and many more, including their captains, were *hors de combat* from their wounds. They had beaten off and damaged several of the Spaniards. One brigantine had already struck; but was retaken, and drawn out of the *melée*, by the *guarda costas*. They had slain of their enemies five to one. One stout schooner or *caravel* had been sunk — gone down in an instant; but, spite of all, the result was certain. The English vessels were almost unmanageable. The sailors were nearly exhausted. The work had been too heavy even for British bulldogs; the inequality too great; and they now but feebly responded to the enemy's fire.    He was closing about them; but, like true bulldogs, there was no thought of surrender.    They might be shot to pieces, but were not prepared to haul down the British lion.

At that moment they had succor.    A new champion came into the field almost unobserved.    The Happy-go-Lucky, with the English standard flying fore and aft, darted in between the Spaniards and their prey!    Her approach, such was the blind fury of the combatants, had been unnoted, almost to the very moment when she delivered her fire — both broadsides; and that one fire, of itself, almost decided the conflict, so exhausted were both the parties.    But how came our cruiser here?    Let us look back six hours.

Scarcely had she made her harborage in Stono bay, when the watch cried out —

"*Boat ahoy!*"

One boat, and then another, and another — three, four — all full of wretched fugitives from the Scotch colony of Beaufort.

The Spaniards had sacked the place, and destroyed or dispersed the colonists.    Some had got safely from the island to the main; some were, no doubt, sheltered in the swamps and thickets; and others had fled, like these, with oars and sails, taking the inland passage for Charleston.

By the time this news was digested, Harry Calvert was in a stern passion, and it was broad daylight.    The sails of the Happy-go-Lucky, just furled, were once more spread to the wind.    Fortunately, the wind was sufficiently favorable; and, by noon, as we have seen, the little cruiser had reached the scene of conflict, and, as we know, not a moment too soon.

All hands had been sent to quarters without beat of drum; the guns shotted and run out; everything made ready: and, as she darted between the Spaniards and the two exhausted bulldog Englishmen, who were the only parties that did not know they were beaten, the effect was magical.    Ranging alongside two of the largest of the brigantines, she delivered her powerful broadside from her big-mouthed brass pieces — the Long Tom thundering over all and through all, with terrific effect!    Then, forging ahead, she tacked in a twink, and poured in a second broadside from the other battery, before the Spaniards could bring a gun to bear.    Down went royal, top, and mainmast; then crashed the timbers; then rose up, in awful clamors, the cries of mangled men, while the joyous shouts of the Dragon and Thunderbolt shook the welkin!

The two ships, thus battered, lay almost as helpless as their British enemies. The third brigantine sheered off, clapped on all sail, and strove by agility to escape vengeance. But the saucy cruiser was upon her next, and fastened to her as closely as the *remora* to the whale. A sharp and sanguinary action followed. The Spaniard showed good blood, but she had already been partly crippled by the Dragon, and she worked heavily. In twenty minutes a cloud mantled her; then came a hiss; then a roar; and the skies were darkened, and the deeps shaken to their very hollows, by the explosion! She was blown to atoms; and incontinently all the smaller craft, the *guarda costas* and *caravels*, were in full flight, gliding off for the shores and shallow water.

Calvert ranged once more beside the two half-disabled consorts of the perished brigantine, prepared to renew the punishment; but their flags came down at his approach! Drawing nigh the English ships, he demanded, through his trumpet, if they had men enough to man the prizes, which were now drifting beside the conqueror.

"Ay, ay! give chase — give chase!" was the answer; while both Thunderbolt and Dragon sent their boats to secure the prizes. Calvert hauled off to a decent distance, and waited just long enough to see that they had full possession, when he cried again, through his trumpet —

"Do you want any help?"

"No! thank you! no! But what are you?"

"The Happy-go-Lucky privateer, of England, Captain Harry Calvert!"

"The h–ll you are!" roared Pogson of the Dragon.

"Ah! very curious — very mysterious — by my faith!" cried Sir Everard Holly.

And both captains began to order their men to the guns, as about to commence a new action.

But the Happy-go-Lucky was again on the wing, in seeming pursuit of the fugitive vessels of the Spaniards. But Calvert had no real purpose of pursuit, and followed not far. He simply sought to fetch a sufficient compass about the English ships — to lose them briefly — so that his own course should not be conjectured. He knew that the work of securing the prizes, and refitting, was one to consume some time; and naturally enough concluded that, this done, the consorts would immediately proceed — however ungenerous the duty — in pursuit of himself! He ran out to sea, accordingly, till fairly out of sight, and on the edge of the gulf; then put about, and shaped his course, as fast as he might, for his secret harborage in the Stono.

# CHAPTER LI.

### THE NIGHT-MARCH.

> "They pass from sight, but whither? Let the stars,
> That watch the march in silence, make report."
>
> *The Seminole.*

CALVERT returned in season, as he believed, to his anchorage in the Stono. The vessel was made fast to the shore. It was night, bright starlight. Our rover lost not a moment in making all his preparations for a night-march. He called his lieutenants, Eccles and Hazard, into his cabin. Thither also, at his bidding, came Belcher and Franks. The door of the cabin closed, and all parties seated, Calvert said:—

"Gentlemen, you are probably all aware of the task that is before us. I have every reason to be assured of a rising of the red men. I am satisfied almost of the very night which they have agreed upon. I have made my arrangements accordingly, and at two points at least I shall be prepared to encounter them. On this business I shall speed myself. I shall take with me some fifty of the crew. I shall leave thirty-five with the ship — forty all told. These will be quite enough for her working, and defence from any foe whom you will be likely to encounter in these waters. When I depart, you will haul off from the shore, and put yourself in cover from the sea, between the islets. There you will escape notice from ships of size passing along the coast, while you will be safe from all danger from the savages, unless they venture, as is hardly likely, to attack you in their canoes. Not only will they not dare this, while you are in deep water; but, as I have reason to think, there will be none but their women left along the shores. The warriors will be busy enough with the settlements. But this must not make you neglectful. You

will need to watch just as closely as if you had a present foe
threatening you from every quarter.  We know not, indeed, but
that the Spaniards *have* left a large force in *periaguas*, after the
destruction of the Cardross colony, to penetrate the bays and in-
lets, and co-operate with the savages even to Charleston.  In that
event, you will be directly in their route.  With thirty-five good
men, and in deep water, you will be quite equal to all their *periaguas*.  I know that you have the strength and courage.  It is
for you to show that you have the vigilance and intelligence also.
You are young men both, and the whole future reputation, honor,
and profit, of your lives, may depend upon the independent command which, for these three or four nights following, I shall trust
to your hands.  I hope to be absent no longer.  We shall run up,
to-night, as far as the Wappoo entrance, after I have taken on
board a guide who is to meet me here within the hour.  Thence,
when I have landed, you will return to this bay, and take your
position as I have counselled.  My signal, when I return, shall
be three muskets; and, if at night, three rockets also.  The men
whom I leave with you shall be all true men.  I shall take with
me all (as far as we know them) of those whom Fowler had seduced, in the hope that they will feel the need to do good service,
to wipe out old scores of ill conduct.

"And now, gentlemen, there is one thing further.  The expedition upon which I go will necessarily be one of peril.  It may
be that I shall never return.  In regard to my own fate, I have
contemplated all the results and necessities.  Let us now consider
yours.  I need not tell you that our present commission, as a privateer, has been revoked by the king; nay, more: under the ma-
lignant influence of Spain, and his own weakness, he has made
that pursuit a crime which he had once authorized as a duty.  It
behooves me, therefore, if possible, to place you in such a condition as to enable you to return with honor to the service of England, and to escape all evil consequences from the king's late proclamation.  Take these letters.  They are addressed — one to Sir
William Berkeley, my uncle; one to Sir John Colleton, who was
my father's friend; and the third to Sir Edward Berkeley, the
cassique of Kiawah, in this province, who is my brother."

The young officers both started with surprise.  He proceeded,
without heeding their looks of inquiry :—

"These facts, hitherto, were only known to my faithful friend and servant, Belcher. I do not wish them to be made known now to any but yourselves, nor until I shall have failed to return. Should this happen, you will communicate immediately to Sir Edward Berkeley, if he should be living; for this adventure, which involves *my* danger, will in like manner involve *his*. Should he perish, then run over to England, without fail, and rely upon these documents to plead for your safety, and secure your future employment under the crown. You will carry with you a sufficient argument besides. You will, of your own free minds, make a gift of a noble ship, and of a brave crew, and good officers, to the royal marine. I hold these documents — which contain a full narrative of our adventures, and a complete statement of our case — to be ample for your security, though they might not be for mine. I can do no more. The rest is with you, and in the hands of God! And now, gentlemen, see to the ship as if she were the apple of your eye: I must proceed at once in my own preparations. Belcher will call off, by name, all the marines that are to go with me. Let ten of them carry muskets, all of them cutlasses and pistols, and a few tomahawks."

He dismissed them with an affectionate embrace. Will Hazard, with tears in his eyes, entreated to accompany him; but Calvert was firm in his refusal.

"No, my good boy, you are better here. Eccles may need all the help you can give him; and I feel that I can trust your vigilance, no less than your skill and honor."

When they were gone, he had a long conference with Belcher and Franks, in respect to Zulieme and other subjects of interest. Neither of them knew that Zulieme had been withdrawn from the city, and been confided to the custody of the cassique. So far as she was concerned, Calvert felt himself secure. The only question was, how she should be got away from Charleston; and it was arranged that Franks, who was to be left with the ship, should contrive it, by a midnight expedition, in a boat through Wappoo. She was then — assuming that Calvert was no more — to be carried home to the *hacienda* of her father, on the isthmus. Briefly, every arrangement was made for each necessity and object which human forethought could conceive. Old Franks, by-the-way, did express the suspicion that Zulieme might be imprisoned for her husband, if suspected; and that the cunning of Sylvester might lead him even to this.  But Calvert dismissed the suggestion with a —

"Pshaw! — What! the council of the lords-proprietors seize upon a woman, and on such pretext?  Impossible!"

And no more was said.  Calvert at once went on with his preparations.  He clad himself in the hunting-shirt and leggins of the backwoods hunter, with cutlass, pistols, and tomahawk.  Belcher was likewise habited.  Similar suits of *blue* homespun were provided for all the party, the better for concealment in the woods.  Nothing was allowed to be worn which could attract by glare or glitter — nothing white, nothing shining.  The men were all ready, and even eager.  They always relished a cruise on shore, even though a battle stood awaiting them in the highway.

In less than an hour, there were certain hoots of the owl, and certain sounds as from the gong of a night-hawk, that signalled them from the shore.  Then did Calvert know that Ligon had reached in safety the place of appointment.  So it was: the guide awaited him.  He was taken on board, and the little cruiser run up the Stono to its junction with the Wappoo.  Here the party landed, and the cruiser put about after an hour, the tide then being at its turning.  But Calvert and his company were gone from sight before the vessel left the place.  They were soon buried in the thick darkness of the night and forest.  But Ligon was such a guide as few could equal in the country, and went forward with ease and confidence.

He brought little news, but this was interesting.  The Indians were about in small parties, all tending to one or more centres of gathering.  One had attempted entrance at Gowdey's castle by artifice, but the old sailor was too much for them.  He found out that they were eighteen or twenty in number; but they made no absolutely hostile demonstration — unwilling, perhaps, by any premature showing, to put their victims on their guard.  But that they would ultimately attempt the castle, and all other exposed settlements, there was no doubt.  Such was Gowdey's own opinion; but the old sailor-hunter was, as he deemed, well prepared for them.  Of what was doing in the town, Ligon knew nothing.  He had heard that there was much military stir, and that Florence O'Sullivan was preparing to build a small castle on the island, at the entrance of the harbor, which was to carry heavy cannon against shipping. This was to be held by O'Sullivan himself, who was a doughty man of arms, a Celt of characteristic courage, nowise bashful, and by no means wanting in skill and cunning for deeds of war. Beyond this news, Calvert got little from his guide.

But we must not linger. The night-march sped. Ligon, the guide, spite of the darkness, went forward with sufficient boldness; the whole party moving silently, and in the well-known order called the "Indian file," a mode of progress natural to the forester, where the path is at once single and narrow. It is, indeed, because of this narrowness of the beaten road in the thickets, that the red men set their feet down in a right line with the body, the toes rather turning in than out; and not because of any peculiar formation of foot or ancle. Dark, indeed, and dense was the forest through which our party had to march. It lay in the original condition of Nature; at least of a growth which had been unbroken for five hundred years. Great oaks, each spanning its half-acre; gigantic pines, that seemed to rush up into the very heavens; magnolias, quite as gigantic, and more beautiful from their depth of green, and the rich varnish of their leaves, now covered with their great snow-white flowers; and a vast variety, besides, of other trees, each the noblest of its kind, all now thickly spread with the green garniture of spring advancing to summer; and woven together, as by veins and arteries, with enormous vines, that wound about their boughs, and bound them as in loving embrace of leaves and blossoms. The atmosphere was thick with the scent from shrubs and flowers, "too numerous and too humble to have names."

It required no ordinary skill to pilot our party through such a wilderness. But Ligon had learned to thread his way through this and other like regions, in the darkness as in daylight; so that he had won the *sobriquet*, among the Indians themselves, of "The Horned Owl." He was an old hunter and scout, though not yet an old man. He was silent, and cold, and stern, like the red men; had fought them in various forests, and entertained for them a mortal hatred, which was due to a history of most bloody massacre, in which his younger brother, a mere boy, had perished and lost his scalp. Many, and as bloody revenges, had Ligon taken for this massacre; and now he never forewent the opportunity to deal sharp and sudden judgment upon the red-skins. But of all this history Calvert knew nothing; and perhaps Gowdey, who had sent him to Calvert, was just as ignorant. All that he knew was, that Ligon was a scout of the greatest excellence and skill; and this, in Gowdey's judgment, was being a person of most admirable virtues.

Leading the way, with Calvert following close, and the whole company keeping together, though in a long, single line, Ligon made a rapid progress through the wood, as he well might, turning neither to one side nor the other. But, at length, as the night advanced, he beheld a great light, as of a fire shining through the thickets on the right; and this was at a point nearly the same distance from Gowdey's castle as from the barony of Kiawah, and lying somewhat below them, and near the course which the party had to pursue. The guide stopped them where they stood.

"Now," said Ligon, "you must stop here, captain, while I go and reconn'itre. You must keep the men still."

This was the custom; and the party of Calvert shrouded themselves in the woods, well hidden, and mute as mice, while Ligon went forward. He was gone, perhaps, the most of an hour. When he came back, he said:—

"Now, captain, we have a good chance at these bloody red-skins! There's some thirty of the cussed savages; and they've been drinkin' and dancin', as is the way with 'em, when they git a chance at the liquor, and are in high hope of somethin' better. They are 'camped on the side of a thick *bay*, full of water; and they are, by this time, pretty well rum-fuddled. We've only got to fetch a compass round the bay — I'll show the way how — and we kin have 'em in a net, and not a fellow go off without losin' a sculp."

"Have they any prisoners among 'em?" asked the captain.

"Not as I see," was the answer.

"Then we will let 'em alone. We have too much at stake now to risk anything."

Ligon was discomfited by this reply. Surprise of an enemy was, to him, an always-pleasant performance. He walked about a little in a sort of reverie; but anon he spoke:—

" Let me go take another and closer look at 'em, captain. Ef they have prisoners, I did n't see 'em; but I did n't look for 'em. It may be they *have* some prisoners in the thick of the camp. I 'll take a sharper look, ef you say so."

" Go!" said Calvert. " If they have prisoners, we must rescue them at all hazards. But bestir yourself, and waste no more time than is necessary."

Ligon set forth again without delay, and was soon out of sight. He was absent this time quite an hour. He had seen and done something, during this interval, of which he made no report to Calvert. But there were no prisoners. Ligon had approached so nigh, that he could see the whole camp, and was able to hear the cries of the warriors, but not to distinguish their words. There were no women among them. But they were very merry, nevertheless; full of strong waters and sanguinary appetites. The rum had been asserting itself with no little potency; and, as Ligon had suggested, it would have been easy to have surprised and destroyed the whole party, which had no reason to apprehend any hostile force near them, and was accordingly careless of any watch. There was merry laughter and jest among them, uncouth dances, and wild song. Some had stretched themselves out for sleep, the Jamaica having had its full effect. These were the older men. The young were still drinking, and gaming with acorns, a sort of game carried on by guessing, and called in their tongue " *Kerakee-lakee-kee*"— " The Cheater," or " The game that cheats." On this game they were betting fox and deer skins. One young fellow, at length, jumped up from the ground, and flung a skin, which he had lost, to another opposite. It was his last, yet he gave it up good-humoredly. Then stretching himself, with arms aloft, he began to sing the famous " Crow-song" of the Yemassee, as he walked off from the crowd, approaching the very spot where Ligon was crouching in watch, and singing as he went:—

> " Ackelepatee madee,
> Indewanta chaoboo :
> Opamola indola,
> Kittee bana sapawak —
> Caw-chee-chow—chow! chow! chow!
> Caw — caw — caw ! — chow! chow! chow!"

Thus singing, the young warrior passed into the thicket, quite out of sight of his companions, who still kept on their play. You could hear their voices, dealing in execrations, or exultation and laughter, as the parties severally won and lost. He drew nigh to Ligon. The scout quickly detached his *couteau de chasse* from his girdle, a heavy and sharp instrument, and stood up close beside a great oak at the edge of an old path. Here he waited, while the red man strode on, still singing his catches and bits of song. Ligon suffered him to pass, then made a single evolution of his arm; and the young warrior, with a solitary gasp, fell forward on his face. He sang no more! There was a sound, as of a heavy body falling upon the dried leaves, that made the players in the camp lift their ears, look up, and listen. They spoke to one another; but soon resumed their game, and finally, one by one, stretched themselves out for sleep. Ligon returned to Calvert as quietly as when he had gone forth. He reported the red men to be sleeping, and with no captives. He had nothing more to communicate.

When the savages awoke next morning, one of their number was missing. This was the young warrior who had gone forth into the thickets from the camp, singing the song of the crow. They wondered a little at his absence. He should not be absent at such a time, as he was one of their " braves ;" and, after a brief search, they found him, lying along the " path," about eighty paces from the camp. He was quite dead, and his scalp gone — so dexterously taken off, that it might have been the work of an Indian. He had been slain by a broad knife, with a single, well-directed thrust, right through the heart. The murderer was never known. Ligon kept his own counsel. He had no passion for fame, but was making privately a collection of scalps.

The march proceeded, without further incident. But day dawned, and the party was still some distance from the barony. Calvert led his men into a close swamp-cover, where, having first set watches all about the encampment, they proceeded to take a very necessary rest, in a dense wilderness, quite impenetrable to any passing espionage. Here they slept for several hours, and ate with good appetite at awakening. It was not till night that the progress was resumed; but, long before midnight, the party had reached the barony of Kiawah.

Having covered his men temporarily in the woods, Calvert, accompanied only by Belcher and Ligon, all well armed, approached the open grounds. The place lay fair in the bright starlight, and silent as the grave. There were no sentinels. Not even a watch-dog bayed. A light faintly shone through one of the curtained windows of the dwelling; but there was no sign of anything stir-ring. All was calm and peaceful, as if Massacre were not gliding, by hourly approaches, with the step and cunning of the tiger, to the unconscious household. Calvert tried the fastenings of the house. The bolts were shot, it is true; but they were slight. From the main dwelling he proceeded to one about a hundred yards distant. This was a "block," windowless, and with but a single door. The fabric was small and square, but lofty.

"This," said he, "is the armory and magazine. To make it securely accessible in the event of danger, there should have been a covered way to it, of pickets, from the dwelling. The pickets have been begun, but are unfinished; they are useless. An ene-my could cover the space between, and cut off all connection with the house. You have brought the key, Belcher?"

Belcher produced it — a skeleton or master key, devised cun-ningly for the purpose of opening any lock. Calvert was as well prepared to be a housebreaker as a pirate. Belcher applied the key; and the lock, which was large enough, was not intricate: its wards readily yielded. A ship's lamp, which Belcher carried with him, enabled them to see some fifty stands of arms, good English muskets, a few cutlasses, a score or two of pistols, and as many small barrels of gunpowder. There were bullets, also, ready cast.

"A pretty good armory," said Calvert. "We must take pos-session of it. Go, Ligon, and bring the ten men whom I set aside with Craig. You see that the walls are pierced for musketry on all sides. Ten men can keep the house, unless fire shall be used upon the roof. This is the point of most importance."

Ligon brought up the men, and they were posted; food was supplied them, and a means of egress; but they were bade to be close, and keep unseen.

"Now," continued Calvert, "we must see to the laborers. They occupy a building on the other side, some two hundred yards off. We must put them in condition to make a defence. In all prob-ability, they have taken no precaution, and sleep with open doors;

but take the key along, Belcher: we must put them in a state of preparation."

Sure enough, as Calvert conjectured, some twenty workmen slept in a building, remote from the mansion as the arsenal, and with open doors. But their house was a strong block, pierced for musketry also, where a good defence might be made. Calvert suddenly appeared among the laborers, rousing them from sleep.

"Who is the chief man among you?" he demanded, as they started from their beds. There were five, or more, sleeping in the same chamber. The house consisted of four apartments. Never were people more surprised. Had the red men been the visiters, not one of them would have saved his scalp; and Calvert could not but meditate seriously upon that amiable insanity of his brother, which, because of his humane theory about the Indians, had exposed all these people to be butchered in their sleep.

A sturdy English laborer came forward — strong, well built, and no doubt courageous — who proclaimed himself the foreman of the people. His name was Grandison, possibly a descendant of Sir Charles: such are the reverses of fortune.

Calvert made the danger apparent to him in few words; made him get his people dressed, and, conducting them to the block-house, supplied them with the necessary weapons.

"Everything must be kept secret," said he. "We are to be prepared simply for whatever happens; all your people — every quarter of your house. It is pierced, I see, for musketry; and you will assign each man his weapon. You have a certain number to each chamber?"

"Yes, sir — ten to two; and six in each of the others."

"But one half must go to work to-morrow; and they must carry pistols, well concealed. The other half must be on the watch, to give their succor at a moment's warning. The red men may attack to-night or to-morrow. The dawn is a favorite time with them. Or they may attack at "nooning," when nobody is prepared; or they may defer the assault till night. I am sure that they will be on you some time within the next thirty-six hours. See that you follow my directions! I am Captain Harry Berkeley, the brother of your master, the cassique."

The workmen touched their heads. Calvert continued:—

"I shall be at hand to succor you. I have fifty men within hearing, all well armed. So, fear nothing, but do your duty, like good Britons, according to your best manhood; and — one thing — should you see the red men running, under your fire or ours, do not seek to pursue! Keep your post. If they are to be pursued, our foresters, who know the woods, are better at that game than you. Be prudent. I shall probably see you again. But put yourselves in readiness *now ;* and, if you sleep, fasten your doors and windows, and set a watch first, to give you warning, whatever happens. The night may possibly pass off without alarm. If so, to-morrow, or to-morrow night, is the time of danger. But you are warned in season."

With this, Calvert left the workmen, and, with Belcher, made his way back to the block-house, where he had already installed the ten musketeers. Having seen this done, he took possession of the carriage-house and stables, both log-houses, where in the loft he established another squad of ten. These were all to lie *perdu*, and to wake only at the proper moment. Calvert then returned to the woods. These he well knew. He had explored them often enough. His solicitude now was, that the Indians should not get into the rear of his party; and some time was consumed in calculating the probabilities with regard to the route and manner of approach of the red men. He took for granted that the course of Cussoboe would be from below, and that, fetching a circuit about the settlement, he would proceed directly to the tree, in the hollow of which the sheaf of arrows had been deposited. They would tell their own story; and, no doubt, by their numbers, embarrass the old warrior. Of course, he would infer his son's neglect of duty. To place his men in such position as would enable them to cover the open grounds and buildings, yet keep them from discovery till the last moment, was Calvert's object, and one of some difficulty; but the points were finally chosen, after due consultation with Ligon and Belcher. This and many other matters having settled, he said to Belcher :—

"I must now seek and see my brother. I leave the charge of the men to you and Ligon. Keep them from straggling. I shall be with you before daylight."

He took the skeleton-key from Belcher, and left him, pursuing the straight route to the mansion-house.

# CHAPTER LII.

### WHAT THE SAD HEARTS SAID TO EACH OTHER.

"How the notes sink upon the ebbing wind!"—SHELLEY.

THE cassique of Kiawah was perhaps not the only sleepless watcher that night in his mansion-house. He was, for some time, however, and at the period when we prefer to look in upon him, the only one who sat watching in the chamber of his wife. Her condition, now utterly hopeless, rendered that sort of watch unnecessary which is expected and needed to afford occasional succor and relief. She was dying, certainly; but by those slow and almost imperceptible degrees which belong to most cases of irremediable decline. The strife was over with the hope; and, if her assured fate had not produced a feeling of perfect resignation in all hearts, it had yet brought to every hea l in the family a full instinct of submission. Nothing more could be done for the sweet victim, but to tend upon and simply note her successive changes; and, slight though they were, the cassique did not fail to discern and to feel them all. She herself appeared to be something more than resigned, in her perfect consciousness of her hopelessness. It would seem as if her spirit had become altogether satisfied; as if the brain, no longer fevered, had subsided into calm. She had certainly become freed from all that spasmodic and excited impulse which had caused her uncertain moods and restless energies before. Her exhausted *physique* did not now permit her to wander about, even if her mental nature had still occasioned the desire. But such was no longer the case. Her mind had become comparatively placid; her temper serene and sweet. There was now no impatient, discontented thought; no lingering, living hope, striving at satisfaction, and refusing to be comforted, seeming to exist in that soul which was simply hovering on the confines of life, and needing but the severance of a few strings, to soar to abodes of sweeter peace and happier existence. Her consciousness was clear; had been growing clearer for some time; even as her frame had been sinking with exhaustion. She no longer sang those fitful snatches of song which formerly burst from her in spasmodic gushes of pain, or passion, or a maddening fancy. The delirium had gone off entirely, and all her faculties seemed to grow bright as she drew near to the close of her sorrows. Her eye was strangely brilliant; her voice was low, but how exquisitely sweet in all its tones! Her skin was transparent; the blue veins as clearly drawn upon it as if defined with the pencil. Her hearing had become wonderfully acute. She could distinguish, from a distance, the approaching footstep, however lightly put down. Nay, she could say who it was that came. All now knew that she was dying. Even the mother, who had deceived herself so long in regard to her daughter's condition, had resigned all hope; and the final issue was simply a question of time, and that short, as between one hour and one week! How long could that exhausted and attenuated frame hold the struggle with the mighty enemy who had already taken possession of all the strongholds of her life — who was in her heart, as in the citadel of her strength, undermining all its props and powers? There were moments when, so still she lay, with eyes closed, and lips scarcely seeming to breathe, though parted, that those around her fancied the event had taken place, and that she had sunk into the sacred slumber, as suddenly and quietly as the child, after a violent play, sinks into natural sleep. But, as they drew near to see, then would her eyes open with that marvellous brightness of gaze; then would the faint smile mantle over her pallid lips, as a sudden sunbeam flushes with color a curl of drifted snow.

This night, after long-protracted watching, the mother had fallen asleep beside her couch at an early hour of the evening. She and the housekeeper were both exhausted. The cassique gently awakened them, and persuaded them to retire. Olive understood him, and laid her thin, wan fingers upon her mother's head, and smiled her wishes, as in support of his; then murmured them, to the same effect.

The cassique was left alone with the dying woman. When all

were gone, and the room was silent, she motioned him beside her; then said, in a whisper:—

" Will you raise me a little, Sir Edward? — another pillow, if you please."

Never did loving hands more dutifully or gently minister than did his.

" Sit beside me, Sir Edward, if you please, a little while."

He would have restrained her from speech.

" You will fatigue yourself, dear Olive."

" No, my husband — not so. Sit quietly, and let me speak. I must speak now, if ever !"

" You know how I should love to hear you, dear Olive — how I have always loved to hear you; but you are so feeble now — so—"

" I am strong as I shall ever be, dear Sir Edward." And her voice now grew louder, though still low. " You do not deceive yourself, you can not deceive me, as to my fate ! What strength is left me I must use, to acquit myself to you, and to entreat your forgiveness for my most unfortunate offence !"

" Oh Olive, *my* forgiveness ! Dear wife, you need make no such prayer to me ! Alas ! it is *your* pity, *your* forgiveness, which *I* should implore ! I who—"

He could not finish the sentence, save by sobs. His voice faltered, and he laid his head down on the couch beside her to conceal his emotions. Her hand gently sought his head, and she suffered it to rest beside rather than upon it, detaching a lock of his long hair, and holding it between the fingers. A deep sigh followed — a brief pause — and then she spoke, in low, sweet, murmuring, but decided accents :—

" No, Sir Edward, the wrong is all mine. It was not for me as a maiden — not now for me as a wife — to reproach him who sought me with love, and who has striven to nurture me with love! It was for me to have said frankly, and with all the boldness of an earnest passion : ' This heart is wedded to another — it is not mine to give; it can never be thine !' "

" Ah ! would to God, dear Olive, that thou hadst so spoken !" ejaculated the cassique, with a deep groan.

" I was a child — weak where I should have been strong — and I yielded to a mother's prayers, when it would have been a thousand times better to have yielded to God! And yet, Sir Edward, I yielded not against my own will. If it had been possible that my heart should have gone to another, having lost the one to whom it had been consecrated, it had gone to you in preference to that of any other mortal man. I could love you, Sir Edward — I *do* love you, next to him whom I loved first and best of all, and more than I have ever loved any human being. As I am living now, Sir Edward, though so very soon to die, I pray you to believe what I tell you!"

He caught her hand in his and carried it to his lips, covered it with kisses, and sobbed over it convulsively, replying with a choking and husky speech —

"Oh, how I thank you and bless you for this, dear Olive!"

"Yes, it is true, Sir Edward; never speech from woman's heart more true! In so much did you resemble *him;* in form and face; in look and action; in tone and thought; in the generous warmth of your affection; in the lofty disinterestedness of your love — oh, I should have been worse than blind and foolish, dear Sir Edward, could I have been insensible to your virtues, your devotion, your generous forbearance, your kind indulgence! I felt it all — ah, my husband — I call you so now — I felt how near I was to loving you, at the very moment when I most shrank from contact with you!"

"I understand it, Olive! Oh, yes, I have long understood it."

"But you were not *he!* alas, no! and I felt that I could not love you enough — not as I ought — and that I had deceived you. I still too much loved another. I had done you wrong."

"No, no, no! Say not that, Olive!"

"Yes! oh, yes! For, Sir Edward, I still loved him — still thought of him — still moaned for him with a heart as much dissatisfied as was my conscience, which perpetually chided me, as a wedded wife, for the passion which I could not help but feel for him! My heart was making my conscience daily more and more dissatisfied. I felt — knew — very soon, that something had not been told you, which ought to have been told; which I should have told you, if nobody else had done it, before I consented to become your wife. But, indeed, dear Sir Edward, I thought it had been done. Forgive me, my husband, that I did not assure myself of this — that I spoke not till it was too late!"

" Not too late, Olive !"

" Alas ! yes ; too late for both of us — too late *for all three !*"

Great tears gathered in her eyes, and for a brief space she was silent. The cassique strove, meanwhile, to murmur out his broken assurances — to soothe after a fashion, and console ; and perhaps he was successful in due degree, as his own emotions forbade that he should be coherent in his speech. When he was silent, she resumed :—

" O Sir Edward, judge of the sense of guilt and remorse — of useless repentance — in my bosom, by the agonies I have endured ; by the temporary madnesss which I suffered ; by the rapid wasting of strength, youth, and health ; by the wreck, so soon to be utter ruin, of what you see before you ! If I erred, dear Sir Edward, the error has been fearfully atoned. And I did err ! Oh, weak, weak ! very, very weak !"

His groan alone answered her.

" Yet, I was so young — am so young ; and — and — and he ! Oh, forgive me, my husband, that I am forced to speak of him !"

" Speak of him, dear Olive, with all your heart ! Oh, my poor Olive, do believe me, that if, by my own life, I could give you back your youth, and put you where you were before the cruel Fates had made *me* your fate, I should now know no greater gladness than to die for you, and in the last moments of consciousness to be able to place your hand in the hand of Harry, my brother — my noble brother — whom, as well as yourself, I have so cruelly but unwittingly destroyed ! Yes, on my life, on my soul, Olive, this would I do, and die ; though, even in doing it, Olive, I should still be free to tell you that the heart of Edward Berkeley was no less sworn to you than that of the more fortunate Harry."

" I believe you, my lord — my husband ! It is so sweet, now, though so late, that we understand each other ! We can sit in the darkness together, dear Sir Edward. Do cover that light. Let there be no light. Sit here, then, and we will commune further. You will not see my face ; and I shall hear you just the same."

He obeyed her — covered the light in the chimney, so that it shed no gleams over the chamber ; then came back and resumed his seat beside her : and she feebly put forth her hand and grasped his, somewhat nervously, between her attenuated fingers.

"And now, dear Sir Edward, I have a prayer to make to you in behalf of my mother.  Her love for me—her desire to see me well established—these have led her into grievous error, which has hurt both of us to the soul.  But she meant me good; she designed you no evil: she has only been guilty of a very sad mistake.  It is one upon which I do not wish to dwell.  It is the saddest of all my thoughts.  I feel sure that no words of mine can express fully my own sense of her shocking error.  Perhaps you will feel it even more painfully than I do.  But, nevertheless, I pray you, at this moment, when my little lamp of life is about to be extinguished—I pray you to forgive her!—"

"I do!  I do, Olive—my poor Olive!  I do forgive her, though she has crushed us both!"

"Do I not feel it?  Never was so fatal an error!  Thanks for this mercy—this kindness!  May I plead for more, dear Sir Edward?"

"Speak, Olive.  Your prayers shall be my laws!"

"I would rather have them your *loves*."

"Loves they shall be to me, and with perpetual regard to you, Olive!"

"It is enough!  You will shelter her, Sir Edward?  She is poor—has no resource now but in your bounty; and, unhappily, she is one of those who live in that foreign world which rather asks a palace for the eye than a home for the heart."

"I know!  I comprehend you, Olive.  Say no more.  She shall be well provided for.  Briefly, dear heart, I will do for her as if she were my own mother.  She shall return to England—"

"Ah!  And you?—"

"Will remain here, Olive, where I will make my temple and my tomb!  Your mother will not need me, nor I her!  In England she shall have 'The Willows' during her life; and I shall make such provision for her there, that there shall be no lack of means essential to that social position which she has always so much valued."

"Alas! yes!"—with a deep sigh.  "I could hope no more, dear Sir Edward; I did not dare to ask so much.  Thanks—thanks!"

"What more, Olive?  Speak, dear wife, and do not fear.  Believe me, I so thoroughly understand all your necessities, that—

I never loved you more than at this moment, when to speak of mortal love is such a mockery!"

"Say not so, dear Sir Edward, when we feel how sweetly it harmonizes hearts between which the chasm has been hitherto so deep and wide; when it strengthens *me* to speak with a courage such as I never knew in the days of my health and youth; when it moves *you*, who have been so sadly wronged, to be so merciful — so nobly loving — with such magnanimity and grace! Ah! how—"

"No more, Olive, I pray you! I—"

"Suffer me, Sir Edward! Yes, on the edge of the precipice — on the verge of the grave — I must plead for the beauties of that mortal love — vanishing as it may seem — which I hold to be still sweet, however faint it gleams from that fountain of Immortal Love which is promised to the pure hearts in a sphere where there can be no loss! I believe in my own heart, Sir Edward, and in yours, and in *his* — your brother's! I believe that yours and his have been equally capable of that heart-sacrifice upon which Love hath need to feed for life! And — I may say something for my own! O Sir Edward, I am now dying for it!"

His head bent over, and was hidden upon the shrouded bosom of the speaker. She resumed :—

"I shall die happy, knowing this! This love, which mortal life has never satisfied — could never compensate — must be immortal; for there must be, under a God of love, justice, mercy, a necessary principle of compensation. How I loved Harry, your brother, HE, the good God, alone can know; how Harry loved me, I have felt and feel! And, dear Sir Edward, I know *your* heart — how true, how pure, how constant, how magnanimous, in all its dealings with mine; and, at times, when it was impossible for me to plead, or you to comprehend, the miseries and the mysteries of mine! Only believe now, my lord and husband, that my heart would have been quite satisfied with yours, would have been devoted to yours, had it not been for the earlier call of love which it first heard from his! And had his not continued to call — as I deemed, from spirit-lands — I had probably as gladly yielded my affections to you as I should have done to him. But there was a power — it is so strange to think of it! — a perpetual voice, as from the tomb, appealing to my heart, and suggesting the doubt — nay, the absolute denial — of his death! Was it *his* voice? How could it be? He was living, and perhaps thousands of miles away! Whose was it, then? There is a wondrous mystery in it, Sir Edward! Surely, there must have been a spiritual presence here, admonishing me of the truth, against all mortal evidence! What else should I believe, or think? Then, he came — in sooth, was living; had me in his embrace; and — but you know all!"

"All! all! Say no more, Olive, my wife! And yet, but for your feebleness and pain, I would have you speak on for ever!"

"Alas! it can not be. It requires some effort to lift my voice. Yet — our boy — *our* Harry! I would —"

Her voice faltered.

"What, my Olive?"

"Oh, I would have *our* Harry beloved by *him*, your brother! Do not let him avoid or dislike the child. Pray him, for my sake, dear Sir Edward, to love *your* child — and mine!"

And, with a sudden burst of sobbing, the dying woman sank back exhausted! The cassique was terrified, thinking the moment of trial had come. He called loudly; and from an adjoining chamber, Zulieme, who had promised Mrs. Masterton to assume the watch at midnight, suddenly made her appearance, and brought some drops which had been provided for these exigencies. The little wife of the rover had all at once begun to be useful — nay, to feel a sort of pride and pleasure in proving so. Olive soon revived under her ministrations; but, as she kept her eyes shut, and appeared desirous of repose, the cassique left her in Zulieme's charge, and proceeded to the hall, where, all in darkness, he threw himself upon the sofa, yielding himself up to the sweet and bitter thought which naturally grew out of his situation.

Here a sort of oblivion of all things seized for the time upon his senses. He had watched nightly; had toiled daily; was enfeebled by fatigue. He had brooded, as he thought, for a long time, in the darkness and solitude of the hall — meditating the mysteries of that chamber which he had so recently left. Perhaps he slept; but he could scarcely persuade himself of this. He was awakened. He fancied he heard the shooting of bolts, but he stirred not. At length, he detected a footfall — slight, like that of a woman. He thought of Olive. She might be dying. She

might be dead.   He started up and rushed into the passage-way,
whence he would have made his way to her chamber, when he
felt himself encumbered — clasped firmly in the hands of a strong
man.   His instincts prompted the instant use of his muscles.   He
would have thrown off the intruder, but found himself firmly
held ; while a voice, which he at once knew — though subdued to
a whisper — said, hurriedly :—

"It is you, Edward — I am Harry.   Do not be excited.   I
come with love — with a brother's love.   Conduct me to a private
room, and bring a light !"

" Harry, my brother, you come at an awful moment !"

" And I am glad that I come at a moment when Edward Berkeley acknowledges awe.   But lead me, and get a light.   I have
that to say which will suffer little time."

Taking him by the hand, the cassique led his brother into the
hall which he had just left, and conducted him to the sofa.   Here
he seated him, while he went to bring a light.   We can easily
conjecture how Harry had effected his entrance.

# CHAPTER LIII.

## VOICES OF THE NIGHT.

"Look! look! One fire burns dim. It quivers — it goes out!"
                                                    *Thalaba.*

THE cassique was not a little surprised by his visiter. As requested, he procured candles, two of which Calvert lighted instantly, and placed in front of a window which was visible from the forest where Belcher and Ligon had been left with the marines. He then proceeded, as briefly as possible, to report to his brother the affair which had brought him, the danger as it appeared to his mind, and the force which he had arrayed to meet it. It is probable that, filled with the peculiar griefs which then distressed him, the cassique would have given little heed to his brother's apprehensions. He was quite as favorably disposed to the red men as ever; it was difficult to disabuse him of his impressions; but when he with some degree of indifference began to declare his doubts, the other said abruptly, and somewhat impatiently :—

"Edward Berkeley, you have no right to trifle with other lives than your own. You have been so long in the habit of indulging in your passion of philanthropy, that you fail to see things with your natural good judgment. But, the danger is no longer questionable. It is not now a thing of speculation, but of positive evidence. I have myself made a circuit, only last night, of a camp of fifty warriors, all well armed, and not quite twelve miles from you. The place is evidently a rendezvous, where, by this time, there may be from two to five hundred more! There has been a gathering of a thousand on the Savannah river; and are you to learn, for the first time, of the utter destruction of the settlement

of Lord Cardross, at Beaufort, by the Spaniards, no doubt assisted
by the Indians?"

"Good God! is it pôssible?"

"True, every syllable! These things are certain. But where
is your Indian boy—the hunter? Is he on the premises?"

"I suppose so. He has a little lodge to himself, within fifty
yards of the dwelling, where he sleeps."

"Ah! does he sleep? We must see if he is in it."

"But, what of him? He is a mere boy."

"So is a powder-monkey: but he may fire a magazine! He
has been put with you, by old Cussoboe, for this very purpose.
He is a spy; something more, indeed, if my suspicions be well
founded. By his hands, no doubt, your keys, especially of your
armory and arsenal, are to be delivered to Cussoboe, at midnight,
when you all sleep!"

The cruiser then narrated all that he knew of the habits of the
boy—of the concealed sheaf of arrows, and how he had supplied,
on several occasions, the place of the arrows which had been
broken, so as to disorder the mutual calculations of chief and
boy.

"The keys!"—the cassique hurried away to hunt them up.
"They are all here," he said, returning. "And when do you
expect the savages?"

"This very night, according to the original count of arrows, or
to-morrow night at farthest. It *must* be one or t' other. Not
knowing whether the arrow *first* broken was counted inclusively,
or from, it is not easy to say positively which is the night. We
must prepare for both."

"To-night? Why, it is already midnight."

"True, but 'the *ides* of March' are not over! It is at the very
hour of the dawn that the red men most frequently choose to begin the attack. But never you fear"—seeing that the cassique
was starting away, full of excitement—"I have anticipated their
movements quite as well as you could have done, had you known
sooner of the affair. I had, indeed, made preparations that you
should know. Have you not heard from Gowdey?"

"Not lately. He gave me some warnings, some time ago; but
I made light of them."

"You were wrong. Gowdey is an authority, *in his province*,

who might save all your governors and councils. But, did he send you no letter from me?"

"None."

"It is well, then, that I relied upon no other agency than my own. Had your governor done as I counselled, Cardross and his colony would have been saved. It is lucky I am not too late here."

The cassique was now quite willing to listen to his brother.

"Before disturbing you," continued he, "I made all preparations for your defence. I have brought a strong force with me; have taken possession of your armory, which I have garrisoned with half a dozen stout fellows. I have converted carriage-house and stables into fortresses also. I have roused your laborers, and armed them; given them instructions what to do; and these lights are designed to apprize a party, which I have in the woods, that you are ready to receive a score of well-armed men in your mansion-house. You have a closed basement, I perceive, which I take to be unoccupied. We must put them there, without their presence being known. I will now withdraw the lights. They have served their purpose. My men will be here in a few minutes more."

The cassique was full of wonder, but he had hardly time to express it; a muffled sound, as of heavy footsteps, at that moment being evident without. Stealthily the door was opened; and, in as much silence as possible, Belcher entered with his squad. Not a moment was lost in hurrying them down into the basement.

"And, now, see if the hunter-boy is within-doors — within his cabin," said our rover. "Possibly he is, for my substitution of the new for the broken arrows will have probably deceived him thoroughly as to the time for the rising. He may be there, but it is just as well to see."

The two went forth together. Twenty minutes sufficed for the examination. But the boy was *not* in his cabin. This was conceived to be, in some degree, a confirmation of our rover's suspicions. But it did injustice to the boy. He, poor fellow, was at that moment buried in the deepest slumbers of an exhausted frame, scarcely a hundred yards from the spot where Ligon and the rest of the marines and sailors were crouching out of sight, in closest harborage. Iswattee had been pursuing his regimen for more

24*

than a week; hence the appearance of illness which had so impressed the cassique and Grace Masterton. His body had become enfeebled by potent draughts of his bitter-root decoctions; while his mind, as he slept, was disordered by wildest dreams, the result of his equally potent narcotic beverages, through which he expected to obtain his revelations from the Great Manneyto, or Master of Life. Alas, for the poor, simple savage!—shrinking from the cruel duty imposed upon him, from which the red boy was seldom known to shrink—stubborn, usually, as the Spartan; and recoiling with horror from those sanguinary deeds which his imagination had so vividly painted to his thoughts; too gentle a nature for the destiny before him; assigned by the Fates to an ordeal for which they had failed to endow him with the requisite characteristics of a wild and savage blood, and a cold, obdurate, inflexible heart and will!

Will the Great Spirit help him in this ordeal? Will he descend with shadowy wings upon his slumbers, and so clear his vision and arm his will as to enable him to find a way out of the deadly labyrinth—the snaky folds of his destiny? His trial is near at hand! Let us leave him where he sleeps, and follow those only who are all awake to the exigencies of the time.

The cassique, now made fully conscious of the perils of his situation, roused up all his energies, which, once afoot, were as stirring and pressing as those of his brother, whom he so greatly resembled.

"My poor Olive!" he exclaimed; "and at such a moment! O Harry, she is dying! Your Olive! my Olive! Perchance this very night—this very night!—"

He could say no more, but fell into his brother's outstretched arms. For a moment the two clung together—a life of meaning in the deep silence which followed. Neither had speech. Neither saw the other's tears, or heard the suppressed sobbing. He only felt his own; and the deep throes of his heart stifled all hearing.

For a moment! And then the cassique drew himself up, and out of our rover's embrace, and said:—

"We must be men! But, O Harry, it is terrible to think that, in the midst of strife, and storm, and bloodshed, her pure, sweet spirit shall go out!—"

" Edward, enough ! Let me close these shutters. Go you to Olive's — to your wife's chamber — and close in every shutter. Gently ! No noise ! We must, so far as we can, spare her every sound of strife without. Let this be your present task. Take no further care or trouble touching this danger. I have prepared — will prepare — for it all. See to her ; cling to her side ; let her not lose you" — a long pause — " lose you, at the last !"

" Nor you ! O Harry, it is your right, even more than mine !"

" I will be *here*, Edward ; and, if it may be so, will be there also. We know not yet at what moment we may be summoned by the cry of battle without — the cry of death within ! Go, now, and see to all the fastenings : close all the windows in Olive's chamber."

The cassique again clasped his brother in his arms.

" Alas, my brother, that we should meet thus !"

" As God wills ! And we are stronger for this meeting, even thus ! The terrors of the grave, which surround us, are only so many clues to a wondrous mystery, to which heart, and soul, and mind, must equally rise, if we would assert a proper manhood. Go, now, my brother, and do as I have told you. If we are to be assailed to-night, the moment of trial can not be far off."

The cassique was about to go ; but was arrested, even at the door, by a third party coming upon the scene. Let us, to explain the interruption, anticipate his visit to his wife's chamber. We are summoned thither.

It will be remembered that, when the cassique withdrew from the chamber, he had left the little Spanish wife of our rover in charge of Olive. She was joined, in a while after, by the Honorable Mrs. Masterton. This maternal lady would have dismissed Zulieme to her chamber. But the latter would not consent ; professed her anxiety to remain, and declared that she had had sleep enough for the night. The mother was talkative, and, after a space, Olive became restive. Mrs. Masterton approached her bed :—

" What can I do for you, my child ?"

" There are footsteps — voices : some one comes !"

" No, my beloved, there is nobody. The house is perfectly still."

564 THE CASSIQUE OF KIAWAH.

The mother smiled — shook her head — and tried to soothe her.

"I can hear, mother. There are voices. Where is my husband — Sir Edward?"

"He has gone into the parlor, dear señora," quoth Zulieme.

"It is there I hear the steps — the voices."

"Impossible, my child; you have dreamed it. I rather think Sir Edward has gone to lie down."

"I have dreamed nothing. I see everything. Life itself is but a dream with me now; but it is such a dream as makes me see and hear more than ever. It is as I tell you, mother: there are footsteps — voices."

"I think I *do* hear voices," said Zulieme.

"No!" sharply rejoined the mother. "It is all a notion. The house is perfectly quiet."

"Ah! quiet — quiet! That is death! Death is a great quiet, mother. But I know that there are men moving and talking in the house. Ah! — lift me a little. Hark, mother!" — in a whisper; and, as her mother bent to her, she said, "*He* is here!"

"He! Who, my child?"

"Harry — Harry Berkeley!"

"My dear child, I tell you, you are only dreaming. It is impossible."

"And I tell you, mother, that I *know* he is here! I hear his voice—"

"What! when we can hear nothing?"

"I hear his footstep!"

The mother smiled, shook her head, and tried to soothe her.

"I *feel* his presence, mother! He *is* here! Will you not go and see, and bring him to me?"

"Bring him, my love?"

"Ay, bring him!"

"Impossible! Why, my child, only think!—"

"Think? How think? Why should I think? Why should you not bring him?"

"What! *after all?*—"

"Yes; *after all!* That is the very time — after all! There can be no doubts or suspicions *now*. Do you still think of such a life as this, that I am leaving? Do you not see that I am no more one of you? — that the world is going from me? — that life, society, all those things that made us ever so sadly think, are departing? I beg you, mother, bring Harry hither. Bring my husband with him. They are there together. I feel it — almost see it — hear his voice — know his step! Ah! why will you deny me?"

"But, my child, I assure you that there is no stranger in the house."

"As if Harry should be called a stranger! But he *is* here!"

"Let me go see, señora," said Zulieme to the mother. "It can do no harm."

"No, no! you are right, my dear girl," murmured the sufferer; "it can do no harm. Go see! — go bring him!"

"Well, go if you will!" replied the mother, a little too impatiently for such a scene and situation. But she had taken a sort of dislike to Zulieme, from the first moment of her coming, and this was her mode of expressing it. And Zulieme went.

She opened the door of the hall, at the moment when the brothers were embracing, as if the better to share their sorrows. The lights had been placed in the chimney, when Calvert had taken them from the window. At the opening of the door, the brothers turned their faces to the intruder; and, even as he turned, the gleams from the candles were thrown full upon the face of the rover. His air, figure, face, were unmistakeable by one who so well knew him as Zulieme; and, forgetting every consideration but the one vivid memory and feeling, she sprang upon him — with no power of self-restraint — threw herself upon his bosom, her arms almost vainly stretching up toward his neck, and cried aloud:—

"O Harry! you great brute of a Harry, you are come for me at last!"

The rover was as much confounded as the cassique. He lifted her in his arms, till her lips were on a level with his own, and she smothered him with kisses. The cassique recoiled in consternation. The rover said—

"Why, Zulieme! you here, child?"

"Didn't you know it? Haven't you come for me?"

"N—o! not exactly! But, it's just as well. I am glad to find you here. It saves me much pain and peril."

" What's just as well?" she demanded, quickly.

He did not answer her; but, still holding the little woman close-ly to him, with much more apparent tenderness than we have seen him show before, he said to his brother:—

" Go, Edward, and see to the windows.   All this shall be ex-plained hereafter."

The cassique disappeared, leaving the parties, but only for a brief space, together.   When he reached Olive's chamber, and heard from Mrs. Masterton what a wild notion his wife enter-tained of the presence of Harry Berkeley in the house, he was astounded.   He could readily conceive how acute might the senses become, where the heart was deeply concerned; but that the soul should be so quickened, while still holding possession of its frail tenement of clay — should so quicken the sensibilities — was a mystery of marvellous significance.   As he paused in silence, suddenly struck with the wonder of the thing, Olive said to him :—

" Surely, it is so, Edward — Harry is here?"

" He is, Olive !   Shall I bring him to you, my love?"

" If you please.   He has come in time."

" He belongs to us both, Olive : he shall come to you."

" It will kill her, Sir Edward !" murmured Mrs. Masterton, in tones which, as she thought, were inaudible to any ears but his. To her terror, Olive said:—

" Have you anything to make me live, mother? — Bring Harry to me, Sir Edward, if you please."

The cassique obeyed her.   The scene had occupied but a few minutes, and he returned promptly to the hall where he had left Harry and Zulieme.   A few words sufficed to say what was want-ed, and our rover hastened to obey; the little wife still eagerly hanging on his arm, and whispering:—

" I see it all now, Harry.   This lady was *your* Olive !"

" Hush ! child — hush !" he whispered in reply, pressing her hand, and passing on, while the cassique led the way.   At the entrance of the chamber, Zulieme, with a certain vague instinct of propriety, held back; but, this time, our rover detained her hand, as if to say, " You shall see and hear all. '   Then he en-tered, closely following the cassique, who went at once to the bed-side.   So did Harry ; and, without a word, he knelt down beside

the dying woman.  Her eyes were closed — she did not look at
him — but she knew he was there; and stretched out her thin
fingers, which he took within his grasp, and carried to his lips.
Then she said:—

"You are here, Harry!  I am glad!  I shall be happy now!
— My husband, Sir Edward—"

The cassique leaned over her; and, possessing herself of one
of his hands, she laid it in that of Harry.

"Am I right?" she continued.  "Brothers — always brothers!
Love me both when I am gone!  In that world to which I hasten,
I shall love you both, over all living men!  I shall watch your
loves!  You have been very dear to me both.  Oh, be always
dear to one another, in remembrance of my love!"

The brothers were now both kneeling beside her.  Their grief
was swallowed up in silence.  The mother, however, suddenly fell
into a passionate sobbing, which once more aroused the dying
woman:—

"O mother!" she exclaimed — "peace, now!  God is overshadowing us with his mighty presence.  If you could see, as I
see, who are about us, you would grow dumb — you would shut
all your senses!  Do not — do not!"

The cassique tried in vain to pacify the matron; but, finding
words unavailing, he led her from the room.  She struggled feebly, but finally submitted.  When she was removed, he returned
and closed the door.  None but Harry, himself, and Zulieme,
were now in the chamber.  Zulieme was kneeling at the foot of
the bed.  Harry remained beside Olive — close by, on one side
— her hand still clasped in his.  The cassique knelt opposite.
Her eyes were now shut.  There was no pressure in her fingers;
but her breathing was audible, though faint.  By this only did
they know that she still lived.  She seemed to slumber like an
infant.  Not a word was spoken for many moments.  The silence
was full of sacredness and awe.  Yes! they all felt that the overshadowing presence of a mighty Spirit was there, sovereign over
pain, death, and the grave!  And under his wings they were
subdued into silence; each seeming to hold his breath, as if waiting for some signal, significant of that approaching Power whose
potency they already felt!  And, even as Olive seemed breathing
herself gently away, as the zephyr dies along the empurpled

waves of a retiring sea; even as they held their own breathing suspended with a hush, waiting upon hers — there *was* a signal — a fearful one in that hour, and under such influences — but not that for which only they then looked and listened!

Wild was the cry which suddenly echoed through and shook the chamber! It was the war-whoop of the painted savage, howled forth, as by a thousand wolves, raging furiously around the dwelling.

# CHAPTER LIV.

### THE BATTLE OF KIAWAH.

"Ring out the alarum! for the foe is on us."

SHAKESPEARE.

THE harboring-place in which Calvert had posted Ligon, with his remaining body of marines, had been chosen with singular circumspection; at once with reference to concealment, and to the maintenance of a watch upon the hollow tree in which the sheaf of arrows had been hidden. He well apprehended that the first visit of the old chief, Cussoboe, would be made to the tree, to ascertain if his commands had been obeyed by his son; and, probably, with the hope to meet him there, bringing the keys of the barony and of all its offices.

Ligon, an old Indian-fighter as well as scout, lay close, grim as death, and not so impatient for his prey as to peril his prospect by any premature exhibitions. He had distributed his men along and within a thick piece of underwood which formed a boundary, as it were, between the original forests and the opened grounds of the barony. He could there behold all who emerged from the former, and yet obtain sufficient glimpses of the latter. His people crouched low, or lay at length, in a line, almost within touch of each other. It may be that some slept, in the two or three hours of watch and weariness which they were compelled to endure.

But Ligon himself never closed an eye, but kept scouting in short circuits, as the panther does about the farmyard. None of his own men knew when he departed or when he returned, so stealthy was his footstep; but in these circuits, which he continually enlarged, he came upon the sleeping boy, Iswattee. The starlight, feebly penetrating the massed boughs overhead, enabled him to discover the prostrate boy only when he stood beside him; for it was to one of the deepest covers of the thicket that the youth had gone in which to pursue his regimen. Perhaps Ligon would have failed to detect him when he did, had he not set his foot down upon a small pile of smouldering ashes which were still warm, and overturned the little earthen pot in which Iswattee had made his root-decoctions. This led our scout to a close scrutiny, and conducted him to the Indian boy, who was wrapped in sleep, and murmuring in some fearful dream.

The first instinct of Ligon was to brain the sleeper with his tomahawk; but he paused, reflecting that this stroke might lead to a premature exposure of his presence and his party, and possibly defeat the purpose for which his ambush had been set. Besides, he knew not how many more sleepers might be found in the same dense harborage. A stroke which should merely hurt — one cry of the wounded youth — would awaken all! Our scout, governed by these considerations, forebore the stroke, and contented himself with removing the hatchet, knife, bow and arrows, which lay beside the sleeper. These he bore away with him, moving back to his ambush with as much caution as before, but with more decided steps, as he discovered that the boy was sleeping uneasily, had shown some restlessness while he was withdrawing the weapons, and would probably soon awaken. Our scout regained the copse in which his men were crouching, and, with a touch of the hand on each shoulder, roused them to preparation. He naturally fancied that the red men were all about in the forest cover; and waiting, as is their wont, for the near approach of dawning, to begin the assault. As the morning hour is usually that when the deepest sleep falls upon men, so do they train themselves to waken at that hour, the better to take advantage of their enemies.

It might have been three quarters of an hour after this event, when a dry branch was heard to break, and the dry leaves to crinkle, as under an approaching footstep. Soon, Ligon beheld a warrior, fully equipped, Indian fashion, for strife and massacre, emerging from the shade and passing over a brief open space in the woods, in the direction of the hollow tree. He was followed by three others, who came out severally from the forest. The first who appeared was old Cussoboe himself; the others were all of them chiefs, and one of them his brother, well known to the whites of that day for his prowess. This was Ocketee. He has left his name to a swamp and river.

The old chief searched the tree, and uttered an exclamation of rage and disappointment. He had grasped the remaining arrows in his hand, six or seven in number, and held them up to his companions. A perfect torrent of execrations, in the dialect of his people, burst from his lips. A long and animated discussion followed between the party; but, though Ligon knew the language, he was not sufficiently near to distinguish the words. He could only hear the sounds; and these, he observed, were warm, violent, and very savage. The old chief crushed the arrows in his hands, and dashed them to his feet. Then, as if the conference had reached a conclusion, he put his hands to his mouth, and uttered a deep, wailing cry, like that of some sea-fowl, in unison with its own melancholy, and its wild abode of foam, and storm, and ocean.

Such a cry, at once deep and shrill — well mistaken for that of a sea-bird — might reach the barony, and the ears of all its inmates, yet occasion no surprise to senses not familiar with the capacity of the red men for imitating the cries of beast and bird, and their habit of employing these as signals in stratagem and war. Ligon readily concluded that the cry had some such signification. It was easy for him, where he stood with his men, to have rushed out upon the chiefs and butchered them, or to have shot them down; but he knew not how many savages were harbored in the woods, and was well aware that the first sound of strife would bring forth all their myrmidons, supposing them to be at hand. He itched to be busy with them, but had schooled his passions to a wonderful patience and forbearance.

The cry of Cussoboe brought forth his warriors, perhaps two hundred painted savages in all, and one group dragged along with them the boy Iswattee, whom they had stumbled over, as Ligon had done, and in less than half an hour after he had left him.

Iswattee came forward staggering, feeble with his regimen, and perhaps half stupid still from his narcotics. He was bewildered, but approached his father, who, at first, seemed not to know him. Some one said, "Iswattee!" At the word, Cussoboe caught up

the broken arrows, still in the sheaf of rattlesnake-skin, and thrust
them in the very face of the boy; then, ere any one could conceive his purpose, or interpose, he raised his hand suddenly and
smote him on the head with the hammer of his stone hatchet,
bringing him to the earth at a blow.  He was about to repeat the
stroke, when Ocketee, the uncle of the boy, darted between, and
defended the body.  Some sharp words passed between the parties, and there was every chance of a violent quarrel, for old Cussoboe raged like a tiger; but several of the other chiefs put in,
and appeased the disputants.  Three of the red men took up the
senseless boy, and, after searching him — as Ligon supposed, for
the keys of the barony — they bore him away from his father's
sight, and hid him in the thickets, where one of them remained
with him.

A hurried consultation then followed among the chiefs, the result of which was that three of them, old Cussoboe still in the
lead, emerged from the forest, taking the direction of the woods
and grounds about the barony.  Suffering them to go ahead some
hundred yards, the main body of the red men advanced also, and
planted themselves along the very edge of the open grounds,
gradually spreading out on each hand; so that, at a given signal,
they might contract their wings, and cover every point of the settlement.

Watching every movement, and suffering the whole force of
the enemy to leave the forest, Ligon set his own squad in motion,
but halted them as soon as he had got them in line and order,
keeping them close in hand and still in cover.  He then stole forward himself sufficiently far to ascertain that the red men were
still in the wood, just on its edge, and perfectly concealed in its
shadows from the settlement.  Subsequently, when they advanced
toward the houses, as they did at the signal of the chief, he brought
his men forward, so as to occupy the very place they had left,
on the edge of the woods, the background of shadow giving them
ample security from sight.  Here he examined the priming of
every musket and pistol.  All had been provided, from the cassique's armory, with guns.  Their pistols and cutlasses they had
brought with them from the ship.

"And now," said Ligon, with a low chuckle, "ef we haven't
got these rascally red-skins in a tight place, then I never seed a

wolf in a steel trap. Only go to it, fellows, with a will, and you'll see the red feathers fly!"

Old Cussoboe, with his two companions, proceeded to the examination of the several houses of the settlement. They stole, like ghosts, silent as the grave, from tree to tree, always taking shrewd care to secure a cover when they could. They went round the armory, which was to them a special object of attention. In the rear of it they had a long consultation, which the marines within could hear, but not comprehend. They tried at the lock, but it was fast. There was also some heavy weight, some bulky article, against the door. This was a surprise to them. It argued that some one slept within; more than one was not thought of. There were holes in the sides of the building, which was pierced for musketry; but no windows, no outlet but the one door. After some minutes spent in consultation here, they stole, in like cautious manner, to the dwelling-house, and that of the workmen. The carriage-house and stables were left unexamined. They seemed to know the grounds well, and up to a late moment had evidently had their spies upon it. They found all the buildings securely fastened; that is to say, so securely as to require some degree of violence to break in. But they also found all silent as death or sleep could make them. They could see no lights, except in one chamber of the main dwelling, and this gleamed only through a crevice in the shutter. It was in the chamber of Olive; the windows had been quietly fastened by the cassique, at a moment when Harry Calvert was kneeling by Olive's bedside, after his first arrival.

As if satisfied with what they had seen, the old chief, Cussoboe, gave a signal which brought up his men, two hundred at least, who came forward into the open grounds as cautiously, one by one—taking the trees severally for cover, the fences and houses—as if their leaders had not already felt the way. They divided into three parties, under as many chiefs. One party completely encircled the dwelling, and squatted close to the basement around it, waiting the word; another surrounded, in like manner, the building where the workmen were stationed; while a third, old Cussoboe at their head, placed themselves about the armory. This building was especially their object, and here they made their first demonstration. There was a small party that squatted be-

side the line of unfinished pickets, which formed the beginning of
the covered way from the dwelling to the armory; and others,
again, individuals, occupied here and there a tree. After a few
words, three stalwart Indians advanced from Cussoboe's division,
and with their hatchets began to work, as quietly as possible,
upon the fastenings of the log-house. They had scarcely commenced, however, when a pistol blazed through one of the musket-
holes, tumbling one of the three incontinently over.

Then rose the whoop from the whole band, as if by a common
instinct — that fearful whoop of death, which had so suddenly
startled all in the chamber of the dying Olive, as we have already
seen. She had not so completely sunk into the lethargy which
was overspreading all her faculties, as to be unconscious of those
fearful howlings which had sent a thrill of horror through all the
rest. She started from her seeming sleep — for sleep she did not:
her eyes were only shut, while her mind enjoyed a sort of sweet,
dreaming reverie, strangely sweet and peaceful, as assured that it
was Harry Berkeley's hand which held her own. And, in this
consciousness of her mind, her fingers had failed to note that the
hand had been withdrawn. She started, and cried aloud:—

"Oh, that horrid noise! Ah, Harry, Harry! where are you?
Do not leave me, Harry! — not now! Hold me still, Harry!"

He was already at the door. He could hear, though the tones
were very feeble. One sad look did he give toward the couch;
then, dashing his hand across his eyes, he hurried away to the
basement. The cassique followed him as rapidly as possible.

"It is no time for tears, Edward. Yet, oh the horrors of such
a conflict, now — *now!* That such a blessed angel should take
her flight from earth in such a tempest!"

"Happy that she flies from all tempests, my brother!" answered
the cassique, solemnly.

At that moment Zulieme, who had followed both, caught our
rover's arm.

"O Harry, is it the red savages?"

"Yes, child! But get you back, out of danger, and keep away
from the windows. Do not leave Olive now, if you love me."

"And you *wish* me to love you, Harry?" whispered the little
wife, pulling him down to her, while she threw her arms round
his neck and kissed him.

" To be sure, child! Yes, yes, Zulieme; if I have heart for anything now, I love you."

And, as if suddenly reflecting that, in the vicissitudes of the night, he might be cut off, he was even tender in his embrace — more tender than we have usually seen him; and when he put her away, it was with a kiss.

" Now, back with you, child, and cling to Olive! You know all now. Go, if you love me, and cherish her with love to the last; and catch her dying words, her dying breath, and bring them to me hereafter."

She obeyed him without pause — was now quite satisfied to obey. Poor little urchin! love — even her brute-husband's love — was fast growing to be a necessity with her heart; a great craving, at all events.

This episode occupied but a few seconds. When she was gone, the cassique said :—

" I know none of your plans, Harry. There must be hundreds of these savages, from that whoop !"

" There are ! My arrangements are very simple, but, I think, sufficient. We have, as so many citadels, your house, the armory, the house of your laborers, and the carriage-house and stables. These are all made tolerably secure, and each has its well-armed garrison : judge if the Indians can penetrate here, without suffering great slaughter. In addition, I have at least twenty sailors in the woods, well armed with musket, pistol, and cutlass. The red men have no firearms, unless they have procured them by some depredation. They are not yet skilled in the use of them. Our various posts cover all the space between the several houses. Our force in the woods will reserve their fire to receive them, when we shall have beaten them off. They know nothing of our defences, and it must be rather a massacre than a fight. But it is better that it is so. We must fill them with sudden terrors, by a terrible punishment. Sharp punishment, at first, will shorten the war. And now, leave it to me, Edward. I would beg you to go and keep with Olive, but that I know—"

" How can you propose such a thing, Harry !"

" I do not propose it. I know that to propose it, to a man of character, would be an insult. I should so hold it myself. What I mean is this : that everything has been so thoroughly arranged,

you are not needed.   I, in fact, am scarcely needed, but for sig-
nalling."

"Hark! they are hammering at the entrance; and, save that
single shot, your men do not give fire."

"I have ordered it so.  I wish them to come on in body.
Your door is well bolted and barred now; though, when I first
came, it was so simply locked, that with a key I found entrance.
They will hardly find entrance so easy now.  But they need to
be watched.  Do you keep and watch the passage, while I go
below.  If you find them making any rapid progress, which they
could only do with a two-pounder or a battering-ram, let me know.
Watch here, Edward, where they seem to be at work."

Our cruiser went below, leaving the cassique in the passage.
The latter was armed — had caught up pistols and gun; his sword
was at his side.  He was eager for strife, if only to escape from
thought; the silence of his wife's chamber still as solemnly calling
to him as did the clamors of the savages without.  He was impatient of the inaction which his situation forced upon him; and, for
awhile — so feeble was the agency employed by the assailants of
the door — they made no seeming progress.  The door was a panelled one, but heavy, and made of hard pine.  The Indians, smiting with their stone hatchets, did not aim, as the white men would
do, at the panels; but struck without discrimination, here and
there, and as frequently upon the cross as the panel.  The door
was secured by a bar of lightwood as well as by the lock.  But a
white man, with axe or hatchet, could have hewn it through in
twenty minutes.  Our cassique listened to the strokes with growing impatience; and, as if to answer his impatience, it was soon
evident that new assailants had come to the work.  The blows
were now harder, made with a heavier implement, and delivered
with more judicious aim upon a single panel at a time.  Watching this progress, he at length hastened below, where the whole
body lay *perdu*, grimly silent, waiting their moment.  Harry Calvert met him at the door, and they spoke together in whisper.
The cassique said:—

"Their hatchet-strokes are telling above.  The splinters begin
to fly.  They have already beaten a hole through one of the
panels."

"Ah! well, I am rather glad of that, for we may soon get a

chance at them, which we have not here. Situated as we are, we do not command the immediate entrance, only the space five or six feet from it. See here!—"

And he took him to the front, and, through a crevice, just wide enough for the muzzle of a blunderbuss, he showed him the area, where the red men were sufficiently visible, and scattered, skipping about the scene, dotting the grounds in all directions between house and arsenal, and in perpetual motion.

"You see," said the cruiser, "that we should shoot unprofitably while they are thus scattered. We have too few shot to throw away any. We must make each bullet tell. I wait to see them massed together. They wait to gain some advantage—to effect an opening; and, this done, you may look to see them rush, in headlong crowds, to the point. *That* will be our time. It is for this we wait. Now, I shall be quite willing that they shall beat in the panels. It will have two good results: we shall be able to crack at them through the opening, and from the passage, where for the present we can do nothing; and it will bring on their masses tumultuously. Once let us have them massed! See this blunderbuss! it carries a pound of slugs. I have another like it here. Two blunderbusses and ten muskets, all crammed with slugs, will be apt to create a sensation among the rascals."

"Good heavens, Harry, it will be a massacre!"

"Exactly! If we do not *make* it so, we are lost! They can overwhelm us with numbers — fire the house above our heads — utterly destroy us — unless we can make it a massacre! We can not afford to fight with them man for man. No! our hope is to bring them on in masses, assailing every one of our garrisons at the same time. With this object, I have specially instructed our several leaders to reserve their fire, or so to fire as to persuade the wretches that we have but a man or two in each. Now, let them gain an opening, or get the promise of one, and they grow mad with excitement; and you will see in what swarms the red devils will rush toward us! Then, they shall have it!"

And he slapped the great brass barrel of the blunderbuss which he carried, with an exulting and determined action.

"The miserable wretches!" groaned the cassique.

"Hark ye, good brother of mine, none of your philanthropy now! Blood is the law of battle! We must show tooth and

25

nail. We must bite and rend. Get you above, Edward, and report progress. Or, stay here, and keep my place, while I go see."

Without waiting for an answer, he stole up-stairs, advancing cautiously along the passage, until he sheltered himself in the left corner near the door, his right hand free. The passage was almost wholly dark, save a little gleam from an opening which the assailants had beaten through one panel. They were still at work upon a second, which was yielding in splinters under their stone hatchets. Calvert watched his moment, and lifted his blunderbuss; but he instantly put it down.

"Not this!" he muttered to himself. "I must not waste its contents upon a man or two."

He pulled from his belt one of the ship's pistols, thrust it suddenly forward, and drew the trigger. Down went the stalwart savage who had been hammering at the door, with a brace of bullets through his head. He was dead ere he fell!

What a yell followed from a hundred throats! There was a rush of a score or more, some of whom eagerly seized the corpse and bore it off, while others darted with their shoulders against the door, as if to break in by the mere weight of their bodies; and others, again, with their hatchets, renewed the strokes upon the panels.

To two of these sturdy assailants the rest yielded the labor. Only two could work profitably at the spot. But the crowd had increased without. Enraged by the loss of one of their stoutest warriors, they were yet encouraged by the fact that only a single shot had been fired. This argued the presence of but one defender, and perhaps but a single weapon. They had cut off the connection with the arsenal and the house of the workmen; and, though seemingly well aware that the garrison of the latter was strong, they counted upon the helplessness of the two other places. This emboldened them in their attacks. Calvert congratulated himself on the approach of the moment when he could effect the havoc which he desired.

"Thick grass," he said, as he again went below — using the very language of the Hun against Rome — "thick grass is easier cut than thin."

He said to the cassique, as he got below :—

"Now, Edward, get to your post again! Keep in cover, and use your pistols only, and only when you can make your mark. I have had a chance, and have used it. These red rascals will be apt to come on now. They are thickening; they are getting feverish and impatient. Just so soon as they get thoroughly enraged, shall we have them on us; and then! — But go! Keep in cover, for these fellows will deliver their arrows through a key-hole."

The cassique promptly obeyed. Though quite as brave as his brother, he yet, with all others, tacitly felt and acknowledged that superiority of resource, that authority in command, which, in the case of the latter, was the fruit of a long experience in strife. Calvert had a motive for hurrying the cassique back to the passage, the entrance to which he saw would, for some while yet, baffle the assailants. But he also foresaw that the red men could not much longer curb their impatience, and that they would almost unconsciously accumulate about the several points of attack, in numbers, irrespective of the commands of their leaders. They were hammering at the door of the arsenal, even as at that of the mansion. They had simply been stung and irritated by the single shot from each, which had taken down its victim. Calvert felt sure that he would soon enjoy his desired opportunity, in delivering all his fire upon their masses.

"Two blunderbusses," he counted again and again to himself— "two blunderbusses and ten muskets!" He did not desire his brother to be present at the discharge. He respected the error (as he held it) of philanthropic tenderness for the red men which the cassique entertained. He whispered all around among his men:—

"They will soon make a rush! Wait my orders, and fire low! You are on a line with them; your muzzles range with your hips, and will cover their bodies. That will do. Shoot exactly level, and just where the crowd is thickest. Blunderbuss"— to the fellow who carried this second formidable weapon—"fire *last*, and as they scatter!"

He had hardly spoken, when the rush was made, at once upon dwelling-house and armory. The crowd pressed the persons before them, mounted the steps of the dwelling to the door, and the rear still kept thrusting on the front. There was a great shouting

—the war-whoop—a flight of arrows at every window, and tomahawks were hurled against the shutters, in their rage. Calvert watched every movement impatiently. His moment came at last!

"Now," said he, "let them feel you! Give it them!"

And, as he spoke, a burst of fire followed, which was echoed seemingly from the several garrisons.

It was no echo! Each of these places had been assailed, in the same manner, at the same moment; and each had poured forth its treasured volley among the swarming assailants, with like terrible effect. It was the first notification that the savages had of any formidable force in preparation for them. They were confounded. For a moment all was confusion and consternation. One universal groan went up; cries of pain; shrieks of terror; while, in front of each of the garrisoned places, lay one or more piles of slain and wounded: the slain, prostrate on face or back; the wounded, writhing to extricate their limbs from incumbent bodies, and draw themselves, if possible, out of the *melée*. Ocketee, the chief, had fallen, slain outright. Cussoboe, however, was unhurt; and he came on again, raging like a tiger, and striving to bring up his warriors a second time to the conflict.

But this was no easy matter. The red men quickly feel their losses. They count a single warrior slain, as a defeat. They stood appalled. They now felt that the barony had been prepared against them, and with such a force as they hardly believed to be anywhere embodied in the colony. But, as the cries of the sufferers reached their ears; as the wounded dragged themselves out of the scene, and became known to them; as they counted and missed the persons slain — they grew furious; smote their enemies in the air; howled to their gods in imprecation; practised a thousand contortions; and strove to work themselves up to a renewal of their frenzy, and a repetition of the attack.

Suddenly, a wild woman came among them from the rear, and howling with the fury of a demon. She had followed or accompanied the party, and her son was among the slain; and, with dismal shrieks and imprecations, she rushed among the combatants, exhorting them to havoc and revenge. She was powerfully seconded by one of their *Iawas*, or priests — a conjuror, a magician — who, gashing himself with a huge ocean-shell, and drawing the wofullest sounds from a great conch, invoked upon their heads the terrors of all their savage gods if they did not wreak vengeance on their white enemies.

The appearance of this Iawa was frightful in the extreme. He was of immense size and stature, nearly seven feet in height, muscular and well limbed, but of little flesh, and he wore a head-dress of buffalo-horns in a fillet of feathers. His age was greater than that of any of his people, yet not one exhibited such wonderful agility, was so lithe, rapid, and powerful of limb and movement. His contortions, savagely frantic and fantastic, as he threw his hands up in air, and whirled through the masses, gashing his breast till the blood issued from every part of it, struck awe and terror even into the souls of those who had been wont to behold his previous displays, and who had long been familiar with such savage rites. With the woman as a Fury, such as haunted the footsteps of Orestes, and the Iawa as a terrible necromancer, calling up the dead and dismal inhabitants of the infernal abodes, we may not wonder that a sort of madness seized upon the warriors as they heard their invocations; and they rushed headlong, as it were, upon Fate!

But what could their stone hatchets, *macanas*, or war-clubs, avail against the defences of the white man? Again did the fiery vengeance, from mansion-house and arsenal, hurtle terribly through their ranks, rending, maiming, and destroying! The savage woman, rushing desperately to the front, as the warriors came on, was among the first to perish; falling, with one wild shriek, upon her face, while the torrent of warriors, passing over her body, trampled out what little life remained in her.

"It is a horrid massacre, Harry!" said the cassique, as it seemed reproachfully.

"Can we escape it, brother mine?"

"No! I see no way. Nevertheless, it *is* horrible!"

"Very! But it is their blood or ours! Give it them again, men! Now—rake the line of pickets, where you see them huddling together! One more round, and we shall disperse the wolves!"

And it blazed—that fiery tempest—blazed, charged with scores of smiting bolts, from gun, and blunderbuss, and pistol, that swept through the line of crouching savages, sending those who were not stricken down, scattered and screaming over the area! Another broadside from the arsenal; a third from the fortress of the workmen; and the affair seemed to be at end. All was disorder and panic among the savages.

Then it was that Cussoboe, that fierce old chief, who had hitherto escaped every shot, though as much exposed as the meanest of his followers, came rushing among them, perilling his person everywhere, reckless of danger, and even smiting down the fugitives with his stone hatchet as sternly as he had smitten down his son! In his own wild gutturals, he cried to his people:—

"Ha! do you fear the white man? Do not be afraid. Be strong! be strong! Kill! kill! Let us drink the blood of the pale-faces; let us tear off the scalps from their skulls! Kill! kill!"

But his appeal helped them little—failed to restore order; and they were still scattered and without purpose, until the savage conjuror, the great Iawa of the tribe, reappeared upon the scene, howling and practising those grotesque, almost demonic contortions, which usually excited them to madness. Armed, now, with an enormous *macana*, or war-club — a huge mace, five feet long, of the hardest wood, into the sides of which were let, nearly its whole length, double rows of sharp flint-stones, like arrow-heads, but thrice as large and quite as keen — he led them himself against the dwelling-house, from which so many fearful streams of fire had issued, and, darting against the door, smote it with thundering effect for entrance.

"We must get rid of that conjuror," quoth Calvert to his men. "Pick him out! give him half a dozen of your muskets at once!"

The fire was delivered; but the conjuror seemed to bear a charmed life! He stood unmoved, tall as a tower, among the crowd, smiting still as fearlessly as ever; and ever and anon crying out to the band to avenge their gods and people. At that moment, there rose a shout among the savages, as if stimulated by some new cause of hope; and Calvert saw with anxiety a runner approaching from the rear, who carried aloft a ball of blazing tow, coated in the gum-turpentine, fastened to the end of a spear, and burning furiously; while another followed him, with a bundle of arrows similarly dressed with gum and tow, not yet lighted, but ready for use!

Our cruiser at once understood what these preparations meant.

"See that every gun and pistol be charged," he said to his men, "and be prepared to follow me!"

Then, taking off his hunting-shirt, he made one of the sailors wrap it tightly, in several folds, about his left arm. This done, he grasped a heavy tomahawk, and, bidding all his men follow, ascended from the basement to the passage-way. Here he met the cassique, to whom he said:—

"We have a new danger to contend with, and the worst yet! The rascals are about to assail the house with burning arrows! We must end this matter as soon as possible, and by a desperate effort, or we are lost!"

"What do you propose to do?"

"Make a sally. We must now make these red rascals feel us, hand to hand! We might destroy many of them, shooting from our defences, yet not prevent others from sending their flaming arrows to every roof in the settlement. There is but one way to prevent that. This conjuror, who seems to defy our bullets, must be met. If we can slay him, we shall probably disperse the rest. At all events, we can only disperse them by a concerted charge."

"I will go with you, Harry!"

"You shall *not!* Who will defend the house, close the door, make good the entrance, if you leave it? No! you must stay, and keep the garrison. Remember Olive! .... When I have sallied out with these men, secure the door after us, as before. Then use your judgment for the defence! And — God be with you, my brother!"

They embraced. It might be a final parting. The cassique chafed; but there was no remedy. He felt that he could not leave the dwelling. He shed bitter tears at the necessity. He, too, was ready for death.

"Where is your horn?" said Calvert to one of his men. He produced it from under his arm.

"The moment we sally forth," continued he to the fellow, "do you sound it thrice, with all your wind! Now — be ready to second me! I will grapple with the conjuror. Do your work among the masses. When you have delivered your fire, rush on them with your cutlasses."

The three bugle-blasts were a signal, agreed upon before, announcing a common sally from all the garrisons. In a moment, and while the Iawa was still thundering at the door with his *ma-cana*, the bar was quietly removed, the bolt shot back, and the door thrown open — the Iawa staggering forward, only to receive a heavy blow from Calvert, upon the shoulder, which drove him out again.

Then the two met in conflict, at the very entrance, and upon the steps of the house. The *macana* swung in air, a terrific weapon, but difficult to manage. Calvert kept his enemy at close quarters, the better to prevent its stroke, and for the more effectual use of the short-handled tomahawk which he bore. It was in vain that the Iawa receded, in order to deliver his blows. Our rover clung to him closely, and drove him before him, with sharp, sudden blows, frequent but slight, as not given with the full swing of his arm. And this difficulty was one not easily overcome — since, to avoid the formidable *macana*, Calvert, who had no shield, but the coat wrapped about his left arm, was required to employ his agility to the utmost, either by getting within the length of his enemy's arm, or by dodging his club in its descent. One well-aimed stroke from such a mace, falling upon head or arm, would slay or disable him for ever. It was a battle of the middle ages. The Iawa was no match for him in agility, however he might be in strength. Calvert pressed him with his keenest purpose, restrained simply by the necessity of keeping the closest watch, and eluding every blow: no easy task, amid the din, the imperfect light, and the sudden glare in his eyes from the blazing tow-balls, which were now to be seen waving in several parts of the area.

But the single combat between the two leaders, though grimly watched by many, on both sides, with all that gloating anxiety which marks the spectators of any great gladiatorial conflict, was not suffered to keep the rest idle. So far, it had been the work of a few seconds only — the two rushing into conflict from the moment when Calvert had emerged from the dwelling. But, so soon as his ten musketeers could make their way out, and spread themselves on either side of their chief, they delivered their fire, full in the thick of the excited crowd! The two blunderbusses roared and emptied their slugs; the muskets, huge enough, in that day, of themselves, had also formidable masses of leaden mischiefs to scatter abroad; and they did so, with most mischievous accuracy of aim! Terrible were the shrieks and groans that followed; and then, even as they had been ordered, the sailors drew their cutlasses, and rushed among the bewildered masses, hewing right and left with their sharp weapons and powerful arms!

But ere this movement was made, and just so soon as their volley was delivered, the bugler thrice sounded his charge, the spirit-stirring notes imparting a new life to the scene of death and massacre.

At that signal, for which the other garrisons had been impatiently waiting, volley after volley was poured forth from each; the combatants following up the effect of a most murderous discharge, with their cutlasses, even as Calvert's party had done.

The red men who still kept their feet, and the field, found themselves assailed, on all sides, by a force that seemed to spring out of the earth. A wide-spread consternation seized upon their host. Old Cussoboe raged in vain; and, even while delivering his war-cry, was hewn, to his very teeth, by the cutlass of a common sailor!

It was a curious illustration of that chivalrous instinct which characterizes all truly brave people, that no one, of either side, sought to meddle in the fight between Calvert and the Iawa. It was seemingly a tacit understanding that the two champions should have fair play. No single stroke or shot was aimed at either. Their conflict constituted the closing scene of the contest. All was fairly over, in the rest of the field, ere it closed with them.

Never did Indian warrior or Magian more bravely or fiercely, or with greater prowess, wield weapon for his gods or country. His tall form was pre-eminent, even above the height of Calvert, which was considered great among the whites; and his mighty *macana* was whirled about in air, the whizzing sound of its motion being heard for thirty feet or more! Its every descent made the heart shrink and shudder — expecting to hear it crashing, the next moment, among the bones of the head which it threatened! But, hitherto, with the exception of two slight injuries, where the club had grazed his bandaged arm, Calvert had escaped unwounded; and he had succeeded, thrice, in giving more decided hurts to his enemy. The Iawa was evidently growing feeble. His strokes were less frequent. He raised his *macana* with more effort and more slowly. He was staggered — twice by the strokes

25*

of the tomahawk; and once, from no apparent cause. But he made a final and powerful effort. He felt that it was probably the last he could make; and, with a wild cry, uttering certain guttural words in his own language — doubtless addressed to his false gods — he whirled the *macana* about his head, and it sung fearfully in the air as it descended!

It required all Calvert's dexterity to elude the blow, which grazed him narrowly, smiting the cap from his head!

The force thrown into the stroke, bore the Iawa completely about; while the heavy end of his mace sank in the ground. Before he could recover himself, lift his weapon, or again meet the *eye* of his enemy, the tomahawk had descended once, twice — the first blow stunningly, the last fatally; the heavy steel crunching deeply into the brain! The conjuror sank forward, with a single yell, which found many a fearful echo among his people. Down he went, like a great tower, and in his fall the conflict ceased. The red warriors had no leader left. Subsequently it was found that he had three musket-balls in his body. Yet he had not faltered once!

All now was flight and confusion. Two or three flights of fiery arrows had been discharged at the roof of the mansion-house, but with such haste and excitement, that they went over it in every instance. The red men were not suffered time to repeat the attempt. The sally of the several garrisons was made at the happy moment; and we have seen the effect. The tow-balls, all on fire, were left blazing on the ground, and, by their ghastly glare, served to light up the horrors of the closing scene. Old Cussoboe, as we have said, was killed by a common sailor. When told whom he had slain, he was so proud of the achievement, that he cut off the old chief's head as a trophy, not having any adequate experience in taking scalps. Ligon, afterward, bought the trophy from him for a bottle of Jamaica, and performed the operation *secundum artem*. But this aside.

All was not yet over with the wretched savages. They naturally fled to the shelter of the thickets whence they had emerged, only to be torn, and shattered, and sent howling to still farther forests, by a deliberate volley — muskets and pistols doing fearful execution — from the party which had been left "in air," under the charge of Ligon. In twenty minutes after the fall of the

Iawa, not a red man was to be seen upon the field, those only excepted whose flight and battle were alike over; or such as had
been too severely wounded to hobble out of the action.   More
than thirty were slain outright, twice as many wounded.   The
dead were buried in the neighboring woods, by the whites, in three
several pits, and the earth heaped upon them into mounds, which
some of our antiquaries are prepared to ascribe to a far earlier
period.   And thus ended the fierce battle of Kiawah, one of the
most sanguinary of the thousand fights of the old colonial periods
in our English settlements.

It is not our purpose to narrate the events of this petty war,
which the historians describe as " The War with the Stono Indians."   It does not belong to this history.   Enough, if we mention that the timely provision of Calvert saved old Gowdey and
his fortress on the Ashley.   He, too, was attacked the same night,
by a strong force of the savages; who, not suspecting his resources in men, exposed themselves in numbers to his fire, and
were beaten off in like manner with those at Kiawah, with considerable loss.   Elsewhere, the settlements were not always so
fortunate.   Several were broken up, like that of Lord Cardross
at Beaufort.   The traders were butchered in large numbers; but
the rangers taking the field, and the Spaniards disappearing from
it, the insurrection was soon suppressed.   The curious reader must
consult other pages if he would learn more of this history.   Let
us confine ourselves to our own.

# CHAPTER LV.

### THE SHADOW PASSES — THE MOON RISES.

"Who comes from the bridal chamber?
It is Azrael, the angel of Death!" — SOUTHEY.

"It is a sudden presence that makes dawn
In the dark chamber.   This is Isfrael,
Angel of Life and loving harmonies!"

THUS ended the battle of Kiawah; a conflict for which the red men were entirely unprepared, and which, but for the fortunate presence of our rover upon the scene, must have ended, as did many other similar attempts, in the massacre of the whole settlement.   With the fall of their chief, Cussoboe, and of the *Iawa*, whom they held to be invulnerable to the weapons of the white man, the savages fled incontinently; but only to encounter the reserve of marines under Ligon, whose unexpected fire, as they rushed confusedly to the forests, took bloody toll at every passage.

Harry Calvert forbade pursuit.   He had done, with *his* men, all that could be expected at their hands; and, once on the alert, and well armed, the cassique and his English workmen were now fully able of themselves to defend the barony, in the event of any renewal of the assault.   He did not find it so easy to restrain Ligon, however, whose passion for scalps would have rendered the pursuit of the fugitives an unrelenting one.   He reluctantly forebore, at the imperative command of the rover; and, thus disappointed, abruptly declared his desire to leave the barony.   He had served the purpose for which he had been employed — had safely guided the party; which could now easily find its way back to the ship: and he was anxious to attach himself to some body

of men less scrupulous in hunting down the savages to their
ruin.

Ligon was an old scout, and knew in what lay the profits of
the business.   He could gratify his passion for scalps, in those of
the warriors; and appease his cupidity by selling captives to the
English, who needed their labor, as slaves, in the West-India
colonies.   This business was an old one, practised pretty generally from the Plymouth rock to the capes of Florida; by the Pilgrim Fathers as by the Cavaliers; and, indeed, the example of
setting the red men at loggerheads, slaughtering the warriors, and
selling their wives and children into slavery, was set by the virtuous people of Massachusetts Bay, who justified it from Scripture,
in numerous delectable texts, at the cost of the heathen.

This old Indian-fighter knew the warfare well; knew that, now
the war was broken out, the rangers would be called into service;
and, among these, an old scout, like himself, could carry on a
very profitable business.   He no sooner declared his desire to
leave the party, than Calvert paid him the twenty pounds sterling, which was the reward of his services.   Without word of
farewell, pocketing his money, Ligon braced his belt about his
waist, primed his weapons, adjusted his knife, grasped his tomahawk, and darted into the thickets, taking the direction for Gowdey's castle and Charleston.   We shall dismiss him from our
future regards, assured that he will be in at the death, wherever
the vultures shall be gathered to the prey!

We are to assume, from what we know of Calvert, that he did
not suffer any time to be wasted, or any military necessity to be
neglected.   The force at the barony was immediately arrayed,
counted, and stationed about the settlement, in proper positions
to discover the approaches of an enemy, and to co-operate against
assault.   His own force of marines and sailors he gathered *in
hand*, with orders to prepare for instant marching, if necessary.
Of course, they were fed and refreshed.   The cassique, just so
soon as the red men were dispersed, had sent out provisions for
them — not forgetting a certain keg, of formidable size, containing
a potent supply of Jamaica.

Having seen his marines gathered and counted; ascertained
his losses (and some had been slain, and others wounded); having done all that might be done to secure equally the party and

the barony, Calvert once more turned his eyes and footsteps upon the dwelling where lay the objects of his solicitude. What was he to learn on reaching that dwelling? What *could* he learn? The condition in which he had left Olive Berkeley, at the beginning of the conflict, led him to but one conclusion. She was dead! That morning star of his youthful fancy — that light still shining upon his soul, and casting a wan but precious moonlight over its darkest recesses — that light was now dimmed for ever to his eyes! The delicious voice of his heart was hushed! It was an echo in memory only. He should never more hear its music!

Such were his melancholy meditations as he slowly approached the house. It was now bright sunrise. The sun was rising upon the closing scene of the conflict, when the reserve, under Ligon, was pouring in its unexpected fires upon the scattering parties of the red men. The light of day had never dawned more cloudlessly, never looked brighter or more peaceful; as if there were no bloody strife, no wild, inhuman passions horridly at work, and heedless of its bright, stern, penetrating glances!

From the eyes of Calvert had gone the wild and savage fires of battle. His face was now wan, his eyes and form were drooping. The passion of the Hun had given place to the saddest expression of a lost hope; the weary, wo-begone look of a humanity which could tremble, and could no longer strive!

His brother met him at the entrance, and silently led him into the parlor. They both sat in silence. But that silence was full of speech.

That last wretched midnight in the chamber of Olive, when the conflict was raging around, and the sharp shot of the marines and the wild whoop of the red men were making the welkin ring! The Death, so busy without, wore no such touching aspect as that within, where he was doing his work in music!

Yes, music! For such is the low, sweet, broken chanting, from those dying lips, through which the soul is about to escape for ever. Hers are so many sweet, throbbing tones of the soul, as string by string is broken, of the beautiful instrument of life!

"Those are strange sounds which I hear," said Olive in a broken whisper to Zulieme. "They almost drown the song! But

I hear the song too, in spite of the clamor. Its music is very close to me. It sounds within my very ears, and seems to thrill through my brain. It comes and goes. It is like a rill in the forest — a low, sweet murmur, as if among green leaves and sunny flowers. If I could only shut out the noise of that shouting, I should hear it all. Where is Harry? He will quiet the noise. He is a charmer, Harry, and speaks the very seas into calm."

And she seemed earnestly to listen.

"I think I know it now! Yes — yes!" with a low sigh. "I know it. There is no pain now! But I do not see you all well, and — I do not now see Harry! Where's Harry — and — Sir Edward? They ought not to leave me now!"

The mother said something in a whisper.

"I know that these are angels. 'I believe in God, the Father Almighty, maker of heaven and earth, and in Jesus Christ, his' — ah! call him — call Harry! — and Sir Edward — my husband."

This was spoken somewhat wildly, and she made a feeble effort to lift her head from the pillow. Zulieme composed her — adjusted the pillow, and tenderly clasped her wan fingers in her own.

"The old willows at Feltham — the old Feltham willows! Ah! I knew that I should see them again. How cool is the shadow, and there are the swans in the lake; all looking so sweet and peaceful! It is time for peace. We shall never have the pain and trouble more! There shall be no storm. Ah! now I see Harry, where he crosses the stile. He is bringing me flowers; and we shall have a sail on the lake. My brave and noble Harry!"

"Olive, my child! — " interposed the mother, in tones of expostulation.

"Yes, my mother, we will come in soon. Harry will spend the evening with us. He says he will not go to sea again. So we shall hear no more about storms and shipwreck. I hear you — yes, I hear! ... But — where is he gone? Come back, Harry; oh, be not so impatient, Harry! I did but jest. It was a child's jest; it should not make you angry. Yes, you shall go to sea, if you wish, and I will go with you. I know there is a beauty in the sea. I know all about the Bermoothes, and those isles of the South, where there are grottoes and caves, with bright, sparry walls — stalactites, you know — and the coral-groves, with the dolphins, like so many living rainbows, gliding in between the walls, so deep down in the clear sea! You may see the very floor of the ocean; and the glistening sand-beds; and the bright gems and jewels — the spoils of the ship — and the beautiful forms of men — 'these are pearls that were his eyes!'—"

So rhapsodizing, in frequent breaks and pauses, with a brain wandering off to all the fancies of her childhood, she suddenly cried out, gasping, as with sudden fright:—

"No, no! Harry! Harry! Where are you? Come back to me, my Harry! Oh, come back! I will not think that you can drown! You are too strong a swimmer! Yes, O Harry, come back to me at once, my Harry — at once, or I shall die with terror!"

A convulsion followed — exhaustion! The pulse flickered wildly — feebly; now here — now there. It is gone — the eyes closing slowly, even while the fingers of the mother are gliding up the arm, as if to follow and arrest the flight of that fluttering, birdlike thing which, at length, afforded the only evidence of still-remaining life. The eyes continued shut; the lips silent, though parted as for speech; and the mother eagerly fastened her ears to them, while her fingers still followed the slight pulsation in wrist and temple.

"It is gone!—no! it is here!"

"It is gone!" said Zulieme.

And the mother threw herself upon the floor, sobbing violently. Zulieme, whose tears fell fast, bowed her head down upon the pillow, beside the silent Olive, conscious of a grief and growing sympathies and sensibilities which had seldom stirred in her little heart before.

The cassique heard the cries of the mother, and came from below into the room. He could now leave his post: the savages were fled! He looked silently — looked — with what eyes of deepest self-reproach and tenderness! — on the pale, sad, highly-spiritualized face, which seemed to smile from its lips; then clasped his hands in mute prayer, but did not venture to approach. He would have kissed her, but he dared not. How many thoughts and sorrows, at that moment, combined to make her lips sacred!

"They are not for me!" he thought to himself. "They belong to Harry now! My poor, poor Olive!"

And, to conceal the burst of tenderness which he felt rising in his bosom, he hurried below, threw wide the entrance, and stood looking forth upon the scene of blood; and here he waited for his brother, whose bugles were sounding on the edge of the wood. It was thus waiting that Harry met him on his return.

For a few moments they sat silent together in the parlor. Suddenly the cassique lifted his hand, and, without looking at his brother, waved it toward the chamber of death. Harry rose and left the room, then quietly passed into the chamber. The mother still lay sobbing upon the floor. Zulieme kept her position beside Olive on the bed. The rover approached and gazed for a moment on the inanimate figure. And this was the sad close of his earliest and sweetest passion!

"How beautiful," he murmured to himself — "how beautiful is death!"

And, even as he thought, he bent over Zulieme, and kissed Olive's parted lips — glued his own to them, as if the right to do so had come to him from Death; and, even as he pressed them, the eyes of the supposed corse opened beneath his own! He started back, his whole frame quivering with excitement.

She spoke — Olive spoke:—

"Harry!" was the single word from the lips, and then they were sealed for ever. The mother started up with a shriek. Zulieme fell back, terrified. But there was no other sound. The eyes were again closed as before — the lips silent, though still parted, with a smile of innocent and childlike sweetness.

"Who spoke? Who called 'Harry'?" demanded the mother. Calvert pointed silently to the corse.

"My child! my child! speak to me once more — but once, my Olive! Tell me — oh, tell me! Let me hear you but once more!"

But there was no response. The face was sweet, very sweet; there was a happier expression upon it now, as if a last want had been gratefully satisfied; and life, it would seem, had lingered only for that last look and word of tender farewell to the beloved one; and, that won, it had detached itself from the mortal dwelling, with as little effort as makes the leaf when detached from the tree in the gusts of the sere November.

The cassique had fixed a place of family sepulture, almost at the first moment of settling the barony. He had certainly chosen the site among his first performances. About a quarter of a mile from the house, on a slight crest of earth, small and nearly circular, his eye had distinguished a noble group of patriarchal oaks, each of which was probably a thousand years old. Their limbs were of the thickness of ordinary forest-trees. The sacred misletoe was imbedded and green in numerous boughs, a strange but not unnatural or unseemly grafting; and the gray moss streamed from the gigantic arms, waving in the wind like the great gray beard of the Druid bard, as described by Gray, when he thundered down, from his heights, his prophetic imprecations upon the march and barons of the imperious Edward! Each of these great oaks of the cassique stood up mightily, with outstretched arms, as giving benediction as well as shelter. And around these a circular line had been drawn; and the axe and hoe had been at work upon the underwood; and the spot had been consecrated to its sacred purpose, though no walls had yet circumscribed it, and no vault had yet been built. A few years later, and the place was duly cultivated and consecrated; and the old vault of the Berkeleys — beginning with the cassique of Kiawah — may even now be seen by the antiquary, looking ancient as Death himself. It is now a venerable ruin! Yet here sleeps, peacefully, all that earth holds of the beautiful but unhappy Olive.

To this spot the solemn procession of the dead bore her pale and delicate form. It was a solemn service, though there were no sacred rites, no stoled priest to officiate in the ceremonial. The war was in progress; communication with the city was cut off, unless under an escort of armed men. Even the burial, so near the fortress of the cassique, required the presence of a military force for its protection. At least, it was a proper precaution to provide one. The workmen of the cassique, the marines of Calvert, were all under arms, and present. They were grouped in order about the grave. The mother of Olive, Grace her sister, the servants, all clung close to the coffin, which was of cypress, without ornament or decoration, if we except a few pale roses, and some wild flowers, which had been gathered by the hands of loving servants. The cassique read the burial-service, standing above the coffin and beside the open grave. He read with subdued but unfaltering voice, his whole soul schooled to the degree of strength necessary for the performance of so sad and unwonted a duty. Calvert, with his face pressed close to one of the great oaks, sought in this way to conceal the show of emotion which he could not well subdue. The strife over, and no call upon his will and courage, he was weak as any woman.

But when his brother's voice no longer reached his ears; when he knew that the last painful duty was at hand, of hiding from human eyes the form of the beloved one — then he turned, made his way through the group, and stood for a single moment gazing down upon the lidded coffin. His eye seemed to pierce the cover. He shuddered with a sharp convulsion, and, with a groan which he could not suppress — which, indeed, escaped him unconsciously — he wheeled around, and was about to make his way into the forest, when a savage cry was heard, a bustle, a rush from without, and, darting through the circle with a succession of bounds, the Indian hunter-boy, Iswattee, dashed in among the group, even as a tiger leaps from the jungle among the brooding or browsing herds.

Never was there a more striking picture of mixed famine, misery, and insanity, than he presented to the gaze. He was meager with long starvation; his eye was full of idiotic fury; his hair was long, wild, and floating black from his shoulders. His shoulders were bare — his arms; the clothes seemed to have been torn from him in desperate struggle with wolf or wildcat. In his hand he brandished a tomahawk; and, with shriek and yell, heralding his descent among the party, his appearance was well calculated to strike terror into every breast. For a moment, all seemed paralyzed. Not a soldier put forth his hand; not a weapon was uplifted; not a word spoken; not a foot advanced to meet the intruder, so sudden was the surprise, so formidable the spectre! In another moment, he had seized upon the form of Grace Masterton, grasped her fiercely with his left arm about her waist, while his right waved his tomahawk, as he cried in his own dialect:—

"Annegar! I come for thee. Annegar — pretty white bird — Cussoboe, the great chief, says, 'Come!'"

It was a grand scene for the dramatic painter. The young savage dragged the damsel with him, heedless of her screams and struggles, his tomahawk waving all the while in the faces of the party. The cassique sprang toward him, across the grave; but, ere he could reach the spot, the hand of our rover, with a single buffet, had felled the wild assailant to the earth, and rescued the girl from his clutches. The boy was taken into custody, and fast fettered. With the one effort he had no power for further struggle; he was exhausted. He was a madman. His constant narcotic potations, his frenzied dreams, his wild and hopeless passion, the misery occasioned by his own consciousness of treachery to his people, and the stunning blow of his father's tomahawk upon his head, had utterly wrecked an intellect which, under other circumstances, might have made him the bard or prophet, the orator or statesman, of his people. As soon as his condition was ascertained, he was treated with constant care and indulgence, but closely watched. In a week he was dead, his last words being a call to the "Annegar"—the little white bird—which had been to him the bird of destiny!

In another day, the cassique and our rover had a final conference. The former had been pleading with his brother to remain with him.

"I pledge myself for your safety. I have power, as you know. Your pardon shall be procured—"

"Pardon!" cried the other, with indignation. "I sue to no man, to no king, for pardon! As for him who sits upon the throne of Britain, he should rather sue to me! He has betrayed, has dishonored me! He should sue to me, were he but half conscious of the true virtue that lies in manhood! No, Edward, I can suffer neither myself nor you to descend to the meanness of prayer or petition in such a case, or to such a sovereign!"

"But, Harry, unless you receive this pardon—which is really a mere form—you can never return to Britain."

"Unless, like Raleigh, to be sacrificed by a coward to a national enemy! But, my brother, I shall never return to Britain. I have been too long a freeman with Nature, in America, to endure willingly the caprices of any European despotism, whether of government or society. No, that Old World, with all its rotten con-

ventions, is no longer world of mine! Wretched as I have been,
am, and may be still, the sense of my present freedom is still my
acutest and most precious sense of life.    Here, manhood, if it so
wills, can live in every vein and muscle, in every beat of heart
and brain.    And here I can maintain my manhood — the noblest
of all mortal conditions; though I may not be able to escape pain
and privation; though I may never more hope as I have done, or
realize those passions which made the glory of my youth.    Still,
I shall be free; still I shall enjoy the sense of manhood; and this
will arm me to endure pain without a murmur, and privation
without impatience, and the denial of my best hope without seeking any vain substitute in the vices or frivolities of society.    No,
no, Edward!    No more Europe for me.    Were I to receive an
unsolicited *pardon* for offences which were once thought virtues,
I should still no more return to England."

"But, Harry, my brother, your people — your followers — are
you prepared to lead them into outlawry, or keep them in it?"

"No!    There you touch me nearly.    But I am safe from your
reproach.    I shall provide for their safety, and their return to
the securities of society.    I have, in some degree, provided already.    The documents are prepared, addressed to our uncle, and
to others, which will no doubt secure their safety from the operations of that decree which puts their leader under ban.    You, too,
can assist in obtaining their pardon; and I have referred my lieutenants and Belcher to you, in the event of anything happening
to me.    The ship herself I shall formally convey to the crown of
Britain."

"And whither will you go, my brother?"

"You shall hear from me on this head hereafter.    Nay, when I am
once fixed, as I expect to be somewhere upon the Spanish main,
looking down from noble mountains upon the broad Pacific, you
will come and seek me."

"Perhaps — perhaps!    But I have much to do here at Kiawah."

"You are right!    Make it a world to itself, and *your* world.
You can transplant civilization to the wilderness, and so train it
as that refinement and art shall be triumphant without excess or
sensualism.    That is the nice point for the study of the philosopher — how to secure the blessings of the higher moral of society,

involving the full development of the best human powers, without endangering or degrading the essential manhood of the race. But you must abandon all your wild notions of philanthropy. You will never reform or refine the savage. You must subdue him. The colonial government will need to follow up this war to the extermination or utter expulsion of these miserable tribes."

" I fear so !   But—"

" Yes, Edward, enough of this !   One thing: what will you do with your boy — Olive's boy ?"

" He shall go to England."

" What ! will you trust his infancy to this old woman ?"

" No !   He shall be consigned to our aunt Craven."

Abruptly — " Give him to *me*, Edward !   Let him share my fortunes !   I will make a man of him.   I have wealth.   He shall be my son as well as yours."

" Ask me not, Harry.   Were he twelve or fourteen years of age — but now — an infant—"

" You forget, I have a wife — who will most probably never bear me a child.   She is not wise, but she is virtuous; not thoughtful, but faithful; and with some really noble traits.   She will be very happy to have your boy; and I—"

" You would make him *yours*, I know !   But this is the very thing I would avert !.   Harry, my brother, I am selfish: I would have him wholly *mine*.   I would rather keep him from *you* than from any other, since I should feel sure that you would wean him from me."

" Enough !   All is said between us, Edward, except that love which no words can ever say or show.   Let us part !"

And, after a fond, repeated embrace, Harry Calvert tore himself away.   They were brothers now, in every sympathy, as in blood.   Zulieme, of course, accompanied her husband, the marines forming a sufficient escort; though the forest-march, from the barony to the Stono, was performed with as great a degree of caution as when pursued before.   They met no enemies, and gained the ship without interruption.

" All's well !" was the cry on board the Happy-go-Lucky.

Soon the anchor was weighed, and all sheets spread to the favoring breeze which bore them south; soon the white sails of the gallant cruiser were perceptible from the shores only as a speck — the wing of a curlew dipping the far crests of ocean. She will never, in her present keeping, revisit these shores.

Once more alone together in their little cabin, Zulieme caught her husband by the arm — got her arm about his neck, drawing him down to her.

"O Harry, stoop down! I have a secret to tell you!" And she clung to him till he bowed, and his head bent to her mouth, which she fondly kissed; then, beginning her sentence with a whisper, she ended it with a scream:—

"Harry, you dear brute Harry, I have something to tell you — to *make* you love me!"

"I do love you, Zulieme."

"Ah! but not as you loved poor Olive."

He was silent. She continued:—

"But when I tell you this, you will love me as you loved her."

"Well, well!. But do not speak of her, Zulieme. What is your secret?"

"I am going to have a baby, Harry! There! I've told it to you the first person!"

"You!" he exclaimed, looking at her almost incredulously, but with an expression of tenderest interest — "you!"

"Yes! why not? Now you will love me, Harry! You great, big, brute English Harry! you will love me! You will call me a child no longer. I am a woman now. I sha'n't dance again for months."

"No! you will always be a child, little one, though you had a dozen children! You a woman, indeed! You are only a pet — a plaything!"

"But *your* pet, Harry. You will make me your pet, won't you?"

"Perhaps!" And he stooped to her, and kissed her mouth tenderly, and drew her up to his bosom with a degree of fondness such as his stern course of life, for a long season, had not suffered him to show.

"And now, my child, that you are delivered of your secret, get your guitar, and let us go on deck. The moon shines softly, and the breeze is fresh and sweet. You shall sing me one of your

600 THE CASSIQUE OF KIAWAH.

Spanish ballads — 'The Loves of Fatima and Reduan' — 'The Moor who lost Valencia' — something — anything."

He unbuckled the sword from his side, put away his pistols, and, with something of a sigh, murmured :—

"My wars are over now! I must lose myself, if I can, in dream and moonlight."

And in the delicious moonlight of the South, while the good ship sped on her course like a wingéd creature, and the breeze fanned her sails lovingly, our rover, half reclined upon the deck, hearkened to his child-wife, as with exquisite effect she sang those wild, romantic ballads of the Moors of Granada, which appeal so sweetly to the heart and fancy.

And the breezes grew stronger; and more swiftly the vessel sped; and still the music rose and fell upon the delighted air — Calvert yielding himself to those seductions with which Love subdues War, and makes even Ambition forgetful of his aim! And thus, with fair breezes and a grateful sky, the Happy-go-Lucky passed out of the precincts where she had made herself felt in storm and thunder, and gradually disappeared, coasting along other yet sunnier shores, which she was destined no longer to disturb with violence; but going with swanlike aspect and motion, a harbinger, as it were, of halcyon seas and skies, and of a more genial and loving Humanity. Peace be upon her course, and upon the fortunes of those who have so long beguiled our interest! Their world has put on a brighter aspect; and Saturn and Mars no longer rule in the house of Venus!

THE END.